Praise for
the Award-Winning Series
'The Gauntlet Runner'

"Bailey has a talent for description. His words paint such a strong, vivid picture of the era that the reader will feel as if they are there."

Anne Boling. for Readers Favorite

"S. Thomas Bailey is truly a gifted wordsmith that paints such a vivid picture of time and place that I actually feel like I step back in time with this series..."

Brenda Castro from WV Stitcher review blog

"I have become a big fan and can't wait to find out what happens..."

King Bennett, Gettysburg, PA

"Not since Allan Eckert has an author captured the interest of the reader in frontier history."

Patrick J. Baier, Amazon.com review

"I must say, these books are so well written that anyone who loves history and the American frontier will be truly mesmerized by Mr. Bailey's books."

Mr. Bill Miller, Hagerstown, MD

"The reader will be able to hear the wind blowing through the lonesome trees of the frontier and feel the fear of the impending disaster which lingers throughout the story..."

Bil Howard for Readers Favorite

"You can't help but get absorbed into the lives of the characters."

Muzzleloader Review May/June 2014 Publication

Books by S. Thomas Bailey

The Gauntlet Runner Series

The Gauntlet Runner-A Tale from the French and Indian War
ISBN 978-1-4620-5123-6

Shades of Death-The Gauntlet Runner Book II
ISBN 978-1-4602-1879-2

Forest Sentinels-The Gauntlet Runner Book III
ISBN 978-1-4602-3161-6

Awards for
The Gauntlet Runner Series

The Gauntlet Runner-A Tale from the French and Indian War

2012 NABE Pinnacle Achievement Book Award
Best in Historical Fiction

2012 Reader's Favorite International Book Award
Honorable Mention in Action Fiction

Shades of Death-The Gauntlet Runner Book II

2013 NABE Pinnacle Achievement Book Award
Best in Historical Fiction

2013 Reader's Favorite International Book Award
Gold Medal in Adventure Fiction

Forest Sentinels-The Gauntlet Runner Book III

2014 NABE Pinnacle Achievement Book Award
Best in Historical Fiction

2014 Reader's Favorite Five Stars

Produced by:

FriesenPress

Suite 300 – 852 Fort Street
Victoria, BC, Canada V8W 1H8

www.friesenpress.com

Distributed to the trade by The Ingram Book Company

Blood
Lines

The Gauntlet Runner Book IV

S. Thomas Bailey

Dedication

To Maria, my best friend and the first person to believe and encourage me to keep writing; thank you for your unyielding support. To Madison, my light, who taught me not to worry about the little things and to smile more. To Kennedy, my star; I love the way you look at the world. I love you guys and thank you for being my inspiration.

Author's | **Notes**

Jacob and Maggie's story continues, as does my journey. I am now an award-winning author and Blood Lines is the fourth book in The Gauntlet Runner series. Blood Lines takes place in 1757 and moves the story into the New York territory. The title represents Maggie and her steadfast attempts to reunite with her family, Jacob and James' struggles to renew their relationship; as well as another disastrous campaign for the British and their colonial allies.

Blood Lines was easily the most challenging book so far to write. My biggest issue with covering the story of the siege of Fort William Henry and the events that took place after Munro's surrender was that the basic storyline has been covered in several novels and movies already. I wanted to write a slightly different version and that is why I wrote from the view of the battle and through the eyes of the men sitting a few short miles at Fort Edward. I knew of Webb's deficiencies as a leader, but after researching the days before the main siege, I learned how he ultimately was the cause of the disastrous defeat.

The best part of writing Blood Lines was I finally had the opportunity to introduce one of my favorite participants in the war, Robert Rogers. Easily the most fascinating person during the time period, Rogers has always intrigued me. Watch for him to play a role in future books as his budding friendship with Jacob continues. His life was amazing and I encourage you to read the many excellent books on his life.

My fascination and appreciation for the French and Indian War period has grown even more since spending time with many fellow authors, re-enactors, living historians and artisans through a great year promoting my first three novels. Even after endless hours of reading and researching to prepare myself, I have found the best way to learn about the time period is to visit the historical sites that are covered in the series. Walking the same trails as my characters and seeing the countryside that I write about has been invaluable.

I honestly can't believe this is already the fourth book in the ongoing series surrounding the Murray family. Please enjoy Jacob and Maggie's struggles and hardships as they continue to fight to reunite and survive.

I would like to extend a special thank you to artist Andrew Knez Jr. for providing the artwork, 'Proofs of Our Courage', for Blood Lines cover. Please take the time to look or order a piece of Andrew's work at www. andrewknezjr.com. He participates in several events throughout the season, and his work has been used for a number of magazine covers. You can always find Andrew at an event either manning his booth, displaying his fine work or busily taking pictures of the re-enactors for a future piece.

Also, thanks to the people at Friesen Press who had a big hand in pro-ducing this novel.

To Catriona Todd, my editor and friend who is invaluable in making my manuscript and book the best it can be! We make a good team and she is a big part of my success.

A new member of my team is Sweet World Media. Elaine and Jason did a wonderful job on redesigning my website, Sandi and Holly did all my new marketing materials for The Gauntlet Runner series, and Elaine produced the two fine maps for Blood Lines. They can be reached at www.sweetworldmedia.com.

Please watch for future novels in The Gauntlet Runner series and be sure to explore, visit and read more about this great time in our history. To stay updated with news about the series and schedule book-signings, check my website at www.thegauntletrunner1754.com.

"When a white army battles Indians and wins, it is called a great victory, but if they lose, it is called a massacre."

~Chiksika, Shawnee warrior

"...The General (Webb) thought proper to give you this intelligence, that in case he should be so unfortunate from delay of the militia not to have it in his power to give you timely assistance you might be able to make the best terms as were left in your power."

~Part of letter written by Webb's Aid de Camp to Munro
that was intercepted by the French, 1757

"...hardly able to conceive of a woods without end."

~William Smith, 1765

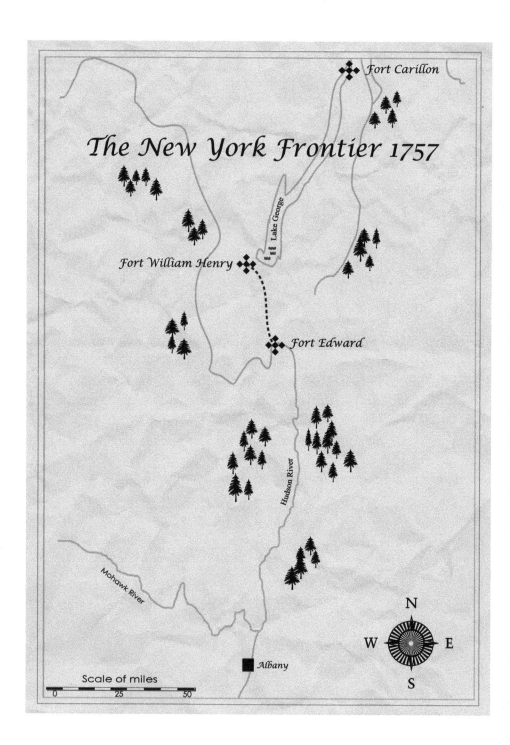

The New York Frontier 1757

Fort Carillon

Lake George

Fort William Henry

Fort Edward

Hudson River

Mohawk River

Albany

Scale of miles

0   25   50

N
W   E
S

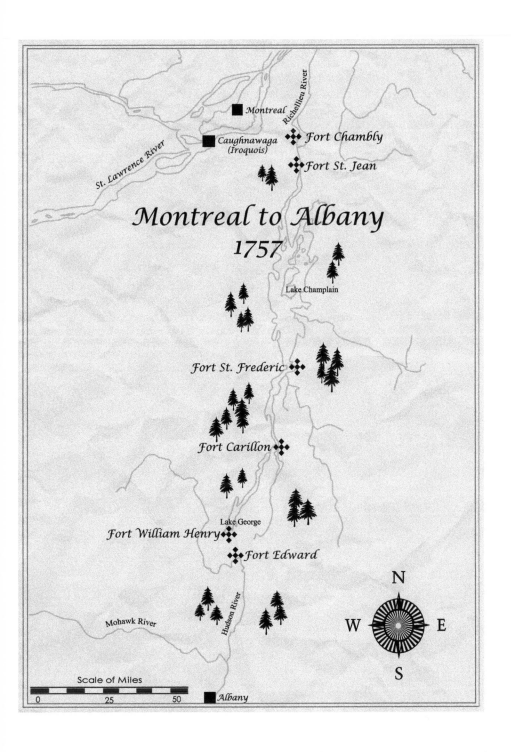

Montreal

Caughnawaga
(Iroquois)

St. Lawrence River

Richellieu River

Fort Chambly

Fort St. Jean

Montreal to Albany
1757

Lake Champlain

Fort St. Frederic

Fort Carillon

Lake George

Fort William Henry

Fort Edward

Mohawk River

Hudson River

N
W   E
S

Scale of Miles

0   25   50   Albany

Chapter | **One**

$\mathbf{M}$aggie had lost all track of time.

She forced her eyes closed, praying this was all just another bad dream. Her thoughts drifted back to the small cabin that she and Jacob had built together on the remote edge of the Pennsylvania territory. Maggie could almost hear Jacob calling out to her from the tree line after returning from a successful trip checking his trap lines. She smiled as she imagined him with a pack full of freshly skinned pelts strapped over his shoulder, and a proud smile engulfing his face as the children rushed to give him welcoming hugs.

It felt like a lifetime since Jacob had departed to support the poorly-organized colonial militia under the command of the reckless Colonel Armstrong. The colonel had been intent on seeking revenge on the ruthless Delaware leader they called Captain Jacobs, and was determined to attack the main Delaware village of Kittanning in the northern wilds of Pennsylvania.

Captain Jacobs had led vicious raids on the settlers and fortifications erected to stop such attacks and had even killed Maggie's own brother-in-law, but she still knew that the arrogant Armstrong was marching his men blindly into the deep wilderness. Despite her objections, Jacob decided she should remain behind with the small, inexperienced garrison at Fort Stevens. The fort had become a safe haven for most of the isolated settlers in the surrounding area.

Maggie could still see Jacob waving to her as he marched away. Behind closed eyelids, her thoughts were besieged by horrific memories of the brutality shown by the French and Delaware during their attack on the vulnerable fort.

She tried desperately to push the images from her mind, but they only gave way to the echoes of the panic-stricken settlers' cries and whimpers as the Delaware set fire to the walls. The men and some of the women had tried their best to hold back the attack, but the sheer number of savages overpowered the fort's defenses. Warriors flooded the damaged fort and began scalping, murdering and pillaging the survivors. The lucky ones were killed outright, while most of the women and children were dragged from the burning fort and tied together to await a grim future. A handful of men were also taken prisoner.

She forced her eyes open when her nostrils began to fill with the smell of burning wood and dead flesh. The vivid sights, sounds and smells of the attack faded away, leaving her with the reality of the forest around her and pain in her feet as she moved up the trail.

Once again, she was the prized captive of the Delaware.

Maggie sensed that they had been moving for several days, but the dimly lit forest made it difficult to judge. She decided it was more important to keep moving and survive than to keep track of details like time, so she focused on assisting the younger captives to keep pace with the others.

Her horrible experiences as a captive of the Huron had taught her that savages had little patience for stragglers or anyone who displayed weakness of any kind. To keep the main pack moving, they would simply sacrifice the weaker captives and push the others to the brink of starvation and exhaustion.

She constantly encouraged the children to remain silent and their families to keep moving. Maggie was blunt and direct in reminding everyone to keep up, saying things like, "If you stop or cry, they will kill you and leave you to the wild beasts to feast on your entrails."

For the most part, things were exactly as she expected. The Delaware pushed the prisoners mercilessly hard despite the number of women and children among them. The accompanying French regulars did nothing to impede the brutal tactics of their allies and turned a blind eye to whatever inhuman treatment the Delaware initiated against the defenseless captives.

The one unexpected aspect of this ordeal was that soon after they entered the darkness of the woods, the Delaware removed the traditional woven rope lines that had bound the captives' hands and kept them in line. Maggie figured it meant the French and Delaware were worried about the possibility of being overtaken by a rescue party and didn't want to waste any time in leaving the fort.

They were so deep in the interior of the wilderness that if any of the tired and hungry captives contemplated escaping, they would have no place to go. They were using less traveled paths that most of the settlers didn't even know existed.

Not long into their forced march, over half of the families were systematically split up. Young children were forcefully torn from the crying mothers' arms and husbands and wives were ripped apart.

Although they were all still close enough to see and hear each other, the Delaware made certain they remained apart. They appeared to relish the pain and heart-wrenching effects the forced separation had on the captives.

Maggie realized that this was a similar activity among all of the savage tribes she'd dealt with. She assumed they did it not only to organize the young children to be taken away, but to weaken the resistance of the adults.

She kept herself busy by making sure the children didn't stop moving. She offered them encouraging hand signs to help them remain strong. Maggie also did her best to console the traumatized mothers left without a child to hold or small hand to comfort.

Pushing her fellow prisoners almost as hard as the Delaware, Maggie did her best to keep the long line moving. The Delaware permitted her to walk freely amongst the women, obviously impressed by the strong white woman. She watched for anyone showing signs of injury or extreme fatigue and kept them ahead of her.

To one of the older mothers she urged, "Please keep going for your children. If the Delaware notice you are not keeping up with the rest of us they will take you into the woods and kill you. All that will be left of you is a bloody scalp hanging from one of these savages' belts."

The mother simply replied, "I have no children; the Indians have made them their own. What do I have to live for now?"

Maggie had no answer, but did her best to encourage the woman to keep walking.

Watching over the others kept Maggie's mind off of what might be in store for her and her fellow captives. She could feel the strengthening grip of early winter flexing its grip over the area. With most of the low-hanging trees losing their leaves, it made the trail treacherous to travel on. The packed-down, slippery combination of leaves and mud made the trekking difficult, especially since all the captives were hungry and tired.

She noticed that the French had begun to slow their pace and were having several conversations with the Delaware leaders along the trail. At one point, they came to a full stop to speak amongst themselves. Maggie had no way of knowing what they might be contemplating, but she prayed that they would be stopping soon for the night.

Instead, a couple of hand torches were lit and they pressed on through the cold night towards the northern territory. Maggie could see that even her captors were becoming noticeably slower than before.

By the time the sun began to fight its way above the high ridge the next morning, she and the others were spent of all their energy. They were hungry, tired and frightened at what might be next for them.

Maggie received word from a French officer who appeared to be sympathetic to the prisoners that an advanced Delaware scout had located an old abandoned Seneca village just a few miles ahead. She looked forward to getting off her feet and eagerly passed word to the others that they should be stopping shortly. This news appeared to give some of the captives renewed energy, and the sight of the village encouraged them to keep moving forward.

The old Seneca hunting village was no more than a few collapsed wooden buildings and an overgrown field of rotted corn stalks. As they entered, Maggie prayed that they would be fed since they were finally stopping, but her prayers went unanswered.

Maggie could sense that the Delaware were upset about something as there appeared to be a heated conversation happening between the French officers and two of the Delaware leaders. Soon after they stopped speaking, several warriors walked amongst the prisoners and forcefully removed the few men that remained with the group.

Her first reaction was to protest, but Maggie immediately recognized the Delaware were in no mood to be questioned by her. She thought it was better to let them take the men and comfort their still separated wives and children who were forced to watch their husbands, fathers and brothers taken away. Maggie knew only a couple of the men by name since most had arrived at the fort only a couple days before it was raided and captured.

It all happened so fast.

The men's hands were secured with heavy pieces of hemp rope. One of them was separated from the group and pulled by the hair towards the main body of screaming warriors. The French did nothing to stop them, but merely stood back and watched the horrific scene unfold.

The frightened man struggled to fight back; unfortunately, most of his strength had been diminished from the lack of food and water. Maggie could barely watch as two of the warriors mockingly toyed with the defenseless man, laughing at his feeble attempts to defend himself.

The captive women screamed and cried out to God, but several of the Delaware approached them and threatened them with raised war clubs and tomahawks. Maggie bravely interceded this time and boldly stood between the visibly upset warriors and the grieving prisoners. Frustrations grew as the Delaware vainly tried to force their will on the weakened captives, but Maggie's resolve made them finally back down and return to their fellow warriors.

The man who was being dragged away continued to struggle as he was pulled into the nearby woods and out of sight of the other captives. After only a few long minutes, an ear-shattering scream echoed throughout the dense forest making all the other prisoners stop their crying. As soon as the echoes died off, a sickly moan reverberated along the trail.

A deathly silence then engulfed the prisoners until a small, unnerving breeze swept through, making the few dry leaves left on the trees whistle and shake. Maggie attempted to walk forward but was instantly blocked by several warriors.

"Let the poor woman be; they have been put through enough already," a voice called out in French, prompting the Delaware to stop and step aside.

"Madame, please accept my deepest apologies for my Delaware brothers," the owner of the voice continued. He was a middle-aged French officer who bowed politely and removed his gold-trimmed hat, exposing his nearly bald head. "They come by their manners naturally. To them, a prisoner is a prisoner, no matter if they are a man, woman or child."

Maggie didn't bother to respond and focused her disgust towards the Delaware.

Seeing her anger, the French officer attempted to calm the situation by introducing himself, "Madame, my name is Corporal Chabot and I am with the Troupes de la Marines out of Quebec."

Maggie finally turned her attention to the polite Frenchman and said, "Monsieur, thank you for your assurances, but these savages can do little else to scare me."

She then moved towards the Delaware and screamed in French so she could be sure they would understand, "They should fear for their sorry lives once they are under my husband's knife!"

Other than slight confusion, the Delaware offered no response or emotion. Chabot, however, was impressed. "Your French is very good for an Englishwoman," he pointed out.

"I can understand and speak enough to know not to trust you or your heathen allies," Maggie shot back in broken French, surprising even herself how well her language skills had improved. Her time with Fredrick and French speaking savages had afforded her an opportunity to pick up a number of words and phrases. Far from fluent, she had more problems understanding the language than verbalizing the bits and pieces she had learned along the trail.

Chabot motioned to the Delaware to leave him with the prisoners and join the others up the trail. He also ordered several of his men to set up an informal guard around the traumatized prisoners.

"I suggested to my Delaware brothers to look for a better place to camp and get your people some food to eat," Chabot said as he looked at the crying and scared collection of women and children.

Maggie accepted his kindness and turned to her fellow captives, urging them to accept the word of the French officer and do whatever he asked of them.

"Merci, madame, for explaining to your friends; if you please, what may I call you?"

"Mrs. Maggie Murray," she replied.

She softened her defiant attitude, but remained stoic. While she had told her fellow captives to trust Chabot, she remained suspicious of his friendliness.

"Well, Mrs. Murray, I can see you are a person who does not like to waste her words," Chabot responded. "As you can see, there are many more Delaware than I have men. I hope you understand that my hands are somewhat tied when it comes to offering protection for your unfortunate people."

Maggie remained silent. She had realized long ago that the French preferred to turn their heads the other way when it came to the actions of their allies.

"So be it, madame," Chabot sighed, tired of her silent defiance. "It appears you have no use for our protection."

He was about to motion to his men to move forward when Maggie finally replied, "What is the 'price' for your protection, monsieur?"

A broad smile consumed his round face at the sheer bluntness of her question. Before he answered, Chabot put his left hand up to stop his men from moving.

"My intentions are all honorable, you can be assured, madame. All I ask from you is to keep your people in order and quiet. I will speak with the Delaware to clarify their plan for all of you."

Maggie nodded to him, accepting his deal. She truly could not sense if this Frenchman really was honorable or was just playing with her emotions. Regardless, she had learned one thing from her past experiences; every opportunity was worth considering in order to survive. She knew if she held on long enough, Jacob would come for her and free her from all of this.

Before anything else could be said, six Delaware warriors appeared out of nowhere and seized three young boys from the group of youngsters and dragged them up the trail.

All Maggie could do was to put her finger against her lips to remind the frightened boys to remain silent and brave. She then turned her attention to Chabot and his men.

Chabot immediately protested the treatment of the boys to a disinterested pack of warriors who just stood back and watched as the young prisoners were led away. It did appear to Maggie that he was, at the very least, vainly trying to ease his prisoners' tension and find out what was happening.

It was clear to her that Chabot and his men could do little to stop the Delaware from doing whatever they pleased. In fact, the outnumbered French soldiers seemed just as terrified of the savages as the prisoners were. Their protection was limited to diplomacy and bouts of discussions with uninterested Delaware leaders.

As the savages once again disappeared farther up the trail, Chabot slowly walked back towards Maggie and the confused prisoners. He was wiping his hand through his thinning hair and speaking with a few of his men.

After their brief conversation, Maggie stood and watched as the small French unit moved into a defensive position. They did their best to surround the prisoners, keeping their muskets at the ready.

Their actions made most of the women hunch down in fear. Maggie's first thought was that they were going to start shooting the prisoners, and she instinctively stepped towards Chabot.

He turned to her and in an effort to ease her fears and calm down the clearly upset captives he said, "The Delaware are very upset and I fear they want to exact revenge on you and your fellow prisoners. They told me that several scouts just returned from the village they call Kittanning and reported it has been attacked by a large army of white settlers. The village has been burned to the ground and their leader, a man you English call Captain Jacobs, and his family were killed by the raiders.

"They are blinded by vengeance and care little that you and the rest of the captives had nothing to do with it. I will do what I can to keep them from killing all of you, but you must see that we are only a few against a much larger force. If they don't get their revenge and collect scalps to honor their dead, they will be shamed along with their families and villages."

Maggie could see that Chabot was just as concerned as the captives were as he continued to watch the upper trail for any signs that the Delaware might return in force. The situation was volatile and could explode at any moment. Scanning the handful of French marines that barely encircled the captives, Maggie knew that if the Delaware decided to kill them all, Chabot and his men could do little to stop them.

"What can we do, monsieur?" she asked. "If the Delaware want to kill us, there is little you can do. Do your men really want to die just to protect a few, unimportant English settlers?" Maggie fell silent, not expecting an answer.

Chabot made no response and focused instead on better organizing his men in defense of the captives. As the men straightened their lines to the front and rear of the group, Maggie thought that if the Delaware wanted to attack, they could easily move through the forest to outflank them on both sides. As if Chabot could read her thoughts, he immediately strengthened the protection to each side of the trail.

"We need to just stay back and pray they might calm themselves down," Chabot finally responded. "I did inform them that you were under the protection of the King of France, and that he would not look on them kindly if they hurt his war prizes."

Such a proclamation did little to lessen the captives' fears.

"Can you fire a musket, madame?" Chabot called out to Maggie, taking her by surprise.

"I have never liked your French-made muskets, but I can manage," she answered, getting a brief laugh out of Chabot and his men within hearing distance.

Once Maggie took her place with the others and had her musket loaded and at the ready, the odd collection of French marines and English settlers waited.

It was cold and a heavy dampness filled the surrounding wilderness. Maggie could feel the threat of either rain or early snow hanging in the air and thought it could only add to their suffering. Most of the captives had proper clothing to protect them from the cold, but had little to keep the rain from soaking them.

"Do you know what they did with the men and the three young boys they took?" Maggie asked, finally breaking the eerie silence and moving beside Chabot who leaned on an old tree stump that sat close to several large birch trees.

"I fear they paid for the raid," he said, keeping his voice down so the others could not hear his ominous prediction. "The boys, I was assured, were taken to a nearby Delaware village to our west. The first gentleman was sacrificed. As for the others, I am not sure, but I do fear the worst. We must also consider that they might want a few more of these captives to appease their sorrow, but we will deal with such circumstances if and when they play out."

Maggie turned to look over the small group of captives. Some were sitting on the cold ground while others were on their knees praying. She noticed that since the Delaware turned their focus to the men, most of the children had managed to make their way back to their mothers. She knew that the reunion would be short-lived before they were ripped apart again, but for now the children slept, oblivious to what was happening around them.

She still had a difficult time grasping why these French soldiers would risk upsetting their much needed allies for a small group of dirty, destitute prisoners. Chabot appeared to an honorable man and the fact she now held a loaded musket in her hand convinced her that the French were just trying to survive as well.

Maggie's thoughts were interrupted when the trail ahead suddenly filled with a number of Delaware warriors. Chabot shouted in French for his men to shoulder their muskets, and Maggie took up her position by the defenseless captives.

The silence on the small trail was striking as all Maggie could hear was the whisking of the warriors' deer hide moccasins scraping over the layer of soggy leaves.

She shouldered her French-made musket, taking aim at the lead warrior as he confidently strode forward towards the tense group of French marines and English captives. She wondered what the Delaware thought of such an odd sight of their French brothers protecting prisoners from their own allies.

The French soldiers did their best to keep themselves between the approaching warriors and the huddled mass of prisoners. A few of the captives stood beside Maggie, holding what they could find to offer some defense against the savages.

Chabot noticed this latest display of self-defense and called to Maggie, "Madame, please keep your people back so they do not join in any forthcoming attack. Hopefully, just the sight of your willingness to defend yourselves will make them reconsider whatever it is they have planned for you. My men will do what we can to keep the Delaware from harming any of you."

Maggie could see that Chabot was worried the situation might explode into an all-out massacre, and he did his best to keep his men calm.

The Delaware were clearly angry as they came flooding onto the trail. The lead warrior walked very close to the French, slowing but not stopping.

Chabot raised his arms and called out in French, "Please my brothers, let us talk."

His simple words appeared to work. The warriors in the front stopped, and those positioned behind did the same. Maggie watched, with her musket still at the ready, as the warriors waited for their leaders to return.

Chabot and two of the older Delaware warriors had walked to a small, natural clearing just a few steps off the trail. They were too far away for Maggie to hear anything, so she watched their gestures and expressions on their faces for any clues.

Chabot had his back to her, but she could see that the two Delaware respectfully listened to him and nodded on several occasions. From where she was it looked like they were conversing relatively calmly, with the Delaware each speaking in turn.

The rest of the French soldiers remained with the captives, not giving any ground to the Delaware. A few of the warriors walked around the perimeter of the trail, trying to frighten the captives. Maggie stood her ground and matched each of their menacing glares with one of her own. She could see that they were confused that she had been given a musket. One in particular positioned himself directly in front of her, almost daring her to shoulder the weapon.

She gave the young warrior little satisfaction and returned her attention towards the three men still conversing just beyond the tree line. The conversation seemed to be going well and Maggie noticed that they were looking and pointing towards the group of prisoners on a few occasions. At one point, she even managed to catch the eye of Chabot, but he gave her no clue at how the conversation was going.

There were a couple moments when the Frenchman was rather animated, appearing to disagree with some of what the two Delaware leaders were proposing. Maggie had the uneasy feeling that the longer the conversation continued the more difficult Chabot was finding it to convince his Delaware counterparts to leave the prisoners unharmed.

Maggie remained diligent in keeping track of where the other Delaware were. Some had returned to the main group, but the one young warrior remained nearby staring at her, treating her like she was some prize to be taken once the presumed attack took place.

The three leaders suddenly split up, with the two Delaware walking together towards the main body of awaiting warriors. Chabot headed immediately to where Maggie stood, bypassing his own men to speak directly with her.

She could see from the look on his face that the news was bad. She said nothing, but simply waited for him to explain their fate.

"Madame, the news is good for your fellow people," Chabot began uncomfortably.

Before he could continue, Maggie's attention was caught by the sight of most of the Delaware unexpectedly pulling back and disappearing into the forest. Only the two leaders who had spoken with Chabot remained with a small contingent of warriors. Maggie's young warrior was amongst them and he continued to watch her as she spoke with Chabot.

Chabot continued, clearing his throat, "The Delaware have agreed to leave the prisoners with me, as long as I escort them to the fort at Niagara."

Maggie immediately interrupted, "Monsieur, this is unexpectedly good news. Please let me tell the others that we will be saved from the Delaware."

"Madame, please...there was one request from the Delaware. Despite my objections, they demanded one condition. I am sorry; I tried to offer them a cart full of pelts and supplies, but they were rather adamant that we meet their only request."

Confused by Chabot's uneasiness, especially since it appeared to be good news, Maggie did not understand why he was acting so nervously. She knew that they were still prisoners and would most likely be no better than slaves at the fort, yet it was definitely preferable to be under the protection of the French than be left with the unpredictable Delaware.

"I am sorry, madame, but they insisted that the 'strong white woman' stay with them." Chabot could not hide the guilt he felt at being unable to negotiate a better deal.

Maggie's usually quick mind was struggling to understand the implication of his words. She stared at him silently.

Chabot stared at the ground as he attempted to clarify what the Delaware wanted, "Madame…I am so sorry. They want you to go with them."

Maggie went numb.

She could see that Chabot was ashamed that he would be forced to leave her with the Delaware. He had barely been able to finish his words.

"Why me?" she cried.

"I am sorry, madame," Chabot said again, continuing to avoid looking directly at her. "You have displayed such courage that they see great value in you."

Suppressing her tears, Maggie tried to get Chabot to explain what they had planned for her. "Will they kill me or trade me like I am some prized horse or cow?"

Maggie watched as Chabot nervously looked towards the waiting Delaware. He turned back to her and said, "We must finish this before they change their minds and decide to kill you all."

She looked over the sad state of her fellow captives and knew what she had to do. "Will you get them some food and let them get some rest before you march them to Niagara?" she asked in a tone that sounded more like an order.

"Certainly, madame, and the Delaware gave me their word that you would be treated honorably. I hope you will believe that I did everything in my power to keep you with us…"

Chabot's words just blended into the dense woods, lost in the moment. Maggie stood, trying desperately not to collapse or break out in a panic. She kept telling herself to stay calm and not give the Delaware the satisfaction of knowing she was frightened at the prospect of being their lone prisoner.

She looked at the other prisoners who had all risen to their feet. Although Maggie and Chabot had been speaking too quietly for them to hear, the rest of the captives had observed the departure of most of the Delaware and assumed that it meant the French had saved them after all.

Maggie could not think of anything to say to them. Her emotions were torn between happiness that most would be spared and a deep fear that she would not make it through the winter. She turned her gaze to the southern end of the trail, and silently prayed that by some miracle Jacob would rush out of the wilderness and rescue her from all of this.

Chabot politely interrupted her thoughts and said, "Madame, if you please, the Delaware need you to go with them."

Maggie stood motionless and watched as her fellow prisoners were escorted towards a small side path that would take them north. A few of them looked at Maggie, confused that she was not immediately leaving with them. She managed a slight wave and offered them a feeble smile.

One of Chabot's men whispered something in his ear and then left with the others. Chabot removed his hat and bowed his head saying, "Please stay well. I assure you, I will return in the spring to negotiate further with the Delaware to purchase your freedom."

Before Chabot departed, he retrieved the musket from her shaking hands. His last words meant little to her now.

The trail was empty and the slight murmurs from the departing French and their English prisoners were all she could hear. She was alone with the small band of Delaware waiting just behind her.

She closed her eyes and, for the hundredth time, prayed that she would wake to find that all of this was just a bad dream caused by too much of her home-made beer. She would open her eyes and find herself safe and sound beside Jacob back at Fort Stevens.

Maggie stood motionless, considering her options. She entertained a brief thought of running madly into the woods or down the trail in hopes she could lose the Delaware somewhere in the wilderness, but without a weapon or means to survive, she figured she would be dead before the sun set.

Once again, her thoughts were shattered as a cold hand seized her arm. The same warrior who had watched her earlier pulled her forward. Instinctively, she jerked back but realized it was useless to waste her energy.

"Come with me," was all he said before escorting her to the small party of waiting Delaware.

Positioned in front of the two leaders who had negotiated for her, Maggie had never felt as vulnerable as she did now. The two looked at her and signaled the warriors to move out.

Alone again, she was left to walk with her Delaware captors. Maggie continued to watch the endless line of trees in hopes Jacob might jump out and rescue her. With each passing tree, her optimism diminished into the sea of wilderness.

The small band of ten warriors and two leaders said nothing to her and simply continued up the trail as if nothing had changed. Maggie did her best to keep up her energy, but the emotions of the past few hours had weakened her spirit and she just blindly walked forward.

The little sunlight that fought through the trees was by now waning and she prayed they would soon stop for the night and get some food.

Wondering where the rest of the much larger group of Delaware had gotten to, Maggie continued to follow her escorts well into the night. Stumbling several times in the darkness, she refused to accept any assistance and kept pushing forward.

By that time, she had not rested for almost two nights and her stomach ached from not having food or water to diminish her pains. Her feet felt as if they might just snap off, and she feared what they would look like whenever she would finally have an opportunity to let them rest.

The Delaware finally stopped at a small stream and before she found a comfortable spot to sit, a large fire was spreading its heat around the camp. The light provided her a good look at her escorts and the surrounding terrain.

Maggie was tired and hungry. She watched as a couple of the warriors walked to the edge of the shallow stream and began to scoop up a few small fish. They also trapped a few dozen little crayfish and three or four large frogs that were all placed by the fire to cook up.

Small branches, inserted in the captured creatures, helped prop them up just enough the get them sizzling over the fire. Maggie enjoyed the smell of the fire, and the wonderful aroma of the bite-sized meal made her stomach ache even more.

She struggled to remember if she had ever eaten the little crayfish that inhabited most streams and creeks throughout the territory. She did know that they smelled wonderful as they cooked. Frogs were always a nice treat, especially the thick, muscular legs, and she was almost overcome by the possibility she might be offered some small morsel to feast on.

Once the small meal was ready, she was shocked that after the two leaders ate, she was offered a whole frog on a stick and three cooked up crayfish. Maggie ate up the frog as quickly as it arrived, and once she figured out how to peel the shell from the crayfish, she was surprised at their wonderful flavor.

It was nice to finally have some food in her stomach. She was surprised again when her young admirer brought her a tin cup of hot water with a handful of winter berries and root herbs mixed in.

She offered a brief smile to him but received nothing in return.

One of the leaders also directed a warrior to give Maggie a beautiful blanket made from a deer hide and a new pair of knee-high moccasins to replace her worn out pair.

Maggie was mainly surprised at how thoughtful her captors were being compared to how they had acted towards the larger group of prisoners. She felt much warmer with her new footwear and finally got some much needed rest just out of reach of the fire sparks.

With her stomach somewhat satisfied and the heat of the tea warming her cold, damp body, Maggie closed her eyes and was soon fast asleep.

Chapter | **Two**

Jacob did his best to ignore the splintering pain that shot through his arm with the jostling of every step. His wrist was swollen and bruised, but he had tied a small piece of cloth around it as tightly as he could to give it support and keep him from moving it. He prayed it was only sprained and not broken; he knew that he needed the use of both hands if he was to be any value to the loyal men that had decided to come with him.

After initially heading northeast, Jacob and his lead scouts lost the tracks of the main Delaware party who had taken his Maggie. Before they managed to walk too far east, Jacob spoke with Joshua and made the decision to turn west and head towards the Allegheny River. Joshua was certain that the river would take them deep into the New York territory and then they could cover the remaining distance on foot.

Jacob was aware that if they reached it before the heavy snows hit and the water froze, they might be able to get to New York and catch the Delaware before they reached the French fort at Niagara.

The three men of the advanced scout were ordered to keep up a good pace and watch for any possible ambush points and to clear the trail of any fallen trees or other debris. They carved markers in the trees to assist the main body of men to guide them, as well as, warning them of possible areas to watch out for ambushes.

Jacob was pushing the main body of thirty men hard and, at times, was at a full run. It was a particularly treacherous place to traverse; they not only had to dodge the endless unearthed roots and half-buried rocks, but watch for potential places where they could be ambushed.

As usual, he relied heavily on his advanced scouts to alert him to any trouble ahead. If he stopped seeing their regular markers along the trail, Jacob would be forced to either send more men ahead to check on the scouts or slow the pace down to a crawl. Even with a skilled advanced guard, the men knew that the possibility of running into the enemy sat around every corner and blind spot in the trail.

Joshua and James did their best to keep up with Jacob's torrid pace, but there were times when they were forced to stop for breath, letting others rush past them. As soon as Jacob got out of their sight, they pushed themselves to start running again as fast as they could.

"I hope he doesn't run us so hard we pass the scouts," Joshua said between deep breaths during one such pause.

"He might kill us all from exhaustion before the Delaware have a chance to attack us," James said with a brief smile and started to sprint again.

Most of the other men struggled as well. They were weighed down by fatigue and the emotional impact of what they had left behind at the fort.

"Sir, hold up before you run yourself to death or, God forbid, into the waiting war clubs of the Delaware," Joshua called out as he neared Jacob.

Joshua's voice made Jacob stop immediately. He looked behind him, finally noticing his men were dangerously strung out in a long line almost a mile to his rear.

Fighting off the sharp pain that ran up both sides of his legs, Jacob leaned against a mossy boulder. He was careful to hide his discomfort from the men, not wanting them to slow down because of him. He had either not noticed or chose to ignore the fact that his feet were covered in sores and blisters. Stopping and waiting caused them to swell, and he was close to collapsing. Added to his foot pain was the ever present throbbing in his wrist.

He waited, finding it difficult to conceal his injuries while the others struggled to catch up. His uncontrolled pace had forced many of them to discard anything that added weight. A long line of packs, cooking pans and other heavy items had been dropped along the trail. A Delaware or French party tracking them from behind could easily stalk them by following the debris left along the trail.

"For God's sake, sir, we can't rush blindly ahead," Joshua gasped, barely able to get out the words before he dropped to his knees and struggled not to release the meager contents in his stomach.

"Damn their slowness, lad," Jacob shot back. "We are just wasting time and letting the Delaware put more miles between us." By now he sat propped up on the boulder letting his sore feet dangle over the edge.

Managing to get back on his feet, Joshua spoke with uncharacteristic bluntness saying, "The men are tired, sir. They have been on the march, non-stop for almost two whole days. They fought a battle before being forced to watch their home burn to the ground. You will lose most of them before we have any chance to find Miss Maggie."

James remained quiet but chose to stay beside Joshua.

Jacob turned his attentions to his son and pleaded, "Boy, if we don't keep moving we might lose your mother forever."

James once again remained silent and offered nothing to his desperate father.

By the time Jacob tried to continue, most of the men had staggered into the small clearing where Jacob sat. It was clear to him now that the men were dangerously tired and in much need of a rest.

"You don't think the Delaware are resting as we speak?" Joshua asked, "They must be in the same shape as us, despite their desire to move the prisoners as far as they can into the wilderness."

Jacob was going to offer a rebuttal but noticed that Sinclair had arrived with his rear guard. "Mr. Sinclair, did you see much behind us?" he asked.

Sinclair hardly offered a smile and wiped off his sweaty brow as he said, "We spent most of our time keeping the men moving and picking up whatever they decided to drop on the trail. A few of the men collapsed from exhaustion, and I think a handful decided to just turn back and head home. I can only pray they made it home instead of being captured by the Delaware or Shawnee."

Jacob said nothing, but took a moment to scan the small mass of men that had shown him their unconditional loyalty. He felt guilty that his blind rage had pushed them so hard that they were practically useless.

"Sir…sir…what should I do with the men?" Sinclair asked, interrupting Jacob's thoughts.

Joshua, Sinclair and James stood by him waiting for their orders.

"Sorry, lads, I fear I pushed you all far too hard. My emotions got the better of me." Jacob felt it was a poor explanation of his actions, but he didn't know what more to say.

"No need to justify, sir," Joshua offered as he stepped forward. "Most of the men understand and would follow you anywhere, but they need some rest and a bite to eat."

"Should we set up camp here, sir, or find a better, more secure spot for the night?" Sinclair asked again.

"Thank you both. Joshua, take a couple of the men and search up ahead for a good place to spend the night. If you please, Mr. Sinclair, re-organize the rear guard and have them set up a picket detail just in case the damn savages surprise us. I fear they are still lurking about, so we need to remain diligent in our duties."

As Joshua and Sinclair moved to fulfill their orders, Jacob watched as the men got some energy back once word spread they were going to stop for the night. James remained standing in place, still not speaking or displaying any outward emotion.

Jacob had noticed James' odd demeanor earlier, and before Joshua got out of earshot said, "Joshua, take James with you. He picked a fine spot back at Kittanning and maybe he can find us another."

Without responding to the compliment, James simply turned and walked towards Joshua.

Jacob was bewildered by James' whole attitude and almost called out to ask him what was wrong, but decided this was neither the time nor place to do so. There were far more pressing issues to deal with first.

His thoughts turned to trying to think of what they could do to cover more territory in an effort to catch up with the Delaware. He assumed they would have to be slowed by the number of captives they had taken.

It was only a few minutes before two of Joshua's scouts returned with the news that they had found a good spot that sat on the banks of a nice sized river. The news excited the men, and Jacob did not have to say much to get them up and moving once again.

He followed the two scouts for a brief walk through a natural gap along a small mountain ridge. They soon stepped into a narrow clearing and saw the winding river that flowed towards the horizon.

Joshua and James were busy clearing a spot in a protected wooded area that sat just across from the western banks of the river. By the time the main body of men arrived and poured into the makeshift camp, they were greeted by a roaring fire pit and several fallen trees moved close enough to sit and feel the heat emanating from the fire.

Impressed by the swiftness and efficiency the two young men displayed, Jacob could hardly hold back his appreciation and said, "Lads, you did a fine job, a fine job."

Walking down by the river, Jacob stood alone and watched his tired men file in and grab a warm place around the fire. Most of them propped themselves up on their packs, while others just collapsed and were fast asleep almost as soon as they hit the cold, damp ground.

Personally, Jacob would have preferred to press on through the night, but he could not risk losing more men to fatigue or desertion. He stared off to the north, straining to look up the winding river for any signs that the Delaware might have used the river as an escape.

The nights were longer now, and a man could see his breath with every exhale as the darkness ate into the useable daylight. Jacob was growing concerned; he knew too well that once the first of the snows hit, he would have a difficult time pushing the men northward. He had never been as far north as the New York territory, but had heard the stories of the frequent, massive storms that would sweep down over the lakes and dump so much snow it would drift over most men's heads.

The fear of being stranded in a strange territory with no shelter and possibly no allies to lend them a hand deeply worried him and he silently prayed that the snow would hold off until they were closer to civilization. Joshua had told him of a large Mohawk village that rivaled the size of Kittanning. He had said it was near the shores of another lake that was as large as the great lake that sat to their northwest.

The village was their target for the winter. Joshua had assured him that the residents were friends to the English and would provide the men good shelter for the worst part of the winter. He mentioned that when he was with the Huron, they would add several days to their trips just to pass by this well-situated village.

Jacob was heading towards the fire to warm himself when he saw Sinclair clamoring up the trail, making enough noise to alert the Delaware for miles. He was about to shout to quiet Sinclair's men until he saw that they were carrying two large bucks tied to poles.

An air of excitement settled over the small camp as soon as the rest of the men spotted the scouts walking out of the woods with their trophies. Even the men who had been fast asleep awoke refreshed and enthusiastic.

The men would eat well that night and Jacob knew that full bellies would give them all some much needed energy. He also knew that this might just be their last good meal for a while and he wanted the men to enjoy it.

Sinclair walked over to Jacob and could hardly hide his smile as he said, "Found these two fine creatures just milling about."

The makeshift encampment of tired, cold men desperately needed such prizes to boost their spirits, and several of them quickly fashioned a spit over the campfire from three solid branches. Ignoring their fatigue, the rest of the men built a second large fire within minutes and set up a similar spit to mount the other animal.

Jacob was happy at the sight of the men's newfound energy. They were so excited he was surprised they even bothered to cook the deer. They had the two animals skinned and already cooking over the fires before Jacob and Sinclair made their way up to the camp.

"Thank you, Mr. Sinclair," Jacob said, patting him on the back and motioning him to a seat by one of the fires. "You may have saved some of these poor souls' lives. I feared we would find a few of them dead in the morning from starvation."

Sinclair smiled and gladly took a seat with a couple of the men, enjoying the fire and the wonderful aroma exuded by the two roasting bucks.

Jacob looked around for Joshua and James and noticed them working hard to gather more wood to feed the fires. Others were busily stacking the wood and making sure the fires kept roaring as they waited for the beasts to cook.

Two of Sinclair's men went to the effort of discarding the two deer heads deep in the forest, so they would not attract any coyotes or wolves in search of an easy meal. Jacob laughed inwardly that the aroma surrounding the camp was probably more likely to attract any wild beasts for miles, not to mention any Delaware in the immediate area.

The men who disposed of the deer heads had first removed the brains to use to tan the hides, packing them into a small sack. They also presented Jacob with the two bucks' impressive antler racks. He obliged the men and gladly accepted their bloody trophy, calling on Sinclair to take one of them as thanks for bringing such a needed prize to the men.

After all the horrors of the past few weeks, Jacob was glad to see the men showing some signs of life and happiness. He was content just to let them have their fun and decided to take the first shift of picket duty.

He sat close to the river bank enjoying the sights and sounds of the men eating and laughing.

A few of the men grabbed the two sets of antlers and mockingly fought each other, charging headlong towards one another. They swerved just before making impact, drawing loud laughs and cheers from the others. Normally, Jacob would have told them to keep the noise down with the understanding that they could be heard for miles, but the men needed such freedom to enjoy the moment.

Jacob agreed with Joshua that the Delaware were probably just as tired. The odds that another raiding party in the area would risk attacking such a large party of well-armed men were slim. One of the only good things about this time of the year was it tended to restrict movement and most of the savages in the area should have moved to their winter hunting grounds.

He simply let the men have their fun…they had earned it.

The men gorged on the unexpected feast and Jacob even got a laugh from watching Joshua taking a turn at charging one of the other men with the antlers. James just sat by the fire eating a few slices of deer meat but still showed little emotion despite Joshua urging him to join in.

James' demeanor greatly worried Jacob. He was clearly not happy, but Jacob was not sure what he could do to change that. He thought it would be best to just let him be for the time being. He honestly missed the little boy that would follow him everywhere, trying to keep up with him on the trails or when they went out together to check on the trap lines. He hoped Joshua could get him into a better state since they had so much in common and Jacob knew that James had always wanted an older brother. The two seemed like they were bonding, so he did not want to do anything that might jeopardize their budding friendship.

At first, Jacob had thought his own strong relationship with Joshua might have been part of the problem, but he didn't feel comfortable broaching the subject. If James felt threatened by his connection with Joshua, Jacob realized he could do little about it. He hoped James' problems stemmed from his readjustment to his English roots after his time spent with the Delaware. Jacob prayed that time would heal whatever wounds James was holding on to, and that they could get back to the way their relationship was before.

Jacob also knew that Maggie could bring the old James back, which made him push that much harder to find her.

Once the men had eaten and enjoyed the occasion, Jacob noticed Sinclair, Joshua and James walking towards the river where he sat on an old tree stump. Sinclair was carrying a nice hunk of thigh meat, which he presented to Jacob before they began to talk.

"Thank you again," Jacob said, "it is certainly good to see the men happy and fed."

The four men looked back towards the glowing fire and could see that some of the men had already fallen asleep where they had eaten, while others diligently kept the fires fed with the piles of wood gathered earlier. Still others worked at cutting thin slices of the meat to hang over the fire so they would have dried meat to carry on their journey.

Biting off a small chunk of the greasy meat and swallowing it, Jacob continued, "Now, for the business at hand. Do any of you lads know what river this might be? Honestly, my bearings are messed up and I am too tired to think straight."

James once again remained silent while Joshua just looked out into the darkness.

"My guess is it might be a runoff river," Sinclair offered. "It looks wide, but I fear it might just be from mountain runoff and will not take us west."

"My initial thought was that it might flow into the Allegheny River," Jacob responded, "although I think that might just be my hopefulness talking. We can't afford to waste more time, and I think we risk losing most of the men if we keep trudging through the woods. If we use the rivers and portage when necessary, we should be able to cover more ground."

Joshua immediately added, "We have to think the Delaware will do the same. They must be concerned about the approaching winter. If they have any hope to reach Niagara or any other French outpost in New York, their best bet would be to get to the Allegheny."

Jacob stared out into the blackness and listened to the last of the frogs serenading them. A couple of owls were calling out to each other, breaking the silence of the four men.

"What are your thoughts, boy?" Jacob asked, looking at James. His son's head was down and he appeared disinterested in the conversation. "You know these people better than any of us."

Initially hesitating, James finally spoke, "What Joshua said sounds right; they will want to use the rivers. If you don't get their trail soon, you will never know if they are heading to the north or south towards their winter hunting grounds."

Jacob smiled at James, but was given nothing in return.

"Let's sleep on it and at first light we will decide what our best course of action should be. My opinion is that we should think about heading west and getting to the Allegheny. Most of the French are either garrisoned at the forts or have already left to winter in Quebec. Still, James brings up an interesting point that the Delaware might be heading south. That certainly would present us with a problem." Jacob paused and waited for any of the others to add to his thoughts.

No one said a thing, so Jacob continued, "Mr. Sinclair, what are your thoughts of taking some of the men and heading south? You could scout around the Virginia territory to search out any signs of the Delaware and spend the winter at Fort Cumberland. You might even want to spend some time at the fort our Captain Stevens was stationed at back in Maryland. You and the men could join back up with us in the spring. We will leave you some markers to follow our trail north."

Two new men arrived to take the next shift on picket duty, and Jacob remained behind for a moment as the others slowly walked back towards the warmth of the fires.

He gave a simple nod to the two men, who took up position near the stump he had used during his shift, and said, "Stay warm, gentlemen, and keep your eyes and ears open. Don't let the silence lull you into thinking we are all safe; the Delaware are out there and we certainly don't want them to sneak up on us just because we let our guard down."

With that warning, Jacob retrieved his small haversack and the carving knife he'd been using to carve his powder horn. He looked around and was happy to see that six of the men had already set up similar pickets around the perimeter of the camp.

He walked behind Sinclair, Joshua and James and could hear them muttering something, but he was too far behind to make out what they were saying.

As they arrived at the fires, Jacob was happy to see that the men had finished their work on the bucks and were once again disposing of the carcasses deep in the interior of the woods. They even went so far as to hang them over a couple of large branches.

Most of the men scattered around the fires had already gone to sleep. Jacob waited for Joshua and James to take a seat beside him around the fire. Before he returned to carving up his powder horn, he quietly said, "James, I will need you to lead us through this territory. Do you feel we are better off going by the river or by land?"

Jacob expected James to display some excitement at the prospect of leading the men, and hoped this might help him return to the old James that he loved.

"Do you trust me to take you the right way?" James asked without showing any outward emotion. "Aren't you afraid I might lead you into an ambush?"

Taken aback by his tone and his insinuation, Jacob immediately shot back, "At the moment, lad, I care little about how you feel about me, but I expect you would do everything in your power to help me find your mother."

Once again, James lapsed into silence with a blank expression on his face. Even Joshua looked on him with some hesitation.

"Get yourselves some sleep and we can discuss things at first light," Jacob said, ignoring James' odd behavior and keeping his focus on Maggie.

He left the younger men by the fire and walked back to the river to rejoin the two pickets. James' reaction confused and angered him, yet he knew that time should bring him back around. If not, then he would be forced to deal with him sooner rather than later.

The two men had positioned themselves closer to the river bank, so Jacob gave them a quick wave and settled on the same tree stump he had used earlier. He relished in the silence and took comfort in the glow from the fires. The peacefulness of the river was enjoyable and he just sat and looked out over the dark water, listening to it hitting the banks where it sent small splashes of spray onto the nearby grass.

With enough light from the two fires, Jacob pulled out his scalping knife and began to carve into his horn again. It was nice to be alone with his thoughts; he was able, for a moment, to push aside worries about his men and James.

Rubbing away most of the dirt and greasy residue of his horn, Jacob dug his knife into the hard shell and began carving a small heart. He was no artist, but he roughed in the shape and filled it in with lines. Blowing off the horn to clear it of the dusty filing he had just carved, he then held it up until he could see his handiwork in the flickering glow of the fires.

The detailed work drove shots of pain up his arm, but after adjusting the make-shift bandage on his sore wrist, Jacob continued on. Slowly he scraped the letter 'M' and continued until he had spelled out 'Maggie'.

Brushing off the dust once more, he stopped and just stared at her name. It made him think of simpler times. Each morning, Maggie would get up ahead of him to brew nice, hot cups of herbal tea, and they would enjoy them at the small wooden table he had built for her birthday.

Seeing her name also made him feel the deep prong of guilt that he could not seem to shake. Jacob asked himself why he had left her behind at the fort. He should have never gotten himself involved with the foolhardy Armstrong. Had he been thinking straight, he would have just remained at the fort despite his orders and kept her close to him. He had the urge to scream as loudly as he could in some off-chance that she might be able to hear him.

He knew he would just be wasting his breath…

His brief moment of silent reflection was interrupted when he noticed a shadowy figure walking around the camp. Standing at first to get a better look, Jacob grabbed his musket and slowly walked towards the two fires.

After only a few paces he realized it was James. Clearly unable to sleep, the boy was wondering around the perimeter of the camp. He stopped to speak with a couple of the men on picket duty and then continued on with his late night wandering.

Before he could get too far away, and being careful not to disturb the sleeping men, Jacob called out to him, "Boy, come and join me."

James was at first startled by his father's voice, but once he caught sight of him, he made his way directly over.

"I didn't know you were still out here," James said and sat beside Jacob on the cold, hard ground.

They sat a few minutes in silence, listening to the ever-present noises that echoed from the woods, struggling to be heard over the intensive snoring of the men.

Jacob could see how much James had grown up over the past couple years. The innocent boy he had left behind was almost a man and had, realistically speaking, already experienced more in his life than a person twice his age. Jacob admired his son's strength, yet at the same time, he could see that James had lost his innocence and had become harder and stoic.

"Get yourself off the cold ground and share this stump with me," Jacob offered, shifting over to give James some room to sit. "It is probably just as uncomfortable as the ground, but it will keep you dry."

Waiting for James to change position, Jacob looked at the rough carvings on his horn and confided, "Sorry if I seem too tough, lad, but I feel I let the family down…If I had just stayed home, we would still be together now." It was difficult not to break down and cry; only he did not want James to see him display such weakness.

"Father, you did what you had to do for us. You had no control over what the French or the Huron were doing. If you remained behind, they might have still raided our farm, and most likely would have killed you…then what?" James spoke with the wisdom and honesty of a much older person.

"Can't do much now except try to keep you safe and find your mother," Jacob said as he put his powder horn down beside his musket. "I just have to stop your Delaware friends from reaching Niagara before winter."

James innocently picked up the horn, noticing the small etchings on it. Holding it up towards the light, he strained to read the name of his mother and the rough heart design. Gently placing it back beside his father's musket, James had a slight smile on his face.

Jacob noticed his smile and realized that this was one of the first times he had smiled since being rescued.

"I think the Delaware will take her directly to the fort at Niagara," James said openly. "Some of the war party will head south, others will stay with the main French army, but I am certain a group of the strongest and fastest warriors will accompany the captives to the fort. The French will also have a small party of regulars traveling with them."

Happy they were finally having a civil conversation, Jacob once again asked, "Will they most likely head to the great lake and then take the portage past the falls to the fort?"

"They might, although the lake is a terrible place to travel this late in the season," James explained. "The Allegheny is longer but far easier to canoe and transport captives. They will have to portage once the river ends in the north country and take some of the smaller rivers, but it will slow them down. They will have to push hard to reach the fort at Niagara before the heavy snows arrive."

Jacob knew if they could cut them off before they got too far up the Allegheny, they just might have an opportunity to rescue Maggie and the other captives. His only hope was that with the number of women and children they were moving, their pace would be severely slowed.

"Do you feel that we might have an opportunity to catch them, considering the large group of captives they took?" Jacob asked, happy that James finally appeared to be coming around.

"They will only take the ones that will keep up. The slow and old will be killed so they won't hinder the others."

Shocked by James' frankness, Jacob was just about to scold him for his insensitive response when he noticed he had slouched over and was fast asleep. Knowing that his son needed the rest, Jacob removed his own coat and placed it on the ground. Gently he lifted James down onto it.

Jacob resumed his study of the river, fighting the heaviness in his eyelids. He was no longer on duty, but he still sat amongst the pickets and wanted to set a good example for the men. The first rule for a man on picket duty was never to fall asleep, no matter how briefly. If a man was caught sleeping, it was punishable by lashes or, depending on the severity of the offense, hanging. This being not an official-military venture, Jacob would never administer such punishment, but he certainly did not want to be a poor example for his men or cause them to be ambushed because he couldn't keep his eyes open.

The bright morning light covered most of the area and exposed an unexpected light dusting of snow that covered most of the ground. The men did their best to get on their feet and keep the fires going to provide some warmth before they headed north. A large pot of water was already boiling over one of the fires, waiting for the men to grab a nice hot cup of tea and enjoy some of the freshly dried and salted slices of deer meat.

Jacob had managed to get some rest, albeit only a few hours. He had remained by the river to sleep next to James. His feet were tender, as were most of the men's. He knew the ground they needed to cover would just make them feel worse, but all he could do was to rest them when time permitted and make sure he kept them dry while he slept.

He stretched his limbs as he looked around the camp, and was happy to see the men up and readying themselves for the next leg of the journey. Jacob dusted the unwelcome snow from his shirt and noticed a particular ache in his wrist from the cold and re-adjusted his wet and dirty bandage. Despite a deep, multi-colored bruise that covered most of his hand and extended halfway up his arm, most of the swelling had gone down and he was beginning to get back some of his mobility. All in all, Jacob was satisfied that it was close to mending.

Before he walked over to grab himself a cup of tea, he noticed James was up and standing alone down by the river.

"He has been down there for a few minutes, sir," the nearby picket said, nodding towards James.

Waving to the picket, Jacob said, "Thanks. Go get yourself some tea and get warmed up."

The man was happy to do so and was gone before Jacob had worked his way down to the sandy bank.

"Get much sleep?" Jacob whispered to James, not wanting to startle him.

"Enough to keep me moving; how about you?" James answered, not bothering to look at his father.

"Not much, I find it difficult to rest when your mother is out there in the hands of the Delaware."

James said nothing more and Jacob decided to leave him to his thoughts. As he made his way towards the camp, he was greeted by Joshua's cheerful, "Good morning, sir," as the young man handed him a cup of steaming tea. Jacob inhaled deeply and enjoyed the strong aroma of berries and pine needles.

"Thank you, lad; the bloody snow caught me off-guard. You know it is coming, but when it does it certainly hits hard."

"Aye, sir, it was not a welcome sight when most of the men got up," Joshua agreed, sipping his own drink as they walked around to the far side of the clearing.

"Did we lose any of the men last night?" Jacob asked as he looked back towards the river to see if James had moved.

"From what I can see, it looks like most of them decided to stay with us," Joshua replied. "We can take a quick roll call to see."

"No bother, lad, I don't want the men to feel obligated to stay. If any man needs or wants to leave, then he should be able to do so." Jacob spoke distractedly, clearly focused on what James was doing.

"He doesn't seem too happy to be with me," Jacob confided once he noticed that Joshua had followed his gaze.

"It's difficult to experience both worlds and realize one is much better than the other," Joshua tried to explain.

"How so, lad?" Jacob asked in bewilderment. "I thought he was more English than savage."

"His experience with the Delaware was a good one. He told me they treated him well and his adopted family was very kind to him. I could see how such a young boy, who thought his parents were both dead, could prefer such a life. Now all of a sudden, his life is thrown back into confusion. He not only regains his parents, but loses the other family that cared for him over the past two years."

Jacob nodded his head slowly for a moment when Joshua had finished speaking. "Please keep your eye on him, lad. He doesn't talk much and I fear he might decide to run back to the Delaware."

"I will, sir, but give him some time. He has been through more than a boy his age should ever have to. He is probably more confused than angry; just give him some time."

"I can see you both have bonded, so I will look to you to help keep him safe," Jacob said quietly as he turned his eyes back to James at the river. "I can only pray he might return to his old self."

Before they could continue their conversation, they were interrupted by a question from Sinclair, "Sir, have we decided what our next course of action will be?"

"Good morning, Mr. Sinclair. What are your thoughts?" Jacob was still unsure what direction they should travel.

"I always hated traveling by water," Sinclair offered, hesitating slightly to gage the reaction from Jacob. "It is admittedly faster, yet I fear we would expose ourselves to being ambushed from the land."

"I must be honest," Joshua said, "I find it strange and disconcerting that we have lost the trail of such a large party slowed down by women and children. I can't even remember the last good tracks we saw."

Jacob turned to face the river and said, "This dusting of snow reminds us how vulnerable we are just sitting around waiting for something to happen. My thoughts are to send Joshua and James to take out ten of our best trackers to scout up ahead. My gut feeling is that the Delaware have already taken to the river, so we should stay close to it and hope to find some decent tracks. Mr. Sinclair, your point about the vulnerability of using the river is well noted, but I think the weather and time will dictate our way." Jacob looked at Joshua who gave an accepting nod of his orders.

At Jacob's dismissal, Joshua poured the rest of his tea on the ground and ran over to inform James of their next task. Jacob remained with Sinclair as they both watched Joshua pick his scouting party and lead them off towards the trail that would hopefully take them to the familiar Kittanning trail. With a quick wave they disappeared from view.

Jacob was satisfied that Joshua and James would be able to find something to confirm which direction the Delaware had taken. He was willing to bet that the river would turn out to be their best option, so he turned to Sinclair and asked him to gather a crew to cut down some small trees to begin construction of enough rafts to hold all the men and supplies.

"Tie ten to twelve good-sized trunks across with some sturdy saplings and then have some of the men test them on the water. That should put us in good shape if it turns out the river is the best way to travel. I don't want any accidents once we are on the water since the water temperature must be close to freezing; I'm sure no one really wants to go for a swim."

Sinclair smirked at Jacob's last comment and moved off to fulfill his orders.

Jacob's sprits were renewed with this course of action and, after gulping down the rest of his tea, he joined the men in constructing the rafts. His men also appeared to have the same renewed energy. They seemed even more determined this morning to locate the captives and fight the Delaware. Of course, revenge was a great motivator, and the men still had fresh memories of seeing their beloved fort torched and their friends dragged off by the enemy.

Jacob tried to keep himself busy so he didn't stand around waiting for word from Joshua that they had found something. During their wait, the men built and strapped together three good-sized rafts. Each had been tested and checked over by Sinclair and Jacob personally. Jacob decided that he could have a small scouting force remain on land to monitor the rafts and defend them if indeed they did run into an ambush.

"The men did some great work," Jacob beamed. "I think these rafts will turn into a great option for us."

The only problem was that after all the work they had put in, it was already well into the afternoon. The late autumn sky was struggling to hold onto the hours of useable daylight, and Jacob now had to decide if they should leave without word from Joshua or wait until they received a report from the scouting party. The thought of getting on the river and heading out blind was a big concern for both him and Sinclair.

Not wanting to waste the entire day and all the men's hard work, Jacob initially thought to send out another scouting party to find Joshua. However, if the first group had gotten into trouble, he would only be sending more men into the same trouble.

Revisiting James' original idea that there was a chance the Delaware might have moved south, Jacob decided that Sinclair should take six men towards the Virginia territory to scout the area for the possibility the captives were taken south. He wrote out his orders and an introduction to the commanders at Fort Cumberland and the Maryland fortification to offer accommodations to his men. If Sinclair decided to use one of the forts as a base, then he should be so provisioned. He also requested that Sinclair take with him the men who were most familiar with the southern territories to aid him with his scouting.

The scouting party worked quickly to pack up so they could leave immediately.

"Keep yourself well, Mr. Sinclair. Actually, I have been meaning to ask you, what is your given name? The formalities of Mr. or Private are getting old, and we have been through too much together to be anything less than friends."

Jacob could see that Sinclair appreciated his confirmation of their friendship as he replied, "Thank you, sir; my name is actually Robert."

"Well, Robert, it is only fair that you call me Jacob. Please take care of yourself and these men. We both know that the Delaware are not the only people moving south towards better hunting grounds. Keep a watchful eye out for the Shawnee and Seneca on the main trails, and especially at night. Keep the men in order; safe travels to you." Jacob respectfully offered his hand and Sinclair graciously accepted it.

"You keep safe as well, Jacob," Sinclair replied.

"I will. We will see each other again in the spring. I will wait for your arrival at the Mohawk village that Joshua spoke about. I got him to sketch a map that will help you find us."

Sinclair gave a slight salute, folded the small map and placed it in his coat pocket.

Jacob called out just before the scouting party disappeared into the forest, "Robert, if I get word from Joshua soon, I will get a message to you."

Sinclair waved and walked into the deep woods out of sight.

Jacob turned his attention back to the few remaining men and knew they could not wait around much longer either. After a few more minutes of intense hoping that Joshua and James would reappear, Jacob decided to get the men moving.

Despite the hard work they had put into building the rafts, Jacob made the difficult decision that it would be better to travel overland with such a small group. He figured that they could head towards the Allegheny

River via the same old Kittanning trail they had just used to raid the Delaware village.

The men reluctantly beached the newly-crafted rafts and covered them with branches to conceal their location. Jacob voiced his concerns with the men about leaving themselves exposed to an attack from the shoreline since they had no men to cover the overland route. He was also worried that if Joshua ran into trouble, he wouldn't be able to get word of it if they were on the water. Being on land and following the same trail as the advanced scouting party would make it possible to offer any necessary reinforcement.

Jacob estimated that the Allegheny River was within one and a half days' hard march, if the weather co-operated. The possibility they might run into parties of migrating savages moving southward was worth the risk in his mind. He still knew that the longer they waited, the more the miles would add up between him and Maggie. With every mile, finding her became more impossible.

Jacob was left with twenty men remaining in his party and decided he would send three men ahead to scout the forward trail and watch for any signs of Joshua and his men. Two more men were placed at the back to form up a rear guard to ensure they would not be overtaken from behind.

Two additional men were left behind at the camp, just in case Joshua sent back word of their activities. Jacob gave them strict orders to leave no later than first light the next morning to catch up with Jacob, whether they heard word or not.

Keeping the men on alert, he instructed them to remain spread out. They walked in single file and kept their muskets primed and ready in case they ran into a possible ambush.

Jacob led the men westward over the easiest mountain gap, understanding that the higher mountain trails might be clogged by early snow that normally hit the region well before this time. He prayed that they would be spared any inclement weather at the lower elevations until they made their way to the river.

It wasn't long into their march that word was sent back by the advanced scouts that an unidentified party had been spotted from a high ridge overlooking the trail.

"Sir, we noticed a small party of men, maybe roughly ten to twelve, heading directly towards us," the messenger explained. "They were seen from a couple of high boulders, but we couldn't make out if they were French, English or savages. One thing's for sure, sir, they were moving quickly and had no visible scouts sent ahead."

Cautious, yet oddly excited at the same time, Jacob sent word back to the men in the rear and rushed forward at double time with the messenger in the lead.

Breathing heavily, Jacob called out to the scout ahead of him, "How far is the place you spotted them?"

"Not far, sir, maybe half-mile or so," the man said without missing a step.

Surprised at how fast they covered the distance, Jacob immediately weaved his way up to the lookout once he saw the other scouts waiting and watching the trail below.

"Anything new to report, gentlemen?" Jacob asked as soon as he took a look over the steep ridge. "Are they still advancing towards us?"

"Nothing more, sir," one of the men answered without taking his focus from the lower trail, "we lost sight of them once they hit the heavier forest canopy area just under us. I think they should be making their way up the ridge in a few minutes."

With the expectation of encountering the still unidentified party, Jacob ordered his men to take up positions on both sides of the trail and to keep their heads down. Two men were sent ahead to attempt to identify if the approaching men were English or an enemy party.

"Be careful and do your best to find out who is coming. If they are English, identify them as such and bring them directly to me. If they turn out to be French or any of their allies, then let them pass and try to give us some warning sign before they are on us." When Jacob finished speaking, the two men darted up the trail.

His first thought was that the men might be Joshua's scouting party, but he had never known Joshua to be so foolish as to not have any advanced scouts ahead to warn them of an ambush. Jacob kept two men on the high ground to watch any further activity on the lower trail.

Taking up position by a large boulder, Jacob could hear the pounding footsteps of men running up the trail. Word was fast to reach him that it was the two scouts he had just sent ahead.

They reported directly to him, "Sorry, sir, but we almost ran right into the buggers. We could hear them coming and unfortunately couldn't get any glimpse of them. They were right on our tails and will be here any second."

Thanking the men and directing them to move to the rear to join the others, Jacob stepped back behind the boulder and took a deep breath.

It wasn't long before he could hear the noise of several men rushing towards them. Jacob signaled to his men to shoulder their muskets and await his order to open fire. To protect himself and his remaining men, he had no choice but to attack. He just prayed that he wasn't about to kill some of his own men.

A fallen branch snapped as the first of the approaching party finally came into full view. Something made Jacob hesitate just as he was about to drop his arm to motion to the men to fire.

Chapter | **Three**

Maggie walked slowly with the small group of warriors. She felt tired and weak; it had been a couple of days since her meager feast by the river.

She watched as a handful of warriors suddenly departed and took a small side path just to her left. The warrior who had kept such a close eye on her since she was taken from the French was thankfully one of those who departed. Maggie was used to how the Indians would come and go as they pleased; her captors now numbered only six warriors.

The remaining warriors didn't bother to secure her hands, but they did make sure she was positioned between them in case she took advantage of their kindness and attempted to run. Maggie knew that the Delaware really had nothing to worry about. This deep into French and Delaware territory, any escaped English captive, especially a woman, would never make it far alone.

The Delaware did not speak to her. They simply moved at a steady pace, keeping her moving until they reached the flat shore of a small, shallow creek. The warriors took a moment to grab a handful of water and rest on the cold, damp boulders that littered the sandy creek bed.

Maggie splashed some of the icy cold water on her face and soaked a small cloth she kept around her neck. The weather wasn't particularly warm, considering the time of year, but their pace had caused her to sweat nonetheless. She sat on a flat rock and watched as one of her escorts searched the nearby overgrown bushes for some late-season berries.

Most had already been picked over by the many animals that were preparing for the long winter, but after diligently pulling back on the branches, she was surprised that he returned with a pouch full of mixed berries. He gave most of the better fruit to his fellow warriors, but did offer what was left to Maggie. Starved and willing to eat practically anything at this point, she accepted the meager tidings with a brief smile.

Her stomach reacted very unkindly to the harsh, tangy taste of the over-ripened berries, and she washed the rest down with a couple handfuls of water. Maggie enjoyed the fresh, cold water; once her stomach accepted the small treat, she sat back and put the cold cloth over her face.

Just as she stretched out to let the berries settle in her belly, the warriors were up and motioned to her to do the same. Her brief yet welcomed rest was over.

Sticking to the creek bed, they followed the meandering stream for several miles. Maggie had no idea where they were and did her best to keep up with the three warriors leading the way. She could see that her captors were beginning to slow and they continuously stopped to look ahead of them, almost as if they were lost.

Maggie found the sandy creek bed difficult to navigate. It was spattered with small, slippery rocks and much larger boulders that she was forced to climb over. She hoped that with the sunlight dwindling, they might just stop for the night.

Sadly, they continued to push west. Before long, just as the sun set leaving them only a little light to watch for rocks and other obstacles, the shallow creek opened up to a much wider, rapidly moving river. The signs of the impending winter could be seen plainly in this place. A thin layer of ice along the banks crackled each time the wavy water crashed into it. Thousands of leaves had amassed behind an old tree trunk that formed a natural but narrow bridge across the river. The leaves had kept the water from moving freely and ice had begun to form over them.

They stopped just near where the creek seeped into the river. It was completely dark by the time one of the warriors took her gently by the arm and directed her to a large rock where she could rest. He remained by her side as the others quickly got a large fire going.

Using the light from the fire, two of the warriors started to cut and peel large pieces of birch bark from the numerous mature white birches that inhabited the area, rolling them into large bundles. Once the bark was removed, they hacked down the bare trees and dragged them towards the light.

Two other warriors had their hatchets out and began to cut down a few of the younger saplings. They also collected a number of the fallen trees that seemed to be everywhere.

The remaining warrior kept busy arranging the de-barked trees and methodically trimming off the branches. He wove a small basket from some of the smaller branches and collected some black, tar-like syrup from the trees.

Maggie sat and watched how efficiently the Delaware went about their work despite the limited light. Once the first two warriors appeared to be satisfied with the amount of trees and rolls of bark they had collected, they carefully began to bend and mold the pieces into a rough frame. They ran the pieces over the fire to make the wood more pliable, and she was amazed to see their work already taking form.

When the other two warriors had finished with their saplings, they eyed one of the larger fallen trees their comrade had been stripping branches from. Maggie guessed they were inspecting it for rot and possible signs of insect infestations before vainly attempting to move it. Its sheer weight and size made it impossible. They straddled the trunk and appeared to be checking it for size and balance. Both seemed satisfied with the tree and climbed back down.

Maggie looked back towards her silent guard; she thought of offering him a smile, but she knew it would be lost on such a stoic, uninterested savage. He just remained behind her and observed his fellow warriors at work.

Returning her focus to the two with the tree trunk, she watched them clean the dirt from the newly-exposed wood. One of the warriors had walked away but returned with a lit torch. Subsequently, both ends of the massive tree were set on fire. He carefully watched both ends to make sure the fire didn't spread and ignite the entire piece. The other Delaware continued to chip away at the center of the trunk, slowly hollowing out a long, deep burrow.

As Maggie had watched the men with the birch bark work, she he been immediately able to see the framed piece taking shape and knew it was to be a good-sized canoe. With this tree, it took a bit longer to tell that it was also going to be a canoe; it was a different style and much bulkier.

The Delaware who was working hard to carve out the trunk finally removed as much as he could. Standing almost ankle deep in the debris he had hacked out, he inspected his work. He had dug out enough room for three to four warriors to sit and paddle. She watched as he climbed inside and could see that he would need to make it deeper and slightly wider to accommodate the paddlers comfortably.

He quickly gathered some of the branches they had removed and piled them into the dug-out center. He carefully moved a large ember from the charred remains at one of the ends of the canoe and placed it among the branches. With a few good breaths, he got the ember to light and began to monitor the fire inside the trunk. Meanwhile, the other Delaware had successfully burned off each end to cut down the size and make it more manageable to move. He was now busily carving the two ends to slowly reveal the recognizable canoe shape.

Soon, both men stood back to look at their handiwork. Smiling and saying something to his partner, the man who had worked on the inside of the canoe began shifting the pile of burning branches between the two ends. Maggie could see that he was trying to level out the dug-out center and soon appeared to be satisfied that his task was completed.

Maggie was once again impressed by their skill. They had been without transportation earlier, but now they had three brand new canoes. She had also been so fixated on the warriors working on the dug-out canoe that she missed the process that made the beautiful birch bark canoes, but now she watched with fascination as they floated them in the water to make sure the thick black seal spread over the seams was watertight.

Once the two warriors with the birch bark canoes were satisfied with their work, they all sat by the fire to begin carving several paddles for their trip. As they worked, they set another batch of the thick tar over the fire to boil.

The smell of the black syrupy liquid was almost unbearable and Maggie found herself covering up her nose with the wet cloth she wore around her neck. Even the Delaware could not take the smell; once the thick liquid was boiling, they were quick to carry it down to the canoes for one last layer of waterproofing.

Although she had no idea what they were saying to each other, Maggie could see that the Delaware appeared to be much more relaxed. Even her guard joined the others, while she still remained on the rock. The rest did her body good, despite the fact that she was still hungry. The small portion of tart fruit had done little to satisfy her appetite and her stomach ached painfully with each breath.

As Maggie watched the canoes bobbing in the creek, she thought of her previous terrifying experiences on the water. Most recently, she and her traveling companions had been forced to abandon their canoes in the face of a sudden ice storm. Even more unsettling, though, was the trip across the great lake from Presque Isle. On that journey, she and One-Ear had nearly died. The idea of possibly returning to the scene of such a narrow escape made her reluctant to even set foot in one of the canoes.

Thoughts of One-Ear made her recall her dear friend and she prayed that he was somehow alive and maybe even out in this godforsaken wilderness searching for her. She so vividly remembered him telling her of how treacherous the big lake would get in the winter, and that his people would never be foolish enough to venture too far into its clutches.

He had told her that every winter the lake would devour fishermen who did not respect her power; she would just swallow them up and they would never be heard from again. As she tried to rid herself of the memory of the horrific waves and her struggles to reach the rocky shoreline with One-Ear, it made her wish she had the courage to just run and hope she could be swift enough to outrun her captors.

Maggie was lost in thought until she saw movement down by the river. Two of the Delaware were getting ready to try out the birch-bark canoes; she watched as they briskly stepped into the icy cold water and jumped aboard the boats. The much larger dug-out canoe was being dragged by the remaining warriors towards the water's edge. Straining desperately, they stopped several times to call out to the two warriors still sitting in the other canoes. Maggie guessed they were asking for some assistance, but all they got were screams and laughter.

With renewed determination, the warriors finally dragged the heavy, flat-bottomed canoe down to the water, leaving a deep track in the sand. Maggie's initial thought was that the canoe would hit the water and sink like a rock, but to her surprise it glided impressively over the water amid cheers from the Delaware.

One of the men jumped into the boat and mockingly paddled around both of the smaller canoes, sending a large wave that rocked them until they nearly capsized. They all laughed and once the water settled, one of the warriors motioned to Maggie to come to the shore line.

She really thought they Delaware would be too exhausted from working through most of the night, but they appeared to be anxious to depart. Despite a lack of sleep herself, she was caught up in their excitement.

The other warriors jumped aboard the canoes and Maggie went directly to the much larger, and clearly sturdier, dug-out canoe. She was offered a hand and then was pulled over and landed in its surprisingly smooth bottom. She was careful not to get herself wet and was soon handed a paddle.

Maggie did her best to keep pace with the much more experienced warriors. Once she adjusted to their rhythm, she did an impressive job of driving her paddle into the clear water. The spray from the front paddler was cold but refreshing.

The early morning sun did its best to fight off the low clouds and provide some light for their travel. She soon noticed that even with an extra paddler in her canoe, the two birch bark canoes were well ahead of them. She pushed on, despite her aching arms; with each stroke, she told herself not to show any weakness.

Maggie felt torn between relief at being off her feet and the knowledge that the only reason they stopped to build the canoes was to put more space between them and any rescue party that might be looking for her. Maggie could do little to stop their progress. Her only hope was that Jacob would think to do the same and be tracking them along the same river.

She remained wholly focused on keeping pace with her fellow paddlers, sparing no time to glance at the shoreline or take in her surroundings. It became noticeably cooler, yet she had a steady bead of sweat on her forehead that she had trouble shaking off as she paddled. She could tell by his movements that the warrior ahead of her was dealing with the same issue, trying to wipe his brow without missing a stroke of his rhythmic paddling.

It felt like a few hours had passed while they paddled. Sometimes they slowed their strokes to take a much needed breathier, but they never stopped paddling. The last time they slowed, Maggie could see that the nearest of the lighter canoes was ahead of them by almost thirty canoe lengths. The lead boat was barely visible. Maggie could not imagine how they could ever catch up unless the two smaller canoes pulled to shore and waited.

To complicate their travels, the sky suddenly darkened and almost immediately opened up with a mixture of cold driving rain and ice pellets. It mercilessly pounded down directly into the exposed canoes, quickly filling up the interior shell. Maggie was completely drenched and was struggling to fight off an uncontrollable shiver that hit her entire body.

The combination of rain and ice made it impossible to see more than a few feet in front of them, making paddling all the more dangerous. Over the noise of the storm, they could barely make out screams from the distant shoreline; the other warriors had pulled their canoes onto the relative safety of land.

Once they caught a brief, blurry glimpse of the other Delaware warriors frantically waving at them, Maggie and her fellow paddlers quickly turned their canoe and pulled towards the shore. It was almost ten minutes before Maggie and the others managed to navigate the rain-soaked canoe alongside the others. Thankfully, the river was shallow along its sandy banks; once they beached the heavy canoe, they all ran across the muddy shore to the tree line where the others stood waiting for them.

Although they stood amid a heavy wall of trees, the rain easily pounded past the leafless limbs and continued to soak the cold, wet party. Maggie knew they couldn't stay there. The Delaware were vulnerable to an attack since they had no opportunity to keep their muskets and powder dry. Left with only their hatchets and knives for defense, Maggie simply waited for them to decide what they needed to do to get out of this rain and reorganize.

They were forced to leave the canoes beached on the sandy embankment and to move inland to find some shelter. The storm showed no signs of weakening and even seemed to increase in intensity since they had made it to shore.

She watched them talk amongst themselves. After the brief exchange, three of the warriors braved the relentless weather to explore farther up the trail for some much needed shelter.

Now with only three warriors left behind to guard her, she thought it might be the best time to run…if only she had the energy. Her soaked clothing clung to her and added more weight to her already fatigued body. The strain of managing to get the heavy dug-out canoe to shore had taken its toll; she could only sit and listen to the rain pouring down from overhead. Even the remaining warriors were in poor shape and paid more attention to getting a small fire going than watching her.

The circumstances were certainly in her favor. The Delaware were just as tired as she; at this point, she thought, they might not even bother to pursue her. If she gathered a small burst of energy and could get through the first line of dense trees, Maggie imagined it might be possible to outrun any Delaware who did decide to track her. Even with the weather so intense, if she used it as her cover, it just might work.

With most of the nearby woods waterlogged from the unrelenting storm, the Delaware finally succumbed to the impossibility of finding dry wood to start a fire. The fatigue must have been clouding their minds, because it had already occurred to Maggie that even if they had managed to get the fire going, keeping it lit would be far more of a challenge.

She was careful not to draw any attention to herself. With her captors no longer fixated on the fire, she would need to act fast if she wanted to escape. She slowly shuffled around to the far side of the tree, rubbing her cold arms to maintain some circulation. She hoped the Delaware might just think she was trying to keep out of the rain or finding a dry patch of ground.

Her heart was racing and her only thoughts were to run, keep running and not to look back. With a deep, steadying breath, she counted…one…two…

She never made it to three.

Thankfully, out of the corner of her eye she caught sight of the shadowy figures of the three returning Delaware. She calmed herself down and was grateful she hadn't run since they had a much better angle to run her down than the others.

She stood still and watched the six warriors talk with each other. At the end of their brief discussion, she was directed to get up and follow them. She was a bit surprised that they just left the canoes behind; they did not even bother to pull them into the woods or cover them for a possible later trip.

Maggie felt even worse than before. She knew she had lost a great opportunity to run. When she got up and felt the weight of her wet clothes, she imagined that she could not get any more soaked. The lost opportunity weakened her spirits and she could barely even take a step. Her already worn down moccasins added to her sore feet, but after catching herself from falling, Maggie fought through the pain.

As they moved farther into the woods, the thickness of the trees and patches of remaining leaves helped to provide a bit more protection from the storm. The trail was still wet and full of clinging mud, but being some-what sheltered made the trudging a little more bearable. As they slowly dragged themselves along the decent-sized trail, it was clear to her that the Delaware were in just as much discomfort as she was.

Despite her fatigue, disappointment and an unusual lack of focus on her part, Maggie had an odd feeling that she had been on this trail before. Tired as she was, her instincts proved to be spot on. As they pushed farther, Maggie realized that the Delaware had stumbled upon the same village where she had been left by her previous captor.

This was the place where she had lived in fear that Pontiac would return to take her back to his land to the west. It was the place where Fredrick had so kindly helped her to escape. With a sinking feeling she remembered that this was the same village where she had left the adopted white woman, Anne, unconscious and locked in an old storage hut.

Maggie slowed her pace, somehow thinking that she might be able to delay the inevitable. She suspected the village would not welcome her openly, especially Anne and her Delaware husband.

Overwhelming fatigue washed over Maggie, and she became too tired even to fear what might happen next. She followed her captors reluctantly into the small village and spent the first few moments looking around.

The storm had clearly taken its toll on the village. The icy rain had damaged most of the winter corn that was now a tattered mess of stalks and soaked corn husks. Maggie stayed back and let three of the Delaware walk ahead into the center of the deathly silent village square. Her first thought was how strange it was that no one was there to greet them, despite the torrential rain that showed no signs of letting up.

The eerie lack of noise around the village was what really struck Maggie as odd, and she finally realized that she had not heard the barks of one of the many wild dogs that were once everywhere. Even the birds that were always busy around the nearby woods were absent. It was like every living thing had deserted the village.

The three Delaware quickly fell back towards the others and Maggie could see that they were concerned about something. Once again, the warriors talked amongst themselves, pointing and gesturing as they spoke.

The once peaceful, thriving village now appeared to be abandoned. Although it was not out-of-the-ordinary for a tribe of Delaware to migrate south for the winter, a village of this size would normally still be inhabited by the elders and others who were needed to maintain the land through the winter.

Just as the warriors were deciding what they should do, the storm that had hit so suddenly now appeared to ease up. The sun struggled to extend a few sparse rays through the thick veil of clouds and mist that remained.

As the weather began to clear, Maggie caught a brief glimpse of a small figure leaning part way out of one of the house's half-rotted doors. Whoever it was seemed to be trying to catch a glimpse of the visitors.

Three of the warriors walked forward cautiously again until they reached the main fire pit that had long since been extinguished. They just stood and waited to be formally greeted by the villagers now that the storm was over. The door screeched the rest of the way open and all eyes lighted on a ragged-looking villager who remained in the shadows.

The Delaware seemed nervous and mesmerized by the reluctant villager, who in turn was clearly frightened by the arrival of the small party. Eventually, one of the warriors plucked up enough courage to walk towards the house to speak with the villager.

Maggie had been standing back watching the strange scene unfold and had begun to wonder if the warriors' confusion was enough of a distraction to allow her another opportunity to run. Before she could set her sights on the small trail Fredrick had used when he had taken her from this place a few months earlier, she suddenly thought she recognized the mysterious villager.

A brief ray of sunlight had cut through the shadows just before the dirty, ragged figure made a mad dash back into the house it had come from. Maggie waited as the same warrior forcefully pulled the person out of the house and towards the fire pit.

Pushing her way past the two other Delaware warriors who still cowered by the village's central fire pit, Maggie shouted, "Anne…?" She forgot that Anne's reaction to her return might be strong, and moved boldly towards the ragged villager to confirm her identity.

Maggie's Delaware escorts did nothing to stop her advance. They simply stood in place and watched.

"Anne, my God, is that you?" Maggie asked again.

The villager said nothing, barely raising her head to see who called out to her.

As Maggie moved closer, she got a much clearer view of the ratty-looking girl who appeared to be more like a wild animal. Her hair was knotted and very dirty, and her face was blackened by weeks of filth, as were her legs and arms. The clothes that she wore hung off her frail body as though they were several sizes too big. She reeked horribly; as soon as the Delaware got wind of her odor, they moved farther away, and refused to even touch her.

Maggie ignored the smell and reached out to this deathly thin figure. It was Anne, although she was now just a shell of the young Englishwoman Maggie had attempted to convince to escape with her all those months ago.

Her outstretched hand was guardedly accepted and Maggie gently guided Anne towards the fire pit and the rained-soaked tree trunks they used as seats. Motioning to one of the Delaware to find a blanket to comfort the poor girl, Maggie took a seat beside her.

"What happened here?" Maggie asked gently. Her Delaware captors stood around confused by her strange attraction to this filthy, ghostly villager.

When Anne made no reply, Maggie tried again; "Anne, do you remember me? It is me, Maggie. Can you speak?"

Maggie motioned to the remaining Delaware for someone to fetch water from the nearby stream and bring it for Anne. Surprisingly, one of them did so without a shred of hesitation. He immediately ran down to the stream and collected some water in one of the abandoned reed jugs scattered around in the mud and dirt. His fellow warriors did nothing but stare at the villager, curious but not willing to get too close.

When he returned with the small jug of cold water, Maggie offered the young warrior a brief appreciative smile and poured some of it on Anne's parched lips.

As she did her best to comfort the shivering and frightened young woman, Maggie noticed that the Delaware continued to stand nervously watching them. It was almost as if they were afraid to move or that they sensed a great spirit at work in the poor village. She called to them in English to urge them to look for any other survivors of whatever had happened here.

"Thank you, Maggie," Anne said slowly. Her voice was so soft that Maggie had to move closer for her to make sense of what she said.

Maggie took off the soaked piece of cloth she had around her neck and attempted to clean some of the caked dirt from Anne's face. She didn't want to press too hard, but the dried mud was very thick. If Maggie hadn't known it was Anne, the poor girl would have been next to unrecognizable. Even her once shiny blonde hair was so full of clumps of crusty mud that Maggie couldn't see much of her natural hair color.

"Can you try to speak some more, Anne?" Maggie continued gently. "We need to know what happened here."

She could see that Anne was starting to come around and relax ever so slightly. The water clearly helped and Maggie fervently wished that the piles of firewood around the village were dry enough to start a fire and add to Anne's comfort. Unfortunately, the warrior sent to find a blanket had no luck, so Maggie did her best to keep Anne warm by wrapping her arms around her.

She didn't want to press Anne, so she turned her attentions towards her captors while they were searching through the buildings for signs of any other villagers. She could see that two of them were out in the far cornfield, pushing aside the stalks with their musket barrels. Maggie could tell that these men were so concerned about what happened here that they were hesitant to walk around within the village.

"They started to die almost a month ago," Anne suddenly murmured, drawing Maggie's attention back to her.

"How did they die?" Maggie calmly asked. "Where are the rest of the villagers?"

Anne got to her feet and started to speak in a louder voice, "The elders were the first to die. It happened after our village was visited by a small group of French traders and one black-robed priest. A couple of them appeared to be ill, but nothing so bad as to result in this." Anne's voice was so much clearer now, as she did her best to fight off tears and stand on her weakened legs.

"Anne, please don't get upset," Maggie said as she stood and walked to her side, "I know this must be difficult."

"My husband died a week or so after that. He had only been sick for few days. It was like a dark cloud covered us and squeezed the life out of this place."

Maggie still had no idea what exactly had happened. There were no bodies. The village was still relatively intact, and most of their belonging still remained. The only thing missing was the rest of the inhabitants.

She thought that maybe most of the villagers had departed so quickly that they only took what they needed.

By this time, the Delaware warriors had returned and were speaking amongst each other again. They did little to hide their concern, and their faces displayed a fear that Maggie had never seen on these proud warriors before.

They were close enough that Maggie could hear them, so she asked Anne to translate, "What are they saying?"

"They are afraid and fear the village has some curse on it," Anne said, concentrating on making out what they were saying. "They are talking about burning it down and finding a safer place to sleep."

Maggie worried that they might decide to sacrifice Anne to appease their gods. They did not hide the fact they were very nervous and didn't want to be here.

"I wouldn't blame them if they torched this place," Anne said with quiet apprehension. "Something truly evil is present here; the villagers that were lucky enough to leave will never return."

"Why did you decide to stay?" Maggie simply asked.

"Most of the healthy people departed before my husband died, and I couldn't just leave him here to die alone. After he passed, no one left was healthy enough to leave. I had no place to go to. I spent most of my time burying the dead. In fact, the last of the bodies were buried just before you arrived." Anne's voice displayed little emotion as she pointed her thin hand towards the open field just beyond the tattered remains of the corn.

Seeing that she was tired, and not wanting to weaken her further, Maggie asked, "When did you eat last?"

She took the young woman by the hand and walked towards the home she thought Anne had shared with her husband.

"Maybe a week ago," Anne replied. "I really can't be sure. What food we had stored was taken by the others when they left."

Maggie knew that if Anne didn't get something in her empty stomach she could be the next to die. She tried to get the attention of her Delaware captives, but they were far too scared to move.

"Anne, call out to them to get you some food," Maggie suggested.

Anne did as she was told, but she was ignored as well.

"They are afraid of me and will not help," Anne said. "I expect they want me dead in hopes the evil spirits might just leave with me."

Maggie decided to take matters into her own hands, saying, "Do you have a musket I can use?"

Anne pointed to where she had once lived with her husband and spoke softly, "My husband has a good musket, but you will have to go in the house to get it…I can't go in there…"

Maggie guided Anne back to the fire pit and motioned to one of the Delaware to try to get a fire going. At first he didn't move, but once he saw the look on her face he did.

Maggie could tell that the warriors were really frightened because they had reached the point where they showed no concern for what she was doing or where she was wandering to. Without a reason to fear their objections, Maggie walked directly to Anne's home and slowly opened the dislodged front door. The first thing that hit her was the pungent smell that hung like a thick fog inside the small room. It was clear that Anne had not been inside since being forced to bury her husband.

Maggie couldn't imagine the pain of watching one's husband die. The sheer helplessness would be unbearable, and the overwhelming loneliness was something she prayed she would never experience. The image of Jacob dying in her arms and then being forced to bury him with her own hands made her eyes water as she searched quickly to locate the musket and get out of the house.

Thankfully, she found it leaning in the far corner, along with a small pouch and a powder horn. On her way out she spotted a bow and a full quiver of arrows which she quickly tossed over her back.

Without a thought for what her Delaware captives would think of her weaponry, Maggie ran over to Anne to check on her. A small fire was slowly trying to eke out some heat as the warriors remained busy gathering enough branches and small pieces of wood to keep it burning.

Maggie placed the musket beside Anne and tested the nicely-crafted bow's tautness. She even took the time to place one of the arrows on the string and pull back on it. It felt good in her hands and reminded her of hunting with Jacob in a much simpler time.

"Keep this musket by your side, just in case the Delaware decide to do something foolish," Maggie said. "It's loaded and ready to fire. I'm going to see what is around for food, but I should be back soon." With that, she ran towards the open cornfield.

As she expected, the Delaware merely watched as she ran into the field with the hand-made quiver on her back and the bow in her hand. A slight movement in front of her made her suddenly stop and crouch down.

Already having her bow drawn, Maggie spotted a large flock of wild turkeys sitting just by the far edge of the field. They were over a hundred feet away and she knew she needed to approach them cautiously. If they retreated into the woods, she would never be able to track them down.

The field was almost too open, but she did her best to work her way to within fifty feet, closing the distance with well-placed steps. Oddly, the earlier downpour that had hindered their movements had also provided the soaking wet ground that masked any noise she might have otherwise made. She could see that the gobblers were bobbing their heads up and down with every one of her steps, but they appeared to be oblivious to her presence.

Maggie still had the bow drawn and just as she moved into a good position, she heard a loud commotion over her left shoulder. One of the Delaware warriors had decided to join her and made enough noise to alert all the animals within a mile.

She turned her head just in time to see the turkeys begin to scatter. Remaining calm and understanding she only had one chance, Maggie set her sight on two large birds that were heading to one of the high upper branches. Slow flyers at best, the two wild birds struggled to take flight and with one quick release, Maggie drove the hickory stocked arrow deep into one of the turkey's breast. It immediately fell to the ground while its partner continued to move into the branches. Just as she was about to approach and retrieve her prize, an ear-piercing shot rang out from behind and she saw the other bird fall straight to the ground almost on top of her own twitching bird.

Without bothering to look back, Maggie ran to her turkey. After pulling out the arrow, she picked it up by the neck and was impressed by the size and weight of it. These turkeys had clearly begun to pack on extra weight to survive the coming winter. She guessed it must be a flock from the north that was just moving south to better ground and dryer, warmer weather.

The Delaware shooter walked past Maggie without looking at her. Once he reached his bird, it was clear that it was much smaller than Maggie's, most likely a hen. She did her best not to gloat as she watched the frustrated warrior move closer to the edge of the woods, apparently searching for a better prize.

Satisfied her bird would provide more than enough meat to feed both her and Anne, Maggie tossed the nicely crafted bow over her shoulder and walked proudly back into the village.

The rest of the Delaware remained in a group, watching her but saying nothing. Surprised that they didn't confiscate her bow, Maggie was happy they just left her alone with Anne.

Maggie held up the large wild turkey and smiled when she saw the girl's eyes light up. "This should fill your stomach, Anne," she boasted, knowing that her captors' eyes were all on her trophy.

It wasn't long before her hunting escort returned with his measly bird. Although Maggie couldn't understand their words, it was clear that the warrior was being ridiculed for the poor rewards of his effort.

Maggie handed the turkey over to Anne who immediately worked on pulling the mass of feathers off. She had obviously done this many times before, and Maggie warmed her fingers over the fire as she watched Anne methodically remove the layers of feathers and carefully set them to one side.

"Maggie, there should be something near my house to hang this over the fire," Anne directed her, clearly energized by the thought of finally having a meal.

Maggie did as she was told and quickly returned with a couple of thick branches that each had a natural 'v' shape at the top. She drove the branches in the ground and Anne suggested using an arrow as a spit to pierce through the bird. In no time, they had the turkey roasting over the fire pit. It was much smaller with the feathers removed, but it would still have more than enough juicy meat to keep both of them fed for a couple days.

The meat had already started to cook up and the greasy skin dripped streams of juice into the fire. The snap of the fire and the wonderful aroma appeared to relax Anne as she finally got some color back to her still dirty face.

Maggie had been so transfixed with the roasting bird she had failed to notice that the sun was already beginning to set. The sky was still a haze of thick clouds that hid the moon from view, causing the darkness to spread quickly across the village.

The darkening sky made the village seem even more frightening, so it was no surprise to Maggie that the Delaware had chosen to remain on the outermost boundary. Thankfully, their more in depth search of the village had turned up some blankets, of which they gave one to the women to share.

When their turkey was finished over the fire, Maggie and Anne excitedly pulled large chunks off to eat. They noticed that they had become interesting to the Delaware who had ignored them for the most part. The warriors had set up another fire pit to cook their smaller bird, but it had not provided much meat to be shared among all of them.

"You should take some of our meat over to them," Anne suggested as she pulled another juicy piece from the well-roasted bird, "they would appreciate such a gesture."

"Why would I share my food with them when they cared little for my stomach?" Maggie shot back, "They deserve to feel the pain of hunger."

"Do what you think is best, but..." Anne tried to continue, only to be stopped by Maggie.

Tired of being a prisoner and how she was ill-treated by the Delaware, Maggie didn't give Anne a chance to justify their actions, "If it wasn't for rotted berries and a couple tiny crayfish, they would have not even bothered to feed me, so why should I feed them and take food from my own mouth? I want them weak and hungry; it will finally give me the advantage."

"Am I to assume you will be escaping in much the same fashion as before?" Anne asked, finally touching on the subject of Maggie's actions before she left with Fredrick.

"I did what I had to do and, honestly, how has your life turned out?" Maggie shot back, not thinking about the coldness of her statement.

Instead of replying, Anne just looked around the shadows of the once vibrant village and began to weep.

Maggie felt guilty for upsetting the already distraught girl and offered, "Once the Delaware fall asleep, I am leaving. This time I am taking you no matter what you say."

Anne made no reply.

Maggie took the rest of the bird off the arrow, which she placed back over the fire. She then pulled some more thin pieces of white meat off the turkey and hung them over the fire to dry. When she was done, she took the arrow-pierced remains of the bird over to the Delaware to finish off.

They accepted her gift and handed her a cloth with some winter berries and a small sack of water. Without a word, she took their offerings, walked back to Anne and sat down.

"They appreciated your kindness and the small offer of their food meant they recognize that you are a good hunter," Anne briefly explained.

"I care nothing for their gestures or recognitions. Their kindness has already been over-shadowed by their savage treatment of my friends and neighbors." Maggie would accept no explanation that made them out to be civilized.

"Once they fall asleep, we will leave," Maggie continued. "They probably won't bother with a guard overnight; besides, with this musket and bow, we have little to fear from them."

Anne looked at her, but gave her no verbal approval or any indication she might indeed leave with her.

Shortly after the Delaware devoured the leftover meat, they simply huddled on the blankets and fell asleep. As she had predicted, they neither set up a guard nor bothered to disarm Maggie.

Anne too was fast asleep before Maggie could continue their conversation. The air was not as cold as the previous nights and, with the fire, it was strangely comfortable. Maggie found it difficult to keep her own tired eyes open and thought it wouldn't hurt to get a little rest before making her escape.

She knew that any escape attempt was still foolhardy even now that she had some weapons to defend herself and hunt with, but Maggie felt this was the best time to run. Anne's condition gave her some concern, but she could not leave the young woman behind. She was unsure if the Delaware would keep Anne with them or just kill her.

As her eyes opened, the early sunrise blurred her vision and Maggie knew she had missed yet another opportunity. Her fatigue had gotten the better of her and she had slept right through the night.

When her vision cleared, Maggie looked around and noticed that some of the Delaware were already up. As she got to her feet, she realized that something was wrong. Two of the warriors seemed to be frozen with fear as they looked down at three of their fellows, still apparently sleeping in their blankets.

Maggie looked at Anne who was just getting herself up as well. "Anne, what do you think is happening with the Delaware?" she asked. "They seem shaken by something."

Anne got to her knees and tried to hear what was being said between the Delaware.

After a few minutes, Anne said, "Their friends appear to be sick. The one mentioned that they have been sweating and shaking uncontrollably."

From the look on Anne's face, Maggie already knew the answer, but she asked, "Is it what your people had?"

"I'd have to see them close up before I could say," she replied. "But if it is, your plans for escape will be far easier soon enough." With that she walked towards the warriors.

Maggie stayed back and watched as the Delaware stepped aside so Anne could see for herself what might be wrong with their comrades. She could hear Anne conversing with them; once she had taken a good look at them, she returned to Maggie.

"I told them to give them water and let them rest," Anne explained as she sat by the fire and slowly rocked back and forth. "I fear they will be dead by the day's end, and I think the two others will soon meet the same fate. One of the others already has the marks on his face; he will most likely be dead by tomorrow's light."

There was no sign of the sixth warrior, and the two women looked around to locate him.

"He might have already died," Anne explained. "Maybe they have taken him into the field to bury him later. They must be frightened by how fast this has killed their friend."

Maggie knew that this was the same thing that killed Anne's husband and infected most of the villagers. "Can we do anything for them?" she asked quietly.

"No," Anne whispered. "They will all soon start to get little bumps all over them and will start to empty their stomachs of what they enjoyed last night. It will continue until they have nothing more to give. Then they will heat up and hopefully die before they suffer too much. It would be best to let them be and keep our distance." Anne kept rocking and began muttering something in her adopted tongue.

It was a bittersweet situation for Maggie. She would have to witness the suffering decline of her once strong captors, but soon she would be free once more.

"How did this happen?" Maggie asked curiously. "Why did you not catch this illness?"

"I have heard of entire villages suffering the same illness. Your people call it 'the pox', but we have no name for it. The Delaware think it is some black spirit that is sent to punish us, maybe for dealing with the French priest."

Maggie had heard about the pox infecting white people as well, but not to the same fatal effect it seemed to have on the Indians. She had heard that the Indians could not fight it off because of their inferior builds.

Anne continued to speak in both English and Delaware, making no sense to Maggie who did her best not to look towards the dying warriors.

"I think it was the blankets they used last night," Anne stuttered between bouts of incoherent grunts and whimpers.

Maggie gave no reply and began to plan what she needed to do next. If possible, she hoped she might be able to leave before she would be forced to sit back and watch them all die. There would be a point when they would all be far too weak to do much and then she could just leave them.

She had a rough idea of where she was and the distance it was between the village and the burned-out remains of Jacob's fort, but Maggie wasn't certain if she should move south or continue to move north in hopes of reaching the English-friendly village she and One-Ear had visited. She also felt certain that as long as Jacob was alive and free, he was tracking her. She just wished she had some idea of where he might be.

Anne was right. The symptoms of the merciless disease rapidly attacked the already weakened bodies of the Delaware. Maggie could hear their desperate moans and the convulsive reactions that jerked their bodies.

Maggie stayed back, but Anne was quick to keep the Delaware as comfortable as possible by providing them water and keeping cold cloths on their heads. By mid-afternoon, one of the three sick warriors was already dead and two others were now near death as well. The two remaining did their best to comfort their dying friends, but it was clear to the women that they would soon succumb to the same disease.

Anne returned to sit with Maggie. She looked tired and frustrated because she could do nothing more to ease their pain.

"I think it is time to leave, Anne," Maggie said in a firm voice that would brook no argument. "If we go now, we can move north towards the lake. I know of a small cabin that might be able to keep us safe for the winter. Do whatever you still need to do for them then gather up what you feel you can carry. We leave in ten minutes."

When Anne didn't respond, Maggie added, "If we wait longer, the winter snows might keep us here and force us to live amongst all this death for the next several months." She looked into the north sky and prayed that it would just give them time to get away from this place.

Chapter | **Four**

Hold your fire, men!" Jacob screamed loudly. "Hold your fire!"

Even as he prayed that he had given his men enough time to react to the change in plans, Jacob ran to the middle of the trail to stop a possible disaster. Thankfully, all the men held their fire and could now see that it was Joshua, James and the remains of the scouting party; they were running up the trail at full speed.

Jacob screamed again, "Joshua, stop…"

Joshua kept running all out with James right on his heels and called out, "Get yourselves back into the woods, the French are right on our backs!"

Motioning the scouts into the woods to his right, Jacob pulled both Joshua and James behind the rock he had used to keep himself out of sight. Realizing there really wasn't time for an explanation, he simply asked, "What did you two get yourselves into?"

Joshua knelt down to catch his breath and peer around the rock to see if the French were near. "We just ran into them," he said. "They were marching up the trail and walked right into our two forward scouts. We held our ground until we could get organized, but there were too many of them. We decided to retreat to better ground; they have been chasing us for almost three miles."

Calling up to the two men still posted to the upper trail, Jacob said, "Keep your eyes peeled for the French and give us fair warning when they come into sight." The men nodded and returned their focus to the lower trail.

Finally catching his breath, Joshua added, "One last thing, they have prisoners with them. Not sure if they are part of ours, but I did see a couple of women and children."

This news complicated everything.

Could Maggie be with them? Were the French foolish enough to just charge head long into a possible ambush? Were there Indians amongst their ranks? If there were, Jacob had to be concerned that they might flank his position and take them from behind.

There was no time to think through all the possible scenarios.

"Here they are, sir!" one of the men shouted from overhead. "I'm not sure how many, but they are running like the devil."

"Do you see any prisoners with them?" Jacob immediately asked.

After taking another look, the scout called back, "No, sir, I suspect they might be well behind the main party."

"I want one of them alive, preferably one of their officers," Jacob called out, but he was unsure if any of his men heard him over all the noise of the onrushing enemy.

Before Jacob could calm his men or repeat his orders, the first wave of French ran blindly into a wall of gunfire from both sides of the trail. The volley did so much damage to the forward men that the French in the rear stopped in their tracks and immediately dropped their muskets.

Another call from above the ridge, "They are stopping, sir, and surrendering," made Jacob step out onto the trail to get a better look. While he slowly walked ahead, some of his men pounced down from the woods onto those French soldiers who were so unfortunate as to still be alive after the murderous volley.

One of the men shouted at Jacob before he got too far down the trail, "Sir, I have one of their officers. He is in bad shape, but he can still speak."

Jacob rushed over, but before he introduced himself to the severely injured Frenchman, he called to the men facing him, "Joshua, take these men down the trail and bring the captured French soldiers to me. Set up pickets on both ends of the trail, just in case there are savages lurking in the woods."

Joshua nodded and asked, "What about the English prisoners?"

"Bring the prisoners here then take some men to search the upper trail," Jacob replied.

When Joshua walked away, Jacob leaned down to see how the badly injured officer was doing. "Bonjour, sir, what is your name?" Jacob greeted the officer as kindly as the circumstance dictated.

Swallowing deeply, the officer spoke in English, "My name is Chabot."

Their conversation was cut short by Joshua's quick return.

"Sir," he said breathlessly, "there were only two French soldiers left, and we can't find the English prisoners."

"As I asked earlier, take some men and search the trail. Don't get too far; I don't want you to get separated from us just in case there are more of them out there." Jacob motioned for James to go with Joshua.

Returning his attention to Chabot, Jacob realized that the man had a fist-sized, gaping hole in his side that was bleeding uncontrollably. "My apologies for the interruption, sir, but we are afraid there might be more of your men lurking in the woods."

"I can assure you that you have all of my men," Chabot replied, shifting his body to get as comfortable as possible. "Most of our Indian escorts have departed our company."

Jacob looked ahead to try to hear any noise from his advanced scouts. "What do you see, lads?" he shouted up to his two lookouts.

"We can see the young lads and the rest of our men, but no sign of the French or the damn Delaware around," one of the men shouted down.

"Good, I expect the search party back shortly," Jacob replied before turning his attention back to Chabot whose breath was barely steady anymore.

"As for you, monsieur," Jacob continued urgently, "I can't do much about your wound. Nonetheless, I need some answers. What of the English prisoners you reportedly have?"

"They are in good order, just north of this place," Chabot forced out in a faint voice as he quickly began to fade. "I asked them to wait for us to come back for them and they did as we asked. You can find them about a mile back, near a hill. They are in the boulders just off the trail."

Seeing he had little time to waste, Jacob pressed for more details from the dying officer, "What do you know of a Maggie Murray that was taken with some of your captives? Is she still with them?" Jacob wasn't really sure if he wanted the answer.

"Maggie…she was the strong one…the Delaware kept her despite my pleas to keep her with me," Chabot did his best to speak clearly, but he was quickly declining and his eyes remained shut with the effort of speaking. "I fear she will be taken to Niagara. The Delaware saw great value in her…"

Jacob started to ask one last question, but Chabot's body gave a final jerk and his head tipped backwards. A ghastly breath spat out, but no inhale followed.

Chabot was dead.

Before Jacob could think, Joshua had sent back one of the men to report that they had found a group of English prisoners near a hill. They were in relatively good health, but were in desperate need of some food and water.

Jacob stood up and looked at the small clump of dead French soldiers. His men had picked their bodies clean of anything that was of value or could be used to aid in their trek.

As they had no time to properly bury the dead, he ordered a few of the men to drag the bodies off the trail into the cover of the woods. Not only did Jacob not want the prisoners to be upset by the sight, but he did not want any migrating Delaware or Seneca to know that they were moving northward.

Anxious to speak with the freed prisoners, Jacob ran ahead of his men to be the first to greet them. He told his two lookouts to remain on watch and also increased his rear guard by five, telling them to get word to him if there were any signs of the enemy.

His heart pounded with the thought of speaking with people who had just seen her, but he also feared that the news would not be good. If the Delaware had decided to keep Maggie and were taking her to Niagara, the time he just spent at this insignificant place might have meant he lost her forever.

If she reached the French fort, how could he get her back? It was most likely that she would soon be shipped by the lakes to Quebec and sold into slavery.

Shaking the image from his mind, Jacob ran as fast as he could towards a place on the trail where he could see Joshua standing with James.

"Lads, where are the captives?" Jacob called out, doing his best to mask the fear in his voice.

The two turned to greet Jacob, but from the look on their faces he could immediately see that the news was not good. Reaching them and taking a quick look around the area, Jacob didn't wait for them to explain as he rushed up the hill to check on the captives.

Joshua and James followed him. As soon as he made it to the secured area where the freed captives were huddled, Jacob got the confirmation he so desperately didn't want.

"She is not with them," Joshua said before Jacob could say anything. "A couple of them explained that she was taken by the Delaware north towards the great lake."

Unable to tell them that he already knew of her fate, Jacob stayed silent so he wouldn't display the true emotions that were overtaking him.

"Sir, you should come over here, there is someone you might want to speak with," Joshua spoke up.

James, as usual, said nothing and just followed the two of them.

"We captured this one guarding the captives," Joshua continued as they reached a tall tree where a young French private was sitting with one of the scouts guarding him. "He didn't put up much of a fight and has been very co-operative."

Rising to his feet as soon as he saw Jacob approach, the clearly terrified private offered a feeble salute.

Jacob greeted him with a returned half salute and said, "Bonjour, monsieur, can you speak English?"

The man nodded a confirmation that he could, and Jacob motioned for the private to walk with him alone.

"Joshua," Jacob said as he moved away, "please make sure the women and children are in good order and see if they need some water. I want to speak with this one alone."

Walking up the small hill until they reached a landing that opened up to a peaceful panoramic view of the lower valley, Jacob asked, "What is your name, lad?"

Jacob could see that the Frenchman could have been no older than eighteen and was finding it difficult not to cry, let alone speak. Softly, Jacob reassured the boy saying, "Don't be frightened; I have no plan to kill you or hurt you in any way. I am Captain Sims, and I just want to ask you a few questions." Jacob stumbled over his assumed name, but waited patiently for the boy to speak.

The young man appeared to believe Jacob and after he calmed himself, he responded, "My name is Henri, Henri Lessard."

"Well, Monsieur Lessard, as I said you have no reason to be afraid; I will not hurt you. I just wanted to get some privacy with you to ask about a woman that was part of the original group of prisoners from the fort but is not with them now. Her name is Maggie and I was told by one of your officers that she was taken to the fort at Niagara."

"Yes, I do know her," Lessard answered immediately. "She was a very strong woman who stood up to the Delaware. They took her after the officers negotiated to keep the others."

Trying to keep his emotions in check, Jacob attempted to change the topic. "Tell me, how did you learn to speak English so well?"

"One of my family's servants was English and she taught me and my sisters how to speak it," Lessard explained, noticeably relaxing after Jacob showed no signs of hurting him.

"Do you mean an English slave that your father purchased?" Jacob snapped, immediately changing his tone.

"I don't know, sir," Lessard offered, taken aback by Jacob's sudden change.

Returning to why he originally wanted to speak with this young French soldier, Jacob refocused and asked for some further details. "Do you know for sure where the Delaware planned on taking Maggie?"

"What some of the others were saying was that they planned on taking her to the fort at Niagara. I can't be certain though; the savages can change their minds like the wind. I think they planned on selling her to one of the officers garrisoned there."

Jacob just looked over the sea of snow-capped trees, mixed with browns and the dark greens of the numerous pines that seemed to overtake the landscape and create massive canopy that stretched as far as a man could see. He thought to himself how he could never tire of such a sight despite how this territory could easily kill the best and experienced trapper or hunter. It was breathtaking all the same, and he still dreamed of the day he might be able to enjoy it once more with his Maggie and their children.

"Sir, what happened to the rest of my unit?" Lessard broke the uncomfortable silence.

"I am sorry to be the one to tell you this, but they are all dead," Jacob said in a cold voice. "They ran into my men just over the pass a mile south of here."

After a quick pause, Jacob decided to change the topic once again before the young man asked for more details. "Can you take us to the last place you saw the Delaware and Maggie?" he asked.

"I think I can, sir," Lessard replied.

"Good, now let's get back so we can get moving," Jacob said, letting the young French soldier lead the way back down the slight decline.

Just as he started his way down, Lessard asked, "Sir, may I ask who this Maggie is to you?"

"She is my wife," Jacob replied calmly and directed Lessard to continue down the hill.

Joshua and James were waiting on the trail with the captives after moving them all from the hill. Jacob greeted the newly freed settlers and could see how relieved they were to have escaped the clutches of the Delaware. Jacob could see some familiar faces, but most of them must have arrived at the fort after he had left for Kittanning.

Joshua reported that there were fifteen settlers. They consisted of seven women of various ages and eight girls. They were all in good health considering their ordeal.

"I did ask where the men and boys were," Joshua told Jacob quietly, "and they explained that the Delaware took them away. They had heard some of the men being tortured and assumed the boys were taken to some of the nearby villages, but they were not certain."

Jacob was not certain what to do with the newly freed women. He offered them a pleasant smile and led them back to the rest of his waiting men.

The smell of death was all around as some of the women shielded the younger ones from the gruesome sight of the dead French soldiers thrown on either side of the trail. Jacob ordered his men to escort them past the carnage and closer to the boulders that formed the ridge they used to monitor the lower trail.

Jacob walked with the young French prisoner and just as they reached the place of the ambush, Jacob said, "You might want to keep your eyes forward; we had no time to properly bury your friends and decided to leave them for the animals."

The honesty of Jacob's tone was well-intended, and Lessard did as he suggested. He showed no emotion, except for wincing at the horrid smell as he walked past the bodies of his friends.

Assigning one of the men to watch over the prisoner, Jacob asked Joshua and James to walk with him up to the lookout spot where he still had two men stationed.

"What should we do with the settlers?" he asked. "They will have a tough time without their husbands through the winter months and I am not sure where the best place to take them is. We certainly can't drag them north with us. We will need to move quickly and can't be slowed by them."

Once again, James had nothing to offer, so Joshua said, "The best choices would be to take them either east over the mountains or to Fort Cumberland. Of course, passing over the mountains this time of year would be dangerous. Once the women were at one of the forts, they could figure out for themselves what they want to do. The small garrison at either fort would probably enjoy the company of the women."

Jacob took off his hat and rubbed his face, thinking what other option they might have.

"You're right, Joshua, the best place would be Fort Cumberland, but I can't just send them with a small handful of men as their escort," Jacob said reluctantly. He knew what he would have to do, but it would mean weakening his own numbers further. "We will have to split up our unit and send maybe ten men to ensure they make it safely. This is French-held territory and we need to make sure they are escorted by men who know the area well."

His options were limited. He couldn't take them with him, but if he waited much longer, the winter would snow them all in and they would all starve to death. Added to that was the reason most of these men followed Jacob was to find the captured settlers and free them from the clutches of the French and the Delaware.

Now that they had accomplished the majority of their goal, Jacob wasn't certain if the men would decide to head back to their homes or stay to help him find his Maggie.

"Joshua, please ask the men for volunteers to go south to Fort Cumberland," Jacob said. "I pray some of the men will still want to continue on until we find Maggie, but please ask them their thoughts and let me know. Make it clear that no man will be looked upon by me in a bad way if he decides to head south. Just be sure to save some of the best scouts for our party if you can!"

Joshua immediately went back to the men and within minutes he had the men split into two parties. One would stay with Jacob and continue north while the other would take the settlers to Fort Cumberland.

"I spoke with the men and they all wanted to continue on with you," Joshua reported happily. "Most of the men that will be accompanying the settlers south have families and I thought it might be good for them to head home and check on them. We have a fine group left to track down Miss Maggie and they are eager to move out."

Jacob looked over the men and assigned a Mr. Wilkens to lead the party south. He knew Wilkens had settled near Fort Cumberland and should know the area well. He briefly went over the details of the journey and reminded him to keep a strong advanced guard. He also reminded him that the young children would not be able to cover as much distance as the men were used to, and thusly to adjust his route accordingly.

Wilkens' party had seven men, a little under what Jacob had suggested. Jacob was happy with the men he had under him and despite thinking he should order some more of them to go with Wilkens, he was assured the numbers were sufficient to get the settlers safely to Fort Cumberland.

"I will have the lads put a couple of sleds together," Mr. Wilkens suggested. "The young ones will enjoy the ride and maybe we will be able to cover a little more ground than expected."

"Make sure you send back word after you have reached the fort," Jacob offered, grabbing Wilkens' hand and giving it a strong shake. "My hope is that you might just run into Mr. Sinclair and his men."

The two parties reluctantly separated and headed in opposite directions. Before they left, all the women and the children gave Jacob and the others hugs and kisses in gratitude for freeing them from the French. A loud cheer could be heard as Jacob lead the way north. A smile came to his face, although he was still deeply saddened by the fact Maggie wasn't among the settlers. He was satisfied that he had helped them escape a potential lifetime of slavery. He was particularly proud that the children would have an opportunity to be with their own people and not end up like his own children.

Jacob still didn't appreciate what the Delaware had done for James. James had told Jacob they taught him to fish, hunt and survive in the harsh wilderness but in his mind the boy had already experienced those things with him. Joshua had explained that the typical Indian village seemed far kinder than the stricter European culture, especially for a child. Even so, Jacob could not grasp why a white boy would prefer to be raised by savages.

Most of the good daylight had been used in organizing the two parties, and as they looked north, they saw heavy rain clouds forming. Jacob was told by one of the men who had some knowledge of such sights that it meant a pretty nasty storm would be heading towards them.

Jacob simply wanted to get away from the site of the ambush, particularly the putrid smell of rotting bodies that was getting much worse with every passing minute. Despite the threat of a bad storm ahead and the darkening skies, Jacob gave the order to move out.

He had informed the men that they would push on through the darkness until they found a good place to rest. Revitalized by the heartfelt appreciation shown by the settlers, the men navigated the dark, cold trail without complaint.

Jacob stayed with the French prisoner and allowed the young man to lead them towards the last place Maggie had been seen. Thankfully, the trail was relatively easy to traverse and the Frenchman appeared to have some knowledge of it. Little was said as the tired men pressed on and continued to follow Jacob.

The reassurance he had felt from the men when Joshua told him they had all wanted to stay with him had given Jacob a great deal of hope in the success of their mission. He had a difficult time holding back his tears when Joshua had first told him. He owed these men a debt of gratitude.

Jacob was particularly proud of Joshua's work and was impressed by the quality of the men he had picked to stay with them. Most of the men were single, young and experienced woodsmen. There were roughly twenty-two;

among them, Jacob noticed the Shaw brothers, Mathew Williams, Jed Larson and young Aaron Stark. The latter was as big as Jacob, despite being only around sixteen, and could fight and shoot like a man twice his age. Jacob was happy to have such a strong unit and knew they would be able to handle the rough-going expected from here on in.

A mixture of rain and snow began slowly partway through the night. Once it got started, though, it pounded them mercilessly. Added to the snow were bone-chilling ice pellets that were big enough to leave a fair-sized welt on any uncovered skin.

The trail quickly became a muddy, slippery mess and Jacob knew they had to get themselves some cover to ride out the storm. He asked Lessard if he knew of any place they could stop for some shelter, but he could not think of any such place.

Jacob decided to send the Shaw brothers ahead to scout out a place that might give them relief from the weather. He halted the rest of the men and told them to try to get some cover under the trees to at least give them a reprieve from the pounding weather.

"Do what you can to keep your powder dry and try to find some decent cover," Jacob said and looked for a good spot for himself. He, like most of the men, had covered the lock of his musket with a thick piece of cow hide to keep it relatively dry. Nevertheless, such an amount of heavy rain soon soaked the hide and threatened to ruin the valuable powder that was their main means to defend themselves. More importantly, the powder gave them a means to hunt and eat.

Thankfully, the high canopy and the fact they were deep enough into the woods, provided them some reasonably good places to shroud them from the rain and ice. Jacob remained with the Frenchman under a massive hemlock tree and they were soon joined by Joshua and James.

The rain pushed through the tangle of branches and what leaves were left on the higher reaches of the trees, mercilessly pelting the desperate men who did their best to stay dry and warm.

Even starting a fire to give the men some comfort was next to impossible in these conditions. The only solace that Jacob and his men could take from the situation was that the Delaware would be forced to experience the same storm, if they hadn't done so already. They too would have been slowed by it; even if the Delaware had taken to the water, Jacob knew that they would have been forced to beach their canoes and get to land for some cover. He thought this might be the opportunity he needed to make up some time and distance between them.

The deafening noise of the rain, made it difficult to even speak to one another. Jacob got as close to Joshua as he could and said, "Do you think we should keep pressing on? We have to assume the Delaware are in the same mess and they most likely have found themselves some place to hide. If we continue on, we might be able to close in on them."

Jacob could see that Joshua did not like the idea of traveling in such conditions, especially at night.

"You should talk to the Frenchman and see how close we are to the place the Delaware took Maggie," Joshua suggested. "We are still uncertain what direction they are heading. If we blindly march on, we might actually get ourselves lost."

Jacob reluctantly agreed and moved his mouth closer to the Frenchman's ear in order to be heard when he asked, "How close are we to the place the Delaware took my wife? Can we make it there tonight?"

The Frenchman looked at Jacob like he was insane, "Monsieur," he shouted into Jacob's ear, "I can't even see my own hand when I hold it in front of my face; how can I know how far this place is from here?"

Tired and unsure what he should do, Jacob was losing his patience. "Look around," he shouted back. "There must be something that might shake your memory."

The Frenchman did so, only to once again state that he had no idea where they were.

Jacob gave up on his idea to continue on, turning his attention back to the weather and where the Shaw brothers might be. Caring little for the pouring rain that continued to drench all of them, Jacob took a walk up the trail to see if there was any sign of the two brothers.

The Shaw boys were from the Virginia territory and Jacob had thought they were twins until he learned that Ezekiel was two years older than Daniel. They had both fought with a unit from the Virginia militia at Braddock's disaster in the wilderness, and since they had lost both their parents, they joined up with Jacob's company and assisted in constructing the fort.

Jacob only had to walk a few long, wet paces up the muddy trail before he spotted the blurry figures of two men walking with their heads down.

He called out to the still unidentified men, "Are you the Shaw brothers?" Not sure if they could even hear him through the noise of the pelting rain, Jacob called out once again.

No reply was given and they still continued forward, unaware that Jacob was standing directly in their path.

Waiting until they were almost ten feet in front of him, Jacob called out as loud as he could, "Stop and identify yourselves."

His voice was now heard, but obviously not recognized as the two men shouldered their muskets and ran to opposite sides of the trail to instinctively take cover.

Not wanting any accidental shootings, Jacob called out once again to the brothers, "Stand down, boys; it's Captain Sims."

Upon hearing the familiar voice, the brothers immediately walked out from the woods and Daniel called out, "Sorry, sir, you startled us! This damn rain makes it next to impossible to see or hear a thing."

"No harm done, boys, just making sure you were not some French advance guard out searching for their mates," Jacob explained, greeting the two men as the rain continued to soak them.

Motioning to them to pull off into the woods, Jacob looked out at the terrible condition of the trail and asked them how their scouting went. "Did you find anything we could use to get out of this hell?"

"We went almost two miles up trail," Ezekiel began, taking his hat off and shaking as much of the rain off it as he could, "but the bloody rain forced us back. The upper trail is no better than a river and we went as far as we could. We did find a nice cluster of boulders and a couple of small caves that might be good enough to get out of this mess."

"Sounds promising," Jacob responded. "Daniel, would you be kind enough to run back and get the others while your brother and I make our way up towards the site?" He watched as Daniel sprinted down the trail, kicking up a steady spray of water with every step he took.

They turned and walked briskly north until they hit a sharp elbow in the trail. Just as Jacob was about to take the blind corner, Ezekiel pointed up and guided Jacob to a far-better-than-expected spot that was nestled well into the woods with a nice view of the trail from above.

"Great spot, lad!" Jacob beamed. "You were far too modest in your description of this place." Jacob walked around the large boulders until he came to two massive caves that could easily accommodate all the men comfortably.

It appeared the rain was beginning to weaken, but even with the cold chill in the air, the thought of a relatively dry night made their predicament a bit more bearable. Regardless of the intense rainfall, Jacob and Ezekiel managed to gather enough dry kindling from the lower branches of a clump of nearby trees to get two small fires going just outside of the two caves. Once the fires were lit and growing stronger, the two carefully placed a couple of larger damp pieces on the fires to see how they would catch.

By the time the rest of the soggy, cold men began to arrive, the two fires were roaring and sending thick plumes of smoke into the dark, clearing sky.

"Nice spot, Ezekiel!" Joshua shouted out as he made it up the short, narrow side path. "I am not sure we should ever leave this place!"

While they were waiting, Ezekiel had pulled out some old debris from inside the two caves and brushed out as many of the spiders and other small creatures that might be attracted to the men as he could. Jacob thought it would be a superior place for the men to get themselves refreshed and dried out.

The two caves were conveniently linked by a large crack in the adjacent wall that was big enough for the men to pass through. The men divided themselves up and appeared to appreciate the space they had to relax.

Not much was said as they all filed into the natural, fort-like spot. Most of them immediately stripped off their wet clothes and hung them on whatever nearby branches they could find. They all took their turns to spread their shirts near the fires to get them partially dry and comfortable enough to wear again. Like most woodsmen, they traveled light. Extra clothing was considered a luxury, something that could be scavenged off a dead Frenchman or, worse, a killed mate.

Jacob was surprised by the mood around the camp. The men had experienced such storms before and appeared to be taking it all in stride. The fires helped ease the coldness in the air, and the fact the rain had all but stopped certainly turned the men around.

They shared what little food they had packed. Once they all ate something, most of the men picked their spots to rest. Jacob decided to take first picket duty as usual and assigned two others to watch from above and to keep the fires going.

Every so often, the wind shifted and pushed a plume of smoke from the fires back into the caves. Despite the inconvenience, once the smoke dissipated, the men just went back to sleep.

Jacob had the Frenchman with him, preferring to keep him away from the men. He took a spot on one of the larger boulders and, once he had wiped off most of the mud and dried it with his hand the best he could, took a seat and pulled the Frenchman up with him. The two sat for a moment, enjoying the darkness and the numerous calls of the owls that serenaded the men to sleep.

"Monsieur," Lessard said, breaking the silence of the night, "we are not far from the spot you asked me to take you to. What will you need from me once we are there? I suspect my usefulness will be limited after that."

"I'm not sure what we will do with you," Jacob replied, uninterested in making any promises he thought he might not be able to honor. "You might still be handy to have around. Most of us have never been this far north, but I do know we are close to your fort and outpost; we do not want to run into any patrols from either one."

Lessard said nothing and looked off towards the northern sky.

"My plan is for you to help us get near the great lake," Jacob said. "Then I can promise you that you will be free to make your way to one of your outposts. I have no intentions of harming you, if you cooperate and help me."

Neither of them spoke another word and Jacob returned to watching the lower trail, praying for a quiet night.

Chapter | **Five**

Maggie struggled to recall the route she and Fredrick had taken the previous year. It felt like a lifetime ago, and the wilderness began to look alike, especially during the bleak transition between autumn and early winter.

She knew that they had escaped north, but this was not the time of year to make mistakes. A wrong turn or poor judgment could result in a long, drawn out death.

Surviving the Huron, Delaware and French, Maggie had no desire to die so far from her home.

Unwilling to stay at the dying village any longer, she had gathered up the muskets that were now useless to her former captors and tossed them as far as she could into the woods. She did keep one, just in case Anne gathered enough strength to carry it. It also had some trade value in case such an occasion arose.

Maggie was concerned by Anne and her weakened state. Now that her stomach was full, she hoped the young woman could keep up.

She also let Anne make sure the remaining Delaware had some water to make their last few hours of life as comfortable as possible.

Understanding they had to get moving, Maggie pulled Anne by the arm and directed her to the trail. Once they were deep into the forest, Anne appeared to accept her fate; she even seemed relieved that she was leaving the home that she had grown to love. It was filled with memories of death for her; without a husband or family to keep her there, Anne knew leaving was her only option.

The two said little as they pushed ahead. Once Maggie got her bearings, she was confident they were heading in the right direction. Anne was weighed down by her musket and initially struggled until she got used to the added weight on her back.

Anne was the first to break the silence between them and simply said, "Thank you for taking me."

Maggie had barely been able to hear her, but replied, "I still wasn't certain you wanted to leave, especially after the last time we had this opportunity."

"I have nothing to keep me there any longer," Anne said frankly.

Not knowing how to reply, Maggie just kept moving and did her best to avoid the massive pools of water that had accumulated all along the trail during the heavy storms. Her feet were still wet from the earlier rains, and her moccasins were noticeably heavier with every step.

Before long, Maggie was forced to stop to attempt to squeeze the water out of her moccasins. Anne stopped her before she removed the first one and handed her a newly-made pair from her pack. They were so soft and dry that Maggie felt guilty even thinking about getting them wet, but they made her sore, wet feet feel much better.

"Thank you, Anne, where did you get these?" she asked as she finished tying them and took a few steps.

Pulling out another pair for herself, Anne said, "I made them and thought we might need a change once we got on the trail. I actually have a couple more pairs if we need them."

Maggie smiled and, once she had tested them out, continued up the trail. They had several hours of useable light left in the day. She figured that if they pushed hard to reach the main trail along the lake, they might be able to reach the small abandoned cabin in two full days.

She prayed silently that the cabin would still be useable. It had been two winters since she had enjoyed her time with One-Ear and Fredrick, but only God knew if it was still standing. It might have been burned out by the raiding Delaware or possibly the Huron. She tried not to think about the chance that the cabin was destroyed, because it would leave them with few options or simply the promise of a slow death.

Making the trek even more difficult was the necessity of stopping several times to let Anne catch her breath and rest. Still, they somehow managed to cover a significant distance. This part of their journey was more about distancing themselves from the village and the stagnant air of death.

Maggie knew the extra weight of the muskets was slowing both of them down, but she refused to be tempted to leave them behind. She knew that they would keep them both alive sooner or later. The quiver she had thrown over her back was light but awkward; it didn't fit her well since it had been made for Anne's husband. She was forced to carry the musket in her hand instead of over her shoulder. After a few miles, the weight of it started to wear her down; she felt she was constantly switching hands to give the other a break.

While they walked, Maggie thought that maybe they should change their course and head east towards the village of the Mohawks. However, she felt the distance might be too far for Anne to travel and that it would be best to spend the winter at a place she knew was a good, safe spot.

They had used as much of the light as they could and she knew that Anne was tiring rapidly. Impressed that the young woman had walked this far considering all she had been through over the past few months, Maggie kept her eyes out for a possible good spot to make camp. She knew that this territory was dotted with enough little coves and rocky crests that they should be able to find ample shelter to keep them warm. The rains had subsided completely and she hoped that the ground had enough time to at least partially dry out.

A fire would be a luxury tonight with all the damp wood around, and her first aim was to get some nice cover for them. She actually felt unusually tired and she had a strange queasy feeling in the pit of her stomach, but she put it down to just being a bit hungry.

Pushing Anne to keep moving, Maggie noticed a small path that appeared to run parallel to the main trail they had been using since they had left the pox-infested camp. She guided Anne along the trail, all the time looking for a decent place to spend the night.

After only a few minutes traveling on the narrow, over-grown path, Maggie suddenly stopped and pulled Anne back into the first line of brush. Straining to listen, Maggie thought she had heard voices on the main trail.

Not wanting to move, just in case her ears were not playing tricks on her, Maggie motioned to Anne to remain quiet. It felt like a lifetime of waiting, but Maggie's senses proved to be true as she saw and heard as clear as day a French patrol.

"What are they saying?" Maggie whispered to Anne once they had both crouched behind some brush at the side of the trail. "My French is limited; when they speak so fast, I can't understand them."

Anne didn't immediately answer, and Maggie could see she was listening to the conversation. It appeared to be a patrol of about five French regulars; there was also one Huron scout that had already passed by their hiding place.

The patrol was only about ten feet away, but thankfully several massive trees sat between them and the soldiers.

Maggie knew Anne had a reasonable grasp of some basic French since her adopted village was frequented by a number of French traders and trappers. The Delaware had dealt with the French for many years and most of their people could speak fluently in the French tongue.

"They are just complaining about having to travel so far from their outpost," Anne translated.

They appeared to care little about the amount of noise they were making. Despite their indifference and lack of usual scouting protocol, Maggie's only fear was they might decide to check on the little used path where she and Anne hid.

Praying they would simply pass, Maggie knew that finding a good spot to rest was now even more critical. Unless this patrol planned on taking the long way back around to their outpost, she had to assume that they would soon be turning around and using the same trail to return north.

Maggie tried to remember which French forts were nearby and where these men might be from. She knew of Fort Duquesne and Fort Machault. One was too far south to have sent such a small patrol this distance, and Machault was such an undermanned frontier outpost that it most likely could not spare the men for such a scouting party.

She wondered if this could be part of an advanced guard and that maybe she and Anne might be walking towards a much larger force. Confused that the French would be moving at this time of year, especially since the remains of the British army had long since departed to the south, Maggie understood they were in a terrible position and needed to find some place to get off these trails.

With so much action around, the thought of enjoying a fire through the night was now just a dream. They had to be careful to move as fast as they could without attracting unwanted attention to themselves.

Maggie knew it would be a long night.

Anne looked exhausted and Maggie knew that she could not walk much more, despite the threat from the French. The thought of making a run for it was out of the question. The two women would have to bide their time and move along the trail slowly and cautiously.

Taking a chance that the French who had just passed were only a small patrol that might just be lost, Maggie urged Anne to get up and start moving. "We must keep moving until we find a safe place to sleep for the night," she said as she helped Anne to her feet. She decided that they should head into the dense woods to look for some place that had some elevation and good sight lines.

Trying their best to keep their noise to a minimum, Maggie pushed her way through the endless branches and thorny bushes that did their best to slash at their faces and dig into their skin. Their muskets were bulky and seemed to catch on every low hanging branch and wild bush that grew uncontrollably on both sides of the trail.

After trudging up a small hill without finding any well-hidden spots that offered full concealment, Maggie decided that all she needed was a simple place to rest her head. She decided they were far enough into the interior of the woods so as to provide them with cover and enough warning if the patrol had somehow tracked them down.

With the sun setting and darkness pushing its way across the frontier, Maggie noticed a nice old tree whose girth was thicker than almost ten men across. Although it was not an ideal shelter, if they cleared the leaves and dirt from its base on the far side, it would give them some comfort and definite protection.

Maggie also started to think that with the onset of darkness, the French patrol would be similarly forced to find shelter for the night. That led her to believe that they must be lost and trying desperately to find their way back to their home base.

After clearing a good-sized space around the massive tree, Maggie piled handfuls of pine needles and a nice bed of leaves for Anne to lie down and get some sleep.

Making sure that Anne was comfortable, Maggie placed her musket against the tree and stood under the tree's high canopy. She also had her bow and quiver at her side and kept her eyes peeled into the mass of greens and browns that had an odd speckle of snow mixed in. Thankfully, this time of the season meant they had little to worry about as far as rattlers and most of the other larger animals that usually stalked the surrounding woods.

With no food and no water, Maggie was happy that Anne was soon fast asleep as it meant one less thing she had to be concerned with. Once the deepest part of the night hit, Maggie could not see much and slumped down against the tree's trunk to get some rest.

When a sudden noise made Maggie jump to her feet, she was surprised to find that the sun had already fought off the darkness and the bright rays shot through the high canopy to give her some much needed light. She was upset that she had slept longer than she wanted, yet again.

Maggie checked on Anne, who was still asleep. Using her bow, she gently nudged the girl and whispered to her to get up and to be ready to head out.

She was still concerned that the French were nearby, so Maggie walked a few steps ahead to listen again for the source of the noise that woke her up. After a few steps, a large rabbit dashed out from the brush and raced directly in front of her. If she had been faster and had an arrow set in her bow, the rabbit would have made a nice morning meal. It was more of a tease since she knew that they could not have a fire and that killing the rabbit would be a waste, unless they ate it raw.

Troubled by the French whereabouts, she continued to walk into the heavy brush and listened for any noises that might give her fair warning if the French were still patrolling the area. She particularly worried more about the Huron scout and his ability to traverse such tough terrain while remaining silent.

Walking back to check on Anne, she heard a scream that instinctively made her duck into the thorny brush that grew just a few paces from where they slept. Straining to see through the thick brush, Maggie finally had a good enough view of the old tree that had provided them such a safe place to sleep.

Another scream made her move to her left on all fours to get a better view of what was happening. Now with a relatively unobstructed view, Maggie felt her heart pound as she saw that the Huron and two of the Frenchmen had somehow managed to find their makeshift camp.

They had Anne by the arms and, although she couldn't understand or make out what they were saying, Maggie could see that they were strangely happy to find such a young woman unescorted in the middle of the wilderness.

The horrified look on Anne's face made Maggie wish she had her musket that still was resting on the tree trunk. She did have her bow and ten arrows in her quiver, but they would be no match against three musket-wielding men.

Anne attempted to scream out again but was quickly slapped across the face before the Huron covered her mouth. Maggie could not just sit there watching these buggers have their way with the poor young girl.

Hoping the element of surprise would give her the advantage, Maggie made sure she was still well covered by the brush and slowly placed one of the arrows into her bow. She gripped the sinew string and pulled it back as far as she could.

Taking aim and a deep breath, she released the arrow. Before it hit anything, she dashed to her right and had another arrow already positioned in her bow. Catching her breath, she looked to see if her shot hit her intended target.

All she saw was the two Frenchmen desperately taking cover behind the same tree that had covered the two women throughout the night. Maggie also noticed Anne just standing, dazed and confused, in the open.

Wishing she could just scream out to her to get down, Maggie had a good angle on the two Frenchmen who were still frightened by her first shot and had no idea where the arrow came from. She released the next arrow, which cut through the early morning air and drove violently into one of the men, striking him in the shoulder. He tumbled back and tried to desperately pull the arrow out of his body, but it had almost passed clean through, with the front half of the shaft sticking straight out his back.

Unable to aid his partner, the remaining Frenchman started to call out to the other men that must have been close by. With her third arrow positioned and pulled back, Maggie boldly stood up and, before the soldier could steady his musket, released the arrow. It whistled through the air before striking the Frenchman who immediately fell to the ground. After a couple of lengthy spastic jerks, the man was dead. The well-placed arrow had hit him just under his left eye and he now was dead on the leafy ground.

Anne had not moved through the entire episode.

Maggie quickly ran from her cover, passing the dead Huron who had taken her first arrow right in the neck. She got to Anne and briefly shook her, telling her to get herself together so they could get out of there before the other Frenchmen arrived.

Grabbing her musket and relieving the dead men of their powder horns and two knives, Maggie made sure Anne was behind her as she rushed back into the brush. Caring little for the thorns that dug unforgivingly into their legs and thighs, Maggie ran wildly through the trees, dodging whatever sat in her way. She constantly looked back towards Anne who was surprisingly keeping pace with her.

Breathing heavily and reaching the narrow side path, their footing was much better now as they ran as fast as their bloodied and bruised legs would carry them. Having no idea how long they had been running, Maggie finally slowed down and reached out to Anne to get her to stop. Both the women had difficulty catching their breath, but once they did, Anne said, "Thank you, Maggie…again."

Standing alone on this desolate trail, Anne handed Maggie a much needed canteen of water. Wiping off around the lip of the kidney shaped container full of cold water, Maggie took a long drink and, after putting the cork cap back into its neck, she asked, "Where did you get the water?"

"I noticed you grabbed the powder horns on our way out. I saw the canteens and pulled them off the dead Frenchmen. I assumed they had no use for them." Anne smiled and took a long gulp from her own captured canteen.

Maggie smiled, then after being refreshed from the water, she took a moment to get her bearings straight.

"Do you know where we are?" Anne asked.

Maggie didn't immediately answer as she once again thought she had heard something and motioned to Anne to take cover.

Kneeling down, Maggie listened for any further noise. She was understandably nervous about the rest of the French patrol being out in the same wilderness. Certainly, once they found their mates dead, they would be bent on avenging their deaths.

"I hope if the other French soldiers find their mates and see the arrows in them, they might just think that they were ambushed by a Delaware raiding party," Maggie whispered. "We just have to pray they decide to head back to their outpost instead of giving chase."

She realized they had to keep moving and try to get as much distance between them and the remainder of the French patrol as they could. She could see that Anne was in far better shape now and with the weather much colder but clear, the two women decided to keep heading northward.

Uncertain of where the side path would take them, Maggie offered, "I think our best choice is to move, keep our wits about us and take this trail as far as we can."

They walked for several hours as Maggie did her best to lead the way. Her goal was to get to the great lake shore trail that should take them to the abandoned cabin where she had overwintered two years earlier.

Thankfully, they had not heard or seen any signs of the French patrol as they maintained their hectic pace. The small path had been a Godsend. It had provided them with the much safer option of staying off the main trail that ran parallel most of the way.

Maggie could feel the wind picking up and the air getting much colder. She was concerned because the clothing they had on was damp and provided limited protection from the elements. If they didn't find some additional layers to keep them warm, she feared they might be slowed by the weather once again.

Her experience had taught her never to let her guard down, so she remained on high alert despite the fact they had not seen a soul for almost half a day.

Maggie was getting tired and she could see that Anne was beginning to slow her pace down as well. They stopped near a ridge and sat down on one of the many rocks that dotted the hillside and trail. Anne took off one of her moccasins to rub her blistered and bloody foot.

Noticing the poor shape her feet were in, Maggie asked, "Are you alright, or do you need me to wrap up your feet?"

Anne took off her other moccasin and poured a little water over her foot to help relieve the pain. "I think I will be fine," she said.

Impressed by Anne's unexpected strength throughout their trek, Maggie was happy she had some company with her and took some satisfaction that she had freed Anne from her misguided life as an adopted Indian.

Thinking they might spend some time resting, Maggie's plan was interrupted by several voices that echoed from behind them.

She helped Anne get her moccasins back on and held her hand to help her up the side of the small ridge and under better cover. The extra height gave them a good view of the trail below.

Maggie wasn't sure if the voices she heard were French or, worse, Delaware or Seneca but she knew she had heard something once again.

It wasn't long after they had scurried up the hill that they both saw another French patrol working its way along the path. Maggie didn't recognize any of the soldiers and had no idea if this was a different patrol or a re-enforcement of the unit she had attacked earlier.

She was upset with herself that she hadn't covered their tracks better. She had been so focused on moving quickly that she hadn't thought that they would be followed on one of the numerous old Indian hunting paths that dotted most of the frontier.

The two women watched as the patrol stopped in the exact spot where they had been resting only a few minutes earlier.

Maggie got on her stomach and motioned to Anne to do the same. She could still see the patrol searching the small area down below. Their voices were much clearer now and in her lowest possible voice, she asked Anne what they were talking about.

"They are looking for us," was all she said.

The two women hugged the ground even closer when they saw that the officer leading the patrol pointed up towards where they were hiding.

Maggie knew that if even a couple of the soldiers ventured up the easily-traversed hill, they had no means to escape. If they made a run for it, their only option was up and Maggie had no idea what the terrain above them was like.

They both knew they were caught if the officer decided to search more of the area. Maggie signaled to Anne to remain silent, and they were both soon relieved as the officer motioned to his men to keep moving north.

He did unfortunately leave two men behind. Maggie assumed this was to watch the backs of the main party. Their presence certainly complicated any plans Maggie and Anne had for leaving.

The two Frenchmen sat on the same rock that the two women had been resting on, oblivious to the fact they were being watched from above.

Maggie knew they didn't have the time to waste waiting for these two to get moving. She had no idea what their orders were or even if they were waiting for another patrol to arrive. Either way she had to do something.

Without speaking, for fear they would give up their well-hidden position, Maggie pointed to Anne's musket and signaled for her to get it ready. The plan was simple, complicated only by the facts that she had to rely on Anne's accuracy and that if they missed even one of their targets, their position would be exposed.

Of course, an additional concern was that musket fire would alert the patrol that had just left northward. Maggie knew that any such sound would have the other Frenchmen running back to check on their mates.

Maggie preferred the well-tuned bow, but had her musket resting beside her on an old tree stump, just in case it was needed. If she missed with any of her arrows, the Frenchmen would be alerted and would call out to the others in the scouting party. At that point, the noise from her musket would matter little.

Much like she had done earlier, Maggie took a deep breath and quietly removed an arrow from her quiver and gently placed it in the bow. She knew if she could fire off two quick shots, they might both hit their intended targets. If she could take advantage of the relative silence of the arrows to hit both men, they could possibly get themselves out of such a bad place and simply use the forward patrol as their own advanced escorts.

With one quick motion, and just as one of the soldiers looked up, Maggie released her first shot. Not even bothering to see if it hit anything, she immediately had another arrow already drawn back. Releasing it, she instinctively readied yet another arrow.

Taking a quick glance towards Anne, Maggie was once again impressed that she was ready and apparently willing to fire her raised musket at one of the soldiers.

Maggie whispered, "Keep me covered; I'm going down to check on these two." She rushed down the hill and hissed back up at Anne, "Shoot at anything that moves."

Hearing nothing, not even any groans from either Frenchman, Maggie blindly rushed directly over the rocks that both men had just been resting by.

Keeping her bow drawn, she found herself back on the trail searching for the bodies of her intended victims.

She saw no such evidence.

Noticing a small blood trail that splattered towards the far side of the trail, she also spotted tracks and a long, flattened out area. Nervous she had missed both men and now they had taken refuge in the woods, Maggie signaled to Anne to get down with her.

Anne took only a few seconds to get to Maggie's side.

"I have no idea where they are or what shape they are in, but we need to find them," Maggie explained. "I need you to stay here and warn me if they make a move."

Walking slowly towards the tracks that ended at the tree line, Maggie still didn't understand why she could not hear anything. She was sure she must have hit at least one of the men, maybe they were not both fatal shots, but one of the arrows had to have hit the target.

The bloody splatters appeared to get thicker as she moved right in front of the last of the tracks. Intensely listening for any noise or rustling of branches or leaves, Maggie crept into the first layer of brush.

By that time, Maggie wished she had her musket loaded. She liked the bow, but at close quarters, a musket was much more deadly.

The woods were ominously silent as she continued to move deeper into the noticeably darker interior. She thought to look back to make sure Anne was still behind her on the trail, but a very slight noise made her turn her head.

Practically stepping on the first Frenchman, Maggie caught her step and moved to her left. She could now see why everything was so silent.

In front of her sat one dead Frenchman, fatally wounded in the neck. The other man was propped up against a tree, bleeding heavily from a wound to his stomach with her arrow still protruding from it.

Maggie could see the pain and vulnerability etched in the dying man's face as he spotted her standing over him. It looked to her that he had dragged his friend, despite his own wound, into the woods for some cover. His friend most likely was dead from the arrow on impact, but the brave young man courageously attempted to help him.

Maggie dropped her bow and got on her knees to try to comfort the Frenchman. As she got closer, it was apparent he was no more than a boy, probably around eighteen or so.

He had tears in his eyes that rained down his face. Maggie removed his canteen and offered him some water.

"Merci, madame," was all he could say as his eyes closed then slowly opened with every torturous breath.

"Don't talk," Maggie said quietly, unsure if he could hear her or even understand what she was saying. "I will help you as much as I can."

Not soon after, Anne made her way to where Maggie sat with the dying young man. Maggie looked silently at Anne. They were in a struggle for their lives and freedom. Maggie did not feel remorse for inflicting the wound, but as a mother, she felt a pang of sadness that he had not died instantly and now suffered. She knew that she could not allow the boy to die alone in this wretched wilderness if she could provide him some comfort.

"What can we do for him?" Anne asked as she carefully sat on the other side of him.

"I know we can't just leave him here alone to die," Maggie said. "We need to get the arrow out and see if we can stop some of the bleeding."

Despite the time of year and the coolness in the air, Maggie was surprised at the increasing number of flies and other bugs that had already come to make the young man's pain even worse. They must have been drawn by the smell that was coming from the dead Frenchman. Maggie knew they would have to move the stiffening body soon or risk attracting deadlier creatures.

"Anne, I need you to help me move the body," Maggie said. "If you would grab a leg, we should try to move him as far away as possible."

The two women grabbed a leg each and, with the weight of the man and the heavy undergrowth, they both struggled to move the body much more than a few feet. The smell alone made it difficult, but the shear dead weight wore them both down quickly.

"We need to move him farther away," Maggie said. "I think if we follow the path he was dragged through originally, it should be easier. We can move him close to the path and hope no one passes by before we can leave."

Struggling again with the man's weight, Maggie could not believe that the young man had done so by himself in light of his severe injury. They managed to get the body far enough away from them, but not so close to the trail so as to be seen.

Fatigued from the struggle they had with the body, Maggie and Anne returned to the surviving Frenchman. He was in and out of consciousness and Maggie knew he would not live much longer. Her only thought was to comfort him in his last moments and not have him die alone.

Anne helped keep him sitting upright and, on several occasions, gave him some water or just poured some over his parched lips.

The young man was holding on longer than Maggie imagined and told Anne not to give him anymore water. She had considered removing the arrow, but at this point it would just add to his pain and prolong his agony.

Unsure of the time of day, Maggie found herself nodding off and was awakened by Anne's little nudges. She certainly didn't want to spend the night here, especially not wanting to wake up in the morning and find the Frenchman dead.

Changing her focus to ending the young man's suffering, Maggie asked Anne to walk with her, far enough away so the injured soldier couldn't hear her words. Stopping a few paces from him and looking towards the path, Maggie just came out and said, "We can't spend much more time with him, we might have to end this soon and get moving."

From the look on Anne's face, Maggie knew she was appalled by such a horrible thought.

"Leave me behind to care for him," Anne said.

Maggie had no answer for her. Just as she was about to put an end to the argument, Anne frantically pointed towards the trail, alerting her that something was amiss.

Immediately realizing what it was that Anne had seen, Maggie called to her quietly, "Let's get back to the boy and keep him quiet. I think it is his patrol returning to check on him."

The body of his mate could easily be found, considering the smell alone would garner at least a short search in the woods. The only thing that stood between them and the patrol was some thick brush and trees that were already stripped of their colorful late autumn leaves.

Once again, they had no place to hide unless they moved deeper into the woods. They couldn't risk moving the near-dead Frenchman, and if they just left him, he still had enough life to direct the patrol to where she and Anne would have retreated.

They were out of reasonable options and understood that the remainder of their trek would be hindered by this patrol that appeared to be determined to find them. Maggie thought quickly and decided to risk pleading for mercy from the patrol. She prayed that they might take pity on them when they saw that they had vainly tried to help their friend.

"We have little choice," Maggie said, "so follow my lead and call out to them in French, if you please."

Confused and reluctant to do so, Maggie once again demanded that Anne follow her suggestion, this time with far more vigor. "Anne, if you want to live, do what I say. We will both be dead if we just stay here and wait for them to capture us…or worse…"

Anne decided that Maggie was right and called out to the approaching Frenchmen, "Messieurs, messieurs…"

At first the patrol stopped, thinking it could be a trap.

"Ask the boy what his name is," Maggie ordered.

Anne spoke to the young man and quickly got him to say his name.

"Call to them and tell them we have one of their men who is in need of some medical attention," Maggie said, already with her bow in her hand.

"Messieurs, we have your Private LeMay with us and he is dying; please help us," Anne yelled out in French, waiting for a reply.

None came.

Within a few long seconds, the two women were completely surrounded. The patrol had their muskets shouldered and pointed directly at them.

The women had no choice but to lay down their weapons and surrender.

Chapter | **Six**

The morning came thankfully soon enough, although the thin layer of wet snow was not a welcomed sight.

Jacob rose well before the others and checked on his prisoner. The Frenchman was still asleep, but Jacob wouldn't have cared if he had escaped. It would have been one less headache to deal with.

He decided to take a brief walk while he thought over what they should do next. He was careful not to let his emotions get the better of him, but it was difficult. He still felt tremendous guilt for leaving Maggie behind, and James' apparent displeasure at being freed from his adopted Delaware family pained him greatly.

As he re-entered the camp, Jacob noticed that Joshua and James were up. He motioned to them, calling, "Good morning, lads! You can certainly feel it in the air that winter will soon be well upon us." His emotions were still running high and he did his best to hide them.

"What is the plan, sir?" Joshua asked immediately, not wasting time with small talk.

"It all comes down to direction, lads," Jacob responded. "Do we risk marching through French and Delaware country or head east to the far more hospitable territory of the Mohawk?"

Joshua was about to answer, but was stifled by Jacob who looked directly at James and said, "I want to know your thoughts, boy. You have said next to nothing for most of this trip. All I want to do is find your mother and then we can deal with all your problems afterwards."

The bluntness of his tone even appeared to shock Joshua, who waited for James to answer.

Taking a moment to contemplate his reply, James simply offered, "I think we should move towards the east. You have to think that the Frenchman might just want you to follow him deeper into French-held territory so we run into a patrol or two."

The logic of James' statement took Jacob by surprise.

"My only fear is that by moving east, we might be heading in the opposite direction of where your mother might be," Jacob said thoughtfully.

James replied without being prompted, "I look at the sky and can feel the winter in the air, if we want to find a welcoming place to spend the winter, then east is our only option."

"What about our prisoner?" Joshua piped in.

Quick to answer, Jacob said, "He is the least of our worries. We can let him go to find his own way back home."

James immediately answered, "We would risk him re-joining another patrol and hunting us down. At the moment, he is the only Frenchman who knows we are out here."

"Are you proposing we just kill him and leave him here?" Jacob said.

"Yes," James said, showing little emotion on his young face.

James' coldness shocked Jacob. After a pause, he said, "We can decide the fate of the prisoner later; our main focus needs to be finding your mother. We need to locate a good place to overwinter and then continue our search once the spring melt starts."

Jacob dismissed them and went back to where he had left the Frenchman. The rest of the men were up and getting their gear ready to move out, but a couple of them had decided to keep their eye on the prisoner.

"Thank you, gentlemen," Jacob said. "I can watch the Frenchman from here. Get yourselves prepared to leave, and please tell the others to do the same."

Jacob was struggling with what to do with the prisoner. The young man was just an innocent player in all of this, and Jacob was uncomfortable with the idea of killing him just because his usefulness had run his course.

"How are you, lad?" he asked the young man. "We need to get moving, so get ready to leave shortly."

Lessard said nothing, but did as he was told.

Jacob sent out a larger-than-usual advanced guard, led by Joshua and James. He knew they were in French-held territory and didn't want to mistakenly run themselves into a French patrol. After taking some time to think about what he should do, Jacob decided their best plan would be to head northeast and get into British-friendly Mohawk country. He had no idea where Maggie might be at that moment, and with the onset of winter starting to grip the region, he needed to get his men to a safe place to ride out the harsh season.

The Frenchman was under the impression he would join the advanced guard, but Jacob immediately told him that he would remain with the main unit. After assigning a couple of the men to watch Lessard, Jacob moved towards the front.

He was uneasy with the fact that he was leaving familiar territory and would have to rely on Joshua and James to lead him. He had no issue with the young lads leading; he just didn't like the idea of not knowing the terrain.

Walking the first few miles with the advanced scouts, Jacob talked over their route with Joshua. The younger man didn't know of a reliable water-route that could be traveled without many time-consuming por-tages. Instead, Joshua suggested that the best and quickest route would be to follow the mountains towards the east. He estimated that if the weather held, they would be able reach the New York territory within a week or so.

Jacob had little choice but to follow Joshua's lead. The only issue left to be decided was what to do with the prisoner. Should he be released, or should he be killed as James so coldly suggested? He was an extra mouth to feed, but for the moment he would stay with them.

The scouts followed a couple old Delaware hunting paths that hugged the foothills of the Alleghenies. The air had grown considerably colder and the nights became so frigid that most of the men huddled together around the campfires all night to keep warm.

The men kept moving through all sorts of weather. Even on the harshest days when they experienced heavy, wet snow, they managed to cover several miles. On those days, they reached points on the trail where the snow was so blinding that the men could see no more than a foot in front of them. Jacob ordered the main body of men to each keep an outstretched arm on the shoulder of the man ahead of him to guide them forward. It worked and kept the men close together, especially during the worst of the snow.

Jacob was proud of his men and how none of them openly complained. They covered miles of unknown territory that provided them very little food along the way. He could see on the men's faces that they had all lost some weight. If he didn't get them into more permanent quarters, he might risk losing some of them.

There was little concern that any of the men might desert since most of them had never ventured this far north before. However, Jacob was worried that some of the weaker men might starve, which would certainly affect the morale of the survivors.

Their eastern route had finally changed to a more northerly direction as Joshua sent a messenger back to inform Jacob that they were moving towards the region near another of the great lakes. Joshua had attempted to describe the lake to Jacob, but told him he would have to see it for himself.

"It is like an ocean of endless water," Joshua had said, "and the Huron said it takes several weeks to paddle from one end to the other. They said if you followed it to its mouth and past the great French village at Quebec, you would find a greater ocean that could devour any canoe with one wave."

The French prisoner had co-operated during the entire trip without causing any problems. Jacob was still struggling with what to do with him. The more time he spent with the young man, the more he had learned to like him.

The young man had helped around the nightly camps, collecting firewood and even assisting in setting a few snares to catch whatever creatures still lingered about so late in the season. Jacob had noticed that most of the other men had grown attached to the hardworking young man as well. Some had even asked him to teach them some French words. It appeared they had forgotten he was a hated French soldier and slowly accepted him into their ranks.

As the party moved closer to the lake region, they noticed that most of the land was already snow covered and that the air was much colder. The land was full of frozen lakes and rivers as well as rows of heavy pine and birch trees that appeared to stretch to the end of the known world.

It had been almost two weeks since they decided which direction to take. Jacob was desperate to find a friendly village or an abandoned outpost to hold up for the winter.

With a large number of the Delaware and Seneca already down south in their winter hunting grounds, there were a number of abandoned villages along the way that sat idle during the long winter months. Whenever one was conveniently located, the men used it to set up camp and take shelter from the colder weather. Unfortunately, none of the villages they had used provided the necessities they required for the winter, most importantly a good defensive position for such a long stay. Two villages had some high palisaded walls, yet were far too small to house the men comfortably through the worst part of the season.

Lessard had informed Jacob that farther east there were a couple of forts that guarded the trade route towards Montreal. "I have never seen the forts," the young Frenchman had said, "but I do know men who have been stationed there. The forts sit on a couple of lakes that directly link the area to Quebec."

During the course of their journey, Jacob had avoided speaking with his prisoner about his fate. As they grew closer to their destination, he knew he could avoid it no longer.

"Monsieur," Jacob said quietly as he fell in step beside Lessard, "we have to talk about what to do with you."

"I am your prisoner, sir, so I have little say in my fate," Lessard said bravely.

Jacob really liked this young man and could not fathom the thought of killing him or just cutting him loose to find his own way so late in the season. He had one proposal that he had been considering for some time and thought he would offer the option to the prisoner.

"This might sound strange," Jacob began slowly, watching the young man's reaction out of the corner of his eye. "In fact, you might think less of me to even make such an offer, yet…what if I asked you to join us? No strings, you can leave when you want and have the same say as any of the others."

They walked a few more paces before Lessard replied, "Monsieur, your offer is both surprising and confusing. What about the men? Have you spoken with them about having a Frenchman amongst their ranks?"

Jacob smiled and offered, "They have no say in who joins us, but if you like, I will speak with them before I ask for your answer."

At the first opportunity he had to talk with the men, Jacob spoke openly and asked what they thought should be done with the prisoner. Other than James, none of the men wanted him killed for just doing his duty. Some suggested they could escort him east and let him go within a couple days' march to one of the French outposts he had told them about. The majority said they would be happy to have him stay with them, at least for the winter. Once the winter broke, he could leave them to rejoin the French if he desired.

Jacob had spoken privately with both Joshua and James about their thoughts and concerns. Joshua cared little either way and said it was nice to have the extra hands, but it also meant another mouth to feed. James remained diligent in his belief that they should just kill him and move on.

"I was under the impression that the Delaware were allies to the French yet you think nothing of killing one of them?" Jacob asked, still taken back by James' bluntness.

"The Delaware dealt with the French because they had to," James explained. "In their eyes, they are no better than the English. Most of the Delaware want both sides to leave their land and let them be. I have no loyalty to the French and have seen how they treated the elders and the women in the village."

"I am sorry, James, but the men want him to stay with us, and I honestly feel the same way," Jacob said. "We can revisit the situation when better weather returns."

Once he was satisfied there would be no problems if the French prisoner remained, Jacob approached Lessard again and said, "The men said they would like you to stay with us through the winter. Your fate can be reviewed in the spring. What do you want to do now?"

"My options are limited, monsieur; I will stay," the Frenchman replied, and it was left at that.

Jacob now turned his attentions back to the matter at hand. Though he was still uncomfortable in not knowing his way in this new land, he was confident that Joshua knew the territory well enough and gave him the freedom to lead the men. The Mohawk and other tribes that inhabited the area were supposed to be friendly to the English, but Jacob could not rely on that as a certainty. He maintained an advanced scouting party at all times and remained diligent in posting pickets each night.

After another long week or so of marching and covering several miles each day in increasingly colder weather, the men remained in good spirits. They had not seen a soul for the last several weeks and this part of the territory seemed even more desolate than the Pennsylvania frontier they so sorely missed.

One day, after several hours of hard marching, Jacob sent word to Joshua that they needed to stop despite having several hours of good light left.

As the season started to shift, the hours of useable sunlight had significantly lessened and it had begun to wear on the men. Jacob was happy that they had not lost a man to desertion or sickness to this point, but he did not want to push them too hard.

The advanced scouts had come across a decaying outpost that had enough shelter to keep all the men out of the elements. Word was sent back that they would be stopping for a much needed rest once the scouts secured the area.

Jacob wasn't sure about the place once he called up the rest of the men. His idea was to possibly stay for a few days to rest the men and re-stock their provisions. He was getting tired of a steady diet of rabbit and salty, dried pork and he guessed the men were feeling the same.

By the look of some of the nearby tracks, the surrounding land was full of brush wolves, winter deer and a few other beasts that braved the long winters. That was a good sign since it meant a good and active food source nearby. An experienced trapper, Jacob was excited about the prospects of setting trap lines and keeping the men well feed throughout what looked like a difficult winter.

He was greeted by Joshua and James as soon as he stepped into the ruins of what must have at one time been a large, impressive Indian village. "This is not a bad place to spend the night," Joshua boasted.

Jacob was not initially convinced, but the men appeared to be happy with it for now. At first, Jacob was worried since the village had clearly been neglected for several years, but after further inspection it was still a fine spot. With a little work, it might be a safe place to wait out the winter.

"It needs some work, but it should do," Jacob guardedly offered.

The interior of the village was spacious and was dominated by two large longhouses covered in thick bark that appeared to be a perfect place to house the men. The center of the village was a great place to build a fire pit and keep the men on guard duty relatively warm.

"It does need some re-enforcement and a few basic repairs, but overall it has some potential," Joshua agreed as Jacob walked around the post inspecting the various structures. "This land has enough trees to provide wood for our fires and timber for repairs."

"Where are we, lad?" Jacob finally asked. "I must admit, I have some strange feelings about this, yet I can't explain why."

While Jacob and Joshua spoke, the men had already begun setting up camp. The two longhouses only needed to be cleared of the snow and overgrowth. Several of the men had already gathered what branches and old wood they could find to make a large fire pit in the middle of the open area between the buildings.

Jacob continued to look around with James as Joshua excused himself and assisted the men in doing what they could to clean up the place. The outer walls consisted of a series of long tree trunks driven into the ground and tightly packed together. It was crude, yet appeared to be effective. There was also another series of inner walls that Jacob thought was used to funnel any attacking enemy into a pre-determined area. It reminded Jacob of a maze and he imagined it would be pretty effective once an enemy got themselves drawn into it.

"What are your thoughts about this place, boy?" Jacob asked James, who had said nothing beyond a simple greeting when he arrived.

"It looks like an old Iroquoian village," James explained. "It's not as large as their traditional villages, but at one time it would have been home to several families. By the look of the longhouses, there were probably close to a hundred people living here at one time."

Peering through the cut tree trunks that must have been at least thirty feet high, Jacob finally noticed a half-frozen lake just behind the village. "There's a good source of water, and it must be stocked with some trout and perch," Jacob said thoughtfully. He began to think this place might actually be able to keep them safe and secure over the long winter.

James did not bother to reply and just pushed on a number of the tall timbers to check on how solid the structure was.

"What are your thoughts about how this place might stand up to an attack?" Jacob asked, trying to get James more engaged in their conversation.

"The timber is pretty dry and we would need to shore up some of the defenses," James said as he continued checking the timbers, "but overall I think it should hold up well. Most of the tribes in these parts are allies to the British, or have remained neutral, so we have no reason to fear them. The French are basically to the north, west and east of here, although we are so deep into the interior that we should not be bothered by them."

The men seemed to be happy with the location and the thought of having enough time to secure the place and go out to set some trap lines. If they stayed, the lake would be an excellent place to hunt beaver, weasels and other winter animals looking for some water. Once the lake completely froze, it would be more of a challenge to fish and collect water, but they were all experienced with gathering winter provision and surviving during the worst of the weather.

Over the next five days, the men worked hard to repair the longhouses and build up the defensive walls around the compound. The plentiful timber allowed them to maintain constant fires to warm the men, especially through the noticeably colder nights.

They were greeted with a fresh layer of snow each morning and, after a week's worth of snow, the surrounding countryside was becoming more difficult to travel across. The men kept themselves busy cutting the endless supply of wood they needed to keep the fires going as well as checking and resetting the trap lines placed in the nearby woods.

The longhouses were nicely constructed, each with two openings in its high ceiling. The builders had hand-cut the two holes and positioned them just above the fire pits to force the smoke out and keep the air inside circulating and reasonably breathable. There was a heavy bear skin pelt that worked surprisingly well as a door cover to keep the cold air out, and the men kept two more reserved to cover up the ceiling holes in the case of extremely bad weather.

One longhouse was adequate enough to hold all the men, so the second was used to store some of the food and dry out the growing number of hides they collected through trapping and hunting. They also built up massive piles of cut wood indoors to keep it dry and usable throughout the winter.

The beds in the house where the men lived had been built up off the cold dirt floor and greatly aided in their comfort. Once they began accumulating their store of fur pelts, those who were fortunate enough not to be on picket duty slept very well.

Joshua spent most of time making sure the trap lines were productive. During just the first week, the traps had brought in a number of beavers, several medium-sized wildcats and so many rabbits that the men used some of them as bait for other traps.

Jacob asked a couple of the men to make as many snowshoes as they could with the deer sinew they had collected. A couple of hunting parties had found that a small herd inhabited the area around the lake.

Having worked hard to get their winter home in shape, the peace around the small village was shattered when one of the frequent scouting parties found tracks in the fresh snow. It appeared that several moccasin-wearing men had been scouting around their post. Some of the tracks were close to the eastern wall, while the majority was found near the edge of the far woods.

Joshua reported the incident to Jacob, saying, "Sir, the last patrol sent out came back to inform me they found a large number of human tracks near the eastern woods. They estimated around thirty men, but said it was difficult to really know."

Jacob did his best to hide his disappointment. He had truly hoped they would be able to make it through the winter in peace, but this news appeared to indicate otherwise.

"Could the men tell if they were Indians or Frenchmen?" he asked, unsure which would be worse. Indians were unpredictable at the best of times, but Jacob had heard rumors that the French sent out Canadian militia to fight during the winter months because they were a very hardy people more used to living in such harsh conditions.

After thinking about his options, Jacob ordered, "Joshua, please go and take a look for yourself. Take ten men out with you and see if you can tell what direction they came from or departed towards. Check down by the lake for tracks or signs they might be moving from the north."

Joshua smiled and took only a few minutes to ready his men and head for the woods.

Jacob stood at the entrance of the first set of palisades and watched the men leave. They looked twice their natural size as most had not only their blanket coats, but layers of furs that had been skinned off the animals they trapped. As they lumbered over the snow with the aid of large snow shoes, they looked like huge beasts walking upright. Jacob imagined that the appearance of his men would frighten even the most experienced Delaware if they met up in the woods.

One important feature that Jacob had requested to be added to the walls was a crudely built tower that was just large enough to have one man observe the countryside. It was normally manned throughout the daylight hours, and it proved to be an effective way to scout the area. He prayed they would have a couple of clear days to construct another tower to face the lake side, but for now having one high vantage point was good enough.

Jacob relieved the man on duty in the tower and remained on watch for the men's return. As time wore on, he began to consider sending out a small search party to find them. His patience paid off, though, when he saw Joshua and his men push across the thigh deep snow and offer an excited wave to all the onlookers.

Jacob scrambled out of the tower and rushed towards Joshua before the young man even reached the first wall. "Good to see you men safe," Jacob said. "How was your trip?"

"Cold and at times miserable, but no worse then what you have most likely experienced," Joshua replied.

"Well, get yourselves into the longhouse and warm up by the fires," Jacob said and led the way into the double-walled village.

Jacob let Joshua dismiss the men to get some food and rest before he began asking questions. The two men sat by the larger of the two fires, and Jacob gave Joshua only the briefest moment to relax his tired feet before pressing him for details.

"What did you find, lad?" Jacob asked.

"There were a number of tracks, but I am pretty certain none were Delaware or any other tribe," Joshua said. "I even doubt if they belong to the French or any part of their militia."

Jacob interrupted before he could continue, "How can you be so sure?"

"The 'visitors' had traveled most of their way on snowshoes, and we walked several miles following their trail and even noticed what looked like the tracks of large, sleds pulled by teams of oxen," Joshua explained. "By their heavy heel marks, they could never be Indians; they are so much lighter on their feet than the English or French. It appeared that they came from an easterly direction; it was a party of twenty, possibly thirty, but no more. My guess is that they might be part of a ranging unit from one of the British forts near Albany."

"Albany?" Jacob repeated. "How far are we from Albany?"

"I said near Albany," Joshua replied. "I meant possibly Fort William Henry or Fort Edward; they are only a couple days' straight march from here. My guess is that only an experienced and well-disciplined scouting party could make such a trek in these conditions."

Jacob was still not convinced that it was a British unit or a colonial ranging company. He wondered to himself why they didn't approach the camp or scout around long enough to see that they were English as well.

"We have to be thankful for now that they have left our trap lines untouched," Jacob said, not bothering to hide his continued concern.

Leaving the details for later, he asked one of the men to get Joshua some food and drink before he dismissed himself to check on the others.

"Get some rest and food in your belly," Jacob said with an appreciative pat on Joshua's back. "I fear we have not seen the last of these fellows, and we might want to make contact with them to determine if they are friends or foes."

It was early December and the camp had been in the grips of winter for well over a month. Thankfully, the snow fell at a steady pace, giving the men the opportunity to clear it as it accumulated. There were a few unusually warm days that gave them the opportunity to spend time setting more trap lines. They even found time to build another look-out tower.

The ample supply of small vermin and the odd deer supplied the men with enough food to live comfortably. The daily routine of cutting wood, scouting and keeping up the maintenance of the village was a tiring one, but Jacob never heard any grumbling from the men.

Despite the comfortable winter encampment they had created for themselves, the men were affected by the yet unseen visitors. The men saw frequent evidence of their presence and knew they were being observed. Jacob sent out regular scouting parties in addition to the hunting parties, and the report was always the same…fresh moccasin tracks in the snow near the camp and signs of sled tracks.

On separate occasions, Jacob had tried communicating with the unseen visitors. He had even gone so far as to ask Lessard to call out in French in case it was a French patrol. These attempts were met with silence and Jacob still had no idea who they were or how many of them were out there.

He was careful not to put his men in a potentially hazardous situation, but thought the situation might prove a good opportunity to get the men out of their mundane routine. It would be good for them to work on their winter fighting skills.

Unwilling to wait much longer in flushing out the unknown party, Jacob sent the men to do what they had done for the last number of days; he sent out a small scouting and hunting party, along with several men assigned to check the lines. However, this time he had Joshua and James take ten men out the secluded back gates of the camp. Strict orders were given to every man to hold his fire until the strangers were clearly identified.

If Joshua and James went unobserved, it would present them an opportunity to take the unknown men from behind. They headed directly towards the lake and had orders to remain in the woods to keep watch in case the strangers were arriving across the frozen lake. It had been noticed over the past weeks that the group may have been using sleds to traverse quickly across the ice and snow.

Two men were positioned in the high towers with orders to signal down if they spotted any movement. They intently kept their eyes on the frozen lake and the surrounding area.

Jacob decided that he would also participate in the controlled attack and took a group of five men to the west. His plan was to loop around to the north and force the others towards his hunting party. He moved with extreme caution as he waited for all the men to get themselves into position.

Keeping his eye on the towers, Jacob soon saw a short signal that there was some movement across the lake. As word spread to each of the groups, and the trap began falling into place, Joshua sent a messenger to inform Jacob that two large sleds, drawn by four oxen, had been seen moving across the lake. It was estimated that there were about twenty men in all. It wasn't long before Jacob caught a glimpse of the men himself.

With all the extra furs and clothing they wore, it was next to impossible to know if they were French or English. The use of the sleds had all but eliminated the threat of Indians from the equation. Though, if they were French, there could have been Delaware scouts with them.

Jacob could see where most of his own men were positioned. Joshua had brought his party around the far side of the lake, directly across where the empty sleds were secured and the oxen were left to feed on two large piles of hay that had been spread over the snow by some of the visitors.

James and two other men had been sent across the frozen lake to cut the sleds' rope lines that secured the massive oxen and was used to steer them. Surprised that no guards had been left behind to stop such actions, Jacob appreciated Joshua's tactics.

Now the visitors were left with no escape route.

The deep snow did little to mask the scuffing sounds of the snowshoes as the men approached. With a quick wave and a hoot owl call from Jacob, the men moved in to trap the troublesome scouting party.

Chapter | **Seven**

Maggie and Anne immediately had their hands bound and were pulled violently towards the trail. Not a word was spoken by their French captors as they were moved quickly, now guided by two Huron scouts.

The injured private was bandaged up on the run and escorted by two of his mates only a few steps behind the two women.

Maggie thought they were heading north, but was not certain. She had lost some sense of direction with all the confusion. Faced with the silence of the patrol, she was left to guess.

Forgetting about their whereabouts for the moment, Maggie turned her watchful and concerned eye towards Anne and their two Huron escorts. The former's frailty had seemed to return, and the latter were clearly unhappy that the two women had killed one of their fellow warriors.

After getting a mile or so from where they had ambushed the two rear guards, Maggie could see that there was another group of soldiers waiting near a small clearing just in front of them. She and Anne were pushed forward to the front of the party, directly to where two French officers were waiting.

"Mesdames, you have caused us some problems that I was hoping to avoid so late in the season," one of the officers said in reasonably clear English as he stepped forward to see them better.

Maggie said nothing and nudged Anne after she appeared to be about to answer the officer.

"Who are you two, and why are you so far north?" the officer began again with some degree of impatience. "I find it odd that two white women would be venturing out alone this deep into this godforsaken wilderness."

The two Huron scouts stood behind Maggie and Anne. When they refused to answer the French officer's questions, the scouts pushed muskets into their lower backs.

"No need for that," the officer scolded the two Huron and motioned them to join the other soldiers who were just standing around waiting to move out.

"Now please, madame," the officer said in a lighter tone, removing his hat and speaking directly to Maggie. "Tell me something so that when we get back to the fort, I can offer at least some piece of information to my commander."

"I am Maggie and this is my friend Anne," Maggie politely explained, once again nudging Anne to stay quiet. "We escaped from a group of Delaware and were trying to find some place to get out of the cold."

The officer looked at the two women and appeared to be contemplating what to do with them. "What will my Delaware brothers think if I take you into the safety of our fort and do not try to contact them about your story?" he asked finally. "You have put me in a terrible position now, but I also must thank you for keeping one of my men alive."

Maggie wished she could think of something to say or offer that would convince the officer to just let them go.

He placed his hat back on his head and slightly touched the rim as he said, "Let me speak with my men and decide what we should do with you two. This damn territory is no place for two women to be out unescorted."

Maggie simply watched as the officer walked back with a junior officer and spoke with some of the men that had found the two women with the injured soldier.

Feeling the stares from the two Huron scouts, Maggie returned their glares and defiantly stood her ground.

"Don't give them any information, Anne," she said softly to the younger woman who stood with her head down. "Let me speak with them. I am not certain what will come of all of this, so let's wait to see what the officer comes back with."

Before they could continue their conversation, the officer returned. His face presented little clue with what was going to happen to them, and he once again removed his hat.

"Excuse my manners, but I failed to introduce myself," he said. "I am Captain Guy and I am struggling with what to do with you two. The young boy you helped happens to be my son, Jean, and he appears to be very thankful that you stayed by his side. At the same time, I must assume one of you caused his injury?"

Maggie noticed over the captain's shoulder that some of the men, including the two Huron scouts, were leaving to move north. Now only four men remained behind.

"Sir, all I can say is that if you would be kind enough to let us go on our way, we will promise not to cause you any further trouble," Maggie said.

"I wish it was that simple, madame," the captain ominously replied.

The two could see that he was extremely distressed by this decision, so Maggie decided to remain quiet and let him speak.

Slowly moving the two women further away from the few remaining men, Captain Guy rubbed his unshaven face and continued, "My training tells me to take you back as prisoners and throw you into the stockades, but the grateful father in me says to just let you go and pray you make it alive out of this place."

Maggie had nothing to add and waited for him to decide their fate.

"My son pleaded with me to let you go," the captain continued. "The others told me to just kill you both and leave you to the animals. I know I can't just murder you and leave you to be devoured by whatever lives out in these woods. I contemplated the fort might be the best place, but I fear no good would come of two young women amongst a garrison of lonely, isolated soldiers." The captain once again took a deep breath and turned to gesture to the soldiers that remained behind.

One of the men leaned two muskets against a tree and hung two powder horns on a low branch. Another did the same with Maggie's bow and quiver before they both disappeared down the trail.

Captain Guy turned his attention back to the two women. Maggie could not comprehend what was happening and instinctively stepped in front of a stiff and frightened Anne.

"Please," the captain said, lifting his empty palm in a stopping motion, "I have no intentions of harming either of you. I only have some advice, if you choose to listen.

"Take your weapons and head east. There is an isolated trail just over this hill that will take you towards British-held territory and a much safer place for the two of you. My men left two sacks of food to hopefully get you on your way, but please move out before the woods become too dark to do so." The captain nodded politely; before Maggie could say anything, he was gone.

Stunned and once again alone with Anne, Maggie slowly walked forward to retrieve her bow and throw the quiver over her shoulder. Anne also moved forward and picked up her musket and powder horn.

Maggie spotted the two packs that the French had left behind and immediately opened them to find several loaves of bread, two blocks of cheese and several large pieces of dried meat.

Satisfied that the French indeed had departed, Maggie finally spoke, "Let's get out of here before they change their minds."

Maggie moved towards the trail Guy had pointed out and made sure Anne was right behind her. The two women understood that they had lost a good part of the day being detained by the French and wanted to push east as fast as their legs would carry them.

The thought of heading deeper into the New York territory without a guide frightened her, but she pushed forward all the same. At least when she had the goal of the little cabin, she had felt like she knew where she was going. What kept her moving east now was the realization that she was heading towards the last place she had seen One-Ear alive.

The two women trudged through the depth of a wilderness that went on forever. The countryside was much like Maggie was used to in southern Pennsylvania. The miles of choking woods were sporadically broken up by a smattering of bogs and swamps. It was just as mountainous as the Scottish Highlands where she grew up, and the trail system that was interwoven with the wilderness appeared to be relatively well laid out.

The one thing both the women noticed as they pressed on was that the weather had become much colder and the snow had accumulated to well past their upper shins. Maggie could feel the change and knew that what they had on their backs was not suitable for this time of year. They had food and supplies to keep them from starving, but now they needed to find some good shelter and get themselves some better clothing.

With the shortened winter days, they found themselves with only a good hour or so of daylight by the time they got back on the trail. Soon the skies opened up again and they were doused with a blanket of heavy snow that greatly hindered their ability to move.

The narrow Delaware trading route was soon covered with several inches of deep, wet snow and, with the added weight of the food sacks, Maggie could feel them both slowing down.

Maggie could barely see a foot in front of her and she made sure that she held Anne's outstretched hand to guide the young woman slowly forward. Desperate to find a safe place to stop and try to wait out the storm, Maggie noticed the terrain had turned very rocky and difficult to traverse.

She helped Anne up and over several of the massive boulders that littered the slope they were climbing, but soon moved quickly ahead when she finally spotted what appeared to be a small cave just a few paces in front of them. With the snow hammering them, they were desperate to get themselves dried and warm.

Maggie let go of Anne's hand and weaved around a number of smaller rocks and boulders to finally get to a large natural crack in the side of a massive foothill, hardly visible through the storm.

Blindly rushing into the cold, damp opening of the cave, Maggie could see that it had been used by some animal that she prayed had long since abandoned it. Maggie turned around and called out to guide Anne towards the cave. Anne took a bit more time to reach the spot, but she was clearly happy to be out of the snow.

"We need to clear out some of this dirt," Maggie said as she kicked some of it to one side to see what the floor of the cave looked like, "but we should first see what we can use to get a fire going."

Another factor that made the cave even better was that the direction of the wind at the moment was blowing across the face of cave, which kept the snow outside.

Working as fast as their tired, cold limbs permitted them, Maggie pushed most of the dusty mess and piles of old animal scat to the entrance while Anne did a good job making a pile of useable twigs and wood pieces so they could start a fire. While she waited for Maggie to finish clearing the floor, Anne gathered rocks from just inside the cave opening to make a fire pit.

"How can we get the fire going now?" Anne asked Maggie, who had found some moss that she was organizing into some bedding to keep their backs from touching the damp floor during the night.

Maggie didn't reply, but immediately grabbed her musket and removed the small leather scrap she had tied around the flint to keep it dry. She pressed the flintlock against some nice kindling Anne had gathered and shot off her unloaded musket. The sparks from the flint hitting the lock quickly fell on the wood and it instantly ignited.

"How's that Anne?" Maggie smiled and enjoyed the blast of heat that shot out from the fire. Getting on her knees she blew the embers to get them to catch.

Anne said nothing but put her hands over the small flame and rubbed them to get them hot.

The storm outside was intensifying and, at times, the two women could not see anything outside the mouth of the cave. Maggie was oddly thankful that the storm was continuing because it would keep most things, man and beast, at bay for the foreseeable future.

Finally having some time to rest their exhausted legs, they enjoyed the supplies they had received from their French captors.

"What are we to do now, Maggie?" Anne broke their peace, not looking directly towards her.

"The weather will dictate what we do," Maggie said slowly as she watched the heavy snow continue to fall. "Now that we can't go towards the cabin, to be honest, I think we have to keep moving northeast. I do know of a large Mohawk village that sits near another large lake, but I can't tell you how far we are from it."

They slumped closer to the fire and stared out into the storm. Maggie said little else to Anne, who soon huddled amongst the thin layer of moss and fell asleep.

Maggie was very tired, but she still didn't feel comfortable enough to fall asleep. The last time she had fallen asleep, the French patrol had been allowed to sneak up on them. Maggie decided this time to keep her musket at the ready and do a better job protecting the sleeping Anne. She started by focusing on the fire and doing her best to keep it going.

The snow had finally lightened enough that she could see as far as the bottom trail they had used. The storm had dumped over a foot of the heavy, wet powder that smothered most of the wilderness. Maggie thought of how easily she or Anne could lose their footing or even snap an ankle on the snow-covered trail.

She also struggled to look as far as she could to somehow jog her memory in hopes she might recognize the landscape. Most of the wilderness just blended into a mass of woods and snow, and she truly had no idea if they were still in the Pennsylvania territory or now in New York. Maggie hoped that once they decided to move out, they might run into some British-allied Indians that would take them in for the winter.

Maggie could feel the fire weakening and her eyes getting harder to keep open, so she thought she might get up and take a look around the cave. She had noticed earlier that it looked like it was pretty deep and she decided to grab a small piece of burning wood and her musket. She did her best not to wake up Anne as she walked into the darkness.

The cold weather had killed off most of the spiders, and any rattlers that might have spent the summer in this cave should have long since found their winter dens. She presented these facts to herself in a stern voice and convinced herself that she had no reason to fear running into either creature.

It was noticeably colder deep in the cave, and the walls were leaking drips of freezing cold water all along its base. Maggie took her time and made sure she had enough light to get herself back out. She had walked far enough into the deep cave that the fire at the opening was barely visible. A light breeze blew on her face and that made her think that the cave might lead to another opening. After walking for what felt like a mile or so, Maggie decided to turn back.

She was very curious and decided that once the sun came out, she and Anne should take a better look at exactly where the cave might take them.

If it proved to be safe, perhaps they could remain in the cave for the time being instead of battling through the deep snow.

Maggie made her way back to the fire that was now little more than glowing embers, and took a seat just by the opening. The cold, damp air was strangely refreshing. With the storm moving out, the night sky became clear and filled with bright stars. The one nice element of winter nights was how the woods were much quieter and more peaceful. The odd brush wolf call broke the silence, but it was still quite pleasant.

By the time the sun wrestled away the cold night sky, Maggie had already eaten a small breakfast and gathered what scraps of wood were close by to keep the fire going. Despite only having a couple pieces of dried meat, Maggie's stomach ached and she felt like she might be getting sick.

Understanding they had little time for illness, Maggie did her best to keep busy and her mind off her sore belly.

"Sorry about resting so long," Anne offered as she finally awoke and rose to her feet. She quickly brushed away pieces of moss from her back.

"You looked comfortable, and we have no real reason to get up early or lose sleep," Maggie replied and handed her a sack of food.

Anne sat by the fire and dug through the sack to grab some pieces of food.

"What are the plans for today?" Anne asked between bites.

"I don't think we would get too far with all the snow out there," Maggie replied, "so I thought we might explore the cave. I walked a bit last night and it seems to go on some. What do you think?"

Anne strained to look into the darkness and replied, "If you think it might help."

Maggie waited for Anne to get herself fed and cleaned up. She found an old branch that she managed to snap in half and made two nice torches to provide them some light for their travels.

Not certain what they might find, Maggie suggested they take the two sacks of food and all their weapons. She prayed the cave would make traveling easier and keep them warmer.

Once again, as the two moved deeper into the cave, it became far colder and a definite breeze blew in their faces. Maggie had suggested remaining as quiet as possible since she guessed any noise would echo for miles.

The two women moved freely through the cave although it narrowed at points, so much so that they had to squeeze sideways just to make it past. It was difficult to know how far exactly they had walked. The farther they moved, the greater the breeze increased; to the point it almost extinguished their torches.

After what felt like several hours of walking, Maggie suddenly stopped.

Whispering as low as she could and motioning to get down, she asked Anne, "Did you hear that?"

Anne listened for a minute but could not hear anything.

Maggie put it down to some animal or the wind and continued on. It was only a couple moments later that they heard what sounded like muffled voices echo down the cave and instantly made Maggie stop again.

"I heard that," Anne said softly.

Unsure what to do with their torches, and afraid they might give up their position before they knew exactly what was ahead, Maggie motioned to get down and wait.

The cave was not easy to follow, and with its narrow stretches and meandering shape, Maggie felt trapped without a plan of action. If indeed they had heard voices, it would be smart to try to identify who they belonged to.

Logically, it might have been a couple of trappers who, like themselves, had gotten caught in yesterday's storm and were just waiting things out.

Maggie had to find out before she decided what they had to do. She was very happy and relieved that they had decided to bring along their weapons. At least they would have some way to defend against a possible hostile encounter.

"Let me move ahead and see who they might be," Maggie whispered to Anne, who just nodded and remained down.

"Stay here unless you hear shots," Maggie called back softly and moved slowly towards the noise.

Keeping as close to the damp wall as she could, Maggie kept her torch by her feet and watched her every step.

It wasn't long until the voices once again started to echo through the cave. As she grew much closer, Maggie could now make out what was being said. She knew it wasn't French and definitely not English, so she guessed it was Indians.

She got down on her stomach and instantly felt dampness seeping out of the cold cave floor, which instantly added to her discomfort. She left her torch resting against the wall and wore her musket around her shoulder. She was careful not to let it rub against the wall or floor to give her position away as she inched forward. She soon stopped to listen for any more noise that might shed some light on who the men were.

Wiggling herself forward again, she could finally see the small shreds of light that streaked across the dripping ceiling from the other opening.

The voices were getting louder and much clearer, but Maggie could not understand the tongue they were speaking. She knew it wasn't the language of the Delaware or Seneca, although she thought there were some familiar words.

Curious but still extremely cautious, Maggie pulled herself ahead to get a better look. One thing that worried her was that she had no idea how many Indians there were. Most of the voices sounded the same and just blended into each other.

Reaching a small, narrow laneway, Maggie peered over and around some loose rocks. She now could clearly see that there were a half dozen Indians sitting around a small fire. They looked like a hunting party more than a raiding party, since most of them were carrying bows and not muskets.

Maggie's eyes were fixated on one of the savages in particular. He was tall and thinly built yet he carried himself confidently. While the others sat around the fire pit, he stood looking over the woods.

She could not yet see his face, but when she heard his voice, it was oddly familiar.

As she slowly propped herself up, the Indian turned to face the others and gave Maggie a direct view of his face. Desperate not to shout out, Maggie pulled herself back and took a big breath.

Her heart was pounding and she was frozen, completely unsure of what she should do next.

Chapter | **Eight**

Jacob's trap was set; his men had managed to fully surround their unknown adversaries. Unwilling to open fire without knowing for sure if they were dealing with allies or enemies, Jacob watched as his men continued to press in slowly as the mysterious party advanced.

From what Jacob could see of the scouting party, their numbers were about the same as his own company. He took up position behind a large fallen tree and waited, watching the men as they advanced completely unaware that they were now being stalked. The party strolled up the snowy shore of the lake in a long single file following the narrow trail that guided them directly towards Jacob and his men.

As they drew closer to Jacob's position, he was finally given more than a mere glimpse of them. He was impressed with their discipline and how their dress blended them into the countryside. He realized they were experienced and began to worry that they might be more than just some wandering ranging party.

Once they cleared the narrow trail, the men quickly reorganized and split into small groups of five. They moved forward slowly, taking advantage of the trees and keeping themselves covered at all times.

Most of the men wore white blanket coats with a plain green stripe near the bottom hem, while others were wrapped in various pelts of deer, buffalo and elk. Their heads were covered with hoods or thick coyote pelts. They glided easily across the snow on snowshoes, though some used thick branches to provide them balance.

They traveled light. Most carried a musket and horn, and Jacob could see that several had simple sashes that held a knife or hatchet. If they had packs, they must have left them back at the sleds. Jacob was impressed with their careful advance and how they used every tree, either fallen or still standing, as cover while they moved forward.

Jacob also thought the advanced group appeared to be more like Indians than part of a regular ranging company. Despite their concealed faces, he was sure they were savages.

He now feared they might be French militia since he knew the British very rarely used Indians as scouts. The memories of Braddock only having a handful of Indian scouts on his disastrous expedition made Jacob extremely nervous now.

As he watched the small advanced guard move forward, Jacob reminded himself that these men could indeed be potential enemies. His own men remained steady, waiting for his signal to engage.

Jacob had positioned his men in a rough horseshoe shape. He was at the center with his back to the village while the rest of the men extended up the two sides of the horseshoe towards the lake. The men stood in pairs so one man could fire while the other reloaded. This would ensure a constant fire and make it appear that they had more men than they actually had.

His only concern was the possibility that another group of the unknown men might have traveled overland and could possibly flank him. He had specifically warned Joshua and James to watch for that maneuver.

Everything appeared to be going as planned until a deafening shout came from Jacob's left.

He swung around and saw a dozen men charging through the snow to hit directly at his exposed left flank. Their advance was quickly halted, however, when Joshua and James led their men and surrounded the surprised party. The attackers had no choice but to raise their arms in defeat and were immediately taken prisoners.

Thankfully, no shots were fired and the confusion soon settled. Returning his attention back to the men moving in from the lake, Jacob was pleased to see one of the men finally leave the security of the snow-capped sea of trees. He was tall and wore a green trimmed-back tricorn hat that was adorned with a large fox tail.

"Stop, gentlemen, we mean you no harm," the man called out in English, holding his short musket above his head.

Jacob waited a moment before he stood and called back, "Identify yourself, sir, or I will have no choice but to have my men fire on you and your men."

"No need for that, sir, my name is Captain Robert Rogers," he responded, still standing in the open. "We are a ranging company stationed at Fort Edward under General Webb."

Jacob waved Joshua to his side and asked, "Have you heard of this officer?"

"No, sir," Joshua responded, "but I had heard rumors of an elite company of rangers from New Hampshire or Vermont. Rogers sounds familiar, but I can't be certain. We know one thing; they are definitely English."

Jacob smiled and called back to Rogers, "I am Captain Jacob Sims of Stevens Ranging Company out of Virginia."

"You boys lost?" Rogers called back, drawing some laughs from his men. "I thought Virginia was south of here."

Tired of this ridiculous exchange, Jacob boldly moved out from the safety of the woods and walked towards the brash ranger standing in the middle of the small landing. Joshua followed directly behind, keeping his musket at the ready.

They quickly reached the tall, impressive ranger. Rogers had removed his heavy blanket coat and stood dressed in a nicely tailored, albeit soiled, leaf-green, thigh-length jacket and well-worn, brain-tanned leggings.

"Sir, I'm glad you finally found it reasonable to show your faces to us," Jacob said, offering a brief salute to show his respect. "We thought you might keep stalking us all winter."

"No need for such formalities, Sims," Rogers said in response to Jacob's salute, "and my apologies for our cautious manner. You have to understand that we don't usually run into unknown colonial or regular troops this far west." Rogers offered a sly smile.

Jacob was still not sure what to think of this ranger, yet he politely offered his hand. His gesture was immediately accepted as Rogers waved to his men to join him in the middle of the small open area.

Both Jacob and Joshua remained guarded as they watched twenty or so similar-looking men walk out of the relative safety of the woods. Rogers' men stood a few feet behind their leader.

"So, Sims, what brings you and your boys to these parts?" Rogers asked.

"Just doing some scouting and seeing what's out in these parts," Jacob said simply. He was honestly not interested in making small talk.

There was an uncomfortable silence, and Jacob figured that Rogers expected him to call his own men out of their hidden perches. Having no reason to expose his men, Jacob attempted to lighten the situation by talking and asked, "How far are we from this Fort Edward you mentioned?"

Taking a look around the perimeter of the forest line, Rogers answered, "Maybe twenty miles due east of here. There is also another British fort we call William Henry that sits fourteen or so miles north of Edward."

"So, the British hold most of the New York territory now?" Joshua stepped up and asked.

Jacob shot a hard look at Joshua for interrupting two senior officers, but Rogers was more than happy to reply to the direct question. "Sims, there's no reason to scold the lad. This is not the British army and every man should be able to voice his opinion."

"As for your question, lad," he said, turning to Joshua, "the British barely hold a piece of this territory, and I fear we might be losing what grip they had. The French have a stronghold on the major lakes and key portage routes. They have a fort called Carillon at the mouth of Lake George and Champlain, which gives them strength in the entire territory.

"It certainly doesn't help when the bloody British officers decide that they need all the best regulars to fight in Nova Scotia. The damn lobsters just received a message from the king that England has just declared war on France."

Jacob immediately commented, "What the hell do they think we have been doing for the past couple years, playing bloody chess?"

Rogers laughed, as did most of his men. He nodded and said, "We have lost a number of good friends already, for this not being a war."

"We should get these men out of the cold and take up a more comfortable place to speak," Jacob said. "Our little village is certainly not to be compared to Fort Edward, but we can get a couple of fires going and keep the boys warm."

Before Rogers replied, he called to one of his men to take five others and set up a picket where they had first encountered Jacob's men. After sending two more men back to check on the sleds and oxen, he motioned for the rest of his men to head towards the village.

"Let's see your village and maybe we can share some coffee," Rogers finally replied and walked beside Jacob and Joshua.

As they approached the entrance, Jacob asked Joshua to retrieve the men and organize a picket to be placed near the opening that led towards the west.

"When you are done, Joshua," Jacob called after the young man's retreating figure, "please come back and join us. Bring along James as well, if you can find him."

As soon as they stepped into the open space of the village, Rogers turned to Jacob and said, "Not sure if you know this, but this place was once an old Seneca village. I think it was a key village to their people at one time. It has held up pretty well considering they abandoned it a few years back. My men usually use it as a safe stopover whenever we venture this far west."

Jacob offered Rogers a seat near one of the fire pits his pickets had set up in the center of the village. Soon after one of the men piled a few larger pieces of dried wood on it, the fire shot out so much heat that Jacob was forced to remove his outer coat.

"So, captain," Jacob began as he poured two cups of bitter root coffee into cups and handed one to Rogers, "you questioned why we are so far east; what about you? Why would you be scouting this far from Edward?"

"Thanks, Sims," he said as he accepted the cup and took a long sip. "That's a good question. There are rumors that the French and their savages are gathering to attack one of our forts and I was asked to scout around to find any sign of them. I think Webb just hates us being mixed with his men and wants us out of his fort."

As the two men enjoyed their coffee, Rogers pulled out a piece of dried pork and cut it in half with the knife he pulled from a sheath he had dangling around his neck. He handed one of the pieces to Jacob and started on the second himself.

"Thank you, sir; please call me Jacob. Much like you, I treat my men with the respect they deserve and not like animals as our English friends do."

"Very well, Jacob, you may call me Robert," he offered kindly. "How are your men holding up?"

Jacob paused briefly and replied, "They have been through a lot over the past number of months, but they are good men and I owe them all a great debt."

"How so?" Rogers piped in before Jacob could continue.

"They are all far from home and they are doing most of this as a favor to me. You see, we built a fort just at the foothills of the Alleghenies, raided a large Delaware village and returned to a burned out fort in which most of the inhabitants were either dead or taken captive. One of the captives is my wife…" Jacob stopped abruptly, not wanting to show too much emotion.

"Damn savages," Rogers said, "the bloody French use them to do all their dirty work and then step back and try to act like gentlemen."

The two fell silent and continued drinking their bitter coffee as they listened to the sounds of the active camp.

"Every time I drink this, I promise myself it will be the last time," Rogers said with a grimace as he dumped the remaining coffee from his cup, leaving a dark streak of melted snow.

Jacob appreciated Rogers' attempt to lighten the mood.

"What's next for your boys, Jacob?" Rogers asked as he stretched out on the log.

"I feel somewhat lost in these parts," Jacob admitted. "If not for the young lad that was with me earlier, we would be in trouble."

"The boy, he is from this territory?" Rogers asked.

"His name is Joshua; he once lived near Albany until the Huron raided his family's homestead and took him captive. He spent a few years with them and then escaped." Jacob explained.

"Damn savages," Rogers spat out again, showing his temper. "I hate them all and wish I could rid them from this country."

"Don't you have a few within your ranks?" Jacob asked, careful not to insult his guest.

"They're Stockbridge Indians; they are civilized and far from the savages we see almost every day," Rogers answered as he got to his feet.

Jacob did the same and said, "I could do with a walk around the lake to check on my men. Care to join me, Robert?"

"Good idea, Jacob; I don't like to stay in one place for too long." Rogers grabbed his musket and was walking towards the entrance even before Jacob had time to retrieve his coat.

Shuffling to catch up, Jacob was thankful that Joshua and James had returned and were speaking with Rogers just at the mouth of the main path. As he approached them, Jacob tried not to show that he was breathing heavily from keeping up with Rogers' sudden spurt of energy.

The conversation between Joshua, James and Rogers stopped as soon as Jacob arrived, and he decided not to read too much into such a reaction. Jacob turned to Joshua and asked, "How are the men?"

"Good, sir," Joshua replied loyally. "I sent a couple of patrols out and they have not returned as of yet. The rest of them are cutting wood and keeping the immediate trails clear of snow and debris."

"Well, gentlemen," Rogers interjected, "I need to take a good look around and see what my men are up to as well. Jacob, I would enjoy your company if you please." Rogers nodded to the two lads and once again started to walk towards the lake trail before Jacob could offer an answer.

"They seem to be good lads, and I must say your men appear to be well equipped to handle this territory," Rogers told Jacob as he slid down a slight slope that brought him down to the lakeside trail.

Doing his best to keep pace with the focused ranger, Jacob replied, "You and your men are welcome to stay with us as long as you'd like."

With that, Rogers suddenly stopped just short of the trail and said, "Funny thing, I was going to offer you and your men the option to come back with us to Fort Edward."

Jacob answered him respectfully, saying, "It sounds tempting, but I think we would rather stay here and keep out of any trouble that might tie us up for a while. If the French are thinking about attacking one of the forts, being stuck there really doesn't get me closer to my family."

For the first time, Rogers looked upset and replied bluntly, "The way I look at it, if you decide to stay here, I fear in the spring I will return with my men and find you either starved out or dead at the hands of the Ottawa or Seneca. How will that help your family?"

Unfazed by his reaction, Jacob said, "We are more than used to living off the land, no matter how strange it might be. My men and I have done well thus far and have little to fear about what the savages in these parts might bring."

"If you think the weather so far has been bad, just wait until you feel the winds and snow in January or February," Rogers said in a voice that had become much more confrontational. "That will certainly be a much better test for your lads. As for the savages, the winter does slow them down; but if they find you here, you will be greeted by cut trap lines and awakened to a burning village."

The two continued on their walk in silence, and Jacob could feel that the tension between them had grown.

Rogers led the way down to the lake and directly to the two large sleds that were left undefended in the snow. As he took a moment to inspect the heavy, wooden vessels, Jacob did the same and was impressed by the fine craftsmanship put into the two sleds. The four heavy oxen were left unhitched to feed on another small bale of hay that one of the men had pulled from the back of one of the sleds.

One of Rogers' men had called him over and was pointing out the damage done earlier by James and his men.

"Damn it, Sims!" Rogers called out as he kicked snow at the front of one of the sleds. "Your men really put me in a bad spot. Why the hell did they cut the steering cord to the runners?"

Jacob offered no reply until Rogers pulled out the rope and held it up for him to see.

"May I remind you, sir," Jacob said tersely, "my men were acting on my orders, and at the time we had no reason to think you were a friend." Jacob felt 'friend' might still be a somewhat loose term at the moment.

"If we can't steer these beasts, we are basically stranded here until one of my men returns from Edward with some hemp," Rogers mumbled, kicking more snow as if it would fix his problems.

"Your men have made my choice easy," he continued while looking at the bleakness of the snow-covered lake. "It appears we will be staying for the immediate future."

Jacob just let him be and kept himself busy by walking the lake's edge, checking for weak spots in the ice to possibly use for some winter fishing.

Before either man could continue, Joshua and one of Rogers' men slid down onto the ice.

"Sir, the men are getting out-of-hand and it looks like we might have a few fights ready to break out," Joshua explained, while the other ranger went directly to Rogers to speak a little more privately.

Jacob did his best to respectfully hide his anger, but Rogers slapped him on his back and said, "Reports have it that one of your boys challenged one of mine. How do you feel about a little fight to keep the men occupied?"

Jacob's first reaction was to send Joshua up the trail and put a stop to all the sudden mischief, but Rogers' outward confidence made him react uncharacteristically.

"My men are not permitted to gamble or fight," Jacob said, "but if you think your lad can give one of mine a good fight, maybe we should see for ourselves." Immediately, he wanted to recant his approval, yet knew it was far too late.

"Joshua, get up there and get the lads to wait for us," he ordered. "I hope the man in question is Larson?" Jacob was satisfied once Joshua turned and smiled in answer to his question.

Jacob felt much better now. Jed Larson was a broad-shouldered Swede and a former blacksmith's assistant who loved to fight. He was a man feared by most of the others within the ranging company. Even though Jacob was four or five inches taller and out-weighed him by almost thirty pounds, he would never want to get in a tussle with Larson. His forearms alone were larger than most men's legs.

Jacob let Rogers and his fellow ranger confidently stroll up to the main trail towards the village. He remained quiet and prayed that the situation would turn out in his favor.

The three men were greeted by shouts and wild cheers. Every available man appeared to be present and they were all forming up a circle around the two combatants just outside the walls of the village.

Both Rogers and Jacob pushed their way through the throngs of men and into the center of the fight. Jacob nodded towards the smiling Larson who returned his greeting. Rogers went directly to his man and was speaking with him like this was a matter of life or death.

Jacob knew he could say nothing of benefit to his man, so he just stood and watched the reaction of the rangers as Larson removed his shirt to expose his muscular forearms and massive upper arms. Larson and his opponent were the same height, but Rogers' ranger was not as big or athletic looking.

Jacob had thoughts to call the whole thing off after seeing the ranger remove his shirt to display a pot belly and a layer of fat that would have made a hibernating bear proud.

Rogers led his man to the informal center of the ring and waited for Jacob to do the same. Jacob obliged and walked with Larson until the competitors were face-to-face with each other.

The ranger looked at the two men and spat a long streak of chewing tobacco across the snow, drawing cheers from his fellow mates. Larson just rubbed his knuckles in anticipation of the forthcoming battle.

Rogers stepped between them and shouted, "Gentlemen, try to make this as fair as you can; this is not a fight to the death. No weapons or such, but the winner will need to get on top of his opponent and hold him there until I count to five. Whoever wins gets his fellow lads the village now occupied by these fine men."

Jacob had not agreed to such terms, but was in no position to back out now. He just shot Rogers a well-intended glare and walked back with Larson a few paces before the fight formally started.

Unable to hold his tongue, Jacob called out to Rogers loudly enough for the majority of men to hear, "I fear you might not be able to count all the way to five, sir; I think Joshua should be the one to count the take down."

Jacob's men cheered but stopped when Rogers spoke up, saying, "Fine with me, Sims; it's really no matter who counts your boy out."

The camp erupted until one of the men shot off his musket at Rogers' signal for the fight to begin.

Just as the two started to circle each other, Jacob called out, "Watch out for his trickery, lad!"

The men on both sides taunted each other and heckled the two men to do something.

Jacob stood back and prayed that his lad could beat Rogers' man; not because he wanted the relative comfort of the village, but more out of spite for the arrogance that the rangers had displayed since they arrived.

Larson was by far the aggressor and attempted to land several punches that were easily dodged by the smaller, quicker ranger.

The beginning of the battle was more of a chase than the fight the men had anticipated. Rogers' man kept moving, obviously trying to tire Larson. Jacob could see that his man was getting frustrated by the ranger's interest in avoiding a fight, but he trusted Larson had faced opponents like this before.

The crowd was also getting tired of the lack of action and showed their unhappiness with boos and mocking cheers.

Jacob could see that Rogers was enjoying his man's tactics and simply clapped his approval. He called out to Rogers, "Is your boy going to fight or just go out for a walk?"

Just as he said that, the ranger charged wildly towards Larson. As though he had expected such a tactic, the Swede easily avoided the man's attempt to drive his shoulder into his mid-section by quickly driving his knee into the lowered face of the ranger.

The force pushed the man's head up and Larson was quick to pounce on the opportunity. He threw two uppercuts before the ranger could cover his face, and ended the fight with three more rapid shots to the man's ribs.

The fight was over. Larson stood over the man who knelt on his hands and knees and was spitting blood. Joshua was quick to count to five and rushed to raise Larson's arm.

Jacob's men erupted in cheers while Rogers' rangers stood silent and stunned by what had just happened.

Before the camp could become a mass of men fighting each other, Jacob and Rogers quickly quelled the possibility of a mob reaction.

Attempting to ease the tension, Jacob called out over the noise, "Gentlemen, we are done here. Get your gear and form up." His men did as they were ordered and left the rangers standing looking at each other.

Rogers screamed, "Rangers, to me."

With the men in order, Jacob continued, "The fight is over and we need to get back to the matter at hand. Captain Rogers and his men are welcome to stay with us in the village, and we must start to treat them like allies instead of enemies."

He waited for Rogers to reiterate his sentiments, but he remained silent. The bloodied ranger was assisted by two of his fellow mates and carried towards the lake.

"Bring him into the village; he can recover by one of the fires," Jacob insisted when he realized that the rangers were about to leave.

None of the rangers, not even Rogers, bothered to react to the offer and they all continued down the trail to the sleds.

Jacob's men stood by his side and watched the rangers leave. No one knew what to say until he ordered them to return to the village.

"Joshua, please take a small hunting party out and check the trap lines. Please also see to the pickets, if you will," Jacob ordered, still unsure of what to make of the reaction Rogers and his rangers had displayed.

As usual, James decided to tag along with Joshua.

As he returned to the confines of the village, Jacob reflected on the reaction of Rogers and his rangers. At the very least, if the rangers left, they would inform the commander at Fort Edwards that there was a small unit of English out in the wilderness. Jacob was pleased by the thought that they were not alone. Once the weather cleared and the trails become passable, he intended to visit the fort with his men.

One of the men remained in the tower that commanded the best view of the lake in order to watch exactly what the rangers were up to. Jacob sat by one of the fires to contemplate what they needed to do next.

"Sir, the rangers are returning up the lake trail," the man in the tower called down. "It looks like they are carrying two large sacks and a few other things I can't make out from this distance."

Unsure what to make of it, Jacob had the men inside the village ready themselves for a possible confrontation. He sent out a man to locate Joshua and recall the hunting party to the fort. He also ordered the pickets to fall back within running distance of the village.

The tension around the camp was high as the man in the perch continued to call out every movement he saw the rangers make. It only took a few minutes for Rogers and his men to clear the trail and return to the small open field just outside the village's first outer wall.

Jacob honestly felt little threat from the rangers and thought maybe this was just an odd way for them to save some face after they watched one of their own get pummeled by what they probably considered an inferior man.

"May we approach, Captain Sims?" Rogers called out. "We have brought some food and drink for the men to enjoy."

Most of the men manning the walls finally appeared to relax. Jacob motioned for them to stay alert as he walked through the winding entrance.

Jacob shouted out a reply before he stepped into the open, "All is clear, sir. Please bring the men into the village."

He stepped out and was the first to greet the returning rangers. Their mood had apparently changed and they happily filed into the intimate confines of the inner village.

Rogers greeted Jacob with a hearty handshake and ordered a few of his rangers to relieve some of Jacob's men on picket duty.

As the rangers made themselves at home inside the village, they dutifully carried in additional cut tree trunks and placed them around the fires as seats. A couple of them constructed two more fire pits and, despite the crowded space, the two groups of men openly mingled together.

Just as Rogers was about to make himself comfortable, he finally noticed there was a Frenchman amongst the ranks of Jacob's rangers.

"What is this?" Rogers said, loudly enough for all his men to hear and to get Jacob's attention.

"He is one of us; we took him prisoner a few weeks back and decided to keep him with us," Jacob explained, unsure why this should pose a problem.

Rogers refused to move and again questioned, "How do you know we can trust him?"

Jacob did his best not to show his displeasure at the line of questions, but answered, "He has pulled his weight and has had a number of opportunities to escape, but he has remained here and proven to be an asset."

Seeing that Rogers was still uneasy about having a French soldier living amongst them, Jacob continued to try to ease his hesitation by saying, "He can speak and translate a number of the savages' languages and works as hard as any man I have seen."

Rogers still didn't appear convinced, and Jacob almost brought up the subject of Rogers' Stockbridge Indians joining in with his men. However, he decided not to push the subject and eventually Rogers seemed to relax.

Thankfully, Joshua and James returned from their shortened hunting trip at that precise moment. Jacob reached them immediately and explained the latest.

With everything settled, Joshua was excited to tell Jacob some news, "We were tracking a good-sized herd of bison. I left two men to keep an eye on them; if we can get one or two, we will have a feast tonight."

"Good news, lads," Jacob said smiling. "Go back and try to get what you can, but return as soon as possible. Please watch the sky and get back here at the first sign of the sun moving below the mountains." Jacob patted both of them on their backs as they excitedly ran back out into the woods.

While he was speaking with Joshua and James, the rangers had opened their two sacks and had already started passing around a couple bottles of rum to the men.

The sacks were also packed with rice, dried pork, deer meat, beans and several smaller bags of corn meal. The rangers were quick to set the rice to boil over the open fires in two pots they had brought with them; they also set out several cakes of corn meal to roast on the rocks placed around pits.

"Thank you, Robert, for returning," Jacob said, as Rogers handed him a tin cup filled with rum. "I prayed we were not going to leave things the way they ended."

He was not much of a hard liquor drinker, but Jacob accepted the rum and took a sip. The homemade rum burned as it went down, and he fought the urge to cough it all back up.

Rogers smiled at his reaction and said, "It takes a bit of getting used to. To be honest, it's not my favorite thing to drink, but it does warm you up when winter is at its worst. The men call this 'New Hampshire Mountain Water', but with one heck of a bite."

Jacob laughed, "Good, I thought it was just me."

The two men shared another laugh and Rogers offered Jacob a seat beside him.

"So what is your story, Jacob?" Rogers asked as he stretched out his long legs, almost putting his moccasins in the fire.

"Well, I have a small plot of land in the southern end of the Pennsylvanian province that my family once lived on. I joined up with Washington's Virginia militia and fought with him at Fort Necessity and Braddock's disaster near Fort Duquesne. While I was away, my farm was raided by the French and Huron, and they took my wife and four children captive." As Jacob spoke, he stopped several times to clear his throat.

"Sorry, Jacob," Rogers said. "I didn't mean to bring up such a tough subject."

"Basically, since then I have been searching the wilderness for my family," Jacob continued as if Rogers hadn't spoken. "I did find my wife, but she was taken again when I was with Armstrong's raiding party at Kittanning. The boy with Joshua is actually my son James, but after spending some time with the Delaware, he is not the same boy I once knew."

Before he could expand any further on his story, Jacob noticed Joshua entering the village with two massive bison. He had them strung up on two large tree branches that were carried by four men to each beast. James took up the rear and, once the other men saw the food, a loud cheers burst from them.

"Looks like we will have a good meal tonight," Jacob said and joined the cheering men.

Rogers followed and was the first to greet Joshua with a handshake and accolades, "Good job, lads! These are two fine bulls that will keep our bellies full for the next week."

Some of the men relieved the weight of the bison from the visibly tired hunters and, within a few minutes, they had them skinned and placed over the two main fires. Four rangers, with the help of a couple of Jacob's men, were busy scraping the pelts and stretching them between two branches. Once the pelts were cleaned and dried, they would make a nice outer coat or, if cut up, some nice winter mitts and leggings.

Everything appeared to be happy within the confines of the once abandoned village. The ordinarily cautious Rogers and his rangers indulged in drink and food that was a special treat at this time of year. Jacob and his men did the same and, completely uncharacteristically, Jacob even recalled the pickets that normally guarded the outer wall of the village.

Little did the usually prudent leaders know that the surrounding forest was full of eyes, and that an unseen force sat back watching…waiting to strike.

Chapter | **Nine**

Maggie knew she had to be sure of what she was doing before she made a fatal error. As she gathered her thoughts, she kept her eyes on the lone Indian as he confidently addressed his fellow warriors.

She feared that standing up might give up her position, so she strained her eyes to make sure they were not playing tricks on her. The warrior in question was very tall and thin; as she studied him, she saw that his build was actually quite muscular.

She could still hear his voice, but it did nothing to help her confirm the man's identity. The fire certainly didn't help either as all it did was light up the faces of the warriors sitting nearest to it. As the speaker was standing, his face was clouded by the shadows, out of reach of the firelight.

Maggie sat patiently by and waited for him to turn his head slightly. She just needed one quick look and that would confirm what she prayed for. Finally, he sat before the fire and the glow of the flames lit his profile.

Exposed in the firelight was the proof Maggie needed and she jumped from her hiding place screaming, "One-Ear! One-Ear! It's me, Maggie… Maggie Murray!"

The reaction from the warrior almost made her step back into the darkness to run, but she knew that such an action could possibly end in her death and Anne's. Anne had remained back, waiting for Maggie to call out to her.

The warriors around the fire were up and covered the space between Maggie and the entrance so quickly that she could not react. They had her arms and she had no time to fight back. They had her prized bow and quiver as well as her musket.

Pulling her towards the waiting warrior, the only thought racing through her head was how wrong she had been. She prayed that Anne remained hidden and would not be dragged into her folly.

Her arms ached from the tight grip the warriors had on them, but she refused to show any signs of pain.

The lead warrior returned to the position where she had first seen him. With his back to her, he stood looking out into the mass of forest that engulfed the territory.

Frightened and upset that her instincts had been so off, Maggie waited helplessly for him to face her and hand down orders for what to do with her. Her heart leapt to her throat as the warrior turned and she saw a smile that brought tears to her eyes.

As he turned toward them, the warriors released their grips on Maggie and she rushed towards One-Ear. She almost knocked him over when she threw her arms around him, but he caught his balance before they both fell.

"My God, I thought I would never see you again!" Maggie teetered between tears and laughter.

"It is good to finally find you, Miss Maggie," One-Ear said, doing his best to keep his emotions in check for the benefit of his warriors. "It has been a tough year without you."

Maggie's relief and excitement were quickly joined by shaking and a burst of tears. One-Ear gently moved her to the fire and sat beside her.

"All is good, Miss Maggie; sit by the fire and warm yourself," he suggested and motioned to a couple of his fellow warriors to gather up some food and water for her.

Her head was spinning and she struggled to believe that she was not dreaming. As she calmed down and took a better look at her friend, Maggie managed to say, "You have changed so much over the last year; I almost didn't believe it was you! I had been watching you for a while, but I just couldn't be certain."

One-Ear just smiled and handed her a carved out gourd full of water.

After she took a drink, a sudden thought came over her and she said, "Anne…I almost forgot Anne. One-Ear, I have a friend who is waiting for word from me. She is waiting back inside the cave. Be careful she has her musket with her."

"Do not frighten her," he said simply as he pointed two of his warriors towards the darkness of the cave. The men nodded and were soon running into the shadows.

"I thought you were dead," Maggie said quietly as fresh tears stung her eyes.

One-Ear laughed and explained, "Me too! It took several moons before I felt better. I was nursed back by one of the elders, but by the time I felt better it had been too long to go and search for you. How did you escape from the Ottawa?"

Maggie took some time to gather her thoughts, but stopped when she heard screams echoing from beyond the darkness. She knew it was Anne and she hoped the girl wouldn't fight back too much.

Returning her attention to One-Ear's question, Maggie gave a concise report of what had happened since they had last seen one another. "The Ottawa left me at a small Delaware village," she began, "but they never returned after the French defeated the British in the wilderness. The French took me from the village, but they were attacked by the English. I was reunited with Jacob and Joshua for a while before being captured by the Delaware again."

One-Ear jumped in, "You saw Joshua?"

"Yes, and he was doing well, though he was worried about you," Maggie replied.

Their reunion was interrupted by the kicking and screaming appearance of Anne. Maggie went to her and tried her best to calm her down. Once she realized all was well, Anne stopped her screams and hugged Maggie with all her strength.

"Anne, all is well," Maggie said, wiggling away from Anne's unusually strong grip. "We are in good hands. This is my friend One-Ear."

Anne smiled weakly but still appeared to be shaken. Maggie guided her to take a seat by the fire and sat next to her. One of the warriors stood near One-Ear with Anne's musket, unsure what he should do with the gun.

"We will have more time to talk later, Miss Maggie," One-Ear said as he stood, "but for now, we need to get out of this cave and back on the trail. The French seem to be out, as are their Huron dogs. We must be careful and silent, so we can reach our village before the winter keeps us here for months." He turned once again and stared out into the sea of leafless trees and thousands of pines that still managed to prevent all but the dimmest light from reaching the forest floor.

Maggie counted ten warriors plus One-Ear, who was clearly their leader, and felt a wonderful feeling of relief and comfort. Being in One-Ear's protection again was nothing like being with Jacob, but it gave her the same feeling of security.

She focused on continuing to calm Anne as she watched a now-mature One-Ear, organize his fellow warriors. He sent out two scouts to see what was happening down below, if there were any signs of movement. He also had two warriors check the end of the cave Maggie had come from to make sure they wouldn't be surprised again from behind.

Maggie was happy that her bow and musket had been returned. Once Anne was feeling better, Maggie asked One-Ear if he needed any help.

"We are good for now," One-Ear said. "I just want to get back on the trail and get home. The weather worries me, as do the French. The sooner we get moving, the better. How are you feeling? Can you move with us? The young girl appears to be weak; I'm worried she might slow us down."

His frankness worried Maggie, but she spoke quickly to reassure him, "We can keep up; I will keep Anne moving as far as you need us to go."

One-Ear just smiled at Maggie's insistence and continued on with the preparations to depart.

It was already early afternoon. Anne and Maggie shared some food while One-Ear sent out some of his warriors to scout the surrounding trail.

Maggie could see that most of the useful sunlight was fading, which would limit how far they could go on trails freshly packed with snow. She hadn't noticed at first, but One-Ear had one of his warriors make two sets of snowshoes for her and Anne. When he finished and fitted them, he took both ladies out to try them on the soft snow.

Despite having hunted and fished throughout past winters back home, Maggie had never had worn a pair before. She was surprised by the light weight of them and once the warrior gave her a fast lesson, she gave them a try. She fell several times and was forced to listen to the laughs of the on-looking warriors. She paused and watched in amazement as Anne navigated through the woods as if she was floating above the snow.

"You have done this before?" Maggie called out to Anne.

"The Delaware taught me the first winter I was with them," Anne replied as she glided effortlessly over the snow. "Most of them learn almost before they can walk."

After watching her and taking further instructions from the warriors, Maggie got her balance and began moving over the snow. She was far less comfortable than Anne, but the more she moved the better she got.

Satisfied that the two women would not slow them down, One-Ear motioned his fellow warriors to move out. Four of them were sent ahead and asked to lay out a good trail and watch for any signs of the French or their allies.

Before the rest of the group moved out, the two women were each given a heavy pelt to keep them warm, as well as a pair of fur-lined moccasins. They were far too big for their small feet, but once strapped into the snowshoes, they fit snuggly and kept their feet dry and warm.

Feeling a renewed sense of relief and strength, Maggie managed to keep pace with her escorts. Anne was just as proficient on the shoes as the men, and at times even took the lead. After a couple of miles, one of the warriors gave Maggie two trimmed sticks to help with her balance.

The line of men and women moved swiftly over the snow. Despite the sun's descent and the lowering temperatures, One-Ear encouraged them to keep moving. It was pitch dark and she was barely able to see the tracks in the snow ahead of her, but Maggie kept herself moving. She almost ran into the warrior ahead of her when he suddenly stopped.

One-Ear decided it was much safer to stop for a rest before heading back out at first light. He moved the group up and over a small rise, into a nice dry camp that was covered by a large overhanging boulder that appeared to be balancing precariously just above their heads.

"We used this place a few days ago and found it safe and a good spot to remain out of sight," One-Ear said.

Maggie could see the burned remains of a fire pit and was surprised when one of the warriors had another fire going before she had her snowshoes off.

"Is it safe to have a fire this deep into the wilderness?" Maggie asked One-Ear, who had taken a seat beside her.

"Most nights we would not, but I fear this night might be colder than most," One-Ear explained. "My scouts said they have seen nothing of the French, so I pray to the spirits that they keep us safe."

Too cold and exhausted to give into any further concern, Maggie was happy to have the awkward shoes off and the warmth of a fire hitting her face.

One of the men opened a sack and shared some dried meat. Maggie did the same with her supply, and the warriors happily enjoyed the bread and cheese she offered.

All was well, and soon everyone in the group was fast asleep. By unspoken consent, everyone seemed to take turns throughout the night, waking to feed the fire.

The sun soon broke over the horizon and Maggie dusted off a thin layer of snow as she sat up and struggled to get her snowshoes back on.

"How far do we need to go?" Maggie asked One-Ear, who was strapping on his own shoes.

"Not far, Miss Maggie," One-Ear replied. "Depending on our efforts today, we might be there by tonight."

Maggie was certainly happy to hear that. Just as she moved to get up, a deep pain in the pit of her stomach wretched at her throat and she spit up all the food she had enjoyed the night before. Thankfully, she was far enough away from everyone and didn't get any of the acidic liquid on them.

The warriors stood around, unsure of what they should do until One-Ear again organized the scouts to move out.

Anne went directly over to Maggie and offered her some water.

"Thanks," Maggie said, taking some water and spitting out a mouthful onto the snow. "I'm not sure where that came from, but I feel better now." She took one last gulp and was ready to move out.

Anne just smiled and was up the trail before Maggie could say anything else to her.

"Are you well?" One-Ear called out.

"I'm fine," she answered, only to be left once again speaking to his back as he raced up the trail.

Taking in a deep breath of cold morning air, Maggie pushed forward. It was one of the first times she had noticed the weight of her musket. Her stomach still ached, but she had nothing more to give up. She trudged through the snow and simply followed the packed line of prints that neatly led the way.

Tired and not completely recovered from her upset stomach, Maggie pushed herself hard to keep up and was happy when One-Ear called to her that they were going to rest and have some food.

It was cold and there was a definite dampness in the air, yet Maggie was happy to stop and take a moment to catch her breath.

Anne moved to her side and asked, "How are you feeling, Maggie?"

"Well, considering the weather and these damn shoes," Maggie replied with a grin, careful not to complain too loudly.

Maggie's first thought was how the tables had turned. When this trek started, she had spent her time worrying about the health of Anne and if she could keep up; now she was the one everyone was concerned about. Her stomach was still sore, so despite the fact that she was actually hungry, Maggie refused the offer of food when asked.

Anne sat with her the entire time they rested, but they didn't say much. As soon as the scouts moved out, Anne smiled at Maggie and quickly returned to the trail also.

One-Ear came by to check on her when he noticed her struggling to get back on her feet. "We are nearly there, Miss Maggie," he said. "The village is just over the small ridge then across an easy pathway."

Maggie did her best to keep her pain hidden and nodded to her friend. The thought of relaxing in the village pushed her forward and she did her best to keep up with the main group. Two warriors, taking up the rear, kept urging her when they got too close.

After moving all day, the ridge One-Ear had pointed to was now at her back. She had struggled through the rough terrain, but once they hit the mostly even ground of a large meadow that appeared to stretch for miles, Maggie got her second wind. The open field now greeted the small party with bone-chilling winds that swept over the trees and kicked up walls of blowing and drifting snow.

She could smell the lake that churned up ice and deathly freezing water just a mile or so to her left. The flat, snow-packed field was much easier to traverse. After the endless miles she had walked, the once hated snowshoes became much easier to use and she was happy to have them.

Even with the snow, Maggie started to recall the countryside and it began to bring back some memories, both good and bad. One-Ear dropped back to her side and they walked the remaining few miles together.

"I can't tell you how happy I am finding you well," Maggie said, breaking the silence that they shared for the first mile.

"Now we have to find Joshua and your Jacob," One-Ear replied and continued to walk by her side.

Once they reached the first of the outer fields of the large village, Maggie got a familiar whiff of the fires and general aromas that permeated around the outskirts of the village's walls.

One-Ear had sent forward two warriors to tell the villagers that they would soon be arriving. The rest of the way was lit by the internal fires that glowed over the sky. The winter night had a deep chill that made one's breath steam and the thought of being under the roof of one of the village homes warmed Maggie.

This was one of the few times that she would be welcomed into a village and not be expected to run the gauntlet of villagers waiting to pummel her mercilessly.

One-Ear soon had to move ahead to greet the village elders; after a brief smile, he was moving briskly forward leaving Maggie to take up the rear just ahead of the two rear scouts.

Anne waited for Maggie to reach her before they walked together into the welcoming village. They were instantly struck by the scene of several of the villagers lined up in parallel lines, ready for the two women to run between them.

"I hope they are friendly to the Delaware," Anne whispered nervously to Maggie.

"You have little to worry about; I think they will look at you as a white woman and not one of their own," Maggie shot back, still upset how Anne saw herself.

Maggie's expectations that she would not have to be greeted in this manner made her look towards One-Ear. He nodded to her and motioned for her to step up and run into the awaiting gauntlet.

Instinctively covering up her face, she smiled at Anne and ran head-down between the lines of villagers. Before she could understand what was happening, the villagers gently slapped her on the back and moved her along the line.

The first familiar face Maggie saw was Morning Sun, the mother of Pontiac, the Ottawa chief who had brutally kidnapped her on her last visit to the village. Maggie stopped in time to watch Anne as she ran the gauntlet and was treated with the same civility. She ran directly to Maggie's side.

Morning Sun smiled broadly as she approached them and said to Maggie, "Morning Fire, you are well. The spirits have listened to my prayers and brought you back to us."

"This is my friend Anne," Maggie said. "She is a friend to the Delaware." Maggie was polite, but remained uncertain about the older woman's role in her abduction by Pontiac.

"You have not eaten well since you were taken from us," Morning Sun said as she took Maggie's hand. She extended her other hand to Anne and said, "Please come and take some of my food and get yourselves strong again." Maggie recognized the house to which she led them as the place where she had stayed briefly the last time she spent time at the village.

"You look well; it is a pleasure to be back," Maggie said politely. She was finding it difficult to face Morning Sun, but decided to enjoy the moment and keep close to One-Ear.

Maggie and Anne spent the night with the rest of the women and their families. Hoping that the morning might afford her some time to speak with One-Ear, Maggie was up well before the others and was out in front of the long house, enjoying the heat from the fire. The morning air was cold and the wind was picking up from the lake, the sky looked darker than usual and Maggie thought the high clouds meant the area would be hit with some more heavy snow.

Her prediction played out; before most of the village was up and doing their regular chores, a massive snow storm hit. Much like the blinding storm that she and Anne had experienced at the cave, the village was pounded with snow and a few bouts of sleet. With the heavy snow halting most of the villagers' activities, Maggie remained inside and listened to the sleet pound the bark covering on the long house.

Sitting on a pile of furs and watching all the children run around, a blast of cold air blew in as the thick bear pelt was pulled to one side and One-Ear stepped inside.

He brushed the snow from his arms as a number of the young children rushed over and hugged him. One-Ear enjoyed the nice greeting and removed his outer fur and handed it to one of the women to hang by one of the fires.

"The season started out well, but I fear this winter might bring us too much snow," One-Ear said. "It might also bring us some hardship; we will have to watch our food and water."

Maggie wasn't certain what she could say; from the look of the weather outside, she feared he might be right. For now, she was just enjoying her time and the peace that it brought.

Since their reunion, the two had found little time to speak about the last time they saw each other. Once One-Ear had cleaned off most of the snow, he took a seat beside Maggie.

"You look well now; how bad was your injury?" Maggie simply said, not thinking that it might be a bad choice of topic until she heard herself say it out loud.

Before he answered, he gave her a heavy fur pelt that did a wonderful job keeping the cold air away. Despite the long house being solidly built, the wind and snow still managed to work its way through the cracks in the bark covering.

"The gods were watching over me that day," he replied. "Thankfully, the Ottawa warrior rushed his shot and it hit me in the side. I remember it bled for days, but once I was bound up and given some time to rest, it was much better. One of the women made a poultice out of some hot bread to draw out the wound and then covered it for a few days. I did get a bad fever and that was what kept me here for several moons."

When he finished his story, One-Ear opened a piece of cloth and handed Maggie a slice of dried meat and corn bread. Sitting in silence, the two old friends enjoyed the small snack together. They both smiled at the children running around and keeping their mothers busy.

"How are Joshua and your husband?" One-Ear asked, finally breaking the peaceful calm.

"We spent a wonderful winter and part of the summer together," Maggie began. Tears once more soaked to her eyes and she became annoyed at this latest in the series of unusual mood swings she had experienced of late.

"Joshua has grown," she continued after a moment, "but I see you have done the same. Jacob, I pray, is still alive and out in this unforgiving wilderness searching for me."

One-Ear appeared to be lost in thought as he sat quietly and took the last piece of bread.

Wanting to change the subject, Maggie observed, "You seem to have gained some standing within this village."

He smiled and almost laughingly replied, "They have taken me in and saved my life. I have just done my share and thank the gods that the village has protected me.

"The Mohawk are a strong and proud people and they have given me some power, which I have been happy to accept. It is actually nice that they have remained out of all the wars between the French and English. That has allowed them to trade with both sides and build up some good stores for the long winter. I do fear that once this bad weather passes, we will have to ensure our stores are still good…this could be a long cold season."

Maggie looked forward to the thought of some relative peace and knew that the Mohawk had good relations with the English. The next several weeks were hectic with most of the villagers preparing for the cold season. They cut down an endless supply of trees and had piles of cut wood stacked in every available corner of the village. One-Ear sent out daily hunting parties who seemed to return each day with a good amount of fish, beavers, rabbits and foxes.

The air had grown noticeably colder. As each shortened day gave way to the darkness, the nights became unbearably frozen. No matter how many furs she piled on, Maggie was constantly cold. Unlike the winters she was used to in Pennsylvania, this territory was constantly cold and the snow seemed to fall every day.

She was housed in the main long house. Despite the constant noise from the number of families that lived in it, Maggie enjoyed the company and all the small children running about. She was happy that Anne appeared to be fitting into the village as well. The two women lived in separate houses, but they spent as much time together as they could.

Maggie's stomach still ached and she did her best to keep as much food down as possible. Thankfully, the women of the village gave her plenty of attention and they let her rest when she needed it. Anne did her best to comfort her and remained by her side on several occasions when Maggie's pains were at their worst.

One morning after several days of her continued illness, one of the older women approached Maggie and said, "You are with child; you need to rest and try to keep some food down."

Maggie did not know how to respond, but after thinking about it for some time, her stomach pains and illness started to make sense. The thought of having a child without Jacob made her long even more for her once peaceful life.

Chapter | **Ten**

Jacob liked Rogers and took particular enjoyment in how Joshua and James had been accepted amongst their ranks.

After a night of eating and drinking, the morning brought more snow and a cold north wind that reminded all the men that the winter had arrived with a vengeance.

After completing a few tasks around the camp, Jacob strapped on a pair of snowshoes and went in search of Rogers. He stopped to speak with the pickets before heading down the well-worn pathway to the lake.

Once he worked his way down towards the lake, Jacob could see that Rogers and a few of his men were talking with a couple of the Stockbridge Indian scouts.

Before he came into their view, Jacob slid down a small embankment and soon found himself losing his balance. He landed on his back just short of where the rangers were talking amongst themselves.

"Jacob, it's nice to see you this fine morning," Rogers called out. "I see you are out for a little snowshoeing practice. Those bloody things are rather challenging to master."

The other rangers did their best not to laugh at the visibly embarrassed Jacob but he could see that they were very amused at his exploits.

"Just out for a little tumble before breakfast, Robert," Jacob laughed as he rose to his feet and quickly brushed the snow from his coat.

"No matter; get yourself over here, Jacob," Rogers said, appearing to be strangely upbeat. "It appears the Redcoats might have some possible fun for us."

Jacob lumbered over to the others and offered a slight salute that was quickly refuted by Rogers, who said, "Damn it, Jacob, this isn't the bloody British army; there is no need for salutes or such."

Jacob said nothing but waited for Rogers to continue.

"Well, my scouts just returned with hemp to repair the sleds and brought along some interesting news," Rogers explained while he watched some of his men re-roping the sleds. "I have orders to head to Fort William Henry on Lake George to get provisions and meet up with one of my lieutenants, John Stark."

Kneeling down to watch his men struggle to align the rope with the large block of wood that worked to steer the sleds and the oxen, Rogers continued, "I am then to head towards Fort Carillon to scout out the area and disrupt the French supply lines. I fear our friends at Fort Edward don't really know what to do with us and decided to have us cause some pain for the French."

"When do you need to leave? I can have some of my men prepare you some food and supplies for your trip," Jacob offered, expecting a cordial reply.

Rogers waited a moment before he answered. He appeared to be caught up in observing his men as they fought with the deep snow and the ever-moving oxen to connect the rope line to the beasts' heavy wooden yoke collar.

"Jacob, I had hoped you and your rangers might join us," Rogers responded in a direct tone, looking at Jacob in disbelief. "I thought some of you could move to Fort Edward to set up winter quarters while the rest would come with me. I received word that I need to take some men north to scout the area between Carillon and Fort St. Frederic at the mouth of Lake Champlain. As for the road between Edward and William Henry, it needs to be patrolled and my rangers are the best suited to perform such duties. The British regulars prefer to stay inside, drink their tea and let us do all their dirty chores."

Jacob was taken aback by the suggestion and, for the moment, was unsure how to respond to the unexpected offer.

"I would have to speak with my men before I commit their services," he said. "They have already sacrificed enough to follow me this far; I could never just order them to head for Edward. I fear most of them are already concerned that we have moved too far from their homes. They will want to return to their farms and families come spring." Jacob waited for Rogers to offer some sort of heated reply.

Unexpectedly, Rogers gave Jacob his blessing instead. "Certainly, you should speak with your men. They can decide what path they want to take and I will be happy to recruit any of them to join me."

Just as Jacob was about to excuse himself, Rogers quickly added, "Remind your men that if they choose to head back, the French and their Canadian militia, are scouting this entire area. Getting past them might prove to be difficult."

Jacob took his final comment as a backhanded warning that if they didn't join his ranks, they would all die without his protection.

Uncomfortable with Rogers' tone and the implication that they could not survive without his assistance, Jacob took his time to walk back to the village. On his way back, he recalled all the pickets and suggested to the handful of Rogers' rangers still loitering around the village that they might want to form up and fill in the vacant picket posts.

The rangers did not take kindly to his suggestion, but they did leave the village to Jacob's men and took up some positions around the perimeter of the forest line.

Jacob immediately asked Joshua to gather the men so he could speak with them.

Most of the men were awake, so it only took a few brief minutes for them to crowd around the main fire pit. Jacob could see that he had their attention and bluntly put what Rogers had proposed on the table.

"Gentlemen, we have all been through hell and back over the past several months, and it appears our journey has still not reached its end. Captain Rogers has offered all of us an opportunity to join his ranks and fight the French from Fort Edward." Jacob masked his own emotions as he spoke, so as not to persuade the men.

"What does it mean to, 'join his ranks'?" one of the men shouted out.

A rumble broke out over the village and Jacob did his best to dispel their concerns, "I pray that is just words and I will get further details once I hear your thoughts on the subject."

Still seeing that the men were speaking amongst themselves, Jacob continued, "Captain Rogers has received word that he has orders to scout the French territory around Fort Carillon and Fort St. Frederic. He is to leave soon for Fort William Henry and then towards Lake Champlain to do his best to disrupt the French. He also mentioned that some of you might be assigned to Fort Edward to set up winter quarters there. What are your thoughts so I can let Rogers know our intentions?"

Once again, Jacob let the men speak amongst themselves as he spoke with Joshua and James privately. "What are your thoughts?" Jacob asked as he continued to watch his men's reactions. "I am not sure of my feelings, but it does give us some food for thought."

For a moment, Joshua and James just looked at each other, both seemingly afraid to offer up their opinions.

"You have nothing to say?" Jacob said, doing his best to get some kind of reaction out of his two most trusted men.

Joshua stepped up and was the first to speak, "Sir, it depends on what we want to do. Are we here to find your wife or here to raid the French?"

James jumped in before Joshua could finish his thoughts, "What about mother? Isn't she the reason you dragged us all through this miserable country?"

Jacob did his best to check his temper towards James and his insensitive comment.

Taking a breath, he explained, "Strength in numbers lads. At this moment, none of us know where your mother might be, but all evidence points towards her being taken north. Fort Edward is north and provides us a more secure base to search for her. Does it not make sense to be amongst men far more familiar with this part of the country? If the winter continues its course, we will have a better chance to survive with Rogers and his men."

"What about the British and even Captain Rogers?" Joshua asked. "Will we be part of their ranks and expected to bow to their wishes? We need to be sure we are not giving up the freedoms that we enjoy now. You have told the men on several occasions that they can leave for their homes whenever they wanted; if we join Captain Rogers does that not make it impossible to do so?"

Jacob had no answer.

From their brief discussion, Jacob gathered that the main concerns of his men would be the question of their standing and the sacrifices they would have to make to spend the winter at Fort Edward.

"Some of us will be garrisoned at the fort, while the rest of will be heading with Captain Rogers to pester the French at Fort Carillon," Jacob finally replied, doing his best to paint a positive picture of what they might be getting themselves into.

He decided Joshua and James should be given an opportunity to think about the situation and left them to their thoughts.

"Sir, before I forget, Mr. Sinclair returned," Joshua said casually.

Shocked by the news and looking around the village to see if he could find Sinclair, Jacob asked, "What happened? Why did he return so soon?"

Joshua simply pointed over towards the long house and added, "He arrived with a handful of men and is waiting for you."

Jacob rushed over to the long house, leaving both Joshua and James standing alone.

Pushing the bear skin back from the doorway, he walked into the warmth of the long house to find Sinclair and four of his men standing around the fire pit.

Sinclair noticed Jacob and immediately rushed over to speak with him, "Jacob, it is good to see you all well!"

Ignoring the niceties, all Jacob could think to say was, "Why are you here?" Understanding how cold and uncaring he must have sounded as soon as the words left his mouth, Jacob was quick to explain his reaction, "Sorry, Robert, but I was not expecting to see you for several months. What happened?"

Sinclair shrugged off the comments and explained what had happened, "We only made it as far as the ruins of our old fort. The damn Delaware and the French were all over the area. We had to fight our way all the way back to you, traveling at night and eating what we could find. This is what is left of our original scouting party. Some of the lads had to be left behind because they were far too weakened to walk from the lack of food."

Jacob could see that the men had experienced some tough going since they had split from the main party. "How did you find us?" he asked.

"You left some good signs that you were here sir," Sinclair explained. We passed by the remains of several dead Frenchmen and ran into a group of former captives with an escort of some of the men. I decided to leave half of my men with the group and suggested they move east towards the Susquehanna. I thought to stay with them, but decided you might need the extra manpower."

Happy that his trusted and reliable friend was back with him, Jacob decided not to press him for more details and suggested that the men to get some food and rest. "Sorry to say, lads," he added, "but we will be heading out to the north very soon."

With that, Jacob asked Sinclair to walk with him outside.

As they walked, Sinclair said, "The lads did well, Jacob. Not a man complained, and they kept moving despite the constant threat from the French."

Jacob honestly did not know how to respond. He offered Sinclair a comforting pat on the back and added, "I am just grateful you've returned."

"I noticed that there is another ranging company here with you. Are they the reason you are headed north?" Sinclair asked.

When they had reached a more private setting, Jacob said, "They are rangers from Fort Edward. Honestly, they know this area better than any of us; we have the option to go with them or spend our winter here. If we agree to join them, some of us might be heading towards two French forts to the north and the rest will over-winter at Fort Edward."

"This place seems like a good enough place to live through the winter; why not just stay here?" Sinclair asked as he looked around. "From what I can see, we have water and endless miles of woods to provide us with some food."

"This place would be a reasonable place to survive the winter, but it is still within French-held territory," Jacob explained. "I think we would fair far better with the rangers at Fort Edward."

"What about Maggie?" Sinclair asked, carefully broaching the subject he knew would be most sensitive to Jacob.

Jacob knew that this was a question all of his men would ask. After a moment he replied, "I fear that we could all die here if the winter gets much worse. We have built up supplies and the men have done a wonderful job preparing this place, but I strongly feel that if we want to continue to look for Maggie once the winter dies down, staying with men experienced with this area makes more sense."

Sinclair did not say anything else.

Both men stood silently and looked around at the desolate village as a long gust of cold air blew past them. After a moment, Sinclair said, "I will get the men ready to leave on your order."

Jacob gave Sinclair an appreciative smile and another friendly pat on the back as he said, "Good to have you back, Robert; make sure you get yourself some food."

When Sinclair departed, Jacob walked slowly towards a group of his men who stood talking around the main fire pit. He knew that some of the men did not see Rogers' offer in the same light as he did. He quickly approached them in hopes he could ease their concerns.

After a subdued greeting from the men, Jacob said, "We are all rangers, so my thoughts are that if we join together and form a larger company, we could cover far more ground. Also, most of us know nothing of this land; if we travel with men who know this territory, we raise the chances that Maggie might be found."

Jacob was particularly uncomfortable that most of this was centered on Maggie and his own needs. When the men gave no reply, he attempted to remind them of the past, "What about fighting the Delaware or the Huron and avenging what they have done to our friends and families?"

This sparked off a new debate amongst the men. As their voices rose, the rest of Jacob's men gathered around to see what was going on. Jacob walked through the crowd and shouted for the men to calm down and remain civil.

"Gentlemen, keep your voices down!" he called. "Let us not act like the savages we all despise."

The echoes of the men's voices had drawn Rogers and a handful of his men into the village. Once Jacob noticed they were present, he knew he needed to speak with them.

"I see the men appear to be struggling with my offer?" Rogers said as he watched the rangers continue to squabble.

Joshua and James were now with the men and stood by listening to their issues.

"They have their concerns and are not afraid to challenge each other," Jacob tried to explain, slightly embarrassed that his men were displaying such undisciplined behavior.

"No need to explain; please let me address them and hopefully relieve their worries," Rogers said confidently and walked towards them.

Climbing on an old tree stump that sat almost in the middle of the village, Rogers shouted above the rumbling of the men, "Gentlemen, please remain calm and let me speak."

As if he was some sort of god, Rogers got their attention and then belted out his plans to them, "I can clearly see that most of you have some serious concerns about what I have put on the table."

To a man, they remained still and were all fixated on the tall, impressive ranger that stood massively over the village. Even Jacob was fascinated by Rogers' bravado and found himself hanging on his every word. The noise and commotion had even drawn Sinclair and his men from the long house.

"My offer is simple," Rogers continued. "Join us and we will do our best to rid this land of all the savages we can. I would be wrong if I told you that it will be easy; in fact, some will lose their lives in the pursuit. Fort Edward is a far better place to spend the long winter than this place. Trust me, once the winter winds hit, being this exposed will make you all pray that you never drifted this far north."

"What about us, sir?" one of the men shouted out. "Will you split us all up and just forget we are Virginians?"

"Pennsylvanians as well, sir," another man shouted out.

"Perhaps I didn't explain all my intentions to your captain, but I can promise that you men can remain together and fight for whomever you want…Virginia…Pennsylvania…the King, or just your families. God knows I care little for why you fight; I just need you to fight." Rogers' voice bellowed over the renewed murmurs of the on-looking men.

Jacob was surprised that Rogers had failed to explain to him that they would remain a unit. He wasn't sure if it was intentional or just something he added to convince the men to join with him.

"What about our captain?" another voice shouted out. "What happens to him?"

Rogers looked towards Jacob and said, "Sir, I would be honored to have you lead your company and fight beside me and my men."

Standing and showing no outward emotion, Jacob simply nodded and let Rogers continue his apparently effective speech.

"Who is with me?" Rogers screamed so loud his voice echoed back almost as booming as his original shout.

Some of the men cheered, while most remained hesitant to commit and waited for Rogers to continue.

Instead of speaking further, Rogers just stepped down from the stump and left as quickly as he had entered. Passing by Jacob, he said, "Come with me, Jacob; we need to talk."

Interested in what he might want to say and unsure if the curious ranger was upset at the reaction from the men, Jacob dutifully followed just behind the fast moving Rogers.

Trying his best to keep stride with him, Jacob almost ran into him as he suddenly stopped and turned back to take a look towards the village.

Watching the two streams of smoke that meandered up into the cold morning sky, dissipating as it reached well above the tree line, Rogers finally offered, "You have some strong and loyal men with you, Jacob. I admire that in anyone."

Jacob knew that there was much more to why Rogers asked him to accompany him and why he was complimenting his men. He waited for Rogers to continue.

"I should have offered you a position as one of my senior officers and for that I apologize," Rogers said, doing his best to reassure Jacob of his intentions. "At the moment, my brother Richard and my good friend John Stark are my two lieutenants. Richard is stationed at Fort Edward with two companies and Stark is waiting for me at William Henry. You can keep your men together and hopefully that might ease their minds."

Jacob appreciated the revised offer and really liked the idea of joining forces with this confident ranger. After a moment, he said, "I hope you understand that most of them are from Virginia and the rest of us are Pennsylvanian. They have followed me this far to help with finding my wife and family, and I feel obligated to all of them to keep them safe. Most of us would prefer to be at our homes, not searching around a territory where we are at a great disadvantage."

"Give the men the opportunity to vote on the offer, but please let them know we will be leaving within the hour," Rogers replied. "If I have to reach the road between Fort Carillon and Lake Champlain by the beginning of the month, I need to get on the move fairly immediately. I received word that John Stark and his company are already waiting at Fort William Henry to meet up with me and head north."

Rogers shook Jacob's hand and then turned to return to his sleds. Before he left, he turned once more and said, "Fort Edward's commander is one of the worst British officers I have ever witnessed, but he leaves us alone to do what we want. My brother Richard is garrisoned there and seems to tolerate General Webb's endless shortcomings. Most of the time, they patrol and scout the area, relatively on their own and without British interference."

Jacob politely nodded to Rogers and quickly returned to find out how his men were doing. Remarkably, the village was relatively silent and only a handful of them remained discussing their options.

Once he was noticed by the men, a small gathering encircled Jacob and peppered him with questions.

"What do you say, sir?"

"Do we stay here or head back home?"

"How do you feel about this Rogers and his men?"

Jacob looked at every man and respectfully listened to all their questions.

"We must decide what to do now, as the captain will be departing shortly," he replied. "Honestly, I am intrigued by his offer. I know we came to this place to search for my wife and family. I am grateful for your loyalty, but we have to look at what might become of us if we remain here without the protection of the British."

"When have the damn British ever protected us?" a voice shouted out.

Jacob continued, "All of you have been steadfast to a fault to me and I will not order or tell you what you should do in this instance. I know I would like to fight alongside Rogers and will most likely join with him. That should not influence any of you; please decide what best fits your life and do not let any man make you feel any the lesser."

Before anyone could accuse him of abandoning them, Jacob quickly added, "I strongly suggest those of you who do not want to join us to fight, should accompany us to Fort Edward and stay there for the winter. You have my word you will be free to leave once the weather permits."

Peering above the crowd, Jacob did his best to catch the eye of Joshua and James to wave them to come join him.

"Where is Sinclair?" Jacob asked, noticing the surprising absence of his friend.

"He is getting his gear together," Joshua said. "He told us that he will be joining with you."

"And you lads?" Jacob asked, waiting for their answer.

"Did you have a doubt what I would do, sir?" Joshua said. "The only time I ever left your side, you managed to get yourself captured by the Delaware. You need me, sir." Joshua had such a broad smile that Jacob did his best to keep from bursting out in laughter.

"Thank you, lad," Jacob said. "You are quiet right that I need you by my side."

"I didn't think I had much of a choice," James said sourly, taking Jacob's moment of joy and tossing it aside.

James' poor attitude kept most of the men at a distance, except for Joshua. Jacob still struggled daily with the pain of the changes in his son. For him, it was worse because he knew what James had been like before all this happened.

Acting on Joshua's advice to remain patient, Jacob offered a smile to his son and calmly said, "So, you need to gather what you can carry and meet me at the entrance immediately."

Jacob watched the two young men walk away and pick up their small packs. He already had most of his gear with him and spent a moment checking over his snowshoes for any cracks or damage to the strings or sinew webbing.

Trying not to look over at the entrance to see how many of the men had decided to join him, Jacob found an empty sled and stacked his gear on it.

When his men first saw how the visiting rangers depended on their oxen-drawn sleds, a few of them had built some crude, hand-pulled models of their own.

Slowly dragging the nine-foot sleds over the packed snow, Jacob finally looked to see how many men were set to take the trip north. He had never known his men to argue in such a way as they had done earlier, so he was really not certain how many he could expect. When his gaze fell upon every single one of his men packed and ready to go, his emotions ran high. Having had no idea how many might go with him, Jacob almost burst into tears when he was greeted by every one of his men. They were lined up and waiting to leave to meet up with Rogers and his men.

Relieved and impressed, both at their solidarity and his own ability to once again suppress tears of relief and gratefulness, Jacob nodded to them and said, "Thank you, lads…"

As Jacob walked past the single file of men, they erupted in a deafening cheer that probably could have been heard for miles.

Taking one last look at the village that had provided them such comforts, Jacob called out, "Mr. Sinclair, please form up the rear guard. Joshua, take five men and inform Captain Rogers we will be joining him."

Releasing a deep breath, Jacob led the remaining men and walked in single file towards the well-traveled path to the lake.

Thankfully, the morning sun was strong enough to melt the first light layer of snow, leaving a nice wet glow on the vast wilderness. The deep silence of winter had already captured the woods and, despite the order to keep their voices down, the men had a renewed sense of energy.

Rogers and his awaiting men finally noticed Jacob's rangers, en masse, coming down the slope towards the lake. A massive cheer broke out amongst Rogers' men, and they continued to clap while Jacob and his men reached the frozen lake.

Once he made it to the flat terrain of the lake, Jacob was greeted by Rogers who said, "Good to see you all here, Jacob. You certainly made me nervous…"

Jacob smiled and turned to make sure all his men had made it safely down the icy slope.

He took one last long look at the village and prayed he had made the right decision.

It was midday by the time Jacob had his men organized and Rogers' own men were lined up to follow his advanced scouts.

The discipline of Rogers' ranging company was immediately evident once the line of men began their long trek across the frozen lake. The Stockbridge Indians made up his advanced scouts and pulled ahead of the main body of men by strapping to their feet blocks of wood affixed with metal blades. When they reached the woods, they removed their blades and again donned their show shoes to enter the woods.

The line stretched from one end of the lake to the other, with Sinclair and his men taking up the rear.

Instead of snowshoes, most of Rogers' men achieved secure footing on the windswept lake by wearing small spiked ice-creepers on their shoes. Jacob's rangers did their best to keep from slipping and watched as their new counterparts swiftly worked their way over the ice. The snowshoes did provide some balance, but they didn't work very well on the exposed icy sections that dotted the lake.

The weather cooperated and gave no sign of snow as the men pushed forward. Once they hit the far woods, the line of men was split up into ten smaller groups that would stay together as they moved forward.

The heavy sleds with their oxen teams pushed forward into the woods and followed the roughly cut trail. Rogers kept a group of men whose sole duty was to keep the sleds moving and assist the drivers if they got stuck in the deep snow. Thankfully, once they moved into the deepest part of the trail, the tree canopy had provided enough cover that the snow was not as bad and permitted the sleds to travel much more easily.

The oxen were clumsy animals at best, yet they were strong and tough beasts. They displayed amazing stamina and only needed the odd rest to eat and take a few gulps of water. Once Jacob's men got used to their smell and watching where they stepped, they found them to be rather useful animals.

Jacob watched Rogers walk ahead and ensure all the men remained in order. Once he was satisfied they understood his plan, Rogers joined Jacob.

"What do you think, Jacob?" Rogers asked.

"I'm excited, to be honest," Jacob replied.

Jacob was not one to trust many people, but he found the similarities between Rogers and himself oddly comforting. They were basically the same height with similar strong builds; Jacob guessed Rogers was not much older than he, and with both men being of Scottish descent, they had formed an instant bond.

"Are you married, Robert?" Jacob asked suddenly, not really knowing why he asked such a personal question.

"Aye, but I think I am sadly not much of a husband," Rogers said. "My travels keep me away for the most part, and I feel sorry that my wife didn't fall for a much more reliable man."

Jacob wasn't sure what to say, but he had the sudden urge to relieve himself of the truth about his past. "I am not completely certain why I feel you need to know this, but my real name is Murray. I was forced to desert a while back and needed to change my name to re-enlist in the army."

Reaching into a dirty pocket inside his coat, Jacob handed Rogers a small folded note, which he unfolded and looked at briefly.

"Jacob," he said after a moment, "I couldn't tell you if most of these men are using their real names or something they made up. My only care is that when the savages are shooting at them or charging head long towards us, they hold their ground and defend their mates.

"I will call you by Sims when it matters, but we will be less formal amongst ourselves…does that sound fair, Jacob?" Without looking directly at him, Rogers refolded the note and handed it back to Jacob, who immediately put it back into his coat pocket.

After a few moments of silence, Rogers asked, "Why didn't you just use the note when you re-enlisted? Most of your troubles would have been over and done with. I have heard about this Stobo gentleman and he is in good standing with both the British and the colonials. The last time I got word about him he had escaped and was causing all kinds of trouble for the French."

Jacob was happy to hear that his old friend was still doing well. "He is a good man," he said. "If God wills it, I hope we meet up again."

The two men walked in silence after that.

As the woods began to narrow around them, their visibility was diminished by the low light that managed to reach the ground through the wind-blown trees. Jacob sent four of his men to form up a vanguard to monitor any movement in the woods alongside the trail.

After several hours of trekking through the ever-changing terrain, Rogers sent word ahead that the men needed to stop for a brief break. Jacob was happy that his men had moved step-for-step with the well-trained rangers and looked no worse for wear once a good spot to rest was found.

With the latest mixture of swampy, half-frozen bogs and forest thick with endless firs, pine and cedar trees, the men had been put to the test. At some places along the trail, the trees had become so overgrown that they were forced to get on their stomachs to get around the heavy branches.

The sleds were far better suited for open spaces and wider trails. In the more confined spaces they became cumbersome. The team of men assigned to keep them moving spent a great deal of their time dragging the sleds out from under trees or pulling them out from knee deep snow piles. The drivers did their best to keep the heavy sleds on the trail and guide them forward.

Occasionally, the men grumbled that they were wasting too much of their energy dragging the useless sleds along the trail and pulling the yokes of the oxen around the trees. Their complaints were met by Rogers' constant reminder that having to carry the supplies on their backs would be a far worse option.

"Sometimes this sorry lot would complain it was too hot and once it rained...too wet," Rogers commented to Jacob, who just smiled and continued on.

The surrounding wilderness was much the same as Jacob was used to back home, except most of the trails were better cut and the men navigating were much better skilled and organized. The winter did provide for a somewhat safer way to travel, especially since most of the Indians were either in their winter hunting grounds or too busy surviving in the poor weather. They concerned themselves with staying alive versus bothering with ambushing a company of rangers foolish enough to be out in the woods at this time of the year.

Rogers' men did keep a wary eye open for signs of the feared Canadian militia. They were known to inhabit the woods from the mouth of Lake Champlain down to the Fort Edward area.

Staying close to Rogers' side, Jacob observed his men interacting with Rogers' men and was happy that they appeared to be getting along.

"Have you heard much about the Canadians, or the Milice as they preferred to be called, and the way they wage their own wars?" Rogers asked while the two men walked along a particularly open boggy area.

"I have seen them fight alongside the French, and they are far worse in many ways than any savages I have ever fought," Jacob replied, watching the far woods for any movement.

"The bloody French just let them run around and do what they please," Rogers grumbled. "I have been told by more than a few prisoners that they are being used by the French to counter my rangers. They have skill, but nothing like my men." Rogers' proud boasting ended with a quick warning whistle to his men ahead to be careful re-entering the woods.

"They like to set up ambushes," Rogers warned and looked back to make sure the men kept advancing.

The scouts sent ahead to locate a good resting place had decided on the cleared ruins of an old cabin that was now just a mound of snow. There was a natural hill that would provide some cover in the unlikely events that the French had a patrol so far south or the Milice were out lurking around. Despite the threat of additional snow, enough space was cleared of the existing snow that the men were able to lay down and get some much needed rest.

Rogers and Jacob walked together into the clearing; at first, Jacob was instantly struck by the sight of an old fence that bordered the old cabin. If he closed his eyes, this place looked much like what he was forced to leave behind back in Pennsylvania. Far off voices of children running around vibrated in his head as he did his best to clear it and walk to where most of his men were resting, visibly tired from the challenging trek.

Jacob decided to leave the men to rest and have a small bite to eat. He walked over to where Rogers was standing staring off into the limitless stretch of tangled woods and frozen rivers.

"Where do we go from here, Robert?" Jacob asked, careful not to startle him.

"I think this is the best place to split up the men and send some of the men to Fort Edward," Rogers said without taking his gaze off the wilderness before him. "If you can spare twenty men to remain with us and send the rest to the fort with a few of my men, we should be able to cover more ground. We cannot afford to be slowed by wounded or sick, so make sure they are sent to Edward as well."

"I will get the men ready and tell them of your plan, but what about the sleds and supplies?" Jacob asked politely.

"I will send them with the men to Fort Edward," Rogers explained. "Honestly, they will just slow us down and I have hopes that Lieutenant Stark will have secured a couple for us at Fort William Henry."

Jacob nodded and turned to go.

"One last thing, Jacob; I don't want that Frenchman to come with us," Rogers said quickly. "He might just betray us all to his own kind and get us all killed."

Jacob had no reason not to trust young Lessard. He had done everything he was asked to do and carried his own weight around the camp. He feared that if Lessard was sent to Fort Edward, he would be thrown into the fort's stockade and be treated like a prisoner.

"I planned on bringing him with us," Jacob said. "He can speak the language and possibly help with any prisoners we secure. The boy has done nothing to make me feel he would run back to his own and give us all up."

"If he should give us up, I will be the first to shoot him," Rogers said bluntly, clearly disinterested in Jacob's reasoning. "Just keep him out of my sight."

Leaving Rogers behind to his thoughts, Jacob went to find Joshua and Sinclair to inform them of the plan. Joshua was sitting with Sinclair, and both men were clearly tired from the trek.

"Gentlemen, Captain Rogers thinks this is the best place to split up the men and send a group to Fort Edward. I think Mr. Sinclair would be best suited to take the men to the fort and Joshua can stay with me and advance towards Carillon. We should be back to Edward by month's end."

After waiting for one of the men to say something, Jacob said, "Any thoughts, lads?"

"How many men do you need for Carillon?" Joshua simply asked.

"Twenty and the rest will report to the captain's brother, Richard, and his unit," Jacob replied. "I was assured that the men will be used as scouts and to keep the road between Fort William Henry and Edward clear of the French or their Indian allies."

"Sir, I would much rather remain with you, but I will take the rest of the men to Edward if that is what you wish," Sinclair said respectfully.

"I haven't spoken with James, but I would like him to go with you," Jacob added. "I don't think he is suited for the potential battle we might face at Carillon."

The two men, especially Joshua, looked surprised that Jacob had decided to send James to Fort Edward. He could see the question in their faces, but decided not to question his decision. Instead, he dismissed the two to rest some and then prepare the men to leave.

Jacob had decided that James would be far safer behind the palisades at Fort Edward. He remembered how James reacted when they fought with the raiding party back at the fort and did not want to expose him to a similar circumstance.

Searching around where most of his men were resting, Jacob spotted James sitting alone on a small fallen tree trunk.

"Everything alright, boy?" Jacob asked as he took a seat beside him.

After a moment of continued silence, James just said, "I'm just a little tired, sir."

"We will be heading out soon, so enjoy the rest," Jacob said. "Captain Rogers needs some of us to head with him to Fort Carillon, but the remaining men will leave with Mr. Sinclair to march to Fort Edward."

Jacob hesitated, not sure if James was even listening or cared what he was saying. "I want you to go with the men to Fort Edward, while I go with Rogers to Fort Carillon," he added.

When James remained silent, Jacob burst out, "You have nothing to say?"

James just looked up at him and said, "Yes, sir; what about Joshua?"

"He is leaving with me, but we should rejoin you at Edward by month's end," Jacob replied. He had neither the time nor the energy to hear any arguments from James, so he got up and patted him on the head before walking away to find Joshua.

Jacob could already see that Rogers was organizing his men and waiting anxiously to leave. As he walked towards Joshua, Jacob called out to Rogers, "I will have my men ready shortly."

Rogers offered a slight nod and returned to check on his men. Jacob finally located Joshua, who had picked out the twenty men to head north.

"Lad, we have to leave," Jacob said. "Captain Rogers looks like he wants to get moving."

"Yes, sir; I have the men ready, so just tell me where you need us," Joshua politely replied.

Jacob smiled and added, "I should talk with the men who are going to Edward."

"No need to, sir," Joshua reassured him. "Sinclair and I already explained the circumstances and the men appear to be in good spirits."

Jacob instantly countered, "Thank you, lad. I am not sure where I would be without you."

"Dead…sir," Joshua laughed and waved to the men to follow him.

Jacob stood uncomfortably for a moment, watching the long line of men move out towards Fort. Edward. It was disconcerting to leave without his entire unit, especially James.

He had spoken privately with Sinclair before the two groups parted. Jacob had been concerned that the condition of some of the men would make them easy targets for an ambush. The ill and injured consisted of mainly twisted ankles and those suffering various ailments like dysentery. He urged Sinclair to keep the men alert and maintain a good rear and advanced guard.

As he turned to catch up with Joshua, Jacob couldn't help himself and turned to take one last glance towards James. The boy walked next to Sinclair, and nothing about his body language suggested he was at all affected by being separated from his father.

James was soon hidden from view by the sleds that followed the column, and Jacob turned back to the trail ahead of him. Fort Edward was within a half day's march and he said a private prayer that his men would arrive without incident.

Guilt ate at him for sending his son out of his protection, but he quickly reminded himself of his duty at hand and focused on keeping his men in order. When he caught up to Joshua, he asked him to stay with the lead group and report back to him if he saw anything of concern.

As usual, Rogers had sent his Stockbridge Indians out as advanced scouts. Despite being uncomfortable in their presence, Jacob was impressed by their skills and loyalty to Rogers.

Jacob soon moved back to walk with Rogers who briefed him on the plan for their movements to the north. They were to join up with John Stark at Fort William Henry and then move as quickly as possible up Lake George towards Lake Champlain. They would stay to the high ridge that skirted Fort William Henry and then descend down one of the mountain passes to reach the fort.

After spending some time walking along with Rogers, Jacob moved forward to walk with Joshua and the rest of the men as they headed north along well-used trails.

"It appears we will be taking the mountain trail around to the fort," Jacob explained. "Captain Rogers prefers to keep to the high ground so he can monitor the lower trails."

"Why have you just stepped aside to let this ranger tell you what to do?" Joshua asked, not thinking how it might come across or sound to Jacob.

Taken aback by his frankness, Jacob appreciated his honesty and did his best to reply, "We are of the same rank, but Captain Rogers holds the advantage of knowing these woods far better than any of us. If we were back in Pennsylvania, I would behave the same way as him and assume my responsibilities as such."

Joshua said nothing and just continued on with the march. Jacob wasn't certain if the others felt the same, yet with the circumstances as they were, he had little choice but to follow Rogers and his rangers. Realistically, all he wanted was to survive the winter and get back to searching for Maggie, he only hoped that his men continued to trust him enough to stay with him.

Rogers moved ahead to remind Jacob to keep his men in small groups of five and keep them in a single file formation he called 'Indian style'.

"We will stop at William Henry for as long as it takes to grab provisions," Rogers said. "I don't really want to spend too much time at the fort before we follow Lake George towards Carillon. Once we work our way north, we will be in French-held territory. They are very active during the winter months, and we will have to remain vigilant for any signs of a possible ambush."

"No need to worry about us, sir; my men have a good sense when it comes to the bloody French," Jacob bragged. He wanted Rogers to know his men were just as good, if not better, then his rangers when it came to wilderness fighting.

Rogers smiled and replied, "Just keep them in order, Jacob. We will soon see how capable they prove to be."

With that Rogers walked back towards the rear guard.

"What do you think of this Rogers fellow?" Joshua asked once Rogers moved out of ear shot, continuing on with their earlier conversation.

"I like him," Jacob answered, keeping his eyes on the thickening tree line. "He is brash and confident, but those are not bad traits if you can control them."

"What are your thoughts, lad?" Jacob asked after a pause. He wondered why Joshua was bringing up these questions now.

"Not sure for now, sir," Joshua answered plainly. "I will answer you after I see him in battle. I still do not like the way he addresses you at times."

Jacob realized that once they made their way to the shore of Lake George, they would have to be extra attentive to their surroundings and cover much more ground.

Rogers had explained to him that Carillon sat at a strategic location between two lakes that provided the French access to move freely between Canada and the lower southern region of the New York province. Jacob was told that as long as the French held such a place, the English would never be able to defeat them in this region. He said that even the Indians in the area knew of the importance of securing the point, and that was one of the main reasons they allied themselves with the French or, in the case of the Mohawks, remained neutral.

The French even held another key location at the southern point of Lake Champlain that sat at the northern tip past the narrows of Lake George. They built a small fortification they called Fort St. Frederic, but Rogers seemed to dismiss its importance. All he was focused on was causing as much discomfort to the French as he could.

The winter air was crisp and the winds were starting to clear the mountains and pour down towards the lake. The deep snow was much more noticeable and Jacob was thankful they had snowshoes to keep them from sinking to their waists.

The terrain was rocky and rugged over the mountains, but once they reached the mouth of the lake, it flattened enough to speed up their march. Lake George narrowed in places and had an endless string of hidden coves and bays along its shores. Some of the narrows were pocked with small islands that were a perfect place for the French to set up an ambush. The French also relied on traversing the lake with sleds and Rogers told Jacob that the track between Carillon and Fort St, Frederic was well used. In the winter, the frozen lakes provided a far easier route to travel on than the deep, snow-packed overland trails.

Jacob finally received his first good look at Fort William Henry. It sat almost directly on the southern shore of the lake. From where he stood, it looked oddly shaped. He noticed the typical bastions but was impressed the engineers had also built a long ditch that worked its way around the land side of the outer walls. It also appeared that the men were working on driving sharpened wooden spikes along the banks of the ditch to impede anyone trying to advance to the walls.

The walls themselves were massive with large tree trunks piled on top of each other and packed thick with loads of dirt and fill. The only entrance to the fort he could see from his vantage point was at its northern side and consisted of a bridge that was placed over the moat. The terrain was dotted with an endless field of tree stumps and heavy earthen works. A large swampy area sat to its eastern shore and had a manmade causeway built across it to meet up with the road.

Jacob was impressed by the fort and thought that with the mountainous countryside, the French would have difficulty dragging siege cannons over the lakes and mountains. The road towards Fort Edward looked fairly clear and, despite its hilly terrain, appeared to be well used.

Thankfully, the message was sent back that they would soon be stopping for the night, just outside the outer reaches of the fort. Jacob and his men were happy to hear the news and could hardly wait to remove the cumbersome snowshoes and have a fire to warm their weary limbs.

By the time they had reached the concealed cove that would provide them much needed cover for the night, the skies opened up and dropped a steady snow down on the men. Jacob immediately noticed the presence of more rangers and, once he got his men settled, he took Joshua to report to Rogers.

It wasn't difficult to find the tall ranger as he stood on a small cluster of rocks and was busy organizing the men. Jacob could see that there was another man directly to Rogers' left.

The man was much older than most of the men, but he had a similar air of confidence that was held by Rogers. He was particularly thin, but not from a lack of food. It appeared to be more from years of trekking through this rough country and living off the land.

Rogers saw Jacob approaching and called out to him and Joshua, "Gentlemen, please come over and meet an old friend."

Jacob led the way and the two men worked their way through the mass of resting men and piles of gear and sleds. A couple fires were already going, but the men were warned that they should enjoy the heat now because most likely would lose the luxury of campfires once they move closer to Carillon.

"Jacob, this is John Stark, a dear friend and one of my lieutenants," Rogers said.

Jacob offered his hand to Stark, who accepted it heartily. "It's a pleasure to meet you, Mr. Stark," Jacob said. "This is Joshua. Like you are to Captain Rogers, he is my top advisor."

Joshua smiled and graciously shook Stark's hand.

"Robert told me, lad, that you were taken captive by the Huron," Stark said to Joshua. "We must talk when time permits. I was a captive of the Abenaki and would be interested in your experiences with them."

"Mr. Stark, did you see much of the French on the road here?" Jacob asked.

"Please call me John," he replied. "My advanced scouts ran into a couple of small hunting parties, but nothing serious. I did get word that a decent sized force was organizing to head towards Fort Edward, yet nothing has been confirmed."

"John also told me that the lake is covered with tracks from French sleds," Rogers explained. "It might present us an opportunity to ambush a small patrol and grab some prisoners to speak with."

The four men took a moment to review the men and consider their next move.

"With Jacob's men and our combined rangers, we have roughly seventy five men to cause the French some problems," Stark said, still looking at the mass of men. "Not a bad number if they all remain fit for duty."

The men in question had already sent out two hunting parties to search out the nearby woods for some game. A group of pickets were already in position to guard against the possibility that the French might be scouting the area.

"I need to visit the fort and get what supplies we will need," Rogers said. "John also mentioned that a few of the British regulars showed some interest in joining us, and I will have to speak with the commander about my orders."

Jacob and Joshua excused themselves to check on their men. They could see evidence that the rangers had used this place before. There were old fire pits with large stones encircling them, along with a couple of stacks of cut wood piled up under a small cleft in the rocks.

The men seemed to be happy with their location, and they found many of them looking over the natural ledge down to the large lake that sat below them. The cove sat between huge mountains that were much steeper than any mountain to the south and a lake that they imagined would be breathtaking during the summer months. Many of them expressed how impressed they were by the fort and the general look of the area.

"If we had the time, I would love to take a crack at doing some ice fishing," one of Jacob's men said.

The man was Daniel Shaw, and Rogers happened to walk by just as the young private spoke. He had just returned from the short trip to the fort and appeared to be in good spirits.

"Are you up to a little trip, lad?" he asked Shaw. "I can have a couple of my New Hampshire boys go along, and I bet they can out-fish you!" Rogers smirked, waiting for the man to reply.

Shaw wasn't sure what to say and looked towards Jacob for some guidance.

"Go ahead, Daniel," Jacob urged the young man. "Show these northern lads that we can fish with the best of them."

Shaw stood up and put on his fur-lined hat and heavy mitts.

"We should make this interesting, Jacob; how about a little wager?" Rogers slyly offered.

Shaw once again looked at Jacob and just shrugged his shoulders.

"First, I don't want to encourage gambling, so maybe we can make other arrangements?" Jacob suggested. "Also, to even the numbers, Mr. Shaw should pick a partner to work with."

By now, most of the men, including Stark, were gathering around to listen to the bet.

"Lad, by all means pick a partner," Rogers said, clearly enjoying their exchange. "Jacob, you are certainly a crafty one. What will you think of next?"

Jacob signaled to Shaw to do as directed.

"I'll take my brother with me, but I must warn you, sir," he said to Rogers, "we have fished since we could walk." Daniel pointed to his younger brother, Ezekiel, and looked much more confident now.

"Lads, get down to the lake," Rogers ordered and watched the four contestants take a small pathway to the ice. "John, please send a few of your boys down to keep their eyes out for any unwelcomed guests. Jacob and I will discuss terms of the wager while you lads take a shot at the lake."

The rest of the men huddled around the rock wall and peered down to the lake below, straining to watch the informal competition.

"Jacob, we can have some fun with this," Rogers said. "My thoughts are that maybe whoever wins gets a sled ride from the opposing team for the first leg of our trip."

Jacob was thinking of a bit more meaningful award to the winning team and countered, "Would you consider putting some of your ice creepers and skates on the table while we ante up some of our finely-crafted Pennsylvania long rifles? My fear with using the sleds is that it might weaken a couple of the men just for the sake of an easy ride."

Jacob sat back and waited for Rogers to offer something else or agree to his terms.

Rogers took a quick look at the activity below and saw that both parties were busily hacking at the ice with their hatchets and bayonets to make a hole to drop a line into the freezing water below.

"Not much of a bet, but we can go with your idea," Rogers reflected. The two made it official by shaking hands.

The men did their best not to cheer out loud as they watched the two groups of men work the small holes in the ice.

It only took a few minutes before Daniel and his brother pulled out a large lake bass from the hole. They held it up to show the on-looking crowd above them, and there was a smattering of low-pitched cheers, which were quickly silenced by the captains. All the same, the men from the Virginia ranging company were all smiles.

The Shaws then pulled out two additional smaller bass. By the time the men representing Rogers' rangers pulled out their first fish, the brothers had a pile of six squirming fish smashing around in the piled up snow.

As the contest quickly became a one-sided battle, Rogers conceded victory and sent down a messenger to retrieve the fishermen.

Jacob could see that Rogers was not used to losing. When Rogers conceded, Jacob signaled his men to keep the celebration to the bare minimum.

"Damn good show, Jacob," Rogers said gruffly. "Your boys certainly put on an impressive display."

"Your lads did very well; luck was just on our side," Jacob said, tipping his hat. "We have both fished, I'm sure, and understand that more often than not, it is simply not an impatient man's sport. Now, let us get the bounty on the fires and enjoy some roasted bass."

Thankfully, the fish provided the men with a good dinner. The two hunting parties had returned emptied handed, except for a couple of small rabbits and a story of a missed opportunity at a large buck.

The men ate well that night and Jacob was happy to finally see the two groups of rangers mingling together. Even the Shaw brothers and their two opponents sat together and enjoyed a couple of plates of the well-cooked fish.

Joshua spent some of the night speaking with Stark, while Jacob sat with Rogers.

"How soon will we reach Fort Carillon?" Jacob asked between pieces of bass.

Rogers offered Jacob a small cask of rum before he answered, "It's not far, if we can use the lake. The French do patrol the upper part of the lake regularly. We don't want to run into a patrol in the center of the lake and be left exposed to an easy attack."

The two men spent some time watching the men interact before Rogers continued between sips of rum, "Tell me, what do you think of this part of the country?"

"From what I can see that is not covered with snow, it is nice," Jacob offered. "It honestly reminds me of my home in southern Pennsylvania. I must admit, the mountains in these parts appear to be much larger though."

"Tell me about this General Webb," Jacob requested, redirecting the conversation.

"The man is an idiot," Rogers frankly admitted. "He is afraid of his own shadow. Any mention of the savages has the poor fool going into some spasm that has him bedridden for weeks at a time."

"Sounds like the typical British officer," Jacob shot back.

Both men laughed and drew the attention of most of the men.

"We sure see the world with similar eyes, Jacob," Rogers added, lifting his small wooden cup as a toast. "I feel we will make a good team against the savages."

The men spent time just sitting and enjoying the heat from the fires. The pile of fish had been quickly reduced to only a few morsels and bare bones. Except for the pickets, most of the men eventually fell fast asleep while the fires shot large sparks into the cold night air.

Jacob just sat and was lost in his thoughts. How was Maggie? If she ever found out that he had let James out of his sight once he'd finally found him again, would it put a wedge in their relationship?

The one thing that ate at him even more was this Webb character. Had he just walked himself and his men into another Braddock-like disaster by having to deal with another incompetent British general?

All he could do now was pray some more…and hope this Robert Rogers was as smart as he appeared.

Chapter | **Eleven**

Maggie sat by herself and contemplated what she should do next. The thought of being pregnant without Jacob by her side honestly frightened her. She decided to not say anything to Anne, just in case the older woman's diagnosis was wrong.

Her emotions were shooting in every direction, and she did her best to still help around the camp in order to keep herself busy. She was happy that One-Ear checked on her almost every day. Most days he remained around the village because the snow was beginning to hinder most travel around the area.

Living in one of the main houses certainly helped her get through the long days. Soon her stomach grew noticeably larger and she could not deny the fact that she was pregnant, to herself or others. When Anne knew, she appeared to be happy for her.

"I heard some news today, Miss Maggie," One-Ear said one day as he came and sat with her. "Did my ears hear the elders say you are with child?"

"Your ears heard correctly; I am with child," Maggie confessed.

"You don't seem excited," One-Ear looked at her belly and smiled. "When one of our women is like you, we celebrate the occasion and hold the woman in high standing during her time. I have asked the women to cook a feast for you and your child to enjoy, and you will get a special blessing from our elders."

"I am happy; it's just the thought of having a child without Jacob here scares me," Maggie explained.

"I am not your Jacob, but please let me help you. Maybe it will make you feel better." One-Ear smiled again.

Maggie could not believe how much One-Ear had matured and grown. He was not the young teenager she had been separated from last spring. He was now an important part of this village. He carried many responsibilities and had a large party of warriors loyal to him.

"Thank you, One-Ear, and please just call me Maggie," she said, reaching for his hand and holding it. "You are family and you should address me as such."

"I will not let anything happen to you; once the winter clears, I will send out warriors to every corner of this land to find your Jacob," One-Ear said and continued to sit quietly with her.

The two were interrupted by two of One-Ear's warriors. They called out to him and One-Ear excused himself and left Maggie alone again.

Soon the long house was busy with several children running around and three families cleaning out their beds. Most of the fur pelts used for sleeping were dragged outside and pounded with sticks to clean off the dust. Maggie attempted to help, but was told not to get up. Her pelts were cleaned for her and returned to her side.

The women made sure she was fed and comfortable. Although she did feel useless at times, Maggie enjoyed the break and really enjoyed the extra attention her pregnancy brought. If she was still back home, her chores and responsibilities would still be expected to be done.

It wasn't that Jacob was cruel or unloving; it was just what came with running a homestead. He had his own chores and duties to do and Maggie was needed to help, despite her situation. If she was to go through this without her husband, it was at least nice to be able to rest and take care of herself and the baby slowly growing inside her.

It had been a several weeks since Maggie realized she was pregnant and once her stomach seemed to settle and she could hold down some food, she slipped into a nice routine around the village.

It certainly helped that the women treated her so well and kept her from doing anything too strenuous. The unusual peace was something she could get used to and with no signs of the French, she was far more relaxed. Even Anne had settled into the village and spent most of her time assisting a young family with their daily chores.

One-Ear came and went, spending days of good weather out in the wilderness scouting and hunting. The weather was inconsistent at best, with days of steady snow and times when the snow blinded the village and forced the residents to remain inside for days at a time.

When the weather was clear, Maggie took advantage of it by taking escorted walks out towards the lake. The cold, fresh air was nice and she particularly loved returning to her house and warming up by the fire.

Her peace was short lived.

One-Ear returned from a long trip and found Maggie before he even bothered to remove his heavy winter, fur-lined outer coat.

"Maggie, I spoke with two French trappers and they spoke of a number of Ottawa warriors in the area. They did not know if they intended to move further south and meet up with the French at their fort between the two lakes.

"I have told my scouts to keep their eyes on the trails and send word back as soon they see any sign of the Ottawa."

Maggie could see that he was very concerned and tried to reassure her young friend by saying, "I don't think Pontiac would want me now that I am with child." She prayed that she was correct and that her condition would alter Pontiac's feelings about her.

"I will not let them take you…even if I have to fight their entire tribe," One-Ear said, keeping his eye on the main entrance of the village.

They both knew that Pontiac, if he was truly in the area, would make it a point to visit his mother.

The tension around the village was noticeable, despite most of the villagers doing their best to maintain their routines.

One-Ear continued to send out daily scouting parties and even increased the number of warriors in charge of guarding the outer walls.

Added to their concerns was a stiffening cold front that whipped down from the lake and made it difficult for the warriors to travel too far before they were forced to return and warm up.

When he was not out scouting, One-Ear remained by Maggie's side, even when she insisted he didn't need to spend so much of his time watching over her.

While the cold front gripped the area, the village received word that a large party of Ottawa was sighted a few miles to the west. One-Ear sent out more scouts to monitor the party, but not to make contact with them. If they were heading towards the village, the scouts were to send a warning to One-Ear.

As he had done for the past several weeks, One-Ear was with Maggie when one of his warriors rushed into the warmth of the long house, saying "The Ottawa are in the outer field."

Maggie's heart dropped as she watched One-Ear get to his feet before the warrior completed his sentence. With his eyes on her, he called to one of the other women, saying, "Take Maggie to a safer place and do not let anyone take her.

Maggie did not know what to do, and once she was taken out into the cold air, she could see that the entire village was in a panic. The young woman pulled her arm and Maggie did her best to keep up through the knee-deep snow.

"Please slow down," Maggie cried out, but her pleas were met with deaf ears.

Thankfully, the woman made a quick turn and took her down a narrow laneway to a small house that had its door already open to greet them. Once she was inside and her eyes adjusted to the lack of light, Maggie heard the familiar voice of her friend Anne saying, "Maggie, just relax; you should be safe now."

Doing her best to catch her breath, Maggie struggled to reply, "What is happening?"

"One-Ear asked me to keep you safe if the Ottawa returned," Anne explained, as she dropped a heavy wooden plank down over the doorway. "The villagers do not want any trouble from the Ottawa, so he wants you to stay here and wait until they leave us."

"So I am no better than a prisoner?" Maggie cried, uncomfortable with her new situation and surroundings. "Did anyone think that the Ottawa might want to spend the winter in the village? What will I do; stay locked up here?"

"We will have to wait and see," Anne replied, appearing equally unenthused about her new duties. "I am sure your friend One-Ear will take good care of you."

The two sat in silence for several long hours as they waited for word from one of the villagers about what was happening outside. Maggie bided her time on a stool, working on a small piece of tanned deer hide with some beads and quills.

The only noise they heard was the wind blowing through the small cracks in the wood and the howling gusts that swept the snow well over the roof.

A brief knock on the door had both women up and waiting by the door. Anne struggled to lift the door plank and opened the door enough to see who was outside.

The door was pushed opened as One-Ear stepped through and closed it immediately behind him.

"They are here, Maggie, but I can see no sign of Pontiac," he said as he stood up against the door. "There are many of them and I fear they will take over the village and eat all our supplies. I have a council set with their leaders and our elders to discuss what they want. I pray to the gods that they leave us alone and just go elsewhere."

Maggie didn't know what to say and certainly didn't want to complain about her new surroundings.

Anne piped up, "What are we to do?"

One-Ear just looked at her and replied, "Stay here until I return or send one of my warriors to retrieve Maggie. Until then, do nothing."

His bluntness surprised Maggie, but she could tell by his voice he was truly worried about the Ottawa. It had been awhile since they had taken her and almost killed him and they both just wanted them to leave.

The two women sat in the small house and said nothing to each other. The outside light struggled to sneak through the small cracks in the aged wood of the small structure, and after hours of waiting, it soon turned dark.

The village was unusually silent; if it weren't for the yelps of the wild dogs that lived around the area, the cold night air would be eerily quiet.

Anne had finally fallen asleep in the corner bed, while Maggie sat up and used a candle made from bear fat, to provide her some light. Unable to sleep, she just did her best to get comfortable in the bed and fought off the cold with several fur pelts piled up to her neck. One of the women had brought some salted meat and a few pieces of fresh corn bread. Though she was being cared for, confinement to such small quarters made Maggie feel like a caged animal.

Just as she was nodding off, she heard a light knock on the door.

Anne barely stirred, so Maggie slowly removed the door brace and opened the door enough to see the shadow of one of the warriors.

"One-Ear needs you to come," the warrior said in broken English.

Maggie was not sure what to do, but layered on a couple of heavy coats and her fur-lined moccasins. She told Anne to go back to sleep and slipped out into the dark, freezing night air.

The warrior said nothing else, but simply guided her to another large house where she knew the elders lived.

Confused and worried that something might have happened to One-Ear, Maggie did her best to keep up with the warrior. Once they got to the entrance, he opened the door and motioned to her to go inside.

Maggie walked into the main room that was well-lit from a number of fires that spit little projectiles of fire high into the air. The snaps from the flames drew her eyes at first, but she soon noticed that the room was filled with villagers and some of the visiting Ottawa.

Unsure what to do, she remained by the door until the mother of Pontiac approached her and offered her a hand, saying, "Come with me, Morning Fire; all will be fine."

Morning Sun's words did little to calm Maggie as she scanned the house to locate One-Ear. She was guided to an empty spot that appeared to be reserved for her. It was near the village elders and directly across from where most of the Ottawa sat.

She sat reluctantly and finally spotted One-Ear. He was in the far corner with a small band of his warriors. She waited anxiously to find out what was happening.

Before she could get herself comfortable, one of the Ottawa leaders stood up and with a deep voice screamed at her. Maggie had no idea what he was saying, but the look on his face made her sick.

The Ottawa warrior continued to speak, frantically pointing and shouting above the ever-present rumbling around the long house. None of the village elders dared to interrupt the ranting guest.

As soon as he finished, the room went ominously silent.

Maggie sat motionlessly with her head down and waited. She had no idea what was happening, but she could tell it was not good. The room soon erupted again when One-Ear shoved past several of the Ottawa warriors and stepped into the center of the room. Ignoring the closeness of the fire pits, One-Ear opened up with a long, heartfelt speech.

Once again, Maggie had no idea what was being said, but she was able to watch his gestures and hear the animation in his voice. She prayed he was defending her and any actions she had supposedly taken against the Ottawa.

One-Ear showed no fear, and several times he even got directly in the face of the Ottawa leaders. Maggie could sense that the Ottawa were not used to being publically scolded and spoken to so directly. She noted that even the village elders appeared to be uncomfortable with the tone that One-Ear was bravely displaying against their feared visitors.

While One-Ear continued his heated speech, one of the Ottawa dared to approach Maggie and attempted to take her by the hand. She resisted and before anyone could lift a hand, the Ottawa warrior collapsed onto the dirt floor just to her left.

He expelled one last breath before going stiff. There was a tomahawk jammed into his spine, buried almost to the hilt. A pool of blood formed on the dirt floor as several of the Ottawa warriors stood up.

The room filled with screams and cries, and Maggie stood up to look for One-Ear. There were far too many villagers between them, so she remained standing and waiting for what might happen next.

Amid the confusion, One-Ear calmly walked over to the dead warrior and placed his moccasin on the Ottawa's tailbone. With one quick jerk, he pulled out the blade of the hawk and wiped the blood onto the man's deer-skinned leggings.

One-Ear turned swiftly to greet the screams from the Ottawa warriors. He stared directly at them and, shouting above their enraged voices, continued his speech.

The room still did not settle and Maggie stood back, waiting for the two groups of warriors to break into a full fight. Even the elders were now shouting at the Ottawa and holding any weapon they had at their disposal.

Amid all the chaos, One-Ear motioned for some of his warriors to guard the doors so no more Ottawa could rush in. Thankfully, when the Ottawa had first arrived, One-Ear had convinced them to take refuge in one of the outer fields instead of within the village. For the moment, most of them remained outside the village wall. Even so, the villagers all knew the Ottawa could take the village if they wanted to.

Just as the room was about to erupt into an all-out war, Morning Sun stood up and waited for the men to notice her presence. Maggie knew that this woman was the village's matriarch; her word, in most cases, was final. Despite the male elders having daily councils, nothing could be settled until she agreed to it. She was also the final voice when it came to choosing the village chief.

Taking One-Ear's place on the floor, her first act was to order the Ottawa to remove the dead warrior's body. After he was moved outside, she waited for the room to go completely silent.

Maggie sat back down and waited for her to speak, confident she would tell the Ottawa to leave and never return.

With a soft, almost inaudible voice, she began.

While Maggie could not understand a word, she was captivated by this strong woman standing amongst a throng of men and admonishing them for their actions. Her speech went on for several minutes and Maggie finally caught the eye of One-Ear. The look on his face seemed to show that he liked what she was proposing. He offered Maggie a brief smile and then returned his attention to what the matriarch was saying.

The smile on his face soon fled and he appeared to be having second thoughts about what Morning Sun was saying. Maggie was confused and grew impatient to know what was happening.

The Ottawa leaders were much happier now, and their smiles displayed some degree of approval for her decision.

As the speech came to an end, One-Ear managed to work his way to Maggie's side. "What did she say?" Maggie asked, as soon as he squatted down next to her.

"She has betrayed us to her own blood," One-Ear whispered, keeping his eye on the Ottawa warriors. "She has decided to give you back to Pontiac, but not until the spring. She wants you to have your child and then be sent to the west country to be with her son."

Maggie was shattered and did not know what to think. She would rather die than go back to Pontiac.

"There's still the issue of my actions in killing one of their warriors," One-Ear continued, pulling her thoughts back to the moment. "They want to torture me as payment for their warrior's murder. Our side wants nothing to be done and for the Ottawa to let us be."

The pair continued to watch the proceedings and waited to decide their next move. Maggie realized that since the winter weather allowed no opportunities to escape, she would be no better than a prisoner for the next several months.

Scared, frustrated and in a near panic, Maggie begged One-Ear, "Please stay with me. I don't want these savages to take me away from you."

One-Ear did his best to shield her and said, "I will stay by you. They will have to kill me before I let them take you."

Those words hit Maggie especially hard as she envisioned the last time they were in a similar situation. One-Ear nearly had lost his life when he had been the only one to step up and help her.

"What about your warriors?" Maggie asked, looking at what they were doing.

"They are loyal but afraid," One-Ear confessed. "Time will tell if they will fight with me or not."

The two friends listened to the debate that flashed back and forth between the elders and the Ottawa. One-Ear did his best to translate what was being said.

Calm finally fell over the house as both sides appeared to accept the decision of Morning Sun.

"It appears I am safe for the time being, but we still must deal with you," One-Ear explained, waiting for additional details. "I think the Ottawa will abide by the ruling and leave you behind until the spring season. I will not leave you until they are gone and out of our sight."

As the crowd started to intermingle, Maggie noticed that most of One-Ear's warriors had made their way around to his side. The Ottawa showed her little attention and they appeared to be content with eating and enjoying the cask of rum that was brought in.

"We need to get you out of here," One-Ear said, watching to see if anyone cared what they were doing with Maggie. "Come with me and we will get you back to your home."

"I don't want to go back to that small room; please take me back to the long house," Maggie pleaded, as she was helped up and taken towards the door.

Just as they were about to leave, a voice called out, "You leave us without sharing a cup?"

It was one of the Ottawa leaders, and he was looking directly at One-Ear.

One-Ear told his warriors to take Maggie with them, but she refused to leave his side. He graciously replied to the Ottawa warrior, "I would, but I do not drink...only water. I thought Pontiac felt the same about rum?"

Laughing at him and ignoring the question, the Ottawa called out again, "What about the woman?"

"She is with child," One-Ear countered defiantly and waited to be challenged by the leader.

Maggie was ready to step forward and defend herself until One-Ear softly held her back with his hand. She did as suggested and slumped back behind him.

One-Ear remained standing and waiting for further questions. Noticing the Ottawa leader appeared to be more interested in another cup of rum, One-Ear looked at Maggie and they took the opportunity to leave.

Visibly distraught with the thought of being back in the hands of the Ottawa, Maggie waited until she was clear of the house before she began to cry. She wasn't sure if the added burden of being pregnant piled on her emotions, but Maggie felt faint and grabbed at One-Ear before ultimately collapsing onto the snow.

Embarrassed for outwardly displaying such weakness, especially to One-Ear, Maggie immediately got herself up and pushed away any attempts by some of the warriors to assist her up.

"Maggie, let's get out of this cold and into a more comfortable place," One-Ear said and led the swelling group of warriors to Maggie's long house. "We need to look at what to do next."

The instant heat welcomed all of them as they stepped inside and got themselves out of the bitter cold.

Gathering herself together, Maggie was the first to speak, "Why did the elder do that to me?"

One-Ear replied and displayed his displeasure at what took place earlier, "I think the village is so frightened by the Ottawa, they would rather give up one of their own instead of facing the Ottawa's temper."

The warriors, crowded into the long house, waited for some decision from One-Ear. Maggie did take some solace in the fact that his men appeared to be just as upset as she was.

Finding it difficult to hold back her temper at the situation, Maggie countered, "Would it save you some trouble if you just handed me over now instead of waiting until spring?"

Her words and obvious doubt, made One-Ear look directly at her and she realized her outburst hurt him. The look on his face brought back a flood of memories from all the situations the two had faced.

Wishing she could take back what she had just blurted out, Maggie spoke again before One-Ear could offer a reply, "I am so sorry, One-Ear. I would never doubt your friendship, but I am so frightened at the thought of being a slave to the Ottawa. I can't see them accepting my child or even wanting to take the child with me...I can't lose another..." Once again doing her best to hold back her tears, Maggie lowered her head and could not continue.

"You will never have to be afraid with me by your side," One-Ear calmly replied. "The Ottawa will never take you away as long as I can hold a tomahawk or musket."

His words made his men erupt with howls and cheers.

Maggie looked up to see their rebellious excitement. For the first time since she had been informed by the leaders she would be given back to the Ottawa, she felt some peace.

"They will have to kill us all, if they want to take you from us," One-Ear shouted, doing his best to rile up his fellow warriors and ensure Maggie that he would keep her safe.

No more words needed to be said, and most of the warriors dispersed to their homes for the night. One-Ear and a handful of his most loyal warriors remained behind.

"There should be no need for you to stay with me every moment of the day," Maggie said in a calmer voice. "After all, the elder did say the plan was for the Ottawa to take me back with them in the spring."

"She did, but I have learned that the Ottawa do what they want," One-Ear explained as he pulled a large fur pelt down to the floor to make himself comfortable for the night. "If they want to take you now, they will try. I would feel better if I stay close by, just in case."

Maggie worried that with the Ottawa celebrating and drinking rum, they might just decide that she should go with them immediately. One-Ear and his band of warriors could easily fight the delegation of Ottawa inside the village, but the bigger concern was that nearly three hundred Ottawa warriors were camped out in the field just a few paces from the main entrance.

The entire village could not withstand such an attack, and the Ottawa could overrun the village with ease. Maggie did not really know what One-Ear had planned, but she appreciated that he was by her side.

Chapter | **Twelve**

Jacob rose early and began packing his belongings for the continued trek north. Ensuring the lock of his musket was covered with a spare piece of deer hide to keep his powder dry, he also slipped his powder horn under his outer coat and strapped his snowshoes over his back.

He noticed that Joshua was up as well and moved to the young man's side as soon as his own packing was finished.

"How was your night; you spent most of the time talking with Stark?" Jacob asked and placed his hands over the small fire that some of the other men had started to make some coffee.

"He was very nice and we spoke mostly about our time with the savages," Joshua said sleepily. "He seemed to have enjoyed the time he spent with the Abenaki and had a great many respectful things to say about them. As you might have guessed, my experience with the Huron was not as nicely painted.

"Mr. Stark also had many things to say about Captain Rogers, and his loyalty to the man was very evident."

"It will certainly be interesting over the next couple of weeks," Jacob said with a humorless smirk. "It appears their plan is to move deep into

French-held territory; these fellows will either cause some troubles for them or get all of us killed."

Jacob helped Joshua get all his gear ready and then the two men did the same with the rest of the men.

Rogers was also up by this time and had already sent out an advanced scout to make sure the trail towards Fort Carillon was safe.

Jacob offered a friendly wave and Rogers called out, "Jacob, bring the lad over; we need to talk."

Working their way through the men and all their supplies, Jacob and Joshua reported to Rogers.

"I hope your men had a restful night," Rogers greeted them as he sat on a snowy tree stump and smoked a small pipe. "It is bloody cold, but at least the skies are holding and a couple of my Stockbridge Indians mentioned the weather should be kind to us."

"The men are anxious to move out, sir," Joshua jumped in and replied.

Not appearing to be interested in any more small talk, Rogers continued, "I have spoken with my scouts and a couple of the men that grew up around this area. It has been suggested that we should think about the mountain route around Fort Carillon. Doing that should keep us from running into too many French patrols. The lake would be much faster, but the likelihood of encountering the French or their Indian allies would be far greater."

Pausing for a brief moment to add some loose tobacco to his pipe, Rogers continued, "What are your thoughts, Jacob? I should add, we received some new orders and we now are expected to concentrate our efforts between Carillon and Fort St. Frederic to disrupt their supply lines."

Jacob waited before he offered his thoughts, just in case Rogers wanted to add anything else. "My men are used to traveling through the mountains of Pennsylvania," he finally began, "but we would rarely take the trails at this time of the year. If we were hit with some snow, most of the passes would be next to impossible to travel on."

"Did I not make myself clear when I told you my scouts had predicted no snow for the foreseeable future?" Rogers flared before Jacob could continue.

Jacob was not used to being spoken to in such a manner, especially by a similarly ranked officer, but he held his tongue until he regrouped his thoughts. The idea of relying on the word of his Stockbridge scouts and taking it as gospel had him rethinking what he thought of Rogers as a whole.

He wasn't entirely certain what Rogers expected him to say, but Jacob figured it matter little what he offered now. The decision was already made and he would just be wasting his breath if he said anything against the plan.

"I suspect the French would never expect you to take such a chance to journey over the mountains," Jacob said. "That alone makes it a worthwhile venture." He was not completely certain that this was the only way to go to avoid the lake, but he didn't want to get on Rogers' bad side...for the moment at least.

"My old friend John Stark had also mentioned his concerns about the mountains, but he came around much like you did once he understood the circumstances," Rogers added, now finished with his pipe and dumping the remaining ashes onto the snow. He stared at the snow that melted under his pipe ash and then refocused his thoughts back to Jacob and Joshua.

"Sir, do you have orders for us?" Jacob asked, trying not to rile up Rogers again, but also unwilling to wait around for Rogers to take his time.

"Jacob, your men will be with the main body and form up in smaller groups of five or six men. I want them to travel 'Indian style', as we did earlier.

"You might want to consider forming up a vanguard to watch the woods as you did yesterday. The mountain trail is very narrow in spots with a number of curves and blind spots; we will all have to be ready for the possibility of an ambush.

"Stark will be taking up the rear and he asked if young Joshua would like to accompany him." When Rogers finished giving his orders, he looked at Joshua for an answer about joining Stark's company.

Jacob did not like the idea of Joshua not being by his side, but left it to the young man to make his own decision and reply to Rogers.

"Respectfully, sir, I would like to help Lieutenant Stark during the first leg of the trip, but I want to remain part of my old ranging company," Joshua answered diplomatically in an attempt not to insult the apparently volatile Rogers.

"Fine, lad, just find Stark and we will organize the men in due time," Rogers replied, dismissing the two men and refocusing his interests on locating some coffee.

Slowly walking back towards their gear, Jacob was the first to speak, "I want you with me, lad, but you might learn something from this Stark. You should report to him and please stay with him. As soon as we get past these mountains, I expect you will move up to join us once again."

Joshua nodded and attempted to lighten the mood by changing the subject, "I assume the bet we won last night will not be paid?"

Jacob just laughed and had already thought the same after they had spoken with Rogers.

Once they found their gear, Joshua respectfully offered Jacob his hand and departed to where Stark and most of his men were milling about.

Jacob spent the rest of his time organizing his men into smaller groups and reminded them all to stay alert and keep up with the men ahead of them.

It took a couple of long days, but the mountains presented a relatively easy way around the outer limits of Fort Carillon. The open, frozen lake would have been physically easier and would have saved the rangers several days of extra travel, but the route would have been thick with French patrols, not to mention their savages.

As the Stockbridge scouts had predicted, the weather held. Despite the higher mountain elevation and its foot of additional snow, the use of snowshoes and the sleds proved to make the trek much easier.

Jacob was proud of how his rangers contributed to the success of the first leg of the mission into French-held territory. He was also very happy to finally be reunited with Joshua who was sent ahead by Stark to join back up with his rangers.

The one thing the mountains did was weed out the weaker men. Rogers was forced to send back a dozen of his own rangers with a mixture of sprains, frostbite and sickness. A couple of escorts were used to take the men back to Fort William Henry, which further diminished the already falling numbers.

Disappointed that he didn't get a chance to see Fort Carillon, especially after hearing some of Rogers' men describe it as such an impressive place, Jacob was happy to get on the other side of the mountains and on to much foot-friendlier terrain.

He had spotted Rogers on a number of occasions through the mountains, as he kept his men moving and dropped back himself to get a report from Stark. Now, as the last of the men cleared the pass, he was down by a small clearing already organizing them to move towards the narrows that linked the northern end of Lake George to Lake Champlain.

Some of the more experienced rangers from Rogers' unit explained to Jacob and his men that Lake Champlain was a long lake that stretched most of the way to Canada. The French used the lake to ship supplies and men from Montreal. Fort St. Frederic was built at the southern end of a narrow strait that joined Lake George to Champlain. What Jacob heard reminded him of how the French used the fort at Niagara as a supply depot for the chain of forts in the Ohio Valley region.

The land in the heavily wooded area running parallel to the lakes was a series of flat areas with some deep valleys mixed in. Jacob's men commented on how similar the land was to the Pennsylvania area, only with more bogs and swampy fields that appeared to not always freeze over. The snow was also higher than most of his men had ever seen. Jacob and his rangers were so thankful they had snowshoes and wondered how any man could survive through such harsh conditions without a pair.

Jacob respectfully reported to Rogers and once again waited for his orders. He prayed that they might be taking the lake trail now, although the thought of running into a large French patrol did not sit well. Any chance to escape would be challenging at best, and if word got to Carillon, they could easily be surrounded with little chance of reaching the much friendlier territory of southern Lake George.

"That wasn't too bad was it, Jacob?" Rogers asked once he noticed Jacob standing near him. "Though, now we should be able to have some fun."

Jacob didn't bother to say anything and just politely nodded his agreement.

Rogers was busily ordering and organizing the men and didn't wait for his entire company to arrive before he sent out additional scouts to search the area.

He turned to Jacob and gave his orders, "We are moving north and will head east to use the lake to move towards Lake Champlain. Tell your lads that we will start to see French patrols all over the area; keep them all on alert."

As Rogers turned to speak with a couple of his men, he surprisingly turned back and asked, "Jacob, how do you feel about leading a small scouting party north to take a look at Fort St. Frederic?"

Not sure about this apparent renewed confidence in him, and doing his best to hide his excitement, Jacob quickly replied, "It would be an honor, Robert. I will have my men ready shortly."

"Be quick and report back if you see anything important," Rogers shouted back and Jacob left to gather the men he wanted to take with him.

Joshua was one of the first men he added to his scouting party before adding ten more men including Lessard. He didn't wait to check with Rogers and just headed north towards the main trail that skirted the lake's western shore line.

Once he reached the southern narrows of Lake Champlain, Jacob could see that the earlier scouting party had crossed over to the eastern side of the lake and continued north. Beside the imprints from Rogers' men, the snow-covered lake was dotted with snowshoe prints and a number of deep pitted sled marks that clearly showed the French were busy exchanging supplies between the two forts.

Looking at the lake, one of the rangers suggested it looked more like a winter road than a deeply frozen lake. The French had done a good job of ensuring the 'road' was cleared of any fresh snow and that a sled drawn by horses or dogs could easily traverse the narrows between the two forts.

Just as Jacob and Joshua stood on the frozen shoreline to get a better look up the narrow part of the stretch that linked the lakes, one of the men shouted the presence of what looked like a caravan of sleds moving towards them.

Running back into the nearby woods and praying they were not spotted, Jacob peered around a massive pine tree to get a much safer vantage point of the approaching sleds.

Before he could decide what to do, the silence of the area was shattered by musket fire and shouts from the scouting party that had been just ahead of them. Jacob could plainly see that the men had attempted to ambush the

French sleds, consisting of four sleds pulled by several wild hounds. They did manage to force them down the narrow part of the lake and directly towards where Jacob and his men were setting up their own ambush.

Desperately racing away from the scouting party that had been easily outrun, the two lead sleds had no warning that they were moving blindly into the ready and waiting muskets of Jacob's rangers.

A deafening blast echoed throughout the small confines of the narrow pass between the lakes. The faces of the men in the two sleds registered surprise as a wall of bullets murderously greeted them.

The results of the accurate volley ended in unmanned sleds that flew past them, out-of-control. A couple of the dogs had also been hit, which sent the remaining hounds across the path of the other two sleds advancing from the rear.

Those sleds were forced to slow down to avoid running into the disabled ones. Jacob had ordered his men to re-load on the run as they watched the last two sleds.

"I want prisoners, so don't kill them all," Jacob shouted over the confusion, praying his men heard what he had ordered. "Get those other two sleds under control before they race all the way to Carillon!"

Looking at young Lessard, Jacob ordered, "Call them to us, boy."

"Messieurs...Messieurs," Lessard obeyed weakly. His call was barely loud enough for even the nearby rangers to hear. Somehow it worked though, and the two lead sleds pulled towards the shore line.

Ignoring the weak effort Lessard had just displayed, Joshua was one of the first of the men to race down and secure the control of one of the sleds from the frightened French. The French soldiers simply threw their hands up and surrendered to the approaching rangers.

Within minutes, all the sleds were captured and seven French prisoners were procured. They were all stripped of their outer coats and bound up separately. The dogs and the well-needed supplies were also gathered up. The other scouting party had arrived from the scene of their first ambush, and Jacob suggested that a couple of the Stockbridge scouts should run the sleds down the lake farther, then up to the trail where they would find Rogers and the rest of the ranging company.

Keeping the prisoners away from one another so they couldn't speak with each other, Jacob led the rest of the combined scouting parties back to the trail.

Jacob took time to speak with some of the men attached to the first scouting party and asked if they had seen any additional sleds. He had an odd feeling that there might have been more than just the four they had attacked. If there were, they would have had time to escape and send word to either fort that there were English rangers in the area.

Before he got too far, Jacob asked four of the men to return to the woods around the lake to keep watch. If any other French troops passed the point, the rangers could send word back to Rogers.

He sent two other rangers ahead to alert Rogers and have him prepare for the prisoners.

Jacob searched for young Lessard and found him escorting some of the prisoners along the trail. Upset with his earlier actions, Jacob called him over and asked, "What was that all about? I asked you to do something and you practically ignored my order."

Lessard was clearly frightened by the look on Jacob's face and did not know what to do.

"Careful, young man," Jacob continued. "There are many around here that would rather see you dead. Next time, when I ask you to do something…do it." Jacob did his best to soften his tone, but he still wanted Lessard to understand that he would only live if he continued to cooperate.

The men were in good spirits and the trek back to the encampment was fairly easy. However, when they were within a mere mile of the first line of pickets, a blinding wall of snow smashed into them and forced them to look for shelter.

"Move into the woods and look for some relief from this mess!" Jacob shouted towards where he figured Joshua stood. Although the young man was only a few feet away, Jacob could barely see him.

The men in charge of keeping their eyes on the prisoners did their best not losing them in the sudden blizzard.

Two of the remaining Stockbridge scouts managed to find a small cluster of pine trees that provided a brief break from the storm.

Jacob finally made his way to them and shouted, "Damn good job, men! I don't know how you can see in this mess, but I am grateful you did."

His appreciation went unanswered and Jacob turned his attention back to ensuring all the men found the place. It took well over an hour for the last of the men to arrive. They all huddled together under the high brush and were forced to wait another half-hour until there was a long enough break for Jacob to organize the men and get them moving again.

Luckily, Rogers sent out a small patrol to locate the missing scouting company, and they helped guide the men back to camp. Once all of his men stepped back into the safety of the camp, Jacob finally collapsed in sheer exhaustion.

"Good scout, Jacob?" Rogers stood over him and asked mockingly.

Getting himself up and dusting off the snow, Jacob smiled and replied, "Nice weather you boys have in this territory. I can see why you like it here so much."

"It's home, mate," Rogers laughed and motioned for Jacob to follow him.

Joshua soon joined them to report about the prisoners.

"All but two of them made it," Joshua began. "I'm not certain what happened to them, but I pray they didn't make it back to the lake. By this time, they would be informing one of the forts of our arrival." Joshua waited for the two officers to give him further orders.

"Thank you, lad," Rogers said. "Have the men get the prisoners ready for me and please keep them away from each other."

"Tell me what you saw and your thoughts about the French," Rogers said as he and Jacob continued their walk.

Jacob hesitated briefly as he watched the men in the camp clean up after the short but impactful storm that hit the area.

"The scout went well," he said slowly. "We noticed four French sleds moving down from the north and we decided to attack them. All the men did a great job and the French were easily overtaken. My only concern is that there might have been additional sleds that were alerted when we sent our first volley into the lead French sled."

Rogers reached his small hut, which had been put up by one of his loyal Stockbridge Indians. He took a minute to add a few pieces of wood to the fire just to his right.

"Get comfortable and I will get one of the men to send over the first of the prisoners."

Jacob did as he was told and took a seat on one of the fallen tree trunks near the fire.

"When the prisoners arrive, please keep your eyes on them as I question them," Rogers said. "You should be able to sense if they are telling us the truth or not. I hope we can get some useable information before we decide what to do with them."

As soon as he finished speaking, one of Rogers' men dragged over a very young, clearly frightened soldier and had him stand directly in front of the two waiting officers.

Noticing Lieutenant Stark making his way over to them, Jacob offered a friendly nod and waited for Rogers to begin the interrogation.

"Get your Frenchman over here, Jacob," Rogers demanded suddenly. "Maybe he will prove to be useful after all."

Jacob waved to Joshua to bring Lessard to him. After a brief moment, the Frenchman reluctantly arrived. He stood beside Jacob and looked briefly at the prisoner as he waited for his orders.

Despite Jacob's knowledge of French and Lessard's availability to translate what the prisoners might decide to tell, Rogers decided to speak with the captives himself. Without notice, Rogers launched into the French soldier with an odd combination of broken French and English.

Jacob concentrated on the prisoner before him. The young man was having difficulty holding back his emotions, and pleaded with Rogers not to hand him over to the Stockbridge Indians.

Rogers listened but still used his scouts as a viable threat. All Rogers asked was the size of the two garrisons stationed at Carillon and St. Frederic. The Frenchman sobbed and although he spoke so low that Jacob could barely make out what he was saying, he did answer the question.

Unfortunately, the answer did not sit well with Rogers or Stark, who by this time had moved much closer.

Rogers motioned for the poor boy to be taken away, amid his continued pleas to be kept alive. Rogers took off his cap and rubbed his hands through his hair.

"I never asked how your French was Jacob," Rogers said, without waiting for a reply. "If you could understand what the Frenchie was saying, then you know that our entire mission might be in trouble."

"What are your thoughts, John?" Rogers asked, turning to his lieutenant. "If the report is true, we might be in for some problems."

Stark did not waste many words and instantly replied, "If he was telling us the truth, then we might want to consider getting back to William Henry."

The three men said little else until the next prisoner was shoved in front of them.

This Frenchman was much older and appeared to be a senior ranking officer. Rogers turned his attention back and immediately asked him about the garrison strengths.

The prisoner stood tall and ignored the question until his escort dug his fist into the small of his back. Quickly recovering from the unexpected blow, the soldier simply replied in surprisingly good English, "All you poor bastards will be dead before the next winter returns. When all our men arrive from Quebec and set their sights on your two feeble forts, all you English will be running home to England as fast as you arrived and took our land."

Rogers nodded to the rangers standing behind the defiant Frenchman. Another quick punch to the kidney felled the man. The rangers pulled him up by his hair and jerked his jaw so he was directly facing Rogers.

"I appreciate your courage, although you will most likely die from it," Rogers spat back and was now face-to-face with the prisoner. "Let me make it clear to you and the rest of your fellow prisoners; it will be your side that will be running home and praying we do not follow you there."

Saying nothing else, the prisoner offered an ill-directed smirk to the clearly upset officer standing in front of him. Losing his patience, Rogers called out to one of his Stockbridge scouts to come to him.

The scout was by his side in a moment and Rogers said loudly enough for all to hear, "Take this prisoner into the woods and see how brave he truly is. He thinks the French are the true owners of this land, and I think you might want to convince him otherwise."

With that, the scout grabbed the Frenchman's arm and pulled him towards several other waiting Indians and soon disappeared into the thick shroud of trees.

"Get the next one," Rogers shouted.

Jacob could see that Rogers was tiring of this and sat back to observe what would happen next.

The third prisoner was forced in front of the clearly impatient Rogers and had little time to breathe before he was asked in French, "What do you have to say about all of this?"

This man wore no uniform and was dressed more like a civilian than any of his fellow prisoners.

Keeping his head down, all the man did was mumble in French. Rogers finally called Lessard over and asked him to get the man to talk.

The young man initially paused until Jacob suggested, "Just ask the man what the captain asked the others."

While Lessard appeared nothing like a fellow French soldier, as soon as he began to speak, the man appeared to relax and talk freely. Once the man stopped, Lessard explained, "He said he is not a soldier. He is basically the owner of the hounds that were stolen. He is frightened that you might kill his dogs."

Rogers acted as if he had heard nothing and continued to ask his questions, "What does he know of the French numbers at either fort?"

Lessard once again spoke with the man. After a short conversation, he simply replied, "He keeps saying he is the owner of the hounds."

Seeing he was wasting his time with this prisoner, Rogers motioned for the ranger to take the man away. Just as the man was forced to move, Rogers shouted, "Let him go so he may find his dogs. Maybe he will be lucky enough to find a few, so he can make it back to Carillon."

The man didn't move until Lessard politely nodded and told him to follow the ranger. The poor man smiled and nervously did as he was told.

Jacob sat and watched as the rest of the prisoners were dragged in front of Rogers and asked the same questions. With varying degrees of detail, they all provided the same information. When the last of them had been questioned, Rogers decided to call a council of his officers and senior men.

The questioning of prisoners had extended well into the night and Jacob was tired from his scout and Rogers' relentlessness as he questioned each of them. He desired only to get some sleep, but reluctantly remained until all the officers had finally arrived.

Rogers addressed them, saying, "It has been a long day and from what we learned from the prisoners, it appears our scouting mission might be complicated. What we gathered from most of them was the French were well garrisoned at both forts with far more men than we expected.

They will be active around the area. While I expect we will have ample opportunities to cause some problems, I fear their numbers might impede our success."

Most of the attending officers looked as exhausted as Jacob, yet they all reacted to the news.

Stark was the first to step up and ask, "What is the plan now? Do we just go on and do our best to disrupt their travels between the lakes?"

"Yes, as far as I am concerned, our mission has not changed…for now," Rogers replied.

Jacob could tell that his tone had altered slightly. His officers seemed to be far less enthusiastic about what was now expected from them.

"I think we need to build up some defensive fortification around this encampment," Rogers suggested. "If we do run into some French patrols, we might want to have this place ready to defend. What are your thoughts of having some of the men stay behind and take down some of the nearby trees?"

Stark spoke up again, "It certainly wouldn't hurt if we took some time to make this camp somewhat more useful."

Jacob sat back, determined not to add anything, but suddenly decided to step up and offer his view after all. "Gentlemen," he said, "we need to consider the French prisoners might have been telling us the truth. If so, having a place to fall back to and make a stand only makes sense. In just the short amount of time I have spent in this territory, I have come to realize that with all the valleys and swampy areas along this trail, it would be hell to have to fight all the way back to William Henry."

Rogers just nodded his head in agreement.

No other man decided to add anything or ask any additional questions and they were all soon dismissed.

Jacob found his way to Joshua and took a seat by the fire.

"What are your thoughts now, sir?" Joshua asked, while he listened to a lone owl call into the night.

Jacob waited for an expected return call from another owl, but nothing came. He looked into the fire and offered his thoughts, "Honestly, I am a bit scared and not certain what all this might mean, lad."

The two men sat for a few more minutes before Joshua said, "I should check on the men and see how the pickets are doing. You should get some rest and we will see what tomorrow holds."

Jacob smiled and watched Joshua disappear into the shadows.

Listening to the prisoners describe what faced them at either of the forts, Jacob's mind wandered to James and how he might be holding up. Jacob silently prayed for all to be well and did his best to get comfortable for the night.

The morning brought additional snow and before Jacob could get himself organized, Rogers found him to plan out the day's actions.

"We need to get moving and have the men out in the woods," Rogers explained. "I already spoke with Stark and he said he would take a patrol down to the lake and run parallel towards the north. I want your men to accompany me across the lake, so we can scout the other side."

Without a pause, Jacob answered, "I will have the men ready, sir."

"We leave within the half hour," Rogers replied.

When their conversation ended, Rogers left to speak with some of his other men. Jacob was excited to get back out and looked at the dark sky, hoping it would break long enough to let them get on the trail.

Jacob looked for Joshua and finally found him speaking with some of the men. "We need to get the men packed up and be ready to leave shortly," Jacob said.

"I heard, sir," Joshua said enthusiastically. "We are all just waiting for word to leave. A couple of the men left earlier with four of the scouts and we should get word from them soon about the condition of the trails and what they might have found."

Jacob checked his emotions and once again prayed that this would prove to be an uneventful day.

A few minutes after Jacob spoke with Joshua, Rogers returned to check on the men and confirm they were ready to head out.

"We are ready, sir," Jacob confirmed and waited for word to leave.

"If you please, Jacob, take out an advanced guard of ten men and move east of here," Rogers ordered. "I have provided you one of my scouts and he can assist you in getting safely across the lake."

Not wishing to waste a second, Jacob asked Joshua to accompany him and pick some of the best men to be part of the scout. Once the men had strapped on their much needed snowshoes, they were well on their way.

Happy to be back in the woods, Jacob reminded the men to remain silent and in single file. The pace the Stockbridge scout set was tough, especially considering the fresh snow that had fallen overnight and the overgrown woods that they had to work their way through.

Making sure the scout didn't get too far ahead, Jacob motioned to Joshua to check for stragglers in the back.

All the men had managed to keep up and Jacob was happy to see that the scout had tracked them all the way down to the lake, waiting for them to catch up.

"Can we make it across the ice or do we need to work our way around the lake?" Jacob asked the stone-faced scout, not sure whether to expect an answer.

"Once all your men have arrived, I will check for tracks on the lake," the scout responded. "It is much shorter to cross the lake than to travel over land."

"I will come with you to the lake and we can check for any signs of the French," Jacob suggested and was greeted with silence and no indication the scout had even heard him.

Soon all the men had made their way to the meeting place and took a short rest break. Jacob briefed Joshua on the scout's plan and ordered him to instruct the rest of the men to turn their attention to the lake.

The scout slid down the narrow trail onto the small opening that brought him to the ice. He turned to look back at Jacob and appeared to be expecting him to follow him.

Jacob did and was by the scout's side as the two men ventured slowly out into the open, watching for any signs the French had passed by. The previous night's snow had covered all the old tracks.

Permitting the scout to lead the way, Jacob stayed a few feet back and watched the southern end of the fairly narrow stretch of the lake. While the wind had forced some of the snow into shoulder-high drifts, it had also exposed some stretches of open ice that proved to be almost impossible to walk on with the snowshoes.

By the time the two men made it across to the wooded landing area on the opposite shore, Jacob noticed that Rogers and the rest of his men had caught up to their scouting party.

A quick wave notified Rogers that all was safe and soon a long line of men were crossing the open ice. Rogers had several of the men form a vanguard to protect the open flanks against the constant threat that a French sled might appear from the north or south.

Jacob and the Stockbridge scout sat and waited. They were unable to do much as they watched their mates stumble and walk gingerly across the lake. Jacob relaxed as soon as he saw Joshua finally make his way across the exposed lake to relative safety.

Rogers had taken up the rear and pushed the men to move quickly. Soon they were all safely across and moving north towards the mouth of Lake Champlain.

"Good job, Jacob," Rogers said. "Your men did well to make it across this damn lake. I didn't relish the thought of spending an extra half-day's walk around the narrows."

"Someone is watching over us, sir, but we are not done yet," Jacob cautioned.

The view from the western side of the lake provided them a nice look at the countryside. After an hour of pushing through heavy brush and heavy, snow-covered branches of the endless fir and pine trees, one of the men sent word back that they could see Stark and his men walking along the distant shoreline.

Rogers handed Jacob his scope and once he had scanned the opposite shoreline, Jacob offered, "I assume this is the peace before the storm."

"I just hope Lieutenant Stark isn't so aggressive that he exposes himself to a possible attack," Rogers mumbled as he took a turn with the scope. "He does tend to be fearless and sometimes rushes blindly into action."

Jacob could see that Stark and his men were a mile or so back of where they stood and Rogers decided to press forward to ensure the French didn't suddenly appear from the northern narrows.

The gap between the two advancing patrols expanded as Jacob and his men slogged through the combined terrain of deep forest and boggy, swampy fields that proved to be far worse than any of the men had traversed before.

Once the patrol had worked their way back to the shoreline trail, Rogers and Jacob once again scoped the opposite shore for any signs of Stark. Rogers had just gotten his scope back into his pack when the shout of "SLED!" rang out along the line of men.

Jacob immediately saw the men pointing at a lone horse-drawn sled rambling over the snow. It was moving quickly and the large work horses kicked up a line of snowy clouds as it dragged the heavily-laden supply sled north along the open lake.

Jacob watched Stark and his men rush to the open shoreline, but they missed the swift target. Stark and his men were left in the open as, without notice, several other sleds rumbled up the same lake trail from around a cove. Seeing the rangers standing in front of them, the drivers pulled back on the horses and desperately attempted to retreat.

Seeing an opportunity, both Jacob and Rogers ordered their men down onto the lake to form up in small groups to fire on the sleds.

The lead sled wildly swerved to avoid the onslaught of rangers attempting to cut off their withdrawal. The driver masterfully maneuvered to the opposite shore. Anticipating such action, Rogers had already stationed four men to halt the advance.

"Fire at the horses or the driver," Rogers' voice echoed across the open lake. "Stop them at any cost!"

The other sleds did their best to follow, but many of the horses became close to unmanageable and fought frantically to instinctively keep moving north.

Standing in a rough semi-circle, the rangers unleashed an unforgiving fire that forced the first of the sleds back towards Fort Carillon.

Just as the men started to celebrate their small victory, Jacob called out to Rogers, "There are more of them coming, Robert."

While the advanced patrol had forced back the first sled, Stark and his men had rushed onto the open lake to take part in the ambush. In doing so, they had alerted a group of eight sleds who immediately turned to head back to Carillon.

Stark and his patrol did their best to stop the retreat and finally managed to cut off the first lone sled, along with two others. Rogers and Jacob had pulled their men forward at a torrid pace, and they were close enough to take part in the capture of the isolated sleds.

Jacob could only watch as the remaining five disappeared south. He knew that they would soon be warning the fort of the ambush. Rogers ran to him and said, "Have your men form up and prepare for a possible counterattack."

He could see that Rogers cared little for the sleds and the couple of prisoners captured, as he stared south. Not even bothering to question the captives himself, Rogers had his Stockbridge scouts take them into the woods after he had Stark speak briefly with them.

Several lone shots rang out across the open lake a few minutes after the scouts pushed the French captives into the woods. None of the rangers said a word. Realistically, they were far too concerned with their own lives to worry about a few captured soldiers.

Once Jacob's men were in position, he ran towards the small cove where Rogers stood talking with Stark. "Robert," Jacob shouted, caring little if he came across as insubordinate, "I think we should get these bloody sleds into the woods and out of sight."

As Jacob approached, he could see bad news written on Rogers' face.

"Damn, I should have listened to that last set of prisoners," Rogers said. "The word is that today there are over two hundred Canadian Militia, plus as many savages that arrived late last night, and more regulars are scheduled to arrive shortly."

Rogers, Stark and Jacob exchanged glances and all three understood they were now left with only one thing to do.

Chapter | **Thirteen**

$\mathbf{T}$he Ottawa remained peacefully within their own encampment, but One-Ear remained diligent in keeping some of his warriors on the high walls, watching for any movement below.

Maggie could not believe that she was once again at the mercy of the Ottawa, specifically, Pontiac. The thought of having her child brought up by these particularly savage people frightened her. Thoughts of ending the pregnancy crossed her mind, but she dismissed them as wild thoughts. Her love for her husband and God would not allow her to kill the only child she still had possession of.

In the days after the meeting, she wanted to be by herself yet at the same time, she loved the constant activity inside the longhouse. Maggie enjoyed that One-Ear continuously made an effort to check on her. Anne stopped by on a few occasions to console her, but found that Maggie was either resting or just didn't want to be disturbed.

The village was on edge with the Ottawa encamped only a few paces away. Although the warriors never bothered the villagers directly, the Ottawa were not welcome neighbors. They hunted the nearby woods for game, basically taking food out of the mouths of the villagers. The sight of a deer or moose roasting over the Ottawa's open fires infuriated One-Ear.

As winter progressed, food would be harder to find and the village would be forced to eat off the supplies they had managed to stock up over the fall and early winter months.

One-Ear kept his warriors on alert at all times. When any of the villagers needed to leave the confines of the village, he made certain some of his warriors provided an escort for them.

The weather brought not only the usual heavy snows expected for the territory, but a mixture of extreme temperatures. Some days were unusually warm followed by nights of unbearable cold. The snow had already accumulated close to two feet in depth; if not for snowshoes, most of the villagers would have been forced to remain indoors. Clearing heavy snow each morning became a tiresome routine that drained the villagers. They took advantage of every moment of sunshine they could get.

Maggie grew tired of staying inside feeling sorry for herself. Her stomach was now noticeably plump and her legs were sore from her inactivity.

She awoke early one morning to take a morning walk around the peaceful village. A thick, misty brew of fog and ice hung in the air, but Maggie was happy to fill her lungs with the cold, refreshing air.

One-Ear was still apparently resting, as were most of his warriors. The upper walls were manned only by a few unfortunate warriors who leaned against the wall. Maggie guessed that the village had finally come to the conclusion that the Ottawa were going to stay through the winter.

The village was basically still; only a handful of women were outside sweeping some snow from around the front of the long houses. If not for the odd howls of the numerous wild dogs around the village, the scene would be one of complete tranquility.

Maggie knew the peace was only masking the threat that sat just outside the tall wooden palisade. She could see the smoke from their fires mixing with the foggy air and could smell the faint aroma of meat that had been roasted the night before.

Feeling reenergized by her walk, Maggie wanted to check on the Ottawa encampment and see what they were up to. Not comfortable enough to go outside the village's walls, she walked to one of the crudely carved out musket slots One-Ear had his men cut into the massive tree trunks that made up the wall.

Instinctively cautious and not wanting to draw attention to herself, Maggie strained to look through one of them and was surprised that she could not get a clear view of the camp. Walking close to the main entrance, she once again searched the outer field for the Ottawa.

An odd feeling struck her, and she immediately found a hand-made ladder that would take her up to the upper wall's lookout. Maggie struggled with her extra weight and felt unbalanced as she moved upwards. Taking her time, she finally made her way to the top of the look-out tower and looked down to see her prayers answered.

Maggie's gaze fell on a field in disarray. An empty clump of half-deteriorated huts and the marks where hastily-dismantled bush tents once stood were all that remained of the Ottawa camp. Uncountable numbers of tracks littered the field and she could clearly see that the main body of the Ottawa party had departed sometime during the night. The prints showed a departure for the south, but Maggie cared little for their whereabouts, just that they were gone.

Taking in another deep breath of the fresh, crisp air, Maggie turned to get a bird's eye view of the sprawling village. There were still only the same handful of women up and doing their daily chores, totally unaware that the hated Ottawa had left. She could not believe that the warriors guarding the upper wall could have missed the departure of the Ottawa until she noticed most were asleep or had their cold faces buried deep inside their winter coats.

It was if a massive blanket had been lifted off her. Maggie fought hard not to scream and shout the exciting news from the top of the palisade, but she decided One-Ear should be the one to announce it to the rest of the village.

Before she could climb down from the wall, she realized that One-Ear was finally awake and was busily throwing several pieces of hardwood on a nearby fire.

"Good morning; come take a look!" Maggie shouted down. Her voice alerted several of the villagers who streamed down to the walls to see what she was so excited about.

One-Ear's face registered surprise at seeing Maggie on the wall, but he gave her a polite wave and did as she suggested. After moving quickly to the village entrance and seeing the empty field, One-Ear found it difficult not to show his pleasure. "Finally, the gods have answered our prayers and sent the Ottawa away!" he called up to Maggie.

Soon most of the warriors, accompanied by several of the villagers, had rushed into the now open field. They celebrated by kicking down the crudely built huts and throwing snow onto the many still-smoking fire pits that dotted the snow-packed field. Screaming and cheering like young children, the warriors danced and shot off their muskets in an odd salute to their gods.

Maggie made her way down the ladder to greet the waiting One-Ear. With a big smile, he reached out to assist Maggie's last few steps down the uneven ladder's rungs and said, "Now we can all breathe and get back to building up our supplies for the winter."

"I have prayed every day that we would be freed from their hostile grip," Maggie said as she reached the ground. Without warning, she grabbed One-Ear in a motherly hug, which he readily accepted.

A moment later, some of One-Ear's warriors approached to await his decision of what they should do next. Releasing Maggie, he told one of his warriors to gather a large scouting party and follow the tracks left behind by the Ottawa.

Maggie understood that he wanted confirmation that they had completely left the area. He had told her before that he suspected the Ottawa had only stopped at the village on their way southward to the French fort called Carillon.

She really didn't care where they were going just that they had moved on without her. As her initial excitement subsided, Maggie realized that the aches and pains she had fought for the past week, seemed to have suddenly dissipated.

Before One-Ear focused on getting the village back in order, he turned to her and said, "Maggie, you need to rest. Go to my fire and I will send one of the women over to get you some food."

Without waiting for a reply, One-Ear walked out into the field and ordered some of his men into the woods to check their trap-lines. Maggie walked slowly across the packed snow towards the fire.

The change in the villagers was immediate. The mood of the entire village was lighter and friendlier. Even before she made it to the fire pit, several of the women offered her a hand and guided her to a seat by the roaring fire. It wasn't long before one of them brought her several slices of freshly-made, steaming corn bread and a wooden cup of hot herbal tea.

Anne caught Maggie's eye and waved. Maggie waved in return and motioned to the place next to her on the roughly carved fallen tree trunk. When Anne walked over, Maggie gave her a hearty smile and said, "Good morning, Anne. I assume you have heard the wonderful news?"

Anne took a seat and replied, "Yes, it has certainly given the village a renewed life."

Maggie gave Anne a nice piece of bread and the two women sat for a moment to enjoy the heat of the fire.

"How are you feeling?" Anne asked after she took the last bite of her bread.

"Much better now," Maggie replied. "Though, my bones have been aching and I still feel tired most days. My hope is that with the Ottawa gone, I can get out and take some daily walks."

Anne just nodded her head and turned back to the fire.

"How are you doing?" Maggie asked quietly. "Does this village make you happy?"

"I like it here, but honestly, it still doesn't feel like home," Anne confided as she stared into the fire. "I miss my old home, despite the fact none of my people are there any longer."

Maggie understood exactly what she meant. No place ever feels like home...except your real home. They sat comfortably amid friendly villagers, but they were still outsiders.

Returning to the moment, Maggie smiled and gave Anne a brief hug.

Anne wasn't sure what to do and finally said, "I stopped by the longhouse several times to see you, but you were either resting or not wishing to see anyone."

"I am sorry for that, but the news of the Ottawa and being betrayed by Morning Sun upset me. I just needed some time to take it all in." Maggie hoped Anne would understand.

"No need to explain," Anne said with a smile. "I knew you just needed some time; I only wanted to make sure you were well."

Just as she was about to continue their conversation, Maggie noticed that some of One-Ear's warriors had returned with what appeared to be a prisoner.

Unable to see what was going on through the villagers and warriors, Maggie stood and said, "Anne, help me walk through the crowd so we can see what is happening."

Anne did as she was asked and the two women walked briskly over to the source of the commotion. There they found one of One-Ear's warriors holding onto one of the recently departed Ottawa warriors, as though he were on display.

The villagers flew into a rage and hurled abuses and threats towards the prisoner. He gave them no indication that he was frightened, and the incensed mob grew violent.

Even the youngest of the villagers joined in as they grabbed sticks, war clubs and anything else they could find to strike the prisoner as he was paraded around the village. Some of the older women just spat or used their wooden plates to throw hot ash over the Ottawa's back. By the time he was dragged past Maggie and Anne, most of his winter clothing had been pulled off and was now only dressed in a thin breechclout and a light trade shirt.

Maggie had experienced running the gauntlet several horrifying times, but this display was far worse. The prisoner was bloodied and bruised by the time he was shoved against one of three poles that stood forebodingly in the center of the village. One-Ear was waiting and immediately tied the warrior's arms and legs against the pole; he appeared to relish the man's pain with every jerk of the thick rope. A final piece of rope was secured around the Ottawa's throat.

In spite of herself, Maggie was impressed by how the prisoner gave no sign of fear or even uttered a noise. His face remained stoic throughout the ordeal, and he only flinched once when One-Ear tightened the ropes around his legs.

She noticed Morning Sun and the other elders standing by in silence. At one point, Morning Sun appeared as if she was going to attempt to stop the torture, but One-Ear defiantly motioned to her to refrain from interfering.

Maggie finally reached One-Ear as he turned away from the pole. "What is happening?" she demanded. "Why did your warriors bring one of them back to the village?"

One-Ear initially ignored her questions and appeared too happy that his scouts had returned with such a prize. "He was found in our woods and my scouts felt he was far more suited to be within our walls than out," One-Ear finally said.

Maggie knew not to press the issue and was surprised to see that the village elders were now speaking with the prisoner. Morning Sun led the contingent and appeared to be the most vocal of all the elders. She even took time to wipe the prisoner's face free of some blood and dirt.

The look on her face was a mixture of fear and anger.

One-Ear quickly made his way from Maggie's side to the group of elders and was immediately set upon by Morning Sun. She ran at him and screamed something in her Algonquin tongue. He listened to her tirade, but offered no response.

Maggie watched and then asked Anne, who had remained with her, what was being discussed.

Anne explained, "The elders are upset that your friend has been foolish enough to take one of the Ottawa warriors as a prisoner. The one called Morning Sun also said this Ottawa is a cousin or some kind of family member to her son Pontiac. She has demanded that he be released and returned with offerings to his people."

Maggie feared that if what Anne had translated was true, the village was in for some harsh consequences either way, but if Pontiac found that the villagers decided to torture and kill a member of his own family, the village would pay heavily for its indiscretions. Maggie wanted desperately to speak with One-Ear and try to convince him that it was the wrong thing to do.

The villagers were not interested in any pleas for leniency towards the prisoner. They had been intimidated by the Ottawa many times and sought to relieve their anger. The elders, led by the clearly insulted Morning Sun, realized that they held no sway over this matter. The villagers wanted their revenge and nothing could be said to change their minds.

Maggie could see that the village had traded peace for unruliness, and at her core, she feared for the prisoner despite her own feelings of hatred for the Ottawa. As One-Ear started back towards her, Maggie saw a look of excitement on his face that showed he was as eager as the rest of the villagers to take vengeance on the prisoner.

"Have you thought this out?" Maggie screamed at One-Ear over the noise as he reached her side. "If you kill him, the entire Ottawa nation will come here to seek revenge. It is not too late to release him and just let him leave."

One-Ear gave no sign that he was listening. The two stood by and watched the villagers scream out in anticipation of the festivities that would last through the night.

"The elders agree with you," One-Ear finally responded, "but I can't just let him go. The Ottawa would look at that as a sign of weakness and still return to seek some form of payment for our actions."

"It is too late…" he added.

"Our peace was short-lived," Maggie said, dropping her head. "Once Pontiac gets word of this, he will bring a thousand warriors from the west and destroy what you have here."

She could see that her words mattered little; the wheels of the tortuous festivities had already been set in motion. The villagers would enjoy a night full of food, drink and killing, but when the morning sun arose, they would realize their mistake and spend the long winter praying to their gods for forgiveness.

As Maggie and One-Ear watched and listened, some of the warriors were already stacking up piles of cut logs around the feet of the warrior. The poor savage's skin had already turned red; if the wind picked up, Maggie imagined he would not survive long enough to be tortured but would simply succumb to the cold air.

One-Ear said nothing more and left Maggie and Anne alone. The two women walked back to the fire pit where they had sat earlier. Anne placed another large piece of hardwood on the burning embers, and the fire once again ignited in a fury of heat and sparks.

"How do you feel?" Maggie asked, once they were both comfortably seated on the log.

"Nothing good will come of this," Anne said ominously, doing her best not to look towards the nearly naked Ottawa warrior.

The excitement of the morning had already given way to the afternoon. The skyline was growing dark enough to force the villagers to expedite their plans. If a storm blew in off the lake, they would lose the prisoner to the weather and not have the satisfaction of seeing his pain.

Deciding to simply torture the Ottawa quickly to enact their vengeance, several warriors started the fire early at the base of the pole. Before the flames reached the prisoner, the clear skies became filled with heavy, snow-laden clouds. The wind picked up and a torrent of flurries began to swirl through the village.

The sudden alteration in the weather forced most of the villagers back into their homes, leaving the Ottawa prisoner alone and exposed to the harsh elements. The weak flames below him sputtered and quickly blew out.

Maggie's first instinct was to find an old animal pelt to wrap around the exposed prisoner, but she had no opportunity to do so. As she was helped to her long house, the flurries gave way to a blinding blizzard that made it impossible to see anything beyond an arm's length. The winds whipped up the already deep snow that already lay on the ground, making it difficult to move even a few paces.

Maggie could not get her mind off the lone warrior strapped to a pole in the middle of the vicious storm. She marveled at the strange coincidence of the weather changing so quickly just as the villagers began to torture their captive.

The villagers inside her longhouse also seemed affected by the circumstances. They were frightened by the sudden storm and, from what she could decipher of their conversations; some felt it was a sign from the gods that they did not approve of their actions.

The idea of assisting an Ottawa warrior made Maggie struggle internally, yet she could not sit back and accept his cruel fate. Even as she conjured thoughts of how to help him, she prayed that once he was free he would not bring back his fellow warriors to invade the village.

The storm refused to let up and most of her house mates had either returned to their beds or were desperately busy attempting to fill any gaps in the wooden strapping to keep the elements out.

It was now dark and much colder outside and the wind could be heard thrashing around the village. Without drawing attention to herself, Maggie began searching for a knife sharp enough to cut the rope tied around the captive's arms and legs.

She moved as quickly as her condition permitted, and found a newly sharpened knife resting on a pile of heavy winter pelts. Concealing the knife in her sash, Maggie bundled herself into a nice fur wrap, fur-lined hat, a pair of over-sized mitts and she tied a loose blanket over her head to keep the wind from blowing directly on her face.

She knew this was a foolish venture that just might lead to her own death, but she could not just sit back and sleep while the poor prisoner was left to die in such a way.

Carrying another long pelt in her arms, Maggie pushed opened the snow-blocked door and pulled back the bear skin that dangled from the doorframe. It did an especially good job of keeping the snow and wind outside, and a slight moan echoed from some of the villagers as a quick gust of wind swept through the opening. Maggie ignored them and stepped into the blur of the heavy, windy storm.

Thankfully, no one tried to stop her.

As she pawed at the air in front of her to find something that might guide her to the captive, she was nearly forced to retreat after covering only a few short paces. Turning to her instincts, Maggie pushed through the wind and the pelting snow to finally reach the open grounds of the village's center. A trip that normally took a few seconds in fair weather, took her nearly fifteen long minutes. The freezing air tore into her like she was also naked, but she soldiered through the wall of snow. The weight of the pelts added to her problems, but she wanted desperately to reach the prisoner.

As she searched blindly for the pole where the he was tied up, Maggie finally felt what she thought was an arm. She pulled herself towards the object and was soon close enough to feel the frozen chest of the warrior. She could feel a very faint heartbeat below his skin.

She immediately threw the pelt over his cold body, and a slight groan eked from his blue lips. Struggling to pull the knife from her inside sash, Maggie was forced to remove her glove. At long last, she finally freed the knife and cut through the frozen hemp rope.

In the brief moment her hand was exposed, Maggie could feel it begin to freeze. She could not imagine how this poor Ottawa warrior had survive so long, bare-chested and exposed to these elements.

The captive almost fell down into the snow, but Maggie braced him slightly by pushing her weight into him. She brushed off as much of the snow from him as she could, and used her own body heat to wake him up.

It only took a few minutes to get some life back into him, and he was soon strong enough to hold the heavy pelt around him. Maggie quickly cut some of the hemp rope to tie the huge pelt around his waist and keep him warmer.

"Please keep moving," she cried as she threw an arm around his shoulder and urged him forward. "If we stop in this snow storm, we will both be dead." She wasn't even sure if he understood her pleas.

He said nothing and just looked at her as if he could not understand why this small villager was trying to help him. The two frozen souls continued forward, doing their best to avoid running blindly into one of the many houses and huts that made up the scattered village layout.

She pulled him towards the outer wall, knowing that if they used their hands they would be able to follow the wall towards the entrance. Thankfully, the storm had forced the lookouts to take cover in their homes, so they moved without fear of being discovered. Ironically, the snow that hindered their movements also provided concealment for the escape.

After what felt like an hour, Maggie was happy to feel the gap in the wall that would lead them to the wide open field where the Ottawa had camped. She could feel the warrior's strength returning. He moved better with every step they took.

At the village entrance, the Ottawa stopped to adjust his over-sized fur pelt and took a final look at Maggie. Her face was now covered in snow and frost, and she appeared more like some snow beast than a woman. He curiously brushed off her face to expose the identity of the villager who had been so brave to help him.

Maggie saw shock register on his face. She thought he was going to speak, but he just remained stoic and looked directly into her eyes. His gaze frightened her, but she prayed he was just doing his best to remember her.

Before she pointed him to the field, Maggie reluctantly handed him her borrowed knife. She half-expected he might just run her through with it, but instead he gave her a kind smile and ran slowly towards the woods. The snow storm covered his tracks almost as soon as he took his first step, and after a couple of seconds she could no longer see him in the darkness.

Maggie breathed a sigh of relief when he was out of sight. She was not completely sure what she would say if questioned about his escape. She once more covered her face and turned to make the slow trek back to the warmth of the long house. While she felt better about the warrior's fate, she prayed that she had done the right thing.

Chapter | **Fourteen**

Jacob could see the concern on the face of the usually confident Rogers and pressed him to make a decision. "Robert, we need to leave or we will be overrun by the French."

Rogers gave no answer, but appeared to be lost in thought. Lieutenant Stark and some of the other senior rangers quickly joined Jacob and Rogers.

"We can't stay here," Rogers finally answered. "I think our best option is to get back to last night's encampment and continue with the build-up of a defensive position. It is midday now, and we are limited by the amount of time left for us. Once night falls, and depending on what the French are doing, we can then possibly work our way back to William Henry."

Stark spoke up and told his friend that he would take an advanced scout to clear the trail towards the camp.

Rogers nodded and then ordered Jacob to get his men in order, "We need to get moving."

Within minutes, all the rangers plus a handful of Stockbridge Indians in charge of the rear guard were deep into the woods. They had the luxury of using the same trail they had moved on earlier, thus presenting them with a relatively well-packed-down path.

Using the same trail they had already traveled on was against everything Jacob was ever told about tracking and trail movement, yet he understood that this situation dictated such unusual actions. The amount of snow that suffocated the countryside made it close to impossible to move over an unused pathway. It was far more important to rush back to the camp where they could wait out an expected attack.

Jacob prayed they would not pay for their decision.

He could see that his men were moving along well and appeared to be in good spirits. So far, there had been no messages sent back from Stark's scouts. The only place that gave Jacob some concern was the couple of deep gullies that they had traversed through earlier. He thought that if the French were around, those would make ideal places to set up for an ambush.

He made his way up to Rogers, who spent most of the trip reminding the men to be ready for the possibility the French might attack them at any moment.

"Robert," Jacob said, "we are approaching a small valley. We might want to send word to Stark to wait for us before he steps into a French ambush." Without waiting for a reply, he moved back to check on his men.

Joshua had remained with him this time. They were moving in single file groups of around five men and appeared to be maintaining a good pace.

Rogers worked his way back to find Jacob.

"I had the same feeling about what sits ahead, Jacob, but thank you for speaking up," Rogers said. "Please rush ahead and find Stark and ask him to wait for us before we enter the valley." He motioned for the men to slow down and have their muskets at the ready.

Jacob pushed ahead and found Stark already waiting in the woods before the small, open valley. The opening ahead was bounded by a steep hill that would cause them an endless amount of problems if in fact the French had already positioned themselves on its heights.

"What are your thoughts, John?" Jacob asked as he crouched beside Stark and scanned the woods around the valley.

"Can't honestly see any signs of them," Stark responded. "If they are waiting for us, they will be able to keep up their fire all day. If we don't clear the valley, we will most likely all die or become French prisoners."

Stark pointed out a small hill that sat just to their left. Jacob saw that it was a good position, but to reach it the men would have to rush into the open.

"That hill holds the key to our success, Jacob," Stark said. "If we can get even a handful of men to it, they can fire down on the French and force them out into the open."

Jacob liked Stark and trusted his judgment of the situation. The valley that faced them presented some serious problems, but if the men wanted to get back to their encampment, they had very few options. The entire area was pitted with peaks and valleys, so if they by-passed this valley, they would face another soon enough.

The snow was also a major concern. Even with snowshoes, it would slow the men down. Jacob could see that the valley floor had a fresh layer, which meant advancing forward would be challenging.

"I'll report back to Captain Rogers, and we can see what he wants to do next," Jacob replied, leaving Stark and his advanced scouts to watch for any movement up ahead.

"Please tell him we need to get the lads up to the higher ground," Stark said as he returned his attention ahead of him. "From what I can see, the French are waiting for us to enter the valley and ambush us from the far end."

Jacob only had to run a short distance before he ran into Rogers and the rest of the main body of rangers. He quickly reported the situation, saying, "Mr. Stark and his scouts are waiting for us, and he feels much like we do about a possible ambush."

"Let's get the men forward and then we can advance as one large force," Rogers boldly suggested.

"He also said that it appears the French were not on the heights," Jacob continued before Rogers could give the order. "He suggested that we move the men up to the higher ground to gain the advantage."

Rogers began walking back amongst his men to give them their orders. He told them to enter the valley in pairs and then each man was to shoot while his partner reloaded. "If we can keep a steady fire by taking alternate shots," he said, "we might be able to hold off a much larger force. The tactic tends to confuse the enemy into thinking they are facing a much larger force." He patted each ranger on the back as he passed by their position.

"Use your surroundings, lads," Rogers added as he continued to work his way along the line. "Every tree or rock can save your life and help you get to the ridge. Check your snow shoes and make sure they are secured properly."

Jacob waited for his men to arrive and echoed the same instructions that Rogers had given his own men. He quickly paired the men up and pulled Joshua to his side once the rest were positioned.

"Stay close, lad," Jacob whispered to Joshua. "I know the bloody French are waiting for us; we will have to fight our way through them."

With the seventy-plus rangers organized, Jacob took another quick scan of the valley ahead. He tried to decide if French were present and where they might be waiting.

The time of day was also a concern. Their encampment was still a few hours' march from their current location, and the French seemed to be determined not make it easy for them.

Jacob watched Rogers as he focused more on the midday sky than the terrain before them.

Once Jacob, Rogers and Stark met up at the edge of the valley, they waited almost a half-hour hoping the French might show themselves. Finally, it was decided that they should advance before they wasted anymore daylight.

"If we get our men to the high ridge area, we can take this valley and force the French back," Stark said again, making certain his point was heard by Rogers.

Jacob was not in full agreement with the idea of blindly walking into the valley and exposing the entire company to a possible attack. He held his men back and watched as Rogers ordered Stark to take some of the rangers around to the elevated ridge that sat nearby.

As the main body of rangers began to advance towards the edge of the forest floor, Rogers asked Jacob to have the Frenchman, Lessard, move to the front and call out in French to see if he might be able to get any French regulars to show their faces. Jacob didn't particularly like the idea, even though he had employed it himself in the past.

He knew that Rogers and his men didn't like Lessard much. Jacob thought about offering his opinion on the matter, but thought better of it.

He certainly did not want to be on Rogers' bad side, regardless of the fact that he really liked the young Frenchman and appreciated his hard work.

While Lessard made his way towards the front of the line, the rangers continued walking cautiously along the path that took them directly into the open valley. Stark had them moving from tree to tree before they entered the cleared area, yet they still saw no signs of the French.

The young Frenchman never had time to call out to his fellow countrymen. As soon as most of the rangers were in the open, the hideous noise of clicking flints echoed throughout the intimate valley floor.

The French stepped en masse from the cover of trees straight ahead at the far end of the valley trail. In swift order, they unleashed a deafening hail of bullets.

Jacob had positioned himself with his men and they were close to the rear, just ahead of four Stockbridge scouts. Having a clear view of the front of the line, he could see the French standing in a half-moon formation and the volley of lead rammed unmercifully into the approaching rangers.

It was difficult to get an accurate count of how many French were up ahead as the smoke concealed their numbers. However, Jacob estimated that with the force of their initial volley, the French far outnumbered the combined ranging company.

At the very first sound, most of the rangers frantically retreated back to the wooded area. Others were forced to fling themselves down to find some useful cover in the open valley.

The French advanced a couple paces and remained in a line to continue their ambush. Fortunately for the rangers, the enemy was hindered by not having snowshoes to traverse over the thick snow.

Jacob and his men were spared the initial slaughter of the first volley, but they were left with the image of several dead rangers and just as many injured. Even Rogers had a slight head injury. Although bloodied, he had worked his way behind a large tree, shielded by the mass of white smoke that filled the valley.

With all the confusion, Jacob lost sight of Lessard and hoped he had also managed to take cover.

After firing off a couple additional volleys, some of the French regulars charged into the first line of rangers who had not been fortunate enough to find themselves suitable cover. They took prisoners and freed the dead rangers of anything of value.

The slight lull gave the rest of the rangers an opportunity to take better cover and reorganize.

Confusion initially took hold, but Jacob and his men took advantage of a number of misfires from the French muskets to scale the open ridge to their left and took a strong position on the hilly area just above the valley.

Taking a moment to judge what was happening and to again estimate the strength of the French, Jacob ordered his men to provide some cover fire for the trapped rangers below. They picked off a few of the French soldiers who had moved into the open on the valley floor and got themselves stuck in the deep snow.

Jacob stood up and fired his musket, hitting a fleeing Frenchman and sending him tumbling into a massive pine tree. The man was dead and left sadly caught up in the heavily branched tree.

Shocked that the French had not equipped their men with snowshoes, Jacob encouraged his men to keep firing and force the enemy back.

Joshua called out that Lessard was still alive but pinned down behind a clump of rocks. Jacob considered sending some of his men down to rescue the young man, but they all knew that it would be a suicide mission. All they could do was watch over him and provide him some cover fire.

Jacob's men continued to pour down fire on the French below, and it wasn't long before Stark had his men move up to the ridge from the valley floor to join them.

It was at that point that the French focused on the rangers firing down on them from the ridge. Before Jacob even had the chance to speak with Stark, Joshua called out, "Here they come, rangers!"

All attention was directed to a large force of French regulars who charged up the ridge, attempting to dislodge the hard-fighting rangers from their position. They were still burdened by the snow and lack of snowshoes, but the regulars valiantly pushed forward.

With the first leg of the battle still raging, Jacob sent Joshua to inform Rogers that he wanted to take some of his men higher up the ridge and set up a better defensive position.

Rogers immediately sent back his reply with Joshua, "Sir, the captain thinks it is a good plan and you should get as many up to that ridge as you can and make sure we can't be flanked from behind."

Jacob took his men up, moving them in small groups so a steady fire could be kept on the advancing French. Stark and his men remained behind to keep the charging French back.

Once Jacob reached the higher ridge, he had his men spread out to use the endless trees as cover.

"Joshua, watch our flank and be ready for the French to try to take us from behind," he ordered.

The first French advance was easily repelled and Rogers moved more of his rangers up with Jacob. Stark also moved his men higher and formed up on the right flank.

Just as the men got themselves organized, one of the rangers spotted a group of French regulars attempting to take the right flank.

Stark screamed above the relentless volley from the French muskets, "Keep them back, lads; keep up your fire and cover each other."

The French appeared to be determined to overrun the outnumbered rangers. They kept up their incessant advances but were repulsed each time. Their superior numbers gave them some advantage, but it was lost to the choice position taken by the rangers.

Some of the French had finally equipped themselves with snowshoes, having confiscated them from a number of the dead or injured rangers littering the lower valley. Even so, their advances were pushed back.

Rogers finally joined the majority of the men on the ridge and spoke directly to Jacob and Stark when he said, "Damn, gentlemen, the French killed a number of good lads."

The three men looked below to see the open valley floor littered with the bodies of the dead and injured rangers.

"They fought hard," Jacob simply stated.

With that, the three officers returned to their positions and waited for the next charge.

Jacob rejoiced at the far superior skills of the rangers as they continued to hold off the advances of the determined French. The valley became thick with clouds of thick, white smoke and it was next to impossible to see any movement along the lower valley floor.

By this time, a band of Ottawa warriors had swelled the ranks of the French, yet the rangers held their ground and poured down what they had left of their quickly dwindling ammunition.

The intense battle extended well into dusk.

Jacob could see that the French had inflicted a great amount of damage on the hard-fighting rangers. He noticed that Rogers had been wounded again; this time he had his wrist wrapped up and was unable to load his own weapon.

Jacob's own men had been seriously impacted by the French volleys as well. A number of the men were dead and a few had been injured to varying degrees. Joshua was nursing a flesh wound to his left side that left him dripping blood.

A lull in the action allowed the smoke to clear, and Jacob was finally able to see clearly that Lessard was dead. The young Frenchman had died still positioned behind the same clump of rocks.

Rogers had sent one of the rangers to call Jacob over for another brief meeting of the three surviving officers. The French were being reinforced with additional regulars, as well as more Ottawa warriors.

Taking advantage of the pause in the fighting, Rogers asked for a quick update of the numbers.

"I have ten dead, a few more injured but still able to fight, and two seriously hurt who are not able to move," Stark responded, removing his hat and lowering his head.

Jacob spoke up next, "I have five dead or seriously injured, and a handful of minor injuries. My remaining lads are still willing to fight."

The surrounding woods had remained silent for several minutes after the apparent ceasefire. Rogers was just about to begin speaking again when several shouts came from the French below.

"Surrender and we will spare you," one of the French called out in English.

"Save your brave men," another voice shouted.

"We will not hold back if you do not surrender," yet another man warned. "We will kill all of you if you do not throw your muskets down."

Unable to hold their tongues, Rogers was the first to scream out a reply, "We still have a full company of rangers willing to fight to the death."

Jacob joined in and stood up and yelled, "We will fight until we are all shot through and dead."

The brash stance was greeted by shouts and cheers from the surviving men. When their screams had echoed down to the French, the woods plunged into a deafening silence.

Returning to the matter at hand, Rogers directed his next comment to Stark, "John, I need you to take a couple men and get to William Henry. If we don't have some sleds to help get us back to the fort, I fear the French will chase us down before we can get back to it."

Stark nodded and offered a smile to Jacob as he left.

Now just Jacob and Rogers sat together, listening to the sounds of the cold winter evening.

"We have to move," Rogers said quietly. "We are running out of ammunition and I suspect the French have already sent for more reinforcements from Carillon. If they reach us by dawn, I expect they will simply overwhelm us by their sheer numbers. We can use the cover of the night to move out undetected."

Jacob wasn't sure if he was to reply, so he just waited.

"We must make it down to the lake," Rogers continued, "so we will only be able to take the able-bodied and the injured that can move freely. We cannot tell the severely injured men left behind of our plan; they might unwittingly expose our movement."

"What about the handful of men we left at the encampment?" Jacob asked.

The look on Rogers' face clearly displayed the answer, but he said, "I sent two of my scouts to check, but they discovered the camp had already been cleared by the bloody Ottawa."

Jacob didn't wait for further instructions and dismissed himself to return to his men. He understood that if they were to move out, it would have to be now or never. He went directly to Joshua's side to relay Rogers' message.

"We need to get back to the lake," Jacob said. "The captain wants us to only take the able-bodied and those wounded men who can move by themselves. How many does that give us?"

"Roughly fifteen men, but only two of the injured are mobile enough to move," Joshua explained.

"Who does that leave behind?" Jacob asked, not really wanting to hear the answer.

"Two men, sir," Joshua said before providing the grim details. "Jed Larson has a bad leg wound; I think his kneecap was shot through. He can't even stand, and it would take two men to carry him. Then Williams is bleeding out from a pretty bad stomach wound. I think he will be dead before we leave."

Jacob put his head down and added, "Get the men in order and ready to leave. Tell them to only take what they need and to keep quiet. The captain specifically ordered us not to inform the injured men that will be left behind. Also, get them to take any ammunition they can find from the dead; we will need it for the trip back."

Seeing that Joshua was going to question the order, Jacob immediately waved his hand to silence him. He waited until Joshua had gone to fulfill his obligations before he went in search of young Jed Larson. Only a few days before, the fit young man had displayed his superior fighting skills.

Jacob found him propped up against a tree. A great deal of blood had soaked through his leggings. Kneeling down to check on him, Jacob gave him a slight nudge to wake him and said, "Jed, how are you, lad?"

Taking a drink from the canteen Jacob offered, Larson did his best to reply, "I'm fine, sir; it just hurts some."

Jacob had known Jed's father, and heard that the elder Larson had died a few years back. The young Swede joined Jacob's rangers just before the attack on Kittanning and had acquitted himself well during that outing.

Barely able to hold back his tears, Jacob looked at the nineteen-year-old's knee and could see, as Joshua had suggested, he would never be able to make it without the support of at least two men. Speed was the key to making it out of the French trap alive.

Jacob found an unused cover and attempted to give the boy some shred of comfort. He handed Jed a knife and hatchet, and could hardly get his words out as he spoke, "Lad, we need to get out of this place...but we can't...take all of you. I am so sorry, lad..."

Jacob couldn't continue to speak and pulled a half-empty bag of lead balls from one of the nearby dead rangers and handed it to the now sobbing boy.

"Can you move, lad?" Jacob asked, struggling not to breakdown. "You might be better off if I drag you around to the other side of the tree."

"No thank you, sir," Larson said bravely, suppressing further sobs. "I would rather see the damn French coming."

"God bless you, lad," Jacob offered, quickly wiping tears from his eyes.

Young Larson managed to smile and said, "I'll kill a few more of them for you, sir. Stay well and tell the lads about me."

Leaving him before his emotions became overwhelming; Jacob went to find Private Williams.

He took one last look behind him and could see that the young Larson boy had organized his weapons and fearlessly waited for the French to attack. He had his coat off and rolled up his shirt to expose his massive arms. Jacob prayed the cold night would take him quickly in his sleep before the French ultimately found him.

Jacob found his other badly injured ranger lying face down in the well-tracked snow. He pulled Williams' stiffened body over and realized in an instant that young man had already died. Jacob was strangely thankful that the man passed before he had to repeat the conversation he had just had with Larson.

Jacob rushed to reach Joshua and the rest of the men, wishing to spend no more time than necessary around the unfortunate injured and dying men.

"Did you find them, sir?" Joshua asked innocently, knowing full well what Jacob had been doing.

All Jacob could do was nod and put his head down to hide his tears.

Joshua did his best to change the topic and said, "We are ready to go, sir. Captain Rogers sent word that we need to leave now."

Jacob nodded again and walked ahead of the survivors of his unit. They were once a mighty ranging company, but were now a mere shadow of their former selves.

He reached Rogers, who pointed towards the pitch black woods and said, "We now can only pray that Stark and his men will make it to William Henry. I fear if John doesn't return with the sleds, we will be overrun by the French. I have confidence in my men, but if the French decide to pursue us all the way to William Henry, we will all be dead well before we reach its outer pickets."

Jacob had little to add to Rogers' dismal prediction. Instead, he crouched in the dark and said a quick prayer.

Chapter | **Fifteen**

Thankfully, Maggie's walk back to the long house was far easier than when she had trudged through the snow with the Ottawa warrior at her side. Before she had moved far from the village entrance, the blinding snow subsided enough that she could see the empty pole where the warrior had been tied.

A wave of relief overtook her, and she hoped that risking her life to help the warrior escape might somehow make the Ottawa display their appreciation by not taking her back to Pontiac. She did fear that the Ottawa might punish the village for their actions and prayed that her lone act of kindness might also stop them from seeking retribution.

Without thinking much about what she would do once the villagers discovered the escape of the prisoner, Maggie stepped back into the house and could instantly feel the heat from the fires. She managed to remove her outer clothes and paused by the fire before moving back to her bed.

Maggie finally fell asleep, but only managed to get a few hours of sleep. She woke abruptly when a number of shouts came from outside. The noise woke up most of the inhabitants of the long house. Many of them had slept with their fur pelts over them and immediately ran outside to see what was going on.

She had not taken the time to dry off her furs when she had crept back into the house, but she quickly did her best to wipe them down and put the damp pelts close to one of the fires to dry them. Just as the noise heightened, One-Ear burst into the house and approached Maggie.

"The Ottawa prisoner is gone," he said frantically.

Seeing the panic on his face, Maggie was at a loss about how to calm him. All she wanted to do was keep the attention from her; she prayed no one suspected her of being part of the prisoner's escape.

"I sent out most of my warriors to search the woods to find him, but I fear he escaped hours ago," One-Ear explained, looking at Maggie.

The look One-Ear gave her made her almost confess what she had done, but instead she asked, "Why not just let him go?"

One-Ear gave her another strange look, but this time it seemed more disbelieving than accusing.

"You know the Ottawa better than any one of us!" he said after a moment. "They will not think kindly that we took one of their own, especially one that is a blood relative of Pontiac. Now he is free to tell them whatever he wants!"

When he finished speaking, One-Ear rubbed his hand on the large fur pelt Maggie had just laid by the fire. Without another word, he simply wiped his hand on his shirt and walked to the door.

Maggie waited for him to say something.

"You look cold," One-Ear said calmly as he looked Maggie in the eye. "Maybe you should warm yourself by the fire." With that, he disappeared back into the cold morning air.

Maggie's mind was racing. Did One-Ear know what she had done? Guilt ate at her and she prayed that her rash act hadn't put the entire village in harm's way.

When she had calmed herself enough to think rationally, she realized that the village would be under threat from a possible attack from the Ottawa regardless if she had helped the warrior escape or not. As soon as the Ottawa warrior was taken captive, the village had exposed itself to the possibility of being attacked.

After spending some time by the fire, Maggie thought she should venture back outside to see what was happening. Her outer pelt coat was now dry and warm, so she dressed and stepped back into the cold.

The initial brightness of the morning sun hit her hard and it took her a few minutes to adjust her eyesight. Once she refocused, Maggie got a good picture of what the village had been doing since the news of the escape.

The storm had dumped almost a foot of fresh snow and created many deep drifts. A good number of the younger villagers were busily clearing pathways from the main homes towards the village center. As she walked she saw the empty post where only a few hours earlier she struggled to cut the Ottawa warrior free and walk him to his freedom.

She also caught a glimpse of One-Ear, who was speaking with a couple of the elders. Their faces all showed deep concern, and Maggie tried to work her way closer to hear exactly what they were discussing.

As she moved to avoid the throngs of villagers working to remove the accumulated snow, Maggie ran into Anne.

"What happened?" Maggie inquired innocently.

Anne was scanning the village and replied, "The villagers are afraid the Ottawa might return and attack the village. With their superior numbers, they could do so with very little effort."

Her voice also showed concern and Maggie felt renewed guilt. If her actions with the prisoner had done anything to save her from being claimed by Pontiac, it may have come at a price. In such a storm, the larger group of Ottawa could not have gotten very far from the village. With confirmation from the warrior that he had been taken captive, what would stop them from returning to enact retribution on the village?

As the two women talked, the first of the scouting party sent out by One-Ear returned empty handed.

"They don't look happy," Anne said.

Maggie found it difficult to hold her tongue and considered confiding in Anne, but upon further reflection, she remained quiet. Anne soon left and went over to help a group of women move a snow-covered wood pile closer to the main long house.

Maggie stood alone until One-Ear spotted her and waved at her to join him. She returned his wave and slowly made her way to him, praying for the whole episode to end.

"Maggie, the elders are thinking of moving most of the women and children east to a small village of the Mohawk," One-Ear explained.

Her heart calmed a bit, but she struggled not to just blurt out and confess. "I am not sure if I would be able to make it through all this snow," she said.

An uncomfortable silence settled between the two friends until Maggie spoke up again, "What did the scouts find?"

"They found nothing," One-Ear replied shortly. "The storm buried any tracks the Ottawa left, and the scouts were too frightened to venture deeper into the woods."

Tired and confused about what she should do, Maggie stood by One-Ear for a short time. When it became apparent that he had nothing further to say to her, she politely said, "I am tired and need to give my feet a rest. Please let me know what is decided, and I will do what you wish."

One-Ear simply nodded his head and left to speak with another group of scouts who had just stepped through the inner walls.

Getting back to the much warmer confines of the long house, Maggie stripped off her warm coat and went directly to her bed. Exhausted by everything that was happening around her, she was quickly asleep.

A soft nudge caused Maggie to sit straight up and she called out through a sleepy haze, "Is everything alright?"

"Maggie…Maggie, it's me, One-Ear," he whispered. "I thought you might want some food. You have slept most of the day."

Struggling to clear her head, Maggie focused on the familiar voice and replied, "Thank you. Food sounds good. How long have I been sleeping?"

"Well, the sun has already set," One-Ear said in a normal tone, trying to get her to wake up fully, "and you have missed some excitement."

Maggie's eyes flew open and her head instantly cleared. "What excitement?" she nearly shouted.

Without another word, he simply offered his arm to help her out of the bed. Maggie moved slowly until she felt the damp dirt floor beneath her feet, and gratefully leaned some of her weight on One-Ear's arm as she rose to her feet.

"Let's get you some food first, then I will tell you what happened while you were resting," One-Ear said as he guided her outside.

The nighttime sky was filled with bright stars and the air was brisk. They walked to a massive fire spewing red hot cinders high into the dark sky; Maggie took a seat and enjoyed the heat flowing from the fire pit. Almost before she got herself settled, one of the women handed her a wooden plate of roasted venison and freshly-baked cornbread.

One-Ear waved the woman away quickly, wishing to speak to Maggie privately.

Before she took her first mouthful of the steaming slice of venison, Maggie asked, "What did I miss?"

"The Ottawa did return, but not to fight or punish us," One-Ear began. "They brought us two large bucks and a message."

He paused and looked at Maggie, who had her mouth full of the freshly cooked meat and couldn't reply.

"Enjoy your food," he said with a grin in response to the impatient glare she gave him. "The message was sent by the warrior we had captured. He sent a young white captive girl to convey his words."

Tiring of One-Ear's penchant to drag out the story, Maggie could clearly see that the atmosphere around the village was more relaxed and upbeat.

Maggie decided to ignore him for the moment. He was clearly enjoying keeping her on pins and needles. She looked around the village and could tell that the fear induced by the Ottawa had greatly subsided.

Finally, she said, "Well, I hope the message is pleasant, because you are certainly prolonging this story!" Maggie smiled as she broke off a small piece of bread.

One-Ear had such a smile on his face that she could not wait for him to explain.

"I spoke with the Ottawa and the young girl that came bearing gifts, and they told me they were thankful we freed the captive," One-Ear said, shooting Maggie a questioning glance. "They seemed to think we had a good reason to let him return to them."

Maggie sat quietly, listening to him. She still did not want to say anything that might indict her. At the same time was getting uncomfortable with One-Ear's hesitation.

"You have nothing to say?" One-Ear asked, though he did not appear upset. "One of the Ottawa wanted us to thank the 'strong white woman' for assisting their brother. Do you know anything about that?"

She still had no desire to admit to her actions outright, but One-Ear looked her directly in the eyes and expected an answer. Choosing her words carefully, Maggie began to explain what happened.

"I should clarify my role in all of this. I did assist the Ottawa prisoner, but at first I wasn't thinking about letting him go. My original plan was just to get him some covers for his naked body. The storm was deathly cold and I feared he might just freeze before your warriors had an opportunity to torture him."

One-Ear took his eyes off of Maggie and looked towards the empty pole where the Ottawa warrior had been tied.

Maggie decided she had said enough and once again waited for him to speak.

"Thank you, Maggie," One-Ear said gently. "Your kindness has saved our village. The Ottawa told me they would be moving on towards the French at Fort Carillon and leave us be."

Unsure how to reply, Maggie just smiled. She looked around the village again and noticed that despite the darkness and the chill in the air most of the inhabitants were out performing various duties and seemed happy.

"Do you know who the young white girl was that the Ottawa used to send their message?" Maggie asked. She found it curious that when the Ottawa were camped in the field, there had been no sign of any white captives.

"She looked familiar, but I struggle to recall where I might have seen her," One-Ear said. "She looked more like an Ottawa than a white girl; if she had not spoken, I would have sworn she was one of them."

"How old did she look?" Maggie asked.

"Hard to say, but maybe twelve or fourteen. She looked well fed and strong."

Maggie's mind buzzed and she immediately wondered if the girl could be her Becky. She pressed One-Ear for more details.

"My eldest daughter is around that age, One-Ear! What color was her hair?"

Not intending to raise Maggie's hopes, One-Ear said simply, "Maggie, I could not see her hair, but she appeared happy amongst the Ottawa. I did find it strange that they had a young girl traveling with them, but maybe she will be traded or sold when they reach Fort Carillon."

His blunt reply shocked her at first, but she understood that he did not want her to imagine anything that most likely wasn't true. Maggie did her best to forget the possibility and put her emotions down to her condition.

"Thank you, you have always been good to me and always did what was best for me," Maggie said after a moment. She said nothing more on the subject, but she still could not get the image of Becky out of her mind.

One-Ear rose to leave, but turned to face her again. "I think you already knew that the warrior you helped was family to Pontiac?" he asked, waiting for her nod. "He must hold some power over his fellow warriors. The message passed on by the white girl said that after the Ottawa have helped their French fathers kill many English soldiers, they will return west and settle back near Fort Detroit."

"You mean they will not be taking me with them?" Maggie asked, cautious not to show too much emotion.

Turning to leave her, One-Ear offered a smirk over his shoulder and said, "Get some more rest and keep your baby safe. I think we will both be here for some time."

Chapter | **Sixteen**

The snow-filled trails were difficult enough to traverse during the midday sun, but with no light and the order to be as quiet as possible, Jacob and his men spent most of the night crawling on their stomachs. Every time a branch snapped or a ranger got the snowshoes strapped to his back caught on a low hanging tree limb, the men stopped and prayed the noise didn't echo down the valley. The slightest hint of noise could cause the French and their Ottawa allies to pounce down on the slow moving rangers.

The night was very dark as most of the stars were obscured by heavy clouds. Without the use of torches, the men did their best not to run into the mass of trees or take a fall down one of the numerous hills or ridges.

Jacob knew the Stockbridge Indian scouts were leading the way and had to be trusted that they knew the terrain well. From what he could tell, the scouts were taking them on a fairly straight line to the lake.

There was also the threat that the poor injured men left behind might scream out and give away their midnight escape; it was a thought that kept the surviving rangers moving. Thankfully, once Rogers felt they had moved far enough away from the valley and cleared any possible French pickets, he passed the word back to Jacob to have his men strap on their snowshoes and keep moving towards the lake.

Jacob's usually warm outer-coat was completely soaked from crawling through miles of snow. He was particularly relieved to finally be standing, and relished the thought of getting to move briskly over the deep snow. He wasn't sure how far they were from the lake, but he still prayed for Stark and his scouts to return quickly with sleds to expedite their escape.

Feeling a little less concerned about making too much noise now that they were moving more swiftly, Jacob asked Joshua, "How are you, lad?"

"I am holding up, sir," Joshua relied quietly. "It looks like we still have all our men, but we won't know how they are doing until we are all resting safely inside Fort William Henry."

"I still can't get young Larson out of my mind," Jacob confided. "I have prayed since we left that the cold might kill him before the bloody French find him, or worse, the Ottawa."

The cold weather did provide them some advantages. The sloppy bogs and swampy areas were finally freezing over, making them far easier to cross. The rangers continued on as fast as they could in the dark with Rogers in front and Jacob and his men taking up the rear.

Cold, hungry and tired from the long trek, most of the rangers held back their excitement when the advanced scouts reported back that the lake was just over a small ridge. They added that there was no sign of Stark or the sleds, but Jacob was certainly happy that their time in the woods was nearly over.

After spending the entire night crawling and walking through the dense woods, the early morning light was most welcome. Unable to have fires to warm them, and running short on food, the men did their best to keep their wits about them.

Jacob had his men form up just around the edge of the lakeshore, using the tree line as cover. Rogers moved a handful of men plus his scouts to the middle of the lake to watch for any signs of Stark. The remaining men were sent to the opposite shore to scout around for a suitable place to set up a camp, if needed.

Although they hadn't seen signs of the French since the fight in the valley, it did not mean that they were out of danger yet. If Stark didn't return soon, Jacob feared they would not be able to complete their escape to William Henry. There was enough French traffic on the lake that they could possibly commandeer a sled or two on their own, but that act presented its own risks.

They could also lay low for a couple days and then go back overland. The only problem with such a plan was the mountain region. They had made it through the mountain pass with relative ease a short time earlier, but with the additional snow that came right on their heels, Jacob assumed that trails the would be completely impassable by now.

Rogers made his way to Jacob to discuss the situation, "Damn, Jacob, I expected John to be waiting for us. If he doesn't return soon, we might have to take to the far woods and prepare for the French and their savages to come after us. If we keep the lake between us, I pray the French would not risk charging across the open lake to attack us."

"Robert, I can try to take some of the men overland and get word to Fort William Henry that we need help," Jacob suggested.

Rogers was too deep in thought to consider such actions and didn't even bother to reply to Jacob's idea.

"I should get back to my men, Robert; it appears our only hope lies with John, so we will wait," Jacob said and walked away.

Trying not to think too far ahead, Jacob found Joshua and joined him on the small ridge above the shore line. From their vantage point, they could make out the outline of the lake narrows that sat a few miles south. The surviving rangers from his company appeared to be in good order, and they all gave a hearty smile as they looked up at the two men.

The sun struggled to break through the clouds, but any shred of light that managed to move through the thick forest branches gave the men a renewed sense of energy. Jacob was worried that the daylight might expose them and he desperately wanted to get his men across the lake to the opposite shore.

The unknown factor was what the large party of French and their allied Ottawa would do once they discovered that Rogers and his rangers managed to sneak past them during the night. Even a poor tracker could easily follow the trail left behind by the escaping rangers. If Stark didn't return soon, they would have to do something to protect themselves.

Jacob made his way to the heavily-wooded area that sat close to the shoreline and provided some excellent cover for the men.

He immediately noticed Rogers was standing alone, still staring off towards the south, waiting for any signs of Stark and the sleds.

"Robert, have you thought about what you wanted us to do?" Jacob asked, doing his best not to startle him.

"Bloody glad we made it, but I fear our escape has only just begun," Rogers replied grimly. "Your lads did well; please pass on my thanks to them."

Jacob was concerned by how Rogers was acting. It was as if they had not spoken earlier, and he seemed confused about what to do next.

Noticing that Rogers was still favoring his injured hand, Jacob asked, "How is your hand, Robert? From the amount of blood, you will have to get someone to look at it and replace the soiled cloths."

"I would be lying if I told you it was fine," Rogers admitted and took a look at the blood stained scarf that was loosely wrapped around it. "I think my wrist might be broken, or just damaged enough that it is next to useless. I can't wait until we get to the fort and have the doctor clean it and bandage it up properly."

"I can have one of my men splint it up with some branches," Jacob suggested.

"I should be alright," Rogers said with an appreciative nod. "I might take you up on it later, but first we need to get these men home safely."

As he looked southward again down the narrows of the snow covered lake, Jacob noticed something moving in the distance.

"Robert, do you have your scope?" Jacob asked abruptly, waiting impatiently for Rogers to pull his viewing scope from a leather pouch. He handed it to Jacob and boldly stepped onto the open shoreline of the lake.

As Jacob turned the scope to try to extend the lens as far as possible and focus, Rogers excitedly asked, "What do you see, Jacob?"

Finally joining Rogers on the edge of the shoreline, Jacob handed him the scope as he said, "There is a sled just to the south of the small bay."

Waiting until Rogers finally had it in his sight, Jacob asked, "Can you tell who it is, Robert?"

Unable to hide his relief and excitement, Rogers kept the scope on the fast moving sled approaching them and said with a chuckle, "That damn Stark has never let me down! If I asked him to bring bloody elephants over the mountains like Hannibal, he would!"

Jacob was not convinced that it was Stark at such a distance. He wanted to make sure that it was indeed the brave ranger and not another French supply sled. Rogers gave him back the scope and left him alone on the shoreline while he planned the rest of the journey. Jacob refocused the lens and waited until the fast moving sled got closer.

A second sled was now visible just beyond the first one. Both were horse-drawn and moving so fast they kicked up huge clouds of snow, which made it even more difficult to confirm their identities.

Rogers returned with some of his scouts, but before he sent them out to intercept the approaching sleds, he asked Jacob's opinion, "Well, are we certain that this is John?"

"From what I can see, it appears to be our men, but at the speed they are traveling I fear they might be in some trouble," Jacob said as he again focused the scope on the far narrows of the lake.

Just as Jacob pulled back the scope, Rogers sent a couple more of his Stockbridge Indians onto the lake to join the other men to flag down the two sleds.

By now, the word had trickled back to the men. They gathered on the shoreline in anticipation that their escape might now be far easier.

Joshua worked his way down to Jacob and joined him. "Are we sure it is Stark?" the young man asked immediately.

Jacob rubbed his eyes and said, "If they turn out to be French, we will have hell to pay. You might want to get the men ready for a possible fight. Either way, we need the sleds to escape this place."

The two men watched as Rogers' small scouting unit, hidden by a large bluff formed by the high winds that whipped around the lake, calmly stepped out into the direct path of the approaching sled to wave down it down.

Thankfully, the lead sled's driver pulled back on the hemp reins, stopping the horse team just short of the awaiting scouts.

One of the Stockbridge Indians then grabbed the nearest horse's bit and pulled it towards the shore. By then it was clear that one of Stark's men was controlling the horses. As the scouts helped guide him to shore, he greeted Rogers with a hearty wave.

Unwilling to wait for his scouts to finish with the first sled, Rogers ran out and flagged down the other sled. This one was being ridden by Stark and two rangers. Jacob decided not to stay on the shore line either and joined Rogers to greet Stark and his men.

"Bloody good to see you, John!" Rogers laughed, patting the horses once they fell into a slow trot. "We were worried you ran into some problems and might have to leave us stranded."

"Good to see you safe, John," Jacob seconded, helping to guide the horses towards those waiting by the shore.

Handing the reins to one of his men, Stark stepped out of the large wooden sled and replied to their kind words, "I am glad to see you both as well. I am happy the men made it."

They had no wish to extend their stay in French-held territory, particularly since the French regulars they had just outsmarted could charge down the ridge after them at any moment. While the horses were given the chance to get some water, Rogers ordered the men to board the sleds. Within minutes, they began the next leg of their escape.

It was already well into the afternoon by that time and the men realized that they only had a limited amount of good light remaining. They had to keep moving.

The Stockbridge Indians and four rangers moved ahead of the sleds and took to the woods to ensure the French couldn't launch an ambush along the route. They had to ensure that if the French decided to pursue the escaping rangers, they could easily warn the sleds of the possible threat.

The added weight of all the rangers slowed the already fatigued horses, but they still made good time. Thankfully, they encountered none of the usual sleds that ran supplies between the two forts.

Jacob finally realized it was Sunday, which explained the lack of French regulars scouting the lake region. The God-fearing French were ardent church-goers, and on most Sundays they spent their time praying and attending mass. Such a break could make it possible to move past the guns at Fort Carillon, since the pickets and guards would most likely be recalled. At the very least, the fort would have a reduced number of guards, which would lessen the likelihood of getting noticed or shot at while passing.

Rogers kept the sleds moving, despite the suggestions from Jacob and Stark that he might kill the horses from exhaustion before they made it to Fort William Henry.

As they reached the narrowest part of the lake, the sleighs slowed enough to make their way past several small islands that dotted most of the upper lake. It was a perfect place to set up an ambush, and Stark called out to Jacob, "Watch up ahead! These islands are a favorite spot of the Canadians and their savages to attack travelers venturing out on the lake."

The islands proved no more than a few inconveniences. The horses quickly built their speed back up to get past the fort that awaited them less than a mile ahead.

Jacob took advantage of the rapidly waning sunlight to study the venerable stone Fort Carillon as it came into view. The heavy guns sat idle and unmanned on the solid stone lookouts, but he was otherwise still impressed by the strategic placement of the fort.

It was massive and its high walls made Jacob pray he would never have to order his men to breach them.

Keeping tightly to the shore, the sleds passed by the fort unnoticed.

As soon as they were out of range of the fort, the sleds were ordered to the western shoreline. The horses were clearly spent and their mouths were foaming from being pushed so hard. They were within just a few hours' ride of Fort William Henry, but both the men and the animals needed a break.

"The poor beasts look like they are ready to collapse," Rogers said as he walked over to Jacob and Stark who stood together next to one of the horses. "We need to take a brief rest and get ourselves organized."

The two officers gave no response. They were still in French-held territory and both men knew that they could not afford to let the men relax too much. The woods were just as thick as they had experienced in the upper lake region, and it would be rather easy for a French patrol to ambush the unsuspecting men along the shoreline.

Once Rogers evaluated the state of the horses and his men, he rejoined Jacob and Stark near the shore. "I sent five men ahead to William Henry to prepare them for our arrival. I also received word from our Stockbridge Indians that they noticed nothing out of the ordinary and will press on towards William Henry as well."

"If we hope to push these poor horses more, we will have to send more of the men on foot to relieve the beasts of some weight," Stark suggested, looking around at the shape of the men. "Sadly, the men look no better than the horses; I am not certain how much farther they can be pushed either."

"Maybe we can take shifts on the sleds," Jacob offered. "Some of the men could walk for a bit and then switch off to let others rest on the sleds?"

"For now, they all need their rest," Rogers said. "I think the threat from the French has lessened this far south, so we can chance a couple of campfires."

Jacob was far more worried about the men's hunger and fatigue than their want of a fire, but he knew that talking would do little to change their situation. He decided to focus on something else.

"How is your hand holding up, Robert?" Jacob asked again. He had noticed that it was clearly troubling him and he still couldn't do much with it.

Shrugging off Jacob's concerns, Rogers replied, "It is worse than earlier, but the doctor at the fort should be able to straighten it out for me."

"Speaking of the doctor, the fort has been hit with a bout of pox and they have lost some men to the damn sickness," Stark interjected.

The three officers exchanged glances. Not only were these men tired and starved, but they were headed towards a place infected with the pox.

"Did you see Richard around the fort?" Rogers asked.

"No, when I was there he was out on a scout," Stark replied. "I did hear that he has spent most of his time moving between Fort Edward and William Henry," Stark replied.

Turning to Jacob with a smile, he added, "I also heard that your boys at Edward were doing well. For the most part, they are all healthy."

Jacob smiled back at Stark in appreciation and relief at this news.

When the horses had been given some time to have a bucket of oats each and some water, they appeared refreshed and ready to move on. The sun was now well behind the mountains and the cold night air was making the trip more dangerous. The men were desperate to get to the relative safety of the fort. Despite looking no better than the horses, they gathered their gear and were ready to leave.

With Fort Carillon now a good distance behind them, Rogers ordered the drivers to keep the sleds close to the middle of the lake to avoid the possibility of being hit by shots from either shore. Thankfully, the lake widened enough to keep the men out of musket range. They moved at a much slower pace to keep the men walking alongside the sleds from falling too far behind and becoming exposed to a possible ambush.

As they moved closer to Fort William Henry, most of the men began to finally relax and looked forward to getting some food and sleep.

Jacob walked with Joshua and the rest of his men instead of staying on the sled with Rogers and Stark. His rangers were in good spirits and relished in the thought of sitting by a fire while enjoying some food and the security of the fort.

With their sights set on the far glow of the torches set on the top of the fort's walls, the peace was soon shattered and the men went back on high alert.

All at once, one of the Stockbridge Indians from the overland scout reported to Rogers that they had spotted what they thought was a French patrol moving along the trail on the eastern shoreline towards Carillon.

Remaining vigilant, the men were relieved when they spotted the two sleds and realized they had been sent by the fort to escort the rangers safely into the bay that sat below it. It was dark and cold and the men were tired, but they were relieved to finally be within reach of the fort.

Jacob saw that Stark and Rogers were speaking with one of the men from the fort and they appeared to be concerned about something up ahead. He motioned for his own men to slow their pace and keep behind the sleds for some cover before returning his gaze back to the other officers.

Joshua quickly made his way over to Jacob and asked, "What is going on sir? Have you noticed the smoke coming from the direction of the fort? It seems heavier than what you'd normally get from a few campfires."

A shot from one of the fort's cannons made them stop in their tracks before they warily trudged forward again. As the fort came into full view, the torches along the lake shed an ominous light on the smoldering remains of several small boats that had been dry-docked by one of the jetties.

Jacob noticed that closer-up the familiar stench of death was also present, comingling with the smoke that rose from the rubble. He watched Rogers and Stark cautiously make their way along the shoreline path towards the fort trail.

"You should go with them, sir," Joshua suggested.

"No need, lad," Jacob replied as the last sled reached the jetty. "I should be with the men and let those two deal with the politics."

Jacob helped his rangers unload the sleds and asked Joshua to have them prepare to make the short hike up the trail over the earthen embankment to the outer works of the awaiting fort. When Joshua walked away, Jacob moved towards the animals that were being unhitched.

The sleds were tied to the posts of one of the unharmed jetties that jutted out into the lake. As the tired animals were being led towards the trail to the stables, Jacob made a point to pat the massive beasts. He admired their amazing strength and stamina that had pulled so many of the men to safety.

The animals moved excitedly towards the promise of a well-deserved meal, and when they were out of sight, Jacob turned towards the fort. The first time he had seen it was only for a brief look, but now he finally got to examine it. Jacob thought it was well-built, but not as impressive as the nearby Fort Carillon. The fort was lit with torches positioned every few feet along the top ledge, but his eyes were drawn to a number of fires that dotted the outer fields.

Unlike Carillon, William Henry was built from the endless supply of mature trees that surrounded it. The height of it stacked up nearly thirty feet in the sky. It looked massive from what he could see; just the sheer appearance of the outer wall would keep the enemy back from the main part of the fort.

Jacob turned back towards the lake and walked between the two jetties where the attack had occurred. He could tell that several of the damaged vessels had been large sloops as well as a number of boats that had still been under construction. A small building that had stood nearby lay in a heap of rubble and smoking ash. Jacob figured it must have been the small workshop for the boat builders.

Within minutes, the men were ready and Jacob led them to the inclined trail. Joshua walked beside him and they soon noticed that Stark was making his way back down towards them.

"John, how goes it?" Jacob called out to draw his attention.

"There is news, Jacob," Stark replied and made his way along the busy trail.

Stark finally reached the pair and continued with his news, saying, "The French have obviously been busy around these parts. One of the officers told me that a raiding party came from Fort Carillon a few days earlier and put torches to some of the newly constructed boats. They managed to burn a few, but overall they did no more than cause a nuisance."

Jacob looked towards the fort and could see some of the rangers he had left behind at Fort Edward. They were standing on the high wall and offered Jacob a quick wave.

"I'm surprised to see some of my men here," Jacob said. "I thought they were stationed at Fort Edward?"

"I think that after the fort was raided, Webb at Fort Edward must have been worried that it could be part of a larger attack," Stark explained. "I noticed some of my men as well, so they must have just moved a couple of units over to reinforce the garrison. The fort was hit with a bad bout of the pox and their numbers were dangerously low."

"How bad was the pox outbreak?" Joshua interjected.

"From what I was told, it was bad. They lost nearly a third of the original garrison and even some of our lads have caught it. Most of the lucky ones were shipped back to Fort Edward. Don't know much more, but I am sure Robert will find out more for us."

Captain Rogers was still making his report of what he had seen and any other information that might help the fort. Jacob knew the picture Rogers would paint was not a good one. The word from the captives they had taken and dispatched was that the French were building up their forces and supplementing their numbers with their Indian allies and Canadian militia. It could only mean that they were thinking of launching an attack on either Fort William Henry or Fort Edward.

Having traveled the nearby forests over the past weeks, Jacob had increased his understanding of the surrounding territory. He realized that if a large, combined force of highly-disciplined French regulars and the English-hating Indians attacked either of the forts, the chances of the fort holding out would be slim.

Walking slowly up the steep trail that took them around to the front of the fort, Jacob, Joshua and Stark said little to one another and just looked out into the darkness around them.

"What are you thinking about, lad?" Jacob asked finally, just as the line of battle-weary rangers filed into the inner wall of the fort.

"Not much, sir," Joshua replied with a grin. "I'm too tired to do much of anything."

Jacob and Stark smiled and led the rangers into the parade ground, where they waited for Rogers to return from his meeting with the garrison's commanders.

"I should try to find some of my boys and then maybe find Robert to see what he knows. Get some food, gentlemen, and I will see you in a bit." Stark quickly walked towards a group of rangers who were already enjoying some food.

"It will be good to see James; I hope he is happier now," Jacob said as he and Joshua walked into the well-lit parade grounds.

"Give him time, sir," Joshua said simply. "Perhaps he is already here with the unit sent from Edward."

Looking around, Jacob was surprised to see that some of the British regulars from the 44th and 48th Foot were part of the garrison. Some of these men would have fought with Braddock at Monongahela; by now, they would be considered veterans amongst the crowds of new recruits and provincial militia. Jacob prayed that none of the veterans recognized him or remembered him from that horrendous defeat.

He sent Joshua to get himself some food and told him he would rejoin him shortly.

Jacob quickly crossed the parade ground and found the men he had seen on the wall. The rangers confirmed what Stark had already told him, that they had spent most of their time scouting the road between the forts.

"Have you seen James?" Jacob asked one of the rangers.

The men looked at each other.

Jacob could see that there was something wrong and asked quietly, "Lads, what is it?"

One of the rangers cleared his throat and without further detail said, "James was really sick, sir."

Seeing that the men were nervous about giving him too many details, Jacob did his best to hide his emotions. "Where is the boy?" he asked.

"He is at the hospital at Fort Edward; the last we heard he was still alive," the same ranger replied. "The pox hit this place pretty hard and all the sick were transported to Rogers Island." The ranger added, hoping the bad news would be lessened by the last part of the news.

Shaken by the news, Jacob dismissed the men and looked for Joshua. He did his best to conceal his panic.

It wasn't hard to find Joshua since most of the men were huddled around the two main fires waiting for the cook to heat up some food.

"Joshua, we need to leave immediately for Fort Edward," Jacob called out.

Joshua had spent enough time with Jacob to realize he was upset. Handing his bowl to one of the many rangers waiting for their share, he went directly to him.

"Sir, what is wrong?" Joshua asked.

"It is James," Jacob said as he walked towards the officers' quarters to speak with Rogers. "I was told by some of the lads that he was sick back at Fort Edward. They said he was still alive, but from the looks on their faces, I could see they didn't want to tell me all the details."

Joshua followed him and stopped just outside the front door of the building that housed most of the senior officers. They were stopped by a large grenadier who attempted to block Jacob from entering.

"Can I help you, scout?" The grenadier asked in a mocking tone, snarling at Jacob's dirty, well-used uniform.

Jacob didn't even bother to stop or knock, but just walked right into the busy room that was clogged with a number of red-coated officers.

The grenadier tried in vain to stop Jacob but was called off by one of the officers in the back of the room. "Let him be, private; he is with me," Captain Rogers called out, leaning against the massive fireplace that graced most of the far wall.

Holding a small glass of what Jacob guessed was port, Rogers simply asked, "What is it, captain?"

Jacob could see that some of the British officers scoffed at his insolence, but he cared little what these arrogant men thought of him. "Sir, I need to get to Fort Edward...it is James...he is very sick," Jacob stuttered, surprised that Rogers had made him explain in front of the entire room.

"Do you even know how to get to Fort Edward from here?" Rogers said, drawing a few snickers from the port-sipping British officers.

Jacob stood speechless in the middle of the room, but he could see that Rogers felt badly for having embarrassed him.

"Gentlemen, I should discuss this matter in private," Rogers said and walked with Jacob to the door. "Please excuse me; I will return shortly."

"Captain, I shouldn't need to remind you that any travel between the forts needs to be approved by me," a thin, well-dressed man pointed out in a thick Scottish accent.

Rogers nodded and opened the door, "I realize that, sir; you will be informed."

The two rangers stepped back into the cold night air, and Jacob offered the grenadier guard a slight scowl.

Joshua, waiting nearby, joined them as they walked just off to the side of the officers' quarters.

"Thanks for rescuing me from those old buggers," Rogers said. "I honestly can't stand being in the same room with them, but my position forces me to do so. So what is all this about your boy?"

Not wanting to waste much more time, Jacob explained, "I have been informed that James is at the hospital on the island at Edward."

"Yes, you said that, but what can you do for him?" Rogers asked. "You both must be tired; it might be best to get some rest and leave in the morning."

Surprised at the iciness of his question, Jacob frankly shot back, "He is my son."

That was all he could think to say.

Rogers didn't ask anything else but excused himself, saying, "I will be right back."

Jacob remained silent and just stood with Joshua, waiting for Rogers to return.

It only took a few minutes before Rogers reappeared. He handed Jacob a sealed note and simply said, "Take this to General Webb at Fort Edward."

Jacob gave Rogers a salute before he and Joshua turned to prepare themselves for their trip. As Jacob grabbed his musket and ammunition and filled his horn with fresh powder, Joshua said his goodbyes to some of his mates. Most of the men were eager to accompany them, but Joshua calmed them down and convinced them to get some rest. He then threw his own small pack over his shoulder and moved to Jacob's side.

As they rushed to the main gates, they found Rogers and Stark waiting for them.

"Jacob, the road to Edward is just to the south and it will take you right to the fort," Rogers said as he looked through the darkness towards the other fort. "You need to follow it up a winding hill and it will then level off slightly. You have about twelve or so miles of small hilly terrain and swampy areas to travel, so be careful. The savages like to set up ambushes along the trail. John has offered to take some of his men with you for the first five miles to provide you an escort."

Jacob offered his thanks and welcomed Stark's company for the first leg.

After they finished with their informal goodbyes, the ten rangers and two Stockbridge Indians were soon over the hill and deep into the forest along the road.

"I'm very sorry for your trouble, Jacob," Stark said as they walked together through the darkness. "I really hope your boy is fine."

"Thank you, John," Jacob replied, concentrating on the roughly hacked, yet well-traveled snowy road.

Rogers had called it a road at any rate, but Jacob thought it was no better than most of the trails he had traveled in his native Pennsylvania. The deep ruts dug into the snow and frozen mud by the oxen-driven transport wagons reminded him of the rough trail Braddock's axemen hacked out on their way to Fort Duquesne.

After they had walked for over two hours, Jacob and the others stopped for a brief rest.

"You should get your men back," Jacob said, eager to keep moving. "Your escort and company were very much appreciated, John."

Stark spoke briefly with the two Stockbridge Indians before sending them ahead. He turned to Jacob and said, "You should be safe the rest of the way. I will have the two scouts take you to the fort. Before I forget, this bloody Webb you will soon have the misfortune of meeting is a fool and a coward. You will most likely find the man cowering under his bed from the fear of meeting any savages. God knows, if he sets his sights on the two Stockbridge Indians, it might just send him into a fit."

Jacob laughed and added, "I have heard of his reputation, and I will take note of it. Thank you again, John, and safe travels. I will return to William Henry once I have checked on James."

Stark took his rangers and, after a quick wave, disappeared into the darkness.

"We should keep moving, Joshua," Jacob said as he led the way. "I hope to reach the fort before dawn."

The lone men walked briskly towards the fort without speaking. They kept their eyes on the dark and desolate terrain that lay before them.

Walking straight through the night and never once seeing the two Stockbridge scouts ahead of them, the two men could smell the fires from the nearby fort. Still tired from their narrow escape from the French the previous day, Jacob kept himself moving by visualizing James in his sickbed and praying he was well.

The two Stockbridge Indians finally made an appearance as they stood at the tree line, just outside the first line of pickets. They said nothing as Jacob and Joshua walked past them.

"Thank you," Jacob offered, but as expected, received no reply.

Greeted by the forward pickets, Jacob explained the situation and that he was delivering a note to Webb from Fort William Henry. He was immediately sent forward to the front gates.

Walking over the massive piles of frozen earthen works whose construction had been halted once the winter weather hit the area, Jacob and Joshua followed the surprisingly cleared trail. Stopped again by another set of guards, Jacob again had to explain his intentions before being escorted through another series of uncompleted earthen works. Finally, they were guided into the traditional wooden fort, nestled within the wilderness and placed on the shores of the Hudson River.

An escort guided Jacob to Webb's headquarters while Joshua met up with several of the men that had originally been sent with Private Sinclair to make up the garrison numbers at the fort.

Jacob was led into Webb's dank, surprisingly small quarters by an old, grizzled British regular who closed the door once Jacob was safely in. Before he left, the soldier had simply pointed towards the officer at the desk.

The man sat at a nicely carved oak desk with his head down. He was too busy signing and sealing a number of letters to lift his head up enough to offer introductions.

There were two clerks working away on their own piles of papers, but they spared brief glances towards the newcomer. Jacob's disheveled appearance caused both men to shake their heads simultaneously.

Wishing to make his delivery quickly in order to get out of this place, Jacob handed the note to the officer he assumed was Webb. After a moment standing at the desk with his hand outreached without the note being taken from him, Jacob finally placed it atop one of the piles of papers.

His actions were received by a fleeting look from the commanding officer. After a struggle to locate his spectacles, Webb broke the wax seal and unfolded the note. Still refusing to lift his head to acknowledge him, Jacob could hear Webb mumble a few inaudible words and drop the note on the pile of letters, waiting to be signed.

Jacob uncomfortably stood, waiting for his orders but nothing came.

After a few minutes, Webb just asked, "Anything else, captain?"

Jacob knew by his tone that it would be smart to just dismiss himself and leave this man to his work. Offering a salute, Jacob simply walked out, still slightly confused by Webb's cold demeanor. He searched for signs of Joshua.

The old guard stood stoically beside the door and said nothing to Jacob as he slowly passed him.

"Where is the hospital, private?" Jacob thought to ask, without expecting him to answer.

To his surprise, the guard replied, "Over on the island sir, but I must warn you, the place is not much of a hospital. I fear the doctor is no better than a blind ox."

Jacob respectfully nodded and tried hard not to let such an ominous description sink in.

"I wouldn't dare to visit anyone there sir," the old man added. "The place is full of the pox, and the lads are tired of burying the poor boys in this frozen godforsaken place."

Leaving the guard to do his duties, Jacob scanned the grounds once more for Joshua.

The sight of him standing next to Sinclair gave Jacob a reason to finally smile.

"Robert, you are looking well!" Jacob called out. "How have things been with the men?"

They were waiting for him by the fort's heavy wooden gates as Jacob slowly approached, finally starting to feel the effects of the miles of wilderness he had covered over the past few days.

The looks on both Joshua's and Sinclair's faces revealed that they had some bad news. Not certain he wanted to hear it, Jacob politely asked Sinclair, "How have the men held up in my absence?"

Their faces still exhibited their concern as Sinclair replied, "The boys did well, Jacob. Webb used us as scouts to make sure the road between the forts was cleared and safe to travel on. We also spend time escorting the endless line of heavy wagons and sleds that transported supplies between the forts."

Jacob picked up on Sinclair's choice of the words 'did well'.

"Gentlemen, please be honest with me," Jacob pressed. "What the hell is happened here?"

Joshua decided to step up and explain, "Sir, we lost a number of the men to the first bout of the pox that hit both forts hard."

"And James?" Jacob felt his voice crack. "I heard from a couple of rangers that he was sick with the pox as well."

Sinclair just put his head down and said nothing.

Joshua spoke up again and said, "Sir, James was really ill, but he managed to fight off the pox."

Jacob interrupted as the two men were clearly hesitant about what was happening, "Well, where is he then?"

"He just left with some of Lieutenant Rogers' men for William Henry," Sinclair explained. "You just missed them."

"Rogers?" Jacob barked.

"Captain Rogers' brother Richard, sir," Joshua replied.

"They left from the island before I walked up here and Joshua found me," Sinclair did his best to explain.

"They must have gotten on the trail while you were in the office with Webb, sir." Joshua added.

Without letting Sinclair continue, Jacob did his best to hold back his frustration. He was tired and hungry and didn't want that to affect his reaction.

"The boy must have been healthy enough to march to the fort then, but I can't believe our luck!" Jacob growled and kicked a pile of snow, sending a cloud into the air. "It is clear why the pox is spreading so quickly between the forts with the constant traffic moving between them! I fear the British do not have the brains to keep the men separated until the pox runs its course."

"Sir, the rangers would never take a man that would slow them down, so James must be in fairly good condition," Joshua suggested, trying to calm Jacob back down.

Confused and furious at the fact he had come so close to seeing James, Jacob briefly walked away from Joshua and Sinclair to stare out into the miles of trees.

"Why did James leave with Rogers?" Jacob asked in a more controlled voice as he walked back to the two waiting men. "I thought he was with you, Robert."

Sinclair went completely silent, unable to offer an explanation.

Joshua finally broke the silence to defend Sinclair, "We both know James is headstrong. If he wanted to go with Rogers, I'm not certain even you could have stopped him."

Jacob's mood changed immediately as he laughed and said, "The boy gets that from his mother."

Sinclair finally added, "Gentlemen, you should get some food and get off your feet. The rangers' island is a safe place to rest and then we can consider what to do next."

Jacob nodded and said, "You are right, Robert. I am tired and have no energy left to walk much more. The two of you might need to carry me to the island so I can get some food and sleep."

Joshua and Sinclair looked at each other and hesitated.

Seeing their confused faces, Jacob laughed again and said, "It was a joke, lads, but if you each wanted to take a leg, I certainly wouldn't stop you."

The three men laughed and walked together to the trail that would lead them to the small island reserved for the ranging companies. When they were fed and rested, they would need to decide what to do next.

Chapter | **Seventeen**

Activity around the village returned to its normal busy pace after the Ottawa threat had departed. The villagers took advantage of days with good weather to complete chores that could not be done in foul weather. With some of the busier trails opening up again, the village began to receive visits from French traders trying to trade their wares. These men normally stayed for only a few hours and moved on to another village.

The last of the heavy snows appeared to be over and winter's push finally started to wane. There was even news that the thick ice that had engulfed the lake was breaking up, and far off the shoreline there was open water. Signs of the spring thaw gave the villagers a renewed sense of energy.

Movement around the area increased. The flocks of birds returned, including hordes of ducks and geese. The trails melted into slushy mud and One-Ear's scouts reported seeing many animal tracks around.

There was word spreading around the village from the traders that the French were busy calling on their Indian allies to join them. It appeared they were preparing to launch an attack on the two English forts that sat to the south near Lake George.

One-Ear remained busy organizing his scouts and hunters. The trails had to be checked for downed trees or anything else that might impede travel. His scouts were sent out daily to find out about what the French were up to. He also had to ensure that the winter stores and supplies were replenished. Hunting parties were out in the woods to set additional traps and to check on the nearby rivers and lakes for opportunities to bring back fish.

Maggie did feel guilty that she was now more a burden than an extra hand to help around the village. The women, particularly the ones residing in her longhouse, treated her kindly and refused any of her attempts to do physical labor. Most of the time they just pointed at her growing belly and told her to rest, not letting her do much of anything.

With every passing day, Maggie could feel the baby rustling inside her. It kicked endlessly and moved constantly. Being at the village was not the worst place to be, except when one needed a doctor.

The thought of having a baby without the assistance of a doctor or someone medically trained frightened her. Even with the best of care, the likelihood of a newborn surviving was always low.

The winter was not the best time to give birth and Maggie was happy to see it finally go. She expected her child would arrive late in the month of March or in early April. As the time grew closer, she found herself becoming uneasy at thought of having her child at the village.

Much of her uneasiness came from her physical discomfort. Soon, not even herbs or roots did much to ease her constant stomach pains, and she found herself unable to keep down very much food. She was thankful that One-Ear was with her and that Anne was around to comfort her.

"I know you wish you were back home to have your baby, but the women in this village are probably far more experienced in helping you than any backwoods doctor you might have dealt with before," Anne said as she tried her best to reassure Maggie.

"I am worried about delivering this child, but I am also concerned about raising it in the village," Maggie tried to explain as she sat outside with Anne and watched as she scraped a deer hide clean. "I've never been comfortable with the thought of my other children being raised by Indians."

"You and your child should feel lucky to live in such a place," Anne said simply as she did her best to remove loose pieces of skin from the stretched hide. "These people will help you raise and teach this child like it was their own."

March finally arrived and Maggie knew the baby's arrival was not far off.

Despite the weather becoming warmer and the sun's rays strengthening, the nights were still relatively cold. Even after the clearest of days, one could awake the next morning to a light dusting of snow. Maggie was warned by several of the women that during this point between winter and spring, the gods might surprise them with a snow storm.

The village elders kept themselves busy by watching the sky and clouds for signs of such storms.

Most of the women around the camp took turns caring for Maggie, and she was grateful for the extra attention. It was not long before the elders decided it was time for her to be moved from the long house to the village birthing hut.

The hut was poorly lit except for a few well-used bear fat candles spaced around the small room. The first thing Maggie noticed was that the hut was built strongly enough to keep out the cold night air. The small hole in the roof provided enough of a ventilated opening to let the smoke escape without back-drafting around the interior of the hut.

There were enough fur pelts and thick woven-hemp floor mats to keep the dirt floor insulated from the frost. The small fire did a good job masking the horrid smell that must have remained from the last woman to use it.

Maggie's biggest concern was to keep the cold weather from her newborn. All her other children were born either in late spring or early summer, so it had been far easier to keep them warm.

She knew all her fears were no more than the worries of a mother. With all the villagers being so kind to her, she knew her new baby would never want for anything.

"How are you feeling?" Anne asked as she stepped through the heavy bear skin that provided a good seal around the door. Anne had been especially caring over the last few weeks.

"I think I am ready to have this child," Maggie answered, not bothering to get up from the comfortable fur-lined bed that had kept her warm over the past week. "My pains have moved down and I think the baby has settled as well."

"Your friend One-Ear has been pacing around the village ever since we moved you to the hut," Anne said with a grin. "The entire village is excited about having a new baby arrive. These people feel it is a good omen to have a new baby grace them just as winter is leaving. I was told that a baby boy, born during this time of year would grow to be a strong warrior and good provider for his family."

She cleaned Maggie's face with a damp piece of cloth then began to spoon some warm broth made from turkey bones into Maggie's mouth. It was a simple food that would provide strength for her upcoming labor without upsetting her stomach.

After feeling Maggie's stomach for a few moments, Anne broke a small loaf of bread and handed some to her, saying, "It will definitely be soon now, Maggie."

"What makes you such an expert?" Maggie asked, curious how such a young childless woman knew so much about giving birth.

"I was young, but I remember my mother having my brother," Anne explained. "She let me help her and I was there when he was born. Also, I was with child two years ago, but the baby died shortly after its birth."

She showed very little emotion as she spoke of her baby, but Maggie said, "I'm so sorry, Anne; I do know how that feels. I was lucky to have four children, but I also lost two little ones during birth."

Maggie's body jerked as a sharp pain suddenly jolted through her. When Anne looked at her, Maggie nodded and said, "This baby is coming."

Before another word was spoken, Anne jumped up and left Maggie alone in the hut. Another sharp pain tore through Maggie, and she slowly but instinctively rose to her knees.

Trying hard not to scream with every deep pain that snapped her hips, Maggie adjusted her position and was on all fours when Anne returned with two of the village's older women.

Speaking in their native Algonquin tongue, the two women directed Anne to pile up some of the pelts and blankets to comfort Maggie. They also called out to the gathering crowd just outside the door to bring some hot water and various herbs.

Anne did her best to calm Maggie and reassure her that all was well. She tried to explain the elders' every move. The two younger women watched as the older women heated up a concoction of roots and bark. They soaked it in water and soon had a hot cup of tea ready for Maggie.

"They want you to drink this," Anne said reluctantly. The two women sat on both sides of Maggie and motioned for to her to sip the putrid-smelling drink.

Maggie realized that the smell in the hut that she had attributed to a previous birth was, in fact, the lingering aroma of this same tea. As she looked at the contents of the cup, she began to think that instead of any healing properties, the smell and taste of the tea were just meant to take her mind off the pain. Once she took her first reluctant sip, she gagged and almost spit everything back into the wooden cup.

The two elders laughed and simply refilled the cup and pressed it back against Maggie's lips.

"They say the root bark tea will help numb your pain once the baby decides to come out," Anne explained. "Every woman who has given birth in this village has partaken in the brew. It does make one think twice about having a baby." She rubbed her nose and smiled.

Maggie was well on her way to having her baby and ignored most of the movement inside the now cramped hut. She did her best to drink most of the root bark tea; once she was used to the horrible taste, it was far easier to digest. She was surprised to find that it really did start to lessen some of her pain.

Two sharp pains struck Maggie back-to-back and gave her little time to react. Anne told her to push, which she did. After relaxing her body back down onto the fur pelts, Maggie heard the wonderful sound of a low-pitched cry. She quickly rolled over onto her back, and a small baby, wrapped in a fox pelt, was placed on her chest.

Anne was in tears as the two elders patted both Maggie and her baby on the forehead, saying something in Algonquin. They soon departed, leaving Anne to clean off the baby and help Maggie nurse her child.

As soon as the women had gone, Maggie asked, "What did they say when they touched us?"

Anne was rinsing out a cloth and after placing it on Maggie's head, she explained, "They were blessing your boy. They named him 'Whispering Wind' because he was so quiet with his cries. They also said they will return shortly to rinse him in the creek."

"What?" Maggie cried. "Why would they do that to a small baby? If I refuse, would they be insulted?"

"Calm down, Maggie," Anne said quietly. "The villagers have done this with every child born here. It was done back at my old village as well. I think they hope it purifies the child and keeps it from getting sick."

"My God, I never even checked to see that he was a boy...Jacob would be so happy," Maggie said, but stopped as she thought about her husband. "What if he never gets to meet his brothers and sisters?" she whispered and began to sob.

Anne did her best to comfort her, but didn't try to stem her emotional release. Instead, she let Maggie cry, hugged her and helped cradle the baby.

When Maggie began to calm down, Anne said kindly, "Maggie, you need to get your baby to take some of your milk. He needs to stay strong and healthy."

After assisting her in feeding the baby, Anne remained by Maggie's side and welcomed the long line of women who wanted to see the new addition to their village.

"Have you thought of a name for him?" Anne asked.

Maggie had thought of a few names, but it felt so strange to give a name to their child without Jacob's opinion. "I was thinking of Israel Murray," She said slowly, as though she were trying it out.

Anne smiled and asked, "Where did you get the name from?"

"It was my husband's twin brother's name; I think Jacob would be happy with the choice," Maggie said as she gently held the sleeping child. As she looked at him, she realized that no matter what the future would bring, a part of Jacob would be with her in this child.

The two elders returned to help with the care of the baby while Maggie got some much needed rest.

One-Ear was not able to enter the birthing hut; not even the father was permitted to enter the hut, so he waited patiently outside until Maggie was ready to move back to the long house.

A few hours after giving birth, Maggie awoke and was anxious to return to the company of the long house. She felt surprisingly healthy and ate a few handfuls of winter berries and a nice warm loaf of corn bread that one of the women dropped off for her.

While Maggie ate, Anne cleaned off the pelts and took them out to hang them in the fresh air. When she returned, she helped Maggie and the baby to get wrapped up in a heavy deer pelt.

"What time of day is it?" Maggie asked Anne while she put some heavier clothes on.

"The sun has already moved close to the mountains and it should be getting dark in a few more hours," Anne replied and checked on Israel one last time.

When Anne pulled back the door cover and Maggie appeared, a loud cheer erupted outside.

One-Ear was the first to greet them and immediately asked Maggie to show him the baby. As soon as he saw the tiny boy, he howled and did a brief dance. Maggie smiled at his excitement; she thought he couldn't have shown more pride if he had been Israel's own father.

Most of the villagers stood in two long lines in front of the hut and Maggie hesitated to walk between them at first. Then she held up her child for all the villagers to view and walked through this new type of gauntlet. Some of them softly touched the baby as they passed by, and others offered small gifts that Maggie graciously accepted and Anne carried for her.

Even Morning Sun and the other elders stood on the other side of the gauntlet and they all touched baby Israel on the forehead. Maggie thought to pull him back from Morning Sun's well wishes, but it was a time to celebrate, not to open old wounds.

Morning Sun smiled and presented Maggie and Israel with a beaver pelt and two finely crafted neck bags that she placed around Maggie's neck.

Maggie returned the older woman's smile and continued to walk through the many well-wishers.

When they finally reached the long house, Anne had her arms full of gifts and Maggie was happy to be greeted by the families inside who had been so kind to her since her arrival at the village.

Once back inside the comforts of the long house, Maggie could see that there were even more gifts awaiting her. She saw nicely beaded fur wraps for the baby, a wooden cradle and so many other items that the thought of going through them all made her tired.

Anne stayed with her and made sure that the baby ate and Maggie regained her own strength with some more food and water.

It was growing late and Anne looked as tired as Maggie did. "You have spent enough time with me, Anne," Maggie said. "You look exhausted; you should go get some sleep."

Anne just smiled and explained, "I am not sure what the word in Algonquin is, but in English I would be called your 'nurse maid'. My role is to remain by your side and get you anything you need."

Holding onto Israel while Maggie got herself more comfortable, Anne slipped a small beaded armband on the baby's tiny wrist. "I made this for your baby," she said, "I hope you like it." Anne handed Israel back when Maggie finally got herself settled.

"It is beautiful, Anne," Maggie said. "Thank you for this and for all the other things you did for me today."

Before Anne could reply, Maggie fell asleep. Being careful not to wake Maggie, Anne gently pulled Israel from her arms. She placed the warmly wrapped baby into the cradle and tenderly rocked Israel to sleep.

Maggie slept most of the night between feedings and well into the late morning of the following day.

When she realized Israel was no longer by her side, Maggie rushed out into the fresh, clean air. She searched frantically for any sign of her baby. She soon spotted One-Ear and immediately rushed over to him.

Interrupting his conversation with two of his scouts, Maggie tried not to shout, "Did you see my baby? I just woke up and he wasn't with me or in his cradle."

"Maggie, all is well," One-Ear said calmly. "The women of the village have him and he is in good hands. You must understand that the young boy is yours, but he is also now part of the village. He will be taken care of by all who live here."

Maggie still wasn't happy that some of the women thought it fine to just take Israel without her permission. She did her best to calm down and asked, "Do you know where he might be?"

"They would either be in the other long house, or possibly down by the water to give the child another cleansing."

"Do the women not think they might harm my child by dunking him in ice cold water?" she asked. Her voice was concerned, but much less frantic.

It was evident that One-Ear was losing his patience with her interruption and unfounded concerns, but he answered, "They will clean him with water for the next two years, each day, despite the weather. Some say it makes us stronger and better able to survive the cold. Now, I must go. We can talk later."

Maggie stood silently as he moved away with his warriors. She decided to first check near the creek. It wasn't a long walk, and the trail down to the creek was much easier to traverse with the snow melted. Once she made it down to the softening mud, she could see that the last of the thin ice that had clung to the edges of the creek bed had also melted since she had last visited.

There were signs that the women had been down to the water already to give Israel his regular morning 'bath'. Just the thought of being submerged in the frigid water made her shiver, but she respected their ways and prayed that it would in fact make him healthier.

Making her way up the small embankment back towards the long house, Maggie spotted Anne using a thick stick to beat several fur pelts that hung over a wooden rail. The dust splattered out from the well-used furs, creating a large cloud so that Maggie could barely make out Anne through the dirt.

"Anne, how are you?" Maggie called out, not wanting to disrupt her work.

Anne poked her head out of the dusty cloud and stopped beating the line of pelts.

"So you finally decided to get up; how do you feel?" Anne asked, putting down her stick and greeting Maggie with a tender hug.

Surprised by her display of affection, Maggie replied after she was released, "I'm well. I feel much more rested, but I can't find Israel."

Anne just smiled and grabbed Maggie by the hand and guided her towards the larger long house.

Pulling back the bear skin and entering the warm coziness of the building, Anne pointed and said, "He is fine. Just look at all the attention the lucky boy is getting."

Standing back, Maggie watched for a moment. Several of the women were busy coddling Israel and passing him along a growing line of villagers eager to hold the newest addition to the village.

"They are fascinated by him," Anne whispered. "They can't believe how quiet he is and that he can sleep through all the noise around the village."

Maggie felt far less worried about Israel's well-being now and could not hide her smile. As soon as one of the older women noticed her standing in the doorway, she was waved over to join them.

Israel was wrapped in a tailored fox skin even though it was noticeably hot inside the busy house. He simply looked around and appeared to be fascinated by all the attention.

Both Maggie and Anne joined the others and as soon as they sat down, Israel was placed in his mother's arms. She kissed him on the forehead, drawing a slight squeal from him. His reaction made all the women cheer and clap with approval.

Maggie was very content with all the help when she realized that it allowed her to relax and heal. She was happy to share him with any of the women who wanted to hold him.

As she looked around at the women as they delighted in Israel's presence, Maggie found herself reflecting on the path her life had taken over the past few years. On that day back on the homestead when the Huron tore her family apart, she would have referred to the women around her now as savages. She would have dismissed them as something less than any white person she knew. While she still did not fully understand all their ways, she had developed a respect for them and had begun to appreciate them as equals. Some of her new friends were in fact much better people than several white people she had crossed paths with.

Maggie remembered the fear that lit in her heart at the thought of her children being raised by the Huron or some other tribe. The pain never went away, but the fear lessened. She ached for her children and wished she could be with them, but she was certain that if they had survived the initial days of the raid, they would be as cherished by their new Indian families as Israel was by the people of this village.

She spent most of the day enjoying the company of the women and it wasn't long until the sun set and a large fire was lit in the village meeting grounds. Soon several of the women began to file outside to start preparing food for a late meal. Maggie followed the women out, leaving Israel with several of the younger women who had no children of their own.

Maggie was enjoying the peace and happiness that surrounded the village over the next several weeks. The men continued hunting and trapping, while the women readied the outer fields for planting. Inside the village, Maggie helped with repairing any damage caused from the long winter. Some of the smaller storage huts had collapsed from the weight of the snow and they needed to be rebuilt.

She was surprised how fast she had recovered from giving birth. With her other children, she rested and took care of them for the first three to four months, without having to do much else. The women in the village encouraged her to keep moving and lend a hand where she could. It was less than a month and she was up and carrying firewood, helping with repairs and washing out her own clothes.

Israel was taken down to the creek every day to be cleaned. Maggie tried to accompany him whenever she could. Every time he was placed into the water he let out a low squeal that brought laughter to the women who had carried him down. Maggie could see that he enjoyed the constant attention.

She was happy that Israel cried very little and had earned his Indian name, Whispering Wind, but there were still times when she was concerned that he might not be crying enough. The villagers urged her to view it as more of a sign of strength than something to be worried about.

One-Ear spent as much time as he could with Israel and even took him on short walks into the woods.

"He is my brother," One-Ear said once when they returned from one of their walks.

Maggie liked being around these people and finally started to see their kindness and how they respected life. Maybe she still thought of the Ottawa or Delaware as savages, but these Indians were far from savage.

With all the snow gone and the air now fresh with the smell of the woods coming back to life, the spring brought the rains.

The rain did well to clean the land, but it made it difficult to do much else. Planting and clearing the fields had to wait, and even the hunting parties found it hard to bring back enough food to sustain the village.

The weather did not stop the women from taking Israel down to the creek, now swollen with the added water.

Maggie did not enjoy being stuck inside waiting for the weather to break, except that it meant she could spend more time with Israel. The villagers encouraged him to play on the dirt floor of the long house and, even though Maggie didn't approve, he spent most of his time naked and having a free reign of the house.

Israel played with the wild dogs that came up to investigate him, and he was endlessly fascinated by the chickens that were let loose in the good weather.

Maggie thought of how Jacob would react to his new son and wished he could be with them. She was thankful that both she and Israel were safe and protected for now.

The rumors of the French and their threat against the British forts were becoming stronger each time a trader arrived in the village or One-Ear's scouts returned from speaking with some of their fellow Mohawks from the east.

The spring meant renewal and a new life, yet it also opened up the trails and waterways to travel. Maggie could feel that her peace would not last long and she could see that One-Ear feared the same.

Chapter | **Eighteen**

The late January morning was cold, and the sun hadn't made an appearance over the mountains yet to warm the area. In the dim dawn light, increased only slightly by a few torches that still burned on the walls of the fort, Sinclair led Jacob and Joshua around the exterior of the fort. They soon found themselves in the outer earthen works that housed the rows of white tents of the provincial troops and a few of the newly arrived British regular troops.

Most of the men were fast asleep, except for a handful of men sitting around one of the fires and the poor souls on perimeter picket duty. The first set of pickets stood just on the other side of the earthen mounds that surrounded the fort on three sides with the frozen Hudson River at its back.

The three lone men headed towards the man-made bridge of bateaux strung together with wooden planks nailed across the top. The eastern channel of the frozen river trapped the bridge in the ice and made for a much easier trip across it. Jacob could see tracks left behind from some of the rangers from the island bypassed the rickety bridge in favor of strapping on steel blades to 'skate' across the frozen water.

None of the three men had mastered the art of gliding across the ice with assistance from the curved blades fastened to wooden blocks. Jacob simply said as he took the first step onto the wooden planks, "Damn foolish if you ask me. I much prefer taking my chances crossing this old bridge then falling my way across this river."

Joshua and Sinclair both laughed and followed right behind him.

"The rangers call this place 'Rogers Island'," Sinclair replied as he walked over the bridge. "It has been home for us since we arrived."

The wind swept over the open bridge and the three men were forced to walk cautiously over its loosely fastened planks. The ice cracked with almost every step, making them stop and wait, unsure whether the entire bridge might collapse into the chilly river.

"I wouldn't want to cross this bridge when the river was open and the wind was blowing along its shores," Jacob said as he pulled his outer coat's collar over his ears.

Joshua and Sinclair just grunted and pushed through the wind.

One of the first things Jacob noticed was the number of dogs waiting on the other side of the bridge. They were thin, sleek-looking creatures that approached the three men without fear.

"What's with the dogs?" Jacob asked Sinclair as he playfully patted one of them on the head.

"The rangers love having them around," Sinclair said, continuing to watch his steps. "They call them wild Indian dogs and they make pretty good guard dogs. Normally, they don't bark unless they sense danger."

Their arrival had attracted a pack of a dozen or so dogs. They were all happy to get their heads rubbed and looked as though they anticipated being fed.

"They also are great for flushing out anything in the woods," Sinclair added. "I have taken a few out on a hunt and they are amazing at spotting things that most of us would never see. I also have seen them used to pull the smaller sleds weighted down with supplies all along these trails."

They were soon greeted by two guards, who had stepped out of a small hut when they heard voices. They were clearly wishing they were still inside and out of the cold air. A small pot filled with wood kept the guards relatively warm, and by their reaction, they had little interest in speaking with the three visitors.

"Where do you lads think you are going this early in the morning?" One of the rangers calmly asked as his partner blocked the path.

Jacob was tired and had reached the end of his patience. Initially, he thought to just push the ranger aside, but he did not want to cause a scene. "I'm Captain Jacob Sims of the Virginia Rangers," he explained quickly. "I just need to get some food in me and hopefully find a comfortable bed to rest."

"Sorry, sir," the guard said, standing a little straighter. "I should warn you that the pox has hit us hard and we don't want it to spread through the entire fort. I have orders to stop everyone and ensure they are not going to expose the fort to any further infections." The ranger spoke politely but stood his ground and began looking at each man for visual signs of illness.

When the guard had finished looking them over, Jacob asked, "Where might the officers' quarters be? I'm looking for Lieutenant Rogers."

"Lieutenant Rogers has left for Fort William Henry with some of the lads," the ranger replied as he motioned for them to pass. "The officers' headquarters is to your right."

Jacob nodded and immediately walked towards the surprisingly dreary looking officers' quarters that sat near the frozen shoreline. He had hoped that there was some mix up and that the ranger would say Rogers was still on the island.

"Just one last stop, sir," Sinclair said as he pointed to another guard house located in front of the wooden porch of the headquarters. The two rangers sitting on stools at the main guard house waved the three men forward without even bothering to ask the reason for their visit.

"Let me run ahead and I will see who is in command in Rogers' absence," Sinclair suggested, running up the trail before Jacob could offer him a reply.

Jacob and Joshua decided to take a brief rest and looked across the wide channel towards the fort. With the sun finally breaking through, the two men got their first clear view of Fort Edward from a distance.

It was typical of most forts on the frontier. Its main feature was the massive, still unfinished earthen works that bounded the entire north-eastern side of its main structure. It did appear that the works had been expanded well into the cleared plain of the fort's outer boundary. The river provided the northwest portion of the wooden fort some good protection and a possible escape route if the garrison needed to depart towards Albany to the south.

The island's only link to the fort was the lone bridge they had just crossed. From what they could see of the main ranger encampment on the island, it was large and provided enough land to house a good sized company of men.

"What do you think of all of this?" Joshua asked.

"I'm impressed," Jacob said after a brief moment to take it all in. "I like how the rangers have their own space and appear to be a separate unit. We have both seen that having the British regulars mixed in with colonial troops never works. It is a matter of discipline over effectiveness, and the British have proven time and again that they have not learned a thing about fighting in the wilderness."

Taking advantage of the increasingly warm sunlight, Jacob started up the road that Sinclair had used. Joshua took up the rear, fixated on the field of crudely constructed wooden huts and tents. Most of the rangers were just rising and getting their fires built up again. The morning air was crisp, and foggy clouds of mist still hung over most of the island.

Some of the rangers stood around staring at the two visitors. Jacob didn't bother to acknowledge the gazes, but Joshua did offer the men a slight wave that went unnoticed.

Spotting Sinclair walking towards them, accompanied by a tall ranger who was struggling to do up his outer coat, Jacob called to Joshua to hurry and sprinted ahead.

Greeting Sinclair, Jacob waited for introductions.

"Captain, this is Lieutenant Warren of the New Hampshire ranging company," Sinclair said as he stood aside and let the two officers formally greet each other.

"I've heard much about you from your men; it's good to finally meet you sir," Warren said kindly as he offered his hand. He was slightly smaller than Jacob and not as athletic looking, but he was still an impressive individual. His mild Scottish accent made Jacob warm up to him immediately.

"Thank you, lieutenant; it's good to meet you as well," Jacob said as he took Warren's outstretched hand. I was expecting to speak with Lieutenant Rogers, but I got word he left for Fort William Henry."

"Aye he did, just before sunrise," Warren replied, still trying to secure the last of his buttons on his coat.

"This is Joshua, my second," Jacob added, turning to Joshua as he approached them.

When Joshua and Warren had shaken hands and exchanged their greetings, Jacob asked abruptly, "What do you know of one of my men, James Murray?"

Warren paused and looked at Sinclair. With his head down, he explained the situation, "The camp, on both sides, has been hit with a serious bout of the pox and we have lost a number of good men..."

Sinclair stepped forward and continued, "James was one of the stronger men who fought off the bloody sickness."

Warren once again replied, "We have been placing the dead as far away from the main camp as our space could afford."

"Lieutenant, Private Murray was sent out as part of a patrol to reinforce William Henry," Sinclair once again interrupted.

"Thank God, it has been difficult to keep track of all the men coming and going. Who is the lad to you, sir?" Warren politely asked.

"The boy is my son; he was told to stay here until I returned, but he is young and headstrong," Jacob explained.

Warren shook his head and chuckled before saying, "It also appears you are the most senior officer now, captain. Though, I did get word that Captain Rogers might be returning with Lieutenant Stark as early as tomorrow."

"I pray Stark joins us soon and gives me the opportunity to get some rest," Jacob said.

"Captain, please excuse me. My morning duties need to be fulfilled, but I hope to continue our conversation shortly. Private Sinclair can give you a quick tour of the island, then you are more than welcome to use Lieutenant Rogers' quarters to rest."

"Thank you, I look forward to speaking with you later," Jacob said and offered Warren a brief salute.

Nothing more was said as the three men walked briskly down a steep embankment and through a field of cleared land that Jacob guessed was used to produce food when the weather permitted.

They decided to walk around the shoreline of the island. It took them some time to finally reach the end of the long stretch of land, moving directly towards the mass of graves that were no more than piles of frozen dirt and rocks.

Jacob said nothing as he continued walking. He was far more interested in exploring the rest of the island than stopping to spend time in this place of death.

The three men continued to walk together and took a moment to check in with the field doctor at a large structure that acted as an isolated hospital for the men inflicted by the pox. Jacob thought it would be best to keep a distance from the doctor until he was needed, yet Sinclair thought it important to introduce the two.

Jacob's first thought when he saw the disheveled, clearly exhausted doctor was what a horrible job he had. Stuck at the end of an already remote island, he was forced to live amongst the sick and dying.

Jacob felt for the man.

Sinclair brought the doctor over and said, "This is Dr. Smith, the head field surgeon from the 44th Foot."

The doctor showed as little interest in the introduction as Jacob. He was clearly far more concerned with his patients than visiting with a ranging officer who looked as bad as he did.

Despite their reluctant meeting, Jacob touched his hat and said, "Dr. Smith, it's a pleasure. How did a surgeon of the 44th make it to an island full of pox-infected rangers?"

Without bothering to answer the question, the doctor simply replied, "Pleasure, sir, but if you would be so kind, I must get back to the men. Webb has been sending these poor souls to me so fast I can barely keep up. I pray for these lads who enlisted in the bloody British army just to die like this. This damn wilderness will kill us all, and you can bloody well mark my words."

Jacob decided not to provoke the doctor any further and respectfully touched his hat. Without saying another word, he let the doctor return to his dingy makeshift hospital and left him to his duties.

"Sorry, sir," Sinclair said when they had departed. "He is not much of a talker."

"Can't blame the poor man," Jacob replied as they continued past the rest of the hospital towards another, much larger graveyard. "I don't believe he expected to end up here after spending so much time at some high-end London medical school."

The three men stopped when more mounds of frozen dirt came into view. Some of the graves had obviously been dug in the early winter; many more were new, having been forcibly shoveled through the frost-laden soil.

Doing a rough count, Jacob could see that there were well over forty graves. They had been marked with rocks and pieces of wooden planks. It was a dreary place; even the ever-present dogs refused to venture there.

Adding in the other mounds they had seen earlier, Jacob figured more than fifty men had died from the pox outbreak.

The river ice around the tip of the island had clearly thawed and refrozen close to shore on a number of occasions. Although the river was a smooth sheet of thick ice, the shoreline was piled with large mounds of broken ice. They leached a dreary sogginess that made the landscape around the graves appear even more miserable and bleak.

As Jacob looked at the graves, he thought of how close James might have come to being in one of them. In an instant, he realized how lucky James was; perhaps his being at Fort William Henry was not such a bad idea.

This was no place for a boy.

The pressure and guilt he had felt during those long months since they found Fort Stevens under siege struck him full force. Standing and staring off into the long, winding river, he covered his face with his hands. His words were muffled as his tears came, "I should have never left him. I should have learned my lesson from Maggie, but…"

Sinclair and especially Joshua found it hard to see their captain break down. At this point, they were not sure what they should do or say.

Joshua finally broke the uncomfortable silence and said, "Sir, we need to find our way back. I don't think we should stay too long here. The smell of death is everywhere. We can always send out a patrol to find out about James."

Jacob looked over the graves, not knowing what to say. He was drained both physically and mentally. It had been almost five months since he lost Maggie and over three years since he left his home and family. How much longer could he go on? What more could he do? He was only one man.

The morning wind still swirled around the bleak point as quickly as Jacob's thoughts spun through his head. He stood rooted to the spot and began to pray for a miracle that would let him find Maggie and the rest of his children, so he could just stop running and searching.

Any further prayers were interrupted by a scout calling out to him, "Captain Sims, you are needed back at the main camp."

Shaken back to reality, Jacob turned to call back, "I will be there shortly, lad."

The scout waved and headed back up the trail.

The three men immediately walked back towards the officers' headquarters and left the terrible place, hoping never to return. As Joshua and Sinclair walked with Jacob, they remained respectfully quiet.

"Thank you, gentlemen," Jacob said quietly. "I am glad you accompanied me, but I am sorry you had to experience all of this."

The two men said nothing, understanding they could not say much to relieve Jacob's guilt-stricken pain.

They made their way up the embankment and were greeted by the sight of additional rangers from Fort William Henry milling about. Jacob was happy to see that the surviving men from his own unit were part of the contingent of rangers.

The three had spent most of the morning touring the island and Jacob had lost all track of time. He guessed it was well past midday and that most of the rangers were likely out on patrol or attached to hunting parties.

He noticed John Stark was among the new arrivals and called out, "John, good to see you well!"

Stark signaled for his men to make their camp by the officers' quarters before walking over to greet Jacob. "I hope all is well with you also, Jacob," he said genuinely. "I honestly thought I would find you fast asleep."

Walking to the officers' headquarters, Jacob said, "You couldn't have gotten much sleep yourself. How did you get here so fast? I didn't see Captain Rogers; did he make the trip?"

Despite protests from the handful of officers sitting around the large fireplace, Stark held the creaky wooden door open until Jacob caught up to him.

"The captain is actually heading to Albany to get his injured wrist looked at," Stark replied as he finally closed the door and offered a seat to Jacob at the lone table in the center of the room. "I was part of the escort who accompanied him this far. He was being transported by ox-driven wagon and should be in Albany by nightfall."

"Where does that leave us?" Jacob asked, careful not to offend Stark's loyalty to Rogers. He did not know what to think about Rogers leaving the area after convincing him and his men to come this far to fight with him.

Before he could answer, Stark was greeted by one of the junior officers and offered a small glass of something that resembled rum or whiskey.

"Pour the captain a glass as well and leave the bottle, lad," Stark said. He raised his glass and offered an informal toast, "To escaping the bloody French…again."

"Cheers to that, John," Jacob said, graciously accepting and raising the drink before emptying it in one quick gulp.

"Easy, Jacob, that is New Hampshire corn whiskey; I have no idea what they put in the stuff, but I know some of the men use it to polish their shoes!" Stark laughed and downed his glass as well.

Lifting the bottle and offering another drink, Stark didn't wait for an answer and happily refilled Jacob's glass.

The two men shared another toast then began to discuss their duties.

"Captain Rogers wanted me to pass on his orders to you and your men," Stark explained. "He wants you to patrol the road between the forts and keep your men stationed here at the island. He regrets you will have to deal with Webb, but as long as you do your duties and keep the road clear, the coward will not have much to do with you. Honestly, Webb far prefers to confine himself to his office and lets us do whatever we feel keeps him safe." Stark's comments drew several laughs from the other officers around the room.

"What about the garrison at Fort William Henry?" Jacob asked, taking a final sip from his glass. "They don't need our extra support?"

"I met his brother Richard on his way to William Henry, and he said he would call for reinforcements if need be," Stark replied. He finished off another glass, which Jacob respectfully declined, and jammed the cork back into the neck of the bottle.

Despite being tired and sore, Jacob was restless. He stood up and politely dismissed himself to attend to his men. "I have to see how my lads are holding up, John. I will catch up with you after I return from our first patrol."

Smiling, Jacob left Stark sitting alone at the table.

Just as Jacob reached the door, Stark called out, "We have strict orders from Webb that we cannot send any patrols as far as William Henry. The general wants us to stay close to him and clear the road of any of the enemy we might run into. The poor bugger is very fearful that the French might attack this fort on the way to Albany."

Unsure how to respond to this latest news, Jacob stepped outside and was surprised to feel the sun grappling with the cold, miserable countryside. He shielded his eyes and searched around to see where his men were encamped.

His mind could focus on nothing but James, the only member of his family whose whereabouts were still known to him. Jacob stood only sixteen miles or a good day's march from knowing his son's condition, and now he was ordered to stay away. He immediately thought to ignore his orders, but he knew that would just be a foolhardy venture that would only get him an appointment from the 'King's Rope'.

Getting himself hanged would not help James or Maggie, and Jacob knew that once again his hands were tied.

As his sense of helplessness grew, Jacob began to grow angry. He was upset with the coward Webb, whose orders had tied his hands. He was angry with Rogers for convincing him to bring his men on this fool's errand in the first place. As usual, he was angry with himself for letting James out of his sight in the first place. He was even mad at James for going against his orders to remain at Fort Edward until he and the rest of the rangers returned.

It wasn't long before he found Joshua and Sinclair. They were standing by a long row of attached log homes. It was just one row amid many that faced each other. Jacob looked at their rough exteriors, which appeared to be no more than piles of logs with angled roofs, and felt a bit wary.

He looked into several of the small sheds and tugged on the wooden frames. He was surprised at how solid they seemed. Each tiny house held up to four men in relative comfort. He was glad to see that his men appeared satisfied with their new accommodations, and Jacob figured that anything solid was a step up from the usual tents that many of the British regulars had to sleep in across the river.

"Jacob," Sinclair said when his captain had completed his inspection of the huts, "we heard of the orders to remain here at Fort Edward. What are your orders for us?"

"You heard right," Jacob replied, looking at Sinclair who was standing in front of twenty men he had chosen for a scout. "We have been ordered to patrol the road between the two forts and keep them clear of any French or savages."

Jacob turned to Joshua and realized the young man had been awake as long as he had. His own emotions were so keyed up that he knew he would be unable to rest, but he looked at Joshua and said, "I want you to get some rest, lad. I will take the men out along with Mr. Sinclair."

When Joshua's face betrayed his disappointment, Jacob added, "Son, we are on an island filled with disease. I need you strong and healthy. If you do not rest, you will leave yourself open to illness. What would become of me if something happened to you?"

Joshua nodded without a word and Jacob patted him gently on the back.

Just as he dejectedly walked away, Joshua turned and quipped, "God knows, if I were to die, you wouldn't last a day without me watching your behind, sir."

Jacob laughed, knowing full well that he was right, "Get some rest, lad, and you can join us later."

Turning to the matter at hand, Stark had suggested Jacob send five of the Stockbridge Indian scouts ahead. He explained they knew the road towards Fort William Henry better than most, and they would be invaluable to Jacob in patrolling the road. There were a number of side paths and little coves that dotted the area around the road and Stark assured him that the Indians knew most of them.

News of the minor raid on William Henry that had left the boats ruined had already spread across the island. There were also rumors that the French had already moved some of their troops down to Carillon to cause continued problems for the fort. It was reported amongst the men that the Ottawa had returned to the area and were scouting with the Canadian militia.

If the rumors proved to be true, Jacob needed all the help he could get.

Continued reports of the French reinforcing Fort Carillon, combined with the much needed break in the cold, snowy weather gave the men a renewed sense of energy. Being stuck behind the walls of a fort, or being confined to their encampments made the men long for some action. They knew that with the French around, they would be in for some.

The only news that upset Jacob was from Albany. Captain Rogers had been expected to return to Fort Edward to join back up with Jacob and Stark once his wound had healed. Instead, he was now ordered to take two companies of his rangers northeast to Nova Scotia. Jacob learned from Stark that the British planned on attacking the French fortress at Louisbourg and needed Rogers to provide his rangers to scout the area.

Jacob heard from a number of the men who had lived in and around the area for most of their lives that March's transition from winter to early spring could introduce some pretty hazardous weather. One of the older rangers explained that he had experienced such drastic changes in the weather that he almost froze one night, only to wake to a sunny and warm morning. By the time the sun set that evening, a blizzard had dumped almost a foot of heavy, wet snow in the area.

Jacob and his men had spent well over a month constantly patrolling the road and scouting around the woods for any signs that the French might be around, or that their savages were in the area.

Jacob was tired of the mundane chores but did enjoy the company of his men and learning from the rangers left behind by Captain Rogers. He did wonder how Rogers was making out with the contingent of British regulars in Nova Scotia. With what appeared to be happening around the two forts, Jacob knew that Captain Rogers would have been a welcomed sight to the rangers at Fort Edward.

Joshua and the rest of Jacob's men remained relatively healthy, except for the usual bumps and bruises. However, the word from Fort William Henry was not so good. The already depleted numbers had been affected by a new bout of the pox, and a good portion of the garrison and the civilians that lived inside the confines of the fort were stricken by the deadly disease.

Jacob had heard numbers as high as seventy men, women and children had died to this point. It was said to be so bad that Webb had renewed his old order that the patrols could go no further than a place the men dubbed, 'Halfway Creek'. He even went so far as to restrict the much needed supply wagons from moving goods between the forts.

Although Jacob had delivered a couple of dispatches to Fort William Henry prior to the reinforced restrictions, he had not seen or heard from James. Joshua had spoken briefly with James on one of his own dispatch runs, but it was no more than a quick 'hello' and 'stay well'. Joshua had reported to Jacob that James appeared to be in good shape and had grown a few inches since they had seen him last.

While Jacob was pleased that James was well, his frustrations mounted with every trip down the road. He could smell the fires at Fort William Henry and, on a few occasions, he could hear the men being drilled and practicing with their muskets.

Being so close gave him some solace, yet he would have much preferred it if James was by his side. The constant rumors of the French plans for an attack on the forts made it difficult not to ignore Webb's direct order and just make a dash up the road to find the boy.

Jacob had already deserted once and still lived with the dishonor. The few men who had attempted desertion from Fort Edward were easily captured and hanged. Their dead bodies were gruesomely displayed above the main gates of the fort as a reminder to the others of what became of deserters. That only reinforced his desire not to meet such a fate.

There had been no sign of the French or their savages over the weeks that followed, although the rumors persisted that they were accumulating troops in and around Fort Carillon.

Jacob still had not heard anything from James. He looked for any opportunity or excuse to head towards Fort William Henry in hopes that his patience might soon be rewarded.

Thankfully, March did not bring horrendous storms, and instead brought in much better weather than they had seen in a long time. Stark took advantage of the improvement and left for Albany to recruit some additional militia for General Webb. That left Jacob in charge to keep the main road clear for travel to Fort William Henry, should Webb ever decide to release any of the men under his command.

Stark had left behind his group of Stockbridge Indians to assist in Jacob's daily patrols, and he continued to utilize them as advanced scouts. After sending them up the road towards Fort William Henry early one morning, Jacob gathered fifteen of his rangers and organized them to move out. Joshua was to remain with Jacob while Sinclair was to take up his usual position at the rear.

"We have our usual orders to patrol no farther than Halfway Creek, but we will judge the situation once we reach it," Jacob informed the group. "I told the Stockbridge Indians to push on ahead to the fort if they have not encountered the French or any savages along the way."

The rough road was now really no better than a roughly cut trail that had been worn down by a number of heavy wagons moved between the forts over the past year. The change in temperature made the already uneven road a messy combination of half-melted snow and pools of mud.

Surprised at how much the road's terrain had changed since he and Joshua slogged through the snow in late January, Jacob ordered, "Lads, the ground is terrible but no worse than the bogs back home. Keep in single file pairs and watch the road ahead. I fear we might make for some easy pickings if the road makes our travel any more difficult."

The patrol left well before dawn and with the days getting noticeably longer, the men could cover a longer distance. They had not seen any evidence of the French or their allies by the time they reached Halfway Creek, so Jacob gave the order to push onward. They almost reached the hilly area at the edge of William Henry's cleared outer field by midday.

The weather had thawed the majority of the ice and snow that had surrounded the forts, but there were parts of the road that were so sheltered by the thick forests that Jacob and his men were still forced to use snowshoes at times.

The going was slow until Jacob noticed a couple of the Stockbridge scouts stopped by a large boulder just off the side of the road. They appeared to be waiting for him, so Jacob ordered his men to fan out and watch both ends of the trail. Word was also sent back to Sinclair that there might be some problems farther ahead.

Jacob and his men had spent several weeks patrolling these woods, often with the support of the Stockbridge Indians, but Jacob was still not sure what he thought of them. They were favored by Rogers and many of his senior officers, but Jacob noticed that the scouts always seemed to have very little interest in what was going on between the British and French. They also chose to live in the woods instead of on the island with the rest of the rangers. Jacob honestly had no idea how many times they scouted the road on their own.

John Stark always reminded Jacob that 'they are not the friendliest of people, but they have proved on a number of occasions to be loyal and that is all that matters to Rogers.'

Joshua accompanied Jacob as the two men approached the scouts, but they made no effort to greet the rangers and simply waited for them to reach the boulder.

Jacob told Joshua to fan out to his left as he stopped just short of the scouts and politely asked, "What is the problem? Have you spotted any signs of the French?"

With a puzzling air of indifference, one of the scouts simply stated, "The French are around the English fort and burning some of the outer buildings."

Slightly stunned that they were not giving him more details, he pushed them to give him a better idea what exactly was happening, "How many French are there, and have they attacked the fort?"

"The French and some of their Ottawa dogs are trying to encircle the fort," the same scout said vaguely.

Frustrated with their display of callousness, Jacob gave it one more try to retrieve some useful particulars before he moved his men forward towards the French threat. "Can we reach the fort?"

"Yes," the scout said without offering any more information. The two scouts were obviously ready to rejoin their mates and had little more to add.

Jacob dismissed the unhelpful scouts and watched them run north towards the fort. He then called his men forward.

"Watch the woods," he said, "I just received word there are French and Ottawa in the area."

Word was also sent back to Sinclair of the situation and Jacob suggested his rear guard stay closer to the main body. He also asked him to send two men back to Fort Edward to inform them of the situation. Jacob suggested they make an effort to speak with General Webb and request him to send forward some reinforcements.

Jacob was aware that the men might be tired since they had marched for most of the morning without a decent break, but if the reports proved to be true, he had to push them ahead. He knew that his dozen or so men might not be able to do much if the French were launching a full scale attack on the fort, yet he had little choice.

As they moved forward, occasional bursts of musket fire echoed back to the advancing rangers. Jacob remained in the front hoping to see any signs of the Stockbridge Indians. He was thankful that the French were more concerned with bothering the fort than sending any of their men down the track towards Fort Edward.

Jacob ordered some of his men to form a vanguard in the forest. The snow was still deep in the shaded areas of the woods, but the snowshoes made it easy to trek along the side trails. He pushed his well-trained men hard and had them running double time. The rangers finally got close enough to the fort to hear steady musket fire and smell burning wood from the number of fires that were sending streams of smoke into the once clear sky.

The sound of cannon fire added to the noise and confusion. Jacob took up a position just short of the rise that edged the open field around the fort. He ordered his men to fan out along the border of the tree line towards the swampy ground near the lake and wait for his signal.

Sinclair finally made his way forward and joined Jacob to find out what was happening. "How does it look, Jacob?" he asked.

"Not sure," Jacob replied. "As you can see, there are clouds of smoke blocking our view. From what I can figure, the French are down by the lake."

Sinclair stood up and tried to get a better look at the field. "If that's where the action is awaiting us, perhaps we can use the swampy area to the east of the outer wall to reach it," he suggested.

"Careful, Robert," Jacob said, pulling his scout back down by his coat tail. "The bloody Ottawa are around; if they spot us, any chance to surprise them will be lost."

Jacob looked at his men and was determined not to march them blindly into action. He asked Sinclair to take two men and try to locate the Stockbridge Indian scouts that were nowhere to be seen. As soon as Sinclair departed, Jacob decided to slowly move the remaining men along the forest line as far as he could without exposing them to the French.

He prayed that Stark would soon arrive with his reinforcements and the echoes from the cannon fire would add to the alert he sent to Webb at Fort Edward. He was also faced with a large open area directly in front of the fort and only one small trail that led to the outer walls of the besieged fort.

It occurred to him that he should try to get word to the fort that they were present and trying to flush out some of the French. He sent two rangers to the fort to locate Lieutenant Richard Rogers and inform him that there was a ranger scouting party in the woods by the road.

Joshua was left behind with three men to wait for Stark by the road. While Jacob and the rest of his men slowly approached the point where the heavy forest met the swampy shoreline of the lake, Jacob got a much clearer picture of what was happening.

He watched as the French regulars, supplemented by Canadian militia and Ottawa warriors concentrated their efforts on setting fire to what was left of the whaleboats and a dozen or so more wooden structures down near the beach area that had survived the first attack. Jacob could also see that a couple of larger vessels that were hoisted up on large rails and near completion by the fort's carpenters were also being targeted.

Jacob felt helpless as he watched the French send small groups to attack the main wall. They were being repelled by the fort's sentries, stationed high on the eastern wall, but Jacob and his men were still too far away to assist the fort. He decided to wait for word from either the fort or Sinclair about the situation.

He did move five of his men forward a bit, taking advantage of a small, slightly burned out building that once housed some of the livestock. Jacob gave them the order not to engage the enemy unless they felt threatened.

The musket fire from the men on the walls and the constant blast from the cannons did a good job forcing the French back and limiting their ability to do much damage. Finally, after an hour of observing the extremely disorganized attack, Private Sinclair returned with word that the Stockbridge Indians were in the fort. He also reported that Lieutenant Rogers had asked Jacob to attack the left flank of the French to draw them away from the boats.

Reluctant to expose his men to a possible counter-attack from a much larger force, Jacob waited and seized the opportunity to advance his men against a small, isolated band of Ottawa.

The Ottawa were known to act as a separate unit and rarely followed orders from the French. Jacob knew that the French usually let them do whatever they felt was best and left them alone to fight.

Before the Ottawa could react to the surprise attack or even shoulder their muskets, Jacob and his rangers charged down a small hill and overtook the dozen shocked warriors. Some did manage to put up a fight, but they were easily subdued by the hard-charging rangers.

The British regulars and rangers who kept up a steady fire from the high walls stopped momentarily to give Jacob and his men a quick cheer. All but two of the Ottawa were killed or injured, and the two survivors were taken captive and moved immediately to the fort.

The attack also drew attention from the French and they reacted by sending a larger party of militia and additional savages to push back the rangers. Jacob responded by ordering his men to form up and offer one massive volley before withdrawing back into the cover of the forest. The effective volley smashed into the advancing party and caused them to halt their disorganized advance.

After being stopped by the original volley from Jacob's men, the French regrouped, advanced and returned fire.

The French regrouped quickly, advanced again and returned fire just as the rangers reached the woods. Jacob calmly ordered his men to return fire at their own accord. Once again, the rangers displayed their prowess with muskets and cut down the next line of Canadian militia and Ottawa still in the open field.

Jacob ordered the men back to the small hill and observed that the badly beaten party was now joined by some French regulars. The rough estimate of the freshly reinforced enemy facing the rangers was between thirty and fifty.

The rangers had only numbered fifteen, but a couple of the men had been injured and were already taken back towards Fort Edward to nurse their wounds.

He understood that his men were in a terrible position. If the French pushed forward and forced him to withdraw further into the woods, the Ottawa and Canadians would be in their element. With their numbers, they might easily overwhelm them.

Watching the French quickly reorganize for another charge, Jacob knew he could not simply wait to be overrun. He thought of ordering a mad dash across the field to his left to seek refuge in the fort, but he did not want to give the French the upper-hand.

Deciding quickly, Jacob called out, "Rangers, we make our stand here! If they advance…fire at will."

His final word had barely left his lips when a massive crash blasted the earth just in front of the French position by the hill. It was followed by a deafening scream that made even the Ottawa warriors run back in a panic.

Once the smoke cleared and the piles of earth sent skyward by the cannon blast rained back down, Jacob and his rangers could see a large company of green-coated rangers charging into the left flank of the confused French. Richard Rogers was leading the charge; as the French fled down the hill to their boats, his men continued to pursue them.

Jacob had immediately recognized their opportunity and ordered his men to advance towards the lake to cut off as many of the French as they could before they reached the water. They were quick enough to kill several of the French regulars and take three more as prisoners.

The Frenchmen who managed to reach the boats quickly boarded and frantically rowed out into the open water, narrowly avoiding several shots from the rangers on shore. Jacob and Rogers called their men back and massive cheers rang out from the rangers and the men on the walls of the fort.

As the rangers began collecting well-earned prizes from the field, Jacob and Richard Rogers met to congratulate one another before ordering their men back to the fort.

"Good showing, captain", Rogers said as he approached Jacob.

"You as well, sir, and please call me Jacob. Your men arrived on the field just in time."

The rangers made it back to the fort with their three prisoners in tow, just as the last of the French finally disappeared northward. The mass of Ottawa canoes also disappeared from view as they paddled past the first of many small coves that dotted the far shoreline.

"Do you think they will return to Carillon?" Jacob asked Rogers, once they were in the safe confines of the fort.

"I assume they will take refuge on one of the islands around the bay," Rogers offered, taking Jacob to the massive fire pit in the center of the parade grounds. "My guess is they will send for more reinforcements and then attack us again, possibly tomorrow."

Sinclair approached the two officers to ask, "What about the prisoners?"

"Bring one of them over so we can talk with him," Rogers spoke up first.

Jacob was tired and was more interested in getting some rest before returning to Fort Edward, than speaking with some French prisoner. He also wanted to find out about James. He hadn't spotted the boy among the rangers who so bravely attacked the French.

Neither man said much to the other as they simply sat by the fire. After a few moments, two of Jacob's rangers pushed the clearly frightened French regular directly in front of the two rangers.

Initially surprised at how young the Frenchman was, Jacob let Rogers take the lead and waited for him to ask the first question.

"Monsieur, what is the strength of the garrison at Fort Carillon?" Rogers asked in broken French.

The prisoner gave no answer and Rogers asked, "How is your French, Jacob? Maybe you can loosen this boy's tongue."

When Jacob had translated the question into better French, the soldier cleared his throat nervously and gave a long-winded answer in a meek voice.

Jacob explained once the prisoner was done, "The garrison has been growing all through the winter. He added that there were many Indians camping outside the walls of the fort. He could only estimate, but his guess was between one thousand to as high as two thousand regulars plus five hundred Indians and Canadians."

"Why have so many French been brought down south?" Rogers asked Jacob to translate to the prisoner.

Jacob asked and let the young man reply.

"There was talk about even more men coming down from Quebec," Jacob translated. "He has only heard rumors but gathers that there is to be an attack on one of the English forts once the snow has completely melted and lake is safe enough to transport the men and artillery. He said he didn't know if it would be William Henry or Edward."

Rogers nodded to the two scouts to take the prisoner away. After thinking about the numbers, he asked Jacob, "Did you see that many French at Carillon when you passed it in January?"

"Honestly, we didn't take much time to look, so I can't really say," Jacob admitted.

The young Frenchman's testimony was soon confirmed by the other prisoners. Their information painted a fairly serious situation. Jacob knew it was only a matter of weeks, if not days, before the lake was clear of most of its ice. The over-land trails were already nearly clear from the long winter's snow.

The numbers reported by the French prisoners left the two English forts in a bad position. In addition to their concerns, the British activity against the French stronghold in Nova Scotia at Louisbourg resulted in the lack of available experienced fighting men. The commander of the British forces in North America, Lord Loudoun, had basically left the New York territory undefended except for two small garrisons at the two isolated forts. The undermanned forts would have to rely heavily on their colonial troops and militia.

When the interrogations were finished, Jacob took the opportunity to ask Rogers about James. "Richard, you brought one of my men with you from Edward and I was wondering how he is holding up."

Rogers initially replied, "I can't honestly recall any of your men joining my ranks."

"He is a young lad named James," Jacob said in a level tone, "he is around twelve and a pretty good scout."

"Yes…yes, young Murray," Rogers finally recalled. "He is a great scout; the boy certainly pulls his weight despite his young age. I was unaware he was one of yours, but he was quite adamant about coming with us."

Jacob just shook his head and continued, "Where is he now?"

Rogers immediately called over one of his men and held a whispered conversation. Once the man left, Rogers replied, "He is presently out on a scout to the north."

Unsure what more to say, Jacob finally said, "Tell him that his father was here and needs him to return to Fort Edward."

Standing, Rogers replied, "I didn't know, Jacob. I will pass on your message."

Jacob stood also and extended his hand to Rogers.

"Well Jacob, our job is done here," Rogers said as he accepted the handshake. "I assume you are anxious to get your men back to Edward, so safe travels and I pray we meet up again." Rogers quickly walked away with several of his own men.

Jacob was exhausted from the day's activities, but also from the long winter. That morning, he had been optimistic that the spring thaw was an indication that he would soon be able to resume his search for Maggie.

With this latest news and the prospects of being attacked by the French, Jacob knew that once again a large French force stood between him and his ability to reunite with his wife.

The rest of March was spent building up the fort's defenses and preparing for the possibility of a French attack. Jacob knew that the forts would be in a panic over which of them would be the central objective of the assault. Jacob expected William Henry would be the obvious target, as it was situated on a lake that the French wanted to control. Fort Edward was far less important by comparison, but if the French took William Henry first, Edward would stand alone and vulnerable to a French attack at their leisure.

Along with warmer spring weather, the garrisons at both forts welcomed the arrival of some additional British regulars. Most of the men were surprised that Colonel George Munro of the 35th Foot took command of Fort William Henry while most of his men remained at Edward. The fiery Scotsman had little experience in battle, but his demeanor made up for it. Jacob spent his time patrolling the road between the forts with John Stark and escorting the continuous supply wagons.

The patrols were being even more diligent about watching for signs of the French or their savages. The garrison at William Henry had reports that the French were on the move and a number of small scouting parties had been spotted.

Jacob still had not had the opportunity to speak with James and was extremely concerned that the young lad seemed to be spending most of his time out scouting. With the French far more active around the territory, James was exposed to the possibility of running into them and Jacob prayed that he stayed safe.

Early one spring morning, Jacob and Joshua were on a short day trip along the road between the forts when they spotted a dozen or so fresh moccasin tracks on a muddy trail that led into the woods.

Following the tracks slowly through the thick forest, the two could smell a fire and soon reached a small clearing. Crouching down on all fours, they crept close enough to get a good view of the Ottawa scouting party.

"Damn, as soon as the bloody weather starts to turn, the French have their savages out skulking around the forts," Jacob whispered.

"Should we go back and get some of the men to ambush them?" Joshua suggested, keeping his eyes on the scouts who sat around the small fire seemingly oblivious that they were being watched.

Considering the circumstances, Jacob thought it might be a good idea. However, they were nearly halfway between the forts and it would take several hours to reach either one. Jacob knew by the time they got some men organized, the Ottawa would most likely be long gone.

"Let's take a look around and see if we can find how these savages got here," Jacob whispered, coming to a decision. "If they used the lake and beached their canoes, I want to find them and destroy them so the buggers will be forced to fight their way all the way back to Carillon." He motioned for Joshua to follow him.

Joshua remained behind Jacob and both men remained alert to the presence of any additional warriors. They knew that the group they just left could simply be the advanced scouts. For all they knew, the entire countryside could be teeming with the main force ready to attack one of the forts.

The journey down towards the lake shore was rewarded after a challenging five mile scout through the thick, swampy forest on paths that had not been cleared since last summer. As the two rangers finally reached the lake, they saw two Ottawa warriors sitting by the shore. They had been left behind to guard the half-dozen birch bark canoes dragged far enough from the shore to be well concealed from any patrols from William Henry.

Waiting for Joshua to take a look at the situation, Jacob said, "We need to get closer to be sure, but if there are only two Ottawa around we should be able to get to the canoes."

Joshua smiled and took a good look around the woods and the swampy shore of the lake.

The warriors did not have a fire since the smoke could be easily spotted by the garrison at Fort William Henry. They did have the benefit of several boulders and the rocky terrain that gave them some cover.

Jacob and Joshua moved slowly along the tree line until they found a spot that offered them a perfect vantage point just over the warriors' backs. It was obvious to both men that if they decided to fire from the woods, the noise would echo far enough that the larger group of Ottawa would be alerted to the ambush.

"My only fear is that there just might be more savages around that we haven't seen yet," Joshua whispered as they watched the Ottawa standing by the canoes.

"Well, if we go by the number of canoes, and it appears there is only enough room for the scouting party we saw and these two savages," Jacob said, hoping his assumptions were correct.

Jacob held up his bayonet to signal Joshua to do the same. Carefully, so as not to make any noise that might alert the two warriors sitting just below them, they affixed their bayonets to the ends of their muskets.

Slowly getting to his feet, Jacob waited for Joshua and they worked their way down along the line of boulders. Luckily, a flock of noisy geese flew over the lake and masked their approach.

Without a word, the two rangers charged down the slight embankment and onto the soft sand of the small beach landing. They were initially slowed by the soft terrain, but they still managed to approach undetected and wildly jammed their bayonets into the backs of the two Ottawa guards.

The initial attack failed to kill the warriors who began to struggle and fight back. Jacob attempted to dislodge his bayonet, but the weapon was caught in the warrior's ribs.

Jacob instinctively let go of the musket and pulled his hatchet from his sash with his left hand. The startled, bleeding Ottawa pivoted and reached for his own hawk, but Jacob quickly dispatched the savage with a viscous blow to his forehead.

Jacob's hatchet was still sunk into the dead Indian's skull as he swung around to assist Joshua with his warrior. Pulling his scalping knife from his quilled neck sheath, Jacob charged towards the two men embraced in a deadly battle.

His help was thankfully not needed, however, as he watched Joshua slash at the warrior's stomach and drive his fist into the man's jaw. Joshua stood up, blood dripping from his knife, and screamed a devilish howl. Jacob shivered at the thought that the dead Ottawa might have made the same sound if the situation was reversed.

"Keep your voice down, lad; do you want the rest of the Ottawa to return?" Jacob called out to the bloodied Joshua.

Not apologizing for his barbaric reaction, Joshua simply wiped off his knife on the leggings of the dead warrior.

Jacob went back to attempt to remove his musket from the warrior he had brutally killed. Still unable to pull the bayonet out, no matter how hard he yanked on the musket, he finally just slid the musket out from the lock of the bayonet and left it sticking out of the warrior's back.

Stepping on the Ottawa's lower back, Jacob easily yanked his hatchet from the dead man's skull. Without bothering to clean off the blood, Jacob continued towards the canoes.

He pulled several of the canoes into the frigid water and slashed at the birch bark just as violently as he had the dead warrior. Joshua was by his side in an instant and began hacking holes in the other canoes. In minutes, every one of the canoes was sunk and left completely useless.

Ignoring the chill from their soaked clothes, both men immediately began running as fast as the narrow paths along the shore to Fort William Henry would allow them. They hadn't spoken since their attack, and they soon cleared the first of the earthen works to reach the first crude block house that housed five Irish guards from the 44th Foot.

Being regular British soldiers, they had their muskets drawn as they greeted the two blood-splattered rangers.

Jacob was tired and sore and had no patience to deal with these Irish soldiers. "Get us to the fort's commander; I have to report some news of the Ottawa," Jacob growled.

One of the guards stepped forward and countered Jacob's request, saying, "Now, that's not how it works, lad. I will be asking the questions to decide what to do with you. First, drop your muskets, gentlemen."

The heavy-set, thick-accented guard was backed by his fellow guards who tightened their grips on their muskets. Jacob knew these bloody Irishmen could easily shoot them and merely explain to their superiors that they were attacked by these two strangers, so he held his tongue and slowly placed his musket on the ground. He nodded for Joshua to do the same.

Left without weapons, Jacob waited for the lead guard's next move. He had never been overly friendly with the Irish, so when the man moved close to Jacob, the smell of whiskey on the man's breath almost knocked him over and he winced.

The guard immediately noticed his reaction and was quick to comment, "Do we have one of those damn bible-thumping Quakers judging us?"

Jacob did his best not to react to the man, but when the guard turned his attentions to Joshua, Jacob lost his patience with the whole drunken group. He pulled his still bloodied hatchet and swung it wildly. He opened up the guard's skull with a direct blow from the hilt of his upturned hatchet.

The rest of the guards had no time to react and were easily overtaken by the two rangers. Now standing in possession of all their muskets, Jacob told Joshua to remain with the five shocked guards. The bloodied and bruised man crawled back with the others, moaning in pain but saying little else.

Jacob ran through the line of earthen works and once he was spotted by the garrison guards, he called to them to find the ranger in charge and have him meet him outside.

It wasn't long before an unidentified man and ten of his rangers joined Jacob and rushed back to reinforce Joshua.

"I'm Captain Jacob Sims of the Virginia Ranging Company," Jacob introduced himself to the ranger who ran by his side.

"Apologies, captain, I'm Lieutenant William Stanton of Richard Rogers' unit," the officer replied, keeping his eye on what was waiting ahead of them.

Thankfully, the five guards had decided not to cause any further trouble for Joshua and were greeted by laughs from the arriving rangers.

Lieutenant Stanton was not so kind to the men and said, "You are lucky that I don't have you all up on charges. Being drunk or even having liquor on your breath when on duty is a hanging offense. Attempting to strike an officer would get you all hanged...twice."

The men all looked frightened. Regulars were not normally afraid of threats from a 'colonial' officer, but they understood they had overstepped their authority. Jacob quickly stepped in to calm down the tense situation.

"Gentlemen, no harm was done except for a little headache. I think we need as many men as we can and these lads were only doing their duty... albeit, a little too eagerly. It's certainly no reason to hang five men."

Stanton agreed and left the men to their duties.

Before they left for the fort, the injured man asked to speak with Jacob.

Agreeing and suggesting he would be in the fort shortly, Jacob waited until the rangers were out of voice range. He motioned Joshua to join Stanton and his men.

"What do you want, soldier?" Jacob asked, not interested in spending much more time with these men.

"My apologies, sir, I was just doing my duty," the man sheepishly tried to explain.

Jacob did not know what to say and only looked over the five men, meekly staring at their shoes.

"My name is Private Ryan and I am sorry for your troubles, sir," the guard continued, offering his hand in an attempt to complete his apology.

Jacob grasped the man's hand and said, "Thank you for your apologies, gentlemen. Please remember in future that the French are the enemy."

The men laughed and the rest of the guards offered their hands to him.

Once all the formalities of the long apology were completed, Jacob excused himself and left the five guards to their duties.

Walking alone with his thoughts, Jacob could not blame the men for trying to drown their pain in rum, whiskey or whatever soothed their ills. The things he had witnessed over the past few years would drive most men to drink. Although Jacob sometimes took part in the odd toast, he never liked anything that clouded his judgment. He lived by his father's words about drinking, 'it makes some men brave, makes some foolish and never makes a man feel good in the morn.'

The fort was far more hectic than the last time he was there. The garrison was much larger and the barracks had spread out into rows of tents in the far cleared field. They were noticeably too close to the tree line for his liking. He noticed more Irish and Scots of the 44th and 48th Foot as well as some provincials and ranger units.

Stanton called out to him once he was inside and Jacob obliged him. They were near the officers' quarters and Stanton asked, "Most of the rangers are out on scouts, but would you like to meet our new commander? He is a fellow Scot, Colonel Munro of the 35th Foot. A good man, but not one with a lot of field experience."

Jacob let Stanton lead the way and was soon standing in front of a grey-haired officer, busily writing out correspondence and signing an endless amount of papers.

"Sir, this is Captain Sims of the Virginia Ranging Company," Stanton politely introduced Jacob.

Signing one last piece of paper, Munro looked up and smiled, "Sims, my pleasure."

Jacob offered a lazy salute and drew the ire of the Scotsman, "Not a formally trained soldier, I see."

"No time for formal training of any kind, sir; the savages care little for it and will scalp you either way," Jacob replied, hoping his attempt at humor didn't upset the officer.

Laughing and standing up, Munro countered, "Aye, the savages are a treat. Never had the pleasure of fighting one yet, but I imagine my time will come soon. If they are even close to what some of the men say, then they will be a sight to behold. Honestly, I suspect they are no worse than some my own relatives who inhabit the Highlands back home."

Munro returned Jacob's salute with a more seasoned example before sitting back down and asking, "Where do you make your home, Sims?"

"I'm with General Webb at Fort Edward, sir," Jacob replied.

Munro nodded and replied, "I don't know Webb well, but what I hear is not encouraging. I only pray that when the time comes for the French to invade, he will be quick to reinforce us and not slump in fear he might be attacked in turn."

Not knowing how to reply, Jacob looked at Stanton who simply nodded and smiled.

Jacob had intended only to report the findings of his patrol to the ranger on duty, but took the opportunity to change the subject by telling both Stanton and Munro at the same time.

"Sir, the reason for my visit was more than meeting you," Jacob began. "I was out on a scout with one of my men when we ran into a group of Ottawa warriors in the woods between the forts. They were maybe five miles south of here and we found them resting. We left them and found their canoes guarded by two additional warriors. We killed those two and sunk their canoes."

Stanton interrupted before Jacob could finish, "Captain, did you notice anything else?"

"We only saw the twelve, plus the two that we dispatched by the canoes," Jacob replied and waited for further questions.

Munro said little and just listened intently to Jacob's report.

Stanton pressed for more details, "Do you think they were just up to no good, or were they part of some advance French force?"

By this time some of Munro's officers and aids had gathered around to listen in on the details.

"I'm not certain, sir," Jacob replied, looking around the crowded room at all the interested men. "Have your men seen any signs of the Ottawa or French recently?"

"Nothing as of yet, but with this information we will have more of the men out scouting the area," Stanton suggested and looked for Munro to confirm. "In fact, we have a number of men already out scouting the overland route to Carillon."

"Well, the rumors are appearing to hold some truth; we probably should increase our patrols for the time being," Munro said, looking at his aid to transcribe some orders reflecting his suggestions.

Jacob had no interest in the conversation beyond his own report and wished to begin the trek back to Fort Edward before completely losing what was left of the daylight. He also hoped that Joshua might have had some luck finding out about James and how he was holding up.

"Sir, I need to get back to Edward and report my findings to General Webb," Jacob politely interrupted and waited to be dismissed.

Munro scrambled around his desk for something and once he found a sealed note, he handed it to Jacob. "Would you be so kind as to deliver this to General Webb?" he asked.

"Yes, sir," Jacob said as he placed the note in his coat pocket. "May I refill my horn and get a few slices of meat before I depart?"

Waving to another aid, Munro said, "See this man has supplies for his trip back to Fort Edward."

Jacob nodded his appreciation and offered a slightly better salute to Munro.

Munro smiled at his effort and replied with his own nod. He quickly returned to the pile of notes and letters piled on his desk.

Stanton and Jacob walked out of the office together.

"As I said, I need to get back," Jacob said. "Where is Lieutenant Rogers? I honestly expected him to greet me initially."

"The lieutenant is ill and in the doctor's quarters," Stanton replied.

"I hope it is nothing serious?" Jacob asked, stopping in his tracks. "We need men like him around to fight the French."

"I don't know much, sir, he took ill only yesterday," Stanton replied.

Jacob didn't know what else to say but earnestly prayed that Rogers would get better soon.

"Get some food for you and the lad you came with, and stay safe," Stanton said. "I think we will be seeing the French soon; then the fun will begin." With that, Stanton left Jacob to resupply and head out.

Joshua was waiting by one of the fires and called out to Jacob, "Sir, we are losing the light; we may want to leave soon."

Jacob finally reached him and replied, "Agreed, let's get some powder and food, then get on the trail."

"Any sign of James?" Jacob added as they walked towards the supply hut.

"Nothing, sir; most of the men thought he was out on another scout," Joshua explained.

"The boy certainly appears to be working hard; I just hope he keeps away from the bloody French," Jacob said, looking up at the late day sky.

"He is a smart boy; from what I have seen from him, he knows how to take care of himself," Joshua said, doing his best to reassure Jacob.

It had been a long and eventful day, and as Jacob and Joshua traveled farther into the woods, the sky above them grew darker. Having traveled the track several times over the past few weeks, the two rangers moved quickly but cautiously. They had no way of knowing what had happened with the Ottawa scouts they spotted earlier.

"I would have loved to have seen their faces when they returned to their canoes to find them at the bottom of the lake!" Joshua laughed quietly as they sprinted along the trail.

Jacob laughed too but offered no reply.

Thinking they were past the mid-point of the road between the forts, Jacob had moved slightly ahead of Joshua before suddenly stopping. Immediately turning, he motioned to Joshua to stop.

"Did you hear that, lad?" Jacob asked and pulled him into the cover of the woods.

Joshua reacted by ducking down and listening intently for any noise.

"It sounds like voices," Jacob said quietly and pointed through the darkness. "Listen...I think they are over there."

They crouched down and stayed as motionless as they could and strained to hear anything that the late night forest might expose.

"We need to try to get closer," Jacob suggested and slowly moved out from the woods and walked ahead of Joshua. "I pray it is just a patrol from Edward and not the Ottawa."

Both men knew that most Indians preferred not to travel during the night, but Jacob wasn't certain the Ottawa followed the same rituals as the Eastern Woodland tribes in the area. Besides, if they had discovered their escape vessels were destroyed, they could have been riled enough to cause some trouble.

It wasn't long before the voices grew louder and the glow of a fire within the forest was easily detectable from the trail. Jacob was surprised by the amount of noise that was being generated; it sounded like the perpetrators were having some kind of celebration. He figured the noise could likely be heard as far away as Fort Edward and was now curious who would be so foolish as to make such a racket.

Joshua stayed right on Jacob's heels and the two moved their way around a sea of trees and thick undergrowth. It wasn't long before they made their way to a spot near a small creek.

Once they got down on all fours and pulled back on some low-hanging branches, they finally saw what all the fuss was about. As suspected, it was the same Ottawa scouting party, but they now had two unidentified prisoners with them. Both men were stripped naked and tied around two posts that each had a pile of cut wood and branches at its base.

"They are going to torture these poor souls and burn them alive…if we don't do anything about it," Jacob said as Joshua scanned the area for any other savages lurking around the perimeter of the woods.

Jacob had no idea how he would rescue the prisoners, but he knew he wasn't just going to sit back and watch the bloody Ottawa have their way with them.

"What can we do, sir?" Joshua asked helplessly. "There are only two of us and the Ottawa appear to be pretty upset."

Jacob thought for a short time and finally said, "Honestly, there is nothing we can really do without reinforcements from Fort Edward. Lad, would you be willing to run as fast as you can to the fort to inform the nearest blockhouse?"

Joshua quickly replied, "It looks like we have no choice but to try. I will go now and hope to hell I don't run into any more of the savages."

Jacob grinned at Joshua's bluntness and gave him a pat on the back as he said, "Godspeed, lad. Go get word back to the rangers."

The noise Joshua made running through the brush was thankfully drowned out by the increasing screams and howls from the Ottawa.

Still confused by the behavior of the savages and their apparent lack of concern about retaliation from either of the nearby English forts, Jacob kept a close watch on the activities. The two captives kept their heads down and made little noise, even after some of the warriors threatened them with their tomahawks. Most of the Ottawa scouts sat around the little fire and enjoyed some roasted meat.

Jacob could not tell if the scouts had gotten their hands on any rum or brandy. He knew the combination of drunken savages and their awareness of the destroyed canoes would make for a long night for the two unfortunate captives.

Doing his best to identify either one of the men, Jacob finally got a quick glance as one of the captives slowly raised his head to see what the Ottawa were up to. His brief look was met with a hard blow to his skull from a war club that left him bloodied and nearly unconscious. Jacob was certain that the man was one of the rangers he had met at one of the guard houses on the island.

The time went slowly and it felt as if Joshua had left hours ago. Jacob knew that realistically, even at a quick run, the distance Joshua would have to travel to the fort and back would take him close to three or four hours. It hadn't really been more than a half hour since Joshua left, but Jacob did not want to wait helplessly and watch while the two captives were brutally tortured to death.

Thankfully, the Ottawa didn't appear to be in a rush to kill the two men and were far more concerned with eating and sitting around the camp. Only a couple of the warriors looked interested in the two men strapped to the trimmed down tree trunks. They took turns threatening the men with their knives or hawks.

Jacob worked on devising a plan to distract the Ottawa and possibly draw their attention towards him. He honestly had no desire to join the two as a captive himself, yet he was not going to just sit back and watch everything unfold.

The one possible weakness Jacob thought he could exploit was that the Ottawa were so bold that they hadn't even bothered to place any scouts around the perimeter of the camp as pickets. Ignoring the close proximity of the main road and both forts that sent scouting parties out on a regular basis, they appeared to be almost daring the English to attack them.

This point was not lost on Jacob.

Estimating that he had enough distance between them and the main track to get a healthy head start, Jacob simply stood up and fired his loaded musket at one of the scouts sitting around the fire.

Not even caring if he hit one of them, Jacob used the cloud of white smoke as cover and ran to his far right as fast as he could.

Desperate to catch his breath, Jacob once again loaded his musket. He pounded down a combination of buckshot and ball into the muzzle. Quickly ramming the deadly contents down the barrel, he primed it and had it shouldered before most of the Ottawa had time to grab their own muskets.

Jacob rarely used buckshot, but he had been convinced by Captain Rogers that it was an effective way to spread your fire. Jacob pulled the trigger and the force of the unusually heavy load forced the butt of his musket hard into his shoulder.

Again, not waiting to see what damage the shot did, Jacob stepped several paces along the trees and had his musket loaded and shouldered once more. This time, he took a moment to aim and fired again into the middle of the confused Ottawa camp.

He could now hear the screams. Some from the injured and others from the surviving scouts bent on stopping the attack. This time, Jacob didn't bother to reload. He ran as fast as the heavily-wooded area would permit and headed straight for the main road.

Unable to hear over his own heavy breathing if he was being pursued, he cleared the woods and was now on the much flatter track. The first part of his plan was working…the Ottawa were now concentrating their efforts on him instead of the two prisoners. Jacob's problem now was that the second part of his plan was not so clearly laid out in his head.

He kept his head down and ran as fast as he had ever gone in his life. The shrieks from his pursuers could now be heard over his shoulder, but he couldn't take the time to look back, fearing he might lose his footing and be overrun.

A musket was fired behind him, sending a lead ball just over his head. The shot hit a nearby tree, sending shards of splinters into the air. His stomach lurched and his legs began to cramp up and slow him down as he continued to run.

A slight bend in the road up ahead looked menacingly dark as he moved headlong into the murky shadows. Just as he made the turn, Jacob suddenly stopped.

He stood with a musket pointed at his forehead. Jacob's breath burned his throat, choking him and causing him to struggle to speak. Knowing he had nowhere to go, he dropped his musket, barely able to stand on his shaking legs and declared, "I am your prisoner."

Chapter | **Nineteen**

It was far too dark to see who had captured him. Their silence made his heart pound even more, and Jacob still struggled to catch what was left of his breath. Almost collapsing to one knee, he did his best not to show any fear.

He assumed it was the Ottawa who outsmarted him and captured him. They would certainly not be happy with what he had pulled off back at the camp, although he had no idea if he had killed any of their warriors. He was not familiar with their language, so he simply repeated slowly in English, "I am your prisoner."

Ducking after two muskets fired just to his right, Jacob thought about diving into the nearby woods until a familiar voice called out, "Sir, you might want to get your musket; the Ottawa are coming up the road and they appear to be upset."

Jacob felt a moment of giddiness. He wasn't sure if he should laugh, cry, or maybe even smack the owner of the voice. Jacob picked up his weapon and followed the rest of the men. They took cover on both sides of the track and waited for the Ottawa to rush forward into their hastily arranged ambush.

"How did you make it back so soon?" Jacob asked as he downed a canteen of ice cold water Joshua handed to him.

"I ran into this patrol a few miles up the trail and they joined me to come and rescue you," Joshua said with a chuckle. "I knew you wouldn't just sit by quietly until I returned."

Jacob slapped Joshua on the back in a friendly gesture and stifled a laugh of his own. Once again, this young man had saved his hide and he was grateful.

He looked around and could make out that these men were all rangers, but he wasn't sure to which unit they were attached. At this moment, he cared little for details but was thankful they were here.

After the two shots were fired, any sign that the Ottawa were still chasing Jacob was gone. Rallying the rangers, Jacob called out, "Follow us, the savages might be retreating to their camp."

Running across the road and into the heavy forest to an old pathway, the rangers followed Jacob as he dodged and eluded the endless obstacles that clogged the roughly cut path. He halted the men to regroup and listen for any noises carrying through the silence of the woods. Joshua kneeled beside Jacob and took a good look into the dark forest for any signs of movement.

"We need to get back to the main road if we want to catch the Ottawa," Jacob suggested. "The bloody woods are next to impossible to work through."

Without waiting, he was up and moving quickly towards the far easier main road that would lead them towards the camp. Suddenly, they reached a cloud of smoke that was extending towards them, swallowing all the fresh air in its path.

"This can't be good," Joshua shouted to Jacob who sprinted ahead of him.

The only positive thing about the situation was that the heavy, oddly sweet smelling smoke led the rangers directly to the Ottawa camp. Slowing to a more cautious pace through the deep woods, the rangers fanned out to encircle the encampment.

The heavy smoke released bad memories that came flooding back into Jacob's mind as they moved. He walked straight into the now abandoned camp and found the two wooden stakes collapsed, but still engulfed in flames.

The rangers all moved in and beheld the sight of two charred corpses, now barely recognizable. A couple of the rangers poured the contents of their canteens on the mess, which just added to the thick smoke that already irritated the men's eyes.

Thankfully, the water extinguished the remnants of the fire. The badly burned bodies of the two unfortunate men practically disintegrated into the ashes right in front of the rangers.

"We need to keep moving, lads," Jacob said as he kneeled down to check the number of tracks that dotted most of the boundaries of the camp. "Do you want to follow the Ottawa tracks or return to Fort Edward?"

The men looked at each other and each waited for one of his mates to step up and say something.

Joshua finally offered, "The Ottawa are several minutes ahead of us and we would need to be wary that they might just set up an ambush for us. Fort Edward appears to be the best choice; we can send out another, fresher patrol once the sun rises."

Jacob agreed. The rangers left the dead men where they laid and headed back south.

The sun was unusually warm the next morning, and it coaxed most of the fort and inhabitants of Rogers Island out of bed early to complete their chores and start their rounds.

Jacob had risen well before the sun had cleared the mountains and sat enjoying a small cup of tea. He was alone and looking across the channel towards Fort Edward. The previous night's episode had tired him out, yet he was intensely focused on seeking some form of revenge on the Ottawa who had so viciously murdered the still unidentified men.

He did like this part of the country. It was much like his native Pennsylvania, although it seemed a bit more untouched and wild. Sitting on an old tree stump, he could picture a cleared field with a small, log cabin nestled in the eastern corner of the lot and a few acres of corn and straw. The sounds of children and a handful of cattle resonated around the peaceful plot of land. The image of Maggie hanging up several basket loads of freshly cleaned shirts and britches made Jacob pause and wonder how he had made it to this place.

In all the excitement, he had almost forgotten the note that Colonel Munro had given him to pass on to Webb. When Jacob rose, he passed the sealed note on to one of the guards to take to the officers' quarters inside the fort.

The noise from newly arrived provincials hammering the stakes around their tents and organizing their encampment echoed around the island and forced him to look past the bridge that linked the island to the outer earthen works of the fort.

With their arrival and a couple companies of the 35th Foot that had arrived just a couple days before from William Henry, Jacob looked over the fort and could see that the British were building up their forces in anticipation that the French would be launching some kind of attack against the two forts.

Lost in his thoughts, Jacob was brutally shaken back into reality by a voice off in the distance.

"Captain Sims...Captain Sims, please join me at the officers' quarters."

He knew the voice and once he cleared his mind, Jacob turned to see Lieutenant Stanton waving at him.

"Yes...yes, lieutenant. I will be there shortly," Jacob called back, took a deep breath and slowly stood up.

He was surprised to see Stanton on the island; after taking a quick look around to see if James might be with him, he straightened up his coat and put on his hat. Walking halfheartedly towards the officers' quarters, Jacob finally joined Stanton on the porch of the well-built building that held over ten officers at any one time.

"Sorry for the intrusion, sir, but I wanted to introduce one of our fellow officers that you missed back at William Henry," Stanton kindly explained before he walked into the quarters.

"When did you arrive?" Jacob asked. "You must have marched through the night to get here."

"I escorted a couple of our supply wagons. With your news of the Ottawa, Munro wanted to be safe and make sure the supplies reached the fort." Stanton replied, rolling his eyes.

Unsure if he should join him inside or stay outside, Jacob did not have to wait long before Stanton returned with another ranger.

"This is Captain Sims from Pennsylvania," Stanton said.

"I'm Israel Putnam of Salem, Massachusetts," the ranger said as he extended his hand.

Jacob shook Putnam's hand but was struck by how cold the man came across. Not wanting to prolong their conversation and seeing the lack of interest that Putnam exhibited in their introduction, Jacob politely said, "Good to meet you, sir, but I should get back to my men."

Putnam said nothing else and slightly nodded then slipped back into the headquarters.

Jacob walked away from the quarters and was soon joined again by Stanton who said, "Sorry about that, captain. Putnam is a strange sort and he doesn't really get along with any of us, but he is a good fighting man."

"No bother, it was kind of you to introduce him to me," Jacob said as he looked around for Joshua or Sinclair.

"He is departing soon for a long scout towards Carillon and I assume his mind is elsewhere," Stanton added. "The French and their savages have us all a bit worried."

Jacob had nothing more to say about Putnam and changed the subject, "What news do you have about the French? With the better weather moving in and the lakes free of ice, I think we will start to see more signs of them. We did run into the Ottawa again last night, but they ran away like frightened dogs."

"Well, we both know the Ottawa have been in the area for some time," Stanton replied. "We got word from a couple French deserters that the French numbers at Carillon are growing, as have their patrols on the lakes. The attacks on our boats in January and March hurt our attempts to keep the lower lake free of them. That is why Putnam is scouting around Carillon and the narrows between it and William Henry."

As the two rangers continued to walk, they both reacted to a massive blast that violently vibrated the ground and kicked up a haze of dust around the camps.

"What the hell was that?" Jacob spat out.

"No trouble, captain, it is just a signal system between the forts," Stanton explained as he watched along with Jacob. "Now with all the enemy activity around, the forts have decided to set up a warning system in case of an attack."

The cannon fire also drew the attention of rest of the rangers, who gathered along the eastern shore of the island to watch the show. Jacob and Stanton joined them and watched the large cloud of smoke rise above the northern bastion.

Spotting Joshua nearby, Jacob elected to excuse himself and said, "Lieutenant, I should be getting to my men."

"Of course, sir," Stanton replied. "I must return to Fort William Henry immediately to continue the scouting of the area."

Jacob smiled and said, "Stay safe. I am certain we will cross paths again soon."

The two men went their separate ways.

Joshua noticed Jacob coming towards him and waited by some of the men. "I have always loved the powerful thunder that the heavy cannons spew," Joshua admitted when he arrived.

"It is impressive, lad," Jacob said as he stood with the men, watching the gun crew re-position the cannon back to its firing line.

Before they could spend much more time enjoying the spectacle, a red-coated messenger approached Jacob and politely interrupted, "Sir, General Webb has requested your presence at his headquarters immediately."

Jacob nodded his acceptance and said to Joshua before he left with his escort, "Lad, get the men ready, I assume we are to head out shortly."

Jacob walked with his escort but nothing more was said. The two men made their way over the earthen works, and Jacob noticed that some of the work details were busy reinforcing the fort's outer defenses, including the sharpened palisades.

As they walked past the fields of empty white tents, Jacob assumed that those among the British regulars who were not on patrol or guard duty were most likely on the parade grounds performing endless hours of their routine marching drills.

When they finally reached the interior of the fort, his escort finally spoke again, "The general is in his office, just past the guards."

The two men walked briskly across the packed grounds and were greeted by two heavily-equipped guards he recognized as men from the 35th Foot, "Halt, sir, what do you men want?"

Jacob did not appreciate their tone but knew that the British regulars did not recognize the colonial troops as anything more than undisciplined thugs. His escort simply nodded his head and the two guards stepped aside.

Once they were in the office, the escort politely pointed towards Webb and motioned Jacob to take a seat. As Jacob had noted during his brief introduction to Webb a few months ago, the desk was still piled high with papers, documents and maps.

Webb didn't bother to look up or acknowledge that Jacob had arrived. A voice from behind made Jacob immediately jerk his head, and he noticed a thin clerk sitting on a stool and sealing a number of letters. The man said, "The general has little time to talk with you, captain, so please sit and he will find a moment for you shortly."

Jacob looked around the room and noticed a small chair by the fire, but he decided just to stand in front of the general's desk instead. Ignoring the glares from the clerk, Jacob waited patiently until Webb decided to speak with him.

Finally looking up at Jacob, Webb said, "We have had several scouting parties report that the road that joins us to Fort William Henry is becoming more treacherous than usual. It appears the French savages have decided to inhabit the woods and have been ambushing our supply lines."

Webb paused, signing several documents before he continued, "I need to keep the road clear. I assume you have heard that the French are reinforcing their efforts around the lakes? I fear they might be considering attacking our forts now that the weather has become a little more predictable."

Jacob had a difficult time listening to the monotone, pompous British officer and fought off several yawns. He assumed that Webb held little regard for the colonials, particularly the 'undisciplined' ranging companies. As such, he decided it would be a fruitless effort to enter into conversation with the general to inform him that he had already traveled the road between the forts many times over the last months.

Not giving Webb any sign he was already aware of the situation, Jacob waited for him to get to why he requested Jacob to report to him.

Still not looking up, Webb continued, "I do not want to weaken my post, but I do need to know what is happening at William Henry. From what I know of the colonial ranging companies, you lot enjoy scouting and fighting with the savages. That being said, I need you to take your men out and ensure our supplies move easily between here and William Henry."

"Will we be reinforcing Colonel Munro at Fort William Henry?" Jacob decided to ask.

Webb finally took some time to look up and scowled at Jacob's rough and dirty appearance. Jacob had respectfully removed his hat, exposing greasy, long hair that made him appear further untamed.

"We need to ensure the French do not turn their attentions on this fort," Webb said disdainfully as he returned his focus to his desk. "If we fail to protect this fort, the French will simply march on Albany and all will be lost. What will their savages do to Albany's fine women and children? Munro is a good soldier and can handle what the French might decide to hand him."

Jacob did not want to continue this conversation. He had learned enough about Webb to know that he only cared about himself and nothing else.

"Take your men out and scout the road for any French or savages," Webb added. "I will need you to send back reports to let me know what is happening."

After handing his clerk a sealed note, which was then handed to Jacob, Webb concluded the one-sided conversation, "Take this to Colonel Munro at William Henry and then keep the road clear of the enemy."

Jacob took the note and placed it in his pocket as he waited a moment for Webb to formally dismiss him.

After a few uncomfortable moments, Jacob figured Webb had forgotten his presence. He gave the general a halfhearted salute and walked past the clerk.

Thankful this ordeal was over, he stood on the small deck that was covered by an overhanging roof and kept the guards relatively dry from the elements. The two guards just looked him over and said nothing more to him. Jacob simply gave the two a brief glance and walked briskly back to the island.

Dodging all the hectic work going on around the fort, Jacob saw Joshua and his men waiting near the entrance of the bridge to the island.

Waving at the men and calling to them to meet him on the fort side of the bridge, Jacob waited for Joshua to join him just in front of the road towards Fort William Henry.

Fort Edward was full of activity, and each day the earthen works around the outer fields were further built up. The fort was becoming very formidable and Jacob wondered why, if the French were to take William Henry, they would bother to attack Fort Edward?

The French were active in and around the upper lake and there were almost daily reports that the Ottawa were increasing their patrols. Jacob had not been to William Henry for a couple weeks, but reports from some of his men patrolling the area mentioned that they too were busy reinforcing the outer works around the fort.

Jacob had his men build a small entrenchment near Halfway Creek, primarily to make it easier to move his patrols between the forts. It backed onto a large swampy area that made it impossible for the enemy to ambush them from behind. Unfortunately, the swamp was home to hordes of mosquitoes and swarming flies, but the men preferred living within the forest because it gave them a place to retreat to if they ran into trouble. By this time, most of the sightings of any savages were to the north of the hills around William Henry. The last time there had been any sightings south of the fort was when Jacob had encountered them.

It was not long into summer before the rangers learned of another outbreak of the pox at Fort William Henry. Jacob told his men not to stay at either fort for too long before returning to their growing encampment at the halfway creek. John Stark and his men also joined him after the pox ravaged Rogers Island. The additional rangers created a large force within the woods that kept the road between the forts clear.

As the news and rumors regarding the French rapidly increased, Jacob learned from a group of British regulars that the French had shipped over a newly-appointed commander from France, named de Montcalm. Neither the rangers nor the British knew anything about the new commander, and thusly had little to fear from him…for the moment.

"What do you think the French are up to?" Jacob asked Stark one day as the two men walked along a long, flat stretch of a parallel side trail that had been cleared and cleaned up by Jacob's rangers.

"The news about them building up their forces causes some worry," Stark replied, "but I am not certain where they might be planning to attack. The bloody rumors have been spreading since the winter. William Henry would be a nice prize, but it would require a long siege to take it. Fort Edward might be the better option because it would give the French the Hudson River and completely isolate William Henry. Such isolation could force the British to abandon it without a fight. Albany is only twenty or so miles from Edward, and that would be a special prize for the French."

Jacob had heard all the rumors but was far more concerned with the lack of savages around the area since the last time he ran into the Ottawa scouting party. If the French could convince all their Indian allies to fight with them once more, the British might not be able to defend either fort.

"I have heard some frightening numbers, between ten thousand or more regulars plus both Canadian militia and savages in and around Fort Carillon," Jacob said, trying not to sound too concerned. "How can we hold both forts?"

Stark reacted to a noise coming from the woods just to his right and replied, "God only knows if we can hold either fort, especially with Webb being in charge of one of them. Munro is a good soldier, but if Webb just hides behind his desk and doesn't offer any support, we all might be dead by the fall."

The ominous words gave Jacob a great deal to think about, and he decided not to talk any further about the future prospects. The two men continued on and spotted two massive carts being pulled by several oxen on the main road. The carts kicked up clouds of dust and dirt, greatly reducing the rangers' visibility, even though they were well off the road.

Stark and Jacob decided to get back to the road to see what news the men might have. The two drivers noticed the rangers and pulled hard on the ropes that guided the oxen. Pulling the packed carts right up beside them, one of the drivers called down, "Mr. Stark, it is good to see you well."

Stark shouted back to the dust-covered driver, "Mr. Gibbons, it is good to see you as well. What news do you have for us?"

Jacob stood next to the oxen and listened as their heavy breathing displayed the weight of the cargo. While the driver spoke with Stark, another man offered the sweating oxen some much earned water.

Barely able to make out what Stark and the driver were saying, Jacob moved closer, stepping past the water-carrying driver's assistant.

"The bloody pox has hit the lads at William Henry pretty hard," the driver was saying. "Your Lieutenant Rogers has been severely sick with it and God only knows if he is still alive. It makes you think twice about even entering the bloody place. I don't spend much time around the fort…in and out, that's what I do, sir…in and out."

Stark glanced at Jacob and asked Mr. Gibbons, "Anything more I should know?"

"Nothing more, sir, but I will let you know if I hear anything else." The driver touched his hat and was soon whipping the oxen to get them moving again.

A brief wave and the carts were well up the trail before Jacob could ask for all the details.

"It doesn't look good for the lads at William Henry," Stark said. The pox is hitting them hard and if the bloody French decide to attack the fort, all could be settled rather easily." He took out his pipe to have a quick smoke.

Offering Jacob a smoke, Stark looked up the trail and took several puffs from his pipe.

"We might want to get the men ready for some fighting and tell them to stay clear of the fort for a while," Jacob suggested. "We can stick to the swamp and the hills and make sure they are cleared."

The two rangers made their way back to their encampment and looked forward to sitting by the shallow, meandering creek that ran alongside the main camp. However, they soon realized that they would have no time to rest.

Almost immediately, one of Stark's scouting parties returned with word from Fort Edward. One of the men handed Stark a sealed note, which he immediately opened. After a few seconds, he handed the unfolded message to Jacob.

As he took the note from Stark, Jacob mused that when lower ranking British regulars ignored his higher rank, it was unacceptable. Among ranging companies, however, it was the way of things. Stark's rangers reported directly to Stark, and Jacob would expect his own men to come to him directly. Besides, although Stark was a lower ranking officer, he was several years older and Jacob had a great respect for him.

Scanning the short note, Jacob looked at Stark for some direction, "Do we follow the orders or choose to ignore them?"

"I think we should get back and see what is happening," Stark replied. "Honestly, with what we just learned about the pox outbreak, it might be better to stay clear of William Henry for now." He took back the note and tossed it onto the small fire that Joshua was tending nearby.

The three men watched the note burn into ashes.

"Joshua, get word to the scouts that we are leaving for Fort Edward," Jacob said.

Joshua initially looked hesitant, but he quickly went off to do as he was told. Once the word was out, the camp was cleared and, within a half-hour, the once busy encampment blended back to one of many small clearings that dotted the swampy terrain.

The two ranging companies departed together with Stark's men taking the advanced guard. Jacob posted Sinclair to the rear and traveled in single file with Joshua remaining beside him for the majority of the trek.

"Sir, is there a problem?" Joshua finally asked curiously.

"What makes you say that, lad?" Jacob replied, keeping his eyes forward.

"Well, if I am not mistaken, neither you nor Mr. Stark had any intention of spending time at either of the forts while we were camped at the creek," Joshua said carefully. "It appears that Stark's message made a decided change to our plans."

"Webb is making his way to William Henry to check on their defenses," Jacob replied. "He wants us to return to help Edward's garrison prepare the fort for a possible attack…we have little choice."

Reaching the outskirts of the first line of earthen works and pickets, the men returned to the island that housed their fellow rangers. After speaking with some of the guards, Jacob learned that the pox had hit the fort again. All the men infected with the disease had been removed to the southern end of the island and isolated to hopefully control the spread of the deadly disease.

In the meantime, the fort was busy still building up their defenses and the carpenters were working day and night reinforcing the wooden structures inside and outside the fort's walls. The colonial troops were used to provide escorts for any working party sent into the woods to work or gather supplies.

Tension was high despite the routine and laborious work being done around the fort. Most of the men expected to see the French charge out of the woods at any minute to launch an attack on the fort. Daily messages were sent between the forts, and the signal cannons continued to be fired off throughout the day.

Webb had also left to visit Fort William Henry and to contemplate what the two forts needed to do to defend their positions against the anticipated French attack.

Jacob and his healthy men were not happy with being confined to the vicinity of the fort. They went out every day patrolling or escorting hunting parties into the deep woods. Their monotony was finally disrupted on an initially peaceful morning when some of the carpenters were attacked near the eastern edge of the wooded area, near the far outer works.

Jacob immediately led some of his rangers across the wooden bridge to assist the pickets in defense of the carpenters. They soon found themselves facing a large force of Ottawa warriors with some Delaware and Seneca in reserve.

A small force of French regulars and Canadian militia were leading the attack and were aggressively moving forward to surround what was left of the carpenters and their guards. Moving into the woods and taking advantage of the trees for cover, Jacob ordered the men to stand two men to a tree, and told them to alternate their fire to keep the savages back.

The Ottawa did their best to force the rangers into retreating, but Jacob and his experienced men held their position and fought hard to keep the savages occupied while the French attackers were forced back by the heavily reinforced pickets.

The welcomed sound of the cannons firing from the gunners at the fort made the Ottawa cease firing. The momentary lull was short lived, and the attackers quickly realized the cannons could do little damage to their position so deep in the woods. The heavy guns merely contributed a lot of noise and a hail of splinters that fell indiscriminately over both sides.

Jacob heard the savages moving once again and looked to his left flank. He immediately realized that during the course of the fighting, some of the rangers had shifted and left a gaping hole in the ranks. He quickly ordered some of the men to fill the gap and had them prepare for hand-to-hand combat.

The Ottawa were spotted moving slowly along a line of cedars. Almost before he could call out a warning, some of the men charged wildly into the midst of the trees. Their undisciplined yet quick actions managed to push the savages back.

Jacob ordered the rest of his men to charge, and they forced the warriors on the flank back towards their retreating mates. Jacob pounded his hawk into the backs of two retreating warriors, while his men continued to push them back.

The restricted confines of the thick woods made it difficult for the rangers to pursue the Ottawa too far. They were careful not to spread themselves too thin, which would make them easy targets for a counterattack.

The sound of musket fire soon lessened into only a few sporadic shots exchanged between the colonial troops and the retreating French. Once Jacob had his men reorganized, the rangers collected what they could from the dead and met back up at the farthest picket station.

"How are you and the rest of the men?" Jacob asked Joshua, who had a trickle of blood running down from a gash in his arm.

"I only saw one of the lads get hit, and it was only a small wound to his left hand," Joshua replied as he checked to make sure the last of the rangers had made his way back. "I think the men did very well; the French and their savages ran like dogs once we hit them hard."

Calling the men to order, Jacob simply said, "Good work, lads, but I fear this is only the start of a much bigger attack."

The rangers checked that the pickets were all accounted for, and some of the colonial troops were left behind to reinforce the boundary around the woods. Jacob decided that his rangers should continue up the road to ensure the attackers had pulled a full retreat and were not simply regrouping.

Jacob knew the fort couldn't let its guard down, but he was convinced that the attack was just an uncoordinated attempt by a French-led scouting party to make the fort aware they were in the area. The rangers followed the trail for a few miles; once they were satisfied that the French had indeed retreated, Jacob ordered them to pull back.

He sent Sinclair ahead with ten of the men to report their actions to Stark and remained with the main body. Jacob moved to the rear and kept his eyes peeled on the surrounding forest. He remained concerned that the French might risk a counterattack.

With this threat over with for now, Jacob decided to keep his men in the woods just outside the first line of pickets.

By the time he had his men positioned and organized, he was surprised to see a large procession of weapons and provincial troops led by two officers riding side-by-side on horses. Behind the officers, several oxen and horses were pulling cannons and a number of whaleboats.

"How have your travels been?" Jacob called out to the officers. At first, he thought they would simply ignore him, but one of the officers stopped the long column and rode up next to Jacob.

"This country is no place to move heavy guns around," the young officer complained, removing his hat and wiping off several beads of sweat that rolled down the side of his face.

Jacob tipped the rim of his dirty cap and introduced himself saying, "Captain Sims of the Virginia Ranging Company; where are you boys from?"

"I'm Colonel Young and this is Colonel Frye," he replied, motioning to the other young man who had ridden up to his side. "Most of our men are from Massachusetts and New York. We are to report to Fort William Henry. I think we were expected a few weeks earlier, but these bloody cannons have been a plague on all of us."

"Your timing is great; we just had a skirmish with a scouting party of French and some of their savages," Jacob explained.

"Bloody hell, we heard from a couple of the other New York lads at Fort Edward that you fought them off and chased them back to Fort Carillon," Young said, now nervously looking around the darkness of the thick forest.

"Thank you, but I fear they might be still lurking about," Jacob said cautiously. "If you would like, I can send some of my lads to escort your column for a few miles."

"No need, sir, we should make good time from here," Colonel Frye spoke up. "We hope to reach William Henry by day break tomorrow."

Not wanting to prolong their trip any further, Jacob stood back and said, "Godspeed, sirs, and stay well."

"I hope to God that they have decided to retreat to Carillon and leave us be," Young said as he moved his horse back in front of the weapons and slowly continued on with the march.

Once the oxen and horses pushed past them and the ground finally settled down, Jacob could see that most of the provincials were young men who most likely had never been outside of their little towns and villages until now. He prayed the poor lads would never have to face the French or especially the Indians.

If they ran into the same party Jacob's men had just forced back, he feared most of them would make easy targets. He wondered if they would make it to William Henry unharmed.

After watching for almost a half hour, Jacob gave a heartfelt wave to the remains of the slow moving rear guard as they finally made their way along the road. He rejoined the rest of his men who were busy building up some fallen trees and branches to provide them some cover in case the French returned.

"The fort is going crazy with rumors and the men are preparing for an attack," Joshua reported after speaking with some of the rangers who had been sent with a return message from Stark.

Waiting until nightfall, Jacob decided that the French were not interested in continuing their fight. He ordered the men to pack up and return to the much safer confines of Fort Edward.

Sinclair was waiting for them when they arrived, and Jacob immediately asked, "Where is Webb?"

Sinclair motioned to the nearby guards and signaled Jacob and Joshua to move to a more private place to talk. "Webb is scheduled to return tomorrow, unless the French capture him on the way back," he said.

"We would not be that fortunate," Jacob replied and tried his best not to laugh.

Webb did return safely from William Henry, but gave no indication what might be happening at the other fort or what his plan was for his own men.

If the recent French attack was any indication, everything was in motion for a larger attack on one or both of the forts. However, Jacob still had no idea what role he would be playing in the impending battle.

"I heard from one of the guards that Colonel Munro has already requested more reinforcements, and Webb has sent word to Albany to call for additional militia to be organized and sent to Edward," Joshua said, as he and Jacob stood briefly on the banks of the river directly across from the busy fort.

Jacob decided he needed to speak with John Stark.

"Joshua, would you be so kind to find Mr. Sinclair and make sure the men are prepared to move out at a moment's notice?"

Jacob left Joshua and went directly to the officers' quarters, but noticed Stark was now down by the shoreline near the bridge. He was looking across the strangely peaceful river, watching the frenzied activity at the fort much like Jacob had been doing moments earlier.

"John, how are things?" Jacob called out, trying not to startle his friend. "I assume you have heard all the news, or should I say rumors?"

Stark didn't turn around, but waited for Jacob to make his way down the small embankment. "I think the rumors are unfortunately true and the French are setting out to attack William Henry," he said when Jacob arrived.

"What can we do about it?" Jacob asked. He stood beside Stark and looked across the river at the cannons that sat idle on the bastions.

Unable to hide his frustrations, Stark replied, "I just spoke with Webb and the damn coward wants us all to stay here. If the numbers are true and the French have brought their regulars, Canadians and a horde of savages with them, William Henry will not be able to hold out very long."

There was an uncomfortable silence between the two seasoned rangers until Stark continued, "From what I know of Munro, the bloody Scot will hold out bravely and expect Webb to send the much needed reinforcements…but I fear Webb will never release us to help."

As Stark spoke, it conjured images for Jacob of the atrocities at Fort Necessity and the Monongahela. At both places, Jacob had experienced firsthand the incompetence of the British army.

Once more, it seemed, the French had set in motion a plan to push the British back to the eastern coast. The vast wilderness and open waterways were the prizes that now awaited the victors.

Jacob could not believe he was once again part of one of the British army's foolish messes. With James still at the endangered William Henry and his beloved Maggie God only knew where, Jacob was anxious for the fight to be over so he could get back to the task of finding his family.

"I'm not certain what your plans are, John, but if the French attack Fort William Henry, I will not just sit here and protect Webb's sorry behind while the French kill all the poor souls in the fort," Jacob said, understanding his words meant disobeying direct orders.

"Aye, Jacob, we will have to do something..." Stark replied, staring across the river, shaking his head.

Chapter | **Twenty**

The winter chill had long since been forgotten as spring flourished. The high forest canopy had filled in with lush foliage that gave a dappled appearance to the sunlight that filtered through, and the weather grew warmer each day.

Maggie usually rose before dawn to nurse Israel; she enjoyed spending the quiet moments with her son before the village started buzzing. After she finished feeding her son one morning, a noise outside the long house startled her. Maggie stepped quickly into the clean morning air and, as soon as her eyes adjusted, saw One-Ear welcoming a very large group of warriors and a familiar-looking white man.

Immediately noticing her, One-Ear waved and called her over to meet with the visitors.

"Maggie, I think you will remember…" One-Ear said before being cut off by the well-dressed visitor.

"Ma'am, I hope you remember me," the middle-aged, immaculately groomed Englishman said, tipping his hat. "We met at a ceremonial meeting here at this village; my name is William Johnson."

As soon as the spark of recognition lit in her mind, she remembered that this was one of the men who had done nothing to assist One-Ear when she was physically taken from the village by the Ottawa.

In a frosty tone, she replied, "Sir, I am glad you have returned."

Once again before One-Ear could intercede, Johnson added, "I fear the last time we were both here, the Ottawa displayed their true colors. I too am happy to see you are well."

Johnson's attempt to smooth over what had taken place before did little to ease Maggie's pain, but she was far too interested in the purpose of his return to retain her resentment towards him. She could see that he had several hundred warriors with him and she found it difficult not to just burst out in a series of questions.

Although Jacob, One-Ear and Joshua valued her opinion much of the time, she understood her place and decided not to interrogate the Englishman. It was apparent that he was a close friend with the Mohawks and village elders.

One-Ear finally found the opportunity to speak and asked, "Sir, do you have news about the English to our south?"

Johnson politely nodded at Maggie and shifted his attention to One-Ear's question. "Aye, the French are on the move again. They have set their sights on our two forts, William Henry on Lake George and the other along the Hudson River," Johnson explained, as he walked alongside One-Ear and Maggie.

He picked up a stick and started to scratch a crude map in the dirt.

"The French are coming directly from the north via Lake Champlain," Johnson continued as he drew the lake and continued to sketch a much narrower lake that he called Lake George.

"This is where the French have their fort and the two English forts sit only a few miles apart. We are here near the great lake, maybe three or four days' walk southwest from us."

One-Ear and Maggie watched quietly as the Englishman continued to add details to his map. Johnson went on to explain, "The mountains sit between us and the forts, so we will need to leave shortly to reach Fort Edward on the Hudson River. I have sent for more warriors from the other nations to the east and expect to meet them at the fort in four days."

When he finished speaking, One-Ear finally asked, "Do you know how many French are coming from Canada? Do they bring their Abenaki dogs with them?"

Johnson pointed again at the upper section of his map and said, "They are many and their Abenaki brothers have joined them as well. I do fear that they have managed to convince many more of their Indian allies to join with them to fight the English this time."

Maggie remained deathly silent as she stared at the dirt map. Another battle was brewing between the English and French and she wondered where Jacob might be. She said a desperate pray that he might avoid the battle and be out searching for her instead.

As Johnson used the stick to quickly erase the map, they were joined by several village elders and half a dozen Mohawk warriors. The group walked towards the large meeting house where they were all ushered inside to talk further about the French situation.

As the mixed contingent entered the large house, Maggie hesitated by the door. She was uncertain if she was allowed to join them until One-Ear said, "Please, Maggie, I want you to hear what the Englishman has to say."

Excited that she would be allowed to partake in the talks, Maggie confidently walked inside and ignored the surprised glares from some of the elders. She quickly took a seat directly on the dirt floor by One-Ear.

When everyone was seated and ready for Johnson to speak, Maggie looked at One-Ear. She noticed he seemed to be happy with what was about to be discussed.

Once the formalities of the meeting and the exchange of wampum and gifts were over, Johnson stood up and addressed the large group, "Thank you for all your kindness and greetings for myself and my Mohawk brothers. I know all my Iroquois Confederacy brothers have remained loyal to their English father in London. Although you have not fought by our sides, you have stayed neutral and not sided with the French."

Johnson talked slowly, waiting for his interpreter to translate the message he was conveying. Maggie watched One-Ear's reaction to what the Indian agent was saying, as well as the reactions of the many elders that sat across from her.

Once his young Mohawk finished his lengthy translation, Johnson continued, "The French are on the move again, and their Canadian, Ottawa and

Abenaki allies are at their side. They have moved down from Quebec and have their sights set on removing the English from the New York territory."

An odd hush came over the crowd as Johnson's message was relayed by his interpreter. It was clear that his speech had the interest of the entire house.

"If we let the French take both forts," Johnson continued, "there will be little English influence left in the area. I have word that the French have strengthened their numbers at Fort Carillon and will, if they have not already done so, launch an attack on the forts."

He paused and looked around the room before adding, "If the French take the forts and remove the English, they will soon turn their attentions on the people of this land that did not take up the tomahawk against the English. They will punish them for their relations…no matter if they fought with the English or simply remained neutral."

Once again, Johnson stood back to watch the reactions of the packed house as his translator conveyed his strongly-worded speech. He looked directly at One-Ear who rose to his feet and walked to his side.

"If the French reach Albany, all will be lost and the French will win control of the entire territory," Johnson reiterated forcefully. "That is why I have come to you today to ask for all your strong warriors to join with me and travel to the English forts to help our fellow brothers fight the French."

All eyes were on One-Ear as he confidently waited for silence. "I have spoken with and listened to our brother and have told him we will send all our warriors to help him," he said.

A large cheer erupted and a number of the people jumped up and displayed their unbridled agreement with One-Ear's grand statement.

Maggie was unsure what to think. She could see that One-Ear was happy, but she was concerned at the thought of how vulnerable the village would be without any able-bodied men. If the French won this engagement, what would become of the village? How could the young and old men defend the women and children against the expected repercussions of the victorious French and their allies?

While most of the crowd dispersed and moved their celebration out into the village's main grounds, Maggie waited to have a word with One-Ear. She watched Johnson walk out with the elders; he was smiling, satisfied with his small victory.

One-Ear had finally managed to work his way to Maggie and, once the remaining few people left the house, he waited for her to speak first.

Unsure where to start, Maggie finally launched into what was on her mind, "Why are you so willing to give up all this peace to fight someone else's war?"

She was so overwhelmed by such a quick change in her circumstances and the reaction of the villagers that was so against her own feelings, she didn't wait for One-Ear to reply. "And what about me?" she cried. "Are you just going to leave me behind?"

"This is best for my people," One-Ear said, appearing to be insulted by Maggie's questions. "If we do nothing, we might just find ourselves an enemy of both the French and English. We have sat back long enough; now we must fight."

Maggie wanted to continue, but from his answer and his tone, she knew he had his mind made up. No matter what she said, he would not alter his stance.

The two friends walked out and saw how the news had already spread around the village. From the reaction of the excited villagers, Maggie said, "You have made them happy."

One-Ear smiled proudly.

"But will they feel the same way once their dead sons, fathers and brothers never return?" Maggie added quietly and left One-Ear to his thoughts.

Deciding to stay back and watch the proceedings, Maggie observed as the women served the men several plates of a freshly slaughtered wild dog that had been cut up and thrown in a large pot with winter vegetables and some leftover fall potatoes.

Maggie stood back and thought over her conversation with One-Ear. If she knew her Jacob, he had likely moved north in search of her after Fort Stevens was captured. If he was anywhere in the vicinity of the English forts Johnson had mentioned, she had no doubt that he too would soon become involved in the latest French entanglement.

For a brief moment, Maggie toyed with the notion of leaving Israel behind with the village women and going with One-Ear. She knew her newborn would be in good hands, and if she went with the warriors, she might be able to find Jacob.

As quickly as the idea struck, she dismissed it. She knew that she could never leave her baby behind, no matter how safe he would be.

Lost in thought, her eyes had remained on the warriors as they enjoyed their meal. As she re-focused on the scene before her, Maggie saw One-Ear get up and move directly towards her.

He had a plate with some fruit and bread on it and smiled once he reached Maggie. "You need to eat some food. I didn't think you would eat the wild dog, so I brought you some bread and dried fruit."

Thankful for his company and the much needed food, Maggie finished off the plate almost as quickly as One-Ear handed it to her. "I thought about asking to come with you," she said, "but I knew I couldn't leave my baby behind. Would you please watch out for Jacob?" Speaking the words aloud nearly brought her to tears.

"He will be happy to know he has another son," One-Ear said, reaching out to touch Maggie's hand in reassurance. "I will look for him and be the one to pass on the good news to him."

The celebration went on for several more hours and Maggie just held onto Israel and watched the village enjoy the news.

After spending most of his time discussing details with Johnson, One-Ear returned to Maggie and reached out to hold Israel. He sat next to her on the small log, and her heart swelled to see him play with her son like an older brother. Despite the doubtful words that always seemed to come out when she was upset with him, Maggie never doubted that One-Ear truly cared about her, and now about her son.

"The young one is happy," One-Ear said, bouncing the ever-smiling Israel on his leg. "I have heard from some of the women that he is not much of a crier."

"He is a good baby, but I can only pray that it will last. Jacob will be happy to add another boy to continue on the family's blood lines." Maggie smiled, trying to lessen the tension.

"He will make a good warrior one day," he continued, not looking at Maggie's reaction. "Strong and silent is good for a warrior's way."

"Maggie, I know you are afraid," he continued after a moment, "but we will stop the French, and then I will come back. Our village has no reason to fear being left alone to defend itself against the French. I will bring back all of our warriors and we will return with many prizes and a number of tales of our great victory."

His confidence was impressive, yet Maggie still had reason to worry. The French and their allies had defeated the English every time they encountered each other. If the French did win once again, Maggie could not imagine what might happen to this village and the people left behind.

Trying not to make One-Ear feel bad about his decision, Maggie continued asking questions, "When do you leave?"

Watching the villagers dance with the Mohawk warriors, One-Ear replied distractedly, "We leave when the sun rises. The Englishman wants us to reach the mountains within a day or two."

She was shocked at how soon they were to leave and hardly knew what else to say. After a moment, she whispered, "You will look for Jacob and Joshua?"

"I will, and I will bring them back to you after we defeat the French," he replied with immediate confidence.

Maggie did her best not to cry or show any other emotions and just enjoyed watching One-Ear play with Israel. After a few minutes of play, he kissed Israel on the head and looked at Maggie.

"I will send a messenger back with news," he said, then lowered his gaze back down to the baby in his lap. "I really believe what I said, but just in case we do not return, the elders have been instructed to leave this place and move towards the land of the Five Nations people. They will protect the villagers from the French."

Neither of them had much more to say after that, but Maggie forced a slight smile as One-Ear handed Israel to her. He quickly left them sitting alone on the log and Maggie was soon comforted by Anne who approached and offered a friendly hug.

Johnson made a point to offer his goodbyes to Maggie as well. "I will keep him safe and ensure all the warriors return," he said, glancing at One-Ear.

"If you are able, sir," Maggie said, "could you enquire about a Captain Murr...I mean Sims? He is with a ranging company and might be at one of the forts."

"I will do what I can, ma'am," Johnson offered and tipped his hat before he joined the band of Mohawk warriors.

"What do you think of all this?" Maggie asked Anne.

"This is what they do, Maggie," Anne replied calmly, betraying no concern whatsoever at the fate of the village. "Before we all came and took their land, the tribes would fight each other over their land or the best hunting grounds."

"I understand all of that," Maggie said, "but what will happen to us if the French win again? Do you not fear that the French or, worse, their allies might find us and see that we have no warriors to protect us?"

Anne had no answer.

Holding onto Israel, Maggie prayed for a French defeat. More than anything else, she feared that being forced to relocate one more time would destroy the last of the hope she held of reuniting her family.

Once the villagers began to return to their homes, Maggie took Israel back to the longhouse. She was very uneasy about the entire plan and prayed that One-Ear might somehow change his mind.

She hardly slept, between feeding Israel and worrying about what might result from the latest developments. She could hardly believe that One-Ear was about to leave her…again.

Maggie rose to see the warriors off and stood outside the village's walls. She watched as One-Ear organized his warriors.

Johnson had already departed with some of his Mohawks before the sun rose. They had the important duty of clearing the trails of any problems. From what she had heard the night before, the trails to the south were a series of poorly-cleared old Delaware hunting paths and some well-used main trails that traversed through the mountains, bogs and swamps.

One-Ear spotted Maggie near the village entrance and crossed over to her. "Do not worry, Maggie," he said, reading the emotion on her face. "I have prayed to the gods that we will have victory and that the village will be protected."

"You stay well, One-Ear," Maggie replied tearfully. "I'm sure we will see you again soon enough and you will be greeted as a hero by your village."

After a quick hug, she stood back and watched him slip into the open outer field with a long line of his hand-picked warriors. He turned back briefly to give Maggie a wave and soon disappeared into the woods.

With One-Ear and most of the warriors absent, the village had an odd assortment of young and old men. Maggie was impressed by how efficiently the women took control of the village and organize all the chores that needed to be done.

Maggie soon came to realize that One-Ear's campaign would likely extend throughout the warmer summer months. She remained busy caring for Israel, but she still managed to help out wherever she could in the village. She valued the friendship and acceptance she felt among the village women and found herself at peace despite her dear friend's absence.

No word had been sent from One-Ear regarding their whereabouts or if they had encountered the French yet.

As the weather turned hotter, the bugs returned with a vengeance. Maggie did her best to keep them from Israel, but she finally relented to the other women and covered his exposed skin with mud to ward off the bothersome insects.

Some of the men left behind received word from a number of traders that the French had great numbers in the south, and would indeed be attacking the English forts.

Maggie's hopes that Jacob might make his way to her weakened with every passing day. Israel was a constant reminder of their love, and she did her best to keep her mind busy.

The next several weeks were unusually quiet and she found joy in watching Israel grow and get stronger. The men did their best to hunt and fish while the women sowed and planted the outer fields with summer corn, squash and other vegetables. Maggie even started her own garden of beans and root vegetables.

Even without the protective presence of One-Ear, Maggie settled into a nice, tranquil routine.

Her peace would not last long…

Chapter | **Twenty-One**

News had finally reached the fort that the French were indeed approaching Fort William Henry.

The reports stated that they had brought with them five thousand savages and Canadians, supplemented with several companies of regulars. They also had full command of the lakes and could freely move their men and artillery from as far away as Fort St. Frederic at the mouth of Lake Champlain.

Jacob could feel the tension rising among the rangers on the island. Stark, for one, was considering disobeying Webb's orders. Jacob could hardly blame him; his own anxiety was multiplied by the thought of James surrounded by enemy raiders.

Joshua kept the men on alert, but Jacob could see that most of the rangers were tiring of waiting for something to happen while their mates sat behind the walls of William Henry awaiting the French.

Jacob had tired of the constant meetings with Webb and his officers. Most of them were far more concerned with protecting their own interests at Fort Edward than assisting their fellow officers trapped at Fort William Henry.

He understood to some extent that Webb's reluctance to send men to reinforce William Henry was due to the belief that by weakening his own fort, the French could simply attack it and move onto Albany. However, it was obvious that the French had their attention set on Fort William Henry, and Webb had truly shown that he had no intentions to send reinforcements.

The arrival of a thousand inexperienced militiamen from New Jersey and New York did little to convince Webb he could spare any help for Munro. Most of the new men were simple farmers, merchants or shop owners and were viewed as no match to go up against seasoned French troops.

The Ottawa and the several other tribes who sided with the French were far more of a concern to Jacob than the regulars themselves. He knew from experience that the French could not control their savages, and that is what scared him the most.

Jacob volunteered his men to be used as messengers between the forts and his offer was reluctantly accepted. The rangers took control of the messages Webb needed sent through the sieging French lines. With most of the allied savages controlling the only usable road between the forts, the runners were now forced to use old hunting trails and swampy, bug-infested paths. Jacob sent out his volunteers in patrols of three men, one carrying the dispatch sewn directly into the inside pocket of his coat, and the others directed to ensure the message made it through.

"Keep moving and stay away from the main trails," he told every trio that volunteered to run the gauntlet between the forts. "The savages are expecting you and they are patrolling most of the paths that run towards the fort. Use the swamps to the east and keep moving through the night. Do your best to protect the messages. Once you enter the fort, resupply yourselves and get home as soon as you can."

The tension and stress at Fort Edward and Rogers Island continued to increase as the noises of the French heavy guns began to echo along the well-traveled road between them. The rangers remained on edge, listening and longing to receive orders to charge down the road to relieve their surrounded mates.

"If the constant thunder from the guns means anything, William Henry will be taken in no time," Jacob commented to Stark, who had made his way down to the frontline pickets.

"I can't just wait for Munro to surrender and do nothing about it," Stark spat in frustration. "What the hell is Webb thinking? He has more than enough men to attack the French. Does he not realize that if he just waits, the French will just push down the road and do the same to this fort?"

While the rangers watched the woods and prayed for the men at the other fort, noise from Fort Edward caused most of them react. Jacob and Stark immediately rushed to the fort to find out what was happening.

Several hundred Mohawk warriors and militia had arrived.

When Jacob and Stark entered the fort, they were greeted by the scene of Webb speaking with the spokesman for the new arrivals. By the expression on the man's face, he was not happy with what Webb was trying to explain.

Caring nothing for protocol, Stark walked directly up to the two men as they argued. Jacob remained by Stark's side and listened as he interrupted the officers.

"Sir," Stark said, addressing the newcomer, "have you brought men who are finally willing to fight the French, or will you also prefer sitting back to hear your mates being battered into ashes?"

"Captain, this is William Johnson from the Mohawk Valley," Webb explained, attempting to hide his disdain for Stark's ungentlemanly behavior. "He is one of our Indian agents and has been kind enough to bring some of his Mohawks to help us."

Johnson stepped forward to introduce himself to the defiant ranging officers, "As your general explained in part, I am William Johnson, but my intentions are to help Colonel Munro with the defense of his fort."

"I am John Stark and this is Jacob Sims. We have been stuck listening to the heavy guns being fired off in the distance, but have been unable to assist our mates." He clearly feared few repercussions from General Webb.

"We all have friends expecting us to help them while they are being sieged by the French," Jacob added.

Webb interrupted to plead his case, "Gentlemen, I must make myself clear; I have been in constant communication with Colonel Munro and have assured him that if the time comes, I will send men forward to relieve his fort."

Jacob pulled Stark back by his arm and whispered in his ear, "We should get back to the men, John; I fear you are only wasting your breath."

Heeding Jacob's words, Stark refused to offer the officers a salute and simply walked away with Jacob.

As they left the fort, Jacob said, "John, it appears we will have to act on our own. Webb will never release any of his men to aid Munro."

The two rangers returned to find their men waiting with the pickets.

Joshua approached Jacob and reported that a few of the men had left to scout up the trail to see if any of the messengers needed their help.

The pounding thunder from the exchange of heavy guns between the sieging French and the brave soldiers behind the walls of William Henry was increasing with every hour. The constant noise was taking a toll on the men at Fort Edward. Jacob and Stark stood among them, watching the woods and hoping that at any moment the men sent out with messages would return safely.

It wasn't long after their first meeting back at the fort that William Johnson made his way down to the picket line where the rangers were now camped out. He brought along several Mohawks, who spoke amongst themselves during most of their visit.

"Gentlemen, this is certainly not the best of circumstances to meet under," Johnson said apologetically as he took up a post by Jacob and Stark. "To be frank, General Webb appears to be afraid of his own shadow, but I pray that common sense will prevail."

"I fear your prayers will be wasted sir," Jacob replied.

Johnson noticed that the rangers appeared uncomfortable being in such close proximity to his Mohawks. He quickly reassured them, saying, "They are friendly and not to be feared. They hate the French and their Ottawa dogs just as much as any man here."

"I spent time as a captive of the Abenaki and they treated me well," Stark replied. "I have great respect for your Mohawk."

"And you, sir?" Johnson asked, looking at Jacob and waiting for his reply.

Giving it a moment's thought, Jacob chose his answer carefully, "My wife and children were taken from me by the Huron, and so my feelings for the savages are different from John's. The Mohawk from the north have fought with the French in the past. How do you know that your savages will raise their muskets against their brothers?"

Surprised by the question, Johnson did his best to defend his friends, "They will fight the French because I have asked them to. As for their northern brothers, I can't honestly say; only time will tell."

When he had finished speaking, Johnson continued looking right at Jacob, and then he appeared to remember something he wanted to say.

"Captain Sims…I think I might have met someone you know. Are you acquainted with a fine lady named Maggie?"

Jacob was shocked by his unexpected question but remained guarded as he said, "Yes, sir…my wife's name is Maggie. How do you know her?"

"I have met her on a couple occasions now," Johnson replied. "The last time was only a few days ago at an Iroquois village northwest of here, where I stopped to gather more warriors."

Jacob did his best to stay calm as he pressed the Indian agent for additional details, "How is she? Was she a prisoner?"

Johnson hadn't expected to strike such a nerve as he hadn't realized that Maggie was asking about her husband. Before he answered, he called over one of his Mohawks and whispered something in the man's ear.

As the Mohawk disappeared, Johnson responded, "She appeared well and she was able to move freely around the village. In fact, she appeared quite active in the affairs of the village."

Interrupting before he could explain further, Jacob asked, "Did you speak with her or only see her?"

"Yes, we did speak; she made a point to ask me to look out for you." Johnson replied.

A strange silence gripped the men and Jacob just stood, taking in the news. His mind was spinning and he was unsure what to say next.

His thoughts were shaken back to the present when one of the rangers called an alert that he had seen someone approaching through the eastern woods. Jacob signaled his men to shoulder their weapons in case it was an enemy approaching.

A few moments later, two messengers cleared the forest line and fell to the ground in exhaustion. Their mates immediately lowered their weapons and offered them some water. When the two gulped down the contents of several canteens, they approached Jacob where he still stood with Stark and Johnson.

"Sit, lads, and catch your breath," Jacob said as he assisted the men onto a massive tree stump nearby and waited for them to speak.

"Sorry, sir," one of the men began, "but we have been on the run for over two days. The bloody Ottawa have most of the upper woods covered and we barely made it past them. They caught Riley; the last we saw of him was with a tomahawk buried in his back. Young Lawson here was struck on his arm just as we entered the woods, but I managed to smash one of the murderers in the face with the butt of my musket and dispatched the savage."

"Get these men some more water and a few pieces of pork," Jacob called out to his men before encouraging the messengers to continue.

Stark stepped up and asked, "How was the fort holding out?"

The messenger looked up and, without saying a word, just shook his head and put it down.

His silent reply made both Johnson and Stark react with further disdain for Webb. His refusal to assist Munro, a fellow British officer, gave them further reason to feel he was simply a coward.

"Are you both carrying messages?" Johnson asked abruptly. When the two men nodded, he said, "Give them to me; I will take them to Webb myself."

Less concerned with the content of the messages and more concerned with what the men could tell him about the events at the fort, Jacob encouraged them to do as Johnson requested.

After they surrendered the small, sealed notes, Johnson thanked them and was off with his Mohawks towards the fort. Stark was right behind them, desperately interested in knowing what Munro's message said.

Returning to the men, Jacob pressed for more news, "How are the men doing?"

The same messenger who spoke before, continued, "From what I could manage to see, the French have been digging their way towards the fort and are pounding the walls without mercy. The bloody savages and some of the militia have formed a half circle around from the lake to the far woods. It is next to impossible to clear their lines."

The news silenced the nearby rangers as they all listened intently to what the man had to say.

"Most of the time the men are just huddled together, keeping their heads down and covering up from all the dirt and mud that the heavy guns have pushed about," the messenger explained. "I feel for the poor families that are trapped at the fort with no place to go."

Curious to hear what the silent messenger had to say, Jacob called over Joshua to ask if he knew the man's name.

"We call him Lawson, but I don't know his given name," Joshua replied. "He is a good shot and basically sticks to himself. I heard his brother was killed during our raid at Kittanning. From the look of him, he needs a doctor."

"Mr. Lawson, how is your wound?" Jacob asked. "Can you add anything to all of this?"

Anticipating Lawson to speak, the men stood by and waited.

"The damn savage caught me on the arm, but it looks far worse than it feels, sir," Lawson finally replied. "I do think the French will take the fort by force unless Munro surrenders soon. The few men I had an opportunity to speak with said they were far more frightened at the thought of the savages running loose around the fort than the bloody French."

Jacob wanted to press the men for more information, but Joshua finally stepped in and said, "Sir, we should let the men have a rest, and Mr. Lawson needs to get his wound dressed. We can speak with them once they are in better condition."

Heeding Joshua's words, Jacob nodded and said to the two men, "Thank you, lads. You need to get some more food and water, and some rest. We can talk later about what you saw. I will send a couple rangers to escort you back to the island."

The two men, clearly tired, nodded their thanks.

Stark soon returned from the fort to tell Jacob what was in the notes to Webb. "Gentlemen, the news from William Henry is not good," he reported. "We will have to decide what we should do to help our fellow rangers trapped behind the French lines."

"Did the note describe the situation?" Joshua asked before Jacob could get the words out.

Stark spoke slowly, choosing his words carefully, "Munro is basically begging for reinforcements. He plainly stated that if Webb doesn't send a relief force, the fort will be lost."

Jacob could barely hide his anger and asked, "What did our Indian agent say about all of this?"

"Webb still appears to be uninterested in sending men and weakening his forces. As for Johnson, he is livid and I left the two arguing about what needed to be done next. Webb said to both of us that he has orders to protect the road to Albany. He suggested that Munro would do well to negotiate the best terms he can with the French."

The three men let this latest report settle in their minds, and quickly realized that their only options were to abide by Webb's orders or ignore him and take the rangers forward to do what they could to help their fellow mates.

"Before I forget, Webb gave me two more messages to be taken to Munro. We have orders to send four messengers to the fort. If all the reports are accurate, we just might be sending four men to their deaths." Stark looked to Jacob for his suggestion.

Joshua stopped the men and pointed out a group of Mohawks that were approaching them along the tree line.

There were six, and just as they came within shouting distance, Jacob said to Joshua, "Lad, look at that savage in the back. Does he not look like your friend you called One-Ear?"

Jacob no sooner got the words out than Joshua called out to the approaching Mohawk, "One-Ear, my brother, is that you?"

A familiar voice called back, "Yes, brother, it is I!"

Jacob watched in wonder as the two old friends ran to embrace each other. He walked towards the two young men and offered his hand to One-Ear, saying, "Are you a ghost or truly the same young lad we last left outside the walls of Fort Machault?"

"Yes, sir, I am the same," One-Ear grinned as he shook Jacob's hand.

One-Ear motioned for the rest of the Mohawk to return to their encampment towards the eastern edge of the fort.

John Stark remained behind and waited to be introduced.

"One-Ear, this is Lieutenant John Stark," Jacob said.

After all the formalities were over with, the four men left the pickets to do their duty and Jacob told them he would send more men to reinforce them. Not wanting to go too far from the front lines, the four men stood on a small embankment that provided them a nice panoramic view of the entire fort's outer works, including Rogers Island.

Jacob had so many questions to ask One-Ear about Maggie, but he managed to control himself and concentrate on the matters at hand. "John, I am going to take the messages to Munro myself," he said. "I cannot truly expect one of my own men to risk their lives for this bloody Webb bastard."

Stark held onto the messages and forcefully replied, "Your place is with your men, not running some message between forts."

"If you will recall, John, my son is at that fort. I cannot forego an opportunity to see him now, especially if the fort is going to fall." Fatherly anguish flashed across his face as he looked at Stark.

"Sir, if you are willing to go," Joshua interjected quickly, "then please let me take the other message."

One-Ear immediately piped in to add, "I will also go with you."

Unable to convince the men that they should send others in their place, Stark relented and handed the messages to both Joshua and Jacob's out-reached hands. "In good conscience, I do this under protest," he said, "but I feel I would just be wasting my breath once again."

"John, you will have to explain to Johnson that we took along one of his warriors," Jacob said as he shoved the wax-sealed message into the pocket of his inner coat.

"I will speak with Johnson and also have one of my men get you sup-plied for your trip," Stark offered, though it was plain by his tone, he was still not in support of their reckless mission.

"John, if you decide to take your lads up the road, please let my rangers join you," Jacob said.

Before he left to get the promised supplies, Stark reluctantly nodded and gave them the same advice Jacob had given all the other messengers, "Stay off the main road and keep to the side trails. What I have heard from the other runners is that they only made it through by running all out and reaching the outer entrenchment on the high ground just outside of the fort. Keep to the swamp and the lake. Godspeed gentlemen; I pray we will see each other again."

Jacob did not know what to say and tried to calm his nerves by asking, "John, do you know what the messages say?"

Stark dropped his head and said, "Webb suggests that Munro take 'the best terms' the French offer him. He also told him he most likely could not get reinforcements to assist him in time."

With that, Stark left and the three men stood waiting for their supplies to arrive. Most of their time was spent checking over their muskets and ensuring they had enough powder to make it safely through the rough wilderness trails that sat between the forts.

Jacob glanced at One-Ear and again all the questions of Maggie rose up in his mind, but this was not the time. His brief conversation with Johnson regarding Maggie had given him hope. Despite the risk he was about to undertake, he prayed he would also find James alive inside the doomed fort.

As he looked at his two young, faithful friends, Jacob wanted to be absolutely sure they were prepared to risk their lives to carry such helpless messages. "Joshua, One-Ear, I would not think any less of either of you if you backed out of this," he said.

One-Ear simply continued to clean his musket and look over his knife and war club while Joshua replied without pause, "We have traveled through far worse, sir. Now One-Ear is with us. I have little to fear from the French or their Ottawa dogs."

Joshua's confidence certainly helped Jacob feel much better. After a short wait, a couple of rangers arrived with two small sacks containing hard bread, salted pork and two sticks of cheese.

Satisfied that they were ready to make the trek, Jacob was somewhat disappointed that Stark had not returned to see them off.

Just as they entered the darkness of the first line of heavy woods, a voice echoed from behind. They saw the shadowy figure of a ranger running wildly across the earthen works towards them until he finally came into full view of the three waiting men.

"Mr. Sinclair, what do you think you are doing?" Jacob called out just as Sinclair ran past the pickets.

Struggling to catch his breath, Sinclair doubled over and spit before he answered, "Lieutenant Stark told me that you were leaving for Fort William Henry and I want to come along."

Jacob didn't know what to say, but they had no time to argue about it. They needed to use as much of the good light remaining as they could. If they pushed hard, they figured they should reach Halfway Creek by nightfall.

"I asked the lieutenant to watch over the rest of the lads and he agreed to," Sinclair explained and smiled at Joshua.

"We will speak about this once we return, Robert," Jacob said, suppressing a grin. "For now, please take the rear and keep your wits about you; I'm certain the French are expecting us."

He was glad to have his reliable friend watching his back.

Sinclair added, "Lieutenant Stark asked that if time warrants, please send him a message as to whether or not you think he should bring his rangers up to reinforce the fort."

Now with everything in order, the four men found a small path away from the main road, which took them directly north. They soon found a small creek that they hoped would lead them to the swampy area by the lake.

They maintained a single file with One-Ear acting as the advanced guard. He kept a quick pace, and all four men pushed very hard.

None of the men had traveled along the tiny trails they were using, but the thunder of the heavy guns and cannons made the ground shake and assisted them in maintaining their course.

The darkening night sky lit up with every blast and Jacob's prayed that each shot would not be the last.

While they were still some distance away, other sounds, including screams from the fort, began to reach their ears. Even the smell of the numerous fires set by the enemy waffled through the air around them.

They pressed on through the darkness for several hours before One-Ear began to have trouble negotiating the narrow, rugged trail. The men were tired and needed to rest before pushing any farther forward.

Jacob stopped and looked around, and he felt that they must be close to the swampy terrain. None of the four felt comfortable traversing such terrain in the dark of night. If they expected to reach the fort and successfully fight through the French lines, they would need to be at their best.

Jacob sent Joshua ahead to see if he could find the encampment his rangers had used a few weeks back. Before long, the two young men led Jacob and Sinclair to what was left of the camp.

Finding a nice tree that had fallen during the winter, Jacob took a seat. He threw his sack on the ground and pointed at it, saying, "Get some food, lads. If we rest for a few hours, we can leave just before first light and make the fort well before noon."

"Would it not be better to wait and attempt to get past the savages during the night?" Sinclair asked, stretching out his tired legs and sitting against a tree.

"Time is not a friend, Robert," Jacob replied. "You are right that using the night as cover would be better, yet we cannot sit around and waste more time."

The four men sat in the dark and shared some of the salted pork and hard cheese. There was a dim glow coming from the direction of the fort, which was due to the relentless heavy guns that fired steadily through the night. The swampy area was close enough that the air was thick with flying bugs and swarms of mosquitoes that showed the tired men no mercy.

"Sir, have you considered splitting up?" Joshua asked abruptly as he slapped his arm to kill several bugs. "We might be able to move faster and meet up at the fort."

The idea had crossed his mind, but Jacob felt far more secure having the others with him and simply replied, "I would only consider it after I can see what shape the fort is in. The savages appear to be more concerned with watching the main road, so we should have a relatively clear run to the edge of the woods. The swamp might slow us down, but if it keeps us away from the savages, then I feel it is the best way. From there, I am not sure what to expect. I like our number; the four of us have a far better chance of surviving together then apart."

Whether any of the others agreed or disagreed with his logic, they didn't say anything more.

With the guns still blasting through the night, Jacob knew that the chance of getting much sleep was slim, but he just tried to get himself comfortable. At some point, the bugs appeared to disperse. Even the mosquitoes seemed to give the men a break.

Joshua and One-Ear were up well before the others, but Sinclair rose soon after. It took several nudges to Jacob's shoulder to wake him, but then he immediately got ready to keep moving.

"I didn't think I would get much rest, but it appears I did," Jacob said sheepishly. He was glad it was still dark enough to cover his embarrassment.

One-Ear headed up the trail while Jacob was still gathering his gear, but soon all four of them were back on the trail with Sinclair in his normal position covering the rear. The men moved along well and could soon smell the musky stench of the swamp.

Their pace slowed as soon as they reached the muddy, spongy ground. At some points, they found themselves thigh-deep in the soggy marsh, and Jacob's original hope of reaching the outer limits of the fort before the sun rose appeared to be impossible.

Ironically, the early morning sky was darkened by the relentless firing of the heavy guns and cannons and therefore provided some unexpected cover for the tired, dirty men. They pushed slowly onward, and eventually the noise of the cannons became steadily louder.

Jacob guessed that they had finally come close to reaching the edge of Fort William Henry's outer field. The field sat just in front of the makeshift outer entrenchment that sat several hundred paces before the fort.

Still deep within the woods and surrounded by the same swamp that had hindered their movement for most of the trip, Jacob was surprised by the fact that they had not run into any French patrols or Ottawa warriors. He called out to both Joshua and One-Ear to wait and reorganize, but they were too far away to hear him. He stopped moving and waited for Sinclair to catch up.

Waiting alone for a few long minutes, Jacob cursed himself for letting Joshua and One-Ear get too far ahead. He had only lost sight of the pair for the briefest of time, but he knew these woods could engulf a person easily.

"Not much is moving, sir," Sinclair confirmed Jacob's own observations.

"Maybe they are concentrating on the fort and have no reason to fear anything from Fort Edward," Jacob suggested, briefly standing up to scan the fields.

"We have sent out a number of messengers that we have yet to hear back from," Sinclair said. "Maybe the French have intercepted a few of the messages and realize Webb will not send reinforcements."

A distant sound of musket fire made both men shoulder their muskets and slowly edge forward along the trail. Jacob feared for Joshua and One-Ear and assumed that they had run into some trouble up ahead.

The musket fire intensified as Jacob and Sinclair slowly moved forward. They moved deliberately, careful not to walk foolishly into an ambush. Soon, Jacob could hear Joshua's voice call out, but he couldn't see him.

Jacob decided to forgo normal protocol and called out loudly to him, "Lad, where are you?"

A brief silence broke the consistent firing as Joshua called out again, "Sir, we are just ahead, but we are pinned down by five or six savages."

Before either man could offer a reply, the trail ahead of them was once again blanketed by another round of musket fire and thick smoke.

"Should we move off the path and try to flank the ambushers?" Jacob asked Sinclair.

Quick to answer, Sinclair suggested, "Let's move to the left and get a better picture of what is happening. The patrol might not think we would use the swamp. We might be able to surprise them."

Nodding in agreement, Jacob led the way. Without the luxury of using a cut path, working through thick underbrush and waterlogged ground was next to impossible. Sometimes getting down on their stomachs, the two men moved along a line of pine trees and finally caught his first glimpse of what Joshua and One-Ear were facing.

They noticed that there were actually far more than six savages firing on the young men. Jacob quickly scanned around the dense woods to spot any additional shooters.

Lying prone under an overgrown pine tree, Jacob motioned to Sinclair that if they could move ahead of the two men pinned down, they might be able to do as Sinclair suggested and flank the left side of the attackers.

Unable to signal or get either of young men's attention, Jacob and Sinclair worked their way around the trees and finally had an unobstructed view of the patrol. They were surprised to find that the patrol was made up of several Ottawa warriors and supplemented by members of the Canadian militia.

As they lay side by side, Jacob asked, "What do you think, Robert? Shall we get closer or just open up on them from here?" The continuing cannon fire masked their voices, and the two were able to discuss their options without threat of being heard and located.

"This is a good spot, Jacob," Sinclair said. "If I fire first then reload, you can then fire and we should be able to keep up a steady volley on them."

"Agreed," Jacob said, shouldering his musket, "but let's get this started. If we wait too long, they will overrun the lads and we will be running for our lives to get back to Fort Edward."

Sinclair shouldered his musket as well and nodded quickly before squeezing the trigger. A large puff of white smoke shrouded any damage the first shot made as Jacob immediately fired off his musket. In no time, Sinclair had his musket primed and took another shot.

The rapid speed of the accurate fire unleashed on the unsuspecting flank of the patrol drove them back and opened up an opportunity for Joshua and One-Ear to make a run for it. Jacob and Sinclair kept up the steady fire until the young men were only a few feet away from them.

As Sinclair took his next shot, Jacob reached out and pulled Joshua and One-Ear down beside them. The four men quickly organized themselves and sent another blast of musket fire toward the confused patrol.

Firing one more round, Jacob motioned for the others to stop shooting and listen. The woods had gone deathly silent; after waiting a few more seconds, the four men moved back and decided to make a run for it to the fort.

They cared nothing about staying in single file and ran as fast as their legs could carry them to the far tree line.

Jacob was the first to reach the thick line of trees that opened up to the far field towards the besieged and battered Fort William Henry. The initial sight of the fort's condition made him stop as if he hit an invisible wall.

The others were right on his heels but stopped too as soon as they saw the desperate sight before them.

"Bloody hell, sir," Joshua said as he looked upon the French position and the guns that had made the earth quake all the way to Fort Edward. "The poor lads inside must be frightened to near death."

Jacob was speechless. The French laborers had pushed enough earth aside to move a line of trenches practically to the fort's walls. There were savages all over the place, running around like bees that had just gotten their hive knocked down. The thought of James huddled under the bastions frightened him and he fought the urge to just dash recklessly through the French lines to rescue his son.

Not a soul could be spotted along the upper walls. If not for a sporadic blast from one of the cannons perched high on the bastions, Jacob would swear that the fort was already abandoned.

From what could be seen of the lake, it appeared the rumors that it was controlled by the French were accurate. With no British vessels available, the French were free to move additional troops in from Fort Carillon.

Jacob noticed that the boats brought by the company of provincials he had met on the road between the forts were now being used for cover by some of the same troops. They were stationed at a make-shift entrenchment a mere six hundred paces from the front of the main fort. The men had dug the entrenchment several feet into the ground and placed the boats around the exterior to give them extra cover, as well as to slow any advance by the French or the Ottawa. They also had six small cannons placed around the inside earthen wall of the trench to keep back any advancement from the nearby enemy.

Jacob wasn't sure why Munro would have some of the men placed outside the fort's walls. They appeared so vulnerable to an attack, but he wondered if they should just make a dash towards the entrenchment anyway.

"What can we do, sir?" Joshua asked, looking also to One-Ear for his reaction.

Before Jacob could answer, One-Ear replied, "The French have the Ottawa and Huron shooting at whatever moves, pinning down any chances the English have of keeping them back."

Keeping down as best they could, the four men could see that to their right sat more of the swampy area they had already struggled through. Beyond it, the lake was under the full control of the French.

They noticed an entrenchment built outside the earthen works and encircling ditch of the nearby fort. It was manned by about hundred men with six cannons used to reinforce the strategically positioned camp. Unfortunately, it was targeted by the Ottawa and Canadian militia, who had the men trapped and incessantly harassed them.

"The French know we are here and will be waiting for us to show ourselves again," Jacob said ominously. "I think they care little if we make it to the fort, but making it back to Edward will be next to impossible now."

"We can't do much from here, sir," Sinclair said. "If the French will let us reach the fort or even just the entrenchment, we should just accept their gift."

The sky was far darker now, and the surrounding air was thick with white clouds and the pungent smell of powder that spewed from the heavy guns encircling the fort. The darkened sky did provide them with some much needed shadow cover, and Jacob understood they had to move or be captured.

The fort was tactically unable to defend itself. The French had most of their heavy guns on the heights and were pouring down constant fire upon the helpless defenders inside the fort.

"How long do you think they can hold out, sir?" Joshua asked.

"Hard to say, lad, but with the French trenches within a few hundred feet of the walls, they will just move up their field guns and blast them until Munro surrenders or the walls are breeched," Jacob said, as he pointed towards the French lines.

Waiting for an opportunity to run across the small marshy field that would take them to an entrenchment full of provincial troops, Jacob took a deep breath and offered, "Keep your heads down and run as fast as you can."

Running all out, the men were almost in the middle of the field before they had caught the attention of the savages.

Jacob was the first to reach the entrenchment, and after receiving aid from the men inside, he immediately fixed his attention on the others.

Joshua was running right beside Sinclair and a few paces ahead of One-Ear, who was bogged down by the lone sack of food and the built-up slope of the terrain.

"Drop the sack and run, lad!" Jacob screamed as a few of the provincials kept up a steady cover fire.

Jacob noticed that there were several Ottawa warriors in hot pursuit, just a few musket-lengths behind One-Ear.

Joshua and Sinclair had already made it to the crudely built wall of entangled trees, dirt and near shattered remains of the boats.

"Damn good to see you lads, but I fear One-Ear might be overrun if we don't force the bloody Ottawa back," Jacob shouted, pointing at One-Ear now within arm's-length of the nearest warrior.

Jacob fired off two shots, missing both moving targets. Before he could reload for a third shot, One-Ear was tripped by one of his pursuers. He tumbled to the ground, losing most of the contents of the sack. Luckily, some of the Ottawa decided to grab the strewn pieces of pork, bread and cheese, giving One-Ear the chance to get back on his feet.

Two other Ottawa warriors attempted to tackle him, but One-Ear did his best to keep them at bay by swinging his fists wildly. He was soon overwhelmed when two others joined in. Even as he was being held by his scalp lock, One-Ear continued to punch and kick at his assailants.

Jacob ordered the men around him to keep firing and attempt to push the attackers back. Sinclair was firing steadily, but his efforts were doing little to stop the Ottawa from dragging One-Ear away.

Jacob tried to hold Joshua back, but was unable to keep him from jumping over the wall. He sprinted across the field, firing his musket towards the four Ottawa that held on to his friend.

Before Jacob could even get his thoughts together, Sinclair was already over the wall and right behind Joshua. "Bloody fools!" Jacob screamed as he vaulted over the earthen wall and joined his men.

The Ottawa were ready for the counterattack, but they could not stop Joshua from driving the butt of his musket into the skull of the nearest warrior. Sinclair was behind him and dispatched another with his musket, sending the savage back into the two surviving warriors.

Now outnumbered and too far away from the main body of the other Ottawa contingent to expect any assistance, the two warriors let One-Ear go free and turned to run.

Out-of-control and blinded with rage, Joshua didn't even take time to check on his friend. He threw his tomahawk towards one of the fleeing men and let the long taut deer hide rope secured to the handle unwind. His former Huron captors had taught him to use such rope in order to retrieve a weapon in case it missed or it needed to be quickly recovered.

Joshua's wild but accurate throw landed just under the warrior's shoulder blade, it knocked the savage forward and lodged deep in his back. Joshua pulled on the rope but couldn't jerk it free.

Jacob was now at full speed and ran past both Joshua and his victim in hot pursuit of the fourth warrior that had attacked One-Ear. By this time, some of the Ottawa had moved forward from the woods to collect the spilled food and decided to turn their attention to the three rangers.

They howled at the warrior being pursued by Jacob to keep running.

Noticing that the rest of the Ottawa were reorganizing, Jacob stopped short and shouldered his already primed musket. He quickly shot at the warrior he had been after.

The smoke from his musket blinded him momentarily, but once it dissipated, he saw the savage down in the grass. Without hesitation, Jacob turned and fled back towards the relative safety of the colonials' entrenchment.

The remaining Ottawa had been joined by several dozen French militia men, and they appeared to be determined to make the four men pay for their murderous attack.

Jacob could see that Joshua had One-Ear close to the entrenchment. Running as fast as he could, the slope of the ground slowed him down and burned his already tired legs.

Hearing and feeling several musket balls pass by him, Jacob kept his head down and focused on keeping his legs moving. He zigzagged up the slope, hoping it would open some opportunities for the men behind the entrenchment to fire on his pursuers. Jacob could hear the men encouraging him to keep running.

His legs finally failed him and he fell just short of the wall. Thankfully, a welcoming arm pulled him up and over the wall. Now in the entrenchment, he lay on the dirt floor and listened to the continuing exchange of musket fire.

Jacob recovered after a few minutes and jumped back up to participate in the fight. He could see that the bodies of the dead Ottawa were being dragged away and the French were now just providing cover fire to aid the savages in retrieving their dead.

The small battle was soon over. Before Jacob could reorganize his thoughts, one of the provincials called out, "You four are either insane or just plain foolish…maybe both."

"Where are you boys from?" another man asked.

"Fort Edward; we have messages for Colonel Munro from General Webb," Jacob explained.

"Well, you have a little further to go yet, sir," one of the men replied. "The fort is over there, but I'm not sure you should risk your lives to get there."

Jacob cared too much for the three men he traveled with to ask them to accompany him on such a fruitless endeavor. He would not risk their lives further.

"Sir, what is the plan?" Joshua asked, keeping his head down. The sky was still full of smoke and whistling cannon shots streaming above them. Sadly, the location where the colonials had built the entrenchment was in direct line with the French cannons placed to the north ridge of the fort. They were peppered with over-shot cannon fire from artillery trying to hit the main fort.

"I need to get the messages to Munro and I have to find James, but I can't rightly ask you lads to follow me," Jacob said in a voice that he hoped would stem any further discussion. "Please wait here until I return. If I am not back by nightfall, get back to Fort Edward and report to Lieutenant Stark."

Sinclair interjected boldly, with the full understanding that he was directly disobeying his captain, "With all due respect, sir, you will never make it alone. I will accompany you to the fort. Joshua and his friend can wait behind for us."

Jacob did not want any of the men to come with him, but he did understand that two men might have a better chance to make it. Reluctantly, he accepted Sinclair's offer, but halted any similar offers from Joshua or One-Ear before they could do so.

"Thank you, Robert," he said. "Joshua and One-Ear, please keep us covered. As I said earlier, get back to Fort Edward once night hits, regardless if we return or not."

Before they left, Joshua handed Jacob the small note addressed to Colonel Munro that he had carried in his jacket. "You should probably take this message along as well. We didn't come all this way to not deliver both of them."

Jacob smiled and placed the note in his pocket with the other message and said, "Thank you, lad."

"Let's go Robert; we need to leave immediately if we hope to return by nightfall," Jacob said, leaving Joshua and One-Ear behind to watch their backs.

With the assistance of the provincials, Jacob and Sinclair were directed to make it to the edge of the swamp and take the old road directly into the fort.

Jacob had barely recovered from his mad dash just a few minutes earlier and slowly climbed over the far wall and ran directly towards the lake. There were only a few hundred long paces of open space between them and fort, so he pushed forward. He could now see how close the French trench-works had gotten to the northwest side of the fort's wall and knew he needed to get inside the fort immediately.

Sinclair remained right behind Jacob as the two men covered the stretch of land relatively easily. Running over a short causeway that joined the two swamps, the two men had to dodge only a few sporadic shots and were greeted by several British regulars of the 35th Foot.

"Gentlemen, get in before the bloody savages pick you off," one of the soldiers yelled.

"Can you take us to Colonel Munro?" Jacob requested as he witnessed the terrible conditions the poor soldiers and civilians had been forced to endure over the past several days.

The situation was very bleak.

Jacob had no idea how many men still manned the fort, but most were huddled together under the darkness of bastions. He could only see the whites of their blinking eyes.

The small parade ground was empty of any movement, except for the few remaining functioning cannons that attempted to reply to the mass of French guns that unmercifully blasted the walls of the nearly shattered fort.

Most of the civilians trapped behind the walls were clustered in and around the barracks. With every blast of the cannons, the women and children openly wept.

No one dared to move.

Ironically, the flag pole still stood proudly in all the confusion, but the flag, waving in the slight wind, was shredded and almost in pieces.

A tall grenadier guarded the remains of the officers' quarters and waved the two rangers past without saying a word.

"Robert, could you please search around for any word of James?" Jacob asked before he walked into the office. "You might want to start with the hospital and move from there. Keep your head down; I will be out shortly."

Munro was pacing around his office, clearly struggling with his options and the burden of the lives of his men and civilians resting in his hands. Two of his officers sat behind two desks reviewing a large map and some other documents.

"Sir, I have two messages from Fort Edward," Jacob said, not waiting for the formalities of the moment.

Munro turned and without much emotion on his face, he accepted the wax-sealed notes from the pocket of Jacob's coat.

"It's Captain Sims, isn't it? How have you been, sir?" Munro did his best to be respectful to the familiar ranger.

Not interested in too much small talk, Jacob simply offered, "Yes, sir; I am doing well considering."

Ignoring his reply, Munro was openly upset with the contents of the messages. He quickly handed them over to one of the officers.

The atmosphere in the office mimicked the rest of the fort and Jacob could sense that they were close to surrendering.

"What the hell I am to do?" Munro said to anyone who cared to listen. "The French are pounding my walls to splinters. Soon they will breach the walls and send in their bloody savages to finish off what is left of my men and the civilians."

Munro looked at Jacob when his own men failed to reply. Jacob had no idea what he should say, so he just put his head down.

"Pardon me, gentlemen," Munro muttered as he finally sat down behind his desk. "The general at Fort Edward keeps promising reinforcements, but I fear once he decides to release them...it will be too late. He basically suggests that I take 'the best terms' the French might offer me.

"He keeps sending me notes, but has not replied to any of my requests for help; now he simply 'advises' me to negotiate the ...the best terms!" Munro ran his hand over his face and said, "I must assume he cares more to defend his own fort than aid this one."

"Sir, General Webb thinks the French have six times the men, and I think that is his hesitation," Jacob tried to explain. "He has sent a number of other dispatches, but we have not heard back from the messengers, so we must assume they have not all made it through the French lines."

Munro appeared like he was going to offer a reply, but he just kept his thoughts to himself instead.

Jacob didn't know if there was anything he could say to make the colonel feel better. Wanting to get back to Fort Edward and tell Stark about the conditions at the besieged fort, Jacob politely asked, "Sir, do you want me to take back a reply to General Webb?"

His question went unanswered momentarily until one of the other officers handed him another sealed note. Offering a courteous salute, Jacob turned and left.

Back in the smoky, dense air, Jacob searched around the grounds to locate Sinclair. The air was filled with the thunder from the heavy guns and the constant dust and shards of wood kicked up from the cannon balls smashing into the thick walls of the fort. Jacob finally found his friend standing with a group of colonial militia.

"Did you have much luck, Robert?" Jacob asked.

Sinclair left the others behind and explained, "None of the men have seen James today, but he is here. I am not sure how much time you want to spend searching him out."

An odd stream of fire slammed past the two and snapped the high mast of the flag pole down. The cheers from the French only a few hundred yards away were answered as the garrison erupted into their own defiant screams of anger.

Seeing the British flag mangled in a heap of wood and splinters made Jacob and Sinclair instinctively react. They rushed over and picked through the debris until Jacob was able to pull the tattered remnant free.

Jacob handed the flag to Sinclair who held it up high and waved it around to the cheers of the men still huddled underneath the bastions.

Another streak of light blasted right over Jacob's shoulder and before he could scream at his friend to get down, a red-hot cannon ball hit Sinclair and tore his head cleanly off his shoulders. Jacob stood frozen as he watched his bloodied and headless body topple onto the remains of the once mighty flag pole.

Jacob stood in the open parade grounds, unable to move or tear himself away from the sight of his Sinclair's quivering, headless body. Finally, he felt a hand grip his arm and jerk him back.

"Keep down; that is why we don't venture out when the guns are firing," a familiar voice said as though it were speaking from a long way away.

Jacob was still in a daze, trying to rid himself of the horrible image of Sinclair and the thunderous noise of the cannon blast. Through the fog, he mumbled his thanks to the man who pulled him away.

"Why did you come here, Father?" the voice asked, from that great distance away.

Clearing his head, Jacob turned to see James sitting next to him, huddled with his hands around his knees.

"I could ask the same of you, boy," Jacob said gruffly. "We need to get away from here."

James rocked back-and-forth after another cannon ball smashed the ground just short of the officers' quarters.

Once the hellish noise stopped for a moment, James said, "I can't leave, sir. I would be a deserter and I could never do that."

Jacob looked at the destruction around him and back at his son. He wanted only to get them both away from the danger. "How can you be labeled a deserter when you are not even old enough to enlist?" Jacob shot back, waiting for James to rebuff him.

"I have done enough work around here with the rangers that most of the men look at me as an equal, despite my age," James replied, pride over-taking the utter fear in his voice. "They have used me as a scout, a translator and I have even assisted the gunners with the cannons."

Jacob was proud of James' sense of honor. As much as his mind shouted that James was a child and subject to his will as a father, Jacob knew the disgrace of being labeled a deserter and could not forcibly subject his son to that.

"I have gotten word that your mother is safe at a village in the Mohawk territory," he said, hoping to coax James into leaving.

"Will Fort Edward send us some relief?" James asked without showing any outward reaction to the news of his mother.

Jacob's temper flared at James' lack of reaction, but he calmed himself to reply, "I'm not certain, lad. Webb is doing his best to call on the militia for help, but I fear it will be too late." Knowing the truth about the situation would do little to ease the men's anxiety, so he provided them a sliver of hope to cling to.

"Lieutenant Rogers is dead," James said without much emotion.

"You mean Richard Rogers...how?" Jacob replied and ducked down when another cannon ball hit the outer wall and kicked up a massive cloud of dust.

James waited for another shot to hit the battered fort's walls before he answered, "The pox. We lost more men to the pox than to the French."

Jacob was filled with renewed desperation to take his son with him. "What if we speak with Colonel Munro?" he asked. "If he releases you, will you come along with me?"

"You can speak with him, Father, but I am sure he will deny your request," James replied.

Not wanting to waste any more time, and knowing that Joshua and One-Ear were waiting for his return, Jacob took James by the hand and guided him towards the officers' quarters. As they entered the confines of the poorly lit room, the colonel gave the two arriving men a brief look and returned to his paperwork.

One of his officers intercepted Jacob before he could get to Munro and said, "May I help you again, captain?"

"I must speak with the colonel," Jacob replied urgently.

Without so much as glancing at Munro, the officer said, "The colonel is busy at the moment."

Jacob brushed the man aside and approached the colonel, saying, "Sir, I respect that you are busy, but I need to ask you about this boy."

Munro took another brief look over his spectacles and said, "Why do you need me, sir? Do you not have a message to deliver?"

Jacob knew that his pleas would most likely be met with deaf ears, but he pressed on. "This young lad is my son and I would like to take him back with me to Fort Edward. He is actually assigned to my company and I need him back with me."

James stood silently behind his father without looking up at any of the officers.

Munro put his quilled pen down and removed his spectacles. Clearly upset with the intrusion, he pushed himself away from the small desk and said to Jacob, "Sir, I trust you understand my situation? Your son has proven his weight around the fort and has been invaluable helping us explain the tactics of the savages that have threatened us over the past several days."

Jacob could see that the situation within the fort's walls was next to hopeless and with a plea in his voice asked Munro, "Sir, do you have children?"

Munro immediately shot Jacob a look that felt like it went right through him, "Sir, I do indeed have children. I am happy they are not here with me, but I have a duty to my men and the King. I arrived at this fort greeted by a sea of wilderness and no useable boats because the French had their bloody savages raid us and destroy them."

Pausing as the French gunners continued their assault, Munro added, "When this siege is over, I will not be able to patrol the lake, so we will need every scout we have to patrol the woods. Despite the boy's age, he has proven himself one of my best."

Jacob looked at James and started to add to his argument but was stopped by Munro, who continued, "Besides, if I permit your boy to leave, what does it say to any of the other men who have family in this territory? I must respectfully deny your request on the grounds that I fear a mass desertion if they see him leave with you."

Munro sat back down and returned to the pile of documents in front of him.

Jacob could think of nothing to say that would not result in his arrest for insubordination. He remained speechless in front of the colonel, uncertain what to do next.

"Did I not give you a message to deliver to Fort Edward?" Munro snapped again.

Jacob still could not move and stood with James, praying that the colonel might somehow reconsider his stance.

"Sir, I suggest you do your duty and permit me to do mine," Munro added before burying himself back into his paperwork.

James tugged on Jacob's coat and finally got him moving. After a slight salute, they walked past the two officers and stepped back outside.

"You should leave while you can, Father...I will be alright and will meet you at Fort Edward when all this mess is done," James said in a wavering voice as he tried not to show his fear.

Jacob was filled with fatherly pride. If not for the message to Webb and the fact that Joshua and One-Ear were waiting for him, he would have remained by James' side.

Another shot made the two duck down, but once the smoke cleared, Jacob asked where he could resupply his powder. James pointed the way to the magazine and Jacob kissed him on the head before walking away.

As he filled his horn, Jacob decided that once he delivered Munro's message, he would call on Stark and the rest of the rangers. Someone had to attempt to end the siege and relieve the poor souls trapped in the fort. If Webb wouldn't order it, they would just have to do it themselves.

Leaving behind his son and the remains of Robert Sinclair was heart wrenching. Fighting hard to not show his emotions, Jacob took one last look at the bewildered, defeated garrison before he made the wild dash back to the entrenchment.

His run was uneventful. The sun was setting and the shadows gave him enough cover to make it to the welcoming hands of Joshua and One-Ear.

"Where is Sinclair?" Joshua asked as he assisted Jacob over the wall.

"He was killed inside the fort," Jacob said between panting breaths.

"How did he die?" Joshua pressed.

"He was standing a few feet from me when a cannon ball hit him and took his head right off," Jacob replied bluntly.

The young men stood in shocked silence.

Jacob saw the last of the sunlight slipping away and knew they had to get moving. He took one last look at the embattled fort and prayed for his son.

The battered provincials offered their support as the three men cleared the wall and sprinted south towards the woods.

They knew the Ottawa were waiting.

Chapter | **Twenty-Two**

The dark sky proved to be a blessing, despite the number of campfires that dotted the French lines. The three messengers took advantage of the dim light and were just able to skirt past a small party of Canadian militia and a few of their savages. Jacob was so close that he could smell their evening meal roasting in a small pot over a fire.

The captivating aroma of boiled meat and potatoes reminded Jacob how hungry he was. His stomach ached, but he focused on the task at hand.

His stomach could wait.

As they finally reached the edge of the swamp, Jacob nearly lost his balance in the dark. He swung around to keep himself from falling and caught sight of the fort.

The French clearly had no intention of ending their siege when the sun went down and continued pummeling the nearly defeated fort.

Momentarily frozen by the hopelessness and the fear of never seeing his boy again, Jacob was shaken back to reality at the sound of Joshua's voice, which called out, "Sir, are you making yourself an easy target?"

Shaking himself to action, Jacob turned and began pushing through the swampy terrain as quickly as he could.

Two quick musket blasts flew over his head, making him immediately turn to look into the dark woods. The three men dove for cover and Jacob motioned to them that the woods directly in front of them were full of approaching Ottawa warriors.

"Our only hope is to move deeper into the swamp," Jacob said quietly. "I think they will give up their pursuit and return their attentions back to the fort. Let's stand up and fire into them; maybe it will stop them for a moment and give us enough time to run."

Joshua and One-Ear both nodded and Jacob began counting down from three.

When he reached one, the three men stood up and fired a volley into the Ottawa. They were only a dozen or so paces behind and the sudden action made the savages take cover behind the maze of trees.

Jacob ran blindly through the darkened, swampy brush, not bothering to look back. He could only pray that the two boys were on his heels, but he had no time to check.

Finally stopping once he heard a screech from just over his shoulder, Jacob knelt down and swiveled to see what was happening.

Thankfully, both Joshua and One-Ear ran to him, and between deep breaths, Joshua said, "I think the Ottawa gave up their chase a mile or so back. I think they were out looking for a couple of easy scalps but decided we were not worth the effort."

"I thought the damn savages didn't fight at night?" Jacob said.

"Only if there is something worth killing," One-Ear shot back.

The three laughed and took a few minutes to rest.

They finally reached the end of the swamp and began following the same old path that had brought them north to William Henry. The three men moved quickly and reached the halfway point after only a couple hours of all-out running.

Joshua and One-Ear had gotten a lead on Jacob and stopped by an old hemlock tree to wait. When he approached, they motioned him to stop so they could talk.

"I thought we lost you a few miles back," Joshua joked when Jacob arrived.

Jacob took a moment to settle his breathing and replied, "Aye, thanks for waiting up for me, lads."

One-Ear was not interested in speaking much and was up ahead watching for any movement in the woods.

"We should rest a bit," Joshua suggested, keeping his musket ready just in case they were ambushed.

"I saw James," Jacob blurted. "He was in good spirits, considering the circumstances…"

When he saw the look on Joshua's face, Jacob quickly added, "Sorry, lad. I know it wasn't what we were speaking about, but…" He dropped his head as his voice trailed off.

"I am glad he is alive, sir, but I am shocked you didn't bring him with you," Joshua said.

"I spoke with Munro, but he would not release him…" Jacob said quietly. He felt shame as a father for not forcibly removing James from the situation, but as a soldier, he understood he hadn't the power to take him without consequence.

"I think we might want to make camp and start up again in a few hours," Joshua suggested, waving One-Ear to rejoin them.

Jacob went uncharacteristically silent and followed the lead of the two younger men. It only took a few minutes to locate a suitable place to rest and Jacob soon took a seat against a half-rotted pine tree.

Since the last of the food had been lost to the Ottawa when they attacked One-Ear, they had nothing to eat. Regardless, it felt good to be off their feet. Everything was still, save for the distant guns back at Fort William Henry.

"I need to go back and rescue him," Jacob mumbled to himself.

Joshua immediately jumped on his guilt-ridden statement and said, "Sir, what could you have done alone? When we get the message back to Webb, we will gather the men and form a much stronger force to relieve what is left of William Henry."

Jacob gave a faint smile but had nothing to add. He slumped down against the tree to try to rest, but he had a difficult time quieting his thoughts. When he finally did fall asleep, it did not last long due to his eagerness to get back on the trail.

As he rose to organize his himself, he was finally struck by the abnormal calmness that overtook the woods.

"Do you hear that, lads?" Jacob asked the young men who had awakened when they heard Jacob moving around.

"No, sir, I can't hear anything," Joshua responded quickly, looking at One-Ear for his thoughts.

"That's my point, lads," Jacob said urgently. "The French have stopped their guns. Did the fort surrender or have the walls been breached?"

"Do we go check?" Joshua asked.

"No, lad, we should get to Fort Edward and then get our boys moved up the road."

Without waiting for discussion, Jacob was back on the path and running as quickly as he could towards the south. As he dodged fallen branches and a number of unearthed roots, Jacob heard Joshua and One-Ear catch up to him.

They continued running without another break and reached the fort just as the sun rose. They offered only a slight wave to the pickets as they passed, and headed directly towards Rogers Island.

Lieutenant Stark was standing on the earthen works just by the bridge. Jacob noticed him and stopped.

Between breaths, he said, "John, it is good to see you well."

"You as well, Jacob; how was your scout?" Stark asked.

"The fort is in a bad way and I fear they will not be able to hold out much longer unless we relieve them," Jacob explained, taking a long drink of water from the canteen Stark held out to him.

"Where is your Private Sinclair?" Stark asked, looking at Joshua and One-Ear who waited beside Jacob.

"The poor man is dead, killed by a cannon shot to the head," Jacob replied. He hoped he hadn't sounded too cold or unfeeling, but it was still a very hard thing for him to talk about.

"Bloody waste," Stark said.

"John, I have a dispatch from Munro. We need to take it to Webb and explain to him the situation at the fort. We must convince him to permit us to help those poor souls."

As Stark began to lead the way, Jacob turned back and said, "Get the men ready and on the trail, Joshua. I will be with you momentarily."

He was hungry and tired, but the vision of James trapped at William Henry made him press on.

"Our friend Mr. Johnson has been fighting with Webb for the past two days, but the coward had refused to relent," Stark said as they walked briskly up the hill. "I fear we will face a revolt if Webb doesn't send some men forward soon."

Just as they worked their way into the fort, Jacob noticed that the gunners around the bastions of the fort were already manning the cannons. Also, most of the garrison was now stationed around the walls, anticipating an attack.

"I see Webb still fears the French will pour down from William Henry and attack this fort," Jacob said.

"I fear the French will have a hard time controlling the Ottawa," Stark responded. "The savages will have little interest in attacking another English fort. If William Henry surrenders, they will want their trinkets and prizes to take back with them. I fear prisoners will not be treated well by the Ottawa and other savages if they have nothing to take back to their villages."

Stark's ominous suggestion made Jacob flinch. Looking at each other, they knew their call to assist the embattled fort had taken a far more serious course now. They felt that Webb would be left with few excuses to keep from sending men to relieve what was left of William Henry.

For the moment, Jacob honestly cared little for the general's opinion on the matter and simply wanted to deliver Munro's message.

Showing no regard for protocol, the two men walked past the grenadier guard without offering him so much as a nod or a glance. Stark led the way and knocked on the wooden door as he stepped into the room. William Johnson was again engaged in a heated discussion with Webb as the two men entered the office.

Stark walked forward, ignoring the general's aids, and interrupted the conversation by saying, "General Webb, Captain Sims has brought word from Colonel Munro at William Henry."

Johnson acknowledged Jacob with a kind smile, but Webb merely scowled at his appearance as he took the folded message from Jacob's hand.

Webb spread the note open, but took only a few seconds to review its contents. He quickly placed it down on his desk and turned his attentions back to the two rangers.

"Gentlemen, I am not pleased by your rude behavior," Webb said aloofly. "Despite any messages you may have for me, it is customary to be admitted, not to just burst into my office."

Before Jacob could reply, Stark said, "Sir, we are sitting idly by and being forced to listen to the siege of our friends at William Henry. I respect your concern about defending this fort, but you do so at the cost of the blood of all who are waiting for our help."

Webb barely looked at Stark, but asserted his authority by saying, "It is a lost cause, gentlemen. I would be ordering more men to their certain deaths. I have my orders to keep the road to Albany clear. If we are overtaken on our way to aid William Henry, then what would become of the fine people in Albany? May I remind you, there are women and children living there; do we just let the French do what they wish to them?"

Just as he uttered the last word, Jacob boldly stepped up, "Sir, there are women and children behind the walls of Fort William Henry as well. Their only hope is that you will send men as promised."

The room went intensely silent.

Johnson attempted to step in and support the rangers, but he seemed tired of all the bickering with Webb. He motioned the two rangers to the door in a manner that suggested he wished to speak with them alone.

Giving up their one-sided fight, Jacob and Stark dismissed themselves to wait for Johnson outside. Webb gave no further acknowledgement as they left and just continued working through his paperwork.

Just as Jacob stepped out into the parade grounds, he was stopped by one of Webb's aids who held out a folded message and said, "Please take this message to Colonel Munro."

Jacob looked at the piece of parchment in the aid's hand and snapped back with a reply that surprised even him, "I will not, sir, risk any more of my men to such a foolhardy order. Tell the general to take it himself."

Stark overheard the conversation and once they were clear of the office, he said, "Bloody good show, Jacob! Maybe now the fool might understand how serious we are."

Jacob just smiled and looked around to find Johnson. The man had slipped past him while he talked with the aid and now stood in the parade ground with several of his Mohawks.

Joshua and One-Ear had also arrived to report to Jacob that the men were ready and willing to move towards the besieged fort. The four men joined Johnson, who began to brief them on his plans.

"Gentlemen, my Mohawk scouts have made contact with some of their brothers who fight alongside the French. They have sent back word that the fort has already arranged terms of their surrender. Montcalm has offered terms that include allowing the able-bodied English to march with their weapons to Fort Edward."

"Aren't the savages upset with such terms causing them to go home with so little to show for their victory?" Jacob jumped in.

"You know the people in these parts well, sir," Johnson replied. "The French have explained and pleaded with their Indians to respect the terms and let the English move freely on the road here."

Stark looked at One-Ear and Joshua and asked them directly, "Lads, will the French allies return to their lands without scalps and prizes from their victory?"

One-Ear immediately answered, "The Ottawa, Huron and Abenaki will not be satisfied without scalps or war prizes, no matter what their French father says."

Joshua simply nodded his agreement.

The men could barely hide their fear and anger. Johnson stepped in again and said, "Speaking for myself and my Mohawk brothers, we have already decided to head up the road and do our best to help the remains of Fort William Henry's garrison. I would not expect any of you or your men to come with us in direct defiance of Webb's orders, but you will be welcomed along. I must also say that I do have the ear of enough powerful men on both sides of the great ocean that we have little to fear from our dear general."

Johnson's words were both impactful yet still spoke of disobeying a direct order from a high-standing general, no matter his level of incompetence. Even though he had already ordered his own men to be ready to move out, Jacob was still leery about taking such actions. If an order was to be disobeyed, he should do it alone and not implicate his men in such actions.

"I will leave you with your thoughts and remind you that we will be departing shortly," Johnson added. "No matter what you decide, I will think of you in no other vein but as honorable soldiers trying to do their duty to the King." With that, he walked out into the outer earthen works with his Mohawks.

The four remaining men stood quietly until Stark broke the silence with what they were all thinking, "Well, gentlemen, we have been given an interesting proposal by Mr. Johnson."

"With the rangers and Johnson's warriors, we could certainly cause the French some trouble," Jacob added.

Moments later, a lone figure came rushing through the woods and burst into the first line of pickets, drawing the attention of the entire fort.

Confusion broke out as both Stark and Jacob ran to find out what happened to the clearly battered man. Making their way down to the picket lines, they could tell that the man was part of one of the provincial militia units that were assigned to Fort William Henry.

The poor man was almost naked, except for his breeches and one left stocking. His body was bloodied, possibly from running through the deep, overgrown woods, but more likely from his experience at the fort.

"What the hell happened to you, lad?" Stark asked when the man had had the chance to gulp some water from a canteen that was handed to him.

"The French have lost control of their savages and are just letting them do what they wish," the man said between gasps of air. "Once the cannons stopped, they attacked the men in the trench outside the fort. They took some of the lads away and stole our coats, shoes and whatever else they saw as valuable. The main garrison has been spared for now, but I fear they will deal with the savages soon enough. God only knows what will become of the sick and injured. Some of the savages entered the fort, but I heard that they did little damage. There was word that we were to leave tonight, but the French changed that and told us to be ready to leave tomorrow."

"How did you manage to escape?" Jacob questioned him before he could explain.

"I was sent to ask for some help, despite the French telling us that they would escort us. There were five more of us, but they were all taken by the

Ottawa. I barely escaped with my own scalp." He touched the crown of his head almost as if to verify for himself that he was speaking the truth.

"The bloody savages did get their hands on some rum and they are all drunk," he added sadly.

Jacob and Stark looked at each, both knowing that rum and Indians never mixed well.

"Bloody hell, lads," Stark managed to blurt out.

Johnson had made it down to the picket line by now and instantly asked the clearly shaken soldier, "What of the French? Are they organizing to attack us here?"

The soldier didn't bother to look at who asked the question as he calmly answered, "The French were busy working out the details of the terms, and most of their Canadians just stood around and watched the entire attack take place. I fear tomorrow's march will be nothing more than an all-out attack on our defenseless men and civilians.

"As for a full siege on this fort, it would take the French weeks to get organized and pull their heavy guns over the road to here. If the savages can't be controlled and the Canadians leave to return to harvest their farms back in Quebec, the regulars would be left with only a few thousand men and could risk losing what they have already gained."

The long-winded yet thoughtful reply took Johnson by surprise. He was at a loss for words until Jacob stepped in, "How many of you were left at the fort?"

With all the questions, the man finally lost his temper and said to all who were listening, "If you continue to stand around and pepper me with your questions, no one will be left! I was assigned to the entrenchment just outside the fort, and now all those men are easy targets for the savages."

His words threw the men into action. Stark ran to organize his men, and Jacob called to Joshua to get the men ready to leave straight away. Johnson did the same and ordered one of the pickets to inform Webb that they were leaving and to suggest that he get his artillery commander to fire off signals to help guide the survivors toward Edward.

The rangers were organized and already on the main road well before the first of the cannon signals blasted into the sky.

Jacob had lost his usual rear guard leader and asked Joshua to take up that important duty. Along with the rangers, Johnson had released a number of his Mohawks to rush ahead as advanced scouts.

It was early afternoon and Jacob knew that even if he pushed the men, they would most likely arrive tired and unable to defend the surrendered garrison in the dark.

He sent back word to both Stark and Johnson suggesting they stop at their previously-used encampment at Halfway Creek. Jacob could tell by their tones of both of their replies that they would prefer to continue on, but they agreed that rested men would be better able to assist their comrades.

Word was sent ahead to the Mohawk scouts so they could ready the camp prior to the larger force's arrival. Thankfully, the road was not being patrolled by the French or the Ottawa, which made the march much easier. No fires were permitted, but most of the men needed the rest above all. Once Stark and Johnson arrived with their men, they could see that Jacob's idea was well received.

"What has become of my Mohawks?" Johnson asked as he scanned the camp. By then, the nighttime sky was nicely illuminated by a huge moon that provided ample light to allow for easy conversation.

Stark had his men positioned a few paces back from the main camp and joined Jacob and Johnson by the side of the road, saying, "Nice enough night; the men surely needed the break. The morning will be here soon enough and then we will be in for some trouble."

"Yes indeed, John," Jacob said. "As for the Mohawks, they have moved further up; I assumed they didn't want to remain with us."

"They do tend to want to be on their own; please take no offense." Johnson replied. "At first light, I will send them out while we get the rest of the men on the road."

The three men all looked up the northern stretch of the dark road. Jacob could not imagine what faced them the next day and prayed that James was still alive. As much as he wanted to assist the survivors of the fort, his main goal was to find his son. He even went so far as to order his men to search for him. An offer of five pounds awaited the man who brought James to him. It was far from a fortune, but he hoped it would entice the men to keep a lookout for him.

Jacob suspected that most of the men got next to no sleep after hearing the rumors spreading around the small camp about the savages and their attacks.

Not much of a sleeper on the best of days, Jacob awoke early enough to hear the Mohawk somewhere outside the camp leaving to scout the trail. Stark soon rose and the two officers enjoyed a few minutes of silence before moving towards the imminent battle.

"I will stay behind your rear guard," Stark suggested. "Once we hit the small hill near the field, I will take my men to the swamp and clear out whatever is left of the French."

Jacob agreed and the two men parted with a brief handshake.

The few Mohawks still remaining back with Johnson were advancing through the far western woods, and Jacob prayed that they would reach the fort before any further attacks were initiated.

The morning was calm and the men were refreshed enough to cover the short trek without incident. Within two miles of the fort, the first of the shrieks and screams could be clearly heard. Jacob called on his men to get into the woods and be alert for signs of either the column of survivors or the Ottawa.

Stark had already moved his rangers to the eastern swamp, leaving Jacob's men to secure the road.

They were forced to stop as large parties of British regulars started to stream towards them from every direction. Although they were in different stages of dress, Jacob could see that they were mostly from the 48th Foot. He managed to slow a couple of the men down to question them and asked, "Lad, what is happening up ahead?"

"God only knows, sir," the private replied. "The savages have hit us again and are killing and taking prisoners. The damn French have no control over them, and we got word that the poor lads at the rear have been hit the hardest. They even murdered the poor bastards in the hospital...God save us."

"Form yourselves up and help us fight the bloody savages," Jacob suggested, knowing that the regulars would never take an order from a lowly colonial ranger, despite his being an officer.

Without a word, the men bolted away and ran south towards the safe confines of Fort Edward.

Jacob was curious why no word was sent back from Johnson or his Mohawks, so he ordered his men to advance slowly. He also called forward the rear guard and was thankful that both One-Ear and Joshua were back by his side.

Their progress was hindered by the throngs of British regulars running past them and clogging the road. More of the 48th and some of the 44th Foot passed by and Jacob began to worry that his men might run themselves into an ambush. Still having no word from the Mohawks, Jacob ordered his men to halt and reorganize.

"We need to get into the woods and try to get around the road," Jacob said as he listened to the distant yells and screams from the fort. "I fear we will run into an ambush or worse, any thoughts?"

"We must get to the fort by whatever means, but the woods appear to be the best option for now," Joshua replied.

"Standing here does not get us to the fort any faster," One-Ear added.

"Of course not," Jacob replied. "Lads, please be kind enough to take a handful of the best men ahead to see what we are facing. The bloody Mohawks are either already fighting or have left us."

As he watched the group of men disappeared into the dense forest, the screams at the fort became much louder. A surge of British regulars scrambled into the woods for cover and hindered the progress of the rangers as they tried to move against the flow of the fleeing men.

"To the woods, lads, and get ready for more survivors," Jacob called to his remaining men. "Shoot at anyone that is not one of ours and keep your heads down!"

Joshua sent word back within a few minutes of leaving that the entire upper portion of the road was jammed with dead bodies, panicking survivors and packs of men trying desperately to fight back.

Seeing the shape that most of the survivors were in, Jacob sent some of his men back as escorts to ensure they made it to Fort Edward. From the increasing noise and screams, he wasn't sure what could be done to rescue the remaining men, but he pushed forward and was met with his first sight of the attack.

There were many groups of half-dressed men desperately fighting off their savage attackers. Some men had made it to the woods, but they were being hunted down and either killed or taken prisoner. Basically unarmed except for empty muskets, most of the men had resorted to swinging them like clubs or spearing at anything that moved close enough to be skewered with their bayonets.

As Jacob looked down towards the lake, he witnessed a number of women and children being secured and taken to waiting canoes down by the two jetties. He could also see that they had taken male captives, whom they had stripped naked and blackened with soot. Jacob knew the savages tended to try to make their captives appear as 'Indian' as possible to fool their enemy.

Groups of French regulars were running around attempting to free the captives and keep the Indians from attacking the remaining column, but their efforts were fruitless. Jacob's rangers immediately moved forward along the road and did their best to assist what men they could.

Most of the British regulars were already past them and well on their way to Fort Edward. It was mostly the colonial troops who remained behind, still trying their best to escape the attacks of the savages.

A few of the men ran past Jacob screaming, "Murder! Save yourselves!"

Jacob finally spotted Stark and saw that his men were trying their best to cut off the Indians moving towards the lake. His men were organized enough to keep some of the drunken, crazed Indians back, but their efforts just forced the savages to focus their attacks on a different group of unfortunate men.

Despite the combined efforts of the ranging companies, there were more Ottawa, Huron and Abenaki than could be defended against.

Jacob soon realized that his own men were coming under attack. As he got closer, he saw that Joshua and One-Ear were among those desperately fighting off the advancing savages. Without thinking, Jacob ran headlong into the heart of the Ottawa attackers and smashed the butt of his musket into the faces and heads of as many of the savages as he could reach. His quick surprise attack gave his men enough time to rush forward and free themselves from their attackers.

Reorganizing and pushing the Ottawa back before they dispersed into the deepest part of the forest, Jacob ordered a number of his remaining rangers to assist the rest of the men and provide an escort to what survivors they could find.

"Lads, I have not seen any sign of James, have either of you seen him?" Jacob pleaded with Joshua and One-Ear. He noticed a French priest rushing around helping as many Englishmen as he could.

Jacob led the rest of his men farther up the road, past another group of savages intent on scavenging anything worth taking. As they got closer to the entrance of the fort, they saw a large number of British soldiers massed together under the protection of a number of French regulars.

A large number of French Canadians and still more Indians were at the two jetties loading up their bateaux and canoes with heaps of coats, shoes, shirts and weapons stolen from the fleeing English. A number of wooden chests and other personal belongings were piled up on the shore-line, waiting to be packed into some of the vessels.

Running towards where the majority of British officers appeared to be congregated, Jacob weaved past two Huron warriors scavenging through the pockets of a dead British soldier. Without stopping, Jacob swung his musket and hit one of the Huron in the forehead. The force of the blow made the savage tumble over the scalped corpse and into a tree.

The other Huron, surprised by the attack, stood up and pointed his musket at Jacob who had already passed by. Just as the warrior was ready to squeeze the trigger, One-Ear drove his raised tomahawk into the middle of the Huron's back. The Huron dropped to the ground and One-Ear briefly stopped to dislodge his bloodied weapon from the dead warrior's back.

The men raced onward and were greeted by a patrol of French regulars positioned in a line formation with their muskets shouldered. Jacob noticed them and called out in French for them to lower their weapons.

They inexplicably listened to his command, and Jacob stopped long enough to explain that his rangers were part of a much larger relief force coming from Fort Edward. Shocked at the unexpected news, the French decided to retreat and race back to the safe confines of the newly cap-tured fort.

Jacob hoped that the word of a large force marching down the road from Fort Edward would alarm the French enough to force them to gain control of their savages.

With their path cleared, Jacob led Joshua and One-Ear towards the growing group of officers and stragglers gathering under the protection of the French regulars and officers. Jacob could see that Colonel Munro was amongst them and was busy calling to more of the men to join their ranks.

"I doubt James would be part of the officers' group," Joshua called out.

"If he is here, he would have been targeted by the Huron or Ottawa because he is young; maybe he is down by the lake," One-Ear suggested.

Jacob stopped short of the road that would take them down towards the lake. He felt exposed with all the crazy activity going on around them. He strained to locate any of Stark's rangers near the swamp land to his right, but they were nowhere to be found.

Finally, it appeared that most of the attacks on the defenseless fort inhabitants were beginning to falter.

Just ahead of them, a young shirtless militia private was doing his best to fight off several attacks on him by a band of roving Ottawa warriors. Without hesitation, Jacob ran forward and used both his hawk and long knife to force the marauding horde of savages to leave the poor soldier alone.

"Are you injured, lad?" Jacob asked, lending his hand to assist the private to his feet.

"No sir, just a slight twisted ankle, but nothing to stop me from getting clear of this place," the still visibly shaken young man said.

"Joshua, get him some water," Jacob called out, and both Joshua and One-Ear ran off to see what they could find. "Get the poor boy some clothes too," he shouted after them.

Calming the private down and insuring he was now safe from any further attacks, Jacob moved the men to a small grouping of trees. Setting up an informal guard around the trees, Jacob offered the private a chance to sit and give him some details.

"What happened here?" Jacob asked. "The French obviously did not keep their savages under control."

"It started last night, as soon as the French had agreed to the terms," the young man explained, flinching several times as a few more distant screams echoed throughout the area. "I assume they informed their savages who didn't like the idea of returning home without anything from the battle. They attacked the fort's hospital and even dug up the recently buried dead men to remove their scalps.

"At first, they just rushed us and started to take our packs. We were told that we would be leaving last night, but that was changed once the French started to lose control over the entire situation. The savages just swarmed us and began pulling off our clothes, stealing our muskets and taking whatever they wanted. We were ordered not to resist, but it was difficult to just let them do what they wanted."

"Rest now, lad. We can talk more about this later. I promise you are safe now; please fear nothing from these animals." While Jacob did his best to console the private, he was far more concerned with finding James.

Ignoring Jacob's words to rest, the young man continued, "The Canadian militia just stood around and did nothing...they just called us dogs and laughed at us."

Joshua returned with One-Ear and a couple of canteens and said, "Most of the action appears to be pushed down by the lake. The savages are now more concerned with filling their canoes and leaving."

Jacob stood quietly and looked at the lake. From where he stood, it was impossible to see much of the activity down by the beach area.

When he didn't get a reply, Joshua suggested, "Sir, would you like me to take One-Ear and look down near the jetties?"

Jacob appeared to have not heard Joshua, so he repeated his idea, "Sir, the jetty?"

Shaking his head as if to clear his mind, Jacob finally replied, "Be careful; the place is still a mess and the savages are still looking for trouble."

Without waiting for further instructions, the two men sprinted down the road that would take them to the water.

Jacob did not want to just stand around and do nothing, so he ordered two of his rangers to escort the private to Fort Edward. Just as they departed, Jacob took his remaining men and headed towards the eastern swamp to hopefully rejoin Stark and his rangers.

Moving quickly to the swampy terrain, Jacob skirted close enough to get a closer view of the myriad of boats docked all along the water's edge. He still could not tell if James was among the men, women and children already being paddled away. He prayed that his son had not been taken; it would be next to impossible to ever find him again.

Jacob halted his men just at the edge of the swamp land near the natural causeway that went to the west side of the swamp. He was relieved to see both Joshua and One-Ear racing across the causeway towards him.

Waving to make sure they noticed him, the two young men appeared to be upset about something.

"What is it, lads?" Jacob called out.

"Get back, sir!" Joshua screamed.

Soon, twenty fast-approaching savages came into view behind them. Jacob quickly ordered his men into a small line ready to fire at the on-charging savages.

"Keep your muskets steady, lads; we don't want to hit our own men," Jacob said as he shouldered his own musket and took aim.

Letting Joshua and One-Ear clear past them, Jacob was almost ready to order his men to unleash their first volley when the crazed savages suddenly stopped and strangely just turned and rushed back to the lake.

Confused yet relieved that the much larger force had decided to retreat, Jacob ordered his men to lower their muskets and draw back.

Turning to look for Joshua and One-Ear, Jacob smiled when he realized why the savages had decided not to continue their pursuit.

Standing in a similar formation to Jacob's own men was a proud-looking John Stark and a large group of his rangers.

"Glad to see you well, captain," Stark barked out.

"You too, John," Jacob replied and walked over to greet his friend with a hearty handshake.

Both the rangers turned to look at the lakefront and Stark said, "What a bloody mess, Jacob. I can't begin to describe to you the sights we've seen since reaching the swamp."

"Us as well, John; I'm just glad we arrived in time to save some of these unfortunate souls. I have sent over half my men back to Fort Edward to escort the survivors."

"We spent most of our time assisting a number of survivors that took to the swamp," Stark said. "Of course, we also had to fight off hordes of savages and French militia in search of prisoners or scalps." He moved to get a better view of the bateaux and canoes down by the lakefront.

"One poor private told us that the bloody savages killed all the sick and injured and even dug up some of the graves…all this for some prizes to take back to their villages," Jacob replied in disgust.

"Maybe they will take along a dose of the pox to their villages," Stark coldly retorted.

Both men just looked around and could not manage to say much else.

"I think we have done all that we can here and should consider getting back to Fort Edward," Jacob suggested, looking around for Joshua. "I am certain that we will run into additional survivors along the trail."

Having given up hope of finding James at the fort, Jacob could only hold onto the hope that his son might have been one of the lucky ones to escape towards Fort Edward.

"Agreed, Jacob; we should get back before the darkness hinders our return," Stark replied and called to one of his senior rangers to get the men in order.

"What will happen to Munro and his officers?" Jacob asked.

"I assume the French officers will provide them protection from the savages and then permit them to leave for Fort Edward once all this mess is cleared," Stark replied.

The two men took one last look back at the battered remains of the fort before returning to their men.

"So you never found your boy, then?" Stark asked after a moment.

Jacob was shocked into silence by the abruptness of the question. With his head bowed, he reluctantly replied, "I fear he is in the hands of the Ottawa or Huron. At the moment, I don't even want to think about how his life might end up. I should have never left him…"

As the last of his words left his lips, John grabbed his shoulder and pointed up ahead.

Standing between Joshua and One-Ear stood a smiling James. Jacob looked at Stark for an explanation, which he readily gave.

"We found him with a group of Ottawa. They had taken him captive and were escorting him towards the lake. We dispatched all of them and freed your boy. He has been fighting alongside us since. He is an amazing young lad and you should be very proud."

Before Jacob could even move, James rushed to him and jumped into his arms.

In the middle of all the chaos and death stood a father and a son, oblivious to all that surrounded them.

Eventually, Jacob managed to utter, "I love you, boy."

James pulled back and, with tears streaming down his face, simply said, "I want to go home."

Timeline of
Important Events
in Blood Lines

1756 December   Jacob and his men encounter Robert Rogers and his ranging company for the first time.

1757 January 23   The First Battle on Snowshoes.

1757 February   The first raid on Fort William Henry. Although minor in nature, the raiders managed to destroy some boats and made patrolling Lake George difficult for the garrison.

1757 March 17   Raid on Fort William Henry. A French and Native raiding party destroys the remaining sloops and boats around the fort resulting in the French having free rein to travel the lakes without fear from the English.

1757 May/ June/July Both Fort William Henry and Fort Edward, work on reinforcing their defenses for an expected attack. Jacob and his rangers keep a constant patrol on the road between the forts throughout early spring and summer. Robert Rogers also departs for Nova Scotia to assist in the attack on the Fortress at Louisbourg.

1757 July-August. Provincial and Colonial troops arrive throughout the period to reinforce the forts.

1757 August 5 William Johnson arrives at Fort Edward with a contingent of his Mohawks. Webb does not let him advance towards the besieged Fort William Henry. The same day the French intercept a message from Webb to Munro suggesting he should take 'the best terms' from the French.

1757 August 3-9 The French, with their Indian allies, attack Fort William Henry and begin their siege until Colonel Munro finally capitulates on August 9.

1757 August 10 Allied French Indians begin to harass, capture and kill several men, women and children from the long line of refuges from Fort William Henry. The French regulars and Canadian militia had agreed to protect the survivors, but provide little assistance to the surrendered garrison once the Indians attack.

1757 August 11-17 The survivors of the siege and Indian attack reach Fort Edward. Guided by hourly cannon fire from the fort to guide them, many staggered out of the woods half naked with tales of the attack.

Author's **Historical Note**

Blood Lines follows Jacob and Maggie into another disastrous defeat. The British hold on North America appears to be in peril and the colonial population is growing tired of the constant losses to a much smaller enemy. The British army has still refused to adapt to fighting in the wilderness and the importance of allying themselves with the local tribes.

After abandoning Pennsylvania, the British were left with to two significant wilderness forts in the interior of the New York territory. Both situated on or near the main route the French used to travel on from the interior of New York and Quebec, Fort William Henry and Fort Edward became the last strongholds of the British.

Much as they had in Pennsylvania, the British basically left the two forts to fend for themselves and provided them only a couple of companies of regulars, supplemented with untrained and raw colonial troops.

The focus was on attacking Nova Scotia and moving up the St. Lawrence to take Quebec. That left the two forts isolated to protect the frontier, especially the important area around Albany, and to keep the French to the north.

Munro, Webb and John Stark were all key players in the defense of the forts, as was Robert Rogers. Rogers only played a minor role and was eventually called to Nova Scotia, missing the main siege.

The major storyline surrounding Fort William Henry, most likely the part remembered by most people because of Hollywood movies, was the circumstances around the surrender and ambush.

There is little evidence for either side as to the details surrounding the so called 'massacre'. The accounts from the French and their Indian allies, tell of only a handful of deaths. There were a number of British and colonials taken captive, but it appears the Indians simply wanted 'souvenirs' of their victory. They had no concept of allowing an enemy to simply surrender without the cache of plunder taken from the defeated army.

Recorded casualty numbers from both sides were grossly different. I put it down to the time period and the desire to feed the emotions of the colonist tiring of the poor showing of the British. The idea of a massacre of innocent, unarmed men, women and children did present a perfect rallying call against the native population. It fuelled the outrage that led to provision of more men and resources to fight the French invaders.

The French reported much lower casualty numbers, as did the Indians. However, there did seem to be a good number of captives taken and transported back to Quebec. There are even accounts that Montcalm used his own funds to pay for the freedom of some of the captives, but the most unfortunate ones spent the remainder of the war as prisoners or were adopted into the many tribes that took part in the battle.

The British exaggeration of the death tolls to whip up emotions was a common weapon used throughout the war and well after; meanwhile, the French appeared to have a more realistic version of the events. It was propaganda at its best and did eventually affect the outcome of the war and how people viewed the First Nations people.

General Webb was an intriguing character and a man that was too much out of his element to be expected to protect the vulnerable New York frontier. His actions before and during the siege demonstrated his inadequacies as a leader. Webb, under the excuse of protecting Albany and the inaccurate information about the actual French numbers, simply left Munro and his garrison to fend off the French led attack. If Webb would had acted swifter and sent forward even some of his men waiting at Fort Edward, the results might have been different. No one really knows, but common sense would dictate that some type of action would have, at the very least, hindered the French assault.

Webb's inaction led to Fort William Henry's surrender and destruction. No one is certain if he was under strict orders to protect Albany at any cost. There is no known documentation saying such. His lack of aid and decision to leave a fellow officer on his own despite having the manpower to possibly alter the outcome seems odd.

History does show that Webb's time in North America was ticking down after his unforgivable actions and he was soon sent back to England. His reputation was severely damaged, yet he had enough influential allies in London to continue his military career. He actually received a couple of promotions in rank over the following years.

Sadly Colonel Munro spent his remaining days in Albany and was dead within a year after his surrender of Fort William Henry.

One last historical note surrounds Fort Carillon. The area around Carillon was called 'Ticonderoga' by the tribes who lived in the area. The fort's name was not officially changed until 1759 to Fort Ticonderoga, after the British captured the remains of the fort. You might read the fort being referred to as Fort Ticonderoga in other books but it was not officially renamed until the French left it burning in the hands of Robert Rogers… but that is a story for another time!

As much as I attempted to stay true to the documented events, Blood Lines is still a fictional account of the period. Most of the documents and historical accounts are one sided and are skewed towards the victors side. First Nations people did not write down their history and instead relied on oral accounts. Their side was never represented, and we were basically left to the writings of their enemies.

Jacob and Maggie's story continue, still separated by miles of wilderness and left between the French and their Indian allies. As in the past, the unpredictable weather, the endless, unforgiving landscape and their enemies, keeps them apart for the foreseeable future.

Acknowledgments

I must continue to express my gratitude to all the living historians, artisans, authors, artists and re-enactors who share my passion and love for this mostly forgotten time period.

Robert Griffing, John Buxton, David Wright, Doug Hall, Todd Price Kyle Carroll, the amazing cover artist, Andrew Knez Jr. plus several other great artists and artisans that have continued to inspire me with their work and dedication. I have had the pleasure meeting many of them and their kindness and friendship gave me a further appreciation for their hard work and commitment to keep this time period alive.

Once again, the great people at Lord Nelson's Gallery in Gettysburg, PA. for supporting my books. Mr. George Lower, who took a chance and carried my first novel, is now a friend and part of my family. Madison and Kennedy always look forward to his hugs and smiles whenever they walk into the gallery. To be a part of History Meets the Arts every June is a highlight both personally and professionally. Thanks to George, Philippe and Marsha who welcomed me and my family into theirs!

To my good friends Roger and Stacy Moore, Jeremy Moore, Tim L. Jarvis, Matt Wulff, Dave Fagerberg and many more people who took time to talk with me over a number of summer events and inspired me to continue on with my journey...Thanks!

Once more, I want to clarify that any depictions of First Nations people in my stories are strictly fictional. It was simply a snapshot in time. They truly were the empire that lost the most and have been unfairly treated, both then and now. I am proud of my First Nation's heritage and my Grandfather Thomas Power.

Jacob and Maggie will continue their own journey in the wilds of the frontier as their story endures. A special thanks to all the readers who have taken the time to phone, send emails or support me at the number of book signings I do throughout the year; your feedback and kind words have provided me the fuel to keep writing and honestly enjoying what I do.

Cheers and best regards to all!

References and
Recommendations

Once again I would be remiss if I forgot to direct interested readers to further materials on the French and Indian War. These are a few of my favorite books and other great resources to consider.

Books:

- Bud Hannings, *The French and Indian War-A Complete Chronology*. McFarland & Company Inc., 2011. Great reference for the War and is particularly interesting for those who need a more in-depth source.

- Fred Anderson, *Crucible of War*. New York. Vintage Books, 2001. The best and most extensive account of the war. Simply a must read for anyone interested in this time period.

- Michael L. Pitzer, *Native Reenacting Made Easy*. Axehead Publishing, 2009. Another great source book for information about the Eastern Woodland Warrior.

- George Irwin, *The Art of Robert Griffing*. New York. East/West Visions. 2000. The follow up, *The Narrative Art of Robert Griffing*, by Tim Todish. Gibsonia, Pennsylvania. Paramount Press Inc. 2007. Once again for their amazing artwork and for putting faces and emotions to a time long forgotten.

- Matt Wulff, *Ranger-North American Frontier Soldier*. Heritage Books. Matt has a series of books on Ranging Companies of the early frontier. They are well written and an invaluable source for anyone wanting to learn more about the men who guarded the vast wilderness.

Other **Sources:**

- *Muzzleloader* magazine, by Jason Gatliff at Historical Enterprises, LLC. An amazing bi-monthly publication that keeps this period alive.

- Lord Nelson's Gallery, est. 1990 in Gettysburg, PA. A great place to visit and purchase artwork depicting the period.

- DVDs on the war include the Paladin Communications great series, *Young George Washington, The Complete Saga, The War That Made America.* PBS Home Video, 2005. Narrated and hosted by Graham Greene.

- Douglas "Muggs" Jones has produced a great series of DVD's from the School of the Longhunter Series. Entertaining, informative and well worth purchasing. For more information check- www.douglaswjonesjr.com.

- Please also pick up a copy of my good friend Tim L. Jarvis' soon to be released book, *Shadow In The Forest, Woodland Warriors of the Mississippi Valley.* Please look for it at your local book store or at www.warriorstrail.com.

Websites:

www.nightowlstudio.net

www.lordnelsons.com

www.kylecarrollart.com

www.paramountpress.com

www.CalumetTradegoods.com

www.doughallart.com

www.friesenpress.com

www.smoke-fire.com

www.andrewknezjr.com

www.brucewoodpecker.tripod.com

I am also a proud member of the CLA (www.longrifles.com) and the NMLRA (www.nmlra.org).

Historical **Sites and Events:**

$\mathbf{P}$lan to visit Lord Nelson's Gallery and History Meets the Arts, Gettysburg, PA in mid-June for great artwork, great atmosphere and great people. Please check www.lordnelsons.com for details.

It's a good idea to plan visits to historical sites when they have a reenactment scheduled. Try Fort Fredrick, MD in late April, Fort Niagara in July and Fort Necessity anytime in the summer for their great atmosphere and historical accuracy. Fort Ligonier is another special place and the staff is second to none!

Visit the reconstruction of Fort William Henry in the Lake George area and while you are in Northern New York, stop and visit Crown Point and Fort Ticonderoga. It is well worth the drive!

If you do attend an event, make sure you visit the tents of the artisans and traders. They are first class folks and their skillful work will make you appreciate the time period even more!

In Canada, make sure you visit the Fortress at Louisbourg and Quebec City. Visiting either place is like going back in time.

Visit a First Nations event in your area. It is one of the best cultural events to attend and they deserve our support. If you visit a historical site during a re-enactment you will see first and how critical the natives were to both sides and how much they truly lost during and after the French and Indian War.

There are a few more great places to visit and my family and I try to include in our schedule every year. Fort Frederick's 18th Century Market Fair in Maryland-visit www.friendsoffortfrederick.com for details and dates. Old Fort Niagara's F&I War Reenacting Weekend in early July is an amazing event (www.oldfortniagara.com). Fort Pitt Museum in Pittsburgh is also a great place to learn about the early years of The French and Indian War.

This is only a snapshot of what is available to the reader interested in expanding his or her knowledge of this great period. Please support our historical sites and buy a membership or plan a visit. Make your own list and remember to read, visit, watch, and enjoy. You will be amazed at what you will learn and what they didn't teach you in school.

If you see me at an event doing a book signing or just enjoying the sites, please take a moment to introduce yourself and say hello.

Author | **S. Thomas Bailey**

About the Author

S. Thomas Bailey is an Award Winning author and independent researcher of early North American life. He is a raw historian at heart, and a writer by choice.

Bailey's own sense of history is enriched by a Mi'kmaq grandfather and a family tree that can be traced back to the young surveyor James Cook, who began his career mapping out the St. Lawrence River system during the French and Indian War.

He resides in a quiet hamlet north of Toronto, Ontario, with his wonderfully supportive wife and two amazing children. His family spends their spring and summer seasons each year visiting French and Indian War sites, attending re-enactments and living history events, and spreading the word about this wonderful period in North American history.

Bailey looks forward to continuing Jacob and Maggie's story. Watch for additional novels in The Gauntlet Runner series, coming soon.

S. Thomas Bailey is always available for signings, speaking engagements or to just talk about his book series. Follow, contact or connect with S. Thomas Bailey for updates, scheduled book signings and events.

www.thegauntletrunner1754.com
thegauntletrunner1754@yahoo.com
and on www.facebook/TheGauntletRunner

CPSIA information can be obtained
at www.ICGtesting.com
Printed in the USA
BVHW071456040119
537053BV00001B/40/P

The NYC Asian American Experience On Stage

Edited by Alvin Eng

Library of Congress Number 99-071850

ISBN: 1-889876-09-7 (paper)
       1-889876-10-0 (cloth)

The text of this book is set in Garamond.

Publication of this book was funded by the National Endowment for the Arts.

NATIONAL
ENDOWMENT
FOR THE ARTS

Cover and book design: Jue Yee Kim
Cover photo by Tseng Kwong Chi © Muna Tseng Dance Projects, Inc. New York
All Rights Reserved

Published in the United States of America by The Asian American Writers'
Workshop, 37 St. Mark's Place, New York NY 10003-7801. Email us at
desk@aaww.org. The Asian American Writers' Workshop is a not-for-profit
literary organization devoted to the creation, development and dissemination
of Asian American literature.

Distributed by Temple University Press, 1.800.447.1656 | www.temple.edu/tempress

CONTENTS

I. Introduction / Acknowledgments

II. The Plays

III. The Verbal Mural

Culled From Interviews Conducted by the Editor With:

• Tisa Chang • Daryl Chin • Frank Chin • Ping Chong • Jessica Hagedorn • Wynn Handman

• David Henry Hwang • Aasif Mandvi • Chiori Miyagawa • Han Ong • Ralph B. Peña • Gary San Angel

• SLANT • Diana Son • Ellen Stewart • Muna Tseng

IV. Contributors

I Introduction/Acknowledgments

ACKNOWLEDGMENTS:

Special Thanks To:

All of the contributors and their colleagues without whom this book would not exist.

Peter Ong, Andrea Louie, Derek Nguyen, Jeannie Wong, Elisa Paik, Nancy Yap, Quang Bao and staffs past and present at the Workshop for believing in and realizing this project through some pretty challenging circumstances.

Designer Jue Yee Kim and copy editor Nina Chaudry for going above and beyond...

Another special shout out to the Workshop volunteers and interns: Hung Dang, Jenny Lee, Marie Avetria, Carlos Gomez.

For invaluable feedback and support: Jin Auh, Daryl Chin, Jessica Hagedorn, Bonnie Rosenstock, Gary San Angel (my original conspirator on this project) and Wendy Wasdahl.

Muna Tseng for sharing her brother's gifts with us for the TOKENS? cover.

Finally, extra special thanks to you for reading this book.

INTRODUCTION:

Most times, a life in the theatre can be such a tenuous proposition at best that even the old "noo yawk" dis' of "that (one's life in the theatre) and a token will get you on the subway" doesn't hurt after a while. In fact, it becomes quite amusing...inspiring even. And in many ways, that is empowerment or "tough love New York City style"--finding the inspiration, resilience and ultimately love in and of your art and nurturing it while the rest of the city (if not the world) swirls around you at a trillion miles an hour with seeming-ly as many simultaneous cultural events in tow. In other words, you know you're up on the big stage, but acutely aware that you're not up there alone. The phenomenon of keeping your head period (not to mention above water) in this dizzying spin is what this book explores--from the unique perspective of "our neighborhood," the New York City Asian American theatre world.

Today, the New York City Asian American theatre is bigger than ever with at least four active producing companies, numerous performing/dance troupes and the occasional (read, one) Asian American play in a "mainstream" venue's sea-son. Yet given all of this artistic growth (and this growth is indeed, an achievement to be applauded), we are still arguably as commercially insular as ever. While there always seems to be that break-out spark or two of a suc-cessful production, that long-awaited day where Asian American theatre becomes another seamless stitch of the supposedly class-free quilt of misfits that is New York City theatre has yet to dawn. So here we are, some thirty years on, still searching for the light of day while being obscured by the foreboding shadows of the same problems that have always plagued our neighborhood. In this murky twilight, one can't help but contemplate "When is a neighborhood a ghetto?" or "How can I be ghettoizing myself when I'm just...being myself?"

Which brings us back to the title of this book, TOKENS? THE NYC ASIAN AMERICAN EXPERIENCE ON STAGE. Yes, a token gets you on the subway, and the subway is the common denominator for New Yorkers in all of the city's greatly varying neighborhoods. But while that token can take you on a trip to anywhere in the city, it does not allow you to stay there. At that point,one feels a strange sensation that is akin to being branded with a permanent asterisk. It is a state of being (or non-being) that Leonard Cohen so eloquently describes as being "there, but ain't exactly real, or it's real, but it ain't exactly there." But one thing is for certain: In that instance, you stand alone, and your token is reduced to tokenism. It is this peculiar isolated cry in the urban wilder-ness that is at the heart of New York City Asian American theatre and all ten plays in this compilation--regardless of whether its characters, theme or premise are "Asian American." Some plays deal with this issue head-on and aim for the gut, some aim for the funny bone, while still others take it to a very different plane that mirrors this point of view without reflecting our physicality. So for the next 4-500 pages, we stand alone together, and our shared struggles become a celebration. A celebration of savoring and documenting our world while overcoming all varieties of obstacles that come with being a part of the New York City Asian American theatre at this tricky turn in the road and of the clocks to a new century where we know not of what lurks around the corner.

As the saying goes, "there's a million stories in the Naked City and this is 'one' of them," albeit composed of ten plays and a "Verbal Mural" of an oral history. Yes, it's admittedly a playwright-centric point of view, but the play is the thing, and these plays, all by New York City-based Asian American theatre artists, were all written and produced during the 1990s, and all but two of them take place in New York. And while reading a play is a completely different experience than seeing a play, reading these scripts will give you a great visceral snapshot of what Asian American theatre was like in New York City in the 1990s, from internationally renowned artists to newly formed ensembles. The "Verbal Mural" features reflections on all of the issues brought up in this introduction and much much more in the form of straight talk from a rich cross section of the playwrights and producers who, for all intents and purposes, founded and maintained "our neighborhood" over the last thirty years of the 20th century (and most of them still live and work here).

Alas, if you're new to these parts, you could think of this book as a talking, walking tour of an area of the city you've only known peripherally. But if you're very familiar with this turf, here's a chance to catch up with new and old friends and be privy to what they really say about the 'hood "in private." But old hand or newcomer, you'll notice that like all neighborhoods, the New York City Asian American theatre is changing... in many unexpected ways.

As neighborhoods in New York and the world begin to change and merge over the next century, will "hyphenated Americans" like "Asian Americans" (a name borne in defense of cultural pride and in defiance of a "mainstream neighborhood" that ignored them) become a relic of the 20th century? In turn, will a token (OK, by then a MetroCard) become a rite of passage to a new, diverse, super cyber highway or will it remain a rite of way down that same ol' grimy, pothole-laden dead end street?... Just as there are a million stories in the Naked City, there are also a million questions, and TOKENS? THE NYC ASIAN AMERICAN EXPERIENCE ON STAGE is one of them.

So yeah, this book may not get you onto the subway, but it will certainly give you a hell of a ride... All aboard!

ALVIN ENG
New York City,
Summer of '99 (the last one of the 20th Century)

II THE PLAYS

TRYING TO FIND CHINATOWN

by David Henry Hwang

This play is an expression of the way in which I believe ethnicity is sometimes a matter of self-identification. I was a jazz violinist for many years and essentially anchored my identity in that world. Similarly, I had met a Seattle stage director who was racially Caucasian, but had been adopted as an infant by Japanese American parents. As our nation becomes increasingly diverse, traditional definitions of race become blurred, and, in the ideal world, we will choose our own identities.

DAVID HENRY HWANG

TRYING TO FIND CHINATOWN was commissioned and received its premiere at the Actors Theatre of Louisville (Jon Jory, Producing Director), as part of the 20th Annual Humana Festival of New American Plays, in Louisville, Kentucky, on March 29, 1996.

Written by David Henry Hwang
Directed by Paul McCrane

Set Design: Paul Owen
Costume Design: Kevin R. McLeod
Lighting Design: Brian Scott
Sound Design: Martin Desjardins
Original Violin Music Composer: Derek Reeves
Dramaturg: Michael Bigelow Dixon
Stage Manager: Julie A. Richardson.

Cast:
BENJAMIN: Richard Thompson
RONNIE: Zar Acayan

Characters:
BENJAMIN, Caucasian male, early 20s
RONNIE, Asian American male, mid 20s

Setting:
A street corner on the Lower East Side, New York City. Present.

Note on Music:
Obviously, it would be foolish to require that the actor portraying "Ronnie" perform the specified violin music live. The score is recorded on tape and played over the house speakers, and the actor can feign playing the violin using a bow treated with soap. However, in order to effect a convincing illusion, it is desirable that the actor possess some familiarity with the violin, or at least another stringed instrument.

Property List:
Electric violin with bow (RONNIE)
Violin case, open, with change and dollar bills (RONNIE)
Coins (BENJAMIN)
Dollar Bills (BENJAMIN)
Scrap of paper (BENJAMIN)
Pack of cigarettes (RONNIE)
Lighter or matches (RONNIE)
Hua-moi (BENJAMIN)

TRYING TO FIND CHINATOWN

Darkness. Over the house speakers, fade in Hendrix-like virtuoso rock'n'roll riffs—heavy feedback, distortion, phase shifting, wah-wah—amplified over a tiny Fender pug-nose.

Lights fade up to reveal that the music's being played over a solid-body electric violin by RONNIE, a Chinese American male in his mid-20s, dressed in retro-'60s clothing, with a few requisite '90s body mutilations. He's playing on a sidewalk for money, his violin case open before him, change and a few stray bills having been left by previous passers-by.

Enter BENJAMIN, early-20s, blonde, blue-eyed, looking like a Midwestern tourist in the big city. He holds a scrap of paper in his hands, scanning street signs for an address. He pauses before RONNIE, listens for a while. With a truly bravura run, RONNIE concludes the number, falls to his knees, gasping. BENJAMIN applauds.

BENJAMIN: Good. That was really great. *(Pause)* I didn't...I mean, a fiddle...I mean, I'd heard them at square dances, on country stations and all, but I never...wow, this must really be New York City! *(He applauds, starts to walk on. Still on his knees, RONNIE clears his throat loudly.)* Oh, I...you're not just doing this for your health, right? *(He reaches in his pocket, pulls out a couple of coins. RONNIE clears his throat again.)* Look, I'm not a millionaire, I'm just... *(He pulls out his wallet, removes a dollar bill. RONNIE nods his head, gestures towards the violin case, as he takes out a pack of cigarettes, lights one.)*

RONNIE: And don't call it a "fiddle," OK?

BENJAMIN: Oh. Well, I didn't mean to—

RONNIE: You sound like a wuss. A hick. A dipshit.

BENJAMIN: It just slipped out. I didn't really—

RONNIE: If this was a fiddle, I'd be sitting here with a cob pipe, stomping my cowboy boots and kicking up hay. Then I'd go home and fuck my cousin.

BENJAMIN: Oh! Well, I don't really think—

RONNIE: Do you see a cob pipe? Am I fucking my cousin?

BENJAMIN: Well, no, not at the moment, but—

RONNIE: All right. Then this is a violin, now you give me your money, and I ignore the insult. Herein endeth the lesson. *(Pause)*

BENJAMIN: Look, a dollar's more than I've ever given to a...to someone asking for money.

RONNIE: Yeah, well, this is New York. Welcome to the cost of living.

BENJAMIN: What I mean is, maybe in exchange, you could help me—?

RONNIE: Jesus Christ! Do you see a sign around my neck reading, "Big Apple Fucking Tourist Bureau?"

BENJAMIN: I'm just looking for an address, I don't think it's far from here, maybe you could...? *(RONNIE snatches the scrap of paper from BENJAMIN.)*

RONNIE: You're lucky I'm such a goddamn softy. *(He looks at the paper.)* Oh, fuck you. Just suck my dick, you and the cousin you rode in on.

BENJAMIN: I don't get it! What are you—?

RONNIE: Eat me. You know exactly what I—

BENJAMIN: I'm just asking for a little—

RONNIE: "13 Doyers Street?" Like you don't know where that is?

BENJAMIN: Of course I don't know! That's why I'm asking—

RONNIE: C'mon, you trailer-park refugee. You don't know that's Chinatown?

BENJAMIN: Sure I know that's Chinatown.

RONNIE: I know you know that's Chinatown.

BENJAMIN: So? That doesn't mean I know where Chinatown—

RONNIE: So why is it that you picked me, of all the street musicians in the City—to point you in the direction of Chinatown? Lemme guess—is it the earring? No, I don't think so. The Hendrix riffs? Guess again, you fucking moron.

BENJAMIN: Now, wait a minute. I see what you're —

RONNIE: What are you gonna ask me next? Where you can find the best dim sum in the City? Whether I can direct you to a genuine opium den? Or do I happen to know how you can meet Miss Saigon for a night of nookie-nookie followed by a good old-fashioned ritual suicide? *(He picks up his violin.)* Now, get your white ass off my sidewalk. One dollar doesn't even begin to make up for all this aggravation. Why don't you go back home and race bullfrogs, or whatever it is you do for—?

BENJAMIN: Brother, I can absolutely relate to your anger. Righteous rage, I suppose, would be a more appropriate term. To be marginalized, as we are, by a white racist patriarchy, to the point where the accomplishments of our people are obliterated from the history books, this is cultural genocide of the first order, leading to the fact that you must do battle with all of Euro-America's emasculating and brutal stereotypes of Asians—the opium den, the sexual objectification of the Asian female, the exoticized image of a tourist's Chinatown which ignores the exploitation of workers, the failure to unionize, the high rate of mental illness and tuberculosis—against these, each day, you rage, no, not as a victim, but as a survivor, yes, brother, a glorious warrior survivor! *(Silence)*

RONNIE: Say what?

BENJAMIN: So, I hope you can see that my request is not—

RONNIE: Wait, wait.

BENJAMIN: —motivated by the sorts of racist assumptions—

RONNIE: But, but where...how did you learn all that?

BENJAMIN: All what?

RONNIE: All that, you know, oppression stuff, tuberculosis...

BENJAMIN: It's statistically irrefutable. TB occurs in the community at a rate—

RONNIE: Where did you learn it?

BENJAMIN: I took Asian American studies. In college.

RONNIE: Where did you go to college?

BENJAMIN: University of Wisconsin. Madison.

RONNIE: Madison, Wisconsin?

BENJAMIN: That's not where the bridges are, by the way.

RONNIE: Huh? Oh, right....

BENJAMIN: You wouldn't believe the number of people who—

RONNIE: They have Asian American studies in Madison, Wisconsin? Since when?

BENJAMIN: Since the last Third World Unity hunger strike. *(Pause)* Why do you look so surprised? We're down.

RONNIE: I dunno. It just never occurred to me, the idea of Asian students in the Midwest going on a hunger strike.

BENJAMIN: Well, a lot of them had midterms that week, so they fasted in shifts. *(Pause)* The Administration never figured it out. The Asian students put that "They all look alike" stereotype to good use.

RONNIE: OK, so they got Asian American studies. That still doesn't explain—

BENJAMIN: What?

RONNIE: Well...what were you doing taking it?

BENJAMIN: Just like everyone else. I wanted to explore my roots. And, you know, the history of oppression which is my legacy. After a lifetime of assimilation, I wanted to find out who I really am. *(Pause)*

RONNIE: And did you?

BENJAMIN: Sure. I learned to take pride in my ancestors who built the railroads, my Popo who would make me a hot bowl of jok with thousand day-old eggs when the white kids chased me home yelling, "Gook! Chink! Slant-eyes!"

RONNIE: OK, OK, that's enough!

BENJAMIN: Painful to listen to, isn't it?

RONNIE: I don't know what kind of bullshit ethnic studies program they're running over in Wuss-consin, but did they bother to teach you that in order to find your Asian "roots," it's a good idea to first be Asian? *(Pause)*

BENJAMIN: Are you speaking metaphorically?

RONNIE: No! Literally! Look at your skin!

BENJAMIN: You know, it's very stereotypical to think that all Asian skin tones conform to a single hue.

RONNIE: You're white! Is this some kind of redneck joke or something? Am I the first person in the world to tell you this?

BENJAMIN: Oh! Oh! Oh!

RONNIE: I know real Asians are scarce in the Midwest, but…Jesus!

BENJAMIN: No, of course, I…I see where your misunderstanding arises.

RONNIE: Yeah. It's called, "You white."

BENJAMIN: It's just that—in my hometown of Tribune, Kansas, and then at school—see, everyone knows me—so this sort of thing never comes up. *(He offers his hand.)* Benjamin Wong. I forget that a society wedded to racial constructs constantly forces me to explain my very existence.

RONNIE: Ronnie Chang. Otherwise known as, "The Bow Man."

BENJAMIN: You see, I was adopted by Chinese American parents at birth. So, clearly, I'm an Asian American—

RONNIE: Even though you're blonde and blue-eyed.

BENJAMIN: Well, you can't judge my race by my genetic heritage alone.

RONNIE: If genes don't determine race, what does?

BENJAMIN: Perhaps you'd prefer that I continue in denial, masquerading as a white man?

RONNIE: You can't just wake up and say, "Gee, I feel Black today."

BENJAMIN: Brother, I'm just trying to find what you've already got.

RONNIE: What do I got?

BENJAMIN: A home. With your people. Picketing with the laundry workers. Taking refuge from the daily slights against your masculinity in the noble image of Gwang Gung.

RONNIE: Gwan who?

BENJAMIN: C'mon—the Chinese god of warriors and—what do you take me for? There're altars to him up all over the community.

RONNIE: I dunno what community you're talking about, but it's sure as hell not mine. *(Pause)*

BENJAMIN: What do you mean?

RONNIE: I mean, if you wanna call Chinatown your community, OK, knock yourself out, learn to use chopsticks, big deal. Go ahead, try and find your "roots" in some dim sum parlor with headless ducks hanging in the window. Those places don't tell you a thing about who I am.

BENJAMIN: Oh, I get it.

RONNIE: You get what?

BENJAMIN: You're one of those self-hating, *assimilated* Chinese Americans, aren't you?

RONNIE: Oh, Jesus.

BENJAMIN: You probably call yourself, "Oriental," huh? Look, maybe I can help you. I have some books I can—

RONNIE: Hey, I read all those Asian identity books when you were still slathering on industrial-strength sunblock. *(Pause)* Sure, I'm Chinese. But folks like you act like that means something. Like, all of a sudden, you know who I am. You think identity's that simple? That you can wrap it all up in a neat package and say, I have ethnicity, therefore I am? All you fucking ethnic fundamentalists. Always settling for easy answers. You say you're looking for identity, but you can't begin to face the real mysteries of the search. So instead, you go skin-deep, and call it a day. *(Pause. He turns away from BENJAMIN, starts to play his violin—slow and bluesy.)*

BENJAMIN: So what are you? "Just a human being?" That's like saying you have no identity. If you asked me to describe my dog, I'd say more than, "He's just a dog."

RONNIE: What—you think if I deny the importance of my race, I'm nobody? There're worlds out there, worlds you haven't even begun to understand. Open your eyes. Hear with your ears. *(He holds his violin at chest level, does not attempt to play during the following monologue. As he speaks, a montage of rock and jazz violin tracks fades in and out over the house speakers, bringing to life the styles of music he describes.)* I concede—it was called a fiddle long ago—but that was even before the birth of jazz. When the hollering in the fields, the rank injustice of human bondage, the struggle of God's children against the plagues of the devil's white man, when all these boiled up into that bittersweet brew, called by later generations, the blues. That's when fiddlers like Son Sims held their chin rests at their chests, and sawed away like the hillbillies still do today. And with the coming of ragtime appeared the pioneer Stuff Smith, who sang as he stroked the catgut, with his raspy, Louis Armstrong voice—gruff and sweet like the timbre of horse hair riding south below the fingerboard—and who finally sailed for Europe to find ears that would hear. Europe—where Stephane Grapelli initiated a magical French violin, to be passed from generation to generation—first he, to Jean-Luc Ponty, then Ponty to Dedier Lockwood. Listening to Grapelli play "A Nightingale Sang in Berkeley Square" is to understand not only the song of birds, but also how they learn to fly, fall in love on the wing, and finally falter one day, to wait for darkness beneath a London street lamp. And Ponty—he showed how the modern violin man can accompany the shadow of his own lead lines, which cascade, one over another, into some nether world beyond the range of human hearing. Joe Venutti. Noel Pointer. Sven Asmussen. Even the Kronos Quartet, with their arrangement of "Purple Haze." Now, tell me, could any legacy be more rich, more crowded with mythology and heroes to inspire pride? What can I say if the banging of a gong or the clinking of a pickax on the Transcontinental Railroad fails to move me even as much as one note, played through a violin MIDI controller by Michael Urbaniak? *(He puts his violin to his chin, begins to play a jazz composition of his own invention.)* Does it have to sound like Chinese opera before people like you decide I know who I am? *(BENJAMIN stands for a long moment, listening to RONNIE play. Then, he drops his dollar into the case, turns and exits R. RONNIE continues to play a long moment. Then BENJAMIN enters D.L., illuminated in his own spotlight. He sits on the floor of the stage, his feet dangling off the lip. As he speaks, RONNIE continues playing his tune, which becomes underscoring for BENJAMIN's monologue. As the music continues, does it slowly begin to reflect the influence of Chinese music?)*

BENJAMIN: When I finally found Doyers St, I scanned the buildings for Number 13. Walking down an alley where the scent of freshly steamed *char siu bao* lingered in the air, I felt immediately that I had entered a world where all things were finally familiar. *(Pause)* An oldwoman bumped me with her shopping bag— screaming to her friend in Cantonese, though they walked no more than a few inches apart. Another man— shouting to a vendor in Sze-Yup. A youth, in white undershirt, perhaps a recent newcomer, bargaining with a grocer in Hokkien. I walked through this ocean of dialects, breathing in the richness with deep gulps, exhilarated by the energy this symphony brought to my step. And when I finally saw the number 13, I nearly wept at my good fortune. An old tenement, paint peeling, inside walls no doubt thick with century of grease and broken dreams—and yet, to me, a temple—the house where my father was born. I suddenly saw it all: Gung Gung, coming home from his 16-hour days pressing shirts he could never afford to own, bringing with him candies for my father, each sweet wrapped in the hope of a better life. When my father left the ghetto, he swore he would never return. But he had, this day, in the thoughts and memories of his son, just six months after his death. And as I sat on the stoop, I pulled a *hua-moi* from my pocket, sucked on it, and felt his spirit returning. To this place where his ghost, and the dutiful hearts of all his descendants, would always call home. *(He listens for a long moment.)* And I felt an ache in my heart for all those lost souls, denied this most important of revelations: to know who they truly are. *(BENJAMIN sits on the stage sucking his salted plum, and listening to the sounds around him. RONNIE continues to play. The two remain oblivious of one another. Lights fade slowly to black.)*

END OF PLAY

SAKINA'S RESTAURANT

By Aasif Mandvi

SAKINA'S RESTAURANT was developed intermittently over the course of five years. It started in the fall of 1992 with me deciding to write a one-man show and writing characters in my living room and performing them at the Duplex Cabaret Space in Greenwich Village. I then moved uptown to Wynn Handman's acting studios at Carnegie Hall. During the time that Wynn and I developed the characters I would bring to his acting class, I not only began to piece together the beginnings of a show but I began to realize what the show wanted to be. Instead of turning into another Eric Bogosian as I had originally thought I would, I found myself writing characters from within the South Asian community, and especially my family. My need to write these characters was never a conscious decision, it's just what came out. I had no statement that I wanted to make about immigrants or South Asians in America, all I wanted to do was write characters from my ethnic background that were real and that had never before been seen on the American stage. The parents in SAKINA'S RESTAURANT are really my parents, the rest of the characters contain aspects of my sister and me.

In 1994, I took these characters to Kim Hughes, and the two of us spent many many late nights rehearsing wherever we could (even in the conference room of her office job). Azgi was born by way of improvising with Kim on my idea that we needed a narrator to bring all these characters together. We first performed SAKINA'S RESTAURANT at the West Bank Downstairs Theatre on 42nd Street. I was terrified, Kim was giddy...The show was a success!! The audience loved it, they got it. It was then that I believed that maybe there was room for a show like this, about these people, about me. Kim and I continued to rehearse and develop the show in conference rooms, storage rooms, basements and now and then, even our apartments. We also continued to workshop it on and off over the course of the next three years at various venues around New York and in other cities. The character of Azgi continued to become more realized and the parables which were originally written for another project entirely found their way into the show and became one of the central themes.

In 1997 Wynn decided he wanted to do the show at the American Place Theatre, and we did the show there as a fundraiser. It was the first time the show was performed to an entirely South Asian audience, it was also the first time that I realized that the characters transcended my family and my experience of them; they were reflections of a community. There was a level of recognition in the audience that I had never experienced, even though the show had played successfully to many audiences before.

SAKINA'S RESTAURANT opened at the American Place Theatre on June 24, 1998. It was a beautiful day, and, for me, the culmination of a dream. The road to realizing this play has been long, glorious, frustrating, cathartic, overwhelming, joyous and spiritual. It has been a true and rare gift in my life to have had the opportunity to perform, share and move people with these characters. They are my friends, they are my family, they are my children, they are my voice, I hope you enjoy them.

AASIF MANDVI

SAKINA'S RESTAURANT had its World Premiere at the American Place Theatre, New York City, where it ran from June 1998 through January 1999.

Written and Performed by Aasif Mandvi
Directed and Developed by Kim Hughes

Scenic Design: Tom Greenfield
Lighting Design: Ryan E. McMahon
Sound Design: David Wright
Production Stage Manager: Richard A. Hodge

For My Parents

SAKINA'S RESTAURANT

Lights up.

We see AZGI standing with his suitcase center stage.

AZGI: Hello, my name is Azgi. I like Hamburger, Baseball and Mr. Bob Dylan. You know, I am practicing my introduction because today is a very important day for me, because today I leave my home here in India and I fly on an aeroplane! *(Motioning with his hands)* And I fly, and I fly and I fly, and then, I land!... *(Motioning with his hands)* And I land and I land and I land and I land, on the other side of the world in America. Oh, I am very excited. Practically the entire village has turned up in my parents' small house to celebrate my departure, can you believe?

(Turning up)

Ha waru me awuchu.

(Back to front)

OK, let's see. I have my passport, CHECK! My ticket, CHECK! You know, I am the first person in my entire family to even fly on an aeroplane... *(Nervous)* I hope no crashing. Oh, and the most important thing I have, a letter!... I read...

(He reads.)

"Dear Azgi,

(To audience)

That's me,

(Reading)

"America is a wonderful place, and as I told you in response to your letters, that since it was your dream to come here, I would help you as soon as Farrida and I could manage. Well Azgi, the time has come. I need help in my restaurant. I can sponsor you, it is hard work, but you can come and work for me, live with us, and get to see America, your dream is coming true."

Mr. Hakim is a very very important man, he own a restaurant in Manhattan! Here is address, 400 East 6th Street...NYC...USA...the World...the Galaxy...the Universe!!!!!!

(Turning up)

Ha waru me awuchu.

(Turning back, he sees his mother.)

Ma, Ma, don't cry. Why you crying, Ma? Listen, listen, You know what, you know what, when I go to America, I will write to you everyday. I will write to you so much that my hand will fall off. Ma, come on. Ma, you know what? When I go to America, I will write to you from the...from the...Top of the Empire State Building!! I will write to you from... from the bottom of the Grand Canyon!! I will write to you from everyplace I go, McDonalds! I will write to you!! Hollywood, Graceland, Miami, F.L.A. everyplace. I will even write you from Cleveland!! Cleveland, Ma! Home of the Indians!... Ma, come on, you know what you know what? When I go to America, one day I will be very rich! And then I will invite you and you can come and stay with me in my big house with my swimming pool, and my Cadillac—

(She hands him something)

What is this? A stone? You are giving me a stone! Ma, the poorest people in our village will give me more than a stone to take on my journey. How can I tell them that my own mother gave me a stone? The story of the river stone? The story of the river stone? I don't remember the story of the river stone. I don't remember, I don't remember—OK, OK, Bawa, I keep the stone. See? I'm keeping it, I'm keeping it.

(He mimes putting it into his pocket and then suddenly pretends to throw it away.)

Oh my God I threw it away!

I'm joking, I'm joking, Ma. It was a joke. Look, I keep it, OK! There it goes in my pocket, OK!

(Turning upstage and then turning back to face his mother)

Ma, I have to go.

(Music cue rises as AZGI slowly does Salaam to his mother, he kisses her hands and then her feet, he then picks up his suitcase and walks off towards America, he looks back at one point and holds up his hand as if to say goodbye. The lights fade and we hear an aeroplane fly through the air. When the lights come up accompanied by the song "Little Pink Houses" or any other appropriate song AZGI is standing on a busy New York Street, he mimes looking at the buildings around him and attempts to speak to people on the street, all of whom give him a very clear cold shoulder, he tries to say hello to people on the subway and the same thing happens until one solitary person speaks to him this it turns out is a bum, AZGI somewhat disappointed gives the man a dime and then is subsequently pick pocketed. He despondently hangs up his coat on the rack upstage and turns to face the audience and a brand new American day.)

(Noticing audience)

Oh, hello, how are you? Here I am! I made it! Oh my God this New York is a crazy place. But welcome to Sakina's Restaurant. This is my new job. I am the Manager here...OK I'm not really the manager... I am the OWNER!!!... No, no, no I am not the owner, I am the waiter here but you know it is such a good job—

(He hears someone off stage.)

Oh, excuse me,

(Speaking offstage)

Yeah?... Oh, OK.

(He begins to set up tables.)

You know Mr. and Mrs. Hakim were waiting for me at the airport when I arrive. I think it is very nice of them to let me stay with them until I find a place of my own. Their two children, Sakina and Samir, are also very nice but they are completely American. Samir, he is only ten years old. He is always playing with his Game Boy. He say to me, he say, "Azgi how are you doing?" I say, "Samir, how am I doing what?" Then everybody start to laugh. Sakina, their daughter, she is older, she is going to be getting married soon. She say to me, she say, "Azgi, don't you worry you will soon Catch On."

I just smile and nod my head and say, "Yes, yes, yes, you are absolutely right," even though I have no idea what any of these people are talking about. But I have found that in America, if you just smile and nod your head, and say "Yes, yes, yes, you are absolutely right," people love you!!!

I have not made any friends yet, because I am here in the restaurant, working, working, working. Mr. Hakim the owner, he is my very good friend, you know when I told him my dream one day to be a American Millionaire, he say to me he say *(Mimicking Hakim)* "Azgi let me tell you something very profound." *(To audience)* So I listen to you know, he say, "In America, Azgi, any ordinary idiot can be RICH, but not any ordinary idiot can be RESPECTED. I am not any ordinary idiot." *(Confused)* I think about this, and then I smile and nod my head and I say, "Yes, yes, yes, you are absolutely right." Mr. Hakim says I will go very far.

When I told Mrs. Hakim my dream to be an American Millionaire, she looked at me and she said, "Azgi, you are smart. Don't be fooled. America can give you nothing that you don't already have." And then she said, "When I was a young girl, I had a dream, just like yours, my dream was to be a classical Indian dancer." I said, "Oh yeah? Show me how you used to dance." She said, "No, I don't dance anymore, but when I first came to America and Sakina was just a baby I used to dance every-day," and then suddenly she close her eyes and she start to do like this—

(He moves his hips.)

I didn't know what to say. I said, "Mrs. Hakim!" But then she say to me, she say, "Azgi, let me teach you how to dance," I say, "No, No, No, I cannot learn, I can only watch," she say "No! you can learn, let me teach you how to make a bird, so I try you know. *(He begins to move his hands in the style of an Indian dance that represents a bird.)* I make a bird, make a bird, make a bird, make a bird... and bird fly away, bye bye bird! Gone!—OK, OK, OK, I do it for real, I'm sorry I was just kidding, *(Seriously now with real intent to learn)* I make a bird, make a bird, make a bird, make a bird, hey I'm pretty good, and then I do like this *(He shakes his hips)* and like this and—"Hey Mrs. Hakim you know what, I'm pretty good at this. I think if I had studied like you, I could have been a dancer myself." *(He gets into the dancing.)* I do a little bit of this and a little bit of this—

(A light change happens simultaneously with a sound cue that sends AZGI into slow motion as he continues to dance, the dance becomes more spiritual as he slowly wraps himself with a pink scarf that he picks up from under the stage, and as soon as he does the lights change and we are in the presence of)

FARRIDA: *(She is surprised by her husband who has snuck up on her.)* Oh my God! You frightened death out of me. Why you have to sneak up like that? OK Hakim, please don't be ridiculous, I don't dance like that, I don't dance like this. *(She wiggles her butt)* I am a very good dancer, OK Hakim you know what, by making fun of me, you are the one who looks ridiculous.

Embarrassed?—Embarrassed! Why should I be embarrassed?—I am not in the least embarrassed. I just think that there is a thing like that called manners, when you don't just sneak up on someone when they are doing something, and then you don't know what I am doing, what if I am doing something I don't want you to see. OK, very funny, ha ha ha. It is not called embarrassment. It is called politeness.

(She picks up her rolling pin and begins to roll out chapati. Throughout most of this piece she is intermittently rolling out chapati as she speaks to her husband.)

Well, there are many things about your <u>new wife</u> that you don't know. I am a very talented and mysterious woman. I can do much more than cook your food.

(He tries to make a sexual advance.)

Chul, chul, Hakim, come on stop, *Are'* come on, you are being absolutely crazy. Oh my God, you see how you get, you see how you get. You see what happens to you—you work in that restaurant 15 hours a day, and then you come home and all you are thinking about is Hanky Panky. Before you eat Hanky Panky! Before you wash your hands and face Hanky Panky! OK, Hakim you know what? I won't cook, I won't clean, I won't do anything, me and you we'll just do Hanky Panky, Hanky Panky, Hanky Panky!

(He pinches her and she turns around and tries to whack him with the rolling pin, he however ducks and she

misses him.)

You are a lucky man!

—That was before, that was a long time back, that was before we came to America. In India, how many friends I had, how much family, anybody to help. Now do you know what I do, do you know? —I cook, I clean, I take care of Sakina, and at the end of the day when she finally goes to sleep, I have five minutes for dance break which you interrupt with Hanky Panky.

—What you brought?—What present? Go away you didn't bring any present for me—Really! You brought present for me? Show no. *Are'* Show no—Come on, you can't bring present and then not show. OK. OK. OK. I close my eyes you show me? You promise, you promise, OK *(She covers her eyes.)* Guess? Guess? I can't guess, come on show no!... OK, OK I guess, I guess... no no no I want to guess.

OK you brought something to eat. No, something to wear? No!—Something for Sakina? No— Something for apartment?—YES!—New curtains!! You brought new curtains!!

(She has taken her hands away from her eyes.)

OK, OK, OK, I'm closing my eyes.

(She puts them up again.)

I can't guess anymore. C'mon, I'm looking—Ready, 1, 2, 3—

(She removes her hands from her eyes on the count of three, and she stands there staring in confusion at the sight before her.)

What you brought? What is this? A FERN? You brought a fern?—Why you brought a fern?—Oh my God, Hakim, Flowers. Flowers. Flowers means roses, flowers means tulips, flowers does <u>not</u> mean fern!—My God, what a romantic Rock Hudson I married! No, no, it's very nice. It's very nice. We'll put it in the window, people will come by and say, "Oh look, this lady's husband, he bought her a bush!"

(He wants her to teach him to dance.)

No, no, I can't teach you—Please Hakim, I can't teach you to dance. Besides, Hakim, that is a woman's dance. If a man dances like that, people will think he is a you know what!? You go, you dance with your fern.

(He seems to insist.)

OK OK I'm sorry, come here you want to learn, come here, OK do like this, like this, make a bird, make a bird, OK? OK, now you are a dancer.

(FARRIDA *pulls on her scarf, so as to give the illusion that he is trying to pull her to him.*)

No, I don't want to kiss you. I don't want to, because I don't want to. Hakim, please don't argue with me, I just don't want to. Because, just because, because you smell like cigarette! Are you happy now?—Then how come I am smelling cigarette in your mouth right now, when you told me after last time that that was your last pack and now I can smell that you are smoking again.

No, no, I don't want to dance with you, I want to know why you broke your promise. Relax. Relax. How can I relax Hakim, when you told me, you told me with your own mouth. You said, "Farrida, because I love you, I will stop smoking," and what did I say? You don't remember, I will tell you what I said, I said, "No. No. You will not, because I know you, and I know the kind of man you are" and what did you say? What did you say? You don't remember, you don't remember what you said, OK I will tell you what you said. You said, *"Khudda ni Kassam."* Do you remember? *Khudda ni Kassam Hakim.* And you are a bloody liar! You lie to me, you lie to God, you lie to anybody.

Mane' tara sathe waat aj nai karwi, tara moma si gundhi waas aweche'.

—How can you say that? If you loved me, I would not smell cigarette in your mouth right now— Teach me to dance. You can't even do one bloody thing for me!

Dramatic. Dramatic. How can I be dramatic? You see me. You see my life. You see my life since I came to this country.—Can you imagine? Me. Me. Hakim, I was the girl in India who was always on the go! Movies, theatre, museum, money to burn. Where have you brought me? Where have we come, to this cold country where nobody talks to anybody, where I sit alone in two rooms all day long waiting for you come home. No friends, no one to talk to, nowhere to go. If I go anywhere, these Americans don't even understand what I am trying to speak.

Look at me, Hakim! I am not even the girl that you married. This is not me, this was not supposed to be my life. I gave up everything for you. For your dream, America! Land of Opportunity! For you, yes. For my baby, yes. For me, no. No opportunity.

—How can you say that, how do you know? Even if we do make it, what happens do we just go on smoking and dancing forever.

(*Soft music begins to play, signifying that Sakina has woken up.*)

See now, Sakina woke up.

(*She looks offstage to talk to the apparently crying child.*)

Na ro bacha Mummy aweche. Na ro.

(She turns back to Hakim, but he is gone.)

That's alright, Hak—you go, I'll take care of her.—You go, smoke your cigarette.

(She turns upstage.)

Na ro, Mummy aweche. Na ro bacha Mummy aweche, Na ro Na ro.

(FARRIDA walks upstage and we see her slowly take the scarf from around her neck and it becomes the baby SAKINA. The scarf is eventually unraveled and we are back in the company of AZGI, as he addresses the audience.)

AZGI: Once upon a time, an eagle and a lark sat on the branch of a giant tree. The eagle pushed out its giant chest and spread its powerful wings, and told the lark of its many adventures. "I have seen the world," said the eagle, "I have seen it seven times over. I have flown over temples and palaces, oceans and valleys, I have swooped down into valleys and I have flown so high that the sun has risen and set below me." The tiny lark had no such adventures of which to speak and it wracked its brain for a story to tell. Finally, it did the only thing it knew how to do. It began to sing. A tiny song, but as it did the tree, the field, the hillside and the entire valley, lifted up out of the earth and rose to heaven.

She doesn't dance anymore. I suppose that eventually she forgot that she could.—Or maybe she simply decided it was not worth trying to remember.

Dear Ma, another day in Sakina's Restaurant. I work, and I work, and I work and I work—but I never dance.

(AZGI is suddenly in the restaurant. He mimes a conversation with a table, tries to clean their dirty silverware, he goes to another table and picks up their plates, he rushes over to the kitchen and screams at ABDUL the cook, who is working behind the line.)

ABDUL!—I need two puri's on table 5! I need two lassi's on table 6, and this lamb curry is COLD, COLD, COLD! Food, Abdul, is supposed to be HOT, HOT! Not COLD! How come you don't seen to understand that?????

(AZGI runs to speak to one of his tables. To first table.)

I am very sorry. In all the time that I have worked in this restaurant, food is NEVER cold, NEVER! He is heating it up right now. I will bring it out in two minutes and you just keep enjoying your... water.

(He moves to the second table.)

Hello, how are you? My name is Azgi, I will be your waiter, How can I help you? Oh yeah, it is kind of spicy, but we have a scale. You see, you can order how spicy you would like one, two, three, four, five. You decide, He'll make it—What?—you want number five?

(AZGI is a little concerned.)

Sir don't take number five, Take number two—No, no, number two is better for you, it's very good, you'll like it very much.—Please sir, don't take number five. Sir I am trying to save your life OK. *(getting angry)* Look, look in my eyes, OK, number two is better for you. OK, you think about it, I will come back OK.

(He runs upstage again.)

ABDUL!—Where is my lamb curry????

(The lamb curry seems to have appeared on the line.)

A-ha!

(He runs over to the first table with the imaginary lamb curry. It is very hot and burns his hands.)

There you go. OK? piping hot—What happened? Why you look so sad? Not lamb?—CHICK-EN—Oh my God!—No, no, please sit down. Where you going? Please don't leave, sit down, I am very sorry, this is a terrible mistake, I will bring out chicken in just two minutes, please don't leave, whatever you do don't leave.

(He runs over to the second table.)

OK, OK, look I tell you what, number three, number three is plenty hot. You don't need number five. LISTEN MAN!! I AM FROM INDIA!!! And even in India nobody asks for number five! It's not a real thing that you can eat, it's just for show. I am not screaming, you are screaming! Look, look, now your wife is crying! I didn't make her cry, you made her cry! OK, OK. Fine, Fine, you want five, fifteen, one hundred five!! I give you OK!

ABDUL!—Listen on dup forty-one, I put number five, but you don't make it number five, you make it number two, OK? And this lamb curry is supposed to be chicken curry—Because I am telling you, that's why. Because I am the boss right now, OK. Listen you give me any trouble no, I will have Mr. Hakim fire you!!!—Oh, yeah? Oh, yeah? Come on, Come on Abdul. *(He puts up his fists.)* I will take you right now! I will kick your butt so hard that you will be making lamb curry for the tigers in India! Oh, yeah? Come on, Big Guy, come on, Big Guy, come on—

(Suddenly AZGI is faced with ABDUL who grabs him by the collar.)

—BIG GUY!

I am joking, man. I am just kidding around, why you take me so seriously?—Please don't kill me.

(Turning)

Every night I have the same dream. I am a giant tandoori chicken wearing an Armani suit. I am sitting behind the wheel of a speeding Cadillac. I have no eyes to see, no mouth to speak and I don't know where I am going.

Mr. Hakim, he come up to me, he say, "Azgi, Azgi, Azgi, you have to calm down, man." He say to me, he say, "Success, Azgi, is like a mountain. From far away it is inspiring, but when you get close, you realize that it is simply made of earth and dirt and rocks, piled one on top of the other until it touches the sky." Mr. Hakim, he is a smart man, but I wonder to myself when God was building the mountain and piling the rock, one on top of the other, was he working or playing?

(He begins to ponder this thought, and then suddenly he smiles and goes over to the first table.)

Hello, my name is Azgi...I am working...and playing.

(He goes over to the second table.)

Hello, my name is Azgi...I am working and playing...how are you?

(He goes over and looks in the direction of ABDUL, and blows him a big kiss.)

ABDUL...I love you man!!!

(Phone rings, AZGI turns and looks at the audience.)

Phone!

(He picks up the phone.)

Hello, Sakina's Restaurant. Azgi speaking. How may I—Oh, oh, Mr. Hakim? No. No. He is right here. I will get him—

(AZGI heads around behind the coat rack as if on his way to find HAKIM, when he comes around the other side, with tie in hand.... he is HAKIM.)

HAKIM: *(Into the phone)* Hello, Sakina's, How may I help you?—Oh, hello Bob! I am very fine.

Business is good, business is good you know can't complain, how about you?—Huh? Dinner for three? Tonight? Oh you must be going to have a big celebration—Usual table? OK—8 p.m. Very good. Oh congratulations, you must be very proud of him. Actually, we are also very proud of our Sakina because—

(He is embarrassingly interrupted on the other end of the line.)

Oh, OK Bob. No no that's fine. I understand. Time is money. Got to go. OK Bob, we'll see you later. OK, we'll see you then, bye bye...bye bye...bye bye.

(Hangs up, and then resumes putting on his tie and grooming himself in mirror and singing a Hindi song of choice. During this, he hears an imaginary knock on the door.)

Come in.

(He turns to see his daughter.)

Hey, hey, hey, hey! Come inside here, close the door, come here. What is this dress?—Oh, I see, I see.

(He talks to his daughter. His distress with his daughter is translated into his ineptness and frustration with his tie that he is trying to secure.)

You think you are too smart, huh?—You think you are too smart.—You think you can go anywhere, do anything, wear anything. You think you have become an American Girl!—You think the world should not care now how you behave, what you wear, how you dress, nothing! You have got all these fancy ideas from all your American friends. You are laughing with all your American friends you are saying, "Oh my parents are introducing me to an Indian man, nice professional Indian man, going to be a Doctor, how foolish of them, right? How foolish they are." All your American friends are laughing. They are saying Hey, Sakina, life is not like that.—Life is easy, marry who you want to marry, Black guy, White guy—who cares, right? Who cares? In America, everything is OK! No right, no wrong, no good, no bad, everything is COOL! As long as I feel good about myself, who cares, right?—Who cares how my father feels, or my mother feels, or my grandfather feels or my grandmother feels. Who cares! It is my business, my life, this is a free country! Am I right?

(Phone rings.)

Hello, Sakina's, how may I help you?—Tonight, dinner for two, Martin...can you spell that? M...A...R *(He notices that SAKINA is leaving and he tries to get her to come back in the room while continuing with the customer on the phone.)* T...I...N. No I got it, I got it, yes we do, yes we do, free popadoms, yes all night long, as many as you want, OK we'll see you then, yes I am excited as well, OK then, bye bye...bye bye...bye bye.

(Hangs up)

Sakina!—Sakina!...Come inside—Close the door. I'm talking to you. Crazy girl, running away.

(He turns to the mirror, notices his tie is completely screwed up and he is a little embarrassed. He reties it.)

"Oh Dad!" You are saying, "Dad! Dad! Dad! What do you know about life in America? You are from India! In America you have to learn to relax, because everybody in America is very RELAXED and very COOL!" Well, let me tell you something, I have seen all of your cool and relaxed friends, and you are not fooling anyone—you will <u>never</u> be an American girl. You can TRY. Oh yeah, you can TRY. You can wear your BIG HAIR, like American hair, and you can wear makeup like American makeup, you can even wear this cheap dress and show off your breasts and your legs and disgrace your whole family—but you will always be an Indian girl, with Indian blood, and these Americans, oh they are very nice, very polite on the face, have a nice day. Have a nice day. Welcome to K-Mart, Very Nice.—They will look at you and say, "Oh, she is so pretty, she looks like Paula Abdul."—But let me tell you something, the minute you steal one of their good ole boys from them, suddenly you will see how quickly you become an Indian again.

(Phone rings. He speaks in Gujaratti.)

Hello Sakina's Restaurant how may I help you? *Aaa Cam cho bhai, are koi divas miltaj nathi...aje, chullo, na na badha ne layaowjo, na khai takhlif nei, chullo pachi milsu...*OK bye bye...bye bye...bye bye.

(Hangs up and faces his daughter.)

We love you, Sakina, you are our daughter. But I will never agree to what you are doing with your life.—Why do you think we came to this country?—For YOU! Why do you think I have this restaurant?—For YOU! Why do you think I am working twelve hours a day?—For YOU and your brother. So that you could grow up in the richest country in the world, have all the opportunity, all the advantages and become something. We are saving every penny for your college, why? So you can run around with American boys...NO!! So we will be proud of you. Indian children make their parents proud of them. Can your American friends teach you that?—Can they teach you about your Culture? Your Religion? Your Language? Can they tell you who you are?... Go ask them. I know, I know, I know it is all fun and games right now, but what will happen? You will marry one of these American boys, have American children, and then what? Then everything will be forgotten—Everything will be GONE.—*Tu kai samje che me su kawchu tane`. Tara Mugaj ma kai jaiche`.*

Answer me, no? No No No No, Not in English. Speak to me in Gujaratti.

(He waits, and she does not respond. She is unable to.)

Can't...! Won't maybe. Look at you, look what you have become. You will not go to this dance tonight. I will show you, I will get rid of this "I want to be American" nonsense—

(Exploding in anger.)

I DON'T CARE! I DON'T CARE, I DON'T CARE IF THIS IS THE BIGGEST DANCE IN THE COUNTRY OR THE WORLD OR THE ENTIRE FUCKING AMERICA!! DANCING IS IMPORTANT, *(He dances around mocking her.)* BUT I AM NOT IMPORTANT!

(The phone rings. He composes himself and answers the phone.)

Hello, Sakina's how may I help you?—Yes, Bob, how are you?—Oh I am very sorry. Oh, no problem, that's perfectly alright, we'll see you another time. I hope she feels better, thank you for calling Bob. Bye-bye, bye-bye, bye-bye.

(Hangs up, and looks back at SAKINA.)

Tell Azgi that the Cohens have canceled, and go help your mother...in the kitchen.

(Phone rings, he watches her leave and then answers.)

AZGI: *(On phone)* Hey Ma, it is me, Azgi. Yeah, Azgi, I'm calling from New York. You know what, Ma? Next month Sakina is getting married, and tonight she is having a Bachelorette party, and I have been invited. I am very excited to be a Bachelorette. Hey, yeah, listen to the music.

(He holds up receiver.)

That's the music ma, You won't believe this party ma, so many people, Ma...I have to go, Ma. I love you, bye.

(He hangs up the phone and comes downstage dancing. He then dances downstage and then talks to the audience.)

Sakina told her parents that if she had to marry who they wanted her to marry, then she was going to have the kind of bachelorette party that she wanted to have. She invited 75 people, all of them would drink, including myself, and then she had a rock and roll band, and just to make sure that her parents would completely disapprove, she paid $200.00 for a "MALE STRIPPER." I told her, "I said for two hundred dollars in India I would run around naked for ONE WEEK!"—She said, "Oh, yeah?"

(The music that has been underlying the previous speech, suddenly becomes very loud and AZGI begins to strip. He speaks as his clothes are seemingly ripped off his body. He is incredibly embarrassed.)

No NO I cannot strip, No I do not do that kind of thing, I am very modest, I am from India, please do not do this, OK OK I tell you what I do this much OK? *(He simply opens a shirt a little.)* La la la la...That's all I can so thank you very much *(His shirt is ripped off him.)* Noooo!!! Because I was the only man, they decided to turn me into a Bachelorette.

(At this, AZGI suddenly runs over to the hat stand and takes the tube dress that has been hanging there. The

dress is slipped over his neck as if it were being done to him by the women at the party.)

No, no, please. I cannot wear this, this is a dress! I am very embarrassed. Please not a DRESS, anything but a dress!

(His protests of genuine embarrassment are unheeded by the women, who after the dress, proceed to finish off the transformation by squeezing a hair band onto his head much to AZGI's amazement and distress.)

AAAAAAAAAAAAAAAAAAAAAAAAAAAAHHHHHHHH!!!!!!!!!!!!!!!!

(AZGI stands center stage wearing a tube dress and a hair band.)

Once upon a time a man asked God for a new face because he was tired of the one he had, so God granted the man his wish. The tragedy of this story is that now every time the man looks in the mirror, he doesn't know who he is.

(AZGI moves over to the table stage left and sits down. We are now in the presence of SAKINA. She primps and preens in a large hand mirror, until she is suddenly surprised by the presence of TOM who is sitting across the table.)

SAKINA: Oh my GOD!!! *(Embarrassed)* I didn't see you come in... Wow you look great, I got your message. I can't stay long...'cus I gotta get upstairs by 7:30.—Well we're having this religious festival at our house and all these people come over and we make this food called Biriani and...Never mind, I just gotta get back upstairs by 7:30 to help my mom get ready for it. *(Pause)* So, what's up?—I'm just surprised to see you because last time we talked you were like, "Sakina we are broke up"...and then you hung up the phone. What?—That's not true!— Is that why you came here, to tell me that? *(She turns and takes a deep breath and then turns back to him.)* No I'm fine, I'm fine, first of all Tom, first of all, Stacey and I are the ones who started this band and Stacey and I are the only ones who can—

(She looks up at the imaginary waiter.)

Hi!—No, I'm not eating...no neither is he, thanks, OK?—Thanks.

(Waiter leaves.)

And Stacey and I are the only ones who can kick anyone out of this band, which is not even a band yet, because Stacey still needs to learn how to play the piano and so you are kicking me out of a band that does not even exist yet!—No, no, no, no, the manager manages the band, Tom. He does not kick people out of the band, that is not his job.—What?—She said that?—She said that! Stacey said that, Tom, look at me, look at me OK, Stacey is my best friend since the 8th grade, and if she said that, Tom, we are totally not friends anymore, so you better not be lying—Oh, my God! I can't believe she said that, I told her why I had to miss those practices, I totally said I have to miss three practices because I have to hang out with that Indian guy that my parents want me to marry—I had to hang out with him—I can't believe she said that, I don't understand, I explained the whole thing to her.

(TOM gets up to leave.)

Where are you going— That's it, that's all you had to say, now you're just gonna leave?

(She reaches for him.)

Wait! Would you please just sit down? *(She stands)* Please, Tom. *(She bends over and becomes cute and coy in order to lure him back to the table.)* Please, just for two minutes, please just sit down. *(He sits back down.)* Hi, What is going on here Tom?—What do you mean, what do I mean?—I mean you come here to tell me that my best friend is kicking me out of my band, and then last week you're like we have to break up 'cus "I need more space," and then this week I find out that you're dating Julie Montgomery, and I'm calling you every day this week and your Dad is like, "Tom? Tom went to the Library"—and I'm like, Tom at the library?...I don't think so—no, I don't think I'd be jealous of her. Because, because, because she's a racist pig, that's why. I can't believe you would even date her.—I was hoping you came here to tell me of her untimely death.—I don't care if I'm not Black. It's still disgusting.—I didn't say that, I just said she's a racist pig and I wish she'd die. You can still date her.—Everyone knows she is, everyone in school knows have you ever heard her mouth?—"Nigger. Nigger. Nigger."

(She suddenly looks around hoping that no one heard her.)

She even called me that word...What's so funny?—You're laughing, yes you are, Oh my God you're sick, Tom. This is retarded, I'm leaving. *(Gets up to leave as waiter returns. She speaks to the waiter.)* Hi!—Yeah I have to leave, I have to go upstairs and *(Directing it at TOM)* THROW UP! What?—I don't care if she's sorry, Tom, my problem is you, my problem is—What? *(Realizing that waiter has taken her seriously.)* No I don't need any PEPTO. It's just HIM, I'm sorry thanks...no no I'm fine, thanks. *(Waiter leaves. She turns back to TOM)* My problem is not her, my problem is YOU. I'm starting to like not know you anymore.—You explained it to her? You explained it to her. OK, fine this should be great, *(Sitting back down)* What, Tom, did you explain to her?—

(She listens and then hears something that makes her suddenly furious.)

Ah ha,—and then?—and?—OK shut up! No really Tom shut up! Tom, Tom, Shut up! Shuuuuuuuuuuuuuuuut uuuuup!—Listen to me. I am NOT IRANIAN!—I am INDIAN! INDIAN! INDIAN! What do you mean? How could you not know that? Look around, Tom. We dated for TWO MONTHS, Tom, TWO MONTHS! In that TWO months, I brought you to THIS Indian Restaurant like a million times. Where you ate all the "OOOOH, it's SO GOOD!" INDIAN FOOD that my Mom put in front of your face. And remember that party I took you to in Brooklyn with all those INDIAN people, wearing INDIAN clothes celebrating INDIAN Independence Day and then you turn around and tell Julie Montgomery, "Hey, Sakina's not a nigger, she's IRANIAN!" Well there it is isn't it, everything is a big mistake to you. Our whole relationship was a big mistake, remember that one?—Oh, my God! I can't believe you, I already explained the whole thing to you. It doesn't mean anything,—I am NOT going to marry him. Because I'm not that's how I know—no no no. My parents can't make me. It's not some kind of medieval thing. It's just part of the culture, that's all. It's just a custom, they are just trying to make sure that I am secure in my life, that's all, they're not American, they're not like your parents—I'm not saying that—Your parents are great! I'm just saying that my parents have a different attitude about things and if you can just accept that and not make a big deal about it?—Well there it is isn't it!! If everyone doesn't think like you, talk like you, believe what you believe, then it's all just dumb, right?

(He takes her hand, music comes on.)

What are you doing? No I can't kiss you...because we are in my Dad's restaurant... What? *(She suddenly starts giggling based on what he has said, she slowly moves toward him, and as the music gets louder she and TOM engage in a big sloppy wet teenage kiss, she pulls away and realizes that she is chewing "his" gum, she takes it out of her mouth.)* What? Why?—No, you're gonna make fun of him. Because you always make fun of him. OK, if I show you, you promise not to laugh?—Do you promise? Say it. Say I promise not to laugh...or make fun of him...OK

(She reaches into her purse, she pulls out of her purse a photograph and puts it on the table.)

When I was seven, my dad, yeah he gave me this picture of this guy that they betrothed me to, and I just kept it.—Because, because, I didn't know I was gonna meet anybody.—When you're young and geeky with a funny name and your Mom makes you wear harem pants and braids everyday it's hard to imagine that you're ever gonna meet anyone.—I don't suppose you can even relate, Mr. Free Throw wins the Junior Championship—So it was a good feeling to have a picture of a guy who was like mine, and even though I was different, so was he, and so we were, like a team.—Jeez, I feel totally stupid. I don't even know why I'm telling you this.—

(He gets up to leave.)

Where are you going? Where are you going?—No No I will tell him, I couldn't tell him last time, I'm gonna tell him next time.

(She snaps the picture up as he reaches over to tear it up.)

Hey!!! I think before I tear up his picture, I should tell him that I am not going to marry him, I think that would be courteous. Would you please come back!! Why is this such a big deal to you?— I'm gonna tell him. Come back, Please come back. Fine! Fine, Tom! Just leave! Just leave the way you always do! *(Pause)* WAAAAIT!!!!

What you don't understand Tom is that it doesn't make any difference, it's just the way it is. You can kick me outta the band, you can date a racist pig, Stacey can be a total bitch, my parents can cry, and I can even tear up this picture and it doesn't make any difference. *(Pause)* OK OK OK OK OK, *(She picks up the picture)* Fine...fine...fine.

(As music builds SAKINA attempts to tear up the picture, but it becomes obvious that she cannot. She holds the picture to her chest, and TOM walks away. she turns and undresses into AZGI again. As the music plays, AZGI picks up the strewn clothes and hangs them up, he then puts his shirt on again as the lights come up.)

AZGI: *(Noticing audience)* Oh Hello!!! Oh you know, Sakina's wedding was wonderful. So many people. She looked beautiful, she looked so beautiful, she looked like a gift. The Groom? He also looked very handsome. In fact, the two of them together, they looked perfect. A little uncomfortable, but perfect. The Groom, he is a medical student and he is also a very religious Muslim man. In fact, even at his own wedding he was studying for his final exam the next day and praying that he would not fail. Can you believe?? By watching him, I also start to pray...But the only thing I could think of to pray after watching him was, "Please God, don't let me spend my whole life just praying and studying, praying and studying, praying and studying..." Oh for their honeymoon, they are going to travel across America. Oh, it sounds very exciting. They will see everything, the Hollywood and the Redwood, they will ride on Wide Open Ventura Highways, and they will see The Grand Canyon, and the Mississippi. I told the groom, I said, "If I could, I would follow you. I envy the adventure you are going to have." And he looked at me, and said, "Azgi, if I could, I would follow you, I envy the adventure you are going to have."

(A sudden light change, AZGI suddenly doubles over in anguish.)

ALI: Shut up! Shut up!—I have to walk, I have to clear my head, and I have to come back. I have to walk, I have to clear my head, I have to come back, I have to walk, I have to clear my head, I have to come back. I have to WALK! I have to clear my head, I have to come—

(Suddenly he looks up as if someone has opened a door and he is staring into their face. He is visibly nervous, his mouth is dry and his hands are sweaty.)

I only have fifty dollars, I don't know if that's enough or not. Oh, that's fine, whatever you do for fifty dollars is fine. I don't know if I want the complete package anyway. It's probably safer that way, in regards to diseases and such. *(Realizing his faux pas)* I'm sorry, I'm not saying that you have any diseases. Oh no I ruined the mood. I'm sorry, it's just that I'm a Pre-Med student, so I'm always thinking about diseases. I don't do this kind of thing normally—NEVER!! Never before actually, I don't know if that matters to you, but it matters to me, and so I just thought I would share that with you.

(Pulling money out of his pocket and handing it to her)

Look, I'll just give you the money and you can put it over there on the dresser, or in your *(Noticing that she put it in her underwear)* There! This is very unlikely for me to be in a place like this—I've actually been trying to deepen my religious faith lately. I'm a Muslim, you know. Do you know what that is?... Yes, it's a type of cloth. What is your name?—Angel?—Really? *(He laughs.)* No, no, I'm sorry. I was just thinking that that's an ironic name for someone who does what you do for a living.—What? No, no, I'm sorry, I'm not a jerk. I'm sorry that was rude, Look I think you're very attractive. In fact, that's even the reason I followed you in here from the street...was because of the way you look...or at least who you look like. Well, you see, you look amazingly like this girl Karen who sits next to me in my Human Anatomy class, and who I cannot stop thinking about, and earlier this evening I was trying to study for my exam tomorrow, but I can't seem to concentrate because I can't stop thinking about Karen, and then when I think about Karen all the time, I think about my parents beating their chests when they realize I've failed all my exams. So I decided to take a walk and pray for some concentration, and that's when I saw you, and you—well, you look exactly like her, and you looked at me, and you smiled, and so when you started thinking to myself that you must be a sign...a sign from God!! That since I'll never be with Karen, I could be with you, and then I could go home and be able to study, and pass my exam and make my parents proud of me!!! *(He suddenly breaks down into tears.)* I'm sorry, I'm really sorry, I think I've made a terrible mistake. You see I just realized that God would never, never lead me to a place like this. I must be losing my mind. I have to study, I have to go! I need some sleep! I have to study, I'm really sorry. I have obviously wasted your time, I'm really sorry but I have to go. *(He leaves, there is a long pause then he returns.)* I think I should probably just get a refund. I don't know what your policy is as far as refunds go. I'm sure that it doesn't come up very often.—What?—Uh, thank you, that's very kind of you— Well I think you're very attractive yourself—No, I can't do that actually, No I can't, No I really can't—Well, because I'm engaged...or at least "betrothed" which is actually more like...engaged!— She's a very nice girl, Sakina!! Would you like to see a picture? I have one,—No of course not. What I'm trying to say is that she really is the perfect girl for me, comes from a very similar family, same religion, same tradition, same values, these things are important, you know. Besides, Karen is just a distraction. I mean, she's American. In the long run she would never accept Indian culture, she would never understand the importance of an Islamic way of life, she would probably want to have pre-marital sex which is something that as a Muslim I could never do. I know that probably sounds ridiculous under the circumstances, but it's true!!! It's not just a religion you know, it's a way of life and I have dedicated my entire spiritual life identity to the complete submission to the will of God. That's what Islam means. So you see, I can't just be running around having sex *(He thrust his pelvis forward unconsciously.)* like a rabbit *(He does it again, with more vigour.)* It would be a SIN!! And that is why I have to leave. What? What is my name?

(He pauses.)

AL!—Really!—OK, OK. It's not Al the way you are thinking of it, like short for Alan or Alvin or something. It's actually the short form of a very religious name, a name I can't even say right now, otherwise it would be a sin—I think. I probably don't even deserve this name.

(We begin to hear the song, "No Ordinary Love." This plays throughout the rest of the piece.)

What are you doing?—No I really don't think you should...REMOVE THAT!!!

(He hides behind his hands so as not to look at her but then he slowly looks.)

You want me to call you Karen?... OK!? Karen, Karen, Karen, Karen...

(She unbuttons his pants and begins to perform oral sex, the rest of the lines are delivered while he is receiving a blow job.)

Oh, my God, this is not me, this is not my life. Oh, shit!

(Looking down)

I'm sorry, I'm trying not to swear. It's hard, you know, to do the right thing, you know.—I'm always asking for forgiveness, because I believe that God understands and he is forgiving, and he knows how hard it is, to do the right thing all the time, even when you want to, more than anything else, and if you fail and you disappoint people, you can just try again, right? And you can have the intention to try again even while you're failing...failing! I don't suppose there is really any chance of me passing this exam tomorrow. I mean, If I'm going to be punished for this, and I'm sure I will be, that will probably be the punishment, because when you're trying to do the right thing and make people proud of you, Satan wants you to fail. And then you end up being a huge disappointment. Well, if I'm not going to be a doctor, I wonder what I will be?—Maybe I will be a bum!—And Sakina will say, "I can't marry him, he's a BUM!!!"

(He is getting quite worked up at this point as he gets closer to orgasm.)

And I will say, "GOOD!!!! BECAUSE THIS BUM WOULDN'T MARRY YOU WHEN HELL FREEZES OVER!" AND HER PARENTS WILL SAY, "HOW DARE YOU TALK TO OUR DAUGHTER LIKE THAT!!! AND I WILL SAY I JUST DID!! AND MY PARENTS WILL SAY, HOW DARE YOU TALK TO HER PARENTS LIKE THAT, YOU ARE A GREAT DISAP-POINTMENT," AND I WILL SAY, "MOM, DAD EAT

(He orgasms.)

SHIIIT!!!!!"

(He falls to his knees in shock, and slowly as if almost in slow motion he doubles over on the floor, unconsciously going into the Islamic position of prayer. After a few seconds, he regains his composure and attempts to stand and button up his pants.)

Thank you Angel, I mean Kar-... I mean Angel.

(He takes off his glasses.)

AZGI: Once upon a time a hunter wandered into a forest, armed only with a bow and arrow, in order to find food for his family. After some time he came upon a clearing, and in the middle of the clearing stood a goat. The hunter, excited by this, raised his bow and arrow in order to kill the goat, but just as he did, the hunter noticed that the goat was crying. The hunter, intrigued by this, asked the animal why it wept. And the goat answered "I weep because God spoke to me and he told me all the secrets of the Universe." The hunter asked the goat to share the secrets with him, and so the goat did, and after he was done the hunter realized...that now, he could never return home.

(Music and lights change, as AZGI slowly sits center stage and contemplates. Suddenly his meditation is broken by a sudden light change and computerized sound, he gets up and finds the sound is coming from and discovers SAMIR's Game Boy)

(Looking off)

Samir!! Samir!! Hey how come you leave your stuff lying around man, I got to clean up!!

(noticing audience)

OH, HELLO!

You know Samir he leaves his stuff just lying around you know, I have to clean up, *(Getting interested in the Game Boy.)* This is a very exciting little game though, apparently the idea is you see if you can just get your little man to the top of this mountain without getting hit by the falling rocks, then you get to go in the space ship and fly away...it's very good *(Playing)* Come on Jump! Jump! Come on you crazy man, come on, Jump! Jump!—

(Looking off.)

HELLO! Oh Samir, yeah there you are, I found your hat and your Game Boy because you leave your junk her in the restaurant and then I have to pick up your stuff—No, no, no, you can't have it, because I'm almost up to the space ship.

(Listening and playing at the same time.)

Sakina? Oh yeah, she sent a postcard? From her honeymoon? Oh yeah? Good for you, good for you.—To me!! To me!! She sent a postcard to me? Oh yeah let me see, let me see!! Come on it's my postcard man. OK, I give you the Game Boy, you give me the postcard, OK? I put it down, you put the postcard down, ready

(He puts the postcard on the table, SAMIR obviously doesn't and AZGI chases him around the restaurant)

Hey!! Hey!! You see how you are? Give me that postcard, come on Samir. Come on, give it to me! Hey!

(He chases SAMIR around the stage trying to get the postcard. At a certain point in the chase AZGI puts on the hat and becomes SAMIR, he squirms around trying to keep a hold of the postcard and then he throws it offstage and runs over to the Game Boy)

SAMIR: *(Playing with his Game Boy.)* It's on the floor—*(picking up the Game Boy)* Hey Cool! You're almost in outer space. You know what, you know what, you know what Azgi? My sister, she is gonna go all over the country for her honeymoon, and you know what, she said that she would send me a postcard from each place she went, but you know what the best part is, Azgi? You know what the best part is? When she goes to Disney World she is gonna send me an autographed picture of the Ninja Turtles...Cool right! Cus that's where they live!!! And we were supposed to go to Disney World last year, but we didn't go, cus my grandmother died and then we had to go to India, *(He pretends to puke)* that Sucked!!! And you know what? You know what? You know what? I got into this huge fight with my cousin Mustafa. Cus you know what, you know what, you know what,

(Light change.)

Dad!!! No I didn't punch him, I didn't punch him, I didn't punch him, no listen, I was showing Mustafa this really cool game, but he didn't wanna play, so then I said...let's play anyway! But he was being a spoil sport and messin up the game, and not playin right, so then I said, "FINE! I'm gonna play Ninja Turtles on my Game Boy," and when I was doing that he wanted to play too! All of sudden! But I said, "No way, Jose!" So then, so then, so then, Mom called me to come upstairs and look at some pictures of Dadi Ma when she was alive and she was really young and you were sitting in her lap and you were just a little baby—Dad Dad Dad, Do you remember that? Dad, do you remember when you were a baby? ....Do ya? *(Realizing he cannot change the subject so easily.)* SO THEN! I said that he could hold my Game Boy for just five minutes. JUST FIVE MINUTES! But then, when I came back he wouldn't give it so I had to give him a Ninja Kick in the head!!!

(He demonstrates a Ninja Kick to the head.)

That's all that happened, yeah but I didn't punch him, I didn't punch him, I didn't punch him, he said I punched him, I didn't punch him. So I don't have to share with a crybaby and a liar if I don't want to. But Dad it's my Game Boy, that I brought all the way from America remember? Remember, you said nobody could touch it, not even Sakina "cus it was the only thing that would keep me shut up," remember you said that? Huh?—So that just means he's a crybaby that's all. I don't have to share with a crybaby—No,—No,—But I'm not even sorry.

(His father slaps SAMIR on the behind. This is done by SAMIR turning himself with his right hand and slapping his own behind with his left hand. Every time that SAMIR is slapped in the remainder of this piece, it is done using this method.)

Hey!!! How come you're hitting me, he's the one who STOLE my Game Boy, how come no one is hitting him? What?—NA-AH—WHY?—Dad no!! That's totally not fair!—No, no, no, I don't want another stupid Game Boy. I just want the one I have. This was my birthday present from Jim's

dad, you can't just give my birthday present to any stupid Indian kid that wants it just cus they don't have any cool toys here.—No, I don't want another one, why can't you buy HIM another one?—I'm sick of this. You know what, Mom already gave him my Ninja Turtle high tops, she already gave him those, yeah the ones with the lights in 'em that go "Kawabunga!" when you jump in 'em, she already gave him those. You're just gonna give him all my stuff.—I hate coming to India, I hate coming to this stupid country—No, no, no, he's not my brother, he's stupid! He smells!!—He can't even speak English! *(He is slapped again.)*
Didn't hurt *(Slap!)*
Didn't hurt more!!! *(Slap!!!)*

(Crying)

Alright! Alright! It hurt!! How come you always hit me when I tell the truth, huh? Yes you do, yes you do, yes you do, everyone in this country is stupid!! And they just want all my cool stuff, cus they don't have any cool stuff of their own, and they're just jealous, cus we get to live in America, and they're stuck here in ugly, smelly old India, and I never, ever, ever wanna come back here ever, and I don't ever wanna go anywhere with you and Mom ever again cus you're just liars! Liars! Liars! Liars!... And you abuse your children too!—Yes you do, yes you do!—You said we were gonna go to Disney World this year, and we were gonna see the Ninja Turtles like all my friends did.—Yeah, well, I don't care. I hate Dadi Ma too!!! I hate her for dying and ruining everything!

(This time SAMIR is slapped on the face. After the slap SAMIR stands in shocked silence as he is about to burst into tears, in that moment he witnesses his father starting to cry. He has never seen this before and is therefore frightened and confused by what he sees.)

Dad? Are you alright? Dad, I'm sorry! I'm sorry I said that about Dadi Ma.—Listen, you know what, Mustafa can have my Game Boy, alright?

(He takes off the hat also, and hands it to his father.)

He can have all my stuff. *(SAMIR reaches out with his hat and Game Boy but his father does not take them.)*

Dad! I'm sorry that your mom died. *(SAMIR begins to cry, slowly he backs upstage and he places both the Game Boy and the hat on the nearest table. He is again AZGI. The lights change and the area where FARRIDA had studios in a pool of light, AZGI enters it as himself.)*

AZGI: "This is not me, this was not supposed to be my life,"...she said *(Moving to the Hat and the Game Boy)* "I thought we were gonna go to Disney World!!!"...he said. *(Moving to where SAKINA had sat.)* It doesn't make any difference, it's just the way it is...she said. *(Moving to HAKIM's area)* Everything will be forgotten, everything will be gone...he said. *(Moving to where ALI had stood.)* "Well, maybe I should just get a refund," he said.

Everyone speaking my voice. Everyone except me, Ma. Where did I go? What happened to the top of the Empire State Building? What happened to the bottom of the Grand Canyon? How did all my adventures and romances end up on other people's postcards?

"I DON'T REMEMBER THE STORY OF THE RIVER STONE"... I SAID... Once upon a time, there was a boy, and this boy was standing by a stream, and by his foot he found a stone. He picked up the stone because he believed it was the most perfect stone he had ever seen. He immediately threw the tiny stone into the stream because in his young heart he believed that as soon as the stone entered the water and sparkled beneath the sunlight, it would become a diamond. As soon as the stone entered the stream, it began to flow with the current, faster and faster and faster and faster, the boy ran along side the stream watching his tiny stone, tossing and turning in the water, always moving, always dancing until...it disappeared and he could no longer see it. The boy panicked. He ran to the end of the stream, where he discovered that his tiny stone had been washed ashore amidst hundreds and thousands of rocks and stones and pebbles, all of which had taken the same journey down the same stream. The boy searched frantically for his perfect stone, picking up one stone after the next after the next, after the next but he could not find it. He searched day after day, week after week, month after month, year after year, until the boy became a man. And then one day he stopped searching, because he realized that the reason he could not find it was because he had never really known what it looked like.

(*He pulls out the tiny pebble from the beginning of the play from his pocket. He looks at it and closes his fist around it, he turns and walks upstage as the music crescendos.Blackout.*)

END OF PLAY

SWOONY PLANET

By Han Ong

In 1991, after working for two years at the Mark Taper Forum in Los Angeles
(reading scripts, taking calls, arranging files), I was let go, a casualty of
downsizing. But the artistic staff, who knew of my work as a playwright and who
also knew that I had no other means of supporting myself, decided to offer me a
commission for a play. Out of this, what I termed my "severance package," came
SWOONY PLANET, which I handed to the theater in 1992. I was twenty-four when I
directed a bare-bones workshop production at the Taper. Nothing came of that
workshop, though there had been polite murmurs of interest from the Taper and
from a scant few quarters. And so, SWOONY PLANET collected dust in my files until
1994 when I stuffed it into a box bound for New York City. I was going to try my
luck not as a writer, but as a citizen, though aspirations toward writerly glamour did hover in my considerations of moving. Once in New York, though, the
play's fate did not change. It continued to collect dust...until 1996 when I was
approached by the Ma-Yi Theater Company and well-known set designer Loy Arcenas,
who was looking to branch out as a director. I handed SWOONY PLANET over to them.
At that time, I didn't think too much about it. SWOONY was simply an "old" play,
one which hadn't been seen in New York, and I was glad that there were still
some people interested in putting my work up.

A few months later, Loy Arcenas got together a group of his friends and acquain-
tances to read SWOONY in the basement of his upper west side building. He wanted,
as did Ralph B. Pena and Jorge Ortoll of Ma-Yi, to "hear" the play. I came. I
listened. And at the end of the evening, the feeling that kept slowly mounting
as I heard the actors speak, became unstaunchable. There was no pushing it back
any longer: I was shocked that I had written this thing. I felt... I felt awakened by the same sense of possibility that I suddenly remembered having suffused
me as I sat down to write SWOONY. I was twenty-four then, more stupid-smart than I
am now, more heedless of other people's opinions about what "worked" and what
didn't, and, as to the prevailing canon of "classics", I almost always unsuccess-
fully restrained a chortle and a raspberry. That was the spirit in which SWOONY
was written but the play had subsequently collected dust for so many years that
I subconsciously and erroneously took that for a judgment of its merits, and so,
during that night of being reacquainted (with my younger self, most of all), I
was, well, nicely reminded that, heck, I was a writer. And I needed to be
reminded because New York turned out to be a big bust. I had been suffering the
dejection of seeing a good production of a play of mine (THE CHANG FRAGMENTS,
directed by Marcus Stern, at The Public) stupidly received, and was living underneath a solo storm cloud of being a failed writer. And so, hearing again the
ambitiousness that I once had, the show-offy language I was once capable of, I
felt...alive. And it'd been a long time since I last felt that way.

I wish that there was some big spectacular movie ending to all this—that we
opened and were a huge success, my bad luck forever reversing itself, etc.—but

all that happened was very simple and very quiet. A few months later, in the spring of 1997, Ma-Yi put up the workshop. We ran for two weeks, not inviting the critics, and playing to a small crowd. But Loy did a beautiful job and I was nonetheless pleased. And among the wonderful actors were two who were old friends from that other, L.A. life, and who had played in the workshop I had directed long ago: Natsuko Ohama and Harvey Perr, reprising their roles as, respectively, Kirtana and Kumar. The collegiality and mutual respect of the whole group was another new, inspiring factor, and basking in it, I was able to finish the third part of the trilogy of which SWOONY was the first: VIRGIN.

Oh, wait. Two months after the workshop closed, in June of 1997, I got a call informing me that I was being awarded a MacArthur "Genius" Fellowship. Now I have no way of knowing if the MacArthur panel had been alerted about SWOONY and had seen it (since their proceedings are kind of hush-hush), but I would like to believe that they did, and that it became a point in my favor. I would like to think that they could see, as I couldn't until much, much later, the difference between collecting dust and being dust. And so, maybe, there is a kind of movie ending after all. And maybe, the trilogy might even be coming soon to a theater near you...

HAN ONG

SWOONY PLANET (Play One of THE SUITCASE TRILOGY)
by Han Ong

Produced by Ma-Yi Theatre Company
Ralph B. Peña - Artistic Director
Jorge Ortoll - Producer
Linhart Theatre, New York
April 1997

Designed and Directed by Loy Arcenas

Lighting Design: Blake Burba
Sound Design: Fabian Obispo
Production Stage Manager: C. Renee Alexander
Assistant Director: Andrew Sachs

Featuring:
Thomas Ikeda
Mia Katigbak
Forrest McClendon
Natsuko Ohama
Harvey Perr
Kaipo Schwab
David Teschendorf

SWOONY PLANET was originally commissioned and given an initial workshop by the Mark Taper
Forum, Los Angeles, CA.

No set at all.

Any environ that parallels abandoned factories shelled-out churches.

This play is dedicated to Jessica Hagedorn

SWOONY PLANET
(PLAY ONE OF THE SUITCASE TRILOGY)

1. *Airport. Bench. Smoke all around. Clouds. A GUARD enters. (An actor who will later play LEONCIL-LO.) Addresses the smoke.*

GUARD: Excuse me

(Obscured by the smoke is KIRTANA, Indian (Asian) woman, mid 30s. She becomes visible in increments, as the smoke slowly dissipates.)

KIRTANA: Please go away

GUARD: There is no smoking here

KIRTANA: I'm not smoking

GUARD: What's all this then

KIRTANA: A woman preceded me to this spot
Why don't you go ask her

GUARD: Four hours ago
Someone was here four hours ago
Since then
You've remained stuck here Alone
For four hours

KIRTANA: I'm collecting myself

GUARD: For four hours?
What's left that still needs
collecting after four
hours? I'll help you
catch it

KIRTANA: This is a public place
It says public
An arrow points here saying, Public
Besides I don't see a crowd

Why should I be cleared out

GUARD: You're a security risk

KIRTANA: You're a cow
You beat your wife
Clear her out of the bathroom
each night after work don't you
so you can rush in there
can't wait to rush in there
to scrub clean the soil
that sticks to your skin
underneath that uniform

GUARD: This is my job

KIRTANA: HOW
You lousy cow
HOW am I a security risk

GUARD: I look at you—

KIRTANA: Your eyeballs wheel
everywhere for a wife substitute
I get the picture

GUARD: And you are a woman—

KIRTANA: Hooray
You are per CEPtive

GUARD: —who's alone
so that's strike one
in this type of environment
where interstate smuggling
is on the rise

KIRTANA: Go away
Please go away

GUARD: Am I breaking you down
Because—
            Good

Because the sooner you get out of here
the safer you'll
         we'll all be

KIRTANA: Please
Just a few more hours

GUARD: Where are you from?
India?

KIRTANA: *(A return to pissed)*
YOU should talk

GUARD: I was born here

KIRTANA: Well hip hip hooray
I'm from
Iowa, I came from Iowa if you wanna know

GUARD: And before that India right

KIRTANA: And before that I have no memory

GUARD: You're a traitor then is that what you are

KIRTANA: Immigrant
How could you possibly claim to have been
born here you don't even speak
the language

GUARD: Traitor that's what we call people like you
I speak English
For you, English says see under: Traitor

KIRTANA: Move off
If I'm a traitor what does that make your parents

GUARD: They were born here

KIRTANA: Well believe me
you are DESCENDED from Traitors

GUARD: If I were your husband—

KIRTANA: Well you're not
I'm a woman who's alone
but not defenseless
I have claws and teeth—

GUARD: You ARE from India
Well if I were your husband
I'd come pretty quick
to collect you
before the jungle reclaims your
manner

KIRTANA: Are you DEAF
I'm husbandless
I don't need one
And if this is your way of applying
for the post, well then
FUCK OFF BUDDY

(Lights dim on them. GUARD leaves. KIRTANA remains.)

2. *Simultaneous: From Stage Left enters MARTIN. White. 40s. From Stage Right enters ARTIE. Filipino-American. Early 20s. MARTIN in white undershirt and white boxers. ARTIE in yellow undershirt and yellow boxers. Each has in both hands a shirt and pants, white. They come in. Stand on opposite sides, facing forward flanking KIRTANA. Tight light on each. Each line they speak is punctuated by an arm being fitted into a sleeve, leg into pant, buttons being buttoned etc.—gestural like dance—movements to lay over this sequence of dialogue:*

MARTIN: When you were young

ARTIE: When I was younger

MARTIN: I used to look at you

ARTIE: You keep looking at me still

MARTIN: And I would open my mouth

ARTIE: You'd open your mouth
Martin I know all of this

MARTIN: Before you go just listen to me
My mouth would open

ARTIE: Into an O

MARTIN: It would curve up

ARTIE: Then down
A little cave
Your words like bats flying out
each one blind

MARTIN: Not the words
But their destination
Which was you

It would curve up
Then down
And I'd say looking right at you

ARTIE: What would you say Martin

MARTIN: I'd say Daddy

I'd peek at you through bars of a crib

ARTIE: I was never in any crib Martin

MARTIN: And I'd say, Call me Daddy
And one day

ARTIE: And one day

MARTIN: You did

ARTIE: All of a day

MARTIN: All of a <u>year</u>

ARTIE: And you said

MARTIN: An entire year hearing
your mouth curve up then down
your voice a junior
saying exactly what I said
saying Daddy

ARTIE: And you said

MARTIN: And I said
all full of joy

ARTIE & MARTIN: Now we're alike

(*At this line, ARTIE & MARTIN have finished dressing and do indeed look alike. White pants, white long-sleeved shirt. Except MARTIN has a band of black around his waist, leather belt, which doesn't fit him anymore.*)

MARTIN: Alike enough to be father and son

(*Struggles with belt. Won't fit. Gives up.*)

MARTIN: Jesus Christ

(*Removes belt. Lifts it up in one hand towards ARTIE.*)

ARTIE: I don't want it

MARTIN: The body fucks up
sneaks up on you
and then one day looking right in the mirror
from crib to middle age in just one glance
That's what a father is for
Take it

ARTIE: I don't want your belt

MARTIN: To tell about the tyranny of the body
That's what a father is for
To give a well-notched belt
each puncture letting a little air out
until

ARTIE: The belt's not my style Martin

MARTIN: Until you float up a little less each year
To make you earthbound
That's what a father is for

ARTIE: Martin
The belt may be the right belt
The story behind it may be the right story
            (Beat)
But you're not the right Father
Somebody else's but not mine
            (Beat)
I'm sorry

(Lights fade on MARTIN. Back up on KIRTANA at the Airport Bench. ARTIE walks to KIRTANA.)

3.

ARTIE: Taken?

KIRTANA: You wanna sit?

ARTIE: I'd like that yes

KIRTANA: Sit

(ARTIE sits.)

KIRTANA: This is Illinois

ARTIE: Are you talking to me

KIRTANA: Do you live here

ARTIE: Not for long

KIRTANA: It's not a big place is it

ARTIE: Big enough to have an airport

KIRTANA: But not too big

ARTIE: Actually quite sleepy

KIRTANA: Restful

ARTIE: *(Beat)* Sleepy

KIRTANA: I've been too awake
So this sounds completely
to me
Some sleep
is more than I've had in the last three days
The plane took three days

ARTIE: Really? Where did you get on

KIRTANA: They keep telling me three hours
but I'll swear to you

it's been three days with no sleep
Iowa We started surrounded by corn fields all yellow and green and by the time the plane tipped this
way all we could see looking down was miles and miles of black

ARTIE: What was black

KIRTANA: Razed grass I think
and structures going up
and it seemed to bode great speed
something far ahead I can't catch up with
like my son
(Sees GUARD approach)
Listen
There's a man coming this way
who's been hitting on me all night
I wanna stay a bit longer
Don't let him clear me out OK
Pretend you're my son

ARTIE: What

KIRTANA: Call me Mom
Say you've come to meet me
and take me home
He won't bother you

GUARD: This is a final warning

KIRTANA: (To ARTIE) That's the man

GUARD: Who is this

KIRTANA: He's my son
(To ARTIE)
That's who's been assaulting me

GUARD: Wait a minute now
Nothing's happened that hasn't been only verbal

ARTIE: Leave my Mom alone

GUARD: This is your Mom?

ARTIE: Didn't you hear what I said

                                I said, Leave my Mom alone

GUARD: A woman alone in an airport is a recipe for trouble

KIRTANA: How
(To ARTIE)
I asked him to be specific and he couldn't say anything

GUARD: That's not true I told you, Interstate smuggling

KIRTANA: I'm not afraid of guns

GUARD: Easy enough to say

KIRTANA: I know what it's like to be in the middle with guns pointed
from both sides
I've been living that way for months

GUARD: It's never the same—

ARTIE: —you don't seem to understand
this is not an invitation to debate
Leave my Mom alone—

GUARD: —A real gun is something else
So's real blood
particularly when it spills onto the whiteness
of airport floors
Never more sobering and redder than then

ARTIE: I really don't see what good all this talk of blood's doing

GUARD: It's my job
to keep it off the floor

ARTIE: Well my Mom's blood isn't on the floor is it?

GUARD: Take her home

KIRTANA: He'll take me home
(To ARTIE)
Let's go home Farouk

GUARD: (To ARTIE)
That's your name?
What kind of crackpot name's that*

ARTIE: I'm calling the cops

GUARD: I am the cops

KIRTANA: (In response to *) It's a king's name

GUARD: (To KIRTANA) A son with a king's name and
Unafraid of guns:
Get down from the clouds where you live lady
(To ARTIE)
Take her home
Lock her up

KIRTANA: (To ARTIE)
Take me home Farouk
Don't ever let me go
(Whispers the following in ARTIE's ear)
Say it back to me
Come on
Say it and he'll leave us

ARTIE: (Not quite sure of all that's transpiring)
I'll take you home Mom
and lock you up

KIRTANA: And you'll never go

ARTIE: And I'll never go

KIRTANA: Give us a kiss

(He kisses her. Slowly)

GUARD: (To KIRTANA) I wish I had a mother like you

ARTIE: (To GUARD) You can fuck off now

GUARD: (To KIRTANA) That's not a mother's kiss You don't fool me
(Exits)

KIRTANA: Do you have a mother?

ARTIE: I have a mother yes

KIRTANA: She's lucky having a son like you

ARTIE: I'm better in the abstract

(LIGHTS dim as an airplane flying overhead is heard.)

4. *Lights return. Same place. Empty. Enter JESSICA. Filipina-American. Early 40s. Cigarette in hand.*

JESSICA: I'm looking for my son
                     (Looks around)
Anyone?
                     (No one)
The thing about hands is
Hands knead
and in the absence of a son (who's
the right kind of dough)
they grope elsewhere
Cigarettes for instance

(GUARD enters.)

GUARD: There's no smoking here
Are you coming or going

JESSICA: Neither

GUARD: Listen it's three AM
and you're not the first crazy lady
I've had to help so if
you've got no business—

JESSICA: I'm looking for my son

GUARD: This is an airport
not an orphanage
And there's no smoking here

JESSICA: He's flying out

GUARD: There you go
He's gone
Will you put out that cigarette

JESSICA: A hand needs a cigarette
I don't do it for the smoke

GUARD: I don't care ma'am

JESSICA: *(Throws cigarette on floor, grinds it with undue emphasis with her feet.)*

I'm sorry
I'm not myself

(Lights fade.)

5. *In the darkness, a song. Sung live by all performers, who are off-stage.*

SONG
Half the world
is packing a suitcase
The other half's
tossing in bed

The first half dies
with no proof or trace
no memory of dinner talk
any remnant of grace
no azure stroll
never a leisurely pace
instead a bolt a run
perpetual longing for Place

Half the world
is packed tight in Samsonite
The other half's
clobbered by sleep

This half lives
underwater not flying by air
that avenue of dreamtime
the long-uncut hair
of the past stretching yards
and years back to where
we once had an estate
       once had a guard dog
       once had a sun
           constant in heat
This half may be rooted here
but all the while
it breathes
the air of
another year
another currency
another God
miles away

Half the world
is doing is making

is acting the act
The other half
is watching is waiting
and forever holds back

(Lights fade up. All characters (7) emerge into a line-up, an inverted triangle whose final point is ARTIE, closest to the audience. The song is sung once more, this time accompanied by the percussion of the singers stomping on the ground, or beating out a rhythm on their chests, or clapping. It should end with a series of claps, or stomps, or beats, speeding urgently then a sudden stop. Everyone deserts the stage, but ARTIE.)

6. *Lights fade tight on him to suggest nighttime.*

ARTIE: It's a motel room in Arizona

                                That much I know

Some numbers splay across a wooden door

Fixing me to:

                <u>this</u> room

                <u>this</u> specific shoebox in the world

                <u>This</u> is where I am

                not lost at all

That much I know

                (Beat)

That I am here

                (Beat)

Here is Arizona

And I've come so far

            so fast

                (Beat)

And I'm still packing my suitcase

And tossing in bed

Packing my suitcase

And tossing in bed

Packing my suitcase

And tossing at sea: those twin feats one must learn

                      to master without a father's precedent

                      without benefit of example

                      in the great

                      American magic act

                (Beat)

Here goes

Watch this trick

Now you see me

(Lights out)

ARTIE'S Voice: Now you don't

7. Lights. Agency. Two chairs, facing each other. On Right, KIRTANA. On Left, notebook in hand, pen too, JESSICA.

KIRTANA: You do see

JESSICA: There are freeway systems in this country
is what I'm saying
And they complicate things beyond comprehension

KIRTANA: He ran away as teenagers do
Nobody beat him

JESSICA: No one's saying you did

KIRTANA: Fifteen

JESSICA: Nobody's going to blame you

KIRTANA: Seduced by the promise of neon and
a constant buffet of hamburgers.

JESSICA: It's foolish to think that
the finger will be pointed at
you here
There are other agencies
the church for example
in which blame is placed
   blame is always placed
on the parent
    the source of all wrongdoing
It's something we don't abide by
in this agency
We counsel

KIRTANA: And track right?

JESSICA: We <u>help</u> track
to the best of our abilities

KIRTANA: I've come very far
    come carried by good word of mouth
       so many mouths talking about this
place you don't know

JESSICA: And they say what? Good things?

KIRTANA: A magic act, they say

JESSICA: The success
when it's come
has come against great odds

KIRTANA: But not—
                    Not insurmountable
People leave tracks
have fingerprints

JESSICA: People do leave tracks—

KIRTANA: Some larger than others yes
And a boy like Farouk
          like no other

JESSICA: But you take a look out any window in any city
and you'd be hard pressed
to second-guess destinations
I mean
I've been here years
                    half a lifetime
and I'm _still_ not used to it
this ludicrous tic-tac-toe of cars
Wheels are like—

KIRTANA: Feet He's left footprints

JESSICA: A little yes
But he _escaped_—

KIRTANA: Not escaped. Left

JESSICA: OK Left
And wheels are the perfect conduit for that
Invented for just that purpose
And yes there are license plates to be written down
Sightings
But those things when they happen are the _exception_
And wheels

The thing about wheels is that
they're better than brooms
Footprints may have been laid down
But wheels sweep them so clean you'd hardly know
anyone had been there
They guarantee
Often they guarantee exits so speedy—

KIRTANA: You're not painting a good—

JESSICA: No not good
Practical
We don't operate on false hope

KIRTANA: *(Beat)*
But where else can I go
If you fail me who else

JESSICA: There are detective agencies—

KIRTANA: They cost

JESSICA: I know
But sometimes they're better equipped
for—
Complications come
in the form of
in many forms
some we're not equipped to handle

KIRTANA: Such as

JESSICA: In the instance of abductions

KIRTANA: He'll escape
I know he will

JESSICA: This has happened to him before?

KIRTANA: Back in India
His father's parents
vindictive
people

They took him away from me
And he came back
Ran halfway across the country
(And it's not—
                    there are hills and haters of children—
                                                        not
a simple matter of running track)
He came back to me
                    (Beat)
And now he's gone

JESSICA: (Beat)
We'll find him

KIRTANA: I know you will
It's our particular fate
Jar the symmetry
Fifteen
and
He'd look at television: Mom we jar the symmetry

JESSICA: You have a local address?

KIRTANA: I'm staying at a motel
The 6 of Hearts

JESSICA: Why don't you go back to Iowa
It could be—

KIRTANA: Weeks, months
Have you heard of the Bob and
Cowboys' Grill?

JESSICA: Yes

KIRTANA: I waitress there
You can put that down
on the form
When no one's looking I sneak some
Indian spices into
whatever's brewing
One day it was beef stew
And the manager

JESSICA: Bruce

KIRTANA: You know him?

JESSICA: The entire female population
has been warned to stay miles away
He hasn't—

KIRTANA: No, no
He's been very kind
Very kind and very stupid Thicklike

JESSICA: And nothing else

KIRTANA: He kept bragging about
the beef stew, calling it
Great American Food
saying how you will never go bankrupt
selling American people
American food (and sure
enough, that batch of beef
stew sold out quicker than
any other before it) but little did he know
those spices
scumming around the top
were mine
all mine
(Beat)
How about you
You're from somewhere else too

JESSICA: Manila
I grew up there
This agency is founded entirely by immigrants

KIRTANA: Manila is
the Philippines?

JESSICA: PI

KIRTANA: What's that

JESSICA: Philippine Islands

KIRTANA: is Marcos?

JESSICA: Was
Not that I keep up
I don't anymore

KIRTANA: You have no family back there

JESSICA: They're all dead

KIRTANA: I have relatives in India

JESSICA: Do they know about your son

KIRTANA: *(Shakes No)*
They're the same as dead
More my husband's family than mine actually

JESSICA: And you're not married now

KIRTANA: I never divorced him
just left
Escaped, to use your word
A suitcase in one hand, a knife in the other,
my boy on my back, we camelled our way
out of there
(Beat)
Are you married

JESSICA: Twelve years

KIRTANA: Is he Filipino too

JESSICA: *(Shakes No)*
American
I meant
I promised I'd stop doing this

KIRTANA: What

JESSICA: Substituting that word for white
My husband is white
It's something my mother did too

even after years of living here
Mom <u>you're</u> American now, I said
but she never quite took to it

KIRTANA: You shouldn't beat your head over
just a word

JESSICA: Yes but—

KIRTANA: There are more important things
(Beat)
Such as a son
(Beat)
Farouk

JESSICA: Is that his name

(KIRTANA nods.)

8. *MARTIN and JESSICA. Patio. Sounds of crickets. Night. Shadows of leaves play.*

JESSICA: He crept in

MARTIN: Crept in how
We invited him

JESSICA: Just snuck up on me

MARTIN: What piece of news was he gabbing on about
You shouldn't have screamed

JESSICA: Look at you Martin
Always the diplomat
He asked what had happened over the weekend

MARTIN: The robbery

JESSICA: The break-in, he kept screaming, tell me
And I said—

MARTIN: —furniture stolen—

JESSICA: —gave him an itemized listing

MARTIN: So why'd you scream

JESSICA: —no suspects, I said
and he kept saying, Any person you know who might
have access to the house, and then and there
I should have known to
stop the conversation dead
but instead I said Carol

MARTIN: That's why you screamed

JESSICA: I said, Carol our housekeeper
and then he asked if we'd put Carol
through some police check

MARTIN: He wouldn't say something like that
He's got this one-of-a-kind brain
that processes (it's what

we use him for)
numbers and diagrams
Where others see crisscrossing
lines of no conceivable use
he sees their application
how to translate them into freeways

JESSICA: The same thing had happened to his
family and they'd done a check-up
on their housekeeper and wouldn't you
know she'd been siphoning loot for
years, at which point that
wife of his
little bird in Chanel
yellow and white teeth
began to crack jokes

MARTIN: What jokes

JESSICA: How can they expect it'll go over well
with me these jokes—Do they think
I'm some sort of
us-not-them kinda gal expecting me to throw
my head back and laugh
The one thing
about you Americans—

MARTIN: We Americans: not that refrain again

JESSICA: you have beautiful teeth but you
reveal them in the aftermath of an ugly joke
Yes we invited him
but we certainly
gave no indication he
had podium rights

MARTIN: You go to work
and see these people
for whom you've developed—

JESSICA: I go to work. Yes.
I bring no one home
And if I did

Not one of them would
think, Carol

MARTIN: —and relative to that kind
of partisanship,
between needy and
sponsor
which is
this cult of
suffering you've built up

JESSICA: A family, Martin

MARTIN: —is nobody can compete
You think
because we're doing
well and belong to this
set—

JESSICA: The smart set

MARTIN: —we become automatically guilty—

JESSICA: Since when*

MARTIN: —as if we were
causing them
misfortune
(*in response to* *)
Since you mentioned it
two nights ago

JESSICA: You talk
because you're missing a son

MARTIN: He's a friend—

JESSICA: I don't want him back

MARTIN: —and he's a—

JESSICA: I said

MARTIN: And I'm telling you what
                          What do you expect me to tell you

JESSICA: I'd rather be robbed
than entertain people like that

MARTIN: I'd much rather do anything but be robbed again
How much more violated do you
want to get Their grubby
hands through our drawers
MY clothes
picking and choosing as if
I were dead
You want a family?
What do you have
One broken lock
And a son out the door.
And now you
don't want friends

JESSICA: The right kind of friends

MARTIN: What do you end up with?
An even emptier house

9. *Hill. BUGLE BOY, young black man. He sings a song, in dim spotlight. Behind him, a field of stars.*

SONG (Outskirts of Town)
Wind blows through
making tin cans rattle
Losers pass through
making each woman tattle
Why don't you
and I take shelter
away from the townsfolk
with their radio and rumor
run out to the tracks
gleaming their poorman's humor
Darling can you
and I try marriage
and be mindful of us only
as we weave and we wear the exile's gown
Sweetheart let's you
and I cast our luck
with hearts that are lonely
who bear and who grieve on the outskirts of town.

(Lights fades on him. He remains there. A silhouette against stars.)

10. *Tight lights on faces:*   *ARTIE, Upstage Left. Standing. JESSICA, Downstage Right. Seated. A phone conversation. Phone receivers may or may not be used. They are both on one half of the stage, as the other half's being occupied by BUGLE BOY.*

JESSICA: You said you'd call earlier

ARTIE: I'm calling now

JESSICA: What's that music Where are you

ARTIE: Arizona

JESSICA: What kind of bar

ARTIE: Mom I'm a fag

JESSICA: Don't get snippy with me

ARTIE: Just stating a fact

JESSICA: You want a fact exchange
This is mine: He ran out on us

ARTIE: I'm still gonna see him

JESSICA: He ran out on you

ARTIE: I know you don't want me to

JESSICA: It's not that I don't

ARTIE: Where you work
You have
Access to information

JESSICA: Access?
This is a man who hasn't called
hasn't written for sixteen years!

(No response)

What's this going to accomplish?

(Lights up on BUGLE BOY. ARTIE is in both scenes.)

BUGLE BOY: *(Points up)*
What's that
Three points that end
No eight
Eight points that tip into
a blade

ARTIE: *(To Jessica)*
What's that star
composed of eight points
which come to a blade

JESSICA: I don't know

ARTIE: Aurora Borealis?

BUGLE BOY: That's not it

JESSICA: Head in the stars
That's where you are

ARTIE: Mom
I gotta go

JESSICA: He's beautiful in the distance

ARTIE: Who

JESSICA: Your Dad
(He doesn't even deserve the name
Martin's been talking about you)

BUGLE BOY: The bear
It's the bear

ARTIE: *(To BUGLE BOY)*
Ursa Major
(To JESSICA)
He's not my Dad

JESSICA: No your Dad shines so much

brighter because he vanished
before you could find him out
for the fraud that he is
That's what I've been
telling Martin:
Abandon him and <u>then</u>
he'll start thinking highly of you

BUGLE BOY: That doesn't sound right

ARTIE: I gotta go

JESSICA: Will you call me

ARTIE: When

JESSICA: As soon as you get to California

ARTIE: I can't promise anything

(Light fades on JESSICA.)

BUGLE BOY: Will you come with me

ARTIE: Where

BUGLE BOY: *(Points)*
See that rainbow down there
Carnival's in town
Only time anyone would
be caught dead here

ARTIE: What do I call you

BUGLE BOY: I told you

ARTIE: —— But it's—

BUGLE BOY: Bugle Boy

ARTIE: Strange name

BUGLE BOY: My father gave it to me

ARTIE: Thinking what
BUGLE BOY: Is there supposed to be a story behind everything

ARTIE: Fathers and sons

BUGLE BOY: What do you do

ARTIE: Mainly I listen

BUGLE BOY: You get paid to listen

ARTIE: Then I sift
Then I write down
What do <u>you</u> do

BUGLE BOY: Certainly not a writer
What do you write
                    You write about your people

ARTIE: Who's that

BUGLE BOY: Privilege

ARTIE: I'm not

BUGLE BOY: You don't work

ARTIE: I'm not rich

BUGLE BOY: What kind of muscles does that give you Writing
Not calves

ARTIE: You're checking out the wrong part

BUGLE BOY: What should I be looking at

ARTIE: *(Lifts hands)* Veins

BUGLE BOY: I like a body to read in the dark
I like to run my hands through skin
and run into
a scar Scars And say This body is not
a stranger to work

                    or discomfort
What I don't like is smoothness
                    and ease
Because it's a world I don't
think I'll ever know
And besides those things
make you flabby
And that's one thing I
don't intend to be

ARTIE: I've earned veins in the right places
And <u>you</u>

BUGLE BOY: Veins in my name   That's one

ARTIE: Tell me the story

BUGLE BOY: I didn't know till my Dad
screamed at me one night:
I called you Bugle Boy direct from
the Bible expecting you to be
                              some sort of angel
                              some herald
of Good News from now on but all your grown-up life
                                              ever since you were thirteen
all you kept trumpeting was a rap sheet

ARTIE: What kind of rap sheet

BUGLE BOY: Petty thievery

ARTIE: Cars?

BUGLE BOY: It's a country dependent on freeways
Cars don't sound petty to me do they to you

(Beat)   I've killed a couple of dogs in my time
Mailman's prerogative
(Beat)
So you wanna come with me

ARTIE: Where

BUGLE BOY: Carnival
A magician who gives late shows

ARTIE: And after that

BUGLE BOY: My place

ARTIE: Where's that

BUGLE BOY: On the outskirts of town

11. *Blue light isolates KIRTANA, standing center.*

KIRTANA: At the University of Bombay where I went
before giving up
thought to be by my husband's
side, a professor told me
You are where history is
going to be made
How absurd thinking yourself
important enough to stencil into books

But I think now
(It's all I do now is think)
Meera Kherjee, the star debater
of the University of Bombay, not
only smart but glamorous, so ripe
for history-making, is
today behind a fat
tyrant she married, a permanent
lock on her lips. From debate to
complicity: no limit to the
perverseness of God's game
plan. And me.
Here in America. History. My footprints so lonely.
So at night to console myself I say,

        But you're making history
      I say,
       repeating after the professor,

            Despite ourselves
            We are history

We lie in bed and toss
Our days are bad and our clothes a mess
still we're history
(Beat)
I say that at night and yet I know inside this heart
I would give up History in a minute in exchange for some
Company
my son back at my side

12. *Carnival: red, yellow, green lights. MAGICIAN (actor who'll later play KUMAR) enters. Stops Center. ARTIE and BUGLE BOY enter Upstage, crouch flanking facing MAGICIAN.*

MAGICIAN: *(Facing audience; takes off top hat)*
In this hat
ladies and gentlemen
my first trick
a rabbit out of my hat
(Beat)
Did I hear a snicker
For what is this
snicker ladies and gentlemen
(Cocks ear)
Lack of originality? Did I hear
someone say, LACK OF ORIGINALITY?
Well let me defend myself: Magic need
not be original The only demand
on Magic is that it be
MAGICAL
I used to be a bus conductor
would you have guessed
all day long I strode the same
narrow corridor which cuts
through the bus's middle yelling
                          All aboard
punching tickets and yelling
                    Come one come
                    All aboard the Homebound Express
                    (what a beautiful word,
                    homebound)
I varied
I <u>tried to</u> vary
              these little choruses everyday
Some days I'd shout
(Singsong)
                    Hey there ho there
                    we're all going home
                    after a hard day's work
                    Clap hands
(He claps.)
                    Clap hands
(He claps.)
Day in day out running after

ORIGINALITY that's what
I'd do
        And did you think I'd get some show of thanks for this? Nooooo
And now you ask me for
ORIGINALITY? After history
has proven to me its
uselessness has proven it
unappreciated? Puh-leeze

A rabbit out of a hat
That's what you're getting so
Shut Up or Get Out
                (*Waves fingers; incantating*)
Yabba dabba doo
Yabba dabba dee
A rabbit a rabbit
                (*Reaches into top hat, pulls out a rose*)
What the
                (*Keeps pulling out rose after rose after rose; into top hat*)
Where the fuck are you
                (*Rose after rose after rose; to audience:*)
OK
You asked for originality
You got it
No rabbit just flowers
Are you satisfied
ARE YOU SATISFIED!

DESPITE MYSELF I'M ORIGINAL!

(*Lights fade on MAGICIAN, who exits, and rise on ARTIE. He rises, wobbles. BUGLE BOY goes to him.*)

BUGLE BOY: Steady

ARTIE: The earth just tilted

BUGLE BOY: You felt the earth tilt

ARTIE: More people with luggage*
got off a plane and we
tilted some more
(*At * MARTIN enters. With him is a small scale architectural model of a strip mall, which he rests on the floor in the exact spot where the MAGICIAN was earlier.*)

BUGLE BOY: You're just swooning

ARTIE: *(Ironic)* Cause I'm in love with you?

BUGLE BOY: Cause you're in love with me
but you don't know it yet

(They exit.)

13. *JESSICA enters.*

MARTIN: You walk around believing you
have a target glued to
your forehead and
think people will
come and bash you in
Ghosts ringing our
doorbell at night now
he's not coming back
It's in his blood

JESSICA: I am not afraid of change

MARTIN: I've been watching you—

JESSICA: You keep watching me

MARTIN: How you rearrange the furniture
preparing for what is it

JESSICA: I've let him go

MARTIN: And this latest
it's change too—

JESSICA: Change flows two ways: forward and
back Which is this, you
haven't even bothered
asking yourself
I never thought
It'd get this complicated

MARTIN: Well it is

JESSICA: It doesn't have to be

MARTIN: Bullshit

JESSICA: The wrong friends, the right friends

MARTIN: What you do is civics, not economics

JESSICA: What I do feeds more
than what you do ever will

MARTIN: It's progress
Where do you stand
With the future or with the past

JESSICA: A wheat field into a mall?
We drive by there every day
A daily reminder

MARTIN: You want the geography to be
impervious to progress just so
we can have a scenic drive

JESSICA: Who are the financiers

MARTIN: What've you got against
the Japanese

JESSICA: I'm a professional sympathizer I have
more than enough sympathy to spare

MARTIN: But not for them

JESSICA: Money

MARTIN: The root of all evil

JESSICA: Doors open when they land
while for my people—

MARTIN: How proprietary

JESSICA: They would love to be thought of
as mine—

MARTIN: Do you teach them to be afraid
like you Your heart skipping
a beat everytime we drive
onto a freeway

JESSICA: —they live here

while the Japanese
leave and don't have to sustain I do

                            I'm the one who has to sustain

MARTIN: A mall
is not a nuclear plant

JESSICA: It attracts listless—

MARTIN: We give them jobs

JESSICA: —aimless youth

MARTIN: Because you're depressed you want
everything around you to spin in
the same circle No change
possible until you're good and ready

JESSICA: You'll end up with a ghost mall How can
we drive past some dead thing by
the side of the road every day   As if we needed
any more reminders

(They stand silent.)

14. *ARTIE and BUGLE BOY bring a bench in. Set it so that it covers the architectural miniature from view. Train station. JESSICA and MARTIN remain. ARTIE, with backpack, and BUGLE BOY, stand side by side, in front of the bench. Sound of a train. They look Left.*

BUGLE BOY & MARTIN: I guess that's it

ARTIE: Here it comes
You have my address*

JESSICA: I guess so

(JESSICA and MARTIN exit. Each on opposite sides.
*BUGLE BOY pats breast jacket pocket .In response to *).)*

ARTIE: Will you call

BUGLE BOY: You're not the kind who should be given
a head start   You'll bolt and then
you'll outrun me

(Beat)   I'll call

ARTIE: Do that

BUGLE BOY: On the road

ARTIE: Handing out telegrams in shorts
to show off calve muscles

BUGLE BOY: Hitchhike your way
to California using veins as bait

ARTIE: Can't get too far on that

BUGLE BOY: Why not

ARTIE: Veins aren't too popular around here

BUGLE BOY: Do I get a kiss

ARTIE: Sure

(BUGLE BOY looks, sees no one, kisses.)

ARTIE: You look then you kiss

BUGLE BOY: You take what you can

ARTIE: And then you run?

(The space between them widens. Mainly it's BUGLE BOY who moves, walking off Right. They wave and mouth the following lines, all drowned out by the boom and hiss of a train pulling in:)

ARTIE: Bye

BUGLE BOY: Take care

ARTIE: I'll see you

BUGLE BOY: Promises promises

IF THERE IS TO BE A BREAK, IT SHOULD OCCUR HERE.

15.

Restaurant. Spill, from off-stage, red-blue off-on neon. Table. Two benches ,similar to train station bench, flank it. KIRTANA: in waitress uniform. JESSICA seated.

JESSICA: Kirtana regarding Farouk

KIRTANA: This is strictly social

JESSICA: This is social

KIRTANA: Unless of course you've news for me

JESSICA: No I'm afraid that's what I was announcing

KIRTANA: As soon as you get news I'm sure you'll tell me

JESSICA: Of course

KIRTANA: But till then we'll be social
We can be social can't we

JESSICA: Of course

KIRTANA: I'll be back with the food and then
you should tell me all about
your life How exemplary it's been

JESSICA: Far from it

KIRTANA: No don't say that Of course exemplary If
not you then who

(She exits, to return with two plates. Sets before JESSICA and herself. Sits.)

JESSICA: This is your concoction

KIRTANA: Beef   I pollute all the stews now
Bruce has no idea why he's doing so well
Just pockets the money and pats
me on my bottom

JESSICA: You should sue

KIRTANA: No

JESSICA: You <u>could</u>

KIRTANA: And then what

JESSICA: And if you don't, what

KIRTANA: More waiting
Case after case tied up in the courts like
a long ball of yarn unwinding
To knit what
                    what kind of fabric

JESSICA: Someone steps on your rights
you have recourse to that

KIRTANA: It's called unemployment

JESSICA: You certainly
don't believe
this is all you have to look
forward to

KIRTANA: What marketable skills do I
possess to begin with

JESSICA: Nothing that training can't remedy

KIRTANA: Night classes

JESSICA: *(Detecting something askew in KIRTANA's voice)*
Yes?

KIRTANA: I've tried them

JESSICA: And what's wrong with night classes

KIRTANA: *(Beat)*
Full of backward geeks consigned
there by pathological social
ineptitude and failure   Impossible to
miss the scent of failure in all

those rooms Don't think I haven't
forced myself to try Night
after night just sitting
hoping to extract some hope from all this

JESSICA: And there is

KIRTANA: This is not what I came for
In just a few nights watching
a roomful of elderly students each
pouched heavy with dismay you
begin to understand this country
It only has time for winners And
What winners need more than
anything else is a batch
of geeks to make them look
winners in comparison
a batch to clean up after
parties and victory
celebrations So the skills those schools
teach, the skills they would
profit from teaching
are service industry ones
of smiling and serving soup

JESSICA: But I don't understand
How is what you're afraid of different
from what you're doing right now

KIRTANA: I went to the University
of Bombay I want you to know that

JESSICA: No one's taking that away from you

KIRTANA: I'm telling you now I come
from a family of proud women
each one bearing pride in a
different manner, but all
equally proud nonetheless
I have pride in my accomplishments
(Beat)
Eat your stew
(Beat)

I'm sorry

JESSICA: This is wonderful

KIRTANA: I wanted to thank you

JESSICA: For

KIRTANA: Introducing me to that group

JESSICA: Are they good people*

KIRTANA: *(Simultaneous with *)*
Who'd have thought in the
middle of Illinois these
Indians

JESSICA: I'm glad you liked them

KIRTANA: I walked through this door
the room all of a sudden
parting in equal rhythm*
to take me in all full
of smiles asking after me
The kind of confidence I can only
associate with having been
born here not boat-tipsy in any
way not like me who's constantly afraid

JESSICA: *(Simultaneous with *)*
I've heard so much about them
but just haven't had the time
to check up

KIRTANA: A group of
people so tip-top they
could've been issuing from
a TV set
Except

JESSICA: Except what

KIRTANA: Well not except really but

There's this guy

JESSICA: Really

KIRTANA: Oh don't smile like that I feel silly enough

JESSICA: An Indian guy

KIRTANA: He wears this ten-gallon hat
and walks into rooms as if preceded
there by a ticker-tape parade
An Indian John Wayne

JESSICA: And

KIRTANA: He's bullish

JESSICA: He's asked you out

KIRTANA: We've gone out

(KUMAR, unseen, enters.)

JESSICA: On a date   Was this a first date

KUMAR: Speak of the devil

KIRTANA: What are you doing here
Walking so stealthy I couldn't
even hear

KUMAR: I thought we had a date

KIRTANA: I don't think so

KUMAR: So you've forgotten

KIRTANA: Maybe it's <u>you</u> who's confused

KUMAR: This was to be our
(Looks at JESSICA) second date

KIRTANA: We weren't talking about you Kumar

KUMAR: I'm Kumar

JESSICA: Nice to meet you

KUMAR: *(Kisses JESSICA on the hand)*
Very nice to meet you
Kirtana speaks highly of you

KIRTANA: <u>Spoken</u> Just that one time
Don't make it
sound like routine

KUMAR: Not yet

KIRTANA: Tell Kumar we weren't talking about him Jessica

JESSICA: I'm afraid we really weren't

KUMAR: My ears were buzzing

KIRTANA: Ear infection   A sign of old age

KUMAR: *(To JESSICA)* She's wonderful isn't she
Always a line for everything

KIRTANA: I've had to

KUMAR: There she goes again

JESSICA: So what is it you do if you
don't mind my asking

KUMAR: I'm into several ventures—

KIRTANA: Speculation   That's
how you described it   Your lips
biting into that word as if
tasting fruit

KUMAR: —real estate being one of them

KIRTANA: It's the perfect word
to characterize his

approach to life—Speculation—Isn't
that right Kumar

KUMAR: My approach to life?

KIRTANA: How you pursue things
romantic and otherwise
mere speculation   You convince yourself
of something long enough you begin
to believe it

KUMAR: Such as

KIRTANA: *(To JESSICA)*
Thicklike
Kumar I don't think we planned
something for tonight

KUMAR: I'm sorry then my mistake
so Should I come back

KIRTANA: Call first

KUMAR: No you're not the kind who
should be given any warning
because you'll bolt and
then you'll outrun me

KIRTANA: Believe me if anyone's bolting
it's not me   If you have to know
I'm practically glued here

KUMAR: So what is it keeps you
glued Certainly not a husband

KIRTANA: *(Acknowledging JESSICA)*
Friends

KUMAR: I have those   The problem with
them is they can only carry so far

KIRTANA: Maybe you have the wrong kind

KUMAR: I know who to surround
myself with One gift of mine

JESSICA: Maybe you should introduce me to some
of your friends

KUMAR: But despite all humaneness they
never seem to know what
to do for lonely nights spent
by yourself in big houses
lightning licking the surfaces
of windows making you feel
like a seven year-old

KIRTANA: Sounds like an advertisement
for a mother to me
(To JESSICA)
Doesn't it

KUMAR: What's wrong with wanting a mother
Perfectly natural tendency

KIRTANA: My hands are full

KUMAR: I don't see any rattles trailing
behind you

KIRTANA: It's the other way around

KUMAR: I don't understand

KIRTANA: You're not meant to
Call next time Kumar

KUMAR: Allright I promise

KIRTANA: You always do but your
promises have a way of never working out

KUMAR: Not the ones that matter

JESSICA: *(Beat)*
Such as

KIRTANA: Jessica

JESSICA: No this is a friend of mine
I'd like to know what intentions
you have Because you seem to have
strong ones and I'd like
to know As a friend

KUMAR: Honorable ones

KIRTANA: Honorable

KUMAR: You sound skeptical

KIRTANA: I haven't heard that word
in such a long time

KUMAR: No It's not a popular word

JESSICA: An Old World word

KUMAR: That's where I'm from

KIRTANA: But not entirely
Something not quite Old
World about you Kumar what
is that

KUMAR: Is that the part you like

KIRTANA: I don't know

KUMAR: But it's the part you don't
mind Because I know you <u>do</u>
mind from the way you
speak, curling your
lips the way you do Not that
I understand why Because I'm fit
if not fitter than most

KIRTANA: It's the part that won't
let me write you off
completely

KUMAR: An amalgam, yes

KIRTANA: Is that what they call it
these days

KUMAR: (To KIRTANA)
Just like you're one
(Beat)
I should leave now but before I
do can I say one other thing
A defense of what you called
my speculative
life which is not true at all
I don't believe in poverty
not for myself it's true
but I don't
I'm not hazy and unforthright either
which is what I understand
speculative to mean
Like I said
I know who to surround myself with—

KIRTANA: Kumar I'm sure Jessica isn't
interested in all this

JESSICA: No I am

KUMAR: Are you sure

JESSICA: Go on Please

KUMAR: You're quite sure?

JESSICA: I don't understand why
you should be so surprised

KUMAR: A history of indifference
from women which as I remarked
is beyond my understanding

JESSICA: You were married before

KUMAR: No never

A lifelong bachelor

KIRTANA: And you want me as a habit-breaker

KUMAR: *(Beat)*
Not when you put it like that no

KIRTANA: And how should I put it Kumar

KUMAR: I don't know Nicely maybe

JESSICA: Go on You were saying something

KUMAR: As an example of my—

KIRTANA: Unspeculativeness

KUMAR: —honorable
(Beat)
habits
What I've been doing
lately I've been trying to convince
these Vietnamese fisherman in
Texas whom the natives
are accusing of encroaching on
their territory, and with
these people who have no conception
of the importance
    the immense need for public representation
(because it's the public who'll vote
on whether or not their fishing
rights are extended) it's
key with these people to
talk, to
illustrate
by improvising ballpoint maps or using
cartoon representations
how this country works
and how if they are ignorant of how
it works they cannot therefore
demand
through legitimate means
what it is that is their due It's a very

jealous age we're living in They have no idea
and must be told
have to be educated
and that's what I do One example
of what I do

JESSICA: That sounds wonderful

KUMAR: But it's an uphill struggle
With these people
you can't be who I am

KIRTANA: Which is what

KUMAR: A dark-skinned
man Can't knock on
their doors and expect ears
to listen attentively,
beg for your
presence You have to
keep coming back and each day
they make damn sure you know
your presence is some form of
encroachment
Who better to cast their
lot with I'm in the
same boat But
Skin always in the way
(Beat)
Thank you for hearing me out
(To JESSICA)
It was nice meeting you

JESSICA: Nice meeting you I
hope we'll see each other again

KUMAR: Kirtana
KIRTANA: Kumar

(He exits.)

JESSICA: Is he who we were talking about

KIRTANA: (nods)
He took me out

JESSICA: Was this a date

KIRTANA: Not a date really   Well
OK a date   He's buying a house

JESSICA: Here?

KIRTANA: This is where he wants to
settle   Originally he's
from Kentucky but
he's buying a house
he wants to buy a house in Illinois
So he took me prospecting

JESSICA: And

KIRTANA: You're smiling   You keep smiling

JESSICA: Isn't this good news

KIRTANA: You've seen him

JESSICA: It's not good news

KIRTANA: He took me out to this wheat field
His hands were dancing wildly the whole time
                conjuring things from the air and
                saying, Here I'm gonna build a recreation
                        room and
                    here the study and
                    here the bedroom
and he held my hand
I mean I've only know him a few days but
he was holding my hand

JESSICA: And you didn't want him to

KIRTANA: It's not that I don't
want him to   It's just
I didn't feel

JESSICA: Give it time

KIRTANA: It's not about time
He took me to this wheat field and his hands were dancing
              and the wheat was dancing
              (a whole field of wheat
              you should've seen how
              beautiful it was Just
              swaying
              back and forth and I would
              love to live there don't get
              me wrong) but

JESSICA: But

KIRTANA: Everything else was swaying and dancing but I wasn't
(Beat)
I have this notion Don't think
me silly but I have this notion

JESSICA: Can I just say something

KIRTANA: No Please
I'm telling you this because I
want you to say something

JESSICA: It seems to me
I don't claim to be an expert on this but
it seems to me
that there are benefits to be had by companionship alone
that people put a premium on romance and then in the process
deprive themselves of other more basic
maybe more important things

KIRTANA: You and your husband

JESSICA: *(Beat)*
No I was lucky
I don't
know what I'm saying You're
right You have to dance
KIRTANA: My notion Can I tell you my notion

JESSICA: Please

KIRTANA: *(Turns her face out to audience, where the windows are supposed to be)* Oh look it's fall
already

JESSICA: I love the fall

KIRTANA: *(Face back to JESSICA)*
My notion is
That it seems to me that one of the inherent promises of
this country
            is that from time to time
                        on a <u>semi</u> regular basis in exchange for all the crap you get
                                    one gets to swoon and I'd like
                                    to be able to do that
I haven't swooned in so long and
I'd like to again
(Beat)
I came to America because you seem to have the patent on
swooning Does that
sound stupid

JESSICA: *(Shakes No)*
Not at all

KIRTANA: And with Kumar I just don't swoon
(Beat)
I just don't swoon

(KIRTANA and JESSICA exit after a beat, taking their plates with them.)

16. *Home for the Aged. ATTENDANT (played by MARTIN, male nurse's uniform on) enters, and throws white tablecloth over table. As soon as the tablecloth is in place and smoothed perfectly on, ARTIE enters. Backpack on.*

ATTENDANT: Under no circumstances are you to
frighten
scare
drop any bombs
He's very excitable

ARTIE: I don't want to scare him

ATTENDANT: And his name's Leoncillo
That's what everyone calls him

ARTIE: He goes by his last name

ATTENDANT: His bingo name

ARTIE: What's he look like

ATTENDANT: You'll see
And under no circumstances are you to say
we helped you find him or anything else

ARTIE: What's he look like
So I won't drop my jaw

ATTENDANT: This is an old person's home
What do you think he looks like
Why'd you come

ARTIE: Excuse me

ATTENDANT: He's not a nice man

ARTIE: I don't know him

ATTENDANT: If he gets nasty
(Points)
press that button by that column

ARTIE: Why's he here

a home for Jews

ATTENDANT: Why should you be surprised

ARTIE: Like I said, I don't know him
(Beat)
If you hadn't seen your father in
years wouldn't you—

ATTENDANT: If only that were so
Instead <u>I've</u> had to labor
under that sonofabitch's shadow
Sixteen years
that little weasel has had
me to marshmallow around
Can you imagine that SIXTEEN
YEARS doing little errands
scooping up after him
Boy oh boy was I glad when
he finally croaked   Except where I
used to wake up with this
intense feeling of aliveness every
morning plugging me up in every
part—this wish for him to just
shrivel up into the ground—now I
wake up empty and I don't know
if that's such a good thing
(Beat)
Go back home
I'm sure you have a nice
family waiting for you

ARTIE: You're not my father are you
Bring him in

(ATTENDANT exits. Pause. ARTIE sits. Rests backpack on bench. ATTENDANT wheels LEONCILLO in to table. ARTIE gets up.)

LEONCILLO: Who is this boy

ATTENDANT: It's your son

LEONCILLO: (To ARTIE)

Who are you

ARTIE: I'm Artie

LEONCILLO: Who

ARTIE: Arturo

LEONCILLO: *(To ATTENDANT)*
Get me out of here motherfucker

ATTENDANT: He just wants to have a talk with you
Not that that's possible if history's
to judge

LEONCILLO: *(To ARTIE)*
I DIDN'T DO ANYTHING
YOU GOT THAT

ATTENDANT: Well in that case you'll have nothing to fear

LEONCILLO: *(To ATTENDANT)*
How much is he paying you

ATTENDANT: It's not the money
Just payback for years
of having to put up
with your crap

LEONCILLO: How much is he shelling out
I'll triple it

ARTIE: I just want to talk

LEONCILLO: Who are you Who is this boy

ARTIE: I'm your son

LEONCILLO: Which one
I have hundreds

ARTIE: Jessica's son
What do you mean you have hundreds

LEONCILLO: I was a handsome motherfucker
Of course I had hundreds
(To ATTENDANT, who's starting to exit)
Where are you going

ATTENDANT: I'll be within distance

LEONCILLO: Ear to keyhole

ATTENDANT: It's a slow news day

LEONCILLO: Come back

(ATTENDANT gone)

ARTIE: I brought you something

LEONCILLO: Listen   You <u>could</u> be my son—

ARTIE: I am

LEONCILLO: —but what could I give you Now
Look at me
I used to be handsome and now
look at me

ARTIE: I just want to talk

LEONCILLO: What'd you bring me

ARTIE: (Reaches into backpack; takes out box, which he gives to LEONCILLO)
Here

LEONCILLO: (Puts it to ear, shaking it)
What's in here Candy?

ARTIE: Some chocolates

LEONCILLO: CHOCOLATES?! Don't you know I have
a weak heart

ARTIE: (Unfazed; reaches hand out)
I'll take it back

LEONCILLO: NO
I love chocolates

ARTIE: I can take it back

LEONCILLO: I said, I love chocolates

ARTIE: I won't be responsible for your death

LEONCILLO: Might as well go with a smile on my lips

ARTIE: Do you want to know anything about me

LEONCILLO: Like what

ARTIE: Like who I am

LEONCILLO: You're my son

ARTIE: Would you like some ID   You don't have to take it on faith

LEONCILLO: You look like me when I was young
God I hate you
You're a handsome motherfucker too aren't you

ARTIE: *(Hands LEONCILLO his ID)*
That's me

LEONCILLO: What is this

ARTIE: My driver's license

LEONCILLO: You drive?
What is this? Illinois

ARTIE: That's where we live

LEONCILLO: You're Jessica's kid?

ARTIE: Did you love her

LEONCILLO: Illinois She stuck it out huh
God I hate the midwest

I loathe the midwest
Rednecks
How's she doing
              she been lynched and tarred

ARTIE: No

LEONCILLO: How's she doing

ARTIE: She's happy
She converted   Left Catholicism Just like you

LEONCILLO: I meant financially
is she happy

ARTIE: Very
Why'd you convert

LEONCILLO: Judaism suits me

ARTIE: How

LEONCILLO: HOW?

ARTIE: I'm curious

LEONCILLO: In the midwest CURIOUS boys stare at you
and say, You're our first
Asian.

ARTIE: Why Judaism

LEONCILLO: *(Beat)*
They know what it's like to be under Foot
(Beat)
It's founded by people who've had firsthand experience
of an exodus and
don't resent the modern-day version
At least I don't think they do

(Pause.)

ARTIE: Did you love her

LEONCILLO: Did she love me

ARTIE: I don't know I'm not her   I can't answer
Did you

LEONCILLO: I've planted so many little
flags in so many different
places Didn't have time
for love

ARTIE: Is that what I am A little banner

LEONCILLO: Like I said, You look like me

ARTIE: I'm not flapping for you
Do you see me flapping for you

LEONCILLO: What's all this then if not
one big flap You're the
flag I'm the sun

ARTIE: Can I have my ID back

LEONCILLO: *(Takes one more look at it)*
I take it back You're not so handsome

ARTIE: I don't care

LEONCILLO: *(Hands ID back)*
You got a girlfriend

ARTIE: I'm married

LEONCILLO: Got any kids

ARTIE: Four

LEONCILLO: You're fuckin' with me

ARTIE: How would you know

LEONCILLO: They got any ID

ARTIE: I killed them all

LEONCILLO: You killed them

ARTIE: Better than abandonment

LEONCILLO: You don't even remember me How could you feel abandoned
Listen Arturo

ARTIE: Artie

LEONCILLO: Artie
Do you want to get to know me <u>Now</u> get to know me?

ARTIE: Don't be ridiculous

LEONCILLO: Did you want to help hold my hand through sunsets

ARTIE: No

LEONCILLO: Did you want to spoonfeed me liquefied food

ARTIE: I came to see you
I came to see California

LEONCILLO: I traveled
Mainly I wanted out of the midwest
Jessica wouldn't
My feet itched And hers were golf shoes
                              spiked into the ground

ARTIE: What are you explaining

LEONCILLO: I traveled so much
Too much I now realize
but that's the price you pay
logged so many lonely nights in exchange for—
                                        in exchange for what? I don't
even remember
                So as not to let this country catch up
lonely nights equal in number to yours
or maybe more
                probably more because I was older

                                        when loneliness and
                                            foreignness feel more
acute
All I have to show
All I have to show
                        is a trunkload of bus and
                                        train chits and
                                        plane tickets all
punched telling: This man has gotten away from hooks
fists
and nooses

I still have it
that trunkload of tickets
Hoping one day for someone to show up
so I could give it away
It's yours Just say the word

ARTIE: What would I do with it

LEONCILLO: Burn it Make a fire
                        or Build a church
the only two choices left in this country
Do you want it

ARTIE: No
(Beat)
What are you trying to explain

LEONCILLO: Why I left You were going to ask me why I left

ARTIE: No she told me

LEONCILLO: Exactly like that?

ARTIE: But without the tickets

LEONCILLO: But you still want to know some other things

ARTIE: I'm not good at this
So I've written
(Takes out notebook from backpack)
down some questions

LEONCILLO: What's that

ARTIE: It's just a notebook

LEONCILLO: Your notebook

ARTIE: Yes

LEONCILLO: She asked you to take notes

ARTIE: It's mine

LEONCILLO: Not hers?

ARTIE: She has nothing to do with me

LEONCILLO: What do I get
If I pass this test

ARTIE: It's not a test

LEONCILLO: Everything's a test

ARTIE: The real test you failed years ago
This is just some post-failure survey

LEONCILLO: I need some incentive
For twenty-five years California was one
Big Incentive Blue sky
                White light
                Invisible Life
What incentive you got to give me

ARTIE: Sorry

LEONCILLO: I need an incentive

ARTIE: If you don't answer these questions
I take the candy back

LEONCILLO: The candy's mine

ARTIE: No I gave it too early

thinking you'd cooperate

LEONCILLO: The candy stays with me

ARTIE: I'm younger
                        stronger
I'm not in a wheelchair
If I want that candy back how much money you willing to bet
I won't get it

LEONCILLO: Is that a threat

ARTIE: I could push you
The wheels would do the rest

LEONCILLO: That's an incentive

ARTIE: *(Looks at notebook)*
First question
Did you think of me

(Long pause)

ARTIE: Did you think of me

LEONCILLO: *(Beat)*
I like watching TV

ARTIE: What kind of answer's that

LEONCILLO: No I didn't think of you
                        I watched TV
                        Plenty of TV to watch No time for memory
Next question

ARTIE: Question number two
Did you think of me

LEONCILLO: That's the same question

ARTIE: No It's question number two
I've crossed out question number one and
I'm looking at question number two

LEONCILLO: What's the difference

ARTIE: The difference is that there's a number two in front of this one
Question number two Did you think of me

LEONCILLO: I have no regrets
Next question

ARTIE: Question number three
If my name weren't Artie what name would you give me

LEONCILLO: *(Beat)*
Junior
I've always wanted a Junior

(Pause)

LEONCILLO: Is that it

ARTIE: Question number four
Would you recommend I go back to the Philippines

LEONCILLO: Why

ARTIE: Don't answer a question with a question
Question four Should I return to the Philippines

LEONCILLO: There's nothing there for you

ARTIE: Have you been back recently

LEONCILLO: You see footage on the news don't you

ARTIE: It's Western eyes It could easily be pejorative

LEONCILLO: Trust me
If there's any good I can do
It's to let you know that there is nothing back there for
you or for me
A book closed when we left You got that?
A book closed You can return and go through the same words
as I have but the story won't change Not even for you It's
the same sad poverty story

ARTIE: Is that why we left?

LEONCILLO: You should thank me

ARTIE: You should answer me

LEONCILLO: If you'd known you would thank me
Why do you want to go back

ARTIE: Maybe this isn't my country
(Beat)
Why did we come here?

LEONCILLO: Word of mouth
(Beat)
People look at you funny?

ARTIE: No

LEONCILLO: They call you names?

ARTIE: (Irritated)
Like what
(No response)
Not that I've heard no

LEONCILLO: They don't give you things you feel you deserve

ARTIE: But I can't say that their reasons are—
I just don't feel—I can't put my finger on it

LEONCILLO: The midwest is like that
makes you fingerless
nothing to point with to say, This is my own piece of land

ARTIE: Is that why you left

LEONCILLO: I've answered that
How many more questions

ARTIE: (Looks at notebook)
Question number six

LEONCILLO: What happened to Question five

ARTIE: You answered it

LEONCILLO: You didn't ask

ARTIE: I didn't have to

LEONCILLO: You think you're so smart

ARTIE: Question number six
I'm six Pretend I'm six
You have an entire day to spend with me
Where would you take me

LEONCILLO: Where would I take you?

ARTIE: Where would you take me

LEONCILLO: Where you wanna g.

ARTIE: Your choice not mine

(Long pause)

LEONCILLO: You're six

ARTIE: And I've never been out in my life

LEONCILLO: Stuck in the midwest

ARTIE: Well maybe once or twice But that's it

LEONCILLO: Stuck and six

ARTIE: I'm still six yes

LEONCILLO: And being six you need a lesson
                                    some kind of lesson

ARTIE: But fun at the same time

LEONCILLO: I thought this was my choice

ARTIE: Sorry

LEONCILLO: *(Beat)*
I would take you to the zoo
I would take you to two cages side by side to learn a
fundamental lesson of this country: On one side a white dove
                                on the other a crow
You know what a crow is

ARTIE: I know what a crow is

LEONCILLO: On one side a dove
on the other a crow
                Both motiveless and acting
                as instinct decrees
And outside these two cages are people
called Americans
And for the dove they applaud
And for the crow they cringe

That's why I would take you to the zoo

ARTIE: I don't understand You're telling me this isn't my country
and yet you're also saying
                        Don't go back to the Philippines

LEONCILLO: I'm not telling you this isn't your country
I'm telling you:
                Know your cage

ARTIE: Know my cage

LEONCILLO: Know your cage

ARTIE: To do what

LEONCILLO: Know your cage well
Memorize its dimensions
            its distinguishing traits
so that when you go to bed
in the instant before you pitch into black
that's what you see the clearest and
you'll know

        if you run or
        if you kill or
        if you—What do you do

(Pause)

LEONCILLO: What is it you do

ARTIE: I want to write

LEONCILLO: if you run or
               if you kill or
               if you write
<u>If</u> and <u>When</u> you remember your cage
you'll know <u>why</u> you run and
          <u>why</u> you kill and
          <u>why</u> you write.

ARTIE: *(Beat)*
Have you ever killed anyone

LEONCILLO: Out of a countryful of sons
how come it was you who
showed up

ARTIE: You don't have to answer

LEONCILLO: There's a young Indian boy
here
changing sheets
Doesn't say a word I told him what
I've just told you
Thought
Of anyone here he'd still
have skin thin enough to
soak things up
Asked him what his name was
and he said Billy
But here they baptize him
Billy Sengupt
Bill Wallah
Billy EM Forster the Kid
anything to get a rise

But he doesn't move
Just goes on folding and cleaning
One day I thought
(just a passing fancy) I'd
adopt him Give him my name
He looked so nameless
(Beat)
But now that you're here

ARTIE: I don't want anything of yours

LEONCILLO: *(Beat)*
Yes I've killed someone

ARTIE: I guess that's it

LEONCILLO: I get to keep my chocolate

ARTIE: *(Nods; rising)*
One more thing
It's a request: Can I take your picture
(Takes out instamatic from backpack; hoists backpack on)

LEONCILLO: You gotta stand far back
Not a close-up

ARTIE: That's fine
(Backs off)
This far?

LEONCILLO: Farther

ARTIE: *(Backs off some more)*
How's this

LEONCILLO: Some more I'm vain I'm a vain man
It's true I don't mind saying it

*(ARTIE keeps backing off until he disappears.
LEONCILLO begins to tear at his box.)*

LEONCILLO: Chocolate Give me my chocolate
(Tears open box:

brings out ROSE after ROSE after ROSE after ROSE:
SIXTEEN in all)
What the hell—
(Pricks himself)
Ouch
OUCH
SOMEONE
I'M BLEEDING

17. *Lights cross fade dim white to ATTENDANT, Standing upstage center.*

ATTENDANT: Listen Billy
fold the sheets
Look at my hands
and do accordingly
fold
the south end
Layer on top of the west
a pie crust
kneaded into place

Now Billy
don't be afraid
of blue skin
how
cold
like some midnight bloom
and the veins
                    Don't be afraid of veins
                        because they're
                        finally at peace
                        If anything you should be
                        afraid when they're still
                        boiling like kettles
And remember to always
close their eyes
because the eyes
are the repository for
hardships little
crime-scene witnesses who
cannot help but look
agitated no matter how peaceful
the life led always some crime
lurking behind there somewhere the eyes refuse to
give in to Death They always lodge
the final protest And when
the relatives come
as they do the day after
obituaries are telephoned
always tell them when they
ask How did he die,
always tell them, Peacefully

Because that word will
carry them through
(Just a simple word but
you can't imagine how
long it'll carry them through
their lives)

It's a good trade to learn Billy
Don't be ashamed
When I leave here
besides a handful
there'll be you

Do as I do Billy
It'll be just like
in the old days fathers
passing trades to sons

Look it's done
The south end over the west
and then tie the knot
It'll never pooch
never loosen
Always remember that

18. *White lightfades to blue.*

BUGLE BOY: It's not often you meet
someone like you
who's young
and confused
and wanting to do something
anything
so I tell myself
What are you afraid of
Bugle Boy
Open up
Open
and meet your match
Love
Love doesn't have to make
you flabby
I'm going
I'm getting there
I have your address

19.

KIRTANA: Farouk?
Your body's so small Farouk
I hope you have clothes beyond
those holed jeans you prefer
or I hope you're
in a warmer climate
Surfing Farouk
Surf back home to me

20.

JESSICA: Artie?

(MARTIN appears.)

MARTIN: I'm here

JESSICA: I was—

MARTIN: I heard you call me

JESSICA: I was

MARTIN: Here I am

JESSICA: That's all I wanted to know

MARTIN: Everything's all right
Let me take care of you
Why don't you just let
me take care of you

JESSICA: Go to sleep

(MARTIN walks out of the light. The blue light holds for a beat on JESSICA, then it widens.)

21. *JESSICA goes and positions two chairs, as in Scene7:Agency. She sits in one. BUGLE BOY enters and stands by the other.*

JESSICA: He looks more skeletal each year

BUGLE BOY: He takes pride in that

JESSICA: Looking thin?

BUGLE BOY: Looking poor

JESSICA: Look at his closet: Nothing if
not the opposite But he goes
around wearing holed
articles instead That's what your
generation likes

BUGLE BOY: I don't know what that word means

JESSICA: They want to project
indifference but one arrived
at by very meticulous means Holes
in exactly the right places

BUGLE BOY: The holes I
have I've worked hard to get rid of

JESSICA: You should talk some sense into him

BUGLE BOY: That's not what I'm here for

JESSICA: You mentioned you were friends

BUGLE BOY: I'm sick and tired of having to educate
people Of constantly being
expected to do that

JESSICA: I'm sorry

BUGLE BOY: And no, not friends I thought
we'd be friends to begin with,
but I don't think it's possible

JESSICA: Was it something I said

BUGLE BOY: I saw your
house Not inside But out Looking
at how the entire thing cuts against
the sky

JESSICA: An empty house

BUGLE BOY: He said he wasn't from privilege But the way he
held himself told a different story

JESSICA: You see where I work
This is it
Does this look like privilege to you
(*No response*)
Does it

BUGLE BOY: Charity work to quiet guilt

JESSICA: This is who I am
Not the house

BUGLE BOY: Your neighbors wouldn't help me
They peeked out from windows and
I expected sirens to
screech their way to where I was

JESSICA: Until recently they did the same to me

BUGLE BOY: What do they have to protect looking at me like that?
Sign of privilege to me

JESSICA: Why do you keep coming back to that
What's it to you

BUGLE BOY: It's not for me

JESSICA: It's not for me either

BUGLE BOY: I'll believe it once I see it
Thanks for your time

JESSICA: What do I tell Artie

(*KIRTANA enters.*)

KIRTANA: You lied to me

JESSICA: Kirtana

KIRTANA: I took in what you said
just staring at that wallpaper
all day long thinking about your
news—

JESSICA: What news

KIRTANA: —before realizing, It's not true
What you were trying to relay—

JESSICA: What NEWS Kirtana

KIRTANA: —when you were trying to relay—
You said possibilities

JESSICA: Our leads?

KIRTANA: Stop using that word Nothing further from the truth
All dead-ends, I'm telling you

BUGLE BOY: I'm going

JESSICA: No no please stay

KIRTANA: (*To BUGLE BOY*)
Don't trust them
They claim omnipotence here
but they lie
    They leak and
                sputter all the while claiming to be Magic

BUGLE BOY: (*To JESSICA*)
Tell Artie—
(*Beat*)
I don't know

JESSICA: That you came?

BUGLE BOY: Good luck with his veins

JESSICA: What's that mean

KIRTANA: It's not him Jessica

JESSICA: *(To BUGLE BOY)*
What's that mean

BUGLE BOY: He'll know

(BUGLE BOY exits.)

JESSICA: Kirtana

KIRTANA: It's not my boy

JESSICA: We have received reports of sightings

KIRTANA: Another Indian boy

JESSICA: This one's clearly a runaway

KIRTANA: Another Indian runaway

JESSICA: *(Impatient)*
Suddenly they've become legion is that it
Early on you said rare

KIRTANA: But not singular

JESSICA: You want a photograph taken would that
constitute concrete proof to you

KIRTANA: Do you have a photograph

JESSICA: It could be arranged

KIRTANA: You'll be wasting your time

JESSICA: Why are you purposely striking down

a possibility

KIRTANA: This is the <u>only</u> possibility you
can offer?

JESSICA: Not the only one—

KIRTANA: What others

JESSICA: —but it's the only one that's
turned into something definite
A track

KIRTANA: Look elsewhere

JESSICA: On what recommendation Yours?
We have sightings, witnesses
What do you have

KIRTANA: A mother knows

JESSICA: Are you afraid of being
reunited is that it

KIRTANA: Don't waste your time on Seattle

JESSICA: It's a <u>substantial</u> lead

KIRTANA: *(Disbelief)*
Male prostitution?

JESSICA: It's a possibility
which doesn't mean Yes
            It means Could

KIRTANA: My son's not a homosexual

JESSICA: Kirtana listen to me
You're not hearing what I'm saying

KIRTANA: No you said
            you clearly said in the last meeting, Mixed up
with male prostitution

JESSICA: If I did that was an unfortunate
choice of words
All I said
All I <u>remember</u> saying was, He's been spotted
in an area in Seattle that's populated primarily
by runaways

KIRTANA: And you said, Male prostitutes

JESSICA: And in these areas—

KIRTANA: Male prostitutes

JESSICA: —male prostitutes and drug dealers
To keep alive yes

KIRTANA: And that's supposed to make
me feel better

JESSICA: We don't paint—

KIRTANA: Not paint no You
scratch away

JESSICA: You asked us to find him
and we <u>did</u> <u>Maybe</u>
Just a name   A spotting
somewhere by witnesses who'd
seen a tacked-up Wanted sheet
with his photograph

KIRTANA: The fact remains—

JESSICA: You asked us to find him not render
him like some story book   We track
the <u>physical</u> body

KIRTANA: The fact remains Farouk is neither
homosexual nor a drug addict

JESSICA: *(Impatient)*
How would you know

KIRTANA: Why are you talking like this

JESSICA: Why are _you_

KIRTANA: I see pictures at night

JESSICA: We all do Kirtana

KIRTANA: Pictures of him floating in some river

JESSICA: Don't be SILLY

KIRTANA: A mother knows these things

JESSICA: You're saying to me what
                              That you'd much rather see him
dead in some river than
alive

KIRTANA: Not if he's in Seattle doing
what you claim   Not that kind
of life he might as well be dead

JESSICA: That's absurd   You're a
sensible woman   Always
you've struck me as being
this sensible person

KIRTANA: I've never told you
my history

JESSICA: History of what

KIRTANA: Premonitions that have come
true one by one   I don't
know whose joke it was to
gift me with this   But I
never asked for it
(Beat)
I'm telling you, My
boy's in some river

JESSICA: Who put him there

KIRTANA: Murderers everywhere

JESSICA: You sit alone watching
the patterns of the wallpaper
all night after work
refusing to socialize—

KIRTANA: With whom
Who do I know besides you
and how do I know you won't
start resenting me
like this dog constantly hanging around

JESSICA: Kumar

KIRTANA: That's not what he wants
To socialize

JESSICA: And pretty soon you can't
tell the pattern of the
wallpaper apart from your life
You see murderers burning into
focus along the corners of the room

KIRTANA: I have to marshal facts at night now

JESSICA: But isn't that what I'm giving you

KIRTANA: Giving me what

JESSICA: Facts

KIRTANA: Facts

JESSICA: The solace of facts

KIRTANA: But not yours Your set
of facts don't provide
solace at all

JESSICA: He can be brought back
Rehabilitated

KIRTANA: That's not what we came here for
(Sits)

JESSICA: Do you want some tea

(KIRTANA shakes No.)

JESSICA: Go back and take the day off Get some sleep

KIRTANA: I quit

JESSICA: What do you mean you quit How
Have you got money saved up

(KIRTANA shakes no.)

JESSICA: What are you going to do

KIRTANA: There's always Kumar

JESSICA: He'll loan you money?

KIRTANA: I'll live with him

JESSICA: Since when

KIRTANA: It got so I wouldn't even
leave the restaurant after work
Just spend the night on the floors

JESSICA: Does Kumar know you want to
live with him

KIRTANA: Believe me he'll be ecstatic

JESSICA: Oh I don't doubt that
But does he know why

KIRTANA: A clean start No son I have
no son Jessica He doesn't need
to know a thing No better qualification
for a new wife than to be without history
Besides he doesn't want

someone to talk
                   tell their story
He wants someone to listen
to <u>his</u>, ears always
buzzing after what he has to say

JESSICA: Do you love Kumar

KIRTANA: You want to know what I've learned

JESSICA: What

KIRTANA: One can't do without diversions   Not
here Not have emotions
so unalloyed like—

JESSICA: One makes do*

KIRTANA: —like me
(In response to *)
Have you

JESSICA: I've made do yes

KIRTANA: But not entirely You have
this house Beautiful and large

JESSICA: Somewhere along the line
I can't even account for
it I lucked out

KIRTANA: Some lottery that I can enter
as well?

JESSICA: You already have
(Beat)
Do you love Kumar

KIRTANA: Does that matter

JESSICA: I thought it did to you

(From KIRTANA's bag, she takes out a cow-noise-maker.)

KIRTANA: This makes me laugh
(*Dips it; It moos*)

JESSICA: Do you love Kumar

KIRTANA: It's this country's main
business isn't it

JESSICA: Toys?
(*Stretches her hand out as a gesture of asking for the toy.*)

KIRTANA: (*Hands TOY to JESSICA*)
The manufacture of diversions Always
something else besides the wound
But never a cure,
just its diversion

JESSICA: It's good to laugh
(*Beat*)
Do you love Kumar

KIRTANA: You keep asking that

JESSICA: Because what you said
about swooning
                why you've held out
stayed with me

KIRTANA: (*A sudden burst of adrenaline;
escalating quickly into mania*)
Believe me
I'm SWOONING all right
I will not change
Do you hear that
This country changes you but
NOT ME It changes you for
the worse but not ME
Not my son either
He's not turning homosexual
Only because it's a new country
If there's anyone who'll change it's
this country
This country and not me

If the food's not to your liking, you change it
COOK IT YOURSELF

Right Isn't that right
If the wallpaper's not to your liking, rip it out
'You have recourse to that': Aren't those
your words? If this country lies
to you
(*Snatches toy from JESSICA and begins to stomp on it*)
If this country lies to you, fuck it
Then fuck it
(*beat;*
more calmly now)
I will not be moved
I will not be moved
I will not be moved

(*Lights fade on everything but the crushed moo-toy, at center.*)

22. *Dim lights Up Stage Center: See Scene 23. Stage Right: KIRTANA, smoking a cigarette. Stage Left: LEONCILLO, sitting in a wheelchair. Lights remain on the moo toy as well. Beside KIRTANA, a phone. Throughout the scene, she plays unconsciously with her hair. Throughout the scene, LEONCILLO coughs.*

LEONCILLO'S VOICE: You want to know what

ARTIE'S VOICE: I remember the carpet

LEONCILLO'S VOICE: Carpet

ARTIE'S VOICE: Green
Like grass chewed off
by horses
I want to know what it
is you remembered about

LEONCILLO'S VOICE: The plane

ARTIE'S VOICE: When we landed
When we first
What you felt

LEONCILLO'S VOICE: And you're writing this down

ARTIE'S VOICE: In my notebook

LEONCILLO'S VOICE: I remember cows
seeing them through porthole

ARTIE'S VOICE: Window

LEONCILLO'S VOICE: I'd never seen cows
I was so excited
What can I say
We're allowed moments of
stupidity But I was so excited
This pulsing Black against white
Never seen these balloon things
Certainly not in the Philippines
Carabaos, they had
You know what that is

(Silence, during which we presume ARTIE shakes No)

LEONCILLO'S VOICE: A Filipino water buffalo
It appears on the flipside of the five
centavo piece in the currency

ARTIE'S VOICE:Of the Philippines

LEONCILLO'S VOICE: In the currency* of the Philippines

(*At this word, KIRTANA's phone starts to ring. She looks at it, impassive. Lets it ring once, twice, thrice, four times, five. It dies. All the while the voice-over continues.)

LEONCILLO'S VOICE: The five-cent piece

ARTIE'S VOICE:And it's called a what

LEONCILLO'S VOICE: *Carabao*

ARTIE'S VOICE:Could you spell that please

LEONCILLO'S VOICE: You want me to spell that

ARTIE'S VOICE:Could you please

LEONCILLO'S VOICE: You want me to SPELL that

ARTIE'S VOICE:*(More authoritative)* Yes I want you to spell it

LEONCILLO'S VOICE: You want me to spell *carabao*

ARTIE'S VOICE:Is there anything wrong

LEONCILLO'S VOICE: You don't know how to spell carabao

ARTIE'S VOICE:Would I ask you if I did

LEONCILLO'S VOICE: You want to hear it spelled

ARTIE'S VOICE:Forget it

LEONCILLO'S VOICE: Maybe you should go back

ARTIE'S VOICE:Just because I don't know how to spell carabao

LEONCILLO'S VOICE: It's C-A-R-A-B-A

(*Before he can say O, an amplified moo-toy sound, or a real cow mooing is heard. As soon as it starts, the lights quickly die on KIRTANA and LEONCILLO. The moo-toy sound fades soon after.*)

23. *The ATTENDANT, Upstage Center, visible in the dimness because of his white male nurse's uniform, and who has been there all throughout, silent, smoking, is now better seen.*

ATTENDANT: *(Sings)*
The first half dies
with no proof or trace
no memory of dinner talk
any remnant of grace
no azure stroll
never a leisurely pace
instead a bolt a run
perpetual longing for Place.
(Speaks)
Don't be afraid Billy
of blue skin
and veins
Everything must end

(He picks up a phone, dials. Rings. JESSICA revealed. She picks up.)

JESSICA: Hello

ATTENDANT: Hello?
May I speak to
Artie Leoncillo please

JESSICA: Who is this

ATTENDANT: Who am I speaking to

JESSICA: I'm his mother
Who is this

ATTENDANT: Oh

JESSICA: He's not here

ATTENDANT: Ma'am

JESSICA: Has something happened to him

ATTENDANT: No ma'am
I was calling

to let Mr Leoncillo know
His father

JESSICA: Yes

ATTENDANT: His father has

JESSICA: Oh my God

ATTENDANT: You have my condolences
Are you his wife mam

JESSICA: No
How
How did he

ATTENDANT: In his sleep mam

JESSICA: So it was

ATTENDANT: It was very peaceful

JESSICA: Thank you

ATTENDANT: He was at peace

JESSICA: Thank you

(*JESSICA remains. Light fades.*)

END OF PLAY

FLIPZOIDS

By Ralph B. Peña

The first draft had twelve characters. Boiling it down to three was a sometimes gleeful, most times excruciating, experiment I under- took with Loy Arcenas, who directed the play's premiere in New York. Later, we were joined by Mervyn Antonio from the Public Theater, who helped steer the play into its quasi-final version.

The character of Aying is a reasonable facsimile of my great grand- mother, a woman who took public buses, drew a chalk line around her seat, and promptly stuck a safety pin into anyone who violated her space. Vangie is a patchwork of observances, mostly from having attended a number of Filipino gatherings in Irvine, California, where a rosary group met every Friday night to pay homage to the Virgin and where, in between a litany of Hail Mary's, the members extolled the merits of Jazzercise. Redford is my sister and broth- er, and a legion of second and third generation kids who questioned their hyphenated tags and who launched into heated arguments over what was more politically correct: Filipino or Pilipino. All these characters are refracted self-images. When I decided to write, I reached for what was then closest.

But I would not have written at all if not for Damien, who makes all things possible.

RALPH B. PEÑA

FLIPZOIDS was first produced in New York City by Ma-Yi Theatre Company. It had its first performance on October 4, 1996 at the Theatre For The New City with the following cast and crew:

AYING: Ching Valdes-Aran *
VANGIE: Mia Katigbak
REDFORD: Ken Leung

*Obie Award for Outstanding Performance

Written by Ralph B. Peña
Directed and Designed by Loy Arcenas

Original music and sound design: Fabian Obispo
Dramaturg: Mervyn P. Antonio
Lighting Design: Blake Burba
Stage Manager: Sue Jane Stoker

To the New Pilgrims who roughed the fickle seas in search of mooring and moss.

Characters:
AYING
VANGIE
REDFORD

Setting:
A beach in Southern California.

A rectangular sandbox dominates the stage. Half buried in the sand, down center, is a large earthen bowl of water. Stage Left, there is a half-sided toilet cubicle, the stained bowl clearly visible. The entire back wall of the playing area is white, on which the names of Filipino-American immigrants are written in black. The walls to the left and right are negative images of the back wall. That is, black walls with white letters.

FLIPZOIDS

Sound of crashing waves.

A beam of white light pierces the dark and illuminates the bowl of water, partially revealing the shadowy figure of AYING standing over it. She is dressed in fin de siecle clothing, and evokes a likeness to a daguerreotype. As she kneels down to touch the gleaming liquid, we hear the sound of a large metal bolt unfastening.

Lights up.

VANGIE and REDFORD enter on either side of AYING. VANGIE has on earphones, listening to a recorded lesson. She wears an immaculately white nurse's uniform.

VANGIE: Excercise One Fifty-Five. The letter D. Dainty. Dandelion. Dandruff. Decapitate. *(She takes out a clothes pin and clips it onto her nose.)* Today's road to the promised land is brought to you by the letter D. Debonair, Desecrate, Donut. Doo-be...doo-be...Do bee-doo.

(VANGIE crosses upstage.)

(Lights cross fade. REDFORD is in the toilet cubicle. He sports the casually hip garb of a Gen-X renegade, and has platinum bleached hair. He carries a shoe string that he ties into knots, before undoing each one and repeating the process.)

REDFORD: *(Peeking at the occupant to his left)*

Hello? Hello...? Nice shoes. I had a pair just like that. *(Pause)* Well, no, not really. Okay, the truth. I wouldn't be caught dead in them. No, no. no. But they look like great sensible shoes. I REALLY mean that. Hello? Hi. Are you reading? Yeah? I thought I heard paper rustling. Hello? Well, you must be busy, so I'll do the talking. You listen. If at any time you want me to stop...just...grunt... or something. What a co-wink-a-dink. I like to read myself. James Joyce is a particular favorite. I just, well...am so drawn to...drunken Irishmen. They're so...manly. Oh yes. I like to read, as you do. Especially the classics. They sweep me off to someplace more sanguine. I often think I was born in the wrong century. Don't you? I imagine myself, living...say...in 18th century England. Oh...all that lace. *(Pause)* Hello? Hello? Are you breathing?

I want to live in Budapest. Or Paris. Maybe join the Black Panthers. Someplace where I can blend in. Oh but Paris. Paris would be nice, huh? I want to change my name. What do you think of... Michel Signoret, or Daniel Piaf? I can be a tour guide at Pere Lachaise. "Let me show you to your favorite dead derelict." *J'suis. J'y reste.*

Hello? I feel very close to you. Do you feel close to me? It's always easier with this metal plate between us. Don't you think? Wouldn't it be great if we all walked around in our own little cubicles? There'd be so much reaching out. Everybody would be so desperate to connect. It might be a less cynical world. Hello? Oh no...don't go. Are you mad? I was just kidding. Don't go. Can I make a suggestion? We don't have to talk. We can just sit here...quietly...just sit here...and be. Hello? *(Pause)* We'll always have Paris. *(He peeks under the cubicle to his right.)* Hello?

(Sound of crashing wave. Lights change. Music. VANGIE crosses down stage. She is carrying a pocket dictionary.)

VANGIE: Domestic. Domicile. Dominatrix. D. Noun. A woman who physically and psychologically dominates. Dominatrix. Hmmm. You see that? I'm putting Webster to memory. So far, I know every word from A to G. That's something, right? Not every nurse can say that. *(Pause)* I can.

Now I'm taking Art classes. Imagine that. Me. The nurses at the hospital say, "Vangie Dacuycuy, art classes?" What do they know? Van Gogh. Van Eyck. Van-Gie. Ha! Today's art is brought to you by the letter V. Everything with a Van. Next week, I'm starting therapy.

Eulogy. Eunuch. Eupeptic. E. Noun. Cheerful. Optimistic. Eupeptic.

Where I come from, you see, there are many flies. Bigger than your thumb. From the boarding house I stayed in with four other student nurses, you had to walk along a narrow plank to get to the main road. If you fell to the right, you landed on a pile of maggots. If you fell to the left, you went through the roof of Mang Dencio's shack and landed next to him in bed. All the girls always chose the maggots. Now I know every word from A to G, so far. And from my Art Classes, I've learned that Rubenesque is the gentler, kinder, classier way to say: Fat. Oh, yes. That's something.

Faith. Fajita. Fallible. F. Adjective. Capable of making a mistake. Fallible. *(Pause)* Oh. (Pause) Erase, erase, erase.

(Sound of crashing wave. Lights cross fade to AYING. Once again, she claws at the sand, searching.)

AYING: Do you like crabs? *Ha?* Plenty here. Sometimes you see them. Then they go away. Hiding. When you see one you tell me. I will try to catch.

(She stares out at the ocean.)

Very very blue the water. You like the water, *ha?* Me, I like. You know why, *ha?* I will tell you. *(She dips one foot in the basin of water.)* It brings me closer to my home.

AYING: *(Pause)* Yes. You do not believe? I tell you. Over there, out there, that is where I come from. When I touch the water, ha, it is almost like touching my home. That is why I like to come here. *(Pause)* You, why do you like?
Trans: J'suis, J'y reste = Here I am, here I remain.

Ay, I will tell you a story. Short only. *Ha?* You like? About the *Milagrosa*. Very nice. Short only.

[Trans: *Milagrosa* = Miraculous]

(Lights change. VANGIE walks over to AYING.)

VANGIE: Stop it Aying. No one is interested in your stories.

AYING: They like. They like.

VANGIE: No they don't. It's not allowed. You scare people. It's illegal in California.

AYING: I do not tell them anything bad.

VANGIE: You don't tell them anything good, Aying. Your stories give people the impression that we're barbarians.

AYING: What is wrong with cutting hair?

VANGIE: Barbarian. Adjective. Without culture. Without refinement. Without Art Classes. Why do you insist on sticking out? Why can't you just blend in?

AYING: I do not know how to do like that.

VANGIE: Melt Aying. Melt. Become part of the Pot, part of the soup. That is what it's all about. Everything we worked for. All of that, so we can become part of the soup.

AYING: Evangelina? Do not be angry, *ha?* But you are becoming crazy already. I tell you something. You listen to me. Do not forget. Always remember. You are the first one in our family to wear a white uniform. Me, I only finished grade four. My grandfather, he sell dried fish. His son, your *Lolo*, he carry sacks of rice all day from the market to Don Mariano's warehouse. Your *Lola*, she wash the mayor's clothes. Me, I learned how to use a Singer Sewing Machine. *(Pause)* Now you wear a white uniform. Do not forget why you are better.

VANGIE: C. Compunction. Noun. Anxiety arising from guilt. Stop it Aying. The white uniform means nothing if you act like you come from a cave. White means nothing if you can't say, emphatically, "I have never eaten a pet." If you can't say that, if you haven't MELTED, Aying, the uniform means nothing.

AYING: You have to go to church some more.

VANGIE: Aying. You know why you're like that? Why you feel sad and alone? Dejected.

Despondent, and…and oh so very…very…BLUE! You know why? Because you won't get out of the grave. You insist on spending your days with the dead. And what? Are they Eupeptic? Euphoric? No. There you go. There you are. Look around you Aying. What do you see?

AYING: I see everything. All color blue.

VANGIE: That's because of your cataracts.

AYING: But I see everything. I smell everything.

VANGIE: And what do you smell? Hmm? Tell me. Do you remember when we used to receive packages from the States? The first time you opened the box, there was this…smell. It was nothing like anything we had back home. The only way to describe it is…better. That smell that came from a box from America was better. And every time I smelled it, it gave me goose bumps, and I wanted to hold it in forever. And I did, until I started turning blue. Now, we don't have to wait for any boxes Aying. Now, we smell like the boxes from America.

AYING: I tell you something. When I first arrived here. I smelled it also. Like leather shoes. Before you step outside. Like that. I made me feel peaceful, that smell. Then it changed.

AYING: After a few months it changed. Now it smells like bad pork. You know what that is like, *ha*? You will not like to have it near you.

VANGIE: Because you choose keep rotting memories.

AYING: You like me not to remember. But I am old already. That is all I have.

VANGIE: Then you'll always be looking in – an outsider. You want that? Every time you're at a department store, people will always ask you: "Do you work here?" We've come this far…

(AYING cuts her off in mid-sentence with a dismissing gesture. VANGIE exits.)

AYING: My daughter. She is changing. She is becoming *Amerikana*. Now I think she will go to hell.

[Trans: *Amerikana* = American]

(Lights change.)

AYING: You see that. Plenty of crabs. You never know where they will come from. *(She looks around.)* *Ay*, I tell you story now. Short only. *Empezar Ya!* You listen *ha*? There is a fisherman who ride his boat to the sea, very early in the morning. You know this story, ha? No. This one is different. I will tell you. You listen and you remember. Do not forget. He ride his boat to very deep water…

we call that *laot*. That is where you catch the biggest fish. He put his net in the blue water, and he wait… and he pray. When he pull the net back into the boat… nothing. Empty. Not even one *dilis*. You know *dilis*? You call it… I do not know what you call it. *Dilis*. Very small fish like that. Could not catch. Not even one.

Poor fisherman. Cannot catch even one *dilis*. *Kawawa*. He stayed there, in the *laot* for three days, never surrendering. After four days, when he could not even open his eyes because of the salt, he see her. Standing inside his small boat. He see her. Dressed in blue and with long gold *belo*. She talk to the fisherman. "You do what I tell you," this one said, and you will catch your *dilis*. "What do you like me to do?," the fisherman ask, and he kneel down because he knows this is not ordinary.

[Trans: *Empezar Ya* = It begins now ; *laot* = deep sea; *dilis* = anchovies ; *belo* = veil.]

AYING: "You take me to every shore, every year, on June sixteen, and wash your spirit with water. Begin again. *Empezar Ya*." She said. And she melt with the waves. The fisherman followed her order, and the fish come back. That is the story of he *Milagrosa*. Do not forget. *Empezar Ya*. It begins now.

(Lights change. REDFORD enters down stage right, carrying a can of spray paint. He begins to write graffiti on the walls.)

REFDORD: There is a small stretch of deserted beach along the Pacific Coast Highway, just north of Laguna called the Red Cove. Nobody goes there. It's too rocky, and the cliffs that overhang the beach block out most of the morning sun. So it's no surprise why it's my favorite spot, along with a handful of other social outcasts who find solace in the company of hermit crabs and the bundles of slimy kelp that litter the shore. From my high perch, which sits atop a sandy dune about a hundred or so yards from the water, I can observe most of the goings on. Why it's called the Red Cove is anybody's guess. There's nothing in the area remotely near the shade of red. *(He crosses to the cubicle area.)* There, just to the left, is a rest area, ostensibly built to provide the public with a place to change and a shower to wash off the sand. Nobody goes in there to change. Or to shower. And it's very definitely not a rest area. People around here call it the Barracks. Once initiated, you are called a cadet. You get the picture.

(REDFORD sits on the toilet.)

I go in here, not to have sex, but to connect. I am most at ease in these fetid fuck chambers. Sitting here, in one of the stalls, I can strip my soul naked to the occupant next door. I can let go. I don't know him. He doesn't know me. Neither has to prove anything to the other. Let's face it. Nobody goes in there with very high expectations. Nobody goes in there looking for a young Kennedy.

(Pause. He peeks at the occupant next door.)

What I'm trying to say is, there is an unwritten sign on the entrance to the Barracks that says:

CHECK YOUR SELF ESTEEM HERE. *(Pause)* I like that.

This is my prison. And my sanctuary. I find a comforting sense of safety in enclosed spaces.

It was early afternoon. I was sitting on my perch at the Cove, quietly running a myriad combination of names in my head. Something exotic. Ivan Sveltskaya. Olaf Pearlstein. Jeremiah Bernhardt. When, suddenly, I was interrupted by this figure walking into my visual periphery. Hold everything. Who is that?

(AYING is heard singing softly to herself, and performing some kind of ritual.)

	AYING:
Empezar Ya. Empezar Ya.	[Trans: It begins now. It begins now.
Dampian ng munting awa	Give a little mercy
Ereng araw na banal.	on this Holy Day.
Hugasan ang kasalanan	Wash our sins
sa Inyong Kapangyarihan	with your Blessed Power,
Panibagong kasaysayan	and help us start
Tulungang Simulan.	a new history.
Empezar Ya. Empezar Ya.	It begins now. It begins now.]

REDFORD: She cut a stark figure on the beach like nothing I've seen before. She wore an ensemble that can only be described as... GOTHIC. Whoa! *(Pause)* I liked her immediately.

	AYING:
Empezar Ya. Empezar Ya.	[Trans: It begins now. It begins now.
Ereng araw, simulan na.	Start on this very day.
Panibagong kasaysayan.	A new history.
Empezar Ya. Empezar Ya.	It begins now. It begins now.}

REDFORD: Suddenly I find myself smack in the middle of a Val Lewton film. *(Pause)* Look it up. I am drawn to her. An enigma. Like me. And though, as a general rule, I don't talk to people outside of cubicles, I sensed this one was different.

(He crosses to the edge of the sand box.)

You there. Yes. You in the period costume. Hi. Hello. I saw you from up there. Hi. What were you doing? Just then, when I saw you?

(AYING does not respond.)

REDFORD: See, from up there, it looked like some kind of ritual. It was very fascinating and seemed fraught with symbols. *(Pause)* It's uh... very... you know... very... earthy. *(Pause)* Delightful stuff…*(There is an awkward silence.)* Angel overhead. The Angel of silence... .it… flies…

(AYING looks at the sky.)

Figuratively, really. It's uh, very hard to actually see.

(AYING looks at REDFORD.)

Just an expression. Chekov I think. *(Pause)* I know, I can be really pretentious. I'll… just uh… walk back to… uh.. where I uh… nice meeting you.

(REDFORD extends his hand. AYING does not respond and continues touching the water.)

REDFORD: You keep doing that.

(REDFORD exits.)

AYING: Howdy.

(REDFORD returns immediately.)

REDFORD: Hi. Hello. What's that you're doing there?

AYING: I am touching my home.

REDFORD: Now, see? That is so charming. I never think to come up with things like that myself. *(Pause)* You were touching what again?

AYING: This water, here, this is the same water on the shore of Pagudpud. That is where I come from. When I feel the water… when I touch it… it is like I am also touching my home.

REDFORD: Right. And home is where?

AYING: Here. Give me your hand.

(REDFORD does not move.)

AYING: I will show you Pagudpud. That is where I come from.

REDFORD: Nah. No. I don't know…are you sure? Really? It seems so personal, and I've never really gotten in touch with my *chakra*.

AYING: Okee dokee.

REDFORD: If you insist. Fine. Okay. What do I do?

(AYING takes REDFORD'S hand and lowers it into the basin of water.)

AYING: *(Pause)* You close your eyes. Please. You close.

REDFORD: Someone told me once I was psychic. I am very sensitive. This is exciting, really.

AYING: You see with eyes closed. *(Pause)* Feel that? There is small town close to the water. Pagudpud. We call it that. Very early, in the morning, you see the smoke from the house of Ka Berting. He is making pan de sal… bread. In the streets, you hear the carabao pulling big carts of rice to the market. That is next to the bus station. Do you see? Where I live, there is a big acacia tree. The biggest in Pagudpud. Nong Peping, my grandfather, he plant it in front of the house.

(She has closed her eyes, and speaks as if in a trance. REDFORD has opened his and watches her, seduced.)

(Music: Strains of a Kundiman. (A traditional Filipino love song))

All around, my mother, Nang Senciang, she put Sampaguita flowers. At night, you smell how sweet they are when you go to sleep. At the back of the house, there is a mango tree. Very low… the branches... very low you can pick the fruit even when you kneel down. We sit under the branches and eat mango until our stomachs hurt. We also have small river. Very small only. When it rains, the water comes out of the river and covers the ground. You can see the fish swimming all around the house. Can you see? It begins now. The rains have started. See?

REDFORD: Yes. *(Pause)* It takes your breath away.

AYING: Yes. Never forget. *(Pause)* I have to go to the bathroom.

REDFORD: *(To the audience)* As depraved and morally bankrupt as I am, I cannot bring myself to point her to the Barracks. *(to AYING)* The closest one is on the main beach.

AYING: What is that? *(Pointing to the Barracks)*

REDFORD: That? It's nothing. It's a...a prison...for...a...very bad surfers. You don't want to go there.

AYING: Okee dokee.

REDFORD: *(To the audience)* I am reeling from this encounter. There is a rush of... of energy... of emotions... it's like... nothing I've ever encountered in the toilet. There is a connection here that I've never sensed with anyone's shoe before. I'm good about things like that. I am a well-honed sensor of connections. This. This is a good connection and, oh my god, the woman is pissing on the beach.

(AYING has lifted her skirt and is peeing on the beach, standing up. REDFORD turns his back and tries to provide some cover.)

I can't help but notice that you can do that standing up. Here. Kleenex?

(AYING takes the Kleenex and wipes her face.)

Not what most people would do either. But like I always say, the face comes first.

AYING: What is the time already?

REDFORD: I don't have a watch. My guess is around three. I'm Redford by the way.

AYING: Howdy. Have a nice day. *(She hands REDFORD the used Kleenex.)*

REDFORD: And you are?

AYING: Rosario.

REDFORD: Like rosary?

AYING: Oh. You go to church?

REDFORD: No.

AYING: You should go to church.

REDFORD: It's not my scene.

AYING: You will go to hell.

REDFORD: I'm there already. *(He starts sniffing)* What's that? You...uh.. *(sniff)* that's... uh... *(sniff)* you smell like.... uh...

AYING: *Naptalina.* Mothballs. That is what old people smell like. When you meet people who smell like that, you better respect them. They smell dead, but they know life.

Who are your parents?

REDFORD: Why do you ask?

AYING: Do they go to church?

REDFORD: No. No they don't.

AYING: You have a very brave family.

REDFORD: I'm an only child. After I was born, my parents channeled all their energies into turning me from a tropical banana into a perfect Macintosh. You know what that is?

AYING: No. But my daughter, she will know.

REDFORD: It's a kind of apple.

AYING: I do not like apple. In Pagudpud, we have *macopa*. Also like apple, but more cheaper.

[Trans: *Macopa* = a tropical fruit, indigenous to the Philippines, usually pink in color and fleshy like an apple.]

REDFORD: Anyway, my mother bought a copy of the Official Preppy Handbook. "This," she said, "this will be our blue print to happiness." It became the spiritual center of our family life, more revered than the Holy Bible.

AYING: You are Jehovah Witness?

REDFORD: No.

AYING: Okee dokee.

REDFORD: Where are you from?

AYING: Anaheim.

REDFORD: No. What country.

AYING: You know Japan?

REDFORD: Yes. *(Pause)* You can't be Japanese.

AYING: No, no, no. Near Japan. The Philippines.

REDFORD: I knew it.

AYING: You know someone who is from there also?

REDFORD: You may find this hard to believe but... well, me. We came here when I was seven.

AYING: You? So you are Pilipino also? *(Pause)* What happened?

REDFORD: *(To the audience)* She can be harsh can't she? *(To Aying)* Here, they call us Flips.

AYING: That is good?

REDFORD: I don't know. *(To the audience)* I've never really thought of it as a pejorative, at least, not in the same vein as say, Catholic.

AYING: You don't look Pilipino.

REDFORD: I've been told that.

AYING: Your parents? They look like you?

REDFORD: *(To the audience)* She says that with just enough contempt in her tone. Any more and I would have been insulted. As it is, I only feel embarrassed. *(To Aying)* Yes. We have similar features.

AYING: Then they do not look Pilipino also.

REDFORD: I'll be sure to let them know that. How long have you been here?

AYING: I came after breakfast.

REDFORD: In America I mean. Have you been in America long?

AYING: Oh yes. Very long, already. And you?

REDFORD: Very long too.

AYING: What is the time now?

REDFORD: I don't have a watch.

AYING: Did I ask you that already?

REDFORD: Once. You asked me once.

AYING: I'm becoming stupid, *ha*?

REDFORD: That's okay. I'm going to hell.

AYING: You like to leave? You can leave if you like.

REDFORD: No. I don't have any plans.

AYING: I like you to stay. Little bit. *Ha*?

REDFORD: Okay. *(Pause)* Do you miss it?

AYING: What?

REDFORD: Your home. Pagudpud?

AYING: No.

REDFORD: Why not?

AYING: I took it with me.

REDFORD: Is there...I mean...I feel really close to you Rosario...

AYING: *(She screams.)* You are a rapist?

REDFORD: *(to the audience)* This is a concern? *(to Aying)* No. Of course not. Do I look like a rapist?

AYING: Why are you asking me? I do not know.

REDFORD: Can I... you know... I want to reciprocate. Can I tell you anything about America? Our land? Our People? This Realm... Orange County?

AYING: *(Pause)* No. *(Pause)* You like it here? America?

REDFORD: Sometimes.

AYING: How come only sometimes?

REDFORD: Sometimes it gets tiring. You know that 3-D game where you stare at a bunch of dots and squiggles and hope something comes of it? Well, America is like that. Sometimes, you have to be a little cross-eyed to see the good stuff. And that gets tiring.

AYING: You have plenty to say.

REDFORD: Do you? Like it here, in America?

AYING: Sometimes also.

REDFORD: Rosario?

AYING: You call me Aying.

REDFORD: A...ying?

AYING: Aying. That is my name also.

REDFORD: Aying. What can I... you know... how do I... can you tell me... what I am? I mean, I know what I am, but how do I... say... get rid of this itch? Can you recommend a book? How do I reconcile myself to... And that's not to say I'm a worthless blob of nothing, because I do have a center of power. I am. *(Pause)* But should I be? Should I even care? Is there, what I'm trying to say is, can I find redemption in public places?

AYING: Okay, you leave now.

(REDFORD looks around uneasily, then exits. Lights change.)

AYING: Evangelina should meet that boy. She will not like to change so much.

(MUSIC: Strains of a Kundiman (Traditional Filipino Love Song))

AYING: I tell you this. Before I ride the airplane, I walk around our house three times. Very slowly, very slowly three times. I stop at the *acacia* tree and stand under her branches, very long time also, so I can count her leaves. I stop by the fence, and I listen to the neighbor's pig. I stop in the middle of my kitchen and I touch the black bottom of my favorite *kaldero*. I stand there, very long time also, and I smell my mother's cooking, I will take this, I say. I will take that. Stop here, for a while. Stop there, a little longer.

This is important. Because I know, someday, you will come to me and say, "I do not remember. I do not smell. I do not feel." And I will give you my heart. "There," I will say, "you look in there. *(Pause)* I keep it all for you." Someday maybe she will look.

{Trans: *kaldero* = cooking pot, usually made from cast iron}
(VANGIE enters. She walks around the perimeter of the sandbox. AYING steps out of the box to follow her.)

Ay, good you are here. I ask you something.

VANGIE: I have advanced. Now H. Homogenous. Homo Sapiens. Hooker. Hoopla. Ha! Today H.

AYING: Where will you bury me?

VANGIE: What kind of question is that?

AYING: I think, in Orange Country they do not let you throw your dead mother in the river.

VANGIE: Do we have to talk about this now?

AYING: You please send my body back to Pagudpud.

VANGIE: Not now. *(Pause)* Why do you want to go back?

AYING: There is nothing for me here. Anaheim is not for old people.

VANGIE: Aying... I'm tired of this. What is it you want to go back to? Ha? Tell me.

(AYING remains silent.)

VANGIE: Tell me. Don't do this again. I want to understand. What do you want that I haven't given you?

AYING: *(She walks back to her place in the sandbox.)* I go back and I work with my Singer Sewing machine. You do not have to send money. *(Pause)* If you like, you can send for Christmas and my birthday, but only if you like.

VANGIE: How do you think this makes me feel? *(Pause)* I don't know what to say anymore.

AYING: *(She takes out a worn letter from her pocket.)* Evangelina, when I receive your letter that you are bringing me here, I show it to all the neighbors. Look, I say, my daughter, she is taking me to America. I was very happy.

VANGIE: It didn't last long, did it?

AYING: *(Takes a long look at VANGIE)* I have different picture in my head.

VANGIE: Do you remember what I used to say. I was what? *Ha?* No more than what? I was no taller than this. And what did I use to say? Do you remember?

AYING: I remember.

VANGIE: I was nine. At night, every night, before we slept…

AYING: I remember.

VANGIE: I used to say… someday… Aying… I will give you better than this.

AYING: You wanted to live in a cement house.

VANGIE: With long, wide stairs and screened windows… and water that came out of a faucet.

AYING: It was the only way you would go to sleep.

VANGIE: I was forcing myself to dream about it. And I didn't just want it for myself. I wanted you there with me, in the big cement house, walking up and down the wide staircase, you and me Aying… all the way up… and then down again… up… and down… and we would never get tired because outside, the neighbors were watching us through the screened windows, their eyes bulging with envy. And they were saying, "Look. Look at them. They are blessed. They have TWO floors and windows that keep out the flies."

AYING: Now we live in Anaheim.

VANGIE: And, it's better. Aying, look at me. It's better.

AYING: Yes. *(Pause)* But I do not belong to your house. I should be outside, with the others and the flies. I think… I feel… in here *(She touches her chest.)*… that is where I am happy.

VANGIE: How do you know that when you've never tried, Aying? You've never made any attempt to appreciate our good fortune. You've never once made me feel like I've done good. Instead, every time I look at you, I'm reminded of my own failure. Why is that? Sometimes, in the morning when I'm brushing my teeth, I would stare at the bathroom mirror and scream, but with no sound so you wouldn't hear me. Is it my fault she's unhappy, have I given her what she wants... am I a bad daughter... sometimes... sometimes... I wish...

AYING: Me also. *(Pause)* Evangelina... you are my daughter... come here. You come.

(VANGIE walks towards Aying, hesitantly. AYING touches VANGIE'S face gently.)

AYING: You have very sad eyes.

VANGIE: What? Where? Me?

AYING: Here, you give me your hands.

VANGIE: Why?

AYING: I show you something.

(VANGIE doesn't move, suspicious.)

You give me. Let me see you hands.

VANGIE: What are you going to do?

AYING: I show you something. You will like.

(VANGIE offers both hands. AYING takes VANGIE'S hands and drapes them around her shoulder. She sings an old Filipino nursery tune.)

AYING: *Buwabo-buwabo*   {Trans: A traditional Ilokano nursery rhyme.
napanan ni inayo   Exact translation not available.
napan tin maki   Loosely translated: A young lad went
idjay adayo manu't pinag- ilo na   to a far off town to take a crap, and washed
sa nga burnay nga suka   his ass with a jug of vinegar.}

VANGIE: What does this have to do with my hands?

AYING: Here. You look.

VANGIE: What?

AYING: We have the same. Same fingers. You see. You have my hands from many years ago.

Strong hands. *(Pause)* Someday, they will be ugly and crooked like mine.

VANGIE: Why do you say these things?

AYING: Here you put your hands here.

(AYING puts VANGIE's hands around her neck.)

VANGIE: What are you doing?

AYING: Here. Now you press hard. Squeeze it.

(VANGIE recoils in horror. She looks at AYING with contempt and runs out.)

AYING: Evangelina. You come back. *(Pause)* Joke only. I thought she was going to laugh. *(Pause)* I tell you something. My daughter, she is good. You do not always see that. This place, it does not let her show that all the time. But I know she is good. In here. *(She touches her chest.)* I know... because she is mine.

(Lights change. REDFORD sits inside the toilet cubicle. He is playing with a rock from the beach.)

REDFORD: Hello? Hello...? Don't get up. I can see your shoes. That's enough. Nice leather. Studs too? Yesiree Bob. Can I call you Bob? Hello? Do this for me, will you? Bob? Close your eyes a minute and imagine a huge... big... oak tree. *(Pause)* You with me? Just to the right, a singing brook... with water like... I don't know... Evian... and... gold fish. Can you see, Bob? In the... spring... when it rains... the water spills all around the house and you can see the darn things swimming around. And... well... that's all I have to say about that.

Do you like apples? Bob? I can never eat the skin. Mama always peeled them for us, as far as I can remember. She peeled grapes too, and peaches. No fuzz for us. Mama peeled them all. Get to the good stuff, she would say. She even took the little seeds off strawberries with a tweezer. *(Pause)* Okay, I'm lying. She didn't do that. But she peeled everything else. Hello? No. No. Don't get up.

Just peel the skin, and reveal the truth. Now isn't that an aphorism to live by? You know it's the largest organ of the body, right up there with the liver. They say you can stretch

Your skin for miles. Is that right? That may be a little overstated. Enough to cover a room anyway. Or upholster a couch. It could happen. Just peel the skin, and reveal the truth. I had this classmate in prep school, Mark Towers, he had acne so bad he couldn't breathe out of his nostrils because they had swollen shut with zits. Everybody said he ate a lot of chocolates and jerked off too much. Fatal combination for a teenager. But Mark was the nicest, most unassuming person in school. Problem is, he looked like raw meat. Just peel the skin, and reveal the truth. This world might be better for it. *(He starts cutting into his skin of his palm with the sharp edge of the rock.)* Something is under there. Something more. We have to believe that. There, you see. *(He holds up his bleeding palm.)* No. No. Don't get up.

(We hear sound of door slamming, and the distant sound of sea gulls.)

Don't get up. This is what you've gotta you do. Expose your true self to the world. None of this superficial bull crud... that just gives them ammunition they'll use against you anyway... Strip. Strip. Strip it all away. This is going to scar. Ooops. Do I frighten you? Hmmm? I don't fit the mold do I? You know what else? This is beginning to hurt. Owwwww. Hello? Hello? Bob? I see you failed to recognize my clear cry for help there. Owwww. Hello? *(Pause)* This is so gauche, I could spit. Hello? *(Pause)* Don't let's ask for the moon.

(REDFORD crosses to the edge of the sandbox, and washes his wound in the bowl of water. Lights change. Sounds of waves and sea gulls. AYING is sitting inside the sandbox, smoking a cigar. She is studying an old photograph. AYING spots REDFORD tending to his hand.)

AYING: What did you do to your hand?

REDFORD: Nothing. *(He notices the picture.)* What's that?

AYING: This is my father.

REDFORD: Can I see?

AYING: *(Hands him the picture)* He used to call me my little *kampupot*. My little *kampupot*. Flower. Yes. I learned many things from him, many stories. You?

[Trans: *Kapupot* = a fragrant flower with dainty petals.]

REDFORD: What?

AYING: You father. He tells you stories also?

REDFORD: My family shares information on a "need-to-know" basis only. You don't know my father. He's... different. *(Pause)* I never once heard him talk about the past. It was always what he was going to be in the future... And there was never any residue, you know... I mean... he never left a trail behind. My father just kept moving forward. Behind him, there was nothing. He is what he is now, and nothing of him is what he was. Does that make any sense?

AYING: No. *(Pause)* I understand a little bit and maybe my daughter will be the same.

REDFORD: Sometimes I'd be standing on a street corner, or be reading a book, or taking a shower, and my skin would begin to itch. Like I'm going to explode. And you know what keeps repeating in my head? Over and over. "I want to go home." I want to go home. Over and over. I want to go home.

AYING: This is your home.

(Silence. AYING senses REDFORD's uncomfortable reaction.)

AYING: I tell you something. I do not know where my daughter will bury me. Okay if she throw me with the garbage on Wednesdays. But I do not think they do that here. Where I come from, if you die poor, they put you in a sack and throw you into the river. I do not mind dying anymore. It does not scare me. You know what I like? Maybe she can send me home to Pagudpud. My mother is buried there. Yes. I would like to be buried next to my mother. We will have plenty to talk about. Nang Senciang, I have been to Disneyland.

Where is that she will say. In Anaheim, Nang Senciang. She will not understand at first, but we have plenty of time. Nang Senciang, in Anaheim, they can cook food faster than you can say Hail Mary. *Dios Mio*, she will say. Yes. But they do not wash their *puwet* with water after going to the toilet. They only wipe it with paper. She will say, Rosario, where is this Anaheim where people cook food faster than they pray but do not wash their *puwet*? And I will say, a place they call Orange Country. *(Pause)* And we will laugh together for a very very long time.

Nang Senciang, I do not think they have too much time for the dead here. What if I do not see you again? I do not know if the soul can ride the airplane. Maybe we can write. *(Pause)* I am not so scared of dying anymore, Nang Senciang. Not anymore. But what will happen to Evangelina?

(AYING looks at REDFORD, as if waiting for an answer. He tries to form silent words with his mouth, but remains silent. There is a long moment of uneasiness, as REDFORD squirms under AYING's gaze. AYING takes out a sandwich from her pocket and offers half of it to REDFORD, who begins to relax. They eat, content with the unspoken, as they stare out into the ocean.)

(Music. Sounds of crashing waves and seagulls.)

AYING: I will die soon. You listen to my stories. They will live with you.

REDFORD: I don't take responsibility well. Besides, I wouldn't know what to do with them.

AYING: You will know.

REDFORD: They could end up on the walls of public toilets.

AYING: You like to help me?

REDFORD: Help you how?

AYING: You help me make my daughter happy.

REDFORD: I can barely keep myself sane.

AYING: You cut my heart and you take it to her.

REDFORD: Say what?

AYING: Take my heart to my daughter and you say, here, Evangelina... now you are free.

REDFORD: Whoa. That is really bizarre.

AYING: Joke only. What? You think I am crazy I will let you cut my heart? *(Pause)* You like to play game?

REDFORD: Like what?

AYING: You know *patintero?*

[Trans: *Patintero* – A game of 'tag' usually played in the streets, along lines drawn on the ground.]

REDFORD: I can't even pronounce the damn thing.

AYING: How about *pitik-bulag*?

[Trans: *Pitik-Bulag* – Literally, "tap the blind," a guessing game.]

REDFORD: What is that?

AYING: You cover your eyes, like this with your hand. I make like this with my hand, then I tap your hand like that, and you make you other hand the same like mine.

(REDFORD just stares at her.)

AYING: You did not understand?

REDFORD: I'm still working on it.

AYING: *Ay, gago.* It's very easy only. You cover your eyes, like this with your hand. I make like this with my hand, then I tap your hand like that, and you make your other hand the same like mine.

[Trans: *Gago* = Stupid]

REDFORD: You want me to guess what you've done to your hand with my eyes closed?

AYING: Yes. Very easy. You cover your eyes now. Go ahead. All the kids play this in Pagudpud.

REDFORD: *(He covers his eyes reluctantly.)* Didn't you have any Barbie dolls?

AYING: *(She forms a fist with one hand, and slaps Redford with the other, hard.)* Pitik-bulag!

REDFORD: Oww! What was that for?

AYING: You try to guess now.

REDFORD: My head is spinning, I could have a mild concussion, how the hell am I supposed to guess?

AYING: You should eat more vegetables. Never mind. We'll play another one. You know hide and seek?

REDFORD: I don't want any more games.

AYING: One more. This one, Evangelina used to play in the back of the church. You know this also?

REDFORD: Yes, yes... I know hide and go seek.

AYING: Good. You hide. I will seek.

REDFORD: You want ME to hide?

AYING: Yes. You go. I will find you.

REDFORD: YOU will find ME? Maybe YOU should hide and I'LL be the seeker.

AYING: No, no. You go. You hide. You.

REDFORD: Alright. If you insist.

AYING: I will stand here and cover my eyes. You hide.

REDFORD: Count to twenty.

AYING: *(She covers her eyes with her hand.) Isa, dalawa, tatlo, apat...*

REDFORD: What are you doing?

AYING: *lima*, six, seven, eight, nine, *sampu...*

REDFORD: Great. Just what I need. A fugitive from *Sesame Street*.

(REDFORD exits.)

AYING: *labing-isa, labing-dalawa, labing-tatlo... apat... lima... (Pause) nauuhaw ako.*

(Lights change. AYING stands frozen. VANGIE enters with a small shopping bag. Cheesy Mall Music. VANGIE'S neck is craned, staring at the ceiling.)

VANGIE: That's what she said. I am thirsty. That's all. *(Pause)* At the mall. The new pavilion... where you can get cappuccino and croissant and watch your reflection on the glass ceiling... oh my goodness, halfway...halfway... not there, but in between... by the drinking fountain.. this is so... I don't know anymore... this is so... THERE... halfway between Eddie Bauer and Baccarat... by a drinking fountain.... in front... IN FRONT AYING... WHY IN FRONT? There were so many people. HUNDREDS AYING... WHY THERE? WHY NOW?

AYING: Why not?

VANGIE: We were just looking... browsing... maybe for a Cuisinart... BUT JUST LOOKING, AYING.

AYING: *Nauuhaw ako.*

[Trans: *Nauuhaw ako* = I am thirsty]

VANGIE: I'm thirsty, she said. Very innocent, like that. Very naive, just like that. And I, what do I know...? You like a glass of milk? How about a coke?

AYING: Tubig lang.

[Trans: *Tubig lang* = Water only.]

VANGIE: I pointed...THERE... conveniently located in between Bauer and Baccarat... in between a lumberjack and a chandelier, AHA! First World accessibility. THERE, AYING, RIGHT THERE.. A WATER FOUNTAIN.

(AYING enters a pool of light. Sound of rushing water.)

VANGIE: STOP. NOW. That's what I should have said. Looking back... that's what I should have said. Instead, I allowed it... I said: RIGHT THERE. GO AHEAD. DRINK. *(Pause)* Well? What? *(pause)* I should have said STOP. But I was distracted. I was absorbed by the pictures in ceiling... lost in the reflection of a perfect world below... the cappuccino and croissant world... and the mirror was saying to me... you're part of it.

AYING: The *Milgrosa*, she say to the fisherman, "You begin again." *(To Vangie)* What is today?

VANGIE: Tuesday Madness. Everything Half-Off. Hurry Aying. Drink already.

AYING: Tuesday what? What is the date today?

VANGIE: RIGHT THERE. RIGHT THEN... But I was distracted, looking at my reflection in the glass ceiling. There I was, standing in the middle of the very classy and the very fortunate... and I was thinking in my head... if you looked up quickly... like that... just a passing glance... like that... very quick... quicker... you could not tell me apart. You could not say... she does not belong... No you could not... I was distracted. *(To Aying)* What difference does it make? There's a sale at Sears. It's Tuesday. JUNE SIXTEENTH.

AYING: Yes. Tuesday. Wash your spirit. June sixteen. *Empezar Ya.*

(*AYING bends over to take a drink from the water fountain. Sound of rushing water. She straightens up slowly, and looks around. AYING begins her ritual dance, and singing. She speaks in almost inaudible tones.*)

AYING: *Empezar Ya. Empezar Ya.*
           Dampian ng munting awa
           Ereng araw na banal.
           Hugasan ang kasalanan
           sa Inyong Kapangyarihan
           Panibagong kasaysayan
           Tulungang simulan.
           Empezar Ya. Empezar Ya.

VANGIE: Oh my goodness. Look at that. HURRY UP, AYING. DRINK.
I Was distracted again. BY THAT. Look at her. Is that confidence? Ha? AYING, HURRY. I was distracted. THERE. See? Her. Her. That one. That dress. The walk. Miss Gucci, or Mrs. Ralph Lauren? Oh my goodness. How much is that?

AYING: Not even one *dilis.*

VANGIE: AYING. And then… and then…I noticed. THERE. Her reflection.

AYING: I see everything. All color blue.

VANGIE: Standing. THERE. By the stainless steel water fountain. I noticed but denied. Who is that? She doesn't belong in my mirror.

AYING: You begin again. That is what she said.

VANGIE: WHO IS THAT? I denied. Again. I should have said, STOP. STOP
NOW. And suddenly, this stranger, this intruder… all of a sudden…HER… the pictures in the ceiling…it was like a dream.

(*Suddenly AYING spits a stream of water at the imaginary shopper.*)

AYING: *Empazar Ya.* I wash your sins away.

VANGIE: From its mouth…the intruder's mouth…shot the venom. Like a stepped-on snake. It burst from the corner of its wrinkled lips…from the flared nostrils…from the small slit of its yellow eyes. I stood there. I could not move. All I could do was trace the stream as it flew across the air…past me…past the potted yellow tulips…and onto the very classy, very confident shoulder of Miss Gucci. STOP. STOP. STOP. STOP. My mother's saliva. Her venom. It was intended for me. She wanted to bite. Me.

AYING: I wash your sins away.

VANGIE: AY! AY! AYING! AYING! DO NOT NOT NOT DO THIS NOT NOT THIS
NOT HERE NOT NOW NOT NOT NOT HER. AYING!

(Lights change. Suddenly speaking with a heavy Tagalog accent, VANGIE drops to her knees.)

VANGIE: Ma'am...ma'am...I am sorry...ma'am. Miss Gucci. *Naku*...ma'am. I...please...ma'am...
you forgive ha? Please...you are so pretty ma'am...so fortunate...and blessed...let me touch your being,
may I? Me. *Pangit ako. Pangit*. I am ugly. Yes. Can I clean you ma'am? I am humble...humble...for-
give...ma'am...forgive. We are worthless...You like, I will clean your house?*Kasi...Kasi...Misis...*Where
I come from...*Doon...*There is so many flies...so many flies...*Kaya...*That is why...you must forgive
ma'am...ma'am?

AYING: Evangelina? What are you doing? There is nothing to forgive. It is June sixteen. Water
will wash her sins away. She has plenty. Begin again. *Empazar Ya.*

Help me remember, Evangelina. Come. We will remember together. *Empezar Ya. Empezar Y*a. The
fish will come back.

*(A waltz. AYING is seen doing a dance and throwing water around her. We also hear the distorted screams of
people running away.)*

AYING: Evangelina! It is like Pagudpud. *Ano?*

(VANGIE looks up at the ceiling.)

AYING: I wash you. And You. And you. And you also. You are clean now. The fish will come
back. Evangelina...it is like Pagudpud.

(Lights change. Sound of voices rising to an excited roar.)

VANGIE: STOP. STOP. STOP. Why here? Now, in front of them? Somebody stop HER. I cannot
anymore. Somebody...anybody...please...please. YOU. YOU. THAT ONE. Mamang Pulis. Mr.
Officer. YOU WITH THE GUN. STOP HER. MAKE HER STOP. SHOOT HER AND MAKE
HER STOP.

(Voices stop suddenly. Lights change.)

AYING: Evangelina...why? Why do you not see? Why do you not want to remember?

AYING: It's water only. June sixteen. *El Viaje de La Milagrosa.*

VANGIE: Take her away. *(Pause)* I do not know her.

(VANGIE exits. AYING stands isolated in the center. She is dazed from the previous encounter, unsure of where she is. She fixes her stare at the direction of VANGIE's exit. REDFORD enters and sneaks up to AYING.)

REDFORD: Boo. *(Lights change)* You're IT.

AYING: You again.

REDFORD: Couldn't find me?

AYING: No. *(Still focused on VANGIE direction)* You are very good. You win.

REDFORD: *(Pause)* You never even looked, did you?

AYING: Did you really want me to find you?

(REDFORD doesn't answer. He sits next to her.)

AYING: I ask you something.

REDFORD: Lay it on me.

AYING: No. I like to stand up.

REDFORD: I meant… never mind… ask me the question.

AYING: Why are we here?

REDFORD: "Why are you here?" *(To AYING)* What the heck kind of question is that?

AYING: Then you do not know also.

REDFORD: I love the way you can be so… concise. It's so… endearing… in a twisted sort of way.

AYING: I ask you something else.

REDFORD: Alright. But start with something simpler.

AYING: No. No. This one is not a question. This one, I ask for your help.

REDFORD: Oh. Okay. What do you want me to do?

AYING: You tell me how I will understand better. Ha? You teach me how to see like you, and Evangelina. Sige na. You teach. Please.

REDFORD: Look at me. I look like a teacher? *(Pause)* I thought you were going to start with something simple.

AYING: When I look at my daughter...my Evangelina...here *(She touches her chest.)*...it does not feel so good. I am like a big heavy stone in her shoes. She likes to walk very fast, my daughter...she likes to run after new things...but she has me inside her shoes...so she cannot. *(Pause)* I think, maybe...she should run very fast is she likes...she can fly if she likes.

REDFORD: I dream that, you know. Flying. Except I never get more that a few feet off the ground.

AYING: You have stones in your shoes also. *(Pause)* Teach me.

REDFORD: I'm not qualified. *(Pause)* Do you like enclosed spaces? *(To the audience)* What am I saying? *(He takes out his shoe string.)* Here.

AYING: What is that?

REDFORD: Take it. Go ahead.

(AYING takes the shoe string. She examines it. Unsure of what to do, she smells it.)

AYING: It does not help.

REDFORD: It helps me. When I'm all knotted inside... when I don't.. as you put it... understand... I use that. I tie it up in knots... you know... like this *(He demonstrates.)* Like that. See? That's what my insides feel like, in here. Then I untie the knots, one by one. It helps me relax. It's a visualization thing, and yes, a nod to triteness. *(Pause)* You can have it.

AYING: Ah...*(Still confused)* Very nice. Thank you.

REDFORD: Try it sometime. It can't do any harm.

AYING: Ah... Yes. Very nice. I keep it. *(She puts the shoe string around her neck.)* What is the time already?

REDFORD: By now, my guess it almost six.

AYING: It is very bright still.

REDFORD: Longer days.

AYING: In Pagudpud, you will hear the church bell ring at six o'clock. We call that *orasyon*. It is time to pray.

(Lights change. VANGIE enters.)

M. Maladroit. Adjective. Awkward. *(Pause)* Tactless.

She should be in a home, with people her own age, where... there's less pressure, I think... to be... I don't know... to be normal. It would be hard, yes in the beginning. Not just for her. But it will be for the best. I'm certain of that. As it is, the way things are... don't look at me like that. Not like that. I can see you think I'm a monster. I'm not. I'm melting. I'm following the rules of the game. *(Pause)* Last night, I dreamt, for the first time, in English. I could see the letters coming out of my mouth, coalescing into perfect words in the air, and everyone around me was saying, "Who is that? Who is that who speaks perfection?"

Don't look at me like that. She spit at Miss Gucci. What do you want me to do? You, what would you have done? Besides, nothing happened. The security man took her to the office, that's all. She was given a lesson, that's all. They asked her to sit in a corner for two hours to think about her sins. Is that so bad? Considering? We're lucky to get away with a only dry cleaning bill. Sometimes, we need to be reminded... that when in Rome, do not do as you would do in Pagudpud.

She can't go back. There's nothing to go back to. I know you probably think, listening to her stories, that where she comes from is a magical place, well it's not. She says to me all the time, "Evangelina, do not forget." *(Pause)* That's exactly what I've done.

(Lights change. VANGIE exits.)

REDFORD: I better go.

AYING: Where?

REDFORD: Away.

AYING: You do not like what I tell you?

REDFORD: It's not that.

AYING: You do not understand?

REDFORD: Not really. I want to.

AYING: I tell you some more.

REDFORD: You should go home. Your daughter will be worried.

AYING: No. No. Short only. One more story. This one you will like. *Sige na*. Short only.

REDFORD: Maybe next week.

AYING: You do not like anymore?

REDFORD: I like. I like. I told you. *(Pause)* It's just that I don't know what to do with your stories. I'm the wrong person....I can't... I don't know how to process these parables...your allegories...whatever...into anything that will make a difference. They're wasted on me.

AYING: You said you like to know about Pagudpud.

REDFORD: I was curious...it all sounded so...exotic. But it's... a can of worms, you know? You... it brings up more uncertainty than answers, and... it's my fault, really.

AYING: I do not understand.

REDFORD: I was convinced that I was deprived of all that. I was sure there was this entire mysterious world...that I felt...I thought...I was somehow tied to...like an umbilical connection. That I was somehow entitled to say, I belong to this...I am part of this. But it's not. It's rings hollow in me. *(Pause)* It's getting late. You should head home. *(He looks at his watch.)* Six o'clock.

(REDFORD suddenly falls to his knees and takes AYING's hand. He touches the back of her palm to his forehead.)

REDFORD: *(Stands)* I don't know why I did that.

AYING: I know. You want to know what it means?

REDFORD: No, I don't *(Pause)* Sorry. I better go.

(REDFORD starts to leave. He stops, and turns back to AYING.)

REDFORD: Teach me a Philippine word?

AYING: Tagalog?

REDFORD: Yeah, yeah. Will you? Teach me one?

AYING: What do you want to say?

REDFORD: I don't know.

AYING: You say that a lot.

REDFORD: I feel it a lot. It's a crutch.

AYING: What do you want to say?

REDFORD: I don't know. Something. Anything, simple. *(Pause)* How about "I love you."

AYING: *(She studies Redford a moment.)* Like this. *"Pangit ako."*

REDFORD: *Pangit ako.*

AYING: *Pa-ngit ako.*

REDFORD: *Pangit ako.* That's "I love you?"

AYING: Yes. *(To the audience)* It means I am ugly. *(Pause)* You are not pretending only? You really do not know how to say "I love you" in Tagalog?

REDFORD: *Pangit ako.*

AYING: *(She smiles, then touches his cheek.)* Me also.

REDFORD: *Pangit ako. (Pause) (He stands up.)*   It was nice meeting you.

AYING: Where are you going?

REDFORD: Around. Here. There. *(Pause)* I'll see you again.

AYING: Yes. Howdy.

REDFORD: Howdy. *(He runs away.)* Au revoir! *(He yells at Aying.)*   *Pangit ako!*

(AYING suddenly remembering, takes out a small camera from her pocket.)

AYING: Wait. *Sandali.* Wait…Red… Red… Redwood!

(She is not able to take his picture. AYING is on the beach, alone.)

AYING: I can see things, all blue. But maybe I should be blind. Where I come from, stories grow from trees. This is what I know.

I will tell you a story. Short only.

There is a very pretty girl who lives in a town far away. Esmeralda. Every boy in this town, they like Esmeralda to be their wife. But she was very choosy, this young Esmeralda. One boy, Santiago, he wanted her more than anything in the world. So one day, he went to her house and said, "What will make you love me, Esmeralda?" And the girl said to Santiago, "You bring me your mother's heart, and I will love you." So, Santiago ran back home and found his mother sleeping, very peaceful, on the floor. He took a very sharp *bolo* knife from the kitchen, and he kneeled down by his mother's sleeping body. He was about to cut her breast, but suddenly, she was awake. "Santiago," she said, very soft...not afraid. "What are you doing, my son?" Santiago said to his mother, "I want Esmeralda to marry me, I need to take your heart." That is what he said. Santiago's mother touched her son's head and said, "Take my heart, and be happy my son." And Santiago plunged the *bolo* knife into his mother's chest and cut out her heart. He wrapped it, still beating in banana leaves and ran back to Esmeralda's house. "Esmeralda, Esmeralda," he said, running, "I have what you want." Santiago opened the banana leaves and showed her his mother's beating heart. Esmeralda screamed. "What have you done?!" "But...but..." Santiago said, he did not understand. "You asked for my mother's heart," he said. "I was only kidding," said Esmeralda. "I cannot marry a man who would cut out his own mother's heart. You get away," she said. And Santiago, very sad, not understanding, walked away with his banana leaves and beating heart. He was crying and could not see very well. This made him trip on a rock. The banana leaves dropped from his hand, and his mother's beating heart rolled out, there, in the dirt. *Sayang.*

Then the heart, it started talking. "Santiago, my son," the heart said, "do not be sad. You took something that was always yours." The heart said this. And then the lightning hit Santiago and turned him into a lizard. That is my story. That is all I know.

[Trans: *Sandali* = Wait ; *bolo* – a machete; *sayang* – wasted]

(We hear the discordant cacophony of voices, murmuring the words to some prayer.)

(AYING looks around her. Very deliberately, she begins to smooth out the sand around her—erasing every evidence of herself—building in urgency as she kicks up a cloud of dust. AYING walks to the edge of the bowl of water. She takes VANGIE's letter and gently drops it into the bowl, as if sending it away with the waves. She does the same with her father's photograph.)

(The cacophony of voices grow louder. Suddenly, AYING plunges her face into the basin of water.)

(The voices peak into a garish scream that lingers as the lights change to reveal VANGIE's silhouette against the back wall, standing next to a chair, and holding a tray with a glass of milk. She waits as AYING makes her

way up to her to sit on the chair.)

(REDFORD has entered and is seated on the edge of the sandbox, down left. AYING is on her chair, tying knots on a piece of string.)

VANGIE: I'm thinking of getting a dog. Not too big, you know. Maybe a small German Shepherd. Something like that...for peace of mind.

(VANGIE tries to give AYING her milk.)

Here's your milk. Aying?

(AYING doesn't respond, but continues tying knots.)

You don't like? *(Pause)* Ha? *(Pause)* Here. *(Pause)* So you can sleep.

(AYING remains silent. REDFORD enters, down Left.)

REDFORD: I have nightmares. I dream I'm some super hero.
I can fly. In this dream, I run. You gotta have to reach speed before lift off.
Back arched...disengage from terra firma...two feet, three feet, and climbing...
I'm a bird.
Then, a great weight pulls me down... Down. Down.
Here comes the crash.
But no impact. It's a soft landing.
I am safe–and–I am pregnant.

VANGIE: *(She kneels in front of AYING, trying to catch her mother's eyes.)* Maybe we'll get a dog. Nice to have around the house. Ha? *(Pause)* We can take it to the beach. You like that? *(Pause)* And we have to name it. *(Pause)* What? *(Pause)* You like to sleep? *(Pause)* OK. *(Pause)* Good night.

(VANGIE walks down right.)

She just stopped. Just like that. One day...just like that. This is what, ha? Punishment? Say something. Go ahead, I said. Yell at me at me if you like. Tell me you wish you had put a pillow over my face when I was in the crib. Tell me anything. *(Pause)* But she just stopped. Completely. Just like that. She never said another word. Not one more word.

And that knotting business. What is that? That's all she does now. And not just on that stupid shoestring. Everything. All around the house. All in knots. The fringes on the table cloth. The tassels on the curtains. My dental floss. I would wake up in the morning to find everything in knots. By the time I get back from work, they would all be untied. What do you do with someone like that? What? And she won't talk.

REDFORD: I contract. Dilate. Whoosh! It's a fuckin' pink baby. We're sitting in a pasture. I know because I can sense a cow nearby. I AM CONTENT. Until it cries, and cries so implacably, I....*(He covers its mouth with his hand.)* SHUT UP. Pink baby turns to Red baby. Red to blue, baby...Blue to purple. OH BABY *(He takes his hand off in horror.)* Good god...what am I...? You hungry? That all? Here. *(He offers his breast.)* Holy shit. I have nothing. IS THIS SOME CRUEL JOKE?

REDFORD: The cow? The cow...Cow, cow, cow...Yes. There, chewing cud under the apple tree. Baby, Bessie. Bessie, baby. SUCK GODDAMIT!

By instinct, it grabs a hold of two udders and drinks. I watch.
Purple progeny turns, first blue, now red, now pink again.
Beautiful pink thing-a-ma-baby.
But it didn't stop there.
Pink to yellow. Come in Yellow.
But paler, and paler and paler still.
Yellow invited White. Come in White. As white as the milk it devoured.
Now black spots form on its tiny hands and feet.

MY POOR BABY IS BECOMING A BARN ANIMAL. Help. *(He tries to pull the baby away from the cow.)* Let go. Let go. But it would not, and I could not. And my child, which has now fully meta-morphosed into a black and white spotted calf, turned to me, as if to say:

VANGIE: All of them say...three different doctors...all of them you're fine. They can't find any-thing wrong. You choose not to talk. Choose? What are they saying? You choose? You can talk but you choose? What is this, ha? What are you doing to me? Ha? *(Pause) Punyeta kayo*!

[Trans: *Punyeta Kayo* – Damn you.]

REDFORD: I turned and I knew it wanted to say:
Don't be sad, Initial Life Giver.
But I CHOOSE to be part of what sustains me.
Only none of these tender words come out.
Instead. Instead of a blessing,
Instead of Daddy,
a long and disgusting MOOOOO.
I wake up with a spoiled taste in my mouth.

I've been coming here, week after week, to the same spot. She never came back. *(Pause)* The three hours we spent together now seem much longer than it was...and each day since seems to stretch those hours into...something more.

VANGIE: My mother died three months ago. *(Pause)* When her heart stopped, I felt her fingers squeeze my hand...not hard...just a little...almost unnoticeable. At that moment, I took a mouthful and air and I didn't breathe for a long time. I just kept it in. I was trying to decide how to feel...

(VANGIE becomes aware, as if for the first time, of her own words. She is unable to talk. She exits.)

(REDFORD has gone back to his toilet cubicle.)

REDFORD: *(He peeks below at the occupant next door.)* Hello....? Hello? I know those shoes. Haven't spoken to you in a while...How've you been? See if this rings a bell. *To be born again, first you have to die. To land upon the bosomy earth, first you need to fly.* Sound familiar? Salman Rushdie. You with me buddy? Hello?

REDFORD: What's there to say? Did I tell you, where I come from. You know, where I've been...stories grow from trees. No, you heard right. Trees. *(He closes his eyes and takes a deep breath.)*

(REDFORD walks out of the cubicle. This time he begins a slow run around the sandbox, building in speed as he jumps into air, hands outstretched as if reaching for a cloud. He steps into the sandbox, falls to his knees, and then lets out a piercing scream.)

REDFORD: *PANGIT AKO.*

[Trans: *Pangit ako*—I am ugly]

(Kneeling down, he makes his way to the edge of the bowl, which is now lit by a single beam of bright white light. Slowly, REDFORD takes his hand and dips it into the water.)

(MUSIC: Broken strains of AYING's kundiman.)

(He closes his eyes, forcing his memory to yield.)

REDFORD: The only thing I remember...from the other side...maybe I was six...maybe seven... the only thing that survives...is a fuzzy picture...a small blue window over a bed. Maybe...over my bed. Lying down, I recall catching a slice of the sky outside and the rusted roof with its peeling blue paint. When it rains, it sounds like...it makes the same sound as when you drop pennies into a tin can. The first few clinks...are like the opening notes...tentative...just before the sky lets loose its change, and you're swallowed by a wave...of...music. There is comfort. There.

(SOUND of metal bolt refastening. Lights off on REDFORD, as the names on the wall are washed in blinding white light. REDFORD remains silhouetted against the names, briefly, before the lights dim into blackness.)

END OF PLAY

PEELING THE BANANA

excerpts from the "PEELING THE BANANA" Troupe

About four and a half years ago, I embarked on an amazing journey
that first began on the "other" coast, the West Coast, in my hometown, the City of Angels. Ten Asian men in a writing/performance
workshop led by fellow performance artist Dan Kwong called,
"Everything You Ever Wanted to Know about Asian Men-But Didn't Give
Enough of a Shit to Ask…" changed my life forever. It was the first
time our community saw Asian Men with bravery, respect and vulnerability. This was the real shit. The real stories. The harsh realities. The triumphs and victories. For the first time, I saw something I could be proud of and there was no turning back.

When I left Los Angeles bound for the Big Apple, I was fucking
scared as hell leaving everything behind for a chance at being on
my own and an opportunity to create a new home called, "Peeling the
Banana." The stories developed by "peeling" over these last three
and a half years are stories that need to be heard and have never
been heard. They are stories that move us and challenge us. Make us
feel pride and shame. But above all, they show truth and honesty.

These "peeling" selections showcase the evolution of this group
from an Asian Men's workshop in 1995 to becoming the first truly
collective and cohesive pan-Asian American performance troupe in
New York City.

I have chosen to arrange the work as an evening of "classic" peeling pieces. They are in no chronological order to the PEELING THE
BANANA timeline but counter point each other to show that we have
distinct and varied life experiences that make us who we are as
Asian Americans. And it is only through our individual stories that
we can truly claim our community as Asians in America.

Warning: The selections you are about to read provide a direct con-
tradiction to any notion of tokenism.

FABA.

-Gary San Angel
 Artistic Director, PEELING THE BANANA

"To My Sisters and Brothers on the West Coast"   —Ed Lin

"Wild Turkey"   —Aileen Cho & Calvin Lom

"Too! Too! Too!"   —Ching-Ching Ni

"P.E."   —Michel Ng

"The First (2)"   —Ngo Thanh Nhan

"Margarita's Kicking Racist Ass Workshop"   —Margarita Alcantara-Tan

"One Cheap Chinaman"   —Ed Lin

"Tough Love"   —Hugo Mahabhir

"A Waiter Tomorrow"   —Bertrand Wang

"Secret M.U.T.A.N.T."   —Gita Reddy

"Asia Files"   —Ed Lin & Ching-Ching Ni

"The Right Stuff"   —Gary San Angel

"Sex 2"   —Ed Lin

"The Voice Behind the Jazz"   —Dave Lin

TO MY SISTERS AND BROTHERS ON THE WEST COAST

Written and Performed by Ed Lin

Spotlight comes up on a man wearing glasses carrying a large red book.

Hi, my name is Ed Lin and I never memorize anything.

(Thumbs through the pages of red book)

I recently traveled to the West Coast and I felt a special kind of kinship to the other Asians out there. I'll be going there in the next couple weeks and I look forward to being in the warm embrace of my sisters and brothers on the West Coast…

(Screaming at the top of his lungs)

FUCK YOU! YOU SUCK!
STUPID THREE HOURS BEHIND, PACIFIC-TIME DUMBASSES. I HEARD YOU EAT RICE-A-RONI INSTEAD OF WHITE OR BROWN, YOU FUCKING SAN FRANCISCO FREAKS. YOU WANT TO LIVE IN 90210 BECAUSE BRENDA LOOKS KINDA ASIAN, BUT YOU CAN PROPOSE ONE-EIGHTY-SEVEN REASONS TO KEEP THE REAL ONES AWAY FROM YOU.
I DON'T EXPECT MUCH FROM YOU SURF-WASHED AND SUN-DRIED BRAINS, BUT YOUR MOMMAS AND POPPAS-SANS BEEN CALIFORNIA DREAMIN' TOO.
RONALD TAKAKI IS JUST TOO COCKY.
I'LL SHOW YOU WHO'S REALLY FAKE, FRANK CHIN. COME OUT TO MY NEIGHBOR-HOOD, YOU'LL BE A DEAD FUCKING DUK.
I WILL NEVER CELEBRATE ACETATE, KRISTI YAMAGUCHI, AND I LOVE MY BEAUTI-FUL BROWN EYES.
YOU SEE, OUT ON THIS COAST, I DON'T HAVE TO MAKE FUN OF MY MOTHER'S ACCENT TO BE ALL AMERICAN, GIRL.
YOU EVER WONDER WHY YOU GOT EARTHQUAKES, MUDSLIDES AND OTHER NAT-URAL DISASTERS AND SHIT?

(Clutches the book like a bible)

BECAUSE GOD HATES YOU, TOO!

(Blackout)

WILD TURKEY

Written and performed by Aileen Cho and Calvin Lom

WOMAN enters a bar stage left and orders a drink from an invisible bartender.

WOMAN: Bartender! Give me a wild turkey please, on the rocks. *(Takes a gulp, addresses audience)* Oh great! Another lonely night on Long Island. I'm going INSANE! There are no decent guys around here, let alone decent Asian guys! They're all dorky engineers! Nobody who relates to me! Where's the perfect guy when you need him?

(MAN enters stage right. WOMAN does a double take.)

WOMAN: Oh my god! He's gorgeous! *(MAN looks at her staring, looks away nervously.)* He's not looking at me! Why isn't he looking at me?

MAN: *(To audience)* Is she looking at me?

WOMAN: He doesn't like me. Maybe he doesn't date Asian women. Maybe he isn't attracted to me!

MAN: *(To audience)* She is so hot! Did she look at me? *(Looks at WOMAN)* She's looking at me! I'm so excited! But why am I so... scared? And intimidated? Bartender...a Wild Turkey please!

WOMAN: Hey...Wild Turkey? Hey! I drink Wild Turkey!

MAN: *(To audience)* Was she talking to me? *(To WOMAN)* Did you say something?

WOMAN: *(Embarrassed)* Ummm...sorry, I didn't mean to bother you. Forget it.

MAN: Did you say you liked Wild Turkey?

WOMAN: *(Hopeful)* Yeah...yeah I did.

MAN: Bartender! A Wild Turkey for the lady!

WOMAN: Thanks?...

MAN: Cal. And your name?

WOMAN: Aileen. Nice to meet you!

MAN: Nice to meet you! Cheers!

WOMAN: Thanks. Here's to...to Wild Turkeys!

(They gulp shots simultaneously and eye each other. They start to move center stage toward each other.)

MAN: So, Aileen, what are you doing out here on Long Island?

WOMAN: *(Grimly)* I ask myself that question every day. No really, I work as a journalist. And you? Are you a...an engineer?

MAN: Yes, I'm afraid I'm the Asian stereotype...but I'm really an artist and a writer.

WOMAN: Really?! I'm a writer...and an artist! There aren't too many Asians out here, let alone ones who are writers...or artists!

MAN: Wow! How about another Wild Turkey! So...are you Chinese?

(They get more drinks.)

WOMAN: Yeah!

MAN: ME too!

(They are visibly excited.)

WOMAN: Well! Here's to being Chinese...

MAN: And artists...

WOMAN: And writers!

(MAN and WOMAN turn to audience simultaneously.)

MAN AND WOMAN: This is too good to be true!

MAN: This is so different.

WOMAN: I feel as if I know this guy already!

MAN: Usually Asian women confuse me!

WOMAN: He looks like me...

MAN: They send me mixed messages...

WOMAN: He's cute! And...

MAN: But this time...

MAN AND WOMAN: (S)He's...interested!

(They face each other, start to move closer with each phrase.)

WOMAN: You know...you have nice hair. It's like mine.

MAN: It's long...and thick...

WOMAN: And our eyes...

MAN: ...Brown...and almond-shaped...

WOMAN: With high cheekbones...

MAN: And smooth...skin...and...

MAN AND WOMAN: ...not white!

(They grab each other fervently.)

WOMAN: I've never dated someone who looks like me!

MAN: You've never gone out with another Asian either?

WOMAN: There aren't too many of us out here to choose from...it gets...lonely...

MAN: ...and isolated...

WOMAN: ...and dysfunctional...

(WOMAN tries to regain control of herself, pushes Man a little bit away.)

So...do you have any brothers or sisters?

MAN: No...I was adopted.

WOMAN: Really? Me too! My grandfather was a famous assassin!

(The two become even more intimate.)

MAN: Me too!

WOMAN: His name was Some Lom Gai.

MAN: Me too!

(They stop suddenly.)

MAN AND WOMAN: Some Lom Gai?

(Beat)

SOME LOM GAI???? BARTENDER! Another Wild Turkey! NOW!

(Beat. They look at each other.)

WOMAN: Brother...

MAN: Sister...

(They take each others hands and leave the bar together.)

(Lights fade out)

TOO! TOO! TOO!

Written and Performed by Ching-Ching Ni

Music rolls: Cui Jian's "Lang Zi Gui: Vagabond Returns." A woman dressed in a red overcoat carries a suitcase on stage, as pillow, baby and airplane. Music fades out. The woman slowly rests her suitcase on floor.

I see my father at the airport. Behind the plexiglass, he looks exactly like he did 18 years ago when my mother flew us out of his life, only a lot shorter and squatter than I remembered. Ba! Ba! Ba! The first thing he says to me is...

(Acting like him, lugging the heavy suitcase back home, and dropping it off on a stool.)

Ayiiiiia! Dai zhema duo dongxi gan shenma? aiya, Zou zou zou! My father loves to remind me that I never learned how to pack light. He even gave me his favorite suitcase, the one he used to travel between military bases playing his clarinet for the People's Liberation Army. Everyday he would stay home and rearrange my things, everyday I would wonder if he thought the lost years of our lives together were some how hidden in the chaos of my suitcase.

(She opens suitcase, starts throwing things out piece by piece and becomes her father again, agitated, waving, pointing, pressing a T-shirt against the body, trying to make it flat and smooth before folding it back into the suitcase carefully.)

Buxing Buxing! aiyha! zhe me da de hai ze lian yifu do bu hui die...The more he fussed over my things, the more junk I brought. It's as if I needed him to touch my things, I needed him to leave his fingerprints on my life.

(Picks up a yellow Chinese toy tiger and pets it close to her face)

What I really want, is to put my father inside my suitcase. Like my Chairman Mao charm.

(Opens jacket to reveal charm)

These cheap souvenirs are luckier than my dad. They get to go all the way to America with me.

(Spins the charm like a plane through the air)

But my father has never been to America. I would look for him, wherever I go. I would find him, every morning in the mirror when I notice my eyes are exactly like his. Why don't they look more like my mom?

(Stretches her big eyes)

I would find him, when I am driving to work, listening to his favorite Peking Opera tape, pretending I am the daughter of a communist martyr, murdered by the imperialist running dogs,

(Shrieks like a Peking opera star)

You killed my father, I will kill you!! I would find him, in every man I've ever loved, searching for the one person who really knows how to pack a suitcase. I would find him, in the old black and white picture of my parents, long before the big divorce turned my life into a frequent flyer program. My father was a poor boy from the countryside, but he was a man in uniform and he was so handsome, he set the standard for all Asian men.

(Proudly displays father's military portrait)

The first time my sister and I went back to China to visit him, we had forgotten how to talk to him in Chinese. So we forced English on him the way we forced potato chips on him. My poor father was gagging on the words, allergic to English. But we kept telling him, Ba, English is good for you. English will make you big and strong. English will help you conquer the world! But wou baba said he's already yo gao yo da and he has no desire to zhanling shijie. The only English he ever cared to remember was something he learned on his own.

(In Ba's voice:)   "Easta, westa, home is da besta."

All we really wanted to do was hear him say, I love you too. But instead we got...

(In Ba's voice:) "ayiieee-la-ayiiee-tu...ayiieee-la-ayiiee-tu...lale-yo-tu...tule-yo-la...ayie-la-ai-tu...tu...tu...tu...tootootoo...."

"too! too! too!"

My sister and I couldn't believe it! Our father has created our own secret love code! "too too too!" We used it everywhere we went. But all these Chinese people were laughing at us because in Chinese, we were saying the words for "rabbit! rabbit! rabbit!" and "vomit! vomit! vomit!"

There's only three people in the whole world who know what it means.

We depend on it, every time we say goodbye.

(Tape 2 rolls : Cui Jian's "Lang Zi Gui: Vagabond Returns.")

(The woman goes back to pack the suitcase, picks it up and walks to center for the departure.)

Too! too! too!

(She starts walking away, waving into distance to Ba.)

Too! too! too!

(She walks away more.)

Too! too! too!

(Pauses in a final goodbye. Music and lights fade out.)

PE 101

Written and Performed by Michel Ng

Lights come up on a row of high school boys who are standing on the school playing field. A whistle is blown. The voice of a gym teacher offstage yells out the order, "Give me fifty!" The Village People's "YMCA" starts up and the boys do a series of exercises–jumping jacks, push-ups, etc.

MICHEL: Of all the classes in grade school, the one I hated most was P.E.—Phys Ed. You know, that dreaded class where boys were supposed to be able to do boy things like dribbling basketballs while running into each other, wrestle with the strength of Hulk Hogan (and those other homos whom we would later discover)...

(The BOYS bond by bumping chests and grunting. When they get to MICHEL, they bump him back and forth like a ping pong ball between them.)

MICHEL: ...and ram into each other with our puny bodies on the field and absolutely love every glorious moment of it...and finally, when it was all over, smell our armpits in the locker room as if the molding smells of decaying lockers weren't enough.

(The scenery changes to the wrestling room. A match begins between MICHEL and the biggest APE of a boy in the class. The APE picks up MICHEL and twirls him helplessly over his shoulders as the other BOYS around cheer. "Kick his ass!" "Get him!" etc.)

MICHEL: P.E. was the litmus test of butchness...the be-all end-all class where you could prove yourself as a man once and for all, or be cursed for the rest of eternity as a flaming mahu. I hated it.

(The BOYS exit to hit the lockers. The sound of water runs as a shadow play of the BOYS in the shower is projected on a scrim behind MICHEL. The BOYS joke around, snapping towels at one another's bare asses.)

MICHEL: I remember having to do sit-ups, push-ups, dribble balls against boys who were two times my size, and wrestling with guys who were ten times my weight. I'll admit, being pinned down can be fun—but not in front of a bunch of closet case high school jocks.

(The scenery changes to the locker room. The BOYS re-enter in towels led by JOCK 1 and JOCK 2. MICHEL stands in the corner silent. MIKE, also in a towel, enters a little behind the rest, drying his hair.)

JOCK 1:   Hey, man. Good game!

JOCK 2:   Yeah, boy! Kicked some ass today.

JOCK 1:   Yo, man, you see that bitch Larry trying to throw the ball? He was like, "Ughhhnn!"

JOCK 2:   You know, they should have separate gym classes. One for real guys who wanna play for real, and one for guys like Larry. It's bad enough we gotta get undressed in front of those queers.

JOCK 1:   No, shit. Yo, I saw Larry checking you out. He almost grabbed your ass on that one play.

JOCK 2:   Shut up. If I ever caught that piece of shit Larry looking at me, I'd have to crack his head open.

JOCK 1:   Yeah, I don't give a shit what fucked up shit faggots do on their own time, but they better not try any shit on me.

JOCK 2:   Don't worry.

(They exit, followed by the rest of the BOYS. Only MIKE and MICHEL are left. Mike is half-naked. They make eye-contact and smile.)

MIKE: Those guys are idiots.

MICHEL: Yeah.

MIKE: I don't even think Larry is, you know.

MICHEL: Yeah, me neither.

MIKE: I mean, even if he was, who cares? Right?

MICHEL: Yeah, I guess. It's no big deal.

MIKE: Yeah.

(MIKE jumps up onto the bench. He flexes his muscles in the mirror.)

MIKE: Hey, man, I've been working out. You think it's starting to show?

(MICHEL giggles.)

MIKE: Oh, c'mon. It's not that bad.

MICHEL: Yeah, it's not bad.

(Pause)

MIKE: Hey, can I ask you something?

MICHEL: What?

MIKE: Never mind.

MICHEL: What?

MIKE: No. Forget it.

MICHEL: C'mon.

MIKE: Well…

(He scans the room for anyone.)

Uh, do you ever…I mean, do you…uh, you know.

MICHEL: Do I what?

MIKE: You know. I mean, you know what I'm trying to say right?

(MIKE begins to move closer to MICHEL, they are more intimate.)

MICHEL: Ummmm. I'm not sure. I mean, maybe. I don't know.

MIKE: C'mon. You know. You know what I'm talking about, right?

MICHEL: Uhhh. I should really get to class—

(They stare at one another. Beat.)

MIKE: I know that you check the other guys out. I do it too. I've seen you check me out. It's OK. Really. Just say it.

(Uncomfortable silence)

MIKE: Say it. C'mon. Don't do this to me. You know what I'm talking about. I'm talking to you because you understand. You know? Just say it.

MICHEL: (Long pause) Maybe. Yeah, sometimes.

(They stare at one another. MIKE has his face a breath away from MICHEL's. MIKE leans in.)

MIKE: Faggot.

(MIKE exits. MICHEL stands alone in the tiny pool of light.)

(Lights fade out)

THE FIRST (2)

Written and Performed by Ngo Thanh Nhan

Dedicated to the killed Paris Commune workers, France.

A spotlight comes up on a man sitting on a wooden stool. He is dressed in black and begins to play his guitar. The music is from "Le Temps des Cierises" (poem by Jan-Baptiste Clément, music by A. Renard, 1866), Music starts for 2 phrases...meticulously.

1. I was twelve when I called his name
from the roster in my class
I vaguely remember him
when my friends called him sissy
and he chased them around the schoolyard
I got to know him the following year
when he sat next to me in the first row...
we became close
when I crossed the railroad tracks
up the hill to his house
his older sister treated me with fried *bánh-chu'ng*...
I remember she giggled
when my eyes never left her face
he smiled and told me she was sixteen
that was our first secret.

(Music continues for 2 phrases.)

2. We rode bicycles
every day next to each other
we held hands in line
walking to class side by side...
I began to draw flowers and girls
and drew his face with his sister's hair and chest
I began to get bad grades for talking in class
I spent a lot of money playing billiard
during the siestas
anyone calling him sissy
also got a revenge from me
we rode bicycles to p.e.
next to each other
he did not like soccer

my friends told me he ran funny
he did not like high jumping
he did not like javelin throwing
he only like to run with me
so I ran with him slowly...
I watched him in the shower
and discovered he grew a few hairs
and I was delighted...
and kept looking...
but knew not why

(Music continues for 2 phrases.)

3. We went to camps together
for many years
I could not bear his absence
even for just one moment
we were together
and we were together
even at night I saw his smile...
we touched each other many times
we played each other's penises
and giggled until both were hard...
we took out a ruler to measure...
and argued as to where they should begin
his was straight and pointed downward
mine curved leftward
and I sighed every time he pulled the skin...

(Music continues for 2 phrases. Tempo a little faster.)

4. We were in bed one night
the summer was hot
and our chests were bare
sweat-soaked underpant shorts
during my sleep I dreamt
kissing him in his cheeks
then on his eyes
then gently on his lips
like lovers on movie screens
he hugged me
and I wrapped my arms around his waist
hearing his heart beats

not wanting to let go
I did not remember how it happened
both our underpants disappeared
our penises were in full blown
I felt excited
and he was trembling as
he pulled down the skin
I immediately came
And...as I was drowned...gasping
I grabbed his penis
like a safety post in a furious tempest
I felt his soft hair soaking wet
and I felt it jumping
and felt the warm juice spurting on my belly
he shook and yelling "ôi!"
and held me tight
I was surprised
I could not shake him off
until much later

(Music continues for 2 phrases relaxing to finale.)

5. We agreed that night
it would be another secret until we die
I learned he went out on a boat
and drown somewhere in the Malaysian Gulf...

(Music continues for 2 phrases, phasing out, clean break.)

(Blackout)

MARGARITA'S KICKING RACIST ASS WORKSHOP

Written and Performed by Margarita Alcantara-Tan

Lights come up on the "Margarita" show sign as the theme music plays and the voice of an announcer introduces the host.

ANNOUNCER: You know her as the best selling author of *"How to Kill 2 Asiaphiles With One Stone,"* and as consultant to the stars. She needs no further introduction.....Please welcome...MARGARITA!

(MARGARITA enters from back of audience with mic in hand. Lights come up on the whole studio audience as music fades.)

MARGARITA: Hello! Welcome to my *"Kicking Racist Ass Workshop!"*

I'll be guiding you through some fun-filled exercises that'll get your heart pumpin' and your Asian self in check! As women, we've all have had some experience with being harassed on the streets. But, as ASIAN women, we get a special kind of harassment, based on our *(Sarcastically)* EXOTIC features, and the overblown fantasies Asiaphile men have because of them.

Who here has been harassed?

(A woman in audience raises her hand. MARGARITA approaches her with mic.)

What's your name?

TAMINA: Tamina.

MARGARITA: ^ well Tamina, tell me—what kind of racist and sexist things have guys said to you?

TAMINA: *(With difficulty)* Did everybody hear her? "Do you girls have slanted vaginas too?"

MARGARITA: *(Nodding with sympathy)* Yes. I've heard that all before myself.

(Switch to upbeat)

But today, I'm going to teach you how to defend yourself using *(Pause)* Pananandata—the Filipino Martial Art of Weapon Fighting.

(She demonstrates.)

You can use sticks, whips, balisongs, or just your pretty little hands!

But first, I'm gonna teach you how to verbalize. Yes. You can defend yourself without lifting a finger. That's the best way to go as a first tactic.

So tell me, girls! What do you say if someone calls you "his cute little china doll with a slanted pek-pek?"

(CHING-CHING, stage L, and AILEEN, stage R, jump out.)

CHING-CHING & AILEEN: FUCK YOU!

(They retreat.)

MARGARITA: I can't hear you!

(CHING-CHING and AILEEN jump out.)

CHING-CHING & AILEEN: FUCK YOU!!!!!!!!!!!

(They retreat.)

MARGARITA: Much better!*(To Tamina)* Tell me, what would you do if someone grabbed you physically, let's say, on the thigh or ass?

TAMINA: *(Pause)* Cry and run in humiliation?

MARGARITA: No!

(She goes to side of front stage to prepare video.)

MARGARITA: Let's see what happened to Stephanie Park of Greenwich, CT. This is a re-enactment of what actually happened...Harry! Roll the tape!

(Spotlight focuses on Stephanie Park a.k.a. NORIKO. "The Mission Impossible" theme song plays. NORIKO walks from stage L to bus stop. While NORIKO walks out, AILEEN passes stage L holding "Re-enactment" sign then retreats. White guy cardboard cut-out held behind curtain, looms out and grabs NORIKO. She freaks out.)

NORIKO: Margarita, help!

(Jumping back into limelight, horrified)

MARGARITA: Help is on the way Stephanie! *(To side)* Thanks, Harry.
(Spotlight off. NORIKO, stage L, and AILEEN, stage R, come out, holding up white guy cardboard cut-outs)

MARGARITA: Here's what you should do if you ever find yourself in ~~Stephanie's~~ unwelcome predicament. Aileen, grab my thigh.

(Demonstrate on cut-outs.)

MARGARITA: Nudge your elbow into their floating ribs, punch the face with the back of your fist, and rake your fingernails down their face to draw blood, get some of that DNA under there!

(To NORIKO, poking eyes of cut-out)

MARGARITA: If ever in doubt, go for the eyes. No matter how big the guy is, the eyes are always vulnerable. Thank~~s girls, for helping me illustrate those point~~s!

(NORIKO and AILEEN exit.)

TAMINA: Have you always been this fearless?

MARGARITA: Of course not!/I too have been the fragile Pacific flower, a product of an Asian household...When I was younger, I grew up in a house where there was a lot of physical violence. But that was then.

TAMINA: You have tattoos and you look tough, so why do you get harassed?

MARGARITA: I know, you can't tell that my mom ever sent me to the Lea Salonga School of Charm, can you? But that's OK, that never stops any of those sexist jerkoffs from harassing a chick of color, especially if they're Asian.

(Sound of a bell)

MARGARITA: I can't believe it, our time is up! This is the end of yet another successful workshop. Let's do our Healing Affirmations—Tamina, I'd like for you to join us!

(TAMINA and the GIRLS join MARGARITA on stage.)

MARGARITA: "I am a wonderful Asian woman!"

GIRLS: I AM A WONDERFUL ASIAN WOMAN!

MARGARITA: "I am strong!"

GIRLS: I AM STRONG!

MARGARITA: "I can kick ass!"

GIRLS: I CAN KICK ASS!

MARGARITA: That's just a little taste of what you can do to defend yourself using the martial arts that's in OUR blood. Our powerful, Asian, female blood.

(Closing theme music plays.)

50

Margarita: Until the next workshop, entitled, "How to Flay Off Those Pesky Neo-Nazis," this is Margarita signing off! And remember: DNA under the fingernails!

(The girls get weapons and pose. Spotlight on MARGARITA, who gets balisongs and plays. MARGARITA freezes on her last move as music fades.)

MARGARITA: Yeah, I'LL show you "china doll."

(Blackout)

ONE CHEAP CHINAMAN

Written and Performed by Ed Lin

Spotlight on man with glasses. He returns once again with large red book.

GODDAMN, HE WAS CHEAP.

He wore size extra large, irregular everything.
He kept a drawer full of dead batteries in case they found a way to recharge 'em, even though they were leaking what looked like a small pool of fried Coca-Cola on his stockpiled pennies.

GODDAMN, HE WAS CHEAP.

He ate low-fat Twinkies and drank diet chocolate-chip soda. He wasn't watching his weight, but they were four for a dollar at Wholesale Liquidators.
He lined his birdcage with subway maps.
He couldn't make plans for the first two weeks of the year because he wouldn't buy a new calendar until the middle of January, 40% off and he got to read "The Far Side" comics he missed when he couldn't find a newspaper for free.

Goddamn, he was cheap, although he fancied himself to be "an educated shopper," like the Syms ads.
He did get ripped off once, though.
He bought a 50-cent used tape which he thought was a Chinese opera star. Instead, he got two white boys telling him and everyone else to "Wang Chung tonight."

He was so cheap, he would take the bus to Atlantic City, watch other people play and ride on the free drinks instead of going to a bar because with the casino bonus plan, the bus ride was cheaper than the subway.

And once and only once, when he was very, very drunk, he played out half his life's savings at the $5 craps table and tipped the waitress with what he could have used as his last bet.

Because, although he was one cheap Chinaman, he never cheated anybody.

(Blackout)

TOUGH LOVE

Written and Performed by Hugo Mulchand Mahabir

Lights come up on a living room with a couch and TV flickering; large group enters dancing to the beating of a bottle and spoon rhythm, all singing a calypso.

GROUP: "Ah goin' down San Fernando
Down deh ha plenty tempo
Pan and steel orchestras jammin' sweet
Ah want to dance up Coffee Street
So leh me go...tempo..."

(They repeat the verse in a soft whisper as HUGO moves center stage. He sings the song as if to himself now, while the rest of the ensemble behind him beats the rhythm softly. He begins to speak his memories.)

HUGO: "Child, where yuh went last night?"
"To a Carnival party, Grandma."
"Deh place was fulla negroes, nah?"
"No grandma...not really."
"Carnival jump ups is full ah dem...dat is their culture...you didn't meet any girls, ah hope!"
"No grandma...not really."
"Leh me tell you something...don't you ever bring any ah dem kaffers home, you know!"
"Yes, Grandma."

FAMILY MEMBER: *(Screams)* Hey, y'all it's Peyton Place...

(The group comes back to life. Everyone shouts and cheers. They rush to the couch, everyone jumps down and sits together excitedly to watch TV. HUGO makes his way to his usual spot on the coach and squeezes in.)

HUGO: We sit on the old couch next to my grandma and cousins and aunties eating the peanuts she has just finished roasting for us, watching TV, it's Peyton Place, her favorite show...Ryan O'Neal and Mia Farrow in a small, snowy town somewhere in America making their drugstore and diner intrigues from Main Street, U.S.A...and us, a bunch of cousins and aunties all squeezed together with grandma on the old couch, brown peas in a Trinidad pod, eating roasted peanuts together.

(He stands up and leaves the others who are still watching TV...faint calypso music can be heard in the background.)

HUGO: But I never could tell Grandma that I had danced with a black girl somewhere at a party in Arima, that she had her hands around me our hips gyrating to the reggae and calypso beats pulling me close to her on the slow songs. That we went out behind the garage, and fooled around all night, kissing and kissing. That I came in my pants, my head lost in the sweet perfume of her neck.

(The calypso music fades out as HUGO walks around his family still entranced by the TV.)

HUGO: But Grandma hated Carnival and Calypso, still I loved her and she loved me...And she cared more about skin color than anyone I know, who was lighter, and who was darker whose hair was straight, and whose hair was kinky separating Indians from Negroes in her Peyton Place world...I had to keep secrets from Grandma if I still wanted to sit on the couch with her. Love and racism, we're all prisoners there.

(He sits back on the couch with his family.)

HUGO: So find your place above the niggers...my brown-skinned grandma forgetting that we were the servants of the empire, then and now in this Peyton Place world...

(As he says the following lines, each person in the group stands up from the couch and moves forward, one at a time, miming the action named, as the group creates a tableau.)

HUGO: Serving tea...
washing clothes...cleaning bathrooms...
cutting cane...dying cotton...picking coffee...
sweeping lobbies...driving taxis...selling newspapers...
Then and now...in this new world...

(From their positions in the tableau, each person mimes a new action, as he says the following lines.)

HUGO: Laboratory experimenting...
computer programming...heart operating...
particle accelerating...AIDS researching...gene splicing...
plastics testing...mathematical modeling...post-colonial theorizing...

(Everyone freezes.)

HUGO: Asians in America...
looking for some place to call home.
Now I walk the streets of this city.

(The group breaks and starts walking around the stage as though they're on a busy city street.)

HUGO: A border child, in between worlds
black, white, yellow, and brown
inside and out,

outcast and castaway...(*Pause*) Am I a ghost?

(*Everyone vanishes from the stage. HUGO is left alone, frantically looking around to see only an empty stage. HUGO slowly moves back to the couch and sits down, looking out into space as if for his grandmother.*)

HUGO: But I did everything right,
Grandma learned the proper way to dress
and cut my hair
the right way to speak
and look at things.
But I am still afraid
like a teenage boy
coming home from a party
afraid to speak the unspeakable,
afraid to say the truth.

Isn't the first duty of love to listen,
listen to your child...listen to your lover...listen to your friend,
that we all have secrets to tell,
that love comes in many forms.

Sometimes...sometimes...I just want you to listen
and hear the whole story.

(*Lights fade out*)

A WAITER TOMORROW

by Bertrand Wang

An East Village Japanese restaurant. Two Asian waiters, BERT and MIKE, are working hard for the money...and some dignity!

ANNOYING HAKUJIN: Excuse me, I asked for extra wasabi.

WHITE GIRL: Waiter, could I have some more water with a slice of lemon?

MR. REGULAR SILVERWARE: (*Snotty*) Can I have some regular silverware please?

ANNOYING HAKUJIN: Excuse me, is all Japanese food raw? I want cooked food. I want some chicken.

MR. REGULAR SILVERWARE: Do you have tea?

MIKE: We have green tea.

MR. REGULAR SILVERWARE: No like regular tea, like Lipton tea.

(Backlit stage BERT and MIKE on break, probably smoking cigarettes—even though they're not good for you— while the restaurant rages on.)

MIKE: Busy night huh?

BERT: Hell, yeah. But at least we'll make money tonight.

MIKE: No shit.

BERT: I really hate being nice to all these...people.

MIKE: I totally know what you mean. We get so many racist and sexist assholes in this place. Did you hear the guy at table 3, asking me for 'regular' silverware? I was like chopsticks are pretty regular to me ASSHOLE!

BERT: Usually, I'm good at shutting off the thinking part of my brain when I come to work. But it still gets to me. Like that sugar in the tea shit. That's just not right, I don't go to their houses and pour fuckin' soy sauce into their Frosted Flakes.

MIKE: I just wish we didn't get treated like, like hired help.

BERT: But we are hired help.

MIKE: I know, but just because people tip us a few bucks doesn't mean they own us.

BERT   :Yup, there is no dignity for the waiting proletariat. We'll be fine as long as you know who doesn't show up.

MIKE: Oh you mean that sushi bar guy? The one that usually comes by himself?

BERT and MIKE: *(Together)*   Mr. Asshole.

MIKE: He is the worst.

(People start calling for the waiters.)

BERT: Case in point.

ANNOYING HAKUJIN: Excuse me, do you have eggrolls?

BERT: No.

WHITE GIRL: Excuse me...Do you have that omelet that they have in Japan. I've been to Japan and they had it, do you have it? Isn't this an authentic Japanese restaurant?

MR. REGULAR SILVERWARE: Are you Japanese? I've been taking Japanese classes and I want to practice.

MIKE: *(Annoyed)*   Actually, I'm Korean.

MR. REGULAR SILVERWARE: Oops, sorry.

(He and his friends laugh off the mistake. Enter MR. ASSHOLE.)
(Music cue: John Woo's "Hard Boiled" score plays underneath scene.)
(MIKE and BERT look at MR. ASSHOLE and then exchange Woo-esque operatic looks.)

MR. ASSHOLE: Two for the sushi bar.

DICKHEAD BUDDY: Did they hear you? Better yet did they understand you?

MR. ASSHOLE: *(Pointing towards BERT)*   Oh yeah, this guy's cool....He speaks English real good. Hey buddy.

BERT: I'll be right with you.

(MR. ASSHOLE and DICKHEAD BUDDY get sick of waiting and seat themselves. Other customers flee to the other side of the restaurant.)

BERT: Do you have any questions?

DICKHEAD BUDDY: What's the difference between a tuna roll and a spicy tuna roll?

BERT: *(Slowly)*   Well, one is spicy...and one isn't.

DICKHEAD BUDDY: I'll have chicken teriyaki.

MR. ASSHOLE: I'll have a Village Jumbo Sushi with a spicy tuna roll and a large sake.

BERT: As long as you know that spicy tuna costs extra?

MR. ASSHOLE: What?! I never have to pay for spicy tuna!

BERT: It's a new policy.

(DICKHEAD BUDDY gets up and MR. ASSHOLE waves his hand to sit him down.)

MR. ASSHOLE: *(Gets up)* I happen to be a close personal friend of Tony...the manager.

BERT: I know who he is.

MR. ASSHOLE: *(Slaps BERT in the face)* Then you won't have any problem finding him. Make sure the spicy tuna is fresh. The last time I was here it was old and no good.

(MR. ASSHOLE and DICKHEAD BUDDY leave and brush past BERT and MIKE. The rest of the customers start to mutiny and demand to see the manager.)

EVERYONE: Waiter! Waiter! I want to see Tony!

BERT and Mike: Let's go get Tony!

(The two waiters leave the chaotic restaurant floor and return wearing dark shades and a new attitude.)

MIKE: You want to see the manager! Here's the manager!

(The Fight: BERT and MIKE reveal guns from their aprons and start killing everyone in the restaurant some in regular speed and some in operatic slow-mo. BERT shoots MR. REGULAR SILVERWARE. WHITE GIRL ducks behind a chair, unveils a gun and tries to shoot BERT. MIKE jumps over the chairs and shoots WHITE GIRL. BERT shoots the cowering customers on stage left. MIKE shoots ANNOYING GWAI LO.

BERT and MIKE back into each other and almost shoot one another but then realize its another 'good guy.')

CANNONFODDER: TABLE for TWO!

(BERT shoots CANNONFODDER.The over the top violence crescendos as customers, flower delivery people, (anyone but restaurant workers) and would be patrons all die in a fiery blaze of bullets. After everyone is dead, MR. ASSHOLE and DICKHEAD BUDDY return from the can. After entering the stage, they all draw guns and assume the classic stand off position. Guns are all up in each other's faces.)

MR. ASSHOLE: *(Unfazed by the situation)* You're one Hard Boiled waiter. Is my sushi ready?

BERT: Oh it's ready!

MR. ASSHOLE: I even told my friend that you were a cool Japanese guy!

BERT: Well, you were half right. I'm Chinese, you stupid fuck!

(At that instant, DICKHEAD BUDDY clicks his gun and shoots MIKE. MIKE shoots DICKHEAD BUDDY. MR. ASSHOLE shoots MIKE. BERT shoots MR. ASSHOLE. MR. ASSHOLE and BERT are wounded.)

MR. ASSHOLE: What do you have against me anyway? I always leave a good tip!

BERT: Shut up and eat this sushi!

MR. ASSHOLE: Wha..?

BERT: *(Force feeds sushi to MR. ASSHOLE.)*   EAT IT!! To you, sushi is part of a bad Japanese joke. But to us, it's a lo-fat, high protein gift from the sea. And you NEVER turn down a gift. EAT!!

(Just as he is about to eat, MR. ASSHOLE spits it in BERT'S FACE. MR. ASSHOLE tries to draw another gun or knife. BERT shoots MR. ASSHOLE.)

BERT: Sayonara asshole...*(Going to MIKE's aid)* Mike, you're gonna be all right.

MIKE: *(Coughing blood)* I don't think I'm gonna make it. I think...I think...I think I'm gonna call in sick tomorrow.

BERT: Don't talk crazy man. You're gonna be fine.

MR. ASSHOLE: *(Comes to life and lunges at the two waiters)* AAAHHHH!

(BERT and MIKE shoot MR. ASSHOLE.)

BERT: C'mon, we gotta bus these tables and set up for lunch.

(Blackout)

SECRET M.U.T.A.N.T.
Written and Performed by Gita Reddy

Lights come up on a small, brightly colored karaoke tape player with attached mic ("Minus One") located down-stage center. Ponytailed and wearing a "Velveeta" T-shirt, a woman enters and exits the stage first in leaps, and then hesitantly. She finally circles the tape player and quickly picks it up. She addresses the audiences via Minus One mic.

Hi. My name is Gita Reddy....Hi. My name is Gita...Josephina Teresita Imeldacita Pinky Bong-Bong Pilar Del Rosario Santos Banaag Arce...Reddy.

(She puts the Minus One down.)

OK, that's not true. My name is just Gita Reddy. Gita...Reddy. Very Indian, my name, just like my dad. Bhaskara Reddy. Unlike...Aida Catalina Florenda Arce Reddy Fusilero. My mom. Very unlike my mom, my name. When I was little, it didn't matter.

(Lights dim as the sweet opening strings of ABBA's "Chiquitita" plays. GITA kneels and walks around as if she is a little kid again. Two women enter and hold her hands, giggling and pretending to chat with others as if at a party. One of them coos "Chiqui-Gita!")

After the divorce, I would dance with all my Titas, all my mom's fellow Filipino nurses, and they would laugh at me because at age nine, I could fit into their dressy shoes.

(She tries on one of her Tita's shoes on her right knee. They laugh. GITA stands and pulls down her long hair.)

But when I got older, they wouldn't dance with me anymore.

(She towers over them. The women look up at GITA in suspicion and whisper to each other. With fake smiles, they quickly take the Minus One and exit as "Chiquitita" fades out.)

So I would dance all by myself.

(She hums the ABBA tune and dances melancholically.)

I mean, I understand. Now my Titas had children of their own, and when they all went on camping trips together to Yellowstone National Park, or balikbayan to the Philippines, they would ask me to...house sit for them.

(People enter and freeze, they pose in joyous family and friend portraits: Christmas morning; high school buddies; singing karaoke at a party. In the final portrait, someone is "singing" into the Minus One's mic. She steps for-

ward, confiding.)

And with no one around, I could pick up and touch all their family photos.

(Excited, she sneaks right up to the first portrait. As GITA speaks, she points to what the girl's holding, then surreptitiously caresses the girl's cheek. GITA touches her own face in reflection.)

Look! Clarissa and her brother Norbert at Christmas! Maligayang Pasko! Look what Clarissa got for Christmas—Clinique loose powder, shade #01...

The lightest shade. That's the shade my mother wears. I wear shade #04....

(She jumps over to the next portrait group and points to everyone, absent mindedly hunching over and covering her skin.)

Oh, they got one of those mall portraits! Clarissa...that's her cousin Jaime, he's on the basketball team, and that's his girlfriend, oh...her name is...Joybelle! Everybody loves her!

(She poses deliriously next to Joybelle, trying to become part of the portrait.)

Look, she's so happy...and so petite! Look at her shoes, they're so tiny! My feet were never that tiny! Never!

(Now also limping, she gathers her last vestiges of excitement to approach the final portrait, drawn by the sight of the Minus One.)

Minus One! Home karoake! Minus One! Minus One! They never let me sing on the Minus One!

(GITA pries the mic out of the person's hand, and sings desperately "I Can't Smile Without You", leaning so near to the Minus One that feedback drowns her out. She grabs the Minus One, clutching it to her defiantly, occasionally caressing it, even talking to it. Hunched over, limping and now sniffling, she makes her way in front of all the portraits.)

I'll never be like them, because they're perfect...perfect Filipinas! Me, I'm just a mutant...a mutant Filipina! Mutant, I'm a mutant! Mutant! You understand, Minus One, don't you! Mutant...

(She accidentally presses "play" on the Minus One and Tito Puente's rousing "Kiss of Fire" begins, which sends her body into uncontrollable shakes. Looking around confused, GITA "transmutates" and feels herself straightening up and standing tall and proud, in response to the beats of the music. She "hears" instructions coming from the Minus One and nervously responds into the mic. Nodding my acceptance, I lift my head and tango with the mic, taking long leaps up to the portraits, dismissing each of them from the stage. They exit. GITA continues the Secret Agent dance to the music, then suddenly stops the tape and addresses the audience via the mic.)

Do you know who I am? They did not know who I am. But I know you know who I am....I am...

(*She spins around and looks back over her shoulder.*)

...Secret Agent...

(*She jumps around and salutes first with the Minus One then quickly extends her mic hand in the air.*)

...Filipina!

(*GITA plays "Kiss of Fire" and dances Secret Agent dance. She stops and peers into the audience.*)

Filipinas? Filipinas anyone?

(*House lights come up. This section varies, and may be completely improvised, according to audience response. GITA walks into the audience, continuing to address them via the mic. She offers them the mic briefly to answer, and then lifts the Minus One deck to her ear as if "hearing" instructions on how she should respond.*)

Are you Filipino? Prove it! What do you have in your pantry right now...do you have SPAM? VELVEETA? Hmmm....I'll have to get a full dossier from headquarters on your...supposed Filipinoness...!

(*GITA plays "Kiss of Fire" and dances Secret Agent dance. She stops and addresses the audience again.*)

Anyone else? Filipinas? Are you Filipino? Prove it! How many shoes did Imelda have when she fled Malaca–ang Palace? Are you sure that's your answer? She had...one thousand, two hundred and sixty...seven! Because she lost one...in flight!

(*House lights fade as she Secret Agent dances to music. She stops to reflect.*)

It is not always fun and games being Secret Agent Filipina, because I have accepted the lifelong mission of being...undercover!

(*She puts down the Minus One and lowers her head, then with a whoosh of her hand lifts her head in presentation, and looks blankly ahead.*)

Example! Operation: covert interaction with the Pilipino public! Location: the Philippine Independence Day Parade—a food booth! My people are...everywhere! But I am...

(*She repeats the undercover gesture.*)

...undercover!

(Relaxing, she excitedly addresses the food booth.)

Hi! I would like...one green mango with bagoong, please! How do I know what green mango and bagoong is?...Don't you know who I am...I am Secret Ag...

(She begins to do Secret Agent salute, but then covers it up.)

...I mean...Why are you laughing? Well, actually I...My mother is from the Philippines. Yes, really! No, I can't speak Tagalog, but...You don't have to laugh. Why are you bringing over all of your friends...? Don't you know...who I am...don't you....

(In a panic, she picks up the Minus One and tries to press play to "hear" instructions. "Chiquitita" plays. Shocked and confused, she clutches the Minus One, and then resigns to put it down. Gathering herself, she addresses the food booth again.)

You don't know who I am? Well...I know who I am! I am...the Filipina who wants her green mango with bagoong! NOW!

(As GITA extends her hand for the mango, her two Titas enter and line up behind her. She turns around and sees them, hesitates then walks back ceremoniously between them. Turning to one, GITA curtsies and takes the back of her Tita's hand to her forehead in respect, and they dance in a tango-esque circle to the music. She turns and repeats the "Mano" ritual with her other Tita, with increasing joy. Lights and music fade out.)

ASIA FILES

Written and Performed by Ed Lin and Ching-Ching Ni

(Stage dark, but not completely black. Dimly lit like the interior of a movie theater. ANONYMOUS CHINESE MAN, in T-shirt and jeans, sits in folding chair in middle of stage. ASIAN MULDER and ASIAN SCULLY, dressed like their television counterparts, run through audience with flashlights as theme from "X Files" plays. Music dies down as ASIAN MULDER and ASIAN SCULLY make way to stage. ASIAN SCULLY and ASIAN MULDER, now at Front Stage Right and Stage Left, respectively, shine flashlights onto each other's faces.)

ASIAN SCULLY: *(In a loud whisper)* Asian Mulder! Where are we?

ASIAN MULDER: *(Whispers)* Asian Scully! We're in the Music Palace, the last movie theater in Chinatown!

(Begins slowly walking to ASIAN SCULLY, behind ANONYMOUS CHINESE MAN's seat.)

ASIAN SCULLY: *(Whispers)* This place smells awful!

ASIAN MULDER: *(Whispers)* Lonely Chinese men come here to kill time.

(Reaches ASIAN SCULLY, stands next to her)

ASIAN SCULLY: *(Whispers)* What's a nice guy like you doing in a dump like this?

ASIAN MULDER: *(Whispers)* I come here to see the beautiful Hong Kong movie stars.

(ANONYMOUS CHINESE MAN slumps over onto ground at ASIAN MULDER's feet and comes to rest on his back.)

ASIAN SCULLY: *(Screams)* Freeze! Federal Asians!

(ASIAN MULDER turns off flashlight, pockets it, lights go up.)

ASIAN MULDER: He's dead.

(Takes ASIAN SCULLY's flashlight and pockets it. ASIAN SCULLY drops to knees and touches ANONYMOUS CHINESE MAN's body.)

ASIAN SCULLY: There's no visible signs of trauma.

(Pulls up ANONYMOUS CHINESE MAN's head a few inches as if to administer mouth-to-mouth. In a knowing way, ASIAN MULDER kneels down, pulls open ANONYMOUS CHINESE MAN's mouth, retrieving note.)

ASIAN MULDER: Except for this suicide note.

(Stands up, reads from note)

ASIAN MULDER: "Goodbye, cruel world. I'm not getting any."

ASIAN SCULLY: Any what?

ASIAN MULDER: Well, he wrote it on an unused condom.

(ASIAN SCULLY opens evidence bag and ASIAN MULDER puts condom into it. Movement is slow and sexually suggestive.)

ASIAN SCULLY: Why would he come to the Music Palace to die?

(Moves to chair, pulling ANONYMOUS CHINESE MAN. ASIAN SCULLY sits in chair, cradling ANONYMOUS CHINESE MAN's head. ANONYMOUS CHINESE MAN is in sitting position on floor. ASIAN MULDER moves to front stage right, looking into distance, as if looking for UFOs.)

ASIAN MULDER: Maybe he wanted to see Chinese men and women in love.

(ASIAN SCULLY pulls up ANONYMOUS CHINESE MAN's shirt, exposing chest.)

ASIAN SCULLY: Look! Look at all this writing on his chest! 'Maggie Cheung.' 'Anita Mui.' 'Ming-na Wen.' These are all women he could never have!

(In a knowing way, ASIAN MULDER walks up to ANONYMOUS CHINESE MAN, back to audience and apparently unzips ANONYMOUS CHINESE MAN's fly.)

ASIAN MULDER: And what do we have here! "Asian Scully"!

(Zips fly back up. ASIAN SCULLY jumps up, runs to front stage right. ASIAN MULDER walks to front stage left. Both face audience, not looking at each other.)

ASIAN SCULLY: Asian Mulder! I have a confession to make! I know this man.

(Sounds a little embarrassed)

We went out a few times...

ASIAN MULDER:	(*Faces ASIAN SCULLY*) He must have been pretty desperate.
ASIAN SCULLY:	(*Faces ASIAN MULDER*) I told him I had a boyfriend.
ASIAN MULDER:	You just don't go for Asians.
ASIAN SCULLY:	My boyfriend's Filipino!
ASIAN MULDER:	Filipinos aren't Asian! Not like you or me. (*Softer*) Or this dead guy down

here.

(*Gestures to ANONYMOUS CHINESE MAN*)

ASIAN SCULLY: Filipinos are Asian enough because they like me!
And Filipinos would never let themselves get so lonely they get stuck at the Music Palace on a
Saturday night!

| ASIAN MULDER: | Sometimes I come here on Fridays. |

(*Arms raised in pleading gesture, walks slowly toward ASIAN MULDER*)

| ASIAN SCULLY: | Asian Mulder, you know I've been looking my whole life for that per- |

fect…Chinese man.

(*Drops to knees at ANONYMOUS CHINESE MAN's body. Pulls ANONYMOUS CHINESE MAN into
upright position.*)

| ASIAN SCULLY: | Someone who can slow dance with me to Chairman Mao love songs! |

(*Pulls ANONYMOUS CHINESE MAN's arms and embraces ANONYMOUS CHINESE MAN's upper
body in a dance partner position. Cheek to cheek with ANONYMOUS CHINESE MAN.*)

| ASIAN SCULLY: | Someone who's not afraid of passion! Someone who understands that |

small is beautiful!

(*Pulls up ANONYMOUS CHINESE MAN's shirt and caresses exposed breasts and then pulls him up on his
feet as they stand face to face.*)

| ASIAN SCULLY: | Someone who will let me look for my father in his Chinese eyes! |

(*Turns ANONYMOUS CHINESE MAN's head to point to ASIAN MULDER*)

| ASIAN MULDER: | You see your father in all Chinese men? |

ASIAN SCULLY: Yes!

(Throws ANONYMOUS CHINESE MAN at ASIAN MULDER. ASIAN MULDER catches ANONY-MOUS CHINESE MAN, stumbles then supports ANONYMOUS CHINESE MAN at shoulder. The two look like a study for a war memorial.)

ASIAN SCULLY: That's why I go for Filipinos.

ASIAN MULDER: Asian Scully, I have evidence that suggests direct government intervention in preventing Chinese men from dating Chinese women!

ASIAN SCULLY: Asian Mulder, you're letting your personal feelings get in the way, again! Where's your proof?

ASIAN MULDER: Asian Scully, I also have a confession to make. I know this man, too.

(Drops ANONYMOUS CHINESE MAN into kneeling position. Walks in semicircle behind ANONYMOUS CHINESE MAN, facing ANONYMOUS CHINESE MAN entire time.)

ASIAN MULDER: We both wanted to be writers, but our parents forced us to go to engineering school. It was like living in a single-sex society. You take classes like "Sexuality in Crime Fiction" just to meet women. But the only thing they teach you is what good writers white guys are. And all the Asian women hooked up with white guys. *(Softly)* And I was the best writer in that class. I was the best FUCKING writer in that class!

(Lets ANONYMOUS CHINESE MAN gently onto back, closes ANONYMOUS CHINESE MAN's eyes.)

ASIAN MULDER: Sometimes people don't appreciate what you've written until you're dead. Even if all you ever wrote was a suicide note.

(Walks back to stage left, faces audience)

ASIAN MULDER: So, Asian Scully, do you still believe the perfect Chinese man really exists?

ASIAN SCULLY: I know he's out there...I can feel him.

(Looks above as if looking for UFOs)

ASIAN MULDER: What does he look like?

ASIAN SCULLY: I don't know...I've never been close enough to find out.

(Walks to ASIAN SCULLY)

ASIAN MULDER: He might be standing right next to you.

ASIAN SCULLY: How would I know he's real?

ASIAN MULDER: *(Softly)* Asian Scully...

(ASIAN SCULLY turns and seems shocked to see ASIAN MULDER so close, so obviously emotional, as if recognizing him as the perfect Chinese man.)

ASIAN SCULLY: Asian Mulder?

(ASIAN MULDER takes ASIAN SCULLY's hands and holds them to his face.)

ASIAN MULDER: Touch me.

(Lights fade out)

THE RIGHT STUFF

Written and Performed by Gary San Angel

A confessional booth glides across the stage. There are no panels. The interior is completely visible. Inside, a priest-like figure dressed in white lights Roman Catholic candles. An Alleluia Spiritual sung by monks can be heard in the distance.

I like…
I like…
To touch…
Myself…
I try to do it at least two times a day.
I don't know why I do it.
I just do.
It makes me feel so good inside.
I remember the first time I touched it.
It was like I was on fire.

I was twelve and I had just finished watching the movie *The Right Stuff*. And all I could think about was this one scene where the nurse asked the astronaut played by Dennis Quaid for a sperm sample. He didn't know how to do it so the nurse threw him some dirty magazines and shut him in a room all by himself. And I began to wonder what it was like and how it…

Felt like…
And that night I could not stop thinking about it. The feeling inside me started to grow and I could not squish it back.

(The confessional begins to creak as it slowly rocks back and forth.)

It began to ask me. Beckon me. And I could not resist.
So I just let myself…
I let myself feeeel…
It…
Ohh… Ahhh…

My whole body became stiff and hot. My legs were sweating and I just kept going. I just could not let go. I wanted to show my right stuff. But then every time I felt it I saw the Virgin Mary and God standing right there with me and they were not very happy. This was not good behavior for someone who is preparing to be an altar boy.

Oh, God. GOD. Ohhhh. GAWWD. Noo. Noooo.

sorreee..

(Begins praying)

HAIL MARY! FULL OF GRACE! THE LORD IS WITH YOU! BLESSED!! ARE YOU
AMONGST WOMEN!! AND BLESSSES!!! BLESSSEED IS THE FRUIT… OF THY WOMB!!
JESUS…
JEESUS!!

(Rocking grows even more frenetic.)

PLEASE!! STOP!!
OOHHHH! GOD! NOOOO… NOOOOO…
YOUR NOT SUPPOSED TO DO THIS!!!
NOOOO! NOOOOOO! NOOOOOOO!
AHHHHHHHHHHHHH!

(Climaxes)

Something started to spill out and it wasn't pee.
It was gooey and it smelled real awful like the stench of Clorox bleach.
Oh God. My mom must have heard me. She was sleeping in the other room. What would she think?
Oh God…
OH!! NO!!
OH, GOD!!
I SPILLED IT ON THE BED!!!
Sh!! Shhhh!!
Be quiet. Don't tell anyone.
Please. Please.

(The confessional turns and becomes the inside of a bathroom. He rubs his hands in front of an imaginary sink and mirror.)

I just went to the bathroom and I scrubbed my hands with soap and hot water and I threw my
underwear at the bottom of the hamper because I didn't want my mom to smell my sex.

(It now becomes the bed. He lies down.)

Before I got to bed I stared at that bed stain.
I laid beside it.
And I began to wonder…
When would be the next time…
I will…

Touch myself.

(Blows out candles. Blackout)

SEX 2
Written and Performed by Ed Lin

A man is seen in the dimly lit shadows of a spotlight. He is speaking gently into a mic. He has no glasses and no red book.

You say I've got a one-track mind But it's only because I've been working on the railroads for so long

Darling, bring your eyebrows to mine
And I will kiss you soft as butterfly nets
And hold you closer than memories
Of a misspent youth

With my—in your—
I promise
It'll be so good
I promise

Think of an island spelled like the letter O
With too many colors to fit in the circumference of the eye
You say I'm just a computer geek
But like a PC
I will go down on you when you need me the most

With your—in my—
I promise
It'll be so good
I promise

Then we'll lie together
And I will kiss you soft as butterfly wings
And hold you closer than Incan blocks
Forever
Or at least until you fall asleep

(Lights fade out)

THE VOICE BEHIND THE JAZZ

By Dave Lin

Fade in. "Blue in Green" by Miles Davis plays in background. Lights come up and we see the silhouette of DAVE, a radio announcer.

DAVE: You're listening to WUSB, Jazz 90.3 on your FM dial. I'm Dave Lin, bringing you the best of the old and the new, from now until 5 AM. Thanks for tuning in. My phone number here is 632-5500. For you cats across the water, that's a 516 area code. Call in your requests, or call just to say, "Hi!" Right now, I'm gonna kick it off with some Miles, from his *Kind of Blue* album. I'll play it first, and tell you what it is later.

(The announcer's face is revealed.)

DAVE: Freshman year was an awkward time for me. In the first few months, I shied away from people. Immersed myself in school and in my college work-study job at the campus radio station as the night-time jazz DJ. I played the music I liked, and people liked what I played. Miles. Mingus. Coltrane. Dizzy. Sonny. Toshiko. I played them all. I had regular listeners. I had   regular callers. Drugged-out jazz hippies...

DRUGGED-OUT JAZZ HIPPIE: *(Sound of inhalation/exhalation)* Dave! Big Dave! What's up, Dave? Here! Yo! My man, settle a bet for me and my buddies... Was Duke's big comeback performance at Newport in 1956 or 1957?

DAVE: Paranoid angry loners...

PARANOID ANGRY LONER: Those microwaves you're beamin' into my head are sendin' me a message. They're tellin' me to come over there and hit you over the head with a lacrosse stick and trash your studio! Whaddaya think of that, Jazz boy? You hip to that, you friggin' be-bop playin' bastard?

DAVE: Sleepless alcoholics.

SLEEPLESS ALCOHOLIC: Hey, Dave. Can you play some Kenny G? I fuckin' love Kenny G!

DAVE: Jilted lovers.

JILTED LOVER: Can you play the next song for my ex-girlfriend Serena? She won't return my calls! Could you say that I won't turn off the gas until she calls me?

DAVE: And occasionally...

SEXY FEMALE VOICE: Hey, Dave. I can't sleep. Can I come over to the studio and hang out?

DAVE: I never took any of those offers. Because I knew from past experiences what would happen if those women met me. But then, one night, she called. USB.

MARIA: Hey, can I speak to Dave?

DAVE: You got me. How's it going?

MARIA: Pretty good. I just wanted to call and say I love your show. I don't usually like jazz, but I've been tuning in for the last few weeks.

DAVE: Let me guess. I'm the only station that comes in on your stereo.

MARIA: (*Laughs*) Well, that is true. But I do enjoy the music you play. And I really like your voice. I'm really glad you quit smoking.

DAVE: How'd you know I quit smoking?

MARIA: Because I used to always hear you blowing smoke and lighting your cigarettes. I haven't heard that for the last couple of shows.

DAVE: 17 days since my last cigarette.

MARIA: Congratulations! I'm glad you quit. You sound too cute to be a smoker.

DAVE: (*Pause*) Are you hitting on me?

MARIA: It all depends. Are you single?

DAVE: Yes, but I don't date my listeners.

MARIA: The station won't let you date listeners? Even me?

(*Pause*)

DAVE: No. It's a personal rule I keep. Hold on for a sec…

That was Miles doing "Blue in Green." This next one's for my man Chris, who's studying late into the night for his organic chemistry midterm. This is a song called "Misterioso" by the great Thelonius Monk. Just remember, Chris, when in doubt, you can always use the Grignard reaction to link anything together. Keep the faith, brother…USB.

MARIA: Dave?

DAVE: Hello?

MARIA: You hung up on me!

DAVE: I'm sorry about that. I'm still learning how to use the phones around here.

MARIA: That's OK. Can I ask you a question?

DAVE: Sure.

MARIA: Is the reason you won't go out with me something to do with my voice?

DAVE: Excuse me?

MARIA: My accent?

DAVE: You don't have an accent. You have a beautiful voice.

MARIA: Thanks! But I moved here when I was six. I learned English as a second language, and it took me a while to speak it. I still have a little bit of an accent.

DAVE: I can't hear it. Where are you from?

MARIA: *(Slight pause)* I'm Chinese. My parents are from Hong Kong.

DAVE: Really?

MARIA: Uh huh. Have you ever been with a Chinese girl?

DAVE: Actually, I haven't. I've never been with a Chinese girl. A strange thing for a Chinese guy to say, huh?

MARIA: *(Pause)* You're Chinese? Are you half black or something?

DAVE: No. I'm all Chinese.

MARIA: Wow. You don't sound like, uh...

DAVE: Like I'm Chinese?

MARIA: You must get that a lot?

DAVE: Not really. I think you're the first listener I've ever told. It's never come up before. I've never had any reason to...hello?

MARIA: I'm still here.

DAVE: Are you?

MARIA: Yeah...listen, this is really going to sound bad...but I thought you were...well, not Chinese. I thought you were probably black, and I really like black men.

DAVE: Well, I'm sorry I'm not.

MARIA: I hope you're not upset with me.

DAVE: Not at all. In fact, I'm gonna play a song for you. What's your name?

MARIA: Maria.

DAVE: Well, Maria, you have a good night. And keep listening...This next song's for my friend Maria, who I sincerely hope finds what she's looking for. This is "Fair Weather" by Chet Baker. I'm Dave Lin. 90.3 WUSB.

(DAVE searches for, finds, and lights a cigarette.)

END OF PLAY EXCERPTS

SILENT MOVIE

By Jessica Hagedorn

SILENT MOVIE is a ten-minute play which was originally commissioned by Chay Yew and the Asian American Theatre Project at the Mark Taper Forum in 1996, as part of a larger piece called THE SQUARE. THE SQUARE involved the contributions of many other playwrights, all commissioned to create their own ten-minute pieces. Han Ong, Maria Irene Fornes, Constance Congdon, David Henry Hwang and Tony Kushner were among the playwrights included. Aside from the ten-minute length, one of the main stipulations was that the plays were to be set in New York City's Chinatown. Each writer was also assigned a specific year and a specific number of characters. Everything else (race, gender, class, conflict, etc.) was left up to the playwright. I was assigned four characters and the year 1920.

JESSICA HAGEDORN

SILENT MOVIE was originally developed in the Center Theatre Group/Mark Taper Forum Asian Theatre Workshop Gordon Davidson, Artistic Director/Producer. It was first presented at the Mark Taper Forum in Los Angeles on December 17 & 18, 1997 as part of the "New Work Festival # 10." with the following cast and crew:

EMMA HANLON: Liann Pattison
LUCY BURROWS: Jodi Thelen
MAN: David Warshofsky

Directed by Lisa Peterson

Dramaturg: Chay Yew
Stage Manager: David S. Franklin
Set Consultant: Rachel Hauck
Lighting Consultant: Geoff Korf
Costume Consultant: Joyce Kim Lee
Sound Consultant: Nathan Wang
Directing Assistant: Wendy McClellan
Literary Assistant: Padraic Duffy
Production Assistants: Anna Louise Paul, Stephanie Schaefer

SILENT MOVIE

A dark, unfurnished room above the curio shop. The only window is covered by a makeshift curtain of flimsy transparent fabric. Lights fade up on EMMA HANLON, a politician's wife, naked and barefoot under her long, black velvet cloak. She is a fading beauty in her late forties—make-up smeared, hair disheveled. EMMA cautiously peers out the window. She obviously does not want to be seen. By the door a couple of expensive suitcases and a worn carpetbag have been set down. Scattered about are Emma's dress, stockings, high-heeled slippers, and an evening purse with its contents spilled—cigarette case, money, gloves, keys, and a silver flask, which EMMA grabs. As she paces tensely around the shadowy room, EMMA sips greedily from the flask. A freak storm rages outside. Sounds of rain pouring down. Distant thunder. Lightning brightens the room, making EMMA jump.

LUCY BURROWS, Emma's personal maid, is sprawled on a pallet downstage. She is in her slip. LUCY is twenty, Emma's physical opposite. Her unpainted face is an inscrutable mask, all angles and planes—her body lean and strong. LUCY seems totally at ease in the dark, sucking contentedly on an opium pipe. Next to her is another pallet, another pipe—possibly Emma's—and drug paraphernalia arranged on a tray. Tiny spoons, a bowl, matches. A short black rubber straw. A razor. The residue of cocaine and gummy opium on a saucer.

EMMA: I told you. We should've waited.

LUCY: No way. Tonight's our only chance.

EMMA: We're in deep shit now. Dear God. Why'd I listen to you? You're just a—

LUCY: What? Yer l'il dumb maid? *(Pause)* Oh, Emma. Stop.

EMMA: Stop? The rain won't stop. And then what?

LUCY: Then nothing. We ain't goin' back.

EMMA: That's right. It's flooding pigshit out there and I'm stuck in this Chinatown shithole with you and can't go home—

LUCY: —because you're high. Face it Emma. You're too high, and it's OK, and you're never goin' back.

EMMA: He'll find us.

LUCY: Shut up. You said he'd be away till tomorrow. *(Pause)* He ain't found us yet, has he? Hasn't figured any of it out, and it's been a whole year. *(Laughing softly)*

EMMA: Don't tell me to shut up. You're getting just a wee bit too cocky, dear. *(Pause)* I know he knows. He's known all along—

LUCY: You're high.

(Silence. EMMA glares furiously at LUCY, who ignores her. A series of low, urgent knocks at the door startles them both.)

LUCY: *(Mutters to herself)* What the fuck.

EMMA: *(Frantic)* Oh Jesus shit. Mother of Mary. I knew it. *(Backs up against the wall, terrified)* What shall we do, Lucy?

LUCY: Will you calm down? *(Struggles off the pallet, then crawls slowly to the door and speaks in a hoarse whisper)* Uncle Wong? Is that you? *(Pause)* Everything OK! We're getting ready to go, promise! Soon as...soon as the weather changes...soon as the sky goes from gray to black...*(Pause)* There. He's gone. Emma.

EMMA: It's not the Chink I'm worried about.

LUCY: *(Offers her the pipe)* Here. Better than your damn whiskey.

EMMA: *(Hysterical, knocking the pipe out of Lucy's hand)* Are you listening to me? It's not that harmless old man I'm worried about. It's my husband! Don't you understand he wants to kill me? And you! *You!*

LUCY: *(Stonefaced)* Don't ever do that again.

EMMA: I'm sorry, Lucy. *(Gets on her knees and crawls around in the dark to find the pipe, which she cautiously hands back to Lucy.)* I'm sorry—

LUCY: Don't ever. *(Refills the pipe, offers it to EMMA. Her tone softens.)* I think you need to slow down and refresh yourself, Mrs. Hanlon.

(EMMA lays on the pallet next to LUCY and reluctantly takes a deep toke. She watches while LUCY snorts cocaine.)

EMMA: That powder's evil. I hate when you get so damn arrogant.

LUCY: *(Amused)* Yeah? And I hate yer damn whiskey breath. And whiskey sweat.

EMMA: *(Agitated again)* Oh, Lucy, sweet Jesus. Let's get out of here. We'll find another way out of town. We will—

LUCY: You just jumpy, that's all. Rain'll let up soon. It's early—nothin' to fret about. We'll get away soon enough. We're halfway there, ain't we? We'll be outta this shithole, soon as the sky... (EMMA *nods off into sleep.*) Dream a while. Yeah. That's it. *(Pause)* I hate you sometimes. Hate havin' to make it all better for you, the way I always do, like I'm expected to. You pay me enough. I s'pose. And you trust me. *(Pause)* I love you too, Mrs. Hanlon. I know how to make you cry, don't I? Stupid pitiful Emma. Beautiful Emma. And you love me back in your own way. Lookit you. Old enough to be my mother. Cow. Beautiful cow. Moo. I love makin' you moo. *(Pause)* But we can't stay here forever, darlin'. Too dangerous. Uncle Wong will most definitely be back. We make him nervous, don't we? I hate the way he scurries around after takin' our...*your* money. Can't wait for us to leave! He's worse than a girl. *(Shouts at the door, waking EMMA briefly.* EMMA *drifts back into sleep.)* I KNOW YOU'RE THERE. YA OLD GEEZER! EAVESDROPPIN' AND PEEPIN AT US! *(Grabs rubber straw and pokes it through keyhole)* ARE YA PLAYIN' WITH YOURSELF AGAIN? I CAN HEAR YA GASPING AND WHEEZIN' IN CHINESE! *(to audience)* "The Chink's scared shitless of my husband," Emma says. *(Pause)* That's milady's favorite word: SHIT. *(Mocking and mimicking)* "*Hurry, hurry, missee. Don't want no trouble. Why you no get stuff from Uncle Wong and just take home? Go home, misses! No safe here! No safe here!*" *(Laughing)* Can you imagine? Emma Hanlon, smokin' goo in the privacy of her bedroom? Makin' hoochie-coochie with me, her little servant, while Mr. Bigshot's at the office? Yeah, sure, Uncle Wong. *(To audience)* She likes goin' to the pictures. That's how it all started. The bigshot husband had no time, but she had all the time in the world.

(EMMA sits up, disoriented.)

EMMA: Come with me to the pictures.

(EMMA gazes out at the audience as if she is watching a movie. As she and LUCY speak, flickering, unfocused images from the 1919 D.W. Griffith film, Broken Blossoms, *are projected on the wall behind them)*

LUCY: *(To audience)* I felt sorry for her. Sure, I said. Anything to get outta cleanin' that mansion of hers. Every damn day the same old grind. *(Image of Lillian Gish as the movie version of LUCY* BURROWS, *in the squalid hovel she shares with her father. She is on her knees, tearfully wiping her angry father's shoes as he stands there glowering at her.)* Dustin' where there ain't no dust, moppin' them already shiny floors, scrubbin' spotless toilets. Fixin' food she don't eat. She don't like food. You wouldn't know it, lookin' at her... Would ya? *(Touching Emma's hip tenderly)* All that *flesh*. *(Pause)* They got a son somewhere I've never seen, sent away to school in another country. She don't like him, either. *(Pause)* I made my eyes real big and round, like this *(Demonstrates)*—"Swell, Mrs. Hanlon. I've never been to the pictures"—

EMMA: Poor thing.

LUCY: Guess she felt sorry for me, too. I acted all meek and grateful. Like my Pa didn't teach me to be. Like my Ma, well—she's dead, so it don't matter. Folks say I take after Pa, anyway. *(Pause)* Anyway. Off we went to the Bijou. *(Pause)* What a dumb picture. *(Movie projection stops.)* I couldn't wait to get outta there. *(To EMMA)* Please, Mrs. Hanlon.

EMMA: It's beautiful. Let's sit through it, again. Please, Lucy. Think of it like a beautiful, scary dream.

LUCY: No thanks. I come from a family of lunatics, and I think you're just like them, Mrs. Hanlon.

EMMA: *(Bursts out laughing)* You're a funny dear. Why don't you call me Emma? *(Stares at her, then kisses her impulsively)* Forgive me. I must truly be out of my mind. Please, dear. Don't tell anyone. I promise I'll never do it again.

LUCY: *(Kisses EMMA)* Then I'll do it. *(Pause)* Emma.

EMMA: I know this place where we can be alone. You ever been to Chinatown?

LUCY: Sure. Once or twice.

EMMA: I grew up there, before the Chinks moved in.

LUCY: I thought you were rich.

EMMA: My husband's rich. *(Pause)* I know this place on Baxter Street, right by where I was born. We'll have fun.

LUCY: Fun. *(Dryly)* I don't know the meaning of the word.

EMMA: I'll show you.

(A thunderclap explosion. Terrified, EMMA makes a move to bolt and run, but LUCY stops her. They struggle until EMMA finally gives up, exhausted and resigned. The two women stare at each other for a moment, the sound of rain pouring down.)

EMMA: *(Sheds her cloak)* Dance with me again.

LUCY: Sure.

(As LUCY and EMMA make love in the dark, specific clips from Broken Blossoms *are projected on the walls, but clearly this time. The entire room is bathed in these black and white images; the images are not shown*

in order, and can be repeated. Richard Barthelmess in obsequious, effeminate pose as "The Chink," his taped eye-
lids perpetually downcast. Lillian Gish as the abused Irish girl, LUCY BURROWS, cowering in terror from
her brutal, drunken father, played by Donald Crisp. The Chink attempting to kiss the terrified White Girl,
then suddenly pulling away from her in shame. The White Girl's immense look of relief. Her subtitles which
read: "What makes you so good to me, Chinky?" The enraged Drunken Father killing his daughter. The
Chink shooting the Father, then carrying the White Girl's limp body back to his curio shop. The grief-stricken
Chink kneeling on the floor by the bed on which the White Girl's corpse lies, then stabbing himself to death in
glorious slow-motion.)

EMMA: *(Disengaging herself from LUCY)* Good. The rain's stopped. We can go.

LUCY: What's the hurry? *(Teasing)* You're hurtin' my feelings, Mrs. Hanlon.

(The naked EMMA starts putting on her clothes. For a brief moment, the room is eerily lit by lightening. A
sound outside the door.)

LUCY: Not again.

EMMA: *(Nervous)* Is that you, Uncle Wong?

LUCY: *(Taking another hit of cocaine)* He don't understand English.

(The door is kicked open by a brawny, fiftyish white man dressed in an elegant suit, overcoat and hat. He points
a gun at EMMA.)

EMMA: *(To man)* I knew you'd find us.

(The man shoots EMMA. She collapses. He shoots her a second time, then a third. Meanwhile, LUCY has
pulled her own revolver from under the pallet. She points it at the man. The man, aiming his gun at her, hesi-
tates.)

LUCY: Go ahead. You'll either die with me—or die first.

(LUCY shoots. The man drops to the floor, near EMMA. LUCY stares down at them for a moment. She runs to
the window and tries to climb out to escape, but realizes how high up she is and loses her nerve. She goes to the
door and peeks out into the dimly-lit hallway.)

LUCY: *(Soft and tentative)* Uncle Wong? Where are ya, old man? *(Pause)* Ah, Mother of God, he
got you too.

(LUCY gets dressed quickly. She rummages through the dead man's pockets and takes his wallet. She starts to
take his gun, then changes her mind. Kneeling down next to EMMA's body, she runs a hand gently over

EMMA's open eyes, to close them. LUCY snatches her gun, EMMA's spilled money, and, after snorting the last of the precious cocaine, takes what's left of the opium. She stuffs everything into the carpetbag and starts to leave, then turns back once more to survey the room. EMMA's luxurious cloak lies on the floor. LUCY scoops it up and wraps herself in it. She slowly backs out the door. Lights fade down.)

END OF PLAY

Jamaica Avenue

By Chiori Miyagawa

In JAMAICA AVENUE, a woman says, "When the lightning strikes a tree in California, monarch butterflies die in Mexico. We are all part of the same web." It is a play about something profound that connects all of us, perhaps not only in this life time and dimension, but beyond, with our ancestors and ghosts and guardian spirits. Everything we do has relevance; we are responsible for each other, for what we have become and for what we will be.

"Seven" punctures the story of JAMAICA AVENUE: the first part spans over seven years; there is a seven-year gap between the two parts; and the second part takes place in seven days. In Buddhism, the number seven has a significant meaning. After death, a soul is supposed to stay in Bardo for seven days. If it does not find a place of reincarnation, it will remain there for seven more days. It can repeat this for seven cycles, up to 49 days. I did not know this as a child growing up in Japan, but I remember whenever there was a death, families officially mourned for 49 days. They seemed to feel a little better after all the rituals that happen during the 49 days following a death were completed. Although in Buddhism coming back to life means suffering, I still view this cycle as a symbol of healing and renewal, a hope in doing it right this time.

My deepest inspiration lives in His Holiness The Fourteenth Dalai Lama of Tibet. I write to keep the promise I made to him: to make small attempts in changing people's mind about hate.

CHIORI MIYAGAWA

JAMAICA AVENUE was first presented at the New York International Fringe Festival in August 1998 at The Soho Repertory Theatre

Directed by Sonoko Kawahara
Dramturg: Judythe Cohen
Lights: Lap-Chi Chu
Costume: Anne Lommel
Set: David Martin
Associate Producer: Michael Yawney

Cast:
CARLOS: Clark Jackson
LAUREN: Anna Wilson
WOMAN/YUMI: Sophia Skiles
INTRUDER: David Altman

JAMAICA AVENUE is scheduled for a workshop at The Women's Project and Productions in the 1999-2000 season. This new version of the play will have songs, lyrics written by Mark Campbell, music composed by Fabian Obispo.

For Kevin

Time:
The play spans over fourteen years of love, disappointments, and hope.

Place:
New York City

Characters:
CARLOS: African American or Latino Man
LAUREN: Caucasian Woman
WOMAN/YUMI: Asian Woman
INTRUDER: voice over when necessary

CARLOS and LAUREN age seven years in Part I. Their physical deterioration is paralleled by that of an emotional one.

Part I spans over seven years, Part II seven days. Seven years pass between Part I and II. LAUREN stops aging at the end of Part I. CARLOS is seven years older at the beginning of Part II, but much healthier.

WOMAN/YUMI remains the same age throughout the play.
In Part I Scene 1 and in Part II, YUMI's speech pattern should be somewhat different from WOMAN's.

JAMAICA AVENUE

Part 1

Scene 1

Two young women stand facing each other. LAUREN is dressed in a ragged fur coat. WOMAN is in summer clothes. Woman holds a large shopping bag.

LAUREN: Excuse me, can I see your bag? Oh, I've heard of that store. They got nice things?

WOMAN: Yes.

LAUREN: What did you get?

WOMAN: Candles.

LAUREN: My father used to tell me about it. He's dead now. He was gonna take me shopping to the store someday. For a fur coat. Do you know what it's like to feel you deserve the best, but fate fucked you up just enough so your father ends up dead?

WOMAN: You'll be alright.

LAUREN: It's funny, you think it's a small thing, but it isn't. It'll never be all right. The empty space gets deeper and deeper in you, and you just can't get out. There are bigger problems. People are starving. Still, your personal tragedy, whatever it is, will ruin you in the end. It won't be alright.

WOMAN: I have to go.

LAUREN: Don't go. What day is it today?

WOMAN: It's Wednesday.

LAUREN: How long have I been crying?

WOMAN: Seven years.

(WOMAN takes a candle out of her bag and hands it to LAUREN. She exits, leaving LAUREN looking at the candle.)

Scene 2

Seven years earlier. A dingy, desolate bar. The TV is playing. CARLOS has been looking at LAUREN who is at the juke box. LAUREN is in her early 20s, dressed "sexy." She occasionally looks over to him. After a while, she approaches him. Woman is sitting next to CARLOS at the bar, listening.

LAUREN: Hi.

CARLOS: Hi.

LAUREN: I'm Lauren.

CARLOS: Carlos.

LAUREN: You live around here?

CARLOS: Flatbush.

LAUREN: You wanna come get some pizza with me?

CARLOS: OK.

WOMAN: Seven years.

CARLOS: What?

WOMAN: Seven years of descent into the deep, dark pit until you find the pink spider.

CARLOS: Do I know you? *(To LAUREN)* Let's go.

WOMAN: Where are you going?

CARLOS: I'm going to the theater. It's the opening night. I gotta get dressed up and pick up some flowers. Does that meet your approval?

WOMAN: I'll see you at the theater.

LAUREN: Is she your girlfriend or something?

CARLOS: I've never seen her before in my life. She must be nuts.

(They exit. WOMAN sits alone and watches TV and drinks.)

Scene 3

The pizzeria.

CARLOS: Do you like pepperoni on your pizza?

LAUREN: It's OK. I really like white pizza. They don't have it here.

CARLOS: What's that?

LAUREN: You don't know? It's pizza with ricotta cheese. No tomato sauce.

CARLOS: That's strange.

LAUREN: It's the new thing. I like it because it looks soft. And nothing drips. Like a perfectly made bed. When I have a house of my own, I'm gonna have all white sheets and comforters and pillows and curtains with wall to wall soft white carpet.

CARLOS: Nice. Where do you live now?

LAUREN: Oh, with my mother. I'm moving out soon. She wants me to get a job at the donut factory or something and pay her rent. She doesn't understand who I am.

CARLOS: My father wanted me to learn refrigerator repair. But I didn't want to be anything like him.

LAUREN: What did you want?

CARLOS: I don't know. My father always said if I didn't get my act together, I'd be fucked up for life. When I didn't make it to the senior year, I thought, shit, I fucked up. There is no way to make it right anyway, so I dropped outta school. After that I stayed home a while. I watched my parents go to work, come home, eat dinner watching TV, and go to bed everyday. I don't spend the evenings there anymore. My father doesn't talk to my mother. I feel bad for her.

LAUREN: Most married people don't talk. My daddy is dead. But when he was alive, he never talked to my mother. He drove the bread truck, you know, the Sunbeam bread. He would leave the house real early to make deliveries. He worked hard. But the bitch slept like a pig and didn't clean the house. My mother is ignorant. If daddy was alive, he'd understand what I'm about.

CARLOS: What do you mean?

LAUREN: I mean I'm nothing like my mother. I'm a freelance artist. Fashion designer. I design celebrities' clothes.

CARLOS: Wow. Who?

LAUREN: Oh, TV and movie stars. But I'm not working right now. Things are slow.

CARLOS: The pizza is on me.

LAUREN: Thanks. Next time, we'll go to Manhattan for white pizza. My treat.

CARLOS: Sounds good.

LAUREN: When I have my white house, you can come live with me if you want.

CARLOS: Sounds good.

Scene 4

Another day. A restaurant.

LAUREN: Try a piece of mine.

CARLOS: What is it?

LAUREN: Raw fish and rice.

CARLOS: Noooo, thank you. I'll stick to my cooked food. Chicken something. Chicken Terayaku.

LAUREN: I can't believe you don't eat sushi. Everyone I know eats sushi. I've eaten sushi with Al Pacino.

CARLOS: Yeah?

LAUREN: Yeah, I used to design his girlfriend's clothes, you know.

CARLOS: Maybe I'll try a little piece.

(LAUREN takes out some pills and takes them. Then she hands CARLOS some.)

LAUREN: Here, take this first.

CARLOS: What's this?

LAUREN: The food will taste better.

CARLOS: Sure. I need something to make raw fish taste better.

(CARLOS takes the pills.)

LAUREN: They are magic pills, Carlos. You'll wake up tomorrow morning and recite Shakespeare.

CARLOS: I've never even read Shakespeare. When I was in school, I couldn't keep focused on math or English. I loved history, though. And I loved my grandmother. I guess once your grandmother dies, there isn't nothing you can do to keep yourself from dying slowly inside.

LAUREN: I know. Having nobody can kill you. That's why you need a white house where you can live forever. This house has everything; and there is a puppy in every room that matches the color of the room. A golden retriever in the gold room, a dalmatian in the polka dot room.

CARLOS: I thought the house was all white.

LAUREN: It's a big house.

CARLOS: A big house can get lonely.

LAUREN: Carlos, I'm all alone in the world. My brother is in jail and my mother hates me. So you are the only person I can live with in my white house.

(The waitress, the same WOMAN from the bar, approaches them.)

WOMAN: Would you like something else?

LAUREN: You know, the sushi wasn't fresh. I'm gonna get sick. I'm not paying for this.

WOMAN: But you ate it all.

LAUREN: So? I feel sick, OK? I'm not paying for this. I'll sue your ass.

WOMAN: And how about you?

CARLOS: Huh?

WOMAN: How did you like your sushi?

LAUREN: Listen, bitch,

WOMAN: The dinner is on the house. *(To CARLOS)* Well? Did you enjoy your sushi?

CARLOS: What happens if I ate a bad piece?

WOMAN: You suffer for seven years.

(WOMAN exits.)

CARLOS: You were mean to her.

LAUREN: Carlos, you gotta take care of yourself in this world. Nobody is gonna help you. We have to protect each other.

Scene 5

WOMAN stands behind LAUREN, but LAUREN does not sense her presence.

LAUREN: I long for things beautiful. I search my memories for a beautiful moment in my life. A song, a dream, an unforgettable feeling of warmth, a smile that fulfilled a small expectation of being alive. But my mother's red eyes block everything else on the other side of my memory. Red from booze, from my father's death, from my brother's stealing. I can't see past the red. It isn't possible that I've had no beauty in my life, is it? I've just misplaced my history. That makes me a child of nothing.

(Pause)

Life should be beautiful, don't you think?

(WOMAN places her hand on LAUREN's shoulder from behind. LAUREN does not feel this.)

Scene 6

One year later. A tenement apartment. There is a knock on the door. CARLOS goes and opens the door. The same WOMAN from the restaurant stands at the door.

WOMAN: Hi. Did you just move in? I'm your neighbor. This package came for you today.

(She gives him a package, invisible to the audience.)

CARLOS: For me? No one knows we are here. We don't even have a phone yet. Hey, haven't I seen you before?

WOMAN: I don't think so.

CARLOS: I used to live in Flatbush. There was a Korean deli around the corner from my parents house...

WOMAN: It wasn't me.

CARLOS: Huh? I was just... Oh, oh, you thought I was gonna say...noooo, I'm not that ignorant. I was just... I guess I was imagining. We've never met before.

WOMAN: Welcome to East Jesus.

(WOMAN exits. LAUREN enters.)

LAUREN: Who was it, Carlos?

CARLOS: A package. It's from my grandmother.

LAUREN: You gave her our address already?

CARLOS: She is dead.

LAUREN: ...Open it.

(He opens the package. WOMAN comes in and dances around CARLOS and LAUREN. CARLOS and LAUREN look in the box. He looks up and sees WOMAN. LAUREN does not see her.)

Scene 7

One year later. LAUREN watches TV in the apartment. CARLOS enters with groceries.

CARLOS: I got food for the week.

LAUREN: Any money left?

CARLOS: A little. Let's go to Coney Island this weekend. I haven't been there for years. They have the best hot dogs.

LAUREN: You're not serious. I wanna feel well this weekend. I'm sick. I gotta get high.

CARLOS: Sure. Whatever you want.

LAUREN: The guy next door got a puppy today. Labrador. He's really cute. I saw him in the hall way. The guy is strange though.

CARLOS: What do you mean strange?

LAUREN: He looks at me all weird. He didn't want me to touch his dog.

CARLOS: Why not?

LAUREN: How do I know? He's just an asshole.

CARLOS: He was probably worried about messing up your white shirt.

(He hugs LAUREN.)

CARLOS: You look nice in white.

LAUREN: It's my color. Not everyone can wear white, you know.

CARLOS: I know. Don't you wanna go outside tomorrow? It's supposed to be real nice this week-end. Maybe we'll see some dogs with friendly owners at Coney Island.

LAUREN: Maybe.

CARLOS: Let's eat now.

(CARLOS takes out a loaf of white bread, jars of peanut butter and jelly, a box of spaghetti, and a jar of tomato sauce.)

CARLOS: The food has to last a week, OK? Monday and Wednesday we eat spaghetti. The rest of the week is peanut butter and jelly sandwiches. Was there any hot water today?

LAUREN: You ask me that everyday. We've lived here for a year now. There has never been any hot water.

CARLOS: What did you do today?

LAUREN: You ask me that everyday. I watched Oprah. Carlos, let's get a dog of our own.

CARLOS: It's expensive to have a dog, you know. I can't even take the bus to work, how can we afford a dog?

LAUREN: But I need company. You don't understand how lonely it gets around here.

CARLOS: Maybe in the future, OK?

(LAUREN cries softly.)

CARLOS: Did you see something sad on Oprah today?

Scene 8

The apartment. Another day.

LAUREN: Did you make sure the ice cream wasn't refrozen?

CARLOS: I'm sure it's OK.

(She opens the ice cream and examines it.)

LAUREN: I can't eat this. It's refrozen. Take it back.

CARLOS: The store was closing already.

LAUREN: Take it back. I'm too good to be eating refrozen ice cream. Who the hell do they think they are? Take it back to them.

CARLOS: Don't start, Lauren. I'll eat it.

LAUREN: What about me? I want some ice cream.

CARLOS: Here. I'll eat the top. It's OK in the middle.

LAUREN: No, it's not. It's not OK. This isn't fair. Do something.

CARLOS: It's OK.

LAUREN: *(Suddenly very sad)* Are you gonna fix it? Are you gonna fix everything?

CARLOS: Jesus. Yes.

(LAUREN sobs silently. The door opens and WOMAN enters. LAUREN doesn't see her.)

WOMAN: Delivery.

CARLOS: What?

WOMAN: One absolutely not ever refrozen strawberry ice cream.

CARLOS: Thanks. I don't know why such a little thing is so traumatic for her.

WOMAN: Why isn't it for you?

CARLOS: Because I'm OK. I had a good childhood or something, I guess.

WOMAN: Didn't you grow up in the house where your parents didn't speak to each other for years?

CARLOS: What do you know about it? It was no big deal, anyway. I didn't take it to heart.

WOMAN: I'm sorry she is so sad.

CARLOS: Yeah.

WOMAN: I know how she feels. A tiny seed from an unknown tree drops in your heart. You try to ignore it, but you can't. It grows to the size of a watermelon in one minute. It crushes your heart. You can't stop it.

CARLOS: Why are you here?

WOMAN: To give you ice cream.

CARLOS: Am I gonna survive this?

WOMAN: I'm not a fortune teller.

CARLOS: Aren't you my guardian angel?

WOMAN: Don't be silly. I have to go now.

CARLOS: Thanks for the ice cream.

(WOMAN exits. LAUREN stops sobbing.)

LAUREN: I guess the middle is OK. I can eat some.

CARLOS: (Tired) That's good, baby.

LAUREN: (As she eats) It isn't possible that I've had no beauty in my life, is it?

CARLOS: How's the ice cream?

LAUREN: The ice cream is OK. I can still have good strawberry ice cream. That's not nothing. Thank you, Carlos.

Scene 9

The bar. CARLOS is drinking beer. WOMAN comes in and sits next to him.

WOMAN: How are you?

CARLOS: Have I seen you somewhere before?

WOMAN: I'm sure.

CARLOS: I can't remember. Sorry.

WOMAN: You look tired.

CARLOS: I mix concrete all day. But I'm glad I have a job. I gotta pay the rent. Sixty dollars a week.

WOMAN: I think this belongs to you.

(WOMAN hands him an object invisible to the audience.)

CARLOS: *(Surprised)* Where did you get this?

WOMAN: Have you been looking for it?

CARLOS: No, not really. I've forgotten about it. I must've lost it months ago. It belonged to my grandmother.

WOMAN: It's possible to find it again, isn't it.

CARLOS: I guess so. Thanks.

WOMAN: Shouldn't you go home?

CARLOS: I don't know. Tomorrow is Christmas, right?

WOMAN: What are your plans?

CARLOS: Are you kidding? For people like us, everyday is the same. No heat, no hot water, the tub is coated black with I don't know what, so I gotta take a drip drip ice cold shower wearing my sneakers.

WOMAN: But you are in love.

CARLOS: Lauren and me, at least we got each other. What do you have?

WOMAN: I don't know. Nothing yet. Years later I may end up dead on a roof of a suspicious hotel in Times Square. Death by suicide or racial hate. Or I may pass by a theater on Broadway one day and be mesmerized by the signs. I'll get a job at the concession stand where *Chorus Line* is so I can see the show many many times.

Scene 10

Two years later. The apartment.

CARLOS: I had a job interview today. For UPS package delivery. This guy from the construction job set me up. It's less money, but I think it's cool.

LAUREN: Less money? Are you nuts?

CARLOS: It's a better job.

LAUREN: How're we gonna get by on less money?

CARLOS: How about you getting a job for a change? You haven't worked in three years!

LAUREN: I'm a freelance artist! Anyway, I heard it's easy to get on welfare. You just have to take some humiliation at the office, that's all. Will you come with me tomorrow?

CARLOS: Forget it. We'll manage.

LAUREN: I'll pay you back everything. I promise.

CARLOS: OK.

LAUREN: So what do you wanna do tonight? We need some money for dope.

(Pause)

LAUREN: Don't worry. I'll get it.

(She goes to the telephone and dials.)

LAUREN: Hi ma? I'm coming over. I need money. I just need it. I'm coming over now. What? It's an emergency. If you don't give me money, I'm gonna kill myself. I'm killing myself for real. You bitch!

(She hangs up.)

LAUREN: Why don't you do something?

CARLOS: I don't wanna get high today. Let's watch TV, baby.

LAUREN: Fuck. I'm gonna kill that bitch.

CARLOS: Stop talking like that about your mother.

LAUREN: She owes me. She lets her boyfriend live in the house. She gives my brother money. She is jealous of me because I'm a fashion designer. I don't care. I had my revenge. Once I took thirty thousand dollars from her. All the money in her saving account. I spent it in two weeks. She didn't notice it was gone for a long time, because she just never notices me.

CARLOS: Come here. (*He holds her.*) My mother, she is always so understanding. She lets me smoke pot and everything. No trouble. I owe my mother. Maybe she will give us some money.

LAUREN: My mother went off on me when she found me smoking pot.

CARLOS: My mother is cool. I wouldn't be here if it wasn't for her. She can be your mother, too.

LAUREN: It's nice to have a mother who loves you.

Scene 11

The apartment. CARLOS and LAUREN are sitting on the floor. He opens a small bag of heroin and puts it into the spoon. LAUREN heats the spoon with a disposable lighter.

LAUREN: I copped it from the same shooting gallery where that guy ODed last week.

CARLOS: That means we are in for some good shit.

(She prepares the syringe. He wraps a belt around his arm. She taps his arm for a vein and shoots him up. She repeats the process and shoots herself. They are relaxed instantaneously. LAUREN picks a short cigarette from an ashtray full of buds and lights it. She is dosing off with a burning cigarette. CARLOS throws up in a paper bag.)

LAUREN: It feels good, doesn't it?

Scene 12

Another day. CARLOS is sleeping. LAUREN is smoking a cigarette. WOMAN is in the room with them, but visible only to CARLOS.

CARLOS: *(Startled)* What time is it?

LAUREN: It's nine-thirty.

WOMAN: It's dried roses crinkle after dream.

CARLOS: What?

LAUREN: Nine-thirty at night.

CARLOS: I had a dream. I was a heroin addict. You, too. We went to cop on Jamaica Avenue late at night. This guy pulled a knife on me because my twenty dollar bill turned into a red balloon. But you protected me from the knife.

LAUREN: It wasn't a dream.

WOMAN: The red balloon popped.

CARLOS: It wasn't?

LAUREN: Do you want some tea?

CARLOS: OK.

(LAUREN exits. CARLOS looks at WOMAN.)

CARLOS: I know you, right?

WOMAN: Didn't you call me?

CARLOS: In my dream?

WOMAN: No, on the phone.

CARLOS: I don't remember.

(LAUREN comes in with tea. CARLOS and LAUREN drink in silence.)

LAUREN: I'm gonna start designing soon. I've got ideas. I'm thinking pink. Do you like pink?

CARLOS: Yeah.

LAUREN: I'm gonna have my own boutique. In Manhattan. What do you think?

CARLOS: Sounds good.

(He looks at WOMAN. She shakes her head no.)

Scene 13

One year later. The bar.

CARLOS: Tell me. What was it that came in the mail from my dead grandmother? Then I lost it for a long time, but you gave it back to me. Remember? What was it?

WOMAN: Don't you know?

CARLOS: I can't remember. We've moved so many times in the past five years. It's lost.

WOMAN: Maybe you'll find it again someday.

CARLOS: When my grandmother died, I stopped drinking coffee. No one could make coffee that tasted like my grandma's.

WOMAN: We lose so much.

CARLOS: I guess. It's no big deal. When will I see you again?

WOMAN: When the seven years are up.

CARLOS: What comes after that? How can life be different now? Don't misunderstand me, this is a pretty good life. I have no problems when I'm doing dope. I'm all right.

Before I started doing dope, things weren't as easy. I was a scared little kid, scared shitless of everything. The nuns at school, the bus driver. Everyday I was so nervous about getting on the school bus after school. So one day I decided to walk home. It took me forty minutes to get home. I guess I was about ten then. I peed in my pants walking home. Because I was too scared to use the bathroom at school before I left. The nuns were yelling at the kids to get on the bus right now.

At home, my parents were always fighting or not talking to each other, but it was no big deal. I had grandma. That's all I needed. Without her, I just didn't think I could make it in this world.

WOMAN: I think I'm from a different place.

CARLOS: I see.

WOMAN: My story hasn't begun yet.

CARLOS: You are like, a vision?

WOMAN: Something like that.

CARLOS: Why do you visit me?

WOMAN: When you are high on heroin, there are already pink spiders crawling all over my future.

CARLOS: I don't understand.

WOMAN: If a lightning strikes a willow tree in California, monarch butterflies die in Mexico. We are all part of the same web.

CARLOS: I don't want to be part of anything. I think whatever potential I had to be something was lost on the day I peed in my pants. I'm tired.

WOMAN: What are you so tired of?

CARLOS: Keeping it up. When I go to Jamaica Avenue to get Methadone, I feel so warm and safe as soon as I have a little cup of metamusel mix in my hand. Sometimes I have to wait an hour until my regular shows up at the clinic. He is on the program, but he sells me his share. You can trust his stuff to be the real thing. He won't rip me off. He's a good guy. I hold the cup in my hand and know everything will be fine in a few minutes. I go across the street to this dive of a diner and order hot coffee. It's supposed to speed up the effect of methadone. When it's gone, I have to figure out how to get some more tomorrow. I gotta do this everyday.

WOMAN: Coffee?

CARLOS: Yeah, I started drinking coffee again a coupla years ago. Drugs helped a lot. It's a good thing I can drink coffee without grandma, right?

Scene 14

One year later. The apartment.

LAUREN: I had another bag.

CARLOS: What?

LAUREN: There. On the side table.

CARLOS: So look.

LAUREN: It's not here. Did you take it?

CARLOS: No.

LAUREN: Who else? Tell me. Why?

CARLOS: I didn't.

LAUREN: Why do you wanna do this shit to me?

CARLOS: I didn't.

LAUREN: It's my share.

CARLOS: You are crazy.

LAUREN: Give it back to me.

CARLOS: Look. I didn't take it. Don't start.

LAUREN: You stupid low life. Gimme back my stuff.

CARLOS: Shut up. I told you to quit crack. It makes you crazy and nasty.

LAUREN: I'm not doing crack. I'm talking about my dope, which you stole from me.

CARLOS: You are hopeless.

LAUREN: Oh, yeah? And there is hope for you?

CARLOS: At least I'm not a crack head.

LAUREN: You are a waste. Don't preach to me.

CARLOS: Crack is a whole different game. It's the devil. I told you to stay away from it. Look at yourself.

LAUREN: Listen you low life.

CARLOS: Call me low life one more time, bitch, you'll be paying for your own dope.

LAUREN: All right. Just gimme back my bag. It's mine. I left it right here. I saw you take it.

CARLOS: What? You didn't see nothing.

LAUREN: I did. I did. I saw you take it.

CARLOS: Liar.

LAUREN: Where did you hide it? Where? Let me check.

(She goes over to him and sticks her hand in his crouch.)

CARLOS: Get away from me, you lunatic!

LAUREN: *(Screaming)* I KNEW IT I KNEW IT I KNEW IT YOU TOOK MY STUFF YOU ARE A LIAR IF YOU DIDN'T TAKE IT PROVE IT TAKE OFF YOUR PANTS

CARLOS: Shut the hell up.

LAUREN: I'll tell your mother. I'll tell her her precious son is a liar and a thief and a junkie.

CARLOS: Yeah, right.

LAUREN: Watch me.

(She goes to the phone. CARLOS goes after her. They struggle over the phone.)

LAUREN: AHHHHHHHHH

CARLOS: SHUT UP!

LAUREN: TAKE OFF YOUR PANTS. IF YOU HAVE NOTHING TO HIDE, PROVE IT!

(Pause)

(He takes off his pants.)

LAUREN: Bend over.

CARLOS: What?

LAUREN: Bend over and let me check your asshole.

(Tense silence. They stare at each other. He takes off his underwear and bends down. She looks quickly and then starts sobbing.)

LAUREN: I'm sorry. I'm sorry. I gotta detox.

(He puts back on his clothes.)

LAUREN: I swear. I'm gonna detox.

CARLOS: What for?

LAUREN: I got nobody. You gotta take care of me. Hey look at these.

(She shows him dark patches on her elbows. Pause.)

CARLOS: Shit. What's wrong with you?

LAUREN: These patches appear and disappear all the time. You don't have them?

(Pause)

LAUREN: It's because I've misplaced my history.

Scene 15

Another day. LAUREN watches TV in the apartment. CARLOS enters with groceries.

CARLOS: I got food for the week.

LAUREN: I need twenty dollars, Carlos.

CARLOS: No.

LAUREN: I swear this is the last time.

CARLOS: I told you no crack. Crack fucks you up.

LAUREN: It's not that. I just need it. I promise I won't ask again.

CARLOS: Here.

(He holds out the bill. LAUREN reaches for it, but he pulls back.)

CARLOS: I want you gone for three hours. Understand? Stay out and give me some peace.

LAUREN: OK.

(She takes the money and exits. CARLOS prepares heroin and shoots up. He lights a cigarette and nods off in front of the TV.)

Scene 16

Another day. LAUREN watches TV. CARLOS enters.

CARLOS: I got food for the week.

LAUREN: I need twenty dollars, Carlos.

CARLOS: No.

LAUREN: I swear this is the last time.

(He gives her the money.)

CARLOS: Here. You know what to do, right? Three hours. Go look for crack for all I care.

(She takes the money and exits. CARLOS shoots up.)

Scene 17

Another day. LAUREN watches TV. CARLOS enters and puts down groceries.

LAUREN: Carlos,

(He gives LAUREN a bill.)

CARLOS: Here. Disappear.

(LAUREN exits. He shoots up.)

(Time passes. LAUREN enters again.)

LAUREN: Carlos, give me five. Please. I swear this is the last time.

(He stares at the wall.)

CARLOS: What's that?

LAUREN: What? What? Shit, I knew it. The cops!

CARLOS: No, on the wall. Over there.

(He attacks the wall. Tries to grab something.)

CARLOS: Did you see that? A Big Pink Spider.

LAUREN: Get the fuck outta here. Com'on, check outside. I think people are following us. Cops, probably. You know what? I think my mother's hired a hit man to kill me.

CARLOS: Why?

LAUREN: Because she is jealous. Because I'm daddy's favorite.

CARLOS: Your father is dead.

LAUREN: Because I'm a fashion designer. Because I'm pretty.

CARLOS: Look, do you see that?

LAUREN: What ta hell?

CARLOS: A big pink spider on the wall.

LAUREN: Forget it. Listen, I think the guy next door is gay. Let's ask him if he is a faggot.

CARLOS: Why?

LAUREN: Why not? It's disgusting. Besides, I think he steals stuff from us.

CARLOS: What?

LAUREN: Stuff. When we leave the apartment, he comes in here and steals. Let's get him.

(CARLOS is examining his arm with horror.)

CARLOS: I got bugs coming outta my arm. Look. What are they?

LAUREN: Carlos, you are just sick. You don't feel good, right? Let's get you a coupla bags. It'll take care of you.

CARLOS: Shit. I got worms or something.

(He scrubs his arm violently.)

LAUREN: I don't believe this. Stop that, you low life. Shit. I had a bright future in front on me. Then you came along. You were my downfall. I was a very successful designer before you messed up my life. I could've had my own boutique.

CARLOS: You never worked a day in your life.

LAUREN: You don't know.

CARLOS: I know. You haven't worked in seven years now. I doubt all of a sudden you stopped working when you met me. You never designed nothing. It's all in your head.

LAUREN: You are a liar. Liar. Liar!

(They get into a struggle. WOMAN enters. Only CARLOS sees her.)

WOMAN: Are you ready?

CARLOS: For what?

LAUREN: What?

WOMAN: Ready to go to the theater. It's the opening night. You have to dress up and buy some flowers.

CARLOS: Right. Yeah, I'm ready.

LAUREN: What's wrong with you?

CARLOS: I've never been to the theater.

LAUREN: What are you talking about?

WOMAN: It's been seven years, Carlos. You survived.

CARLOS: Why?

WOMAN: Because you wanted to take care of somebody. Because Lauren had no one to love her. Because you didn't know what to dream about except for the things you saw on TV. Who knows?

LAUREN: (Punching CARLOS) Don't do that!

CARLOS: Lauren, I'm going to the theater.

LAUREN: Yeah, right.

CARLOS: I've never been to the theater. I think you are supposed to dress up. Isn't it amazing?

LAUREN: What's so fucking amazing?

CARLOS: I've never been to the theater. Amazing. But I can go if I wanted to, believe that? I'll quit dope and save some money. Buy a decent shirt and new sneakers. Maybe even leather shoes. I'll go to Broadway when I have enough money. Look around. Have you ever thought anything that outrageous?

LAUREN: Bullshit. You don't know what you are talking about. I used to go to the theater all the time. People like you don't go to the theater. Because you are nobody. Nobody.

CARLOS: Do you remember what it was I got from my grandmother in the mail seven years ago?

LAUREN: Your grandmother's been dead for twenty years.

CARLOS: I think I know what it was. I thought I lost it, but I didn't. You can never lose something like that. It's yours for life.

LAUREN: Let's just smoke some pot. Just pot, that's all. Let's relax, OK Carlos?

CARLOS: Lauren, I'm going to the theater.

(*WOMAN opens the door for him. He looks back once, then walks out.*)

Scene 18

The same street as Scene 1.

LAUREN: I never had a candle before. I almost always had electricity in my life.

WOMAN: You are lucky.

LAUREN: I ain't lucky.

WOMAN: The candle is scented. It smells like vanilla.

LAUREN: Nice. Is it Chinese?

WOMAN: I don't think so. It's from Bloomingdale's.

LAUREN: I know. But where are you from? Are you Japanese? I used to eat sushi. It's my favorite food in fact. I stopped when I got together with Carlos. He didn't like it much, plus he could never afford it. I've had better boyfriends you know, men with money and respect. With this one boyfriend, I had a new dress every week and we went out to eat sushi all the time. But Carlos needed me. He needed my company. He came from a fucked up family, so I was all he had.

WOMAN: Where is he now?

LAUREN: I had to send him away. He was no good for me. I had to take care of myself. I'm gonna write a book about my life. I can call Al Pacino to play my father in the movie version. I have plans. Carlos was gonna hold me back. What do you think about my idea?

WOMAN: Years from now, you often think about writing this book, but it doesn't matter. You get arrested for trying to walk out of Bloomingdale's wearing a fur coat you tried on. Instead of sending you to jail, they send you to the hospital. You are clean and sober when your mother dies.

LAUREN: What are you, a fucking fortune teller?

WOMAN: You'll be alright.

LAUREN: No, I won't. Don't go. I got AIDS.

WOMAN: What will you do now?

LAUREN: I'm serious. A book about my life. A song, a dream, an unforgettable feeling of warmth, a smile that fulfilled a small expectation of being alive.

WOMAN: Sounds beautiful.

LAUREN: It's a lie. A true book about my life. How fate can fuck you up, and you have two choices. You can either live with the pain or have a little bit of pain killer, you know. To numb you just a little. And what kinda life that would be, living in the fog of high happiness. My tragedy couldn't have been just mine. Right? Right?

WOMAN: I know.

LAUREN: One day, Carlos' kids can read it. They'd have no idea who I was, but they'd be moved by it anyway. I owe Carlos some money. This is how I'll pay him. His kids will read my book.

WOMAN: I have to go. It's time.

LAUREN: Ask me who I am.

WOMAN: Who are you?

LAUREN: A child of nothing.

WOMAN: Again.

LAUREN: A child of a bread truck driver?

WOMAN: And?

LAUREN: A child of...me.

WOMAN: Good bye.

LAUREN: Yeah, take care of yourself.

(WOMAN exits. LAUREN remains.)

LAUREN: I like that. I'm a child of me. Hello, me.

Part 2

Scene 1

Seven years later. A lobby of an apartment building in Queens.

WOMAN/YUMI: Hi. I'm the new tenant in 4C.

CARLOS/DOORMAN: Your name?

YUMI: Yumi.

CARLOS: I'm Carlos. You look familiar.

YUMI: I just moved to New York.

CARLOS: My mistake then. I've never been outside New York.

YUMI: You look familiar, too.

CARLOS: Where are you from?

YUMI: Japan.

CARLOS: Far away. Are you here to go to school?

YUMI: I wish. If I was in school, I would at least have some company.

CARLOS: You'll meet people. It's a friendly town.

Scene 2

Another day. The lobby again.

CARLOS: You never came to visit New York before this time?

YUMI: No.

CARLOS: I feel like we've met.

YUMI: You haven't been to San Francisco, right? I went to school there.

CARLOS: What were you studying?

YUMI: Survival.

CARLOS: Is that like camping?

YUMI: No. English.

CARLOS: Oh. I wish I could go to school. Study history. You know there are people whose job is to restore history. Archeological objects. I saw a documentary on PBS once. People paste together broken vases and statues from ancient time. I didn't know such jobs existed when I was a kid.

YUMI: Do you like your job now?

CARLOS: It's a good job. People are friendly. I watch out for the old ladies in the building. Before I came here, I had a rough time. But life is decent now. It's been seven years. How about you? If you could go to school again, what would you study?

YUMI: Movies. In Japan, I worked in an office job for six years and saved money. I wanted to make movies. But there is no such thing as a woman film maker in Japan. So I spent most of my money studying English in California. My parents think I'm insane.

CARLOS: Why?

YUMI: They are respectable people. My father is a lawyer and my mother is married to one.

CARLOS: But you always wanted to make movies.

YUMI: No. I always loved watching movies. But didn't even know there were such people as film makers. I thought movies just appeared.

(Pause)

YUMI: Most of what's going on in the world is still a mystery to me.

CARLOS: I like it that way. I can't imagine the pain of knowing everything.

(Pause)

CARLOS: Maybe you remind me of Yoko Ono.

YUMI: I do not.

CARLOS: I guess not.

YUMI: See you later.

CARLOS: Wait. Do you ever think of making a book into a movie?

YUMI: Why?

CARLOS: Here, you can have this book. I hear it's pretty good. Take it. I'm not going to read it. Maybe there is a movie in it.

YUMI: *Living in the Abyss* by Lauren O'Neill. I don't know. It sounds like a melodrama.

CARLOS: I heard the author died of AIDS.

YUMI: That doesn't mean she wrote a good book.

CARLOS: But it's her last book. It was published after her death.

YUMI: Why don't you read it?

CARLOS: Because I know it by heart.

YUMI: What do you mean?

CARLOS: It's my gift to you. Welcome to Jamaica.

Scene 3

In her apartment. She is reading the book. Silence. She looks up to find LAUREN standing.

LAUREN: Remember me?

YUMI: ...No. This is my apartment.

LAUREN: It's nice. You need some curtains. White will look nice.

YUMI: You have to go.

LAUREN: Do you like the book?

YUMI: I just started.

LAUREN: True story.

YUMI: Do you need help?

LAUREN: No, I thought you might.

YUMI: I'm fine. I'm going to call down for the doorman, OK? He can show you the way out.

LAUREN: There is no need. I'll go. Enjoy the book.

(She exits.)

Scene 4

In the lobby.

YUMI: Someone came into my apartment unannounced.

CARLOS: Last night?

WOMAN: Around nine.

CARLOS: I'm only here til seven everyday. The door is unmanned at night. The tenants have to be careful not to let strangers in.

YUMI: She wasn't dangerous.

CARLOS: Someone you knew?

YUMI: She looked familiar, but I don't think so.

CARLOS: Maybe it was someone who lives in the building. What did she look like?

YUMI: She was in her thirties, I think. Very skinny and pale. She had a long black hair and a small scar on the corner of her mouth.

(CARLOS is surprised.)

YUMI: Carlos? Is something wrong?

CARLOS: No, it just reminded me of someone I used to know.

YUMI: Maybe it was your friend looking for you?

CARLOS: No. She is dead.

YUMI: I'm sorry.

CARLOS: Listen, be careful at night. Jamaica isn't the best neighborhood. It used be worse. They've cleaned up a lot of drug activities in the past few years. Still, you should watch out for yourself. Don't let a stranger in your apartment.

Scene 5

The apartment.

LAUREN: Remember me, Yumi?

YUMI: Of course. You know my name. Come in.

LAUREN: Did you finish the book?

YUMI: The book? Oh, *Living in the Abyss.* Yes.

LAUREN: What did you think?

YUMI: Have you read it?

LAUREN: Yes.

YUMI: I thought it was good. Sad. Honest.

LAUREN: Maybe someone will make a movie of it.

YUMI: Maybe.

LAUREN: What are you doing now?

YUMI: Nothing... I'm trying to be a film maker. But it's silly. Right now I'm trying to meet some people and get a job.

LAUREN: Years from now, you will be working at the concession stand at the Broadway theater where *Rent* is. You get to see the show as many times as you want. Then you decide to write your own work. You become a poet. Your poems are read by Carlos' children.

YUMI: What?

LAUREN: It's all part of the same web.

YUMI: Why are you here?

LAUREN: Didn't you call me?

YUMI: Maybe I did. Thank you for coming.

LAUREN: You'll be all right.

Scene 6

The lobby.

YUMI: Carlos, I forgot to tell you I finished the book you gave me.

CARLOS: How was it?

YUMI: I liked it. I'll bring it down.

CARLOS: Don't bother.

YUMI: It's no bother.

CARLOS: Maybe later. Don't worry about it now. So what was the book about?

YUMI: It's about a woman whose father dies early in her life. She is lost without him. Later she falls in love with a man who is also lost, and together they become heroin addicts in order to stop the pain.

CARLOS: What...what happens at the end?

YUMI: She dies. He recovers and writes a book about his life.

CARLOS: You mean she writes the book before she dies.

YUMI: No. The man is the one who writes the book.

CARLOS: But the author is a woman. It's a true story about her life. She wrote the book.

YUMI: I guess the ending is fictionalized. I don't know why.

CARLOS: ...I know why.

(Pause. CARLOS is pale.)

YUMI: Carlos, are you feeling OK?

CARLOS: Yeah.

YUMI: Are you sad about something?

CARLOS: No...I don't get sad about too many things. I'm lucky to be alive. I got no right to be sad. How about you? What makes you sad?

YUMI: I feel sad after a mid-day nap that I didn't intend to take. I wake up empty and closer to death. When I finish eating lunch or dinner. Right after the meal, I feel an enormous fear of the time passing.

CARLOS: Breakfast?

YUMI: It doesn't happen to me after breakfast. I think that's because I don't really like breakfast food. So when it's gone, there is no regret.

CARLOS: I like breakfast food the best.

YUMI: I guess we are different.

Scene 7

In Yumi's apartment. She is still unpacking. LAUREN stands behind her (in a reverse position from Part 1 Scene 5).

YUMI: Starting my life over from scratch. I often romanticized it. Moving. Leaving everything old behind. In the land where I know no one, and no one knows me, I can invent a whole new life.

I can dress in long skirts and wrap my head in colorful fabric. But after a certain point in your life, you are who you are. My head wrapped will never feel comfortable. It will always feel like a hundred and nine degrees and itchy and the scarf about to fall off.

The awkwardness that I have carried deep in my body for thirty years is now part of my being. I realize that leaving doesn't mean birth or death. It means negotiation.

My life is in these boxes. In New York City. In Queens. The rent is reasonable. I look at the help wanted section in the Sunday *Times* every week, but I'm not qualified for anything. Qualification means accumulation. You have to stay, not leave. My phone never rings because I don't know anyone. Sometimes I'm overcome by fear. What if I die in this apartment? It will be weeks before anyone notices. I guess that's why people don't often pick up and leave. For the fear of dying alone.

(LAUREN places her hand on Yumi's shoulder from behind. YUMI feels this.)

YUMI: I was just thinking about you.

LAUREN: Have you misplaced your history?

YUMI: No. I still have it.

LAUREN: You are lucky.

YUMI: I'm not lucky.

LAUREN: You'll be all right.

YUMI: Carlos, are there good restaurants around here? Inexpensive.

CARLOS: I don't really know. I live in Brooklyn.

YUMI: Maybe I'll just cook. I hate ending up at a wrong restaurant. It's depressing to pay money for bad food and be upset for not being smart and hip.

CARLOS: You'll get used to living here. You'll be all right.

YUMI: Maybe. The first month I was in California, I picked up some spaghetti and a jar of pasta sauce at a supermarket. Cook the spaghetti for eight minutes. OK. But there was no instruction written on the jar of sauce. I didn't know what was already understood and agreed on by everyone. You just open it and heat it as if that is your birth right. No doubt. No apprehension. I felt so lonely. I called my parents in Japan and asked them to airmail me some rice crackers.

CARLOS: Did they?

YUMI: Yes. Even though they were very angry when I left. I think they were angry with me for most of my life.

CARLOS: It's important to take care of your parents. I had a rough life before I came to this job. But I don't blame my parents for anything. My problems were my own.

YUMI: What kind of problems?

CARLOS: Nothing big. A little experiments with drugs. I started out smoking pot when I was twelve, but my mother was understanding. She didn't try to discipline me. I owe my mother.

YUMI: You came to your senses because she left you alone?

CARLOS: Not until later. She had her own problems anyway. She was young and poor. Besides, I turned out OK. I've been completely clean for five years now.

YUMI: I don't understand. How did your mother help you?

CARLOS: Look. You've got to have something to hold onto. Something good. Home. You can't give it up. You have to believe.

YUMI: I don't think it helps to be in denial.

CARLOS: In Egypt?

YUMI: What?

CARLOS: De Nile. Get it? De Nile River? It's a joke me and my mother tell each other.

YUMI: How nice.

Scene 9

YUMI walks out to the streets.

The sun is setting. She pauses, takes out a small bag of rice crackers from her pocket and eats one. After a moment, she begins walking again. She sees a pizzeria and enters. The woman employee is LAUREN.

YUMI: Is it you?

LAUREN: Can I help you?

YUMI: I don't know... What's that?

LAUREN: White pizza.

YUMI: OK. White pizza, please.

LAUREN: But you don't even know what it is.

YUMI: It looks good. I'll try it.

LAUREN: What if it's a mistake?

YUMI: How can I know that before tasting it?

LAUREN: You had plans for dinner. Pizza. Usually that means a regular slice.

YUMI: I was just passing by to go to the supermarket.

LAUREN: So this isn't even part of the plan.

YUMI: I guess I'm not very good at keeping on a track. I want to see where the side street leads to.

LAUREN: If you detour from the main route, you may die alone.

(Pause)

YUMI: What are my options, then?

LAUREN: A regular cheese slice. Or with pepperoni. Very popular.

(Pause)

YUMI: ...White.

(LAUREN *gives her a slice*.)

YUMI: It's delicious. I have been waiting to taste this all my life.

Scene 10

The lobby. YUMI gives CARLOS the book.

YUMI: Thanks.

CARLOS: I told you, you can have it.

YUMI: OK. I'll get it back from you after you read it.

CARLOS: It's OK.

YUMI: I think you should read it. It's very good.

CARLOS: I don't have to read it.

YUMI: Why?

CARLOS: Just leave it alone.

YUMI: I think you are scared of the book for some reason. It reminds you of a painful time maybe. You don't like that.

CARLOS: If you think I can't face pain, you are wrong.

(Pause)

YUMI: Carlos?

CARLOS: My parents never ate dinner together when I was a kid. Family that eats together doesn't produce drug addicts. That's just basic, stupid psychology. I know my mother should have cared whether or not I was smoking pot when I was twelve. But I lose so much if I held onto that. I have to remember the good times. Otherwise it was all for nothing.

YUMI: I think you'll like the book. You know it's her only book ever.

CARLOS: I'll think about it.

(Pause)

YUMI: Carlos, would you call me on the days you don't see me? Just to make sure.

CARLOS: Make sure?

YUMI: That everything is OK with the apartment. Just on the days you don't see me in the lobby at all.

CARLOS: Sure.

Scene 11

CARLOS is reading the book in the lobby. LAUREN enters.

LAUREN: Hi, Carlos.

CARLOS: Shit.

LAUREN: You look good.

CARLOS: Shit.

LAUREN: You are sober.

CARLOS: Shit.

LAUREN: Carlos, stop saying shit. We won't be able to repeat this. So concentrate.

CARLOS: What are you doing here?

LAUREN: I'm just visiting. You gained weight.

CARLOS: Yeah, I detoxed five years ago. I've been clean since. This is strange.

LAUREN: I just came to say good bye. We never did that.

CARLOS: Lauren, I didn't know you were in the hospital...

LAUREN: I didn't want you to visit me anyway. No one came. My mother had died already. I was clean for her death. She saw me sober... How did you feel when you heard the news?

CARLOS: Relieved. Sad. I took the test so I knew I wasn't infected. It seemed strange not to share that fate after so much.

LAUREN: Do you think we could have done better?

CARLOS: No. We were like two wounded animals. We needed each other in the process of healing, that's how I look at it. We had to do it the way we did. We both came out of it all right. I mean...your book and everything.

LAUREN: Do you go to the theater?

CARLOS: Yeah, I always take my dates to the theater. Sometimes to the opera even.

LAUREN: I'm glad.

(*Pause*)

LAUREN: I should go now.

(*Pause*)

CARLOS: Good bye.

(*LAUREN turns to go.*)

CARLOS: Hey, it's a good book. I like the ending. Thanks.

LAUREN: Carlos, what was it you had that belonged to your grandmother?

CARLOS: Your book, I think.

LAUREN: Thank you.

(*LAUREN exits.*)

CARLOS: (*Reads from the book*) It isn't possible for your history to be ruined completely. One day you are standing out on the streets crying, and a strange woman gives you a vanilla scented candle. From that day on, you will always have a candle in your life. Vanilla scented. When you light the candle, memories of songs, dreams, smiles and warmth will come back to you. You'll go on to have an ordinary life, a job, dates at the theater, and ordinary hope to stop the cycle of personal tragedies.

Scene 12

YUMI's apartment. A knock on the door

YUMI: Who is it?

MALE VOICE:Delivery.

YUMI opens the door. A man rushes in and knock her down breathless. LAUREN appears suddenly and stares at the man. He does not see her.

MAN: Don't move.

(YUMI begins to get up.)

YUMI: red hot splashes of
splintered mirage,
ice cold in three seconds.

behind my left eye,
a hole large enough
to store a cherry or
an acorn.

(MAN fires. YUMI falls backward slowly, holding her left eye. LAUREN goes through the same motion simultaneously. YUMI falls to the floor. LAUREN kneels and holds her head.)

YUMI: I was going to be a film maker. Spent all my money learning English. My parents were angry at me for chasing my dreams across the Pacific Ocean.

LAUREN: Years from now you often think about the movie you meant to make based on the book, *Living in the Abyss*. But your book of poems about seeing the world with one eye is published. Your parents read it when it is translated into Japanese.

YUMI: I was hoping you would come back. I wanted to ask you something.

LAUREN: I have to go now. Help is on its way.

YUMI: Am I supposed to be here? Is this how things should have turned out? Is this right?

LAUREN: There is no design. Only connections.

YUMI: What will happen to me?

LAUREN: *(Kidding, to encourage YUMI)* You are going to make my book into a movie. I suggest Al Pacino for the role of the father.

YUMI: It'll never heal.

LAUREN: Everything heals in seven years.

(Sound of an ambulance and a police car approaching. CARLOS rushes in. LAUREN stands, looks back once, then exits. CARLOS doesn't see her.)

YUMI: my mother calls early
Japanese are being murdered
you have to be careful
spending a dollar a minute
for an echo in the strange place
between Tokyo
and Jamaica

everyday
somewhere in the world
the phone rings
wakening a gray haired couple
hearts pounding
with visions of red

CARLOS: Yumi, Yumi, can you hear me? Just hang in there. Help is coming. You'll be all right.

*(He holds YUMI's head in the exact same position that LAUREN wa*s.*)*

(Blackout)

END OF PLAY

BIG DICKS, ASIAN MEN

By SLANT

While lounging in a sauna with a case of beer and talking about
what the three of us had in common, we were conjuring up names for
our debut show. Thus, BIG DICKS, ASIAN MEN.

What you will read in our script is the SLANT genesis, the first of
five original theatrical and musical works in our repertory to
date-a tapestry of amplified and acoustic music, scene and monologue text, shadowplay, puppetry and choreography that currently
characterizes our performances. In BIG DICKS, ASIAN MEN we satirize
pop and media images of Asian masculinity, share experiences of our
American upbringing while paying homage to the guiding influences
of our Asian heritage.

A big thank you to Alvin Eng for including BIG DICKS, ASIAN MEN. This
is the first publication of our work.

Many, many thanks to our teachers, friends, girlfriends, wife,
brothers and sisters, and the thousands of fans and supporters
we've been blessed with thus far.

Special thanks to Ellen Stewart who gave SLANT a beginning and an
artistic home at La Mama Experimental Theater Club.

And eternal gratitude to our parents and ancestors who showed us
the way.

Peace,

Rick Ebihara, Wayland Quintero, Perry Yung - SLANT

B<small>IG</small> D<small>ICKS</small>, A<small>SIAN</small> M<small>EN</small> had its World Premiere at the La Mama E.T.C. First Floor Theatre, November 30-December 10, 1995.

Written and Performed by SLANT-Rick Ebihara, Wayland Quintero, Perry Yung

Lighting Design: Howard Thies
Police Dispatcher Voice-over: Sarah Boggan
Police Sergeant Voice-over: Christopher Gomez
Sumo Stablemaster Voice-over: Brian Nishii
Dr. U's Receptionist Voice-over: Erin McDonnell
Final End Dance Music Composer: Genji Ito

SLANT is a registered trademark.

BIG DICKS, ASIAN MEN

Vietnamese Muzak of American pop songs play as the audience enters and is seated. Gradually a sound loop of a cheering arena audience takes over as SLANT *plays its opening song. Quickly lights come up from behind the performers so that they appear as a shadow band behind a white screen that is hung downstage of them. The song is a short, lively, grungy rock tune.*

SLANT

(Intro)

S-L-A-N-T, S-L-A-N-T, S-L-A-N-T, S-L-A-N-T

We're not the waiters on TV
Not the model minority
No little dicks for you and me

We're BIG DICKS ASIAN MEN

S-L-A-N-T, S-L-A-N-T, S-L-A-N-T

Turn the channel and burn the paper
Television says I'm a masturbator
Television says I'm a masturbator

We're BIG DICKS ASIAN MEN

(Instrumental break)

We are the product of TV and cable
I have my eyes and penis labeled
Now it's time to turn the tables

We're BIG DICKS ASIAN MEN

S-L-A-N-T, S-L-A-N-T, S-L-A-N-T, SLANT!

(Right after the song ends there is a blackout as police sirens and flashing red lights come up. A female police dispatcher's announcement is heard:)

POLICE SERGEANT *(Voice-over)*: All units in the vicinity of Chinatown please respond. Suspect is a young oriental male dressed in dark clothing, last seen on Canal Street selling counterfeit Gucci purses. Repeat, suspect is young Oriental male dressed in dark clothing wanted for selling counterfeit Gucci purses. All units in the vicinity of Chinatown please respond.

(Lights come up as 3 Asian males enter and take their places in front of the white line-up screen.)

POLICE SERGEANT *(Voice-over)*: Well ma'am, take your time. Identifying a suspect in a line-up ain't easy. We'll get the guy that sold you that fake Gucci bag.

(As the line-up interrogation begins, we hear a short blast of loud feedback. This feedback repeats after each spoken line during the interrogation.)

SERGEANT *(Voice-over)*:   Suspect #2. Yes you in the middle. Step forward please. Turn to your right. Turn to your left. Please repeat after me—Gucci, Rolex, Obsession, check it out. Best deal, check it out.

SUSPECT #2 *(Perry)*:   Gucci, Rolex, Obsession, check it out. Best deal, check it out.

SERGEANT *(Voice-over)*:   Uh, try it again...this time as if you're in Chinatown.

SUSPECT #2:   Gucci, Rolex, Obsession, check it out. Best deal, check it out.

SERGEANT *(Voice-over)*   Suspect #2 please try it again as a Chinese person.

SUSPECT #1 *(Wayland)*:   Oh, hey, can I try? Gucci, Rolex, Obsession, check it out. Best deal, check it out. Heh heh! I do this all the time in auditions man. Check this out--If you can grab the pebbles from my hand you may leave the temple. The wind carries the lotus leaves across the ocean, the mountains, the deserts...*(He is interrupted by feedback.)*

SERGEANT *(Voice-over)*:   Thank you suspect #1. Step back in the line-up please! Suspect #2, where were you at approximately 2:45 PM yesterday?

SUSPECT #2:   Uh.. I was uh...well I went to the post office in the morning *(The other two actors exit.)* and checked my post office box. Then I went to have some coffee at the west side cafe over there on Chambers Street. Oh! 2:45 PM yesterday! I was rehearsing with my band Secret Asian Man. *(He reaches behind his back.)*

SERGEANT *(Voice-over)*:   FREEZE! DON'T TRY IT!

SUSPECT #2:   Hey, it's just my flute man. I was rehearsing with my band. We're working on a new song..."Buddha Blues."

*(He begins playing the flute as the screen rises to reveal a rehearsal space. The other two actors join in with elec-
tric guitar, drums and percussion. The tune develops into a catchy rendition of a Grunge-Bluesy Peking Opera
interpretation of "Heartbreak Hotel." After the song ends, the screen descends gradually as SUSPECT #2 walks
back downstage to the line-up finishing up his last flute melody. The other two actors join him in the line-up.)*

SERGEANT *(Voice-over)*:   Thank you suspect #2. Relax gentlemen. *(Pause)* Now can you all
motion or gesture like you're trying to get someone into a shop. *(Each suspect executes sales hustler gestures interrupted by the voice-over.)* Thank you gentlemen. Suspect #3 step up to the line please. Turn to
the right. Turn to the left. Now do what you were doing and at the same time repeat—Gucci, Rolex,
Obsession, check it out. Best deal, check it out.

SUSPECT #3 *(Rick with an English accent)*:   Gucci, Rolex, Obsession, check it out. Best deal, check
it out.

SERGEANT *(Voice-over)*:   Were you at Mulberry and Bayard at 2:45 PM yesterday?

SUSPECT #3:   Well, yes. I was.

SERGEANT *(Voice-over)*:   Is that the way you always talk?

SUSPECT #3:   The way I talk. Yeah. I've been talking like this since I was 12, when I
saw my first James Bond film *Goldfinger*. *(The other two actors exit quietly.)* It drove my folks crazy. Still
does. Yeah, but when I saw him, Bond, James Bond, I said to myself that's what I want to be. He
was so cool. He had all those great gadgets, all those great cars, that great charisma, making love to
all those great-looking women. Oh yeah, he had a real great...accent. Yea, I know, people tell me it's
strange, you know, me being Asian talking with an English accent. Yeah, but I mean, who wanted to
be Asian. What like Odd Job? Or Dr. No?! Hell no! I wanted to get laid. Now there was Bruce Lee.
He was cool. He had charisma, presence, all those great moves. But did he ever get laid? Did he ever
screw? No. Never screwed in any of his films. That's probably why Asians got labeled with that word
"in-screw-table." Yea, well I never got laid either even with this accent. I began thinking that maybe
it was hormonal, you know, like it was my Asian testosterone that wasn't attracting women to me.
God knows it was making me horny enough. But maybe it just wasn't sending off the right signals,
like it was somehow stopping my pheromones from being released. Well, they say that Asian men
don't smell, maybe that's why I wasn't getting laid. I didn't stink enough. But then along came
JASON SCOTT LEE. Oh yea, in *Map of the Human Heart* making mad passionate love on top of that
huge blimp. And in Dragon where we finally see Bruce Lee getting laid. And in *Jungle Book* being
raised by wild animals, running, sweating naked through the steamy jungle. You know he had to be
smelling pretty good then. Jason Scott Lee gave me confidence, passion, lust, masculinity, got my
testosterone boiling, released my pheromones! I'm Man! I'm Asian!!! Smell me!!! Now if I could only
get rid of this bloody accent.

SERGEANT *(Voice-over)*:   So you were at Mulberry and Bayard yesterday afternoon.

SUSPECT #3:   Oh yeah! Friday night, broccoli with garlic sauce and brown rice.

(SUSPECT #3 disappears behind the screen as the lights fade to black and the audience begins to hear little squeaky sounds, bells, horns and vocal noises in the dark. The screen rises as the lights come up revealing three Chinese food deliverymen on tricycles peddling around and chanting a guttural work rhythm. An a cappella song begins.)

NO MENUS PLEASE (THREE DELIVERY GUYS RIDING IN A CIRCLE ON TRICYCLES)

(Rick) Through crowds of people I ride my bike,
Thousands are eating Chinese tonight,
Free delivery is my life, Send my money back to my wife,
To feed my family went overseas,
Only to read no menus please,
(All) No menus, No menus please *(repeat)*

(Perry) My tuition's due I don't get a break,
How much can I save how long will it take,
Two dollar tips are all that I get, Midterms are soon have to study yet,
I'm failing intro to Cantonese,
Should have took French,
(All) No menus, No menus please *(repeat)*

(All Chant) Soy sauce, and hot sauce, and duck sauce, Hooh!
Lobster sauce, fish sauce, and garlic sauce, Hooh!
White sauce, and brown sauce, and red sauce, Hooh!
Don't matter what color as long as it's good!
Don't matter what color as long as it's good!

(Wayland) I can't stand this goddamn bike,
I'd rather be boning my girl tonight,
Dad says the restaurant needs family, But handing out menus is not for me,
It's for the family I shiver and freeze,
But inside I scream no menus please,
(All) No menus, No menus please *(Repeat)*

(Break—Choreographed cycling, collision and slow motion falls...They sing the final verse at a slower tempo, coming downstage looking disheveled and holding food delivery bags.)

(Rick) Through snow and rain and gloom of night
(Perry) We bring to you your chicken delite
(Wayland) Nothing is ever quite as it seems
(All) We litter your halls with our family dreams,
Delivery is our opportunity
But all that we see is No menus please
No menus, No menus please *(Repeat)*

(Scene ends with the three holding out their hands for tips. One by one each leaves the stage, leaving the bags downstage in three pools of light.)

THREE ANOREXIC SUMO WRESTLERS

After "No Menus Please," the actors enter the stage one by one stripped down to black mawashis (Japanese sumo wrestling "jockstraps"). They execute a brief choreographed unison movement that takes them to the delivery bags that were left downstage in the pools of light from the previous scene. They immediately attack the bags of food, and with loud chewing, slurping and burping sounds, they devour noodles, except for JACK-SAN who is not eating. The three begin their conversation while eating and proceed through their daily ritual of warming up, stretching and wrestling.

TOM *(Perry)*: Hey Jack-san, you better finish up. We only have five more minutes.

(JACK pulls out a cheese sandwich.)

HARRY *(Rick)*: Jack-san! You're not even half-way done. You know how important it is for us to eat. The Oyakata says if we don't put on some pounds he's going to drop us from the stable.

JACK *(Wayland)*: I'm just not hungry.

HARRY: Hungry!? Hungry has nothing to do with it. We need poundage man.

TOM: Jack-san we've all been eating like maniacs for months, you can't fall off your diet now. Hey, look at Harry-san, he's got a nice belly going there.

HARRY: You think so?

TOM: Oh yeah, you're getting a real nice shape.

HARRY: Hey thanks man, I've been meaning to tell you that your butt's getting big.

TOM: Thanks. I thought I was getting bigger, but it's so hard to tell back there.

HARRY: Jack-san, eat. Listen, if you go up against someone like Kitanoumi you're going to need something between you and his 360 pounds. It's not like we got driver-side airbags.

JACK: Linda left me.

TOM & HARRY: Holy shit. No way.

OYAKATA *(Stablemaster Japanese voice-over)*: Meals over! Begin the warm up!

(All three clean up their bags of food, HARRY exits with the bags.)

JACK: I should have seen it coming. I came home last night, all her things were gone, and she left a note on the kitchen table. She even made me meatloaf before she left.

TOM: Your last supper huh?

JACK: She made six.

HARRY: (Enters with a faux rubber sumo wig) See on the way out the door even she wants you to eat. Keikoda!

ALL: Keikoda!

(They get into their respective positions in a circle, warming up.)

JACK: She said she couldn't take it anymore. All the practice. All the traveling for tournaments. She said she needed some stability.

HARRY: I thought she liked the road. Didn't she follow the tour around before you started dating?

JACK: Yeah, but that was three years ago. She said her biological clock was ticking and that she needed to settle down.

HARRY & TOM: Aaaah...the clock.

JACK: Yeah the clock. I told her just wait, baby. Just wait until I get moved up to the next ranking. Then I'll be making more money, I'll be home more, and I won't have to tour these farm towns anymore, just the majors.

HARRY: Can't argue with the clock. There's no snooze button for the nesting alarm.

TOM: Sanban.

ALL: Sanban.

(They reposition themselves and begin a ritualistic tilting movement.)

TOM: That's why I date young, man. The younger you date, the more time you have for your clock to catch up with hers.

(They move in a circle.)

HARRY: Like Biological Savings Time.

TOM: Yeah! Men fall back, women spring forward. Besides, what a lot of women are looking for in relationships are their fathers anyway.

HARRY: Just like a lot of men are looking for their mothers.

JACK: Yeah! My mom makes one hell of a meatloaf!

TOM: Despite all this "Woman of the '90s" stuff, women are still looking for the perfect provider, the bringer of the proverbial pork strips.

HARRY: Goban! (*HARRY signals TOM & JACK to begin wrestling.*)

ALL: Goban!

(*TOM & JACK execute a brief choreographed wrestling routine that ends with a "patty-cake" hand routine and butt slap.*)

HARRY: Yeah but women always go for the loner, the rebel, the inaccessible, the James Dean.

JACK: The Brad Pitt.

TOM: Elvis!

ALL: AH! Elvis-san! Soh-des! Thank you ma'am, thank you very much, thank you ma'am....

(*JACK breaks into hip-swiveling rendition of "Hound Dog" as HARRY and TOM begin wrestling.*)

OYAKATA (*Stablemaster Japanese voice-over*): Jack-san! Bakayaro! What the hell are you doing? Get back to work! Give me 20 push-ups.

JACK: Hai sensei! (*Begins doing push-ups*) Uno, dos, tres...

OYAKATA (*Stablemaster Japanese voice-over*): Count in Japanese!

JACK: Hai sensei! Ichi, ni, san, shih, go.

TOM: Elvis was the shits man. He had it all.

(*TOM & HARRY continue to wrestle.*)

HARRY: Women, fame, he had America in the palm of his hand.

TOM: Charisma, sex appeal, music, the moves. He definitely had what women wanted.

JACK: Yeah. My mother was into Elvis.

TOM: Yeah? My mom too. I grew up listening to her old 45s. "Hound Dog."

HARRY: "Jailhouse Rock." Hikake!

ALL: Hikake!

(HARRY is flung down by TOM)

JACK: Yeah, but when it comes down to an actual relationship that's exactly what women
don't want. *(JACK & TOM collide & begin wrestling)* They want sensitivity, vulnerability, stability.

TOM: Elvis had that too. Remember "Love Me Tender," "Treat Me Nice," "Don't Be Cruel."
Now there's sensitive and vulnerable.

(JACK throws TOM down.)

HARRY: Now that's what women want. The right combination of the spicy, the wild, the passionate, but watered down with stable, sensitive and vulnerable.

JACK: Sounds like Linda's meatloaf recipe!

*(JACK breaks down sobbing uncontrollably like a big baby as HARRY & TOM look dumbfounded. Soon
HARRY and TOM go over to JACK.)*

HARRY: Hey! Hey! *(He grabs JACK.)*

JACK: What?!

HARRY: Would Elvis cry?

JACK: Nooooo...

HARRY: What would Elvis do?

JACK: I don't know.

TOM: He'd eat!

JACK: He'd eat?

HARRY: That's right! He'd eat! Burgers, fries!

ALL: Burgers, fries!

(By this time all three are massaging each other, JACK still kneeling on the floor, HARRY directly standing behind him kneading JACK's shoulders, Tom behind HARRY elbowing HARRYs shoulders.)

TOM: Elvis had it all!

ALL THREE: Soh-des!

OYAKATA *(Stablemaster Japanese voice-over)*: Warm-up is over. Hit the showers. *(They all respond with "Hai sensei!" bow and start to leave.)* Tom-san stay! Tom-san your butt's getting big.

TOM: Uh thanks sensei. I thought so but it's so hard to tell back there.

(End of scene. The screen slowly comes down.)

(TOM stays onstage and begins putting on clothes to transform into a tourist taking photos of the audience with a flash camera. He begins a monologue.)

THE TOURIST *(Perry)*:   I was in Venice, Italy this past summer with my lover. Venice is really beautiful. A city of canals, clean. I had to take a piss really bad and the thing about the Venice was that they had public urinals. There were "toilette" signs all over the place with arrows pointing to the nearest one. So we started following the signs but I really had to go. That's when I got homesick for New York City. Cuz if I was back home in the city I could just whip it out anywhere. We finally got to the toilet and Valentina paid our way in. Italian toilets are just like the ones in China. They don't waste any time sitting. They just squat, do the job, and split. So I'm finished and I'm outside leaning against a replica of Michealangelo's David when I noticed Valentina coming out. She looked a bit disturbed, actually, she was pissed. She came storming out and I chased after her. "Hey baby what's wrong? What's the matter?" She said, "Nothing, forget it!" I'm like come on what's wrong, what is it? It's nothing, forget it! Let it go! Let go of what? What's wrong? What is it? Then she slipped into her Italian mode."*Va bene va bene non valiente.*" Valentina's from the south of Italy. A real southern Italian woman and when she starts speaking Italian and says, "*Va bene va bene non valiente,*" I say forget what! So later on we were cruisin on a gondola through the canals. Vale's in my arms and she says, "*Senti...prima en el bagno...quando c'erano...quei ragazzi.*" Whoa Vale. You know my Italian's not that great. You know earlier at the toilette? Those guys taking the money, one of them said, "I wonder if she's fucking him?" And the other said, "What does it matter? You know Orientals can't fuck." Did they mean the women too? They used the masculine term UN-Orientale. They spoke in Sicilian dialect but I understood them quite clearly. "Aren't you angry?" she said. I said, "Vale, Americans talk about penis size all the time and how our sexuality is measured by the size of it. Black men have the biggest, Asian men have the smallest and everyone else is safely in between. Besides, how can I let a remark by a couple of Sicilian migrant workers taking money from peeing

Venice tourists bother me?" I told her of a saying I once heard from a wise old black man...Richard Pryor. He said, "Take a look at China. They've got 1.2 billion people. Someone over there is doing some serious fucking!"

(Blackout. Gradually the screen rises revealing a darkly-lit setting, we hear the sounds of drilling and hammering.)

Dr. Uehara's Waiting Room

Featuring a "non-traditional" casting:
THICK: A Texan
RODNEY: A recent Chinese immigrant
HOMEE: An African-American homeboy.

RODNEY is nervously pacing back and forth downstage as THICK is down and left of center in a chair facing diagonally up stage left. There is another chair up and right of center facing diagonally down stage right. The chairs are about 3-4 feet apart. Drill sounds continue for a few beats until lights come up.

THICK *(Wayland)*:   *(In a Texas drawl)* Been waitin long?

RODNEY *(Perry)*:   Huh?

THICK: I said have you been waitin long. Are you next?

RODNEY: *(In a Chinese accent)* I suppose to see the doctor at 3:00.

THICK: Listen, you mind if I see the doctor first?

RODNEY: You have appointment?

THICK: Nope, just droppin in.

RODNEY: Just dropping in? Sure, go ahead.

THICK: This your first time here, huh. My name's Johnny. But you can call me Thick.

RODNEY: My name is Wong. Wong Siu Long.

THICK: Shoe Who?

RODNEY: No, Wong Siu Long. I have an American name, Rodney. Yes, it's my first time.

(Drill sound/light flicks off and on and off and on- each time this happens RODNEY reacts jittery and jumpy.)

THICK: Boy, you're real nervous aren't you. Listen Rodney, the first time I came here I was real nervous too in fact worse than you. Yeah I understand cause it ain't like just gettin a nose job, your eyelids adjusted, or even gettin a breast enlargement. It's real serious reworkin' Willie!

RODNEY: (*Quickly sits in chair*) Willie? You been here before!

THICK: Yeah. I'm just here for a tune up.

(*Drill sound/lights flicker to go off.*)

RODNEY: Tune up? What you mean? Like car tune up...change the plugs, check the wires?

THICK: Yeah Rodney. 6 months or 600 fucks whichever comes first.

RODNEY: Aaahyaah. Unbelievable! You busier than Hong Kong stock exchange.

THICK: Yeah!

(*Tool sound/lights flicker on and off and on.*)

RODNEY: This doctor. Is he good?

THICK: Yup. Best in the business. He even worked on Schwarzenegger.

RODNEY: Arnold? Really? You mean *Kindergarten Cop*?

THICK: Yes sir. But you know all them steroids he took back when he was body-buildin really messed him up. Made him even smaller than us. Size of an espresso bean. Doctor's got photographs before and after. Picture this. You got his wife Maria smilin real big next to her new Arnold proudly holdin him up like a firehose. According to Doc, Maria wouldn't marry the man unless he did one of two things. Get an enlargement or become a liberal democrat.

RODNEY: Tough choice.

(*Tool sounds/lights flicker.*)

THICK: Rodney, Rodney don't worry there boy. You're in good hands.

RODNEY: I just want to be sure. I work real hard save my money for something special like today. Thick, all my friends tell me American girls, they like...ahh... (*Motioning to THICKs crotch*)

THICK: Big dick?

RODNEY: Yes yes. BEEG DEEK! In Chinese we say "Dai Lop Churng." You have girlfriend?

THICK: Yup.

RODNEY: American?

THICK: Yes sir. African-American.

RODNEY: She's Brack!? *(Breaks into Chinese—That's unbelievable!)* You brave! I wish I have American girlfriend, blonde goddess like Sharon Stone or nice Jewish girl with big mouth and sexy lips like Barbra Streisand. I tired of Chinese girls. Too traditional, old country, *(Pause)* except the ones from Brooklyn. I never been with brack woman.

THICK: Hey most of us haven't. It's a rare sight you know? Us guys with a black woman.

RODNEY: Yes, yes but maybe after my operation then I can get American girlfriend too!

THICK: You will buddy. Soon as Dr. U. works on you, you're going to have one big...hey boy, how is it you say big dick in Chinese again?

RODNEY: Dai Lop Churng.

THICK: Dai Lop Churng! With your new Dai Lop Churng you'll be fighting off truckloads of women.

RODNEY: Beeg Deek.

THICK: Dai Lop Churng.

RODNEY: Beeg Deek

THICK: | Dai Lop Churng.

RODNEY & THICK: *(They get out of their chairs, move downstage and chant together:)* Big Dick, Dai Lop Churng, Big Dick, Dai Lop Churng *(Repeat as necessary)*

(HOMEE enters carrying a boom box, picks up the chant and continues until he has been chanting at least four times alone. By now the lights have come up even more brightly.)

HOMEE: *(In a thick African-American street accent)* Hey, dis must be the right place. Dat was fun. Why'd ya all stop?

THICK: *(Laughing at HOMEE)*

HOMEE: The name is Wong, HomerWong, but you can call me Homee.

THICK: *(Still laughing)* Homee?

RODNEY: (As THICK laughs) Homer Wong...hmmm.

HOMEE: What's so funny? You laughing at me, man?

THICK: Hey alright, alright boy! Do you have an appointment?

HOMEE: Yeah, I got an appointment! I'm a little late, but I got an appointment.

THICK: Hooowee! Irritable lil "homeboy" aren't you?

HOMEE: Dat's right Jethro.

RODNEY: (Breaking right in) Homer Wong. You the son of Ming-Wa Wong?

HOMEE: No. But I have an aunt named Ming-Wa Wong live ovah deah on Mulberry Shtreet.

RODNEY: Aayaah. This is unbelievable day. Must be destiny again. My name is Wong Siu Long. Rodney! Ming-Wa Wong is my auntie too!

HOMEE: No shit?! Oh you must be the guy dey told me about, some guy come ovah from Guangzhou owns a big Chinese restaurant. Dat's you?

RODNEY: Yeah! You must be my second cousin on auntie's side.

HOMEE: Oh no man. Actually her husband Jo-Long is my mother's older brother.

RODNEY: So then you not directly my second cousin from Ming-Wa. You my cousin still, though, from Jo-Long, brother of your mother, what her name?

HOMEE: Stephanie. Her Chinese name is Shu-Fen.

RODNEY: Ooooh. So your mother Shu-Fen...American name Stephanie, is younger sister of Jo-Long married to my auntie Ming-Wa, who is younger sister to my mother Cheng-Yu, wife of my father Hop Jai Wong.

HOMEE: Yeah, yeah I guess dat's right. I don't know all of dat, but yeah...

RODNEY: So, Homee, your English is so good. What you do? Are you a waiter?

HOMEE: No man. I do a lot of things. In fact I just came from helpin out some kids at the Police Activities League, kind of like the Big Brothers, Big Sisters Program only we call it the Big Homees, Little Homees Project for Disadvantaged Youth.

THICK: Volunteer work, huh? That's quite commendable! But uh, Homee, what is it you do
for work?

HOMEE: You wanna know how I make my cash? Yo it's really none of your business! You probably think I deal drugs, rip people off or some shit like that, huh?

THICK: Well do you?

HOMEE: Fuck you. I'm a rap artiste!

RODNEY: Really! Sing something for me cousin.

HOMEE: Cuz, you gotta be shitting me? In this dress and cap?

RODNEY: I would be honored. I love the rap music, the urban feeling, so simple and strong like
Cantonese opera. Make me feel, how you say, "like one bad motherfucka." Give it up Cousin Homee.

HOMEE: Alright, alright, alright. Let me see. Oh I got an idea! Hey Rodney, check dis
out.*(Begin a vocal rhythm for a little while.)* Now keep this rhythm. Yeah dat's it. Here we go, but you
gotta be ready for your turn alright? Yeah, dat's it. And keep that arm going like dat. Yeah, dat's
good. Alright, here we go. *(Return to rhythm and then begin Rap)* Your mother Cheng Yu, wife of Hop
Jai Wong, sister of Ming Wa, wife of Jo Long, whose sister is my mother, Shu Fen, Stephaneeeeee,
married to my father Frankie Wong, pick it up hey hey...

RODNEY: Hey, hey. My auntie Ming Wa, married to Jo Long, brother of Shu Fen, mother of my
cousin, Homee, Homee, Homee, her name Stephanee...

HOMEE: Ming Wa your auntie too, sister of Cheng Yu, wife of Hop Jai Wong, we the family
Wong, bro we can't go wrong, *(RODNEY joins in and they keep rapping "we the family Wong, bro we can't
go wrong" until THICK breaks in.)*...

THICK: Hey, hey, hey! Quit y'all. That rap music shit drives me crazy!

HOMEE: Chill man. You interruptin us. I don't always get to rap wit a real live fresh off the
boat Chinaman. And rap music ain't shit. It's urban poetry, Jethro.

THICK: Urban poetry? That's bullshit! And by the way there boy, my name is not Jethro. You
call me sir, alright?

HOMEE: Scuse me? You got some fuckin attitude Mr. Tootie-Fruttie. The only bullshit around
here is the crap comin out your mouth.

THICK: You're a real insultin' bitch aren't you, you pathetic piece of street shit. *(THICK &*

HOMEE start circling as they trade verbal punches.)

HOMEE: Weak! Weak! Dat's the best you can do? Hit me again hillbilly boy.

THICK: I don't hit anybody in a dress!

HOMEE: Shit, what's that you wearin?! At least mine matches my cap!

RODNEY: Wait! Everybody relax! Chill! We all here for same pathetic reason!

HOMEE: Rodney, I ain't takin take no shit from this banana ass whitey wanna be.

THICK: You watch your pussy mouth there, homeboy wannabe.

HOMEE: Oh yeah? You wouldn't know a pussy from a fuckin bear rug.

THICK: I know you get no pussy with that little bitty tinkle of yours and you talk like you got a fuckin egg roll up your skinny ass.

HOMEE: So show me what you can do you thick, cock-sucking motherfuckin mama's boy.

THICK: Alright boy. Let's go!

(THICK & HOMEE charge at each other as RODNEY is in the middle and pushes them apart.)

RODNEY: Wait, wait! Stop! I don't understand! *(Breaks into Chinese—Can't we just get along!)* We all Asian! We all brothers! We all Small!

(Sexy female receptionist's voice-over breaks in—"NEXT!")

THICK & HOMEE: You're up Rodney.

RODNEY: Thick, Thick you want to go first?

THICK: You go on right ahead, Rodney. It's your day, boy!

RODNEY: Homee, you want to go first?

HOMEE: Sure! *(Begins to walk off and then turns around)* Hey Rodney, you really nervous about this huh? Hey cuz what if we go in together at the same time?

THICK: Homee, that is a brilliant idea. Make it a family affair! After all—*(Begins rapping)* You the family Wong, boys you can't go wrong, you wanna bigger dong, you want it one foot long, your mama's in the john...

(*RODNEY & HOMEE cut THICK off*).

RODNEY: OK,OK, OK. Thick, Can Dr. U. work on both of us at the same time?

THICK: Yeah Rodney. Like I said he is the best in the business with his special procedure, he's got these big delicate hands to work with, plus he's got this dynamite looking ex-Dallas Cowboy cheerleader blonde assistant named Ingrid.

RODNEY & HOMEE: Let's go bro!

(*RODNEY & HOMEE run off excitedly. THICK pushes play button on the boom box and begins guitar-accompanied monologue.*)

THICK:
There was time when I was like those guys
Couldn't score with the ladies no matter how hard I tried
Then I thought I'd score better if I was different than
Your stereo-typical Asian American man...

I started making up stories, fantastical lies
About my background, my family, that I bungy jump and fly
But the ladies were unimpressed with my overzealous tries
Until desperately I boasted of my larger than average size

Then this long-legged lady at the end of the bar
Started slowly walking, down my way
I froze in my aroused fascination
As she whispered in my ear "Give me a first-hand examination"
And if what you say is true I'll take you up to my room
And make all of your wildest fantasies true too...

I backed down humiliated
I ran out of the bar extremely deflated
Down the street and onto the train
I wallowed in my self pitied pain...

Then I looked up and I saw a sign
Right next to the anal-wart 800 hot-line
All the answers to my problems my head raced as I read
All my hopes, all my dreams
And this is what it said...

(The Dr. U prelude is followed by the Dr. U. theme, sung and danced by all three characters accompanied by the tape player on stage. They enter the stage with phallus props strapped on.)

(Chorus)
Dr. U can do it for you
Dr. U can do it for you
He can make a tree out of a your stick
Dr. Yuhara's penis enlargement clinic.

You say you've got a little problem man
You want a bigger hot dog stand
Dr. U has got the foot-long bun to make you number one

(Repeat chorus)

(The song cycles as each actor comes downstage to do bits of an infomercial.)

INFOMERCIAL SPOKESMAN 1: Are you a man with a small penis? Or perhaps you know some-one. Well, your worries are over. Dr. Uehara has developed his exclusive PEEP system—the Penis Enlargement Effusion Procedure. These men have had their penises enlarged through PEEP and as a result they look and feel much younger.

HOMEE: Before I had the procedure, I used to wait until the gym shower was empty before I went in. Now I go straight in for a shower right after my workout. No more snickers and I can hang out with the brothers.

INFOMERCIAL SPOKESMAN 2: PEEP or the Penis Enlargement Effusion Procedure is a patented system that is completely safe and natural. It is a non-surgical, in-office procedure that will have you back at work the same day.

RODNEY: After I had PEEP my friends came up to me and asked, "Have you been on vacation? You look great!"

INFOMERCIAL SPOKESMAN 3: Once you've had the PEEP procedure there's no lengthy follow up visits. Just drop in for a tune-up and vitamins when you need to. The time varies depending upon individual usage.

THICK: Having PEEP done gave me back my self-esteem. Now my social life is all booked up. Bar-hopping with Reba on Wednesday, mud wrestling with Dolly on Thursday, and off to the ballet this weekend with Sarah!

(All three continue to sing and dance a ballet variation as the Dr. U song keeps playing, and they end with a big bang, pulling and detonating the party popper streamers from their phallus props.)
(Quick fadeout)
(The shadow screen drops down. Two actors stand behind, back-lit, with profiles of their shadows and phalluses still strapped on. They wave at each other and begin to attempt to shake hands in silence. Their big dicks get in the way. A little game of whose phallus is bigger begins as each takes turns stepping upstage to the back light to increase the size of the shadow phallus. The third actor returns with an object in hand that looks like a bigger phallus as the other two begin moving back downstage toward the screen shaking in fear. They all stop in back of the screen motionless.)

(The police sergeant's voice-over returns.)

SERGEANT *(Voice-over)*:   Well ma'am. I know it could be any one of them. Ah what the hell, book 'em!

(Original composed music begins as the third actor in the center turns on a chainsaw and begins to execute a cutting pattern with the chainsaw, and castrates each of the other two shadow phalluses.)
(Fade out lights)

(This is the beginning of a dance/partnering piece, with the actors' pants down around their ankles. It is a dance that is extremely physical, supported by driving percussive music interspersed with strains of Asian instruments and voices. At the end of the dance all three run downstage and stop, as the screen drops down quickly behind them.) (Blackout)

(Lights up for a bow.)

(As the audience applauds SLANT quickly sets up their musical instruments and perform "Secret Asian Man.")

END OF PLAY

The Last Hand Laundry in Chinatown

By Alvin Eng

"You used to have to buy-in, to be an American.
Now you've got to sell-out, to really get some clout."

Just as "What are we fighting for?" was the battle cry for social
change and awareness in the 1960s and '70s, in the down-sizing
'90s, that cry became "What are we working for?" Under the dark
shadow of the corporate cleansing of America (cum the world), where
the eventual outcome seems to be only one big (brother of a) controlling corporation, almost every working person finds it difficult to build up any personal or professional equity and security.
In fact, most find themselves getting ousted from the very institutions to which they have dedicated themselves and built-up.

It is this ghostly landscape, in which America knows what it is
not, but is not exactly sure of-or afraid to admit-what it has
become, in which THE LAST HAND LAUNDRY IN CHINATOWN (A REQUIEM FOR AMERICAN
INDEPENDENTS) is set. Utilizing contemporary "vaudevillian rock &
roll" songs within a traditional musical narrative structure, the
piece focuses on the spiritual, financial and ethical effects of
gentrification on a second generation Chinese American family in
New York City's Chinatown-where ancient, supernatural Chinese spirits have a head-on collision with modern, gritty urban realities.
Within this framework, the musical also explores the legacy of the
pioneering hand laundrymen and women of Chinese America-of which my
parents were two.

ALVIN ENG

Concept, Book & Lyrics by Alvin Eng
Music by John Dunbar

THE LAST HAND LAUNDRY IN CHINATOWN was presented at La MaMa, E.T.C., May 9 - 18, 1996, with the following cast, crew and band

Cast *(In order of appearance):*
BO-GEE: Ming Lee
MARTHA/GHOST: Elizabeth Speck
GEORGE/GHOST: Gabriel Hernandez
JOSIE: Emy Baysic
DYLAN: Rick Ebihara
JUNE: Lori Tan Chinn
CRAZY TOM: Jojo Gonzalez

Director: Bevya Rosten
Musical Director: Miriam Daly
Stage Manager: Alexandra Lopez
Lighting Design: Howard Thies
Costume Design: Linda Keller
Set Design: Joey G. Mendoza
Mask Design: Madeline Slovenz-Low

Piano: Miriam Daly
Guitar/melodica: John Dunbar
Percussion: David Martinez

THE LAST HAND LAUNDRY IN CHINATOWN was first developed in the NYU/Tisch School of the Arts' Graduate Musical Theatre Writing Program.

Dedicated to the spirit of the Chinese Hand Laundry Alliance

Setting: Chinatown, NYC, mid-1990s

Characters
(all characters are Asian American)

DYLAN TOM, Male, mid-30s,

JUNE TOM, Dylan's mom, late 50s.

"CRAZY TOM" (everyone just calls him Tom), Dylan's father, early 60s

BO-GEE (means "newspaper" in Chinese), Late 50s, physically challenged newsstand owner and operator, Dylan's Uncle.

JOSIE TOM, Early-30s. Dylan's sister.

MARTHA & GEORGE / GHOSTS, Singing tourist couple, mid-40s, who also double as Crazy Tom's ghost friends.

Songs

Prologue

      "Ballad Of Chinatown" - BO-GEE

Act I

      Opening Medley: "Chinatown Suite (& Sour)" - TOURISTS & CAST
      "Home Is Where It's Harshest" - DYLAN
      "Ballad Of Chinatown" (Reprise) - BO-GEE
      "I Tried" - JUNE
      "Not For Sale" - CRAZY TOM, DYLAN
      "Family" - BO-GEE, DYLAN
      "Happy Birthday Lily" - BO-GEE
      "Ballad Of Chinatown" (Reprise) - BO-GEE
      "Stand Your Ground" - JOSIE, DYLAN
      "Something For Me" - JUNE, CRAZY TOM
      "Home" - CRAZY TOM

Entr'Acte

      "Ballad Of Chinatown" *(Reprise)* - BO-GEE

Act II

"Things You Can't Forget" - CRAZY TOM, BO-GEE
"Like A Couple In A Great Old Movie" - JUNE, JOSIE
"The Last Hand Laundry In Chinatown" - CRAZY TOM, GHOSTS, DYLAN
"Lament" - CRAZY TOM
"Home" *(Reprise)* - CRAZY TOM, GHOSTS
"Where Is Home?" - JUNE
"Proclamation" - DYLAN, JUNE, JOSIE, BO-GEE

Epilogue

"Ballad Of Chinatown" *(Reprise)*

THE LAST HAND LAUNDRY IN CHINATOWN

(A REQUIEM FOR AMERICAN INDEPENDENTS)

PROLOGUE

Lights up on a rectangular newsstand on a Chinatown street. It is dawn and the street is empty save for a few bundles of newspapers. The newsstand's "window" opens and from inside, BO-GEE sings while opening up for business. As he sets up shop, he emerges from the newsstand in a wheelchair.

"BALLAD OF CHINATOWN"

BO-GEE: THE MORE WE TRY TO STAY THE SAME
              THE MORE WE HAVE TO CHANGE
              JUST LOOK AROUND OLD CHINATOWN
              AND TELL ME WE'RE THE SAME
              AND TELL ME WE'RE THE SAME

("Ballad" music continues as BO-GEE speaks:) This used to be a place called Chinatown. It was a small village of...convenience, shall we say. It was located near the southernmost tip of Manhattan, on the northeastern shore of America. The rest of the country used to think of Chinatown as exotic. But those of us who lived here knew otherwise. Our ancestors were barred from returning to our old homeland of China, yet never fully accepted here. So for them, while Chinatown wasn't quite home, it was the only place they had. So they made the best of it and prospered in spite of their outsider status. Many children were raised, and we got over our need to be accepted here...until recently.

(Lighting change—end of prologue)

ACT I - SCENE 1

"Tourists Music" starts. It is now mid-morning. MARTHA and GEORGE, two tourists enter. They clutch NYC tour guide books.

"CHINATOWN SUITE (AND SOUR)"

MARTHA: WELL IT LOOKS LIKE WE'VE FOUND CHINATOWN
        BOY, THAT CABBY TOOK A REALLY STRANGE ROUTE

GEORGE: LET'S GO AND FIND THAT FAMOUS HOLE IN THE GROUND

MARTHA & GEORGE:
        HERE IN CHINATOWN
        HERE IN CHINATOWN

("Tourists Music" continues as underscore.)

MARTHA: Excuse me, do you speak English?

BO-GEE: Only during business hours.

GEORGE: Sorry, we didn't mean to insult you, but we're just lost.

BO-GEE: I'll say.

MARTHA: Yes, this map is a little confusing... Can you tell us how to find Wo-Hop?

BO-GEE: Wo-Hop? You sure you don't mean the new IHOP?

MARTHA: You have an IHOP down here?

BO-GEE: Well, doesn't IHOP stand for International House of Pancakes?

MARTHA: I guess so, but we have one of them at home, and frankly we came down here to see just how different Chinatown really is.

GEORGE: Plus we've heard nothing but good things about that place. Like this book says, "For a great, cheap meal, you've got to check out that exquisite hole in the ground, Wo-Hop."

(JOSIE enters. Underscore changes to "Stand Your Ground.")

JOSIE: Hurry up, Bo-Gee I'm late!

BO-GEE: Sorry Josie, *The Wall Street Journal* is sold out this morning.

JOSIE: Typical. I'll just have to get one uptown. It's amazing how any business is conducted at all in Chinatown.

(Underscore returns to "Tourists Music.")

MARTHA: THE TRAVEL AGENT KEPT ASSURING US
          THAT CHINATOWN IS STILL A CURIOUS PLACE

GEORGE: MAYBE IT USED TO BE EXOTIC DOWN HERE
          BUT CHINATOWN HAS CHANGED
          CHINATOWN HAS CHANGED

(DYLAN enters. He sports "Hollywood sunglasses" and carries several suitcases. Underscore changes to "Home Is Where It's Harshest.")

DYLAN: Uncle Bo-Gee?

BO-GEE: Dylan!

DYLAN: It's been too long!

BO-GEE: Too long indeed... Hey, nice shades!

JOSIE: Why is it really my big brother, "Hollywood Dylan Tom?"

DYLAN: Why it's the outlaw Josie Tom! How the hell have you been?

BO-GEE: *(To tourists)* Then I hope you enjoy your visit, because Chinatown is really different now—

JOSIE: No, no, no! Chinatown is the same as where you come from, right Bo-Gee?

BO-GEE: Uh, right Josie.

(Underscore returns to "Tourists Music.")

JOSIE: PAY NO ATTENTION TO WHAT YOU'RE SEEING NOW
           THIS TIME NEXT YEAR THERE'LL BE A NEW CHINATOWN
           NO LONGER ROWS AND ROWS OF UGLY OLD STORES
           WE'LL HAVE BRAND NEW MALLS

(JOSIE shmoozes with MARTHA and GEORGE.)

JOSIE: Hi, I'm Josie Tom from the Chinatown Office of Development, C.O.D. for short. And if there's anything we can do to make your visit better just let us know. Here's my business card and our office is right here.

(Lights up on the Chinatown Office of Development, one floor above The People's Laundry. The "C.O.D." sign should overwhelm the Laundry's sign.)

JOSIE: When you come to Chinatown, no matter where you're from, we want you to feel at home. I wish I could show you around personally today, but I've got to run. But I'm sure Bo-Gee will show you all of the new things Chinatown has to offer. Have a wonderful visit!

MARTHA & GEORGE: Thank you.

(Tourists exit.)

JOSIE: Here, Dylan, you get a card too.

DYLAN: Give em hell, Josie!

JOSIE: Bo-Gee, have you given some thought to what me and Mom spoke to you about?

BO-GEE: Can't say I have.

JOSIE: Just remember, money isn't the only thing that's numbered around here. Well, Dylan, I've got to go to work now.

DYLAN: I thought we were in your office already.

JOSIE: Very funny, no wonder you never get any on-screen credit for your writing.

DYLAN: Low blow. But at least they pay me out there, not like the New York theatre world.

JOSIE: But seriously, are you free later? Maybe we can have a drink and catch up?

DYLAN: Well, don't we have that family dinner thing tonight?

JOSIE: Well, how about before that? I'd really like to talk a bit before we sit down with Mom
and Dad.

DYLAN: And I'd really like to drink a bit before we sit down with them.

JOSIE: Great! Then why don't we meet at about 6:30 at Golden Palace?

DYLAN: Wow, that would be just like the old days.

JOSIE: Only this time, the drinks are on you, Mr. Hollywood.

(Underscore changes back to "Ballad Of Chinatown." DYLAN and JOSIE freeze, BO-GEE sings:)

BO-GEE: PEOPLE ALWAYS COME AND GO
            WHAT DO THEY HOPE TO FIND?
            ALTHOUGH WE LEAVE WE STILL MAY SEEK
            THE THINGS WE LEFT BEHIND
            THE THINGS WE LEFT BEHIND

(Underscore returns to "Tourists Music." JOSIE starts to exit.)

JOSIE: Save me a *Wall Street Journal* tomorrow!

(JOSIE exits.)

BO-GEE: So, I hear you're a Hollywood big shot now?

DYLAN: Yeah, if you can call selling one script—after seven years—that they immediately take your name off of and have someone else mutilate then yeah. But I'm getting divorced now, so maybe I'll finally fit in with Hollywood...

BO-GEE: I was very sorry to hear about that.

DYLAN: Thanks, but I think it's ultimately for the best.

BO-GEE: I hope so...So are you back here on business?

DYLAN: Yes, I'm back here to deal with the meanest, dirtiest, least-fulfilling business of all.

BO-GEE: Are you going to work for the Mayor?

DYLAN: No, nothing like that. I'm back here to deal with unfinished family business. Besides, I'm overdue for a visit...and, well, you know my mom. It seems like she writes me every month... and calls me every week!

(Underscore changes to "June's Music." Light comes up on JUNE, who is writing a letter. BO-GEE & DYLAN continue to speak.)

DYLAN: How's my Dad doing?

BO-GEE: Maybe it's best if you just see him yourself.

(A light comes up on CRAZY TOM, who sits near a wall of laundry. He seems to be counting them and talking to himself. Their singing overlaps.)

JUNE: EVERY DAY AND EVERY NIGHT
          HE SITS ALONE IN THE BASEMENT

CRAZY TOM:
          YIT, NGEE, SLOM SLEE *(1,2,3, 4 in Chinese)*
          PRETTY SOON, WE WILL BE FREE

JUNE: DOING GOD ONLY KNOWS WHAT

CRAZY TOM:
          YIT, NGEE, SLOM SLEE *(1,2,3, 4 in Chinese)*
          PRETTY SOON, WE WILL BE FREE

JUNE: I SIT UPSTAIRS WONDERING
          HOW THESE THINGS JUST FELL APART
          WHEN YOU WERE HERE
          THINGS ADDED UP

CRAZY TOM:
          YIT, NGEE, SLOM SLEE *(1,2,3, 4 in Chinese)*
          PRETTY SOON, WE WILL BE FREE

JUNE: NOW WITHOUT YOU
          THINGS SEEM WASHED UP
          I KNOW IT'S NOT YOUR BURDEN
          BUT CAN YOU PLEASE COME HOME?

DYLAN: So I know that taking care of this unfinished family business won't be sweet. But hopefully, it will be as short as possible.

(Blackout on JUNE and CRAZY TOM. Underscore returns to "Tourists Music." GEORGE & MARTHA enter.)

MARTHA: Excuse us again, uh...Mr. Budgie, is it?

BO-GEE: No, Bo-Gee. It means newspaper in Chinese.

GEORGE: Funny, we're Martha and George Carpenter, and my great granddaddy was a—

GEORGE & BO-GEE: Carpenter.

GEORGE: Isn't that something? I bet in all cultures, people's names are always derived from their trades.

MARTHA: George please! I'm sure he's not interested and neither am I.

GEORGE: Oh pardon us, sir, but are you from out of town also?

DYLAN: No, do I look it?

MARTHA: Not really...

DYLAN: Then what? Do I smell like I'm from out of town?

GEORGE: Nothing of the sort. We just saw your suitcases and all.

DYLAN: Well I live in L.A. now, but I grew up around here.

MARTHA: So this is home?

DYLAN: Right over there.

(Lights up on "The People's Laundry" exterior.)

GEORGE: You mean that little building that says "The People's Laundry?"

DYLAN: Yes, I'm afraid I come from a long line of stereotypes.

GEORGE: You know, I think I read something about The People's Laundry in one of the guide books and I thought that it was a museum about communism or something.

MARTHA: George, don't let everyone know we're from Columbus, Ohio.

GEORGE: Martha!

MARTHA: I'm sorry, but we just thought those things didn't exist anymore.

BO-GEE: Well, you're both sort of right. Years ago, laundry owners were the backbone of our community, and The People's Laundry was like Town Hall. But not anymore.

(Underscore changes to "Ballad of Chinatown." All freeze except for BO-GEE, who sings:)

BO-GEE: THIS LAUNDRY WAS A SOURCE OF PRIDE
NOW IT'S FALLEN OUT OF GRACE
NOW IT'S A FAMILY DIVIDE
AND WHAT WILL TAKE ITS PLACE?
AND WHAT WILL TAKE ITS PLACE?

BO-GEE: Yes, they don't make them like The People's Laundry anymore.

(Underscore returns to "Tourists Music.")

MARTHA: Well, as I was saying, Ball-Gee. That "People's Laundry" building over there looks kind of quaint.

DYLAN: Quaint? Yeah, come on into the kitchen, I'll introduce you to my uncle, Hop-Sing, you'll remember him, he used to be the cook on *Bonanza*, and—

(Underscore changes to "Home Is Where It's Harshest.")

MARTHA: All right! Perhaps quaint wasn't the right word, but I meant that as a compliment.

GEORGE: Oh let's go Martha he's just like our kids, no respect for his elders.

DYLAN: Yeah, run along Martha and enjoy your visit now.

GEORGE: Thanks, we will.

MARTHA: You try to enjoy your visit home, too.

(MARTHA and GEORGE exit. DYLAN sings:)

"HOME IS WHERE IT'S HARSHEST"

DYLAN: Home...Home... We'll see about that.
(Sings)

I'M HOME...I'M HOME
I'M HOME...IN THEORY
AND WITH THEORY, ONE MUST ALWAYS BE
A LITTLE LEERY
LEERY OF THE FAILURE RATE LEERY OF THE PLANS YOU MADE
BUT MOSTLY LEERY
OF WHAT THE "EXPERTS" SAY

LIKE THEY SAY: "HOME; IS WHERE THE HEART IS"
BUT I SAY; "HOME; IS WHERE IT'S HARSHEST"

AT HOME; THERE'S NOWHERE TO HIDE
THEY KNOW ALL YOUR SECRETS AND THEY'RE HIP TO YOUR JIVE
YOU CAN'T PRETEND YOU'RE SOMEONE YOU'RE NOT
AND YOU HAVE TO CONTEND WITH THINGS
YOU WISH YOU FORGOT

SO IS HOME; REALLY WHERE THE HEART IS?
NO NO NO; "HOME; IS WHERE IT'S HARSHEST"

AND THERE'S OUR LAUNDRY
"THE PEOPLE'S LAUNDRY"
IT MAY BE THE PRIDE OF THE NEIGHBORHOOD
BUT TO ME, IT WILL ALWAYS BE
THE NEMESIS OF MY CHILDHOOD

STARCH THAT COLLAR
SCRUB THAT CUFF
IRON THOSE SLACKS
THEN WRAP 'EM ALL UP

PHONE CALL FOR ME?
NO I CAN'T GO TO THE MOVIES
I GOTTA WORK IN THE LAUNDRY
NO I CAN'T TRY OUT FOR THE FOOTBALL TEAM
I GOTTA WORK IN THE LAUNDRY
NO I CAN'T HAVE ANY DREAMS
I GOTTA WORK IN THE LAUNDRY

IF THIS SOUNDS LIKE A BAD B-MOVIE
BELIEVE ME, IT IS
SO WHY AM I IN THIS SEQUEL?
IT'S ALL PART OF MY MOTHER'S GUILT TRIPS;
AND BELIEVE ME, HER GUILT HAS NO EQUAL
HER GUILT TRIPS ALWAYS DO THE TRICK
AND WE'RE NOT EVEN JEWISH OR CATHOLIC!

MONEY MAY MAKE THE WORLD GO ROUND
AND LOVE MAY BE ALL YOU NEED
BUT GUILT IS THE TIE THAT BINDS
AND GUILT RULES MY FAMILY AND ME

LIKE I SAY; "HOME IS WHERE IT'S HARSHEST"
YES I SAY; "HOME IS WHERE IT'S HARSHEST"

(DYLAN sees his mother, JUNE, coming out of the laundry.)

THOUGH THAT STILL MAY BE
WHERE THE HEART IS

(Song ends. JUNE and DYLAN embrace.)

DYLAN: See you later, Bo-Gee.

(DYLAN and JUNE exit into the laundry. BO-GEE sings:)

"BALLAD OF CHINATOWN (Reprise)"

BO-GEE: DYLAN'S HOME SO NOW HE'LL SEE
THE WORLD HE LEFT BEHIND
READY OR NOT, IT'S HERE HE'LL MEET
THE FATE HE IS TO FIND
THE FATE HE IS TO FIND

(Blackout)

ACT I - SCENE 2

JUNE and DYLAN in "The People's Laundry."

JUNE: Dylan, you must be hungry.

DYLAN: No, I'm OK mom.

JUNE: Why don't you help yourself to some of those bows and don-tot on the table, while I wrap up these few packages, and we can keep talking.

DYLAN: Mom, I'm not hungry but why don't you let me help you while we talk?

JUNE: Oh, don't worry. I just do these three or four packages and that's it for the day.

DYLAN: That's it?

JUNE: That's it.

DYLAN: How long has business been this bad?

JUNE: A few years now. But Josie is doing some great work with the Chinatown Office of...Commerce, I think?

DYLAN: Development—C.O.D. I saw her in action this morning. She should run for Mayor.

JUNE: Yes, Josie is doing fine...and she can help us do fine.

DYLAN: Mom, look I have no time to play Truth or Dare; What's going on?

JUNE: Look, I keep telling your father we should get out.

DYLAN: Mom, you've been saying that since I was in grade school

JUNE: This time is different!

DYLAN: How?

JUNE: Well you know we never had much money, but now we owe a lot of money...And your father refuses to pay the rent.

DYLAN: So how do you stay here?

JUNE: Somehow, Josie, through her job, has been able to work out an extension.

DYLAN: Extension?

JUNE: The landlord wants to build a new mall here and a few years ago, he offered us a relocation fee that was enough for a down payment on a small house...but your Dad always refuses. But that was before Josie came back. So now we're going to try and strike that deal again. But just in case, I was wondering if you could...

DYLAN: Give you some money, sure, but I could've easily done that from California.

JUNE: Dylan, this time I need more than your money; I need your support.

DYLAN: My support? When Dad practically disowned me when I left, where were you?

JUNE: Dylan...

DYLAN: You didn't face up to him then, just like you won't face up to him now! I know Dad has done a lot of damage; But you've always let him have his way!

JUNE: Dylan, don't.

(JUNE gets upset. DYLAN comforts her.)

DYLAN: Oh Mom, I'm sorry.

          I TRIED

JUNE: OH LIVING'S TOUGH WHEN THERE'S NOT ENOUGH
          AND WORSE WHEN THAT LITTLE BIT IS GONE
          THAT'S THE WAY WE'VE ALWAYS LIVED
          I'M SURE YOU REMEMBER, MY SON

          THIS TAKES IT'S TOLL ON YOUR HEART AND SOUL
          YOU START TO DREAD EVERY COMING DAY
          I KNOW IN YOUR HEART THERE'S A HOLE
          THAT COMES FROM LIVING THIS WAY

          BUT SOMEHOW YOU MADE YOUR WAY THROUGH
          BUILT UP YOUR WRITING AND PRIDE
          THOUGH I WISH WE DID MORE FOR YOU
          JUST KNOW I TRIED

AND NOW WE'RE HERE WITH THE SAME OLD FEARS
THE STRINGS ATTACHED TO OUR HEARTS ARE CUT
NOT FACING EACH OTHER FOR YEARS
THEN HOPING THAT DOOR WOULD STAY SHUT

TO OPEN THE DOOR DOES NOT MEAN WAR
ALTHOUGH I WANT YOU TO TAKE MY SIDE
I FEEL THAT I'M UP FOR THE TASK
OF TURNING OUR FAMILY'S TIDE

SO LET'S TRY TO OPEN THAT DOOR
AND NOT KEEP OUR FEELINGS OUTSIDE
AS FAR AS CONVINCING YOUR DAD
YOU KNOW I TRIED

MAYBE WITHOUT THIS LAUNDRY
THE THREE OF US COULD FINALLY BE
SOMETHING THAT WE NEVER WERE; A FAMILY

(*JUNE takes DYLAN's hand.*)

TOGETHER WE CAN SEE THIS THROUGH
FROM US BOTH, YOUR FATHER CAN'T HIDE
IF ALL OUR WORST FEARS STILL COME TRUE
AT LEAST WE TRIED

DYLAN: OK Mom, I'll help you talk to Dad.

(*Blackout*)

ACT I - SCENE 3

CRAZY TOM sits in dim light of the laundry office, which looks more like an abandoned storage room. He is coughing and counting the packages on the wall. JUNE and DYLAN are just outside, knocking on the door.

CRAZY TOM: *(Sings)*
　　　　　　YIT...NGEE...SLOM...SLEE *(1,2,3, 4 in Chinese)*
　　　　　　PRETTY SOON, WE WILL BE FREE

JUNE:　　　Tom, Dylan is here open up! Tom? Tom, Dylan is here, please open up!

CRAZY TOM: The door's always open.

(JUNE and DYLAN enter.)

DYLAN:　　Dad! *(Coughs)* Dad? Are you in here?

(CRAZY TOM turns on a lamp over his head. He is sitting on a stool, smoking a cigar and occasionally coughing.)

JUNE:　　　Look Tom, Dylan is here!

CRAZY TOM: June, I think I can see that.

JUNE:　　　Well, aren't you going to say something?

CRAZY TOM: When you give me a chance, I will.

JUNE:　　　Tom, we haven't seen Dylan for so long and you're acting like you can't be bothered —

DYLAN:　　Mom, Dad, I don't know what to say. Except that it's good to see you two...together.

JUNE:　　　Why don't I let you two talk?

CRAZY TOM: That would be a wonderful idea, my dear.

JUNE:　　　See what I have to put up with Dylan?

(JUNE exits.)

CRAZY TOM: Welcome home, son...I'm sure you've noticed that things haven't changed much around here.

DYLAN: It's really good to see you.

CRAZY TOM: Good to see you too. Why don't you have a seat?

DYLAN: I guess it's been a while.

CRAZY TOM: Yes, it has.

DYLAN: Dad, why are you sitting here alone in the dark?

CRAZY TOM: This is where I always sit. The basement is good for my asthma.

DYLAN: But that cigar can't be helping.

CRAZY TOM: Well, like you told me, just before you left for college; you said I was "beyond help."

DYLAN: Dad, would you mind if I turned on another light?

CRAZY TOM: Make yourself at home, son.

(DYLAN searches a bit, then finally finds a light that illuminates the whole room and reveals a wall-size shelf of laundry packages.)

DYLAN: Whoa!...It's the "Great Wall of Laundry."

CRAZY TOM: You could call it that.

DYLAN: What is all of this...unclaimed laundry?

CRAZY TOM: Just some things my friends and colleagues have left behind.

DYLAN: It's almost like a cemetery.

CRAZY TOM: I prefer to think of it as a shrine.

DYLAN: A shrine!?...A shrine to what?

CRAZY TOM: Nobody's ever made a movie about this, so you wouldn't understand.

DYLAN: Dad, there's no need to be patronizing—

CRAZY TOM: I was just about to say the same thing.

DYLAN: Well...I guess I have been away too long.

CRAZY TOM: Five and a half years, but who's counting?

DYLAN: I guess it's been a really long time.

CRAZY TOM: The last time you were here the President didn't smoke pot.

DYLAN: Yeah, I think Bush was more of a Prozac kind of guy.

CRAZY TOM: Well, at least we agree on one thing. So what brings you back here?

DYLAN: Well, since you ask, I've been talking to Mom about that possible mall deal—

CRAZY TOM: OK, I get it now. My son, the big Hollywood big-shot, has come back to Chinatown to straighten his loser dad out.

DYLAN: Dad, no one's calling you a loser. But maybe we can get you to reconsider.

        "NOT FOR SALE"

CRAZY TOM:
        SO NOW YOU'RE GONNA SHOW ME HOW TO LIVE?
        TREAT ME LIKE I'VE GOT NOTHING LEFT TO GIVE

        YOU MAY BE RICH, NOW
        WHILE I'M STILL POOR
        BUT THAT DOESN'T MEAN YOU HAVE EVERYTHING
        THAT I'VE STRIVED FOR

DYLAN: IT'S NOT ABOUT HAVE AND HAVE NOT
        THIS IS ABOUT WHY AND WHY NOT?
        I'M NOT SHOWING YOU HOW TO LIVE
        I'M JUST TRYING TO SHOW YOU HOW TO STOP DYING

CRAZY TOM:
        DYLAN, WE NEVER STOP DYING
        RIGHT FROM THE DAY WE ARE BORN
        DEATH IS A REWARD OF LIFE
        JUST AS PEACE IS A REWARD OF WAR

DYLAN: EVEN IN WAR THERE IS PEACE
        BETWEEN BATTLES THERE IS PEACE

        SO FOR ONCE, FOR US
        LET THERE BE PEACE

CRAZY TOM:
        I HEAR YOU SPEAKING OF PEACE
        BUT WANTING TO BUY MY STORE
        AND TO BUY ME OUT
        IS TO ENGAGE IN WAR

DYLAN: I DON'T WANT TO "BUY YOU OUT"
        I WANT TO HELP ALL OF US OUT

(*Spoken*) I know I haven't been around much. And I'll probably never be the son you wanted. But maybe it's time we cut our losses here.

CRAZY TOM:
        THE PEOPLE'S LAUNDRY'S NOT FOR SALE
        NOT TO YOU, NOT TO EMPIRE NATIONAL
        NOT TO ANYBODY
        WE'LL GET OUT OF THIS, ALL BY OURSELVES
        AS LONG AS CRAZY TOM'S AROUND,
        "OUR OWN LAW" WILL PREVAIL

DYLAN: Why are you bringing that up now?

CRAZY TOM:
        YOU CAN'T SELL OUT
        WHEN THE PRESSURE'S TOO GREAT
        YOU MUST PREVAIL AND CARRY YOUR WEIGHT
        ALWAYS CARRY YOUR WEIGHT
        THAT'S WHAT OUR OWN LAW'S ABOUT
        THAT'S WHAT CRAZY TOM IS ABOUT

CRAZY TOM: Dylan, do you remember The Laundry...Allied...Workers; what we used to call "Our Own LAW."

DYLAN: Of course I do! They used to meet right here. You'd stand before them, raising holy hell, like you were in the pulpit or something.

CRAZY TOM: That's right they even called me—

CRAZY TOM & DYLAN: Crazy Reverend Tom.

CRAZY TOM: But after a while, they dropped the Reverend— "Our own LAW" we were an ecumenical bunch.

DYLAN: More like a maniacal bunch. What ever happened to all those guys of "Our Own LAW?"

CRAZY TOM: Well Dylan, this "great wall of laundry"—as you call it, is all that's left of "Our Own LAW."

DYLAN: This unclaimed laundry?

    "NOT FOR SALE (Reprise)"

CRAZY TOM:
        TO YOU, THIS IS UNCLAIMED LAUNDRY
        TO ME, A LEGACY
        THOSE LAUNDRIES ALL WENT DOWN
        NOW THEIR SPIRITS LIVE THROUGH ME
        YOU CAN'T SEE THIS
        CAUSE YOU'RE NOT LIKE ME
        BUT THIS UNCLAIMED LAUNDRY'S WORTH
        MORE THAN YOUR SCREENWRITING FEES
        YOU CAN'T BUY ME OUT
        BECAUSE I AM NOT FOR SALE
        NO, CRAZY TOM IS NOT FOR SALE
        NOT FOR SALE!

CRAZY TOM: Now, leave me alone, I have some work to do.

(DYLAN exits. Underscore: "Home.")

CRAZY TOM: We did well, boys, we did well. I mean, this is what you wanted, right? This is what you wanted, right! This is what you wanted, right!

(Blackout)

ACT I - SCENE 4

DYLAN comes out of the laundry. It is now dusk and BO-GEE is closing up his newsstand. DYLAN goes to help him. BO-GEE throws a magazine at him.

DYLAN: *Basketball Digest!*

BO-GEE: When you were a kid that was your favorite.

DYLAN: Between you and me, it still is. Hey, thanks a lot. It's the nicest present I've gotten since I've been back.

BO-GEE: Well, like they say, you can never go home again.

DYLAN: Well, whoever said that wasn't Chinese, cause when you're Chinese, you always have to go home again.

DYLAN: So, are you living in the same place?

BO-GEE: No, I've moved.

DYLAN: Oh great, so you've finally moved out of Chinatown?

BO-GEE: No, I live right there.

(BO-GEE points to the laundry.)

DYLAN: Uncle Bo-Gee, you're pointing to the laundry.

BO-GEE: That's where I live.

DYLAN: My god, I didn't know that.

BO-GEE: Yeah, my old building on Walker St. went co-op and I couldn't afford it—story of a lot of people around here. Luckily, your father took me in.

DYLAN: I'm glad he did.

BO-GEE: Me, too. "Crazy Tom" is like me, we hate to see what's happening to Chinatown. I bet if he could, "Crazy Tom" would take us all in.

DYLAN: He's always left me out in the cold—I don't know why I came back. In fact, my parents are the best argument I know for never getting married. But did I learn from them? No, of course not!

BO-GEE: Look, Dylan. I'm sure it was not easy for you to come back here. But believe me, despite all the problems, you should be thankful you still have a family to go to.

DYLAN: Oh, then take my family—please!

"FAMILY"

BO-GEE: FAMILY IS LIKE AIR
YOU CAN'T SEE IT, BUT YOU KNOW THAT IT'S THERE
IT FILLS YOUR LUNGS WITH PRIDE
IT'S HARD TO SWALLOW WHEN YOU CRY
AND YOU KNOW IT DOESN'T LEAVE TILL YOU DIE

DYLAN: *(Spoken)* No, Uncle Bo-Gee; *(Sings)*
FAMILY IS MORE LIKE A RECEIPT
YOU PUT IT AWAY, HOPING NO ONE NEEDS TO SEE IT
IT'S NICE TO KNOW YOU HAVE IT
BUT LET'S NOT MAKE IT A HABIT;
MORE THAN ONCE OR TWICE A YEAR—LIKE TAXES

BO-GEE: FAMILY IS A NEST TO US

DYLAN: NO, FAMILY IS A PEST TO US

BO-GEE: BUT IT'S BETTER TO HAVE, THAN HAVE NOT

DYLAN: YOU WOULDN'T SAY THAT WITH MY LOT!

BO-GEE & DYLAN:
AND THAT'S WHAT FAMILY MEANS TO ME

BO-GEE: *(Spoken)* All right, Dylan; *(Sings)*
FAMILY IS LIKE FOOD
AFTER YOU EAT IT; YOU ARE IN A GOOD MOOD
YEAH, YOU MAY SKIP A MEAL,
BUT INSIDE YOU'LL ALWAYS FEEL
THE NEED TO CHEW ON SOMETHING THAT'S REAL

DYLAN: *(Spoken)* No, Uncle Bo-Gee, you be for real. *(Sings)*
FAMILY IS LIKE GOING OUT TO EAT
IT'S TOO EXPENSIVE, AND UNCOMFORTABLE SEATS

THE ATMOSPHERE IS RAW
THE CONVERSATION'S A BORE
BUT WE'RE ALWAYS COMING BACK FOR MORE

BO-GEE: FAMILY IS A NEST TO US

DYLAN: NO, FAMILY IS A PEST TO US

BO-GEE: BUT IT'S BETTER TO HAVE, THAN HAVE NOT

DYLAN: MAYBE A LITTLE, BUT NOT A LOT

BO-GEE & DYLAN:
            WELL, THAT'S WHAT FAMILY MEANS TO ME

BO-GEE: Oh Dylan, you must like your family a little bit.

DYLAN: You know how I would like my family, Uncle Bo-Gee?

BO-GEE: How would you like your family, Dylan?

DYLAN: Over and easy; just like my morning eggs.

BO-GEE: Well, Dylan, then you better wake up and smell the tea.

(BO-GEE smacks DYLAN in the head and sings.)

BO-GEE: FAMILY IS A NEST TO US

DYLAN: NO, FAMILY IS A PEST TO US

BO-GEE: BUT IT'S BETTER TO HAVE, THAN HAVE NOT

DYLAN: JUST MAKE THE BEST OF WHAT YOU'VE GOT!

BO-GEE & DYLAN:
            WHY CAN'T FAMILY BE LIKE US?

(BO-GEE wheels back into his newsstand and then re-emerges with a table and duffel bag.)

BO-GEE: Come here, I want to show you something.

(BO-GEE pulls out incense sticks, oranges, snapshots and a bowl of sand from the bag, and starts arranging *them on the table.)*

BO-GEE: I usually do this alone, but since we hardly see each other anymore. I'd like you to share this with me.

DYLAN: Sure.

BO-GEE: Today is your Aunt Lily's birthday. She would've been 49 today.

DYLAN: I'm sorry.

BO-GEE: She's been gone for almost six years now. And every year, on her birthday, I still write her a letter. And in "hung-ngen," Chinese tradition, I always write her a letter and burn it, so she can read it in heaven.

(BO-GEE lights six incense sticks. He hands three to DYLAN and holds three himself. BO-GEE looks at DYLAN, they both close their eyes and bow their head three times. BO-GEE stands the incense sticks in the bowl of sand and motions for DYLAN to do the same. He does BO-GEE pulls out a letter, which he sings.)

"HAPPY BIRTHDAY LILY"

BO-GEE: HAPPY BIRTHDAY LILY
      YOU WOULD'VE BEEN FORTY-NINE TODAY
      THOUGH IT'S BEEN A LONG TIME
      YOU'RE STILL ON MY MIND
      AND YOUR PICTURE'S NEVER FAR AWAY

      HAPPY BIRTHDAY LILY
      THE NEWSSTAND'S STILL DOING FINE
      THAT WAS YOUR IDEA
      AND NOW I'M STILL HERE
      BUT WHO KNEW WHAT WAS DOWN THE LINE?

      WE OPENED THE NEWSSTAND
      SO YOU COULD TAKE CARE OF ME
      AFTER I COULD NOT WALK
      THEN YOUR ILLNESS STRUCK
      AND YOU COULD NO LONGER SEE
      CARING FOR YOU TOOK ALL OUR TIME AND MONEY
      BUT I'D DO IT ALL OVER AGAIN, HONEY
      I'D DO IT ALL OVER AGAIN

      HAPPY BIRTHDAY LILY

HOPE YOU HAVE A GOOD TIME TODAY
DON'T THINK OF NEXT YEAR
JUST TAKE CARE OF WHAT'S NEAR
CAUSE MY LOVE, I'LL BE THERE SOMEDAY
MY LOVE, I'LL BE THERE SOMEDAY
HAPPY BIRTHDAY, LILY

(BO-GEE burns the letter in the bowl next to the snapshot. He looks at DYLAN, they both close their eyes and bow their heads three times.)

BO-GEE: Here, have some orange.

(They eat oranges. BO-GEE starts packing up his things.)

BO-GEE: Thank you for sharing this with me.

DYLAN: No, thank you. It certainly puts things into perspective.

BO-GEE: I'm glad I could be of help.

DYLAN: Life's just way too short for all of this bickering and bullshit. And Uncle Bo-Gee, I know I'll miss my parents one day, but for now, my parents—especially my Dad—make me as mad as when I was a little boy.

(JOSIE enters.)

JOSIE: Bo-Gee!

BO-GEE: Well, Dylan, I have to go now.

DYLAN: Hi, Josie!—*(To BO-GEE)* Where are you going?

BO-GEE: Excuse me, Dylan, but I really must be going.

JOSIE: Wait! Don't leave yet!

(JOSIE and DYLAN freeze as BO-GEE sings:)

"BALLAD OF CHINATOWN (Reprise)"

BO-GEE: WHEN JOSIE CAME BACK HERE TO STAY
SHE HAD TO GET HER WAY
TO GET HER WAY SHE'LL HAVE TO CHANGE

THE COURSE OF SOMEONE'S FATE

JOSIE: Bo-Gee, me and Mom really need an answer!

DYLAN: Josie, what's going on?

BO-GEE: I'll have to talk to you later!

JOSIE: Bo-Gee!

(BO-GEE gathers his bag and exits into his now closed newsstand.)

DYLAN: Why are you yelling at Uncle Bo-Gee?

JOSIE: Look, you've been away too long, you don't know what he's doing to Mom and Dad.

DYLAN: What on earth is he doing?

JOSIE: Even you must be able to see that the only reason Dad lets him live in the back room—
for free—is just so he can use him as another excuse to stay in Chinatown.

DYLAN: Maybe they want to stay here.

JOSIE: Well, they sure don't act like it.

DYLAN: What are you talking about?

JOSIE: Dad doesn't even pay the rent and he has a little bit of money saved up—

DYLAN: Mom says they're broke!

JOSIE: Dad keeps it all away from her, and the only reason they haven't evicted his sorry ass is
because I took out a loan to pay all the laundry's back rent.

DYLAN: Mom never mentioned this.

JOSIE: She's too proud. Besides, it's my contact with their landlord that's keeping them there
at all. You see, their landlord wants to work with my company to redevelop this block into a mall.

DYLAN: So Dad is the only thing standing in the way of "The Great Mall of Chinatown?"

JOSIE: Hello? This is not a god-damned movie, this is real life! In fact, I'm even getting them to reconsider offering Mom and Dad a relocation fee if they get out this year. That's why we need you <u>and</u> Bo-Gee to talk to Dad about this.

DYLAN: Excuse me, but who died and left you in charge?

"STAND YOUR GROUND"

JOSIE: FOR SO LONG, THE CHINESE WERE PASSIVE
           ALTHOUGH, OUR NUMBERS SO MASSIVE
           WE SEE OURSELVES AS SECOND CLASS
           WE STEP ASIDE TO LET OTHERS PASS

           NOW LOOK WHERE THAT THINKING HAS TAKEN US
           THE CITY, HAS ALL BUT FORSAKEN US
           AS LONG AS IT'S KEPT IN OUR NEIGHBORHOOD
           AS LONG AS WE JUST DO WHAT WE SHOULD
           THEY DON'T GIVE A DAMN AND THEY NEVER EVER COULD

           YOU'VE GOT TO STAND YOUR GROUND
           OR ELSE ALL YOU'VE FOUND WILL BE LOST
           THEY'LL TAKE EVERYTHING YOU HAVE
           AND LOSING FACE WILL BE THE COST
           CAUSE YOU CAN'T TRUST PEOPLE
           NO MATTER HOW NICE THEY SOUND
           SO JUST SMILE AND BE CHARMING
           BUT INSIDE, ALWAYS STAND YOUR GROUND

JOSIE: THAT'S WHY I WORK IN THIS PLACE NOW
           TO HELP CHINATOWN SAVE FACE NOW
           BUSINESS BOOMED LIKE NEVER BEFORE
           HELPED DEVELOPERS TO OPEN NEW DOORS

           IF WE DON'T, THIS COULD BE A GHOST TOWN
           THESE STORES ARE ALL GONNA CLOSE DOWN
           WITH A NEW MALL, WE CAN STAND TALL
           WITH A NEW MALL, WE WILL NEVER FALL
           WITH A NEW MALL, THERE'S NO MORE GREAT WALL

           YOU'VE GOT TO STAND YOUR GROUND
           OR ELSE ALL YOU'VE FOUND WILL BE LOST
           THEY'LL TAKE EVERYTHING YOU HAVE
           AND LOSING FACE WILL BE THE COST
           CAUSE YOU CAN'T TRUST PEOPLE

NO MATTER HOW NICE THEY SOUND
SO JUST SMILE AND BE CHARMING
BUT INSIDE, ALWAYS STAND YOUR GROUND

JOSIE: HELP ME TO TAKE THIS STAND
HELP YOUR MOM CONVINCE YOUR OLD MAN
THAT THE LAUNDRY'S A THING OF THE PAST
AND NOW IT'S TIME TO LEAVE WHILE THEY STILL CAN

SOMETIMES TO STAND YOUR GROUND
YOU GIVE A LITTLE TO GAIN A LOT
AND THIS IS NOT JUST BUSINESS
I AM TALKING MATTERS OF THE HEART

JOSIE: Dylan...no one has to die for someone else to take charge. Will you help me talk to Dad
tonight?

DYLAN: Let's go for that drink first.

(Blackout)

ACT I - SCENE 5

The Tom's dining room in "The People's Laundry." Entire cast is sitting around a dining room table. JUNE proposes a toast.

JUNE: Dylan, we're all glad to have you back. Even if it's just for a week.

BO-GEE: That's right!

DYLAN: Thank you!

JUNE: And hopefully, this will be the last time you have to visit us in this cramped, old place.

JOSIE: Amen!

BO-GEE: What do you mean "cramped, old place?"

JUNE: Excuse me, but am I making this toast or are you?

BO-GEE: Sorry I asked.

CRAZY TOM: Why don't we just drink already!

JUNE: Is that all you have to say?

CRAZY TOM: Well, I think you've said more than enough.

DYLAN: Let's just all calm down and finish dinner.

JOSIE: I guess I'll bring out the dessert.

(JOSIE exits.)

JUNE: Yes, Josie was nice enough to bring dessert.

BO-GEE: Just save mine. I'm sorry, everybody, but I'd like to be excused.

CRAZY TOM: Bo-Gee, you haven't missed a dessert in years.

DYLAN: And besides, the night is still young.

BO-GEE: Thanks for the great dinner, but I have to go back to my room.

DYLAN: Why don't you just stay through dessert?

JUNE: He wants to leave, so let him go!

BO-GEE: To tell you the truth, right about now you two always start to drink too much and say stupid things.

JUNE: I won't tolerate that from a lodger. Not a lodger, a freeloader!

CRAZY TOM: June!

BO-GEE: See what I mean? Goodnight everybody.

JUNE: Not so fast, Bo-Gee I am so tired of having no say in what goes on around here...so until we decide what we're doing I'm moving in with Josie!

DYLAN: Mom!

          "SOMETHING FOR ME"

JUNE: I'VE PUT UP WITH HIM
          FOR YEARS PUT UP WITH YOU TOO
          FOR YEARS HELD SO MUCH BACK
          BUT NOW MY SILENCE IS THROUGH

          TOM, YOU KNOW I'VE ALWAYS STOOD BY YOU
          IT'S THE PLACE I'VE ALWAYS CHOSE TO BE
          NOW I'M ASKING; CAN WE DO SOMETHING FOR ME?

          I KNOW THIS LAUNDRY
          AND CHINATOWN YOU LOVE SO
          BUT YOU HAVE TO REALIZE
          THAT IT IS TIME WE MUST GO

          TOM, I REALLY NEED TO GET OUT NOW
          AND I THINK YOU NEED TO GET OUT NOW
          AND WE HAVE TO ACT WHILE THERE'S STILL SOME WAY OUT

CRAZY TOM:
          YOU FORGOT WHERE WE CAME FROM
          YOU FORGOT THE BAD OLD DAYS
          RIGHT BEFORE THE LAUNDRY CAME OUR WAY
          STRUGGLING TO JUST GET BY

THE LAUNDRY GOT US RIGHT IN STRIDE
IT GAVE US A LIVING AND OUR PRIDE

REMEMBER HOW CHINESE WERE TREATED
EVEN THOUGH ALL OF US WERE BORN HERE
THEY STILL SAW US AS FOREIGNERS
AND LOWLY LEECHES THAT WAS MADE PERFECTLY CLEAR

WE SURVIVED WITH OUR OWN LAW
DON'T FORGET OUR OWN LAW NOW
WE SWORE TO IT LIKE A WEDDING VOW

THROUGH IT, WE BECAME SOMEONE
AND THROUGH OUR OWN LAW, WE EVEN RAISED A SON
THAT LEGACY IS WHAT WE'RE ALL ABOUT
SO JUNE, LET'S NOT THROW IT ALL AWAY NOW

JUNE: TOM THIS IS NOT AN EASY TASK
            AND I'M NOT THE ONE TO SAY YOU'RE WRONG
            BUT THIS HAS BEEN ONLY YOUR DREAM ALL ALONG
            I HAVE BEEN WAITING PATIENTLY
            IT'S AMAZING THAT YOU STILL CAN'T SEE
            THAT I STILL NEED SOMETHING DESPERATELY FOR ME

(Spoken over underscore)

DYLAN: Mom, let's not be so hasty!

JUNE: THIS HAS BEEN BUILDING
            FOR THIRTY YEARS NOW
            SO I DON'T THINK THAT
            YOU COULD CALL THAT FAST
            BUT IT IS HERE NOW, THE TIME IS HERE NOW
            AND I THINK FREEDOM'S REALLY GONNA LAST

JUNE: FOR MANY YEARS NOW, TOO MANY YEARS NOW

CRAZY TOM:
            WE SURVIVED WITH OUR OWN LAW

JUNE: I'VE SACRIFICED ALL TILL THERE WAS NO MORE ME

CRAZY TOM:

                    DON'T FORGET OUR OWN LAW NOW

JUNE: BUT IT IS HERE NOW, THE TIME IS HERE NOW

CRAZY TOM:
             WE SWORE TO IT LIKE A WEDDING VOW

JUNE: AND I AM DOING SOMETHING JUST FOR ME
             SOMETHING JUST FOR ME

(As JUNE gets up from the table, JOSIE enters with dessert.)

CRAZY TOM:
             LET HER GO, JUST LET HER GO
             "CRAZY TOM" IS FINE ALONE
             SO WHY DON'T YOU ALL JUST GO HOME!

JOSIE: Maybe we should take a rain check on dessert?

DYLAN: Josie, how many different scams are you running?

JOSIE: *(Pointing at CRAZY TOM)* Maybe you should ask him that. Come on Mom. Dylan,
perhaps you should come too.

CRAZY TOM: Can everyone please leave the premises!

(JOSIE exits with JUNE, BO-GEE follows.)

DYLAN: Dad, don't worry, it's gonna be all right, I'm just gonna go get Mom settled at Josie's.
I'll be right back.

CRAZY TOM: So will she, you'll see; a bad penny always comes back.

DYLAN: Dad when will you stop!

*(DYLAN exits. Music to "Home" starts. CRAZY TOM pours all of the unfinished drinks on the table into his
glass and drinks it in one sip. He starts toasting "The Great Wall of Laundry" by calling off his old friend's
names. After each name is called, a faceless figure dances out from behind the wall.)*

CRAZY TOM: Chin! You're not forgotten. Wong! You're not forgotten. Yee! You're not forgotten.
Loo! You're not forgotten. "Our Own Law" is still upheld here. "Crazy Tom" calls a meeting of the
officers of the Laundry Allied Workers Society.

(CRAZY TOM dances with ghost friends and sings.)

"HOME"

CRAZY TOM:

      COME ON BOYS, GATHER 'ROUND
      CAUSE SOON WE'RE GOING TO LEAVE
      LITTLE OL' CHINATOWN

      CAUSE THE TIME WILL SOON COME
      WHEN THE MOON WILL OBLITERATE THE SUN
      THE SKY WILL COME CRASHING DOWN
      AND THE EARTH WILL COME UNDONE

      WHEN THAT DAY ARRIVES
      YOU WON'T SEE ME CRY
      I'LL SEE IT AS DESTINY FULFILLED
      AND MY CHANCE TO FINALLY GO HOME

      HOME; WHERE OUR OWN LAW
      IS ALWAYS UPHELD
      HOME; WHERE OUR OWN LAW
      IS ALWAYS UPHELD

      BOYS WE'RE HALFWAY HOME
      WE'VE WEATHERED MANY STORMS
      NOW THERE'S ONLY ONE MORE BIG ONE TO GO
      THEN IT'S TIME FOR US TO GO HOME

      HOME; WHERE OUR OWN LAW
      IS ALWAYS UPHELD
      HOME; WHERE OUR OWN LAW
      IS ALWAYS UPHELD

END OF ACT I

ENTR'ACTE

BO-GEE appears in a single spotlight.

"BALLAD OF CHINATOWN" (Reprise)

BO-GEE: CHANGE IS A NECESSITY
               ABANDONMENT IS NOT
               BEFORE YOU MAKE A MAJOR CHANGE
               BE SURE OF WHAT YOU'VE GOT
               BE SURE OF WHAT YOU'VE GOT

(Blackout)

ACT II - SCENE 1

CRAZY TOM sits alone getting drunk in his office. BO-GEE enters.

BO-GEE: Tom, can I come in a moment?

CRAZY TOM: Sure, come on in. Want a drink?

BO-GEE: No, thank you. I'm sorry about what happened tonight, Tom.

CRAZY TOM: No need to be, Bo-Gee, no need to be.

BO-GEE: Well, I'll only stay a minute, but I just wanted to say, that if you think I'm becoming too much trouble, I can stay somewhere else.

CRAZY TOM: Nonsense! As long as I'm around, you're staying right here.

BO-GEE: You're a good man, Tom. Thank you.

CRAZY TOM: Sometimes. But I did some really stupid things tonight.

BO-GEE: But Tom, you always have, and—

CRAZY TOM: Thanks a lot, my old comrade in confidence.

BO-GEE: Tom, please don't take this the wrong way. What I meant is, everybody does stupid things, but you're one of the few who learn from their mistakes.

CRAZY TOM: That's very nice of you to say that, Bo-Gee.

BO-GEE: Well, it's true. You just have to do that now, to turn things around with June and Dylan.

CRAZY TOM: Well...what have I learned? I've learned that I've slaved here for twelve hours a day my whole life, while Dylan and Josie, and to some extent, June, were free to go see the world. I've never stopped them, and that's fine—that's why I've worked here. But they don't understand that this laundry is my world. It's all I know. And now they want to take that away from me...and if that happens I'll be just like my father and so many other guys here in Chinatown. They leave China, leave their world, come here and become zombies. Sure they make some money, go buy their houses on Long Island. But inside, they're dead...Bo-Gee, I'm not ready to leave my world yet.

BO-GEE: Come on Tom, no one's saying that.

CRAZY TOM: Well you saw tonight. Dylan, Josie and June...My wife and my kids were like complete strangers. They hate this place. They hate me...what have I worked for all these years? What have we lived for all of these years?...Bo-Gee, why go on?

BO-GEE: TOM!...It's going to be OK.

"THINGS THAT YOU CAN'T FORGET"

BO-GEE: I REMEMBER WHEN YOU WERE NINETEEN
YOUNG AND STUPID, EVEN MORE STUPID THAN NOW
AND SO NAIVE, YOU DOUBTED OUR FATHER'S WAYS
YOU WOULD NOT LISTEN TO WHAT HE HAD TO SAY
IN FACT, YOU DIDN'T EVEN WANT TO STAY

THINGS GOT SO BAD
YOU HAD ONE FOOT OUT THE DOOR
THAT'S WHEN I PULLED YOU ASIDE
AND SAID "WHAT ARE YOU DOING THIS FOR?"
GIVE YOUR OLD MAN A CHANCE
CAUSE YOU'RE ALL HE'S LIVING FOR"

CRAZY TOM:
I HAD A HEART TO HEART WITH OUR DAD
THOUGHT, "WELL THIS AIN'T SO BAD"
I STARTED HELPING WITH HIS LAUNDRY
NOW YOU KNOW IT'S BECOME ME
AND THAT'S SOMETHING YOU CAN'T FORGET

BO-GEE: YOU MUST BELIEVE THAT TOM
AND REMEMBER THOSE THINGS RIGHT NOW
YOU'VE GOT A WIFE AND SON
WHO REALLY ARE AWFULLY PROUD
AND WHEN THE TROUBLES START
YOU SAY THINGS THAT YOU JUST REGRET
THAT'S WHEN YOU SHOULD REMEMBER
THE THINGS THAT YOU CAN'T FORGET

LISTEN TO ME, TOM
TOGETHER WE'VE BEEN THROUGH A LOT
BUT HERE IS HOPING THAT
ALL THIS IS ONLY A START
CAUSE IF WE STICK TOGETHER
THERE IS NO NEED TO REGRET

THE THINGS THAT WE CAN'T FORGET
THE THINGS THAT WE CAN'T FORGET

CRAZY TOM & BO-GEE:
      AND IF WE STICK TOGETHER
      THERE IS NO NEED TO REGRET
      THE THINGS THAT WE CAN'T FORGET

BO-GEE: You just have to talk this way to June and Dylan.

CRAZY TOM: I've always said I would give my life for them. And I still would.

BO-GEE: They'd do the same for you, Tom.

CRAZY TOM: Ha! They don't even give me the time of day. They just laugh at me. Laugh at me all the time. Ha! Ha! Ha! Well I'll have the final laugh.

(DYLAN enters.)

DYLAN: Excuse me, was I interrupting...

BO-GEE: No, come in, come in. Good to see you. I was just having a word with your father

DYLAN: Are you sure?

CRAZY TOM: Hey it's Mr. Hollywood!

BO-GEE: Tom, take it easy! (To DYLAN in a stage whisper) He's had a few too many, give him some slack.

DYLAN: I only came back to get a few of Mom's things.

BO-GEE: Dylan, please stay a minute...for me.

DYLAN: Only for you, Uncle Bo-Gee.

BO-GEE: Thank you. So why don't I let you two talk...Good night all.

DYLAN, CRAZY TOM: Goodnight.

(BO-GEE exits.)

CRAZY TOM: I saw that awful movie you supposedly wrote—

DYLAN: Dad—

CRAZY TOM: I stayed to the very end, and your name wasn't even in the credits!

DYLAN: I became an uncredited ghost writer on that one.

CRAZY TOM: So what did you come back here for, to "ghost write" my life?

DYLAN: I just came back to get some things for Mom, that's all.

CRAZY TOM: What's your hurry, they gave out this year's Oscars already. Why don't you have a drink?

DYLAN: Haven't you had enough?

CRAZY TOM: I was feeling deprived.

"THE LAST HAND LAUNDRY IN CHINATOWN"

DYLAN: MOM STOOD BY YOU FOR THIRTY YEARS OR MORE
           NOW YOU'VE PUSHED HER OUT THE DOOR AND WHAT FOR?
           I OFFERED YOU SOME MONEY, BUT YOU TELL ME NO
           NOW I'M READY TO GO WITH MOM AND LEAVE YOU HERE ALONE

CRAZY TOM: Are you threatening me?

DYLAN: Threatening? No. (Sings)
           DAD, WHY DON'T YOU COOPERATE FOR A CHANGE?

CRAZY TOM:
           COOPERATE?
           FOR WHAT KIND OF CHANGE?
           FOR YOUR CHUMP CHANGE?
           THAT COOPERATION JUST MEANS CO-OPT
(Spoken) And co-opt means kaput!

DYLAN: So where are you now, that you can be so proud?

CRAZY TOM:
           DO YOU KNOW WHAT IT'S LIKE
           TO REALLY GIVE YOUR WHOLE LIFE
           TO SOMETHING THAT GIVES YOU NOTHING BACK?
           WELL I HAVE LIVED THAT LIFE

THAT LIFE HAS BEEN MY LIFE
FOR A VERY LONG TIME
SO UNLIKE YOU COMPANY BOYS
OR IN YOUR CASE, STUDIO BOYS
I KNOW HOW TO SURVIVE ON MY OWN
HOW TO TAKE A STAND ALL ALONE
FOR BETTER OR FOR WORSE
I'VE ALWAYS BEEN IN CONTROL
WHILE YOU COMPANY BOYS
MAY FALL INTO FAVOR EVERY ONCE IN A WHILE
MY HEART, MY GUTS ARE ALWAYS ON TRIAL

YOU USED TO HAVE TO BUY-IN, TO BE AN AMERICAN
NOW YOU HAVE TO SELL-OUT, TO REALLY GET SOME CLOUT
BUT I WILL DO NEITHER AS LONG AS I CAN BREATH
SO THE PEOPLE'S LAUNDRY WILL STAY FOREVER FREE
EVEN IF WE'RE THE LAST OF A DYING BREED

THE LAST HAND LAUNDRY IN CHINATOWN
MAY BE DOWN, BUT NEVER OUT
THE LAST HAND LAUNDRY IN CHINATOWN
WILL NEVER GO DOWN FOR THE COUNT

(As before, CRAZY TOM starts toasting "The Great Wall of Laundry" by calling off his old friend's names. After each name is called, a faceless figure dances out from behind the wall.)

CRAZY TOM:
            CHIN'S LAUNDRY; DOING FINE
            WONG & SONS; JUST DIVINE

DYLAN: What's going on?

(CRAZY TOM pays him no mind and carries on with his ceremony.)

CRAZY TOM:
            YEE'S HAND LAUNDRY; GOING STRONG
            LAUNDRY BY LOO; CAN DO NO WRONG
            BUT CRAZY TOM'S PEOPLE'S LAUNDRY
            IS STILL THE MIGHTIEST OF THEM ALL
            I'M STILL THE LEADER OF THE PACK! VROOM! VROOM!

            WITHOUT THE LAUNDRY WHERE WOULD I BE?

WHERE WOULD YOU BE? WHERE WOULD WE BE?
THE LAUNDRY HAS BEEN OUR HEART
THROUGH IT WE BREATH AND BLEED
IT'S ANSWERED ALL OF OUR QUESTIONS
PROVIDED ALL OF OUR NEEDS
FOR YOU, FOR YOUR MOTHER,
FOR YOUR GRANDPARENTS AND FOR ME

(CRAZY TOM and GHOST FRIENDS gesture for DYLAN to join them, he does.)

CRAZY TOM & DYLAN:
THE LAST HAND LAUNDRY IN CHINATOWN
MAY BE DOWN BUT NEVER OUT
THE LAST HAND LAUNDRY IN CHINATOWN
WILL NEVER GO DOWN FOR THE COUNT

CRAZY TOM, DYLAN & GHOST FRIENDS:
THE LAST HAND LAUNDRY IN CHINATOWN
MAY BE DOWN, BUT NEVER OUT
THE LAST HAND LAUNDRY IN CHINATOWN
WILL NEVER GO DOWN FOR THE COUNT

CRAZY TOM:
THAT'S ALL FOR TODAY, BOYS;
CAUSE SOON WE WILL BE HOME;
WHERE OUR OWN LAW IS ALWAYS UPHELD
YES SIR, SOON WE'LL BE HOME;
WHERE OUR OWN LAW IS ALWAYS UPHELD

(CRAZY TOM holds up two glasses, offering one to DYLAN.)

CRAZY TOM: Dylan, don't let them take away "Our Own LAW."

(DYLAN takes a glass and toasts CRAZY TOM. Blackout.)

ACT II - SCENE 2

JOSIE's apartment in a different part of Chinatown. JOSIE sits in her kitchen getting drunk. JUNE enters.

JUNE: You couldn't sleep too?

JOSIE: Nah, I'm the original insomniac...Oh, and uhm...I don't do this every night.

JUNE: Josie, Josie, this is your house. You're a grown-up now and you can do what you want.

JOSIE: I know, but well you know. You're still my Mom. Want to talk?

JUNE: Yes.

JOSIE: All right, don't mind if I have a drink or three? Would you like one?

JUNE: No, thank you, but you enjoy.

JOSIE: I guess I never thought it would come down to this. You staying here with me. Dad, Dylan and Bo-Gee back at the laundry.

JUNE: A lot of things don't turn out the way you think they will.

JOSIE: Maybe that cliché is true that you really don't know what you've got until it's gone.

JUNE: I think there's a lot of truth to that cliché. But on the flip side, you also don't know what you have until you actually have it—especially when it comes to marriage.

JOSIE: My marriage was not nearly as long as yours—and thank God we didn't have any kids—but I know what you mean. It couldn't have been easy for you.

JUNE: Marrying Tom, and now maybe leaving him, have been my two biggest leaps of doubt.

JOSIE: Mom, <u>that</u> cliché is "leap of faith."

JUNE: Whatever.

JOSIE: It's funny, well, not *funny*, but kind of ironic that now that Dylan's getting divorced, we're all in the same boat again. Maybe it's meant to be for us all to be back together in Chinatown.

JUNE: I feel very badly for Dylan. Because he's back in the middle of a struggle he thought he'd left behind years ago.

JOSIE: Let's make this the last cliché of this conversation, but sometimes you've got to go back and clean up where you started before you can move forward.

JUNE: Maybe so, but I look at some marriages and think what were they thinking when they got married.

JOSIE: Mom...can I ask what <u>you</u> were thinking?

"LIKE A COUPLE IN A GREAT OLD MOVIE"

JUNE: I USED TO SEE TOM AND ME
LIKE A COUPLE IN A GREAT OLD MOVIE
NEVER BROKE, NEVER LOW
ALWAYS DRESSED UP WITH SOMEPLACE TO GO
LIKE A COUPLE IN A GREAT OLD MOVIE

JOSIE: SO WHEN DID THE MOVIE END?
MAYBE YOU'RE JUST CHANGING REELS?
CAUSE IF THE MOVIE REALLY ENDS?
WHOSE TO SAY YOU'LL FIND A NEW DEAL?

JUNE: WAS IT ONLY ME, WHO YEARNED TO BE
LIKE A COUPLE IN A GREAT OLD MOVIE?

JOSIE: MAYBE WE SAW DIFFERENT MOVIES
BUT WE SAW STARS ALL THE SAME
I USED TO SEE PAUL AND ME
GOWING OLD TOGETHER—POOR BUT HAPPY;
NOT AS BAD AS MOM AND DAD
MAKING MARRIAGE A JOKE THAT'S HAD
BY A COUPLE IN A GREAT OLD MOVIE

COULD IT BE MY FOLKS WERE RIGHT
YOU CAN'T MARRY JUST FOR LOVE ITSELF
TAKE A LOOK AT ME TONIGHT
ALMOST FORTY AND ON THE SHELF

JUNE: SO MAYBE WE WON'T EVER BE
IN A COUPLE LIKE A GREAT OLD MOVIE
BUT THERE'S STILL TIME FOR YOU AND ME
TO REMAKE SOME GREAT OLD MOVIES

JOSIE: (Spoken) No, we can still be in some great new movies!

JUNE AND JOSIE:*(Sung)*
        LET'S TRY AND MAKE SOME GREAT NEW MOVIES

(DYLAN enters.)

JUNE: Dylan!

JOSIE: Did you talk to Dad?

DYLAN: Well...Sort of!

JUNE: What do you mean, "Sort of?"

DYLAN: Mom, you can't leave Dad and the laundry yet.

JOSIE: Dylan, Mom's already left.

DYLAN: There's something important you're leaving behind. Please Mom, let's just go back to the laundry one more time.

JUNE: I'm never going back!

(JUNE runs out of the room.)

JOSIE: Dylan, how could you do this?

DYLAN: Josie, you don't understand—

JOSIE: No, Dylan, I understand. You choked and sold us out.

DYLAN: I sold out? Now wait a minute—

JOSIE: Look Dylan, I'm not happy with what has happened, but I can't apologize for what I'm trying to achieve for Mom.

DYLAN: There's a lot that you don't know about that laundry.

JOSIE: You left me holding the bag here nine years ago, and now you think you're gonna just waltz back in and take over? I don't think so.

DYLAN: Josie, this is not some real estate power play. This is Mom and Dad!

(JUNE comes back with her coat on.)

JOSIE: Mom!

DYLAN: Oh good, come on Mom.

JUNE: Oh Josie, I have to hear him out.

JOSIE: You're just going to throw away everything I've done for you?

JUNE: Josie, please don't be upset with me.

JOSIE: You should be upset with yourself. But go ahead, go back! Let him walk all over you again!

DYLAN: Josie, that's enough.

(*JUNE and DYLAN exit. JOSIE pushes everything off of her kitchen table and lets out a scream of frustration.*)

ACT II - SCENE 3

DYLAN and JUNE enter TOM's office and turn on the lights. CRAZY TOM is very drunk and singing to himself.

CRAZY TOM:

      HOME, WHERE OUR OWN LAW IS ALWAYS UPHELD

DYLAN: Dad, Mom wants to talk.

CRAZY TOM:

      Who's stopping her? It's a free country!
(Sings)   HOME, WHERE OUR OWN LAW IS ALWAYS UPHELD
      HOME, WHERE OUR OWN LAW IS ALWAYS UPHELD

JUNE: See what I have to deal with Dylan!

(JUNE turns to go, DYLAN stops her.)

DYLAN: Please let's all just try and talk. DAD!

(CRAZY TOM stops singing.)

DYLAN: Dad, why don't you show Mom what you showed me earlier.

CRAZY TOM: Come on June, let's get this over with. You've been trying to get rid of me for years.

JUNE: And you've been ignoring me for years!

CRAZY TOM: You and Roy Orbison; "Only The Lonely" huh?

DYLAN: Dad, come on!

JUNE: Tom, I'm not coming back. I just came here to see if you'd reconsider the landlord's relocation offer.

CRAZY TOM: OK.

JUNE: Do you mean OK you'll reconsider?

CRAZY TOM: No, OK, let's take the God-damned deal. I don't want to hold anyone back.

DYLAN: Dad are you sure you don't want to show Mom what you showed me earlier?

(Music starts for "Home." CRAZY TOM gets up and slowly walks over to "The Great Wall of Laundry.")

CRAZY TOM: No, your Mom is right. Let's sell this useless place. Your Mom is strong, she can stand alone, right June?

JUNE: Tom, I don't want to be alone. I just want to get out of here, I just want to be free of this laundry.

CRAZY TOM: We all do June, We all do.

(CRAZY TOM tries to lift the wall, but it just comes crashing down on him. Music stops.)

DYLAN: Mom, call an ambulance!

CRAZY TOM: Don't call an ambulance!

JUNE: Tom, we must!

CRAZY TOM: PLEASE!...Don't call an ambulance...Just listen to me.

(DYLAN and JUNE finally get the wall partially off of him. DYLAN props him up on his lap, JUNE grasps his hand.)

"LAMENT"

CRAZY TOM:
        I HOPE YOU ALL KNOW
        I NEVER WANTED THIS LIFE
        I JUST WANTED TO BE
        GOOD TO YOU; MY FAMILY

        I GOT TOO CAUGHT UP
        WHEN LAUNDRY OWNERS HAD TO UNITE
        FOR IT WAS US AGAINST THE "NEW WORLD"
        IN A VERY, UNFAIR FIGHT

        SO WE MADE "OUR OWN LAW;"
        THE LAUNDRY ALLIED WORKERS IT WAS CALLED
        TOGETHER, OUR LITTLE VOICES
        MADE A SOUND SO GREAT
        AND THROUGH "OUR OWN LAW"
        SOON WE COULD CARRY OUR WEIGHT

US LAUNDRY OWNERS
HAVE NO MORE MUSIC AROUND
FOR LAUNDRY OWNERS
THERE'S JUST A FAINT SOUND
BUT LISTEN CLOSELY
WHILE THERE'S A CHANCE YOU CAN HEAR
BECAUSE THAT FAINT SOUND
SOON WILL JUST DISAPPEAR

(CRAZY TOM slides off of DYLAN's lap and lands on the floor. Suddenly, CRAZY TOM's GHOST FRIENDS appear and lift the wall entirely off of him. CRAZY TOM gets up and does a slow, processional dance with his GHOST FRIENDS as they escort him out the door. He sings)

"HOME" (Reprise)

CRAZY TOM:
MY BOYS WILL SEE ME HOME
LIKE THEY ALWAYS DO
THROUGH ALL I'VE DONE WRONG
THEY'VE SEEN ME THROUGH
WHEN DEATH HAS CALLED ME UP
 MY BOYS WOULD ALWAYS SAY
"I'M SORRY, HE'S NOT HOME TODAY"
BUT NOW THE TIME IS RIGHT
SO MY BOYS WILL SEE ME HOME

SO STEP ASIDE, MY LITTLE ONES
CAUSE WHERE I'M GONNA GO
THEY DON'T GIVE A DAMN OF WHERE YOU'VE BEEN
THEY JUST SAY "TAKE A LOAD OFF"
THEN LEAVE YOU THE HELL ALONE
SO DON'T WORRY ABOUT ME
CAUSE NOW MY BOYS WILL SEE ME HOME

HOME, WHERE OUR OWN LAW IS ALWAYS UPHELD
HOME, WHERE OUR OWN LAW IS ALWAYS UPHELD

(CRAZY TOM and GHOST FRIENDS exit. Blackout.)

EPILOGUE

One month later. DYLAN, carrying a bunch of laundry packages tied together, stands in front of the laundry with JUNE, JOSIE & BO-GEE. They watch as workers take down "The People's Laundry" sign and erect a huge "Empire National Mall" sign. After sign has been put and workers exit. DYLAN puts a small plaque on the wall. JUNE, JOSIE and BO-GEE set-up snapshots, incense and bowls of sand. Once incense is lit and distributed, JUNE comes forward with a letter.

"WHERE IS HOME?"

JUNE: WHERE IS HOME?
I USED TO KNOW
NOW IT'S TIME TO GO
TO ANOTHER HOME
WITHOUT YOU

WITHOUT YOU
I THOUGHT I WANTED TO BE
NOW IT'S SO HARD TO SEE
SO FAR GONE

SO FAR GONE
TOMORROW THAT'S WHERE I'LL BE
TODAY IS THE LAST FOR YOU AND ME
NOT FOR THE FAMILY
OUR FAMILY

HOME IS NOT JUST SOMEPLACE TO GO
HOME IS HAVING SOMETHING TO SHOW
HOME IS PLANTING SOMETHING TO GROW
AND WE'VE DONE THAT
AS LONG AS WE HAVE THAT
THEN YES, WE ARE HOME

(JUNE adds her letter to the fire, everyone joins hands and bows three times. Then, DYLAN comes forward to read his own letter.)

DYLAN: Dear Dad, We sold the laundry, cause there's no reason to stay here without you. I hope it's all right that I'm taking the remains of the "Great Wall of Laundry" back to L.A. with me. I'll set it up in my writing room as a shrine. Mom and Bo-Gee will be working in the mall...I don't think you would've liked that, but it's the best we can do right now. I'm sure Mom will be O.K., but I'll be coming back to New York regularly to take good care of her. Finally, we're putting a plaque on the building for you. I hope you like it. It says:

"PROCLAMATION"

DYLAN: (*Spoken*) You may say
THIS WAS JUST ANOTHER LAUNDRY
JUST ANOTHER MOM AND POP STORE
JUST ANOTHER FAILED SMALL BUSINESS
JUST LIKE THE ONE BEFORE
BUT THIS ONE WAS REALLY DIFFERENT
UNLIKE ANY OTHER STORE
THIS WAS THE LAST HAND LAUNDRY IN CHINATOWN
AND YOU WON'T SEE IT ANYMORE

JUNE: YOU WON'T SEE THE FAMILIES TOGETHER
GENERATIONS SIDE BY SIDE

JOSIE: GENERATIONS TEACHING EACH OTHER
GENERATIONS SHARING PRIDE

BO-GEE: PEOPLE CARING FOR EACH OTHER
OPENING UP WITH NOTHING TO HIDE
PUTTING THE FAMILY BEFORE THEMSELVES
WITHOUT THINKING IT'S A SACRIFICE

DYLAN: NOW I CAN'T SAY I DID THAT
BUT MY PARENTS AND GRANDPARENTS DID
AND IN MY FATHER'S DYING PLEA
HE SAID THESE WORDS TO ME;

DYLAN, BO-GEE, JUNE AND JOSIE:
"YES, THIS WAS 'THE PEOPLE'S LAUNDRY'
RUN BY THAT TROUBLE-MAKER, 'CRAZY TOM'
AND EVEN WHEN I'M DEAD AND GONE
MY SPIRIT WILL LIVE ON
THE SPIRIT OF INDEPENDENCE
THE SPIRIT TO BE FREE
THE SPIRIT OF OUR OWN LAW
THE SPIRIT OF THE PEOPLE'S LAUNDRY
HAND LAUNDRIES USED TO BE EVERYWHERE
NOW THERE'S NONE TO BE FOUND
SO WHEN YOU READ THIS, REMEMBER:
THE LAST HAND LAUNDRY IN CHINATOWN"

DYLAN: THIS MAY NOT BE OUR HOME, ANYMORE
           BUT IN OUR HEARTS,
           OUR OWN LAW WILL ALWAYS PREVAIL
           IN OUR HEARTS,
           OUR OWN LAW WILL ALWAYS PREVAIL
           AND THAT IS WHERE I WILL CALL HOME

DYLAN: Goodbye Dad. I'll really miss you. Your son, Dylan.

(DYLAN burns letter and places it in bowl near the incense, oranges and snapshots. DYLAN, BO-GEE, JUNE and JOSIE all join hands and bow three times. DYLAN bids goodbye to everyone and exits. JUNE and JOSIE exit into the mall. BO-GEE starts putting away the ritual apparatus.)

BO-GEE: Yes friends, this used to be Chinatown.

"BALLAD OF CHINATOWN" (Reprise)

BO GEE: THE MORE WE TRY TO STAY THE SAME
           THE MORE WE HAVE TO CHANGE
           JUST LOOK AROUND OLD CHINATOWN
           AND TELL ME WE'RE THE SAME
           AND TELL ME WE'RE THE SAME

           PEOPLE ALWAYS COME AND GO
           WHAT DO THEY HOPE TO FIND?

(CRAZY TOM & GHOST FRIENDS enter and begin to sing with BO-GEE.)

BO-GEE, CRAZY TOM & GHOST FRIENDS:
           ALTHOUGH WE LEAVE WE STILL SHALL SEEK
           THE THINGS WE LEFT BEHIND
           THE THINGS WE LEFT BEHIND

(BO-GEE starts to exit into the mall.)

CRAZY TOM & GHOST FRIENDS:
           FATES FULFILLED COME ONLY ONCE
           AND THEN THAT TIME IS GONE
           BUT TIME AND SPACE CANNOT ERASE
           THE FAITH WE CARRY ON
           THE FAITH WE CARRY ON

           SO DEAR FRIENDS OUR STORY ENDS

BUT THAT'S THE SIMPLE PART
AS WE ADVANCE WE MUST RETAIN
THE MEANING IN OUR HEARTS
THE MEANING IN OUR HEARTS

(BO-GEE, CRAZY TOM & GHOST FRIENDS enter the mall.)

END OF PLAY

SlutForArt

By Ping Chong & Muna Tseng

In 1990, my older brother and photographer Tseng Kwong Chi died of AIDS at the age of 39. I was suddenly robbed of an idyllic Chinese childhood we had growing up in Hong Kong, the misery of adolescence spent as immigrants in Canada, and our unspoken, steely alliance as working artists in New York, far away from the disapproving looks of our parents.

SLUTFORART began as an idea of an homage to a brother, and it has taken nine years to realize it. I began collaborating with theater director Ping Chong three years ago, and I asked him to help me with this new visual dance-theater piece. The visuals are built around projections of the now-famous iconic "tourist" snapshots series of photographs Tseng Kwong Chi took of himself, dressed in a Mao uniform, posing as a Chinese ambassador in front of highly recognized landmarks around the world. The text is culled from the hours of interviews with friends and colleagues of my brother's, all movers and shakers of the New York downtown art scene of the 1980s. The music is from his favorite music: from dad's 1950's mambos, to Nino Rota's Fellini hits, to Brooklyn caplypsos.

The choreography is mine, peppered with the insouciant poses and elegant hauteur I recall from a "first-born, number one Chinese son," the first of the last emperors.

The new work includes 98.6:- A CONVERGENCE IN 15 MINUTES, my first collaboration with Ping Chong, which serves as an intro. to SLUTFORART.

MUNA TSENG

SLUTFORART had its World Premiere at Playhouse 91 in New York City, March 2,3,4,6 & 7, 1999 in a joint presentation by The 92nd Street Y Harkness Dance Project, and Muna Tseng Dance Projects in association with Ping Chong & Company.

SLUTFORART Scene list:
1. Mock 98.6
2. Jenny and Hong Kong
3. 1st Cable Release
4. 1st Dance For My Brother
5. 2nd Cable Release
6. Party of the Year
7. Things My Frere Liked Dance
8. 3rd Cable Release
9. Interview with Tseng Kwong Chi
10. Expeditionary Series
11: Last Dance For My Brother/Monologue
Epilogue

with the voices of:
Interviewees:
      ANN MAGNUSON, actress/performance artist/friend of Kwong Chi
      KENNY SCHARF, visual artist/friend of Kwong Chi
      RICHARD MARTIN, Curator of Fashion, Metropolitan Museum of Art
      KRISTOFFER HAYNES, companion
      BILL T. JONES, choreographer worked with Keith Haring & Kwong Chi
      TIMOTHY GREENFIELD-SANDERS, fellow photographer
      JENNY YEE, cousin
      MUNA TSENG, sister
Interviewer: PING CHONG

Choreography & Performance by Muna Tseng
Conceived & Directed by Ping Chong
Projection Design: Jan Hartley
Light Design: Mark London
Sound Design: Brian Hallas
Music Collage: Hong Kong Pop, Nino Rota, Perez Perado, Eartha Kitt, Gustave Mahler
Costume Design: Han Feng
Mao Suit Tailor: Carol Ann Pelletier
Production Stage Manager: Courtney Golden
Stagehand: Hitoshi Yoshiki
Assistant to Ping Chong: Edith James
Assistant to Muna Tseng: Marcello Picone

SlutForArt

Scene 1: Mock 98.6

PING (*Voice-over*):   The things they share
The full mystery of an Other

Eyes, ears, nose, mouth,
The ability to breathe, breath.
You know, the givens:

Billions of cells working in unison
To create a walking, prancing, dancing
Likely to function
Likely to not,
Full fledged, miraculous being,
Him, her, us, them, you, me.

The full mystery of an Other
The things they share.

(*MUNA enters*)

PING (*Voice-over*):   She's 5'1/2" tall, dark eyes, short hair
What one would describe as petite,
Seeming to need protection,
Seeming to not,
Seeming to be assured
And seeming to not,
Hesitating and seeming to not,
Not to be that is.
One thing's for sure: she moves with a buttery grace.

The things they share.

MUNA: An alliance at the altar of Art

PING (*Voice-over*):   The full mystery of an Other.

MUNA: He was my idol. He was my guru.

He was impossible, but I loved him.
He was my brother.

PING (*Voice-over*):   The things they share.

MUNA: The solace in Art as a refuge from pain.

PING (*Voice-over*):   The full mystery of an Other.

(Blackout/Slide out. MUNA exits as soon as blackout occurs. Stagehand removes drum stools.)

nny and Hong Kong

*p from the '50s. Slides: Black & White Hong Kong slide fades up turns to color. After Hong
to color along the top of the image appears over the course of the scene Black & White por-
traits/close-ups of Kwong Chi. During this scene the whole image may flutter once or twice like a flag.*

PING *(Voice-over)*:   You're cousins?

JENNY *(Voice-over)*:   Yes, we're cousins.

PING *(Voice-over)*:   What kind of cousins?

JENNY *(Voice-over)*:   My mother is number 19 and Kwong Chi's father is number 14, because there
are so many aunts and aunties, we don't call names; first of all no respect. And secondly you just
couldn't remember so we all call number by number. And there's number 10, number 14, number
13, number 19, number 8, there are more close, you know. My mother And Kwong Chi's father had
the same father but different mother. Kwong Chi's father is number 2 wife son. My mother is number 3 wife.

PING *(Voice-over)*:   OK, I think that's enough. I don't think anybody can keep up with that.

JENNY *(Voice-over)*:   At that time Kwong Chi, Muna, they all lived there in that big mansion. So
here goes summer time, party time. I remember Kwong Chi then was very like delicate and very
fragile. Kwong Chi's mother, my aunt, is always the nervous type paranoid. Kwong Chi can't do this,
Kwong Chi gotta take a nap, he can't do—you know, Kwong Chi cannot play with you guys, you
know, very restricted. But the minute my number 14 aunt is out the door, like to go shopping, then
we would be dancing and singing, you know. I remember particularly, we were all chasing each
other, running up the stairs with the rest of the cousins, he fell. Big deal, right? You know just tumble down a little bit, no big deal. At that very moment my number 4 aunt walked in from shopping
or something, walked right in. Boy, she freaked out. Everybody got punished and screamed at.

I remember, we used to take Chinese painting together near where he lived and he loved to eat. One
time and we here are sitting with this painting teacher, he's an old guy, he real slow and asking us to
do the—I think we were drawing crabs you know in Chinese painting and he was instructing us how
to do it. Here Kwong Chi and I look at the water we've got to go, you know, finish it up so we can
eat our noodles and rush home in time, in a decent time. So I think our mind was off as a result, the
crab I think is supposed to have eight legs or something like that—I don't know how many legs we
draw. We draw like 20 legs, you know, keep drawing legs you know and the painting teacher looks
at us and says what is this? You know? I remember we go crazy like how many legs does a crab have?

PING *(Voice-over)*:   How would you describe his personality?

JENNY *(Voice-over)*:   Just fun-loving, you know—just loved to play. And even when he was a teenager, same thing. Any time he can have fun he would go for it. He loved to laugh I remember—he was always laughing. He always enjoyed life, I think that's his nature. He's the type that you know, do it today and forget about tomorrow.

(MUNA enters in red dress with cable release.)

JENNY *(Voice-over)*: I think he's very rebellious against his mother, at least that's the impression I got. His mother is always a pusher—push, push, push—his mother is very intellectual. I think that's what she want Kwong Chi to be, an intellectual like her. You know she never want him to be a photographer or an artist. But his father, I think they are very close. Whatever Jojo want, Jojo get. I tell you I really miss him. Every time I go to New York I say gee, I wish Jo was here, especially when you do something crazy—gee I wish he was there, he would have liked this.

(Blackout)

Scene 3: 1st Cable Release

Slides: Squares of light. MUNA is on stage in red dress with cable release.

PING *(Voice-over)*:   How did you meet Kwong Chi, when and how?

KRISTOFFER *(Voice-over)*: We met at Twilight, the only gay Asian bar in NYC at the time.

BILL *(Voice-over)*:   I think I saw Kwong's pictures before I met him.

PING *(Voice-over)*:   What's your earliest memory of Kwong Chi?

MUNA *(Voice-over)*:   I think I remember playing with him and then in the garden, in my grandfather's house in Hong Kong.

ANN *(Voice-over)*:   I can't remember the exact moment when I met him, but I remember we did a photo shoot and it was when I was running Club 57.

PING *(Voice-over)*:   Where and when did you first meet Kwong Chi?

TIMOTHY *(Voice-over)*:   I imagine I met him first—I imagine that I met Kwong Chi first through his photographs. I think he was along with Keith Haring one of the early people in the East Village scene in the mid-'80s.

RICHARD *(Voice-over)*:   I'm not sure actually when I first met Kwong Chi. I remember the first time when we had a really sustained conversation which was the show he did at Semaphore gallery of the, I think, first group of Expeditionary photographs.

KENNY *(Voice-over)*: I think I met Kwong Chi at Club 57.

ANN *(Voice-over)*:   I was running Club 57 between First and Second, it was underneath the Polish National Church. We had a juke box in the corner...so it was a mixture of Motown, old Ventures, singles and new stuff like The Flying Lizard and Devo and X-Ray Spex—that kind of stuff. And Kwong was there, dancing away. I seem to have an image of him with a joint in his hand, kind of swaying around and laughing and just being delighted by everybody. We had a "Tribute to Lawrence Welk" night, we had a hay ride hootenanny. We had an Elvis memorial night and there's a good picture of Kwong with a giant Elvis head. He was very inventive and also everything was always done very professionally, very slick. Nothing Kwong Chi did was shabby!

MUNA *(Voice-over)*: Uh, there was a lot of drugs.

(Stagehand enters and takes cable release from MUNA. MUNA starts to dance.)

ANN *(Voice-over)*:   Cabaret Voltaire and Dadaism and Andy Warhol's Factory...

PING *(Voice-over)*:   It was kind of an innocent time.

KENNY *(Voice-over)* Very innocent! You know, Kwong would just break out dancing. He was always hysterically laughing and making me laugh...it's all like big mush of great feelings. Oh god, he would walk in the room and go like hiiiii B does that sound like him, Muna?

TIMOTHY *(Voice-over)*: But I kind of remember him particularly for his elegance—you know Kwong Chi always dressed so differently from the rest of the scene.

ANN *(Voice-over)*:   He was I think just maybe a few years older than us, I'm not sure, just a couple, but he seemed so worldly. I mean he had so much knowledge both as a professional photographer and as a connoisseur of *(Laughs)* food mostly, of fashion, of beautiful, young people and of life, of music. I think his studio was the first place I heard the sound track of "La Dolce Vita," all the Nino Rota music. Oh god there's so much now all starting to flood back.

(Music: Nino Rota)

Scene 4: 1st Dance For My Brother

Music: Nino Rota. Text slides: Start of identity fugue text

An eternal tourist
A solitary figure
A solitary figure in shades
A deadpan in a Mao suit with shades
A displaced person sugared by privilege
A downtown art scamp
A throw away insouciance
A fixture of the East Village scene in the 80's
A party animal
Mao Tse Tung amid the pines, the glaciers, the snow smeared mountains
A walking cartoon guaranteed to activate stock associations of...
An Oriental
A slippage in geopolitical history
A party animal
Court photographer for Keith Haring
A reflection of...
A mirror of...
An enigmatic knight of one Billion plus
An ambiguous emissary
An objective witness
A subjective interpreter
A robotic Chinese avatar
A Chinese power doll (batteries not included)
A Joseph Tseng who is also a Tseng Kwong Chi
A latter day Caspar Friedrich Monk
An icon of the Cold War
A caricature of the yellow peril
An alter ego
A doppelganger
A SlutForArt
A photographer for Vogue and Gentlemen's Quarterly
An Asian American
An Asian American in a costume
An Asian American in a costume reproaching assimilation

A gay man or a bachelor bystander
A footnote to Keith Haring
A signifier signifying

A fixture upon which a pair of sunglasses rest
A friction between place and person
A figure upon a landscape
A prince in the funk

(*MUNA freezes then gestures to stagehand to bring her cable release.*)

Scene 5: 2nd Cable Release

Start second cable release scene voice-over just before music ends from previous scene. Slides: Continue identity fugue text then squares of light with Keith Haring subway documentation photographs and denizens of the '80s photos appearing in the squares of light.

RICHARD *(Voice-over):*   You know...you know as one looks back...you know as one looks back on the '80s art world, there were such extraordinary things that happened.

MUNA *(Voice-over)*   One day Kwong Chi just said, "Oh I met this really cool guy and his name is Keith Haring and we met on First Avenue."

RICHARD *(Voice-over):*   There were young artists...

PING *(Voice-over):*   For example.

MUNA *(Voice-over):*   Keith was a student at the School of Visual Arts at that time.

RICHARD *(Voice-over):*   There were young artists...

PING *(Voice-over):*   For example

RICHARD *(Voice-over):*   Keith Haring is someone/thing like that—who was immediately catapulted into a kind of fame and recognition.

MUNA *(Voice-over):*   Then he started drawing on the subways on the blank, black paper, before the advertising was put on. Kwong Chi decided that this was such historical, monumental work that Keith was giving to the people of New York and so Kwong Chi started to document and photograph this body of work.

MUNA *(Voice-over):*   Keith was very savvy because the first line he did was the E & F that went through the 53rd Street and 5th Avenue stop, because that's the Museum of Modern Art stop.

RICHARD*(Voice-over):*   Keith Haring is someone/something like that—who was immediately catapulted into a kind of fame and recognition.

ANN *(Voice-over):*   Suddenly we were in Keith's limousine, you know, going off to fabulous parties and, getting to meet Andy Warhol and going to Mr. Chow's.

TIMOTHY *(Voice-over):*   Artists were stars and the art world blossomed.

ANN *(Voice-over):* It was just like eight different events every night so you were always.

RICHARD *(Voice-over)*: He seemingly happened to be there at the right place at the right...

TIMOTHY *(Voice-over)*: And Wall Street was powerful...

ANN *(Voice-over)*: Jumping in a cab, hooking up with people somewhere...

TIMOTHY *(Voice-over)*: And there was money everywhere.

RICHARD *(Voice-over)*:There were these sort of jokes about the youngest artist to be seen in the East Village.

ANN *(Voice-over)*: It was very exhilarating, very intoxicating.

RICHARD *(Voice-over)*: In a sense it is one of those great times in which one has a sense of art can be anything...

TIMOTHY *(Voice-over)*: And there was money everywhere that was the shiny side of the coin and the dark side of the coin was AIDS.

(Music slowly fade up during this scene and with the word AIDS it bumps out. Also with the word AIDS the squares of light flutters and as it flutters—dissolve into Manchu robes in Black & White still fluttering and then the flutter settles and title for next scene comes up.)

Scene 6: Party of the Year

Slide: Identity fugue text continues into this scene. Following text slide appears over Manchu robes image which goes from Black & White to color.

THE MANCHU DRAGON
Costumes of the Ch'ing Dynasty 1644 - 1912

(Fades out. Fades in.)

A Party of the Year.

(Slides of the party appear in a choreographed slide sequence.)

RICHARD *(Voice-over)*:   The Metropolitan Museum party photographs I think are extremely important because it was a party/part of the year for the Chinese costume exhibition that Mrs. Vreeland had done and so in part it was—everybody was dressed up or many of the people were— Adele Simpson and others—in a kind of New York Chinoiserie in which they were trying to sort of emulate this-sort-of world in China. Kwong Chi comes to the party as a representative of "The SOHO Weekly News."He shows up there in the Mao suit and I think no one knows whether this is a member of the press, whether this is, you know, an emissary from the Chinese government.

(MUNA exits)

PING *(Voice-over)*:   Cabinet

RICHARD *(Voice-over)*:   Right! Exactly! Like an emissary from Cathay in an 18th Century European court. Here are all the Europeans or the Americans here, who are dressed up in this extravagant way—trying to be as Chinese as possible and there's this young man who walks among them who is innately and in a way, intrudes upon them and yet is at the same time—you know the one who is observing them, inasmuch as they're dressed up they must have been more captivated by him and by his mystery—than anything that they could, put together as those sort of fake Chinoserie outfits.

KENNY *(Voice-over)*: I remember I wanted to learn Chinese and I was very into Chinese culture and I had made up this language, was part of my paintings and I had made up this big dance with this scarf. It was like a Chinese scarf dance and I was like, you know Kwong was part of that. I would make sounds like—when I would be making a mark, you know? Like crazy. I'd do stuff in Japanese scroll style, like paper scrolls and Chinese landscapes, you know misty watercolors and then you know how they'd have the Chinese writing, telling the story? Well I had my own writing, telling my own story, that kind of thing? And it looked a little, it didn't really look Chinese, it looked Chinese and space age or I don't know. Telegraphic. Do you remember that, Muna?

MUNA *(Voice-over)*: I remember some of those, yeah. You were really crazy.

KRISTOFFER *(Voice-over)*: I don't think that he really enjoyed being Asian so much. Anytime that I mentioned doing anything related to Asian or Chinese culture he would just put it down, he didn't want to have anything to do with it.

MUNA *(Voice-over)*: In 1988 my parents wanted to have a family trip back to China and this was the first trip back to China, since they left in 1948. I took it to be a very important trip of a pilgrimage to my native land and to accompany my parents back from exile after a 40 year absence—to see my mother's sister, who she hadn't seen for 40 years. I thought that Kwong Chi would very much want to come along on this pilgrimage, but Kwong Chi didn't go! And he didn't, he didn't seem to think that was such a missed opportunity.

PING *(Voice-over)*: How did you meet Kwong Chi? When and how?

KRISTOFFER *(Voice-over)*: We met at Twilight, the only gay Asian bar at the time.

PING *(Voice-over)*: What's Twilight like?

KRISTOFFER *(Voice-over)*: Asian men go there to meet Caucasian men and Caucasian men go there to meet Asian men and people drink and try to pick each other up. I thought he looked very sexy in his Mao suit.

BILL *(Voice-over)*: I think he described himself to me once as a snow queen, any person of color who prefers white men and but yet by the same token, he was very aware of the races and the way in which Asian people were viewed, and I think that's what I saw a lot in his work. He was taken aback that I was in a way, before people were really talking about identity politics.

MUNA *(Voice-over)*: He did not want to be identified as an Asian-American artist, he hated that. He said I'm an artist.

BILL *(Voice-over)*: However, his imagery was always the curious, blank Chinese tourist. I would say to Kwong that you don't fool me. I, I know, I can sense protest when I see it. This is a rough conversation we were having, that this blankness was the way in which this culture at large expected him, as an Asian man, to—to exist. So he became a kind of a cipher, a smooth surface that because it was so impenetrable, this persona, it reflected everything!

ANN *(Voice-over)*: I remember going with him to the Vietnam Vets parade, the one that the country finally gave the Vets, you know, like twenty years too late and him photographing. I mean, there was this Asian fellow at a Vietnam Vet parade? In a Chinese Communist uniform? He'd get in the middle of the street and wait till like the last possible second they were as close as they could be before he took the picture. He was fearless. Absolutely fearless!

PING *(Voice-over)*:   You said that he knew that he couldn't pass.

BILL *(Voice-over)*:   ...but we started this by saying if you have in fact, as a bright, intelligent let's say Asian person or even Indian or whatever and you are a nuclear physicist, right? You have tenure at Yale or Princeton. You have everything, the best that the society could offer you, but what you don't have is inclusion in that, that you are not white. And I think now to be white means to be powerful. See that's what I was saying before.

PING *(Voice-over)*:   To be entitled, immediately!

BILL *(Voice-over)*:   Um hum. This young man, educated, I think from a pretty affluent background, right?

PING *(Voice-over)*:   Um hum.

BILL *(Voice-over)*:   What was it that he still didn't have from the culture at large? And it's that inclusion, that's what the question was—why is that fucking inclusion so important to us? Because it represents power, but I'm saying you have power! You have economic power. Intellectual power. What power don't you have? And you're saying there is, there is, there is this entitlement. This I think we can feel it, but he was trying to express it, I think, by this retreat if you will, of maybe this appropriation of this official Other, this stranger, a stranger...He can't be hurt, he needs nothing, he is completely self-contained, he is just moving through. I am just a tourist here, right?

MUNA *(Voice-over)*:   Well this persona in this official uniform gave him access to those various worlds of white power, the first one being the costume, the party of the year at the Met.

BILL *(Voice-over)*:   —Yes, that's right!

MUNA *(Voice-over)*:   I think it was Yves St. Laurent or yeah—Yves St. Laurent said to him because they were speaking in French and he says, you must be an ambassador from China *(BILL laughs.)* to speak French so well!

BILL *(Voice-over)*:   Ah hah!

MUNA *(Voice-over)*:   So there again, it's the whole play of why is this yellow person speaking French so well.

PING *(Voice-over)*:   ...Or English.

MUNA *(Voice-over)*:   Or English.

BILL *(Voice-over)*:   Well, there was something of an aristocrat in his strategy. You know the way that the eccentricities of most of the English aristocrats. They are set apart, they are maybe not comfortable where they come from, they have a—when you're up that high, this is a metaphor—you have a pretty wide view, you know. But by the same token, you're somewhat isolated and off the ground. That's the aristocrat's dilemma in a way. So in a way he made the art feel almost like the art of an aristocrat.

Scene 7: Things My Frere Liked Dance

Music: Eartha Kitt

Slide text: Things Kwong Chi liked plus other layers from previous scene which may be dissolving underneath. This text below is not in presentation order! Just a rough list. MUNA enters dressed in grey Mao suit.

Sole picasso
Federico Fellini's *La Dolce Vita*
Early morning mist, Vermont Lake
Falling foliage
Drunken crabs at Double Happiness
Rita Hayworth's brows
Soca in Brooklyn
Black truffle omelette
7 Lonely Days
Dancing all night at Bahia Carnivale
Marilyn Monroe
Bill T. Jones' physique
Kenny's beach, Ilheus, Brazil
Everything about Elvis Presley
Dinner parties at Mr. Chow's
Noodles
Keith Haring's subway forays
Guilietta Masina
Jean Cocteau's hands
Di Roberti's espresso
Rue du Dragon
Theatre 80's double features, remember Theatre 80?
Maria Callas
Noodles
Montblanc cakes at Patesserie Claude
Je ne regrette rien
DJ'ing at the Michael Todd Room, Palladium
Fred Astaire
Roma
New York
Paris
Afternoons at Cafe de Flore
Whole suckling pig on Chinese New Year
Peres Prado's Mambos
Mighty Sparrow

Gertrude Stein
Buffet lunches at the Mandarin Hotel in Hong Kong
Labor Day Calypso Parade
Brigitte Bardot
Nino Rota
Les Enfants du Paradise

Scene 8: 3rd Cable Release

MUNA remains on stage, stagehand brings on cable release and hands it to MUNA. Slides: Squares of light, text slides from previous scene may still be up. Slide: KENNY SCHARF's installation image comes up.

KENNY *(Voice-over)*: Well he'd always take us out to Chinatown. I remember having the most incredible Chinese food and Kwong would take this whole group of East Village weirdos and we'd all go to this totally Chinese restaurant and this big table and he ordered in Chinese, that was always a fun ritual. We were just such freaks for all the Chinese people in the restaurant.

KENNY *(Voice-over)*: Well, I think he had difficulties with his father. The whole gay thing. I think was really hard on your dad, right Muna?

MUNA *(Voice-over)*: Yeah.

KENNY *(Voice-over)*: Yeah, that was a big issue all through his life, all the way until the end and hey, Kwong was gay! I mean, come on, I mean! I wish that his dad, your dad could have been more...

MUNA *(Voice-over)*: Yeah, he never, I don't think he ever understood it or

KENNY *(Voice-over)*: He never did.

MUNA *(Voice-over)*: ...wanted to understand or accept it, you know.

KENNY *(Voice-over)*: That's always a hard thing, but most of us we're like almost misfits in a way and outcasts from our communities and our families, for whatever reason. And that was, we had adopted each other as our, as family.

(Stagehand brings chair on stage and places it. Then exits.)

KENNY *(Voice-over)*: Yes, he talked about Paris and I think he learned a lot living there and he spoke French very well and it just made him just so much more sophisticated than he already was. Kwong liked the finer things! Didn't he?

MUNA *(Voice-over)*: He demanded the finer things.

PING *(Voice-over)*: But he was also comfortable with a lot of different kinds of people though? He wasn't..

KENNY *(Voice-over)*: Oh yeah, he'd be fine in the jungle, you know, eating bug eyes with, you know Indians.

MUNA *(Voice-over)*: Coconuts

KENNY (*Voice-over*): He'd be equally happy at the Ritz. He was very, very adaptable and you know, had that Chinese thing like he'd go anywhere in the world and just be fine.

KENNY (*Voice-over*): Well, I mean God I spent so much time with Kwong...Kwong was always very into music and anything tropical, in fact Kwong was a very tropical person. He kind of adopted the tropics, the Caribbean and Brazil.

KENNY (*Voice-over*): I remember when, I just had this memory of him in Carnival, everyone dresses up and he was like green. He had a green wig on and a green dress on and we called him—it was such a funny name like China green or I don't remember. And we were just running through the streets, screaming and you know, dancing—it was just fun.

(*MUNA hands cable release to stagehand who comes on to take it off.*)

KENNY (*Voice-over*): I'm very happy to see Kwong getting, finally, what he should have had during his lifetime, which is recognition of his art work. I think it was very frustrating for him—I know it was—especially because everyone was focusing on you know, Keith, John Michel, and me. He really wasn't getting the respect that he deserved. I realized that it's hard to have to listen to someone go on about all the great things that are happening and recognition and then not getting yourself and I could feel that was affecting his, you know, mood. It was, it's hard.

(*MUNA sits in chair with back to audience.*)

PING (*Voice-over*):   Where were you toward the end of his life? Were you still close at that point?

KENNY (*Voice-over*): Yes, I was close and this is the hard, I mean it really-it was very, very difficult, you know, being with him you know every step of the way—all the way, you know I hadn't thought about that for a while. It was very hard.

KENNY (*Voice-over*): I just think he was always celebrating, you know, just life in general. He was such an alive person.

KENNY (*Voice-over*): God I just miss him so much, he's still around in my life!

Scene 9: Interview with Tseng Kwong Chi

Slide: Square of light behind MUNA which turns into the expeditionary series photographs starting with the little house in Provincetown.

MUNA: I take pictures of myself because it is easier for me than having to direct somebody. On the other hand, I always set up my photos by composing perfectly the situation in advance. After that, I can get in front of the camera knowing the rest of the picture is what I want it to be; it leaves me the freedom to do what I wish within that frame, take chances. Also, you must have noticed that on these photos, I wear mirror glasses to block out my eyes; when you can't read the eyes, you become an object; it gives the picture a neutral impact, a kind of surrealistic quality I'm looking for.

The whole idea got started when I read that Nixon was going to China and open a dialogue with my country; a real cultural exchange was supposed to take place between the East and the West, but after a year or so, everything had stayed on a very official level and nothing substantial had been done. Today, the only Americans who are allowed in China are not so much the rich, but the people who, somehow belong to an elite; the visa is given to famous artists, musicians, scientists, politicians. So, I really got disappointed by all this and I thought it would be a good idea to make a statement about it.

(Slide: Provincetown image appears here beginning Expeditionary series images.)

MUNA: In 1979, I went to Provincetown, and I ran into a funny beach house; I happened to have my Chinese costume with me and that is how I did my first self-portrait; then, I took a trip around the USA and being interested in finding out what Americans worship in their country. I followed the trail of the typical places they love to visit. I find the architecture of American monuments quite wonderful; these monuments pretend to be authentic and their perfect realization brings out a kind of beauty; yet, we know they are the imitations of the real thing somewhere in Europe and that brings out the tacky note. The Parthenon in Nashville is a good illustration of my comment.

There's no prerequisite to taste in this country, something which would be unthinkable in Europe. Americans acquire what they want without questioning anything: that is certainly one of the reasons why the country is so dynamic. I find especially fascinating but also alienating in many ways the futuristic quality of their environment, like these new cities. Miami, Dallas or Las Vegas while holding on to very conventional and traditional social values.

When Diana Vreeland's Chinese Costume Show was about to have its opening, I learned that nobody was going to cover it! So, I immediately called their public relations and I explained my project to them. They got very excited over the idea. I put my Chinese national uniform on and I went to the opening taking with me a tape recorder. I interviewed many famous people that evening; I asked them what they were wearing, who had designed their dresses and what they thought of the show; it was the first time I did interviews and I got a good kick out of it. It was very entertaining. Paloma Picasso got her costume all wrong; she has a Japanese kimono on; Nancy Kissinger had purchased for the occasion a $5,000 dress designed by Adolfo and she ran into a woman who was wearing the exact same one. The interesting thing is the attitude they adopt under such circumstances. In France, a woman would feel terribly embarrassed and offended. In this country, they take it rather graciously. I took a picture of those two ladies with me in the middle and they thought nothing of it. I believe a sort of silent complicity took place between them, because wearing the same dress means they belong to the same crowd; it is reassuring.

I would like to go on the road again, but, in a more luxurious way! Perhaps with a mobile home, spacious and comfortable; also, take as much time as I want. There is a trip I hope I will do very soon. I want to go to EPCOT, Experimental prototype Community Of Tomorrow in Florida, the last born project of Walt Disney. Practically everything on Earth has been reproduced in that city: I will be able to do my self-portraits without the burden of real traveling: no taxis, no airports, no jet lag! And it will cost a lot less.

(MUNA exits. Stagehand removes drum stool.)

Scene 10: Expeditionary Series

Slides: The expeditionary series continues without voice-over or anything else. Then the voice-overs begin.

RICHARD *(Voice-over)*:   I think it was about two things. I think it was about two things happening at once, the sense of Kwong Chi himself as the artist who is moving through the world and not really a part of it.

ANN *(Voice-over)*:   I guess in Disneyland, didn't they think he was from Communist China?

MUNA *(Voice-over)*:   Yeah, especially when he had the ID badge on that said, "SlutForArt."

TIMOTHY *(Voice-over)*:   How did he do that? How did he get into some far location, trigger a camera? I mean technically they were incredibly accomplished. Did he have time release shutters?

KRISTOFFER *(Voice-over)*:   That trip was when he first stopped using the squeezing thing and he was so excited he ran down a hill to scout out a location and he lost that squeezing thing and that's when he went further away from the camera because he no longer needed that cord.

ANN *(Voice-over)*:   I think he had more of an understanding of America, had more appreciation of America than most Americans.

BILL *(Voice-over)*:   The world changed in light of this one persona, not the persona changed in the light of the world.

RICHARD *(Voice-over)*:   It's strange that as someone who admired the work and made that admiration clear, in terms of writing about it on a number of occasions and being very enthusiastic about it, I always found that I was more enthusiastic about his work than he was. I was the one overwhelmed and he was barely whelmed.

KENNY *(Voice-over)*: We would all be out and whatever—doing, looking, exploring, and we'd see the elephant and go, "Oh my god" and he'd stop and he'd set up and do me and the elephant.

MUNA *(Voice-over)*:   So he always had his suit with him and things like that?

KENNY *(Voice-over)*: Oh, in the trunk of the car, yeah.

MUNA *(Voice-over)*:   And his camera equipment?

KENNY *(Voice-over)*: Everything!

ANN *(Voice-over)*:   Then when everyone started dying, I felt that I was really operating through a nervous breakdown and it seemed like the whole world was falling apart.

TIMOTHY *(Voice-over)*:　Of course, they were very beautiful—the way that frame them. The way that the light...he captured the light of the environment. They were kind of like Ansel Adams taken to a new level.

RICHARD *(Voice-over)*:　In my experience Kwong Chi was not the 80s artist out to establish his own reputation, at all. If anything he was almost the polar opposite of that.

TIMOTHY *(Voice-over)*:　And then that scene essentially, as Robert Pinkus Whiton said, "That scene turned on a dime." And that scene ended almost over night.

MUNA *(Voice-over)*:　His figure in the last works became smaller and smaller, like Chinese paintings, the classical paintings, man did not matter so much in this, in the wonder of nature.

ANN *(Voice-over)*:　He really unlocked a lot of doors, opened up a lot of windows. I guess as a little hick girl from West Virginia, who, strangely enough, I do get a little timid about going into new territories, and he certainly was an inspiration that way.

ANN *(Voice-over)*:　I remember, I remember Kitty called me up to tell me that he died. I remember where I was exactly. I had an old phone and I remember sitting on the ground just crying, just sobbing, you know. And looking out at the California sunshine and just feeling just such, this bottomless pit of sorrow that everyone died.

TIMOTHY *(Voice-over)*:　You're used to your parents dying, or your grandparents dying, but you're not used to your best friends dying! And, that I think was devastating for a lot of people.

KRISTOFFER *(Voice-over)*:　I get the feeling that he's at peace with himself, and more comfortable with being Chinese, and having his picture taken with that suit on.

(Slide fades out.)

I⋯ ⋯ides. Music: Mahler. MUNA enters after music starts, begins dance until music fades. MUNA on floor upstage left.

MUNA: When his eyesight started to go it really freaked him out. He needed his eyes. He was still talking about all these photographs he was going to shoot in Alaska. He was fighting so hard for life, for something to live for. When his left eye started to go he said, "Oh, thank god I focus with my right eye!"

One day I was cooking him lunch in the hospital, no hospital food for Kwong Chi, and tears were streaming down his face. I said, "What's the matter?" He said, "Oh I just love that song!" It was Edith Piaf singing "Je Ne Regret Rien."

Then on March 10, 1990, in his apartment at 14 Maiden Lane at 4 AM, Kwong Chi died of AIDS. He wanted to be cremated and have his ashes scattered into New York harbour from the Statue of Liberty which made me realize how much he loved New York. At Very Special Flowers on 10th Street, I found some beautiful, Shaker cedar boxes so I bought one, but when I tried to put the ashes into the box it didn't fit. I didn't know a person could make so much ash.

I think Kwong Chi never looked back much. I don't think he thought about the future much either. He always lived intensely in the moment like right here, right now celebrating all that life had to offer.

(Fade to black. MUNA exits. Sound of wind in a canyon.)

Epilogue

(Slide: Slide fades up of image from the expeditionary series of KWONG CHI with his back to the camera looking into the Grand Canyon. The image establishes itself, then Kwong Chi vanishes from the landscape. After a beat or two, Kwong Chi's full name appears on top of the image, dead center and the date of his birth and death, the names of celebrities and friends who died of AIDS in the last decade and a half appear around the image of the Grand Canyon. The memorial names stay up and the Grand Canyon fades away. The house lights go up.)

List of names for AIDS Memorial

Jim Thomas

David Lusby

Gin Louie

John Bernd

Lee Connor

Bill Anselmo

Bob Carroll

Michael Mathews

Robert Sterns

Arnie Zane

Michael Ciccarelli

Julio Galindo

Robert Labiak

Mario Saboya

Charles Ludlum

Georg Osterman

Chip Elwell

Bernard Samilon

Robert & Carole Wolfe

James Driver

Fidelio Bartolomea

Frank McDermott

Frank Moss

James Chumbley

Bill Ford

Gordon Bonwell

Rudolf Nureyev

Huck Snyder

Peter Anderson

Roland Roux

Wayne Springer

Daniel Mahoney

Robert Stark

John DeMonico

Ari Darom

Manuel Alum

Keith Haring

Michael Schwartz

John Sex

Dan Friedman

David Wojnarowicz

Tom Rubnitz

Robert Mapplethorpe

END OF PLAY

III THE VERBAL MURAL

PROLOGUE:
IN THE BEGINNING...

I started what is now called "Asian American theatre" in New York in 1970 with La MaMa Chinatown. Ching Yeh and Wu Gingi, who were a part of La MaMa, told me that they wanted very much to have something in Chinatown. They told me that the only thing in Chinatown was an occasional traveling troupe doing Beijing opera and not really anything else, and would I come and do something? So I did. We were able to get the basement of the Transfiguration Church on Mott Street, and the first La MaMa Chinatown show was THREE TRAVELERS WATCH THE SUNRISE by Wallace Stevens on August 6, 1970. In 1972, we changed the name of La MaMa Chinatown to La MaMa Asian Repertory Theatre. Then in 1976, they asked if they could call themselves Pan Asian Repertory Theatre; I trained Tisa Chang. So I can't say that somebody else wouldn't have come along and started Asian American theatre, but I was the one.

ELLEN STEWART

Out of respect for Ping Chong, I think he was the first Asian American to be produced in New York . I think that same year 1972 he had had something done at La MaMa off-off Broadway. He's been pissed at me for laying claim to being the first Chinese American playwright to be produced in NYC , when he was really the first (laughs). THE CHICKENCOOP CHINAMAN was maybe the first Asian American play produced a step up from off-off-Broadway, but not that much. But if you've ever read THREE TIMES I-BOW by this writer named Carl Crow, he writes that he had gotten a Workcore grant in the '30s to put together a theatre company, I think, called the Jung Wah Players, in New York's Chinatown. He writes that these Chinese Americans were anxious to put on a translation of a Chinese opera. A member of that group, Wood Moy, was a printer in San Francisco and then joined my theatre group Asian American Theatre Workshop in the '70s. Wood said that it was Carl Crow's idea to do this opera and that they were all American born and knew nothing really about China or Chinese opera. They were interested in doing American stuff - whatever that was.

FRANK CHIN

I don't know what he's talking about. Frank Chin is completely paranoid. How could I be mad at him for being the first Asian American produced in New York when I don't give a shit about that stuff! In fact, I think he's the pioneer...on that coast. The first time I ever had any contact with him was when a Chinese journalist said to me, "Frank Chin says that you are an expatriate," and I've never even met this man! So I laughed and said to the journalist, "How can I be an expatriate when I've never even been to China?" I'm a New Yorker. I grew up in Chinatown and went from a public school that was 99 percent Chinese kids to a junior high school that was half Chinese and half Italian kids, to a high school where I was the only Chinese kid and graduated as one of only four Asian kids. Then I went to Pratt Institute where again I was pretty much on my own. So basically that arc, that journey, was one of adjustment of growing up in a very enclosed cultural community to one that I really didn't understand. By the time I started working with Meredith Monk in 1971, and then doing my own pieces starting in '72, I was still working that out and I didn't have any kind of support group or anything because Asian American movements and all that stuff was just starting. It was a very difficult time for me because I was negotiating this identity schism on my own. So from the very beginning, my work was always about the issue of culture and the Other. When I finally met Frank Chin years later, he starts to rant, which is very Frank Chin, and he says "Your friend Erika Monk...blah, blah, blah," I don't remember exactly what he said. But I said "My friend Erica Monk? I'm not a friend of Erica Monk." So he immediately starts off being hostile. Then he goes, "Amy Tan is not Asian American, she's a Baptist." So I said, "Well, you're the first Asian American bigot I've ever met."

PING CHONG

I wrote the THE CHICKENCOOP CHINAMAN to get off Maui. I was on Maui with a bunch of other acid casualty friends. We were doing construction and we were all just too stoned too long and accidents started to happen and I had to find a way off. So I read about

East West Players' in Los Angeles playwrighting contest, wrote THE CHICKENCOOP CHINAMAN, won the contest and got off the island. East West said the play was too difficult to do, or beyond their technical capabilities, so they didn't do it. A friend of mine, Ishmael Reed, sent it to Harry Belafonte Enterprises, and the producer there, Chiz Schultz, sent it to Wynn Handman. Handman called me up and said let's do it.

FRANK CHIN

Since I started the American Place Theatre in the early '60s I had one phrase that guided me: to put voices worth hearing on the stage. So I didn't think that I was doing the first Asian American or Chinese American play on stage. When you do these things you don't know that you're making history. Chiz Schultz was on my advisory board and he sent me THE CHICKENCOOP CHINAMAN'S PREGNANT PAUSE—that was the original title—by Frank Chin because he knew it would be one of my type of plays. It may not have been as fat as the Manhattan phone book, but it was at least as fat as the Queens or Brooklyn phone book. So we proceeded to bring Frank in from California, because we had to get this play down to some size that was manageable, but Frank was a hard man to manage. He had and still has so much talent and anger and fury in him and such a wild imagination that it creates a turbulence that just keeps exploding. So when you ask him to change something in a scene, he comes back with a long prologue when you don't need a prologue. I haven't thought about this for a long time, but ironically, Frank stayed in the apartment of Harold Ickes, on the Upper West Side. We knew Harold, who's now my son-in-law, because he ran the New York state campaign for Eugene McCarthy in 1968, and his father was the Secretary of the Interior for F.D.R.'s administrations known as "The Curmudgeon." The Curmudgeon was the only one in the Roosevelt administration who openly opposed the incarceration of Japanese Americans. My father-in-law would be a hero to Frank...These were my original notes from when I first read Frank's script: "The talent is squandered because the scenes are too loose and drawn out. The writing is excessive. The audience will be too worn out by the time the play is less than half over. It needs focusing, tightening and cutting, but the talent is abundant, original, genuine and full of force needed for drama. This is the 'Chinese Look Back in Anger.' You must know that what we do to minority groups will ultimately produce its anger and then its violence, even with the Chinaman."

WYNN HANDMAN

In the early days, the 70s, it was quite a pejorative term to be called "minority theatre" or "ethnic theatre." Then we got the terms, "ethnic-specific" or "multicultural," and that sort of softened it or made us legitimate. I guess in the early days Asian American theatre felt like the step-child; we were not really fairly dealt with in terms of funding, recognition, press. I think much of that changed due to our Pan Asian Repertory Theater's success. When I started Pan Asian Rep, I just wanted to do something really meaningful to expand the American theatre. American theatre was very much dominated by a WASP mentality since the turn of the 20th century. By the 1970s, I thought we want to have a little chance because we are Americans! I thought the definition of American theatre was a little narrow if you limit it to everybody that's in the Antoinette Perry Awards. So I wanted to expand it to also include the very enriching traditions of the master works of China, Japan and India, but in a way that bridged both Asian and American cultures. Because at that time, the traditional Asian arts were always these pieces that foreign troupes would bring over and you would see them in a museum or lecture hall setting and it was rather boring. I'm not putting the Asia Society down, but I thought why don't I put these works in a truly integrated theatrical environment? So I guess in a way, I was a little revolutionary. And this was way before Peter Sellars and his "Peony Pavilion."

TISA CHANG

By the mid-'70s, things like the National Endowment for the Arts and the New York State Council on the arts and a lot of the foundations that had been giving to the arts were really established for a decade. Once that happened, there were a lot of forms to fill out and in a lot of the narratives for these grant proposals you had to justify why you were getting these grants. And part of this justification had

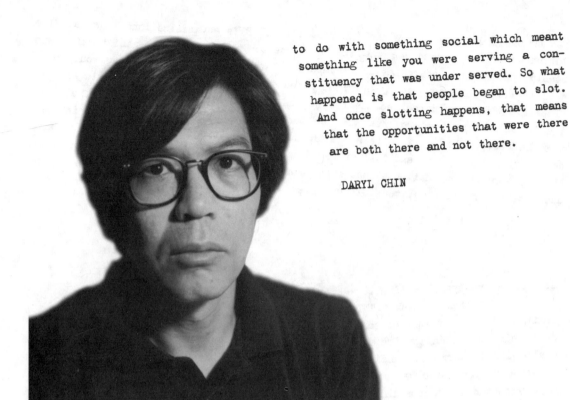

to do with something social which meant
something like you were serving a con-
stituency that was under served. So what
happened is that people began to slot.
And once slotting happens, that means
that the opportunities that were there
are both there and not there.

DARYL CHIN

ACT I:
WHAT BECOMES ASIAN AMERICAN THEATRE MOST?

1. How far have we come?

There are more playwrights now that we can speak about, but I don't know how many more people are getting produced since that 1972 splash when Frank Chin's play came out. David Henry Hwang had his huge success in 1988 with M. BUTTERFLY, and not that Broadway has to be the barometer, because it's such a rarefied arena for anybody, white, yellow, black or brown because the stakes are so high in terms of money. So I'm certainly not expecting all of us to make it there. But there hasn't really been a huge, huge success for an Asian American playwright since then, and that was over ten years ago!

JESSICA HAGEDORN

Having gone through that period now where it's no longer a radical thing for New York theatrical audiences to see a play about the black or Asian experience or whatever, it's important that theatrical institutions and artistic directors begin to understand the context of the work they are dealing with to present it in the best way. The same way that if you were to do Shakespeare that you wouldn't do it without knowledge of the period or meter. You have to have a point of view about it. Theatres that program these ethnic works for token reasons are doing a disservice to their audiences, to themselves and ultimately to the artists and communities from where the plays come. And that probably can be attributed to a degree of tokenism in that the artistic directors of institutions do not feel sufficiently connected or committed to the work of an Asian American author to make that commitment irrespective of how a given work performs critically or commercially.

DAVID HENRY HWANG

SAKINA'S RESTAURANT was written by a student of mine, Aasif Mandvi. He developed all these characters in my class. It ran for 202 performances here and it was very gratifying to see how that audience became more and more Indian. By the time we closed, well over half and sometimes 75 percent of the audience was Indian. I so wanted them to come, because when the experience is shared-the recognition, the laughter, the tears-in an audience between people of different races, the race that is not being represented on the stage learns something about the other people.

WYNN HANDMAN

Now, with large white companies putting Asian American plays into their season once a year how that effects us is that Pan Asian, which is a small to medium theatre with four people on our staff, still cannot compete with The Public Theater in terms of promotion and marketing. When they have an Asian American play, they have a theatre that can sustain it. We still rent our theatre space and we're locked into schedules at St. Clement's. We're locked into what unions will allow us on the contract that we're able to afford. We don't have an 18-million dollar budget like The Public Theater does. In that way I feel a little frustrated. I feel that most of ethnic-specific, multicultural theatres are small to medium-size, and for the price of independence and the price of that originality, hand carved originality, we've given up a lot.

TISA CHANG

Asian Americans have had little or lack of representation within the theatre community. There are only a few major institutions that actually produce and support Asian American works like, for example, The Public Theatre. But they only do one Asian American play a year and other institutions don't even have an Asian American "slot" so to speak. I'm really disappointed that as we approach the millennium, I sense a lack of cohesion between mainstream institutions and the Asian American community because there a lot of talented playwrights, directors and artists who are forced to play in tiny venues where only people from within their own community will see them-be it at the Asian American Writers' Workshop, P.S. 122 or La MaMa. What I notice even more is that what gets presented as Asian American work in mainstream institutions in particular doesn't represent the current stuff that is out there by Asian American artists who try to push the envelope. I think what happens then is that we start to lose our voice even more because we see the one play that goes up. Then when it's not good because it's riddled with issues or it's an immigration story which a lot of folks think is old news, or it's catering to the white audience, no one in the community supports that. Then the mainstream audience sees this and says, "Wow this is really bad. Why am I going to support this crap? I could go see a black play or a Jewish play and it would be much more fascinating than an Asian American play." It's a pretty sad state of reality when David Henry Hwang is not known to the arts community and then he is our only representative. We should have ten people like him. I feel we're in a pretty crappy place, I have to say, compared to other people and artists of color-especially in New York, the center of our culture and theatre.

GARY SAN ANGEL

Benefiting from the groundwork having been laid by the previous generation of superior crafts people, my generation has the latitude to play more. We have a tradition to respond to. The earlier generation, like David Henry Hwang, Philip Gotanda, Jessica Hagedorn, felt the responsibility to first present images of Asian Americans and say "We are here." And I think it is my generation who's going to say, "We are weird."

DIANA SON

2. What does being an Asian American theatre artist mean to you?

Asian American theatre is a relatively new concept if you think about it. We only go back 20-30 years, so we have all of those issues to work through-chief of which is the immigrant experience. Writers need to get this out of their system. It's their most immediate experience of all; growing up, family, generations, racism, gender. We have to get through that before we start getting into all the other iterations of American life. It takes a certain amount of maturity as a writer to hone in on the nitty gritty of relationships and look at other situations, and as we develop Asian American theatre that'll happen.

RALPH B. PEÑA

We have an opportunity that no other people have: to tell people who we are. To show ourselves who we are and we haven't done it. Instead we're saying we're just like you, we're something Other. We're not. We have not looked at our history, and we believe that there are human beings and then there are minorities. No! Any real writer of any worth writes as if "I am the fucking universal man! Anyone who knows less than me is stupid!" Green, yellow, purple, whatever, any real writer writes from that point of view. But here we all are writing in this Christian form of confessional autobiography, pitching, "Please, puh-lease, puh-lease for-give me for being an Asian. Puh-lease I am really a human being." Fuck that.

FRANK CHIN

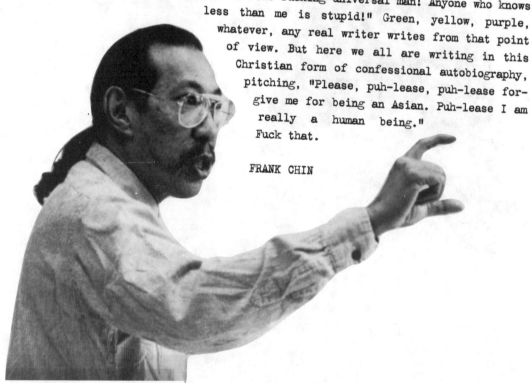

I'm not a "professional Asian American" so I've dealt with it in my own personal way. I've never been a joiner of any one group. By personality or choice I've always been Other. People say he's part of the avant-garde, well the white avant-garde never really academically accepted me. Like with Performing Arts Journal, I never really fit their white theories. Then some Asian American organizations might say, "Oh, he's not really part of the Asian American scene." But then because I have visibility and am needed, then I'm part of the Asian American scene. There's a lot of bullshit in the Asian American scene. The funny thing is that sometimes the people who are saying to me, "You're not Asian American," don't even speak their own language. They're completely American pie really and I don't judge that cause that's just a circumstance of fate. If they happen to be born here and they're third generation, am I supposed to judge them because they don't know anything about their culture? Yet they say to me, "You're not Asian American."

PING CHONG

I'm really not sure what value there is in identifying a writer by their ethnicity. For me, it's mostly an institutional commodity that a theatre can point to and say, "We're producing a play by so and so, who's an African American playwright." It's sort of like a peacock feather. When I see Asian American before the words, "playwright Diana Son," I really question why. My instincts say they are trying to relegate me and make assumptions about what I write about, i.e. generational differences, culture clashes. I am more interested in people who came to New York City from small towns to reinvent themselves as very different from the image that people had of them in their small towns. That comes out of my very specific experience, growing up Korean American in a small American rural town. But for me, it doesn't have to have a Korean American face in order for that story to be told.

DIANA SON

While I'm thankful for the recognition that SAKINA'S RESTAURANT has received, it gives me pause to be thought of as some kind of pioneer in bringing South Asian representation to the stage, because that is not my mission statement. It cannot be, because if it is, then it limits what I do. There's nothing wrong with the label, Asian American. I think it comes from the outside and it's necessary on one level for people, because we need to categorize things. The label just cannot come from the source. I cannot label myself as a South Asian writer because if I start doing that, then it's death for me and it's death for my work. And it's death for any writer or performer or anybody who starts labeling himself after arbitrary things like ethnicity, gender, sexual orientation, whatever.

AASIF MANDVI

There will always be writers exploring issues of identity, whether it's transgender or transcultural or transnational. Some people really have a satisfying life writing for a particular audience and a particular vision. They are not interested in writing color-blind stories. They want to write about what they know well. They're happy doing it and they do it well, so why the hell not? What's wrong with that label on some level? Maybe they don't mind being pigeon-holed or tagged or whatever.

JESSICA HAGEDORN

I was born in Hong Kong, spent my high school and university years in Vancouver, Canada, and then moved to New York to be a professional artist. That was a good twenty years ago. I didn't start thinking of myself as an Asian American artist until 1989 when I went back to China with my parents for the first time to visit "my mother land." When I came back from that trip, I wasn't searching, but this piece, "Post Revolutionary Girl," just poured out. That was the first autobiographical piece I did using my family history as fertile ground for making a dance theatre piece. And I used text for the first time in that piece. H.T. Chen said, "Why don't you do a piece at the Mulberry Street theatre?" As you know, that's smack dab in the middle of Chinatown. So I said yes. I had never connected with a Chinese audience before that. So that was the beginning of my consciousness as an Asian American artist. I was not trained in anything Chinese like Beijing opera, so my methodology and my conceptual thinking is Western, yet I had to find a way of linking that with my source material. I spent many years making work that did not really ring true from a center, or maybe it did at that time. But as I'm getting older and reflecting more and more about my heritage, and how I see life, that whole perspective of being a Chinese person living in the West and being in exile in a way... these issues come out. I think I'm finally reaching a place where I can freely weave the East and the West in me and I like that very much. But I still get calls from people saying, "Oh, can you come and do the 'Dragon Ribbon Dance' on Chinese New Year's?" And I just say thank you very much but I don't do that. So where do you place my work? It's not ethnic as such, but it comes from a place that is clearly from the perspective of a Chinese born.

MUNA TSENG

I don't call myself an Asian American playwright but I don't deny other people the opportunity to do so. It's just occupation modified by race to inform the consumer about the plays I write. But Sam Shepard isn't called a white playwright. He may not be called a white playwright but there are probably other adjectives that precede his description as a playwright. On the minus side, there's a connotation to

"Asian American playwright" of inferior quality, second rate. That's the unacknowledged, unofficial reading of that descriptive. It's just not going to be fashionable to be an Asian American playwright until a playwright comes along who easily shrugs off the label, says "Why not?" and has some modicum of glamour to him. No one is going to own up to being "Asian American" because it's just not a sexy enough term—that's what it all boils down to. And I'd like to think that I'm that figure—I'm just kidding. No I'm not kidding...Who cares?

HAN ONG

If you can't be proud of being an Asian American artist then you need to check yourself. We are not being pigeonholed by claiming and honoring who we are as people. Because all our work, all of our lives have been about suppressing and putting down anything valuable about how we feel about being Asian American. We've squashed it down so much that it's become a negative connotation. Now, when we have the opportunity as leaders in the community or respected artists, we shy away from that. I think it says more about the problematic issues within our community about self-hate, about not really seeing that what we have to offer is so unique and valuable and so beautiful that we should claim being Asian American artists 100 percent. By doing that, we are creating no limitations. It doesn't mean that all of your work is going to be about immigration because let's be frank, we've seen a lot of those plays and we do need to move forward. But it really means honoring all that history and then pushing forward.

GARY SAN ANGEL

3. If a play is written by an Asian American, but does not feature Asian American characters or "Asian American themes" is it still an Asian American play?

That's a phony question. A play is defined by its authorship. If you're an Asian American and you write a play it's an Asian American play. Shakespeare is British. He writes a play about Italians, calls it "Othello." Is it still a British play? But it's set in Italy. Why were the blacks pissed off at William Styron for winning the Pulitzer Prize for THE DIARY OF NAT TURNER? Because he's not black.

FRANK CHIN

One argument is that you're an Asian American playwright and you are part of the Asian American tradition because you are Asian American. But then would you likewise say that "Stop Kiss" does not belong in the canon of gay and lesbian literature because I personally am not living a lesbian lifestyle? I think it's very complex...What are you identifying? The personal life of the playwright or the piece of literature that they've created?

DIANA SON

This is where, frankly, the term "Asian American theatre/culture" needs to become more elastic. The community has changed a whole lot since the term was invented, and we've never really used it very precisely. The original arguments were a) we're going to use the term "Asian" because "Oriental" was colonialist, and b) it was unspecific because "where is the Orient?" But we ended up inventing this term Asian American and we're using it as unspecifically as the old Oriental term was used. Because as we deal increasingly with multiplicity of ethnicities in our community, the spirit of Asian American culture may continue to evolve, but the term may become less and less necessary or useful.

DAVID HENRY HWANG

It's Asian American, you don't have a choice. Your point of view, whether politically correct or not, whether it's of the majority view or not, it's uniquely yours as an Asian American. So when you write something, the roots of the material are Asian American regardless of whether or not your play has Asian American characters in it or if you're talking about an Asian American theme.

RALPH B. PEÑA

Is this a trick question? (*laughs*)

WAYLAND QUINTERO

I can understand the baggage that the term "Asian American plays" carries since we don't refer to mainstream plays as "white American plays."

CHIORI MIYAGAWA

The definition of Asian American theatre has broadened. I certainly think that if the characters are not written for Asian Americans, but the playwright is Asian American, that playwright should absolutely be represented in an Asian American theatre's repertoire. It's an individual case and it depends very much on what the playwright and the theatre want to accomplish and the synergy between those two.

TISA CHANG

I have a really hard time calling anything an "Asian American play" or a "black play." I don't have a clear answer because honestly, I'm almost not interested in that. But if you have to have an answer I guess it depends on the theme of the play and how the audience interprets what's going on on the stage.

AASIF MANDVI

Using painting for an example, everyone says, "That's a Van Gogh." No one says, "Oh, that's a Dutch painting."

RICK EBIHARA

As far as I'm concerned, if you're an Asian American, you have some consciousness about that, and you're writing a play and your characters are not Asian American then it's still an Asian American play. But the key, I think, is consciousness about being Asian American. Cause if you don't know the issues or what it means to struggle with that identity then what you're writing is just like any other play and it doesn't have the heart.

GARY SAN ANGEL

To me, that's not a very important question.

HAN ONG

It's a question of opportunity. In other words, if an Asian American writes it, that's what qualifies it, simply because there aren't too many opportunities out there for anybody. So if that's the only way that people can get their work done, fine. But what that leads to, though, is that there are so many plays that are supposed to be about "the Asian American experience." Then, what does that mean? It's actually a very diverse thing. But from the outside, a lot of regional theatres' definition of Asian Americanism is founded on a very clear idea that they already have from almost stereotyped images of oh, people in Chinatown that always have their extended families and on and on. So you find that they are either consciously or unconsciously looking for those kinds of plays. But what if you wrote about, for example, the fact that out on Long Island there's been these Asian Americans who have lived there for a long time in this almost country club environment that has gone on since the '50s? If you wrote about that, I don't think that that play would get produced, because that's not what people can stretch their imaginations to imagine the Asian American experience as.

DARYL CHIN

It's who the writer is and what that writer's vision is. It's always terribly interesting to see that vision and I think we need to contend with that and include it (Asian American plays) that don't feature Asian American characters or themes. Otherwise, we're all just going to segregate ourselves into nothing. It's going to get so narrow and so tunnelvisioned for everyone -- including white people.

JESSICA HAGEDORN

ACT II:
WHAT'S NEW YORK GOT TO DO WITH IT?

New York is the only place in America where you can work in the theatre and sort of feel like you're in show-biz. If you do theatre in L.A., you're definitely doing art. Because of Broadway and the influence of the commercial theatre here there is a show-biz entertainment aspect which doesn't exist in the other cities. When I started off, I had no idea that I would end up being a Broadway playwright. I just assumed that no serious work gets done on Broadway -- which is, by and large, true. But because I had a Broadway hit it changed my perception of the degree to which theatre can be a part of popular culture and this has changed my approach to writing. Therefore, I probably write more to that now which has its advantages and disadvantages. Struggling to try and create another hit is not a very productive artistic thing to think about. One should really focus on the truth of your work because you can't control if it's going to be a hit or a flop anyway. Yet that virus is part of me for better or worse, and that has affected the way I write.

DAVID HENRY HWANG

I don't think "The Chickencoop Chinaman" reached an Asian American audience in New York. I don't think there was an Asian American audience. I still don't think there's an Asian American audience. I don't think there are very many Asian American writers because everything they write is as if yellow is a disease or an affliction that they have to get over and that really they're white and they're just begging to be white and be accepted as white. Well, more power to them, but they're not Asian American. So whatever they have to say about Asian America is that they despise it. They despise themselves. They despise their history, they don't know it. They make a point of pride in not knowing it. Certainly they won't stand up for it. So here we have Asian American writers writing as if playing to the stereotype as if it's true, as if a yellow having sex with another yellow is an unnatural act, and that's New York. It's exclusive to New York. It begins in New York...Ms. Magazine... the chickens go to New York.

FRANK CHIN

Everyone and anyone is an artist in New York and I truly believe that. If you're in New York you're an artist in your own heart whether you're a doctor or a stock broker because there is this need, there is this hunger, to write your stories and get up and perform on stage, and there's no other place like it. So you have all these people who hunger for this. So when you create a space like PEELING THE BANANA, where it's about being able to tell your stories and share them openly and honestly with the community, as vulnerable as that is, anyone and everyone can be a performer. The workshops that inspired PEELING THE BANANA started in Los Angeles and we even did them on the East Coast in Philly and Boston. But New York is the only place where this work has continued.

GARY SAN ANGEL

We just got a rejection letter the other day from a regional theatre saying that the artistic director thought STOP KISS was "too New York." This is hilarious to me because I will never think of myself as a New Yorker. I always will be the country mouse in the big city.

DIANA SON

If you're a young man of any kind of ambition and you're not from New York and your ambition is to be a writer, sooner or later it will do you well to move out here. There's a certain competitiveness in the air...it's very Darwinian, and I think that, for the most part, it changes your writing for the better. But the best part of living in New York is that I don't have to think about living in New York anymore. It's always this mythic "going to" place. Now that I'm here, it frees my mind up to think about other things. I don't have to constantly think about "one day, I'm going to move to New York."

HAN ONG

When I was living in Florida, I was one of only two Indian kids in my whole school and I was always on the outside of a very white or black world. Coming to New York, there are lots of people who look like me and it maybe a clich , but New York is a city where you can be exactly what you are and nobody's going to judge you for it. It's a great place to experience everything there is to experience about different peoples and cultures and everything down the line. SAKINA'S RESTAURANT is seen as kind of an edgy play in other cities, and it's not necessarily edgy in New York.

AASIF MANDVI

I'm not a big fan of theatre in New York, I think the worst theatre I've ever seen in the world has been in New York and I've seen lots of it. The thing about New York is it makes fun of other places and other regions of the country, and cites very specific regional flavors as a way of demeaning the tastes of other parts of the country. But New York is the most regional place I've been in -- your plays have to have a certain bent to it. If you're Jewish; you have a guaranteed audience. If you're gay; you have a guaranteed audience. If you write about older people with older, more conservative concerns, you have a guaranteed audience. And I think the producers now are getting more conservative. Not as conservative as they were in the early '90s when arts funding was getting cut. The New York Times has a lot do with that. It's not really an arts organ, for me it's like a consumer report. It's like Ralph Nader going, "I've tested this battery and if you want to drive 10,000 miles..." That's all it really is. There's nothing artsy about it. In San Francisco I did two productions of mine that were lambasted by this critic who used to be a sports writer and in a way, I feel that a lot of theatre reviewers in NY and in this country are sports reviewers. They're like, "If I don't see a ball then...the ball has to be here and then it has to go there, and someone has to hit it back," and that's really the extent of theatre reviewing.

HAN ONG

New York put muscle in my work. Just because people here have seen a lot and they're a much more demanding theatre audience because this is one of the few places in America where theatre is taken seriously. More of your peers see your work so there are higher stakes. It also made me reassess my work and myself; is this what I really wanted to do? Do I really want to live here? Because it's a struggle to live here, as we all know, so every artist who decides to stick it out had better love it because it ain't about the landscape.

JESSICA HAGEDORN

Pan Asian would not have survived anywhere else except for New York, simply because in New York you are scrutinized and the expectation for excellence and professionalism is so high, and the competition is world class. There are 300 events going on every night in New York. So you really have to be quite competitive and stay on your toes. I sometimes feel like I'm a pit-bull. I gotta stay as fighting and as fit as a pit-bull walking on a tight rope.

TISA CHANG

I like that the disgustingly rich are right next to the homeless here. That kind of interaction of all these different class levels is a big inspiration for work. Like one thing that's unique to New York are all the Chinese delivery guys, they're like this unsung labor force. And one night I'm cruising along on my bike, you know I have my long hair, my leather jacket. Then this Chinese delivery guy rides up next to me and he says in Cantonese, "Hey, you working late tonight?" I thought, Whoa, he thinks I'm a delivery guy! Then everyone on the street thinks I'm a delivery guy! I thought I look nothing like this guy, yet I felt this connection with him. So I just kind of stuttered back in Cantonese, "No, I'm not actually working tonight." I was so embarrassed, I didn't know what to say. But that really inspired the idea for "No Menus Please" in BIG DICKS, ASIAN MEN. Because I was suddenly connected to them and their plight of what they have to face every day, which is essentially trying to do their job in front of signs that say, "Don't come here."

PERRY YUNG

2. How is the experience of the NYC Asian American theatre artist the same, and different, from other artists of color?

Like other artists of color, we expect to be in the mix, but we've also gotten used to dealing with ourselves as invisible people in the stories that we hear through popular mediums like film, theatre and music-although it's not so true in literature. In this country, there's been a longer and more distinguished history of African Americans and Latinos in the theatre, and subsequently there's been more of an audience and theatre going tradition in those communities. It's been difficult for those artists, but they have a certain visibility and a sense of themselves as part of the theatre. I think we're still scratching the surface.

JESSICA HAGEDORN

I went to see a performance by the Alvin Ailey Company up in Harlem and there was such incredible support from the community. It was a sold-out house that was so enthusiastic to see their friends and neighbors, sons and daughters up there on stage. We lack that as an Asian American community. I remember thinking, it's going to be a long time until we have this kind of support for our own kin. Asians are just not very supportive of the arts, especially not contemporary arts, except for a few classical music prodigies like Yo-Yo Ma or Sarah Chang or Midori.

MUNA TSENG

As far as other folks of color...I think we all need to realize that there's a hierarchy; and the reality is that if you're black, you have a much stronger chance of getting your work out there because this culture is basically black and white. There are just two races, and whether you're Latino or Asian you have figure out your own path. In many senses, I feel like the Latino community is just as lost even though they have much more of a presence culturally than Asian Americans—especially in New York, the heart of a lot of Asian American activism.

GARY SAN ANGEL

I think one thing all writers of color share is this expectation from the mainstream to deliver something culturally specific, and I think this is an obstacle especially because this expectation comes from the mainstream so it's not very enlightened about different cultures to begin with. The difference at this point lies in the critical mass of African American writers and artists as opposed to the very small pool of Asian American writers who are working in the mass media. Because of that, I think it's more likely that a theatre will view Asian American work in a spirit of Tokenism.

CHIORI MIYAGAWA

Initially the similarities are more striking than the differences. Certainly, Asian American political consciousness, out of which the Asian American theatrical movement initially stemmed, was an outgrowth of Third World and African American mentalities and ideologies. Therefore, it's not surprising that a lot of early models drew on African American work, like "The Chickencoop Chinaman" with the Black Jap Kenji character. So, seeing African Americans starting to define their own identities through literature and being an alternative to mainstream theatre is what kicked off a lot of the Asian American theatrical movement. As far as the differences, I think it comes down to the different ways in which different ethnic groups are stereotyped. So with Asian Americans, you end up having more of a sense of what the mainstream audience expects, which is more artistic, more beautiful, more poetic and more exotic than what they expect from plays about the African American experience, which is more sort of street. One of the biggest recent changes, and this actually applies more in film, is that Asian American artists, at least those behind the camera, have been able to crossover much more easily than other artists of color . Directors like Ang Lee, Wayne Wang and John Woo are basically just considered directors now, they're not considered Asian American directors even though a lot of their early work began either in terms of dealing with Asian American themes, as in Wayne's case, or Asian themes in Ang Lee and John Woo's cases. It's often been curious to me why the establishment has not allowed African American or Latino directors to do work that does not deal with their ethnicity. And to me, it seems as if that has to do with the ways in which the stereotype of Asian Americans, as being more purely artistic and more assimilated, works to our advantage at least in this narrow sense.

DAVID HENRY HWANG

3. How is the NYC Asian American Theatre community the same and different from other Asian American communities?

The New York community is, in a funny way, more traditional and more tied to root culture and root culture forms than some of the west coast communities. There are more immigrant groups in New York that maintain a community identity apart from assimilating into the mainstream community. And that means that you have more indigenous theatre groups. The city is supporting more Asian American theatre companies than are supported, to my knowledge, in Los Angeles, San Francisco or Seattle. There's more Asian American theatre going on here of a more diverse nature than on the West Coast, which is odd in a way. You always think of the West Coast as Asians having more influence and a lot stuff comes out of the West Coast, and both of those things are true. A lot of powerful stuff came out of San Francisco in the '70s and '80s, and there's been a great rejuvenation of East West Players under Tim Dang, but there's still a greater variety and greater number of companies here in New York.

DAVID HENRY HWANG

Asian Americans on the West Coast seem a little closer. In Hawaii and California there's a lot of film and TV, and everybody wants to be a celebrity and a star and a beauty queen. Here in New York, you just do your work and if by chance you get to a certain status, great. While the money's great, I can take or leave stardom-whereas in Hawaii and California, it seems to be more of the thing to go for.

WAYLAND QUINTERO

More than in other Asian American communities, the level of training and professionalism here is more exacting. The actors get more experience doing everything from theatre to TV to cabaret to improv, soaps, industrials, etc., so you don't get stuck in a certain mode. You're able to exercise your talents and skill more. Some of the other cities have a slower pace but that can also be an advantage as they have a greater gestation time for developing plays.

TISA CHANG

With the theatre and dance people I worked with in California, the sense that I got is that their work is more content, narrative driven. It's more about conventional plays and it's more about the story. Here in New York, I find that a lot of Asian Americans aren't as concerned with content as they are with form. I see that because there are a lot of Asians from Asia and you don't really understand what they're saying but you see their form of dance or music and how they're approaching their craft. It's like they're investigating how to tell the story more than what the story is.

PERRY YUNG

The Asian American communities on the west coast are much more cohesive than they are on the east coast. In San Francisco, for example, there is a real palpable Asian American community. You know where they are, so arts programming and arts development in theatre is much more community-rooted than it would be here. But the realities of the business in New York make it a completely different animal than it would be on the west coast. Here, we certainly enjoy support from the community, but here, the term "community theatre" is a pejorative term. It means that you're less than par and amateurish and I don't think there's that connotation on the West Coast. In Los Angeles there's no crossover. If you do a Chinese play you only get the Chinese community. If you do a Filipino play you only get the Filipino American community. When FLIPZOIDS was presented in Seattle the audiences were primarily Filipino Americans. We didn't get the other Asian American communities coming to see the play. That crossover we get more in New York simply because the nature and tradition of New York is just so mixed and exposed to the idea of going to the theatre.

RALPH B. PEÑA

4. Did the MISS SAIGON protests change anything?

When I look back on 1990, when the "Miss Saigon" protests erupted, I really feel a little sad because I think we were very misunderstood. 1990 was fifteen, twenty years after we first started picketing and things hadn't improved that much. If the producers had just simply wanted the original actor, Jonathan Pryce, to play the role they should have just said so instead of besmirching Asian American talent by saying, "there is no Asian American actor capable of playing the role." Once that went into print in The New York Times we of course got into arms. The bone of contention by the Asian American community was that we have an equal opportunity to audition and be seen in the lead role of the Amer/Asian character. Somewhere I also feel a little bit manipulated about that whole thing because all of the controversy and P.R. gave that show an awful lot of free advertising and we got a black eye. Pan Asian certainly got a black eye in the commercial arena because we were misunderstood. To this day, I still cannot get the rights to certain mainstream properties.

TISA CHANG

When they went out against "Miss Saigon" they admitted it was a racist play, and what did they want? They wanted Asian America to stand-up for the right of Asian American actors to play racist stereotypes. If they had any sense at all, they would have encouraged a boycott of Asian American actors from that play. It's a racist play so let the white racists play it all! But we won't do that because we're chicken shit. We have become the stereotype.

FRANK CHIN

The protests were confounding to me. We're fighting for the right to be in these plays? But it was an instance where Asians and Asian Americans were not seen as just taking shit. We went out there and gave people headaches and that's good.

JESSICA HAGEDORN

We lost the battle but won the war. For what it's worth Cameron MacIntosh has subsequently always cast that role with Asian actors. Another long term benefit is any producer knows that if they cast a white actor as an Asian they will get a lot of shit.

DAVID HENRY HWANG

To me, the main issue was not just Jonathan Pryce playing an Asian. It was the fact that playing prostitutes in bikinis were still the only roles that Asian women could get on Broadway.

CHIORI MIYAGAWA

ENTR'ACTE:
GROWING UP: ASIAN AMERICAN THEATRE THROUGH THE YEARS

What was your first Asian American theatre experience as an audience member?

Until I was seventeen I only saw Chinese opera because I come from a family of Chinese opera performers.

PING CHONG

There was no such thing as Asian American theatre. There were church groups, and amateur productions of white works. I guess the only thing that could be called Asian American theatre was the Cantonese opera that was big in every Chinatown.

FRANK CHIN

A workshop that Frank Chin ran at A.C.T. in San Francisco.

JESSICA HAGEDORN

Menotti's THE MEDIUM at East West Players in L.A. in 1967. My mother was the pianist.

DAVID HENRY HWANG

I don't remember what it was, but the first time I saw Chinese performers in the West, I remember thinking, "Wow Chinese people can be on stage and not be ashamed." (laughs)

MUNA TSENG

SOUTH PACIFIC at the Dorothy Chandler Pavilion in Hollywood when I was seven. I saw two Asian kids on stage-back then I probably called them "Orientals"-and I actually felt proud. I thought, there are kids like me and they're on stage.

GARY SAN ANGEL

A Pan Asian Rep. production. I don't remember which one, but I went to see some of their shows when I was in college.

CHIORI MIYAGAWA

Local Asian American actors trying to do kabuki in high school in Hawaii.

WAYLAND QUINTERO

David Henry Hwang's FAMILY DEVOTIONS or Philip Gotanda's YANKEE DAWG YOU DIE during the early '80s in college in San Francisco.

PERRY YUNG

In San Francisco during college I saw Philip Gotanda's SONG FOR A NISEI FISHERMAN, and in New York it was Stephen Sondheim's PACIFIC OVERTURES which I consider to be an Asian American work.

RICK EBIHARA

M. BUTTERFLY on Broadway.

RALPH B. PEÑA

Act III:

SUMMATION: NYC ASIAN AMERICAN THEATRE 2000, A NEW DIVERSITY OR THE SAME OL' TOKENISM?

1. What has, and has not surprised you about how NYC Asian American theatre has evolved?

In the '70s there was a real excitement surrounding Asian American theatre -- particularly when Pan Asian Rep. was doing its first productions under the wing of La MaMa. It was new, they were doing new plays, adaptations of classics -- there was a real buzz around it and then that went away because we wore out our novelty. Nobody rode that wave into the next logical step to really establish a solid repertoire of original Asian American works. I don't know what happened. Either the artists lost interest or whatever, but that wave was not seen to its full potential. Now, we're almost starting from scratch again. Part of it was that the initiative was co-opted by the more established theatres. By somehow validating us, they weakened the initiative. Once they said, "Oh yes that is a viable form, we're going to start including you," all of a sudden, within the community was this feeling of "Well now that they're doing it on a much bigger and better scale then we don't have to push as hard." So right now, there's no solid development program out there. That's what's surprising and not surprising. I just thought that at this stage of the game that we'd be so much farther ahead.

RALPH B. PEÑA

I think some of the theatre we see now is what I call "comfortable theatre." It's like people see theatre as this 9-5 thing and you don't really see the blood, sweat and tears and the same degree and intensity of dedication and sacrifice. You don't quite flagellate yourself so hard to get it done. Now I'm not advocating that you flagellate yourself-you'll bleed to death!-but sometimes I'm a little disappointed with the 20-somethings and 30-somethings. Maybe they're just smarter. But I don't think anything that's really worthwhile can be achieved without some bloodletting, without some sacrifice, without something extreme.

TISA CHANG

To me it doesn't really surprise me that there are no Asian American theatre people. What surprises me is that there are. Because I don't think it's part of the acculturation. I never grew up with that which is why, for me, being in the theatre is a very tenuous proposition. I always expect the worst in human nature and most times I'm proven right. I'm mystified by why my plays are not often produced and what it is about the earlier generation of playwrights that makes them as often produced as they are? What is that people see in those works which I find very inferior?

HAN ONG

It's definitely grown to be much more of an identity and a force in giving people voices. I think it's important not to ghettoize ourselves by saying "I'm an Asian American artist and I always make work with that identity and keep it in the community." I guess the ethnic thing is a double edged sword. You've got to use it, but use it to break out of your own ethnicity and get out there and have a bigger voice so people will listen to you whether you're an Asian American or if they don't give a damn that you are.

MUNA TSENG

Young Asian American writers are still writing like Christian missionary school-boys. All the stereotypes that the Christians had put down, if any of them had any guts, they would test the stereotype instead of accepting it. Go out, find the history. See if it's true. But they don't dare do that because deep down in their Christian souls they believe, they buh-lieve! that the stereotype is real. That they are that. And year after year, play after play, autobiography after autobiography that's all they have to say. What happens to those who say, "I am a human being, I am white." Then they write about whites. Then they are white, they live white and we never hear about them, do we? There are these writers out there who've taken white names and don't write about yellow people. Nobody knows that they're yellow from their authorship or the author's name or the subject matter of their book and nobody knows who they are... and who gives a shit? But there they are, supposedly the best of us. Supposedly what we want to achieve. This racial anonymity and just my good looks and my talent alone will lead me to my success. And what kind of success do we have?...Anonymity? The only difference was me. I was the change. I test the history, I don't play the stereotype. I stand up for Chinese culture, I don't tolerate the fake and I am not Christian. I made the change and the theatre got so fucking scared of me that they brought back the stereotype and created Maxine Hong Kingston.

FRANK CHIN

Often times it's perplexing that with Asian Americans and other ethnic groups, like blacks, the form they've chosen to make their theatre with is completely white. So their subject matter might be radical, controversial, whatever, but the form is completely traditional white theatre. So I find it very ironic and funny that there's all this stuff about what I do. Some of my detractors even say I jumped on the Asian American bandwagon because in '89 I started doing all these Asian pieces. I've never had any use for Western theatre, it's never had any influence on me. The biggest influence on my work is Chinese theatre. That's why I find it ironic when people don't recognize that where I'm coming from is not a Western thing.

PING CHONG

What surprises me is that we're still around and that we still want to do this. What it comes down to is who's still writing for the theatre anyway? Why would young people want to write for the theatre? More and more they're drawn to film where you can make a living without ever being produced-you can doctor scripts or something-whereas theatre is really a labor of love. They already know that they're not going to get widely produced so who's going to be attracted to that? You have to be some sort of lunatic to want to do this and put up with all this shit.

JESSICA HAGEDORN

The most surprising thing, and this is true about Asian American literature in general, is that we never expected the literature to become this popular. While at the same time, another thing that's surprising in a negative sense is that there hasn't been another kind of Asian American straight play commercial success since "M Butterfly" by me or somebody else. So the longevity of the footprint of "M Butterfly" in a commercial Broadway sense didn't happen -- it didn't have legs so to speak. Even given that, the popularity of Asian American literature is very surprising. The idea that this sort of subject could end up having mainstream appeal is something that we didn't imagine would happen when things first got going in the '70s and '80s.

DAVID HENRY HWANG

2. Is this the beginning of a new diversity or just the same ol' tokenism?

Han Ong, Alice Tuan, Chay Yew and I joke about who got "The Chink Slot" this year at what theatre. But for me, I really question whether or not I fulfill "The Chink Slot." Was STOP KISS the Asian American play of the season at The Public Theater? Is it an Asian American play because I wrote it? Is it an Asian American play because Sandra Oh was in it? The dominant theme of the play was sexuality, sexual identity and committing and not ethnic identity. So I don't know or care if it fulfills that spot. I would hope that they chose to produce STOP KISS because it was a good play. I can't imagine anyone who would feel satisfied that they got in because they fulfilled "The Chink Slot."

DIANA SON

There's certainly tokenism involved in the programming of these large commercial theatres and there is probably some attempt to diversify the programming of their season. But look at who's getting produced. We're talking about David Henry Hwang, Philip Gotanda, and Chay Yew and once in a while you'll see Diana Son or Alice Tuan slip in there. And what are we doing to insure that there's this continuous flow of work for these theatres or us smaller Asian American theatres to do? Nothing. So what's happening is theatres are taking a very passive approach and letting writers sort of self-develop themselves to the point where they become commercially viable or artistically exciting for these venues so you have to do it yourself.

RALPH B. PEÑA

It's the same old, same old. It's just contingent upon a new batch of people who haven't been beaten down yet by the system to come up and have the hubris to write their play and think, "History will make an exception and reward me because I'm so special," which is the way I thought when I first came along. But all of this is pretty privileged carping because the MacArthur ("genius" grant) has made it possible to remove myself from the to-ing and fro-ing of having to make a living and shaping my plays to meet a certain box office demand. Which is probably why I remain, over the past few years, unproduced.

HAN ONG

To have just one Asian American play in your season is complete tokenism. In some ways, what needs to happen is there needs to be an institution in New York like East West Players that serves the Asian American community and is an umbrella for a huge plethora of work, from experimental to straight plays to musicals. In some ways, Pan Asian is that in New York. But they don't have a home, so that forces them to be in all these other theatres and in some ways that's a metaphor for Asian American artists in New York. We're forced to bring our work to all these other theatres because we have no home.

GARY SAN ANGEL

There's some kind of unspoken quota or formula they're going after. They'll call it a balanced season and I'm sure that it stems from a genuine place. Unfortunately, sometimes the sensibility that selects those plays and the criteria for their choosing it is just, to me, a little whacko or off-kilter. There's no question that someone who's not schooled deeply in Asian American work and artists really can't do a very good job of selecting what is a great script. They'll generally play it safe and do a David Henry Hwang or a Philip Gotanda play.

TISA CHANG

You can argue that affirmative action, if used carelessly, can promote tokenism. But there's also a degree to which tokenism can open doors, but it tends to only open doors to a very small room.

DAVID HENRY HWANG

Token interest? They have no interest. It's a racist industry, it always has been and that's no surprise. They don't care about what we have to say. All they care about is making money and the stereotype makes money. And we have played that game.

FRANK CHIN

There's always room for more Asian/South Asian American plays. It's great that they're doing one play per season and they should do more. So even if it is just a token, so what? If it's good, has value, needs to be seen and it is seen, then who cares?

AASIF MANDVI

It's tokenism on another level because they'll do the one Asian American play a year, but they will not look at the play as merely an American play, but as "the one black play," "the Asian play" "the Latino play." It's better than nothing, but I truly don't like it. I love multiculturalism but I don't think it's been practiced. What I envision for multiculturalism is not like bringing out the "black play" for February or the "Asian play" for April and all that crap. For me, multiculturalism is a vision of how you relook at America and how the land-scape is constantly evolving. When you say America now, you can't assume that it's coming from a blonde, blue-eyed perspective. You have to include the constantly changing communities around you and the fact that America is now composed of these many cultures coming together, colliding, colluding, conflicting but vibrant, alive. There's no pat solution like then it's going to stop and we're going to close the doors to anybody new-although they're trying that. I think that when you look at a theatre season I wish it was no big deal if they would just decide to do plays that reflected this changing mosaic-and I hate to use that word because it makes me think of Mayor Dinkins, but it's a beautiful word. It's just been used to death by politicians. This country and what's wonderful about it on some level is that we're all here, and those collisions make for interesting theatre. Why can't Chay's play simply be part of the season? And why couldn't they do Chay and Han? I mean what's the weirdness of doing three Asian plays in one season instead of the one and making theatergoers deal with it instead of going, "Here's a spe-cial treat now, here's our Asian project for the whole year." Or, "Now we're doing the Latinos because we just did the Asians last year." And I really resent that because I feel like my work is not being looked at for the right reasons. Tokenism is alive and well, not just in the theatre but in everything.

JESSICA HAGEDORN

EPILOGUE:
IN THE FUTURE...

In the '70s '80s and 90s we did a good job of defining ourselves. Now the legitimacy is there, and in the 21st century we need to strengthen and empower ourselves, and take control in every way, and not just artistically... Maybe we need to take some tips from Jessie Ventura!

TISA CHANG

Once at the Playwrights Center in Minneapolis this Asian American moderator was putting me through the grill saying things like, "How come your company is all white? How come you don't work with the Asian American theatres? My answer was, "Cause nobody's asked me! If they ask me, I'll do it."

PING CHONG

Personally I'm interested in going to places where I can be free of limited expectations as an immigrant or Asian American or woman writer, and more and more I'm finding freedom in quite small theatres like Dance Theatre Workshop where it's very artist-focused and not season-focused so they don't have to program it according to what's available and what the subscribers can take. So I think the key is finding people that you like to work with and finding inspiration in the work and not expect the mainstream to change because that will take eons. Small revolutions I believe happen away from the mainstream where the work is more innovative and people have a vision that goes beyond just selling tickets and getting good reviews. So if we ever want to come out of this tokenism we have to create our own world and not copy the mainstream and not try to be admitted as a member of the mainstream and not make that a priority and make the work a priority.

CHIORI MIYAGAWA

The future is going to be much more global and getting out of tribal mentalities and into a global and universal language. At the same time, individual artists are just going to have to be stronger on their own identity. Because given the scope of how easy and open communication and travel is, I think it's important that, somehow, we don't get all homogenized. That we still hold on to our own strengths and identities and at the same time be more open to each other.

MUNA TSENG

The opportunities that exist are a double-edged sword. The larger institutional theatres have to look for Asian American plays . Because of the foundation grants they have to look for diversification. It's good because it will allow people to work, but it's also problematic because often people are just targeted as a token and there's no development that goes beyond that. So far there's not been a single Asian American playwright or director in the theatre that's had a sustained developing career with a major institutional theatre. And I think that's a real problem because if that happened, a playwright could write something specifically Asian American and then experiment with something that was not and all sorts of other themes and ideas, and still find that they would have a place where there would at least be readings and development of their work. But there are more opportunities now.

DARYL CHIN

Asian American theatre never was, and never will be, a token at La MaMa.

ELLEN STEWART

I think tokenism will always be around, but we'll get away from tokenism as we understand it now-based on the particular racial categories that are currently existent; black, Latino, Asian. For instance, there's this whole theory about "The Browning of America" perhaps with the degree of multiracialism it's going to break down into this white/brown mix but there's still going to be African Americans. If so, there will be a tokenism that comes out of that-positive and negative. Both, tokenism in terms of trying to do things, however well meaning, but doing them badly for people who are perceived to be disadvantaged, and also the backlash of hatred and racism and other negative things. It's human nature to divide people into categories, but I think that those categories may change over time into things that we can't anticipate today.

DAVID HENRY HWANG

I think we are very close to the point where we won't be needing these "slots."

DIANA SON

I see no Asian American theatre on the horizon, ahead of me or behind me. Not in my lifetime, definitely not. We're all too busy kissing white ass and that's not Asian American theatre and that's not what passes for Asian American theatre. If Asian American theatre doesn't stand for Asian America, it stands for nothing. And it stands for nothing. I'm not holding the whites responsible for Asian American theatre, Asian Americans are responsible for Asian American theatre. I expect whites to be white racists, now and forever. They will always have their reasons and their reason will always be to make money their way. It is we ourselves who have no confidence in ourselves to make theatre. If there is no Asian American theatre, it is not the white man's fault. It is our fault, period.

FRANK CHIN

IV CONTRIBUTORS

TISA CHANG is the Founder and Artistic Producing Director of the Pan Asian Repertory Theatre. She began her career as a dancer and actress on Broadway and in films. In the early '70s, she started directing at La MaMa, E.T.C., where she specialized in bilingual productions such as RETURN OF THE PHOENIX (later premiered on CBS-TV's "Festival of Lively Arts"), A MIDSUMMER NIGHT'S DREAM, THE ORPHAN OF CHAO and innovative adaptations such as HOTEL PARADISO, THE SERVANT OF TWO MASTERS, and for Buffalo's Studio Arena, THE LEGEND OF WU CHANG. Memorable Pan Asian productions include Cao Yu's THUNDERSTORM, Momoko Iko's FLOWERS AND HOUSEHOLD GODS, Wakako Yamauchi's AND THE SOUL SHALL DANCE, Vijay Tendulkar's GHASHIRAM KOTWAL, Lao She's TEAHOUSE, Kan & Stewart's SHANGHAI LIL'S, and Ernest Abuba's AN AMERICAN STORY, EAT A BOWL OF TEA, CAMBODIA AGONISTES. Tisa is also on the Executive Board of Society of Stage Directors & Choreographers.

DARYL CHIN is a performance/theatre artist who created over 30 works between 1975-1984. Since then, he has worked in a variety of production capacities on independent film projects. In 1977, he cofounded the Asian American International Film Festival; in 1982, he cofounded the Asian American International Video Festival. At present, he is Associate Editor of "PAJ: A Journal of Performance and Art."

FRANK CHIN is a playwright, novelist and screenwriter known for his uncompromising portrayals of Chinese Americans, and for his outspokenness and controversial views on other Asian American authors. His plays, THE CHICKENCOOP CHINAMAN and THE YEAR OF THE DRAGON, were presented at The American Place Theatre in 1972 and 1974, and were the first Asian American plays to be produced on a NYC Off-Broadway stage. His fiction works include the novels, DONALD DUK and GUNGA DIN HIGHWAY, and the short story collection, CHINAMAN PACIFIC & FRISCO R.R. CO, which received the American Book Award from the Before Columbus Foundation. He is also an editor of AIIIEEEEE! AN ANTHOLOGY OF ASIAN AMERICAN WRITERS and THE YARDBIRD READER, VOLUME 3. He is the recipient of the Joseph Henry Jackson and James T. Phelan fiction awards, the East West Players Playwriting Prize, a Rockefeller Foundation and National Endowment for the Arts' Playwright's Grants. He is also the founder of the Asian American Theatre Workshop in San Francisco and was the first Chinese American brakemen on the Southern Pacific Railroad.

PING CHONG is a theatre director, choreographer, video and installation artist. He was born in Toronto, Canada and raised in New York City's Chinatown. He is the recipient of an OBIE Award, six National Endowment for the Arts Fellowships, a Playwrights USA Award, a Guggenheim Fellowship, a TCG/Pew Charitable Trust National Theatre Arts Residency Program Fellowship, a National Institute for Music Theatre Award and a 1992 ("Bessie") Award for Sustained Achievement. Since 1972, he has created over 30 works for the stage including NUIT BLANCHE, NOSFERATU, A RACE, THE GAMES (with Meredith Monk), ANGELS OF SWEDENBORG, KIND NESS, SNOW, NOIRESQUE, BRIGHTNESS, 4AM AMERICA and ELEPHANT MEMORIES. KIND NESS received the 1988 USA Playwrights Award and was published in TCG's PLAYS IN PROCESS and in NEW PLAYS USA. NUIT BLANCHE was published by TCG in BETWEEN WORLDS. SNOW was also published in PLAYS IN PROCESS. At NYC's Artists Space in 1992, Ping created the first production of UNDESIRABLE ELEMENTS, an on-going series of works exploring the effects of history, culture and ethnicity on the lives of individuals living in a particular community. He has created other versions of this throughout the world. It's Tokyo production, entitled GAIJIN or "foreigners" received a "Best Play of 1995" award from the Yomiuri News Company. Ping Chong created an audio version of UNDESIRABLE

ELEMENTS with sound artist Jordan Davis, that is currently available on CD.

ALVIN ENG is a native NYC playwright, lyricist, storyteller and journalist. Eng's stage works include MAO ZEDONG: JEALOUS SON (AN ABSTRACT PORTRAIT), an opera he wrote with composer Yoav Gal, the musical, THE LAST HAND LAUNDRY IN CHINATOWN, written with composer John Dunbar; the solo performance/monologue plays, MORE STORIES FROM THE PAGAN PAGODA and OVER THE COUNTER CULTURE; and THE GOONG HAY KID, his play with rock and rap songs. His plays have been presented throughout the country at venues including La MaMa, E.T.C., The Nuyorican Poets Cafe and Performance Space 122 (NYC), Theatre Mu (Minneapolis), The Group Theatre (Seattle), among others. THE GOONG HAY KID was published in the anthology, ACTION: THE NUYORICAN POETS CAFE THEATER FESTIVAL (Touchstone/Simon & Schuster). Excerpts from THE FLUSHING CYCLE, his autobiographical storytelling play, were published in THE SECOND WORD THURSDAYS ANTHOLOGY from Bright Hill Press. In '89, Eng wrote and co-directed a short film, THE 20TH ANNIVERSARY REUNION CONCERT OF BIG CHARACTER POSTER, in collaboration with Melissa Cahill. His honors include fellowships from the New York Foundation for the Arts, the Corporation For Public Broadcasting and The Harburg Foundation among others. He holds an MFA in Musical Theatre Writing from NYU/Tisch School of the Arts and was named after the Chipmunk cartoon character.

JESSICA HAGEDORN is the author of THE GANGSTER OF LOVE and DOGEATERS, both novels; a collection of poetry and prose, DANGER AND BEAUTY; and the editor of CHARLIE CHAN IS DEAD: AN ANTHOLOGY OF CONTEMPORARY ASIAN AMERICAN FICTION. Plays and collaborative multimedia theatre pieces include MANGO TANGO, HOLY FOOD, TEENY TOWN (with Laurie Carlos and Robbie McCauley), and AIRPORT MUSIC (with Han Ong). Hagedorn adopted DOGEATERS into a play for a 1998 production at La Jolla Playhouse. She is working on her third novel.

WYNN HANDMAN is the Artistic Director of The American Place Theatre, which he cofounded with Sidney Lanier in 1963. The American Place Theatre presented the World Premieres of the Frank Chin plays, THE CHICKENCOOP CHINAMAN and THE YEAR OF THE DRAGON, in 1972 and 1974 respectively, and of Aasif Mandvi's SAKINA'S RESTAURANT in 1998. Mr. Handman has been instrumental in bringing to the stage the early work of many of America's finest playwrights including Ed Bullins, Maria Irene Fornes, Frank Gagliano, Jonathan Reynolds, Ronald Ribman, Sam Shepard and Steve Tesich. The writer/performers Bill Irwin, Eric Bogosian and John Leguizamo also received early recognition for their work at The American Place Theatre. He is a recipient of two AUDELCO Awards for Recognition for Excellence In Black Theatre, the Lucille Lortel Lifetime Achievement Award from the league of Off-Broadway Theatres, a Rosetta Le Noire Award from Actor's Equity Association the Carnegie Mellon Drama Commitment to Playwriting, The Townshend Harris Medal, and The Working Theatre's Sanford Meisner Service Award for leadership in disseminating the arts to working people, among others.

DAVID HENRY HWANG is a playwright, screenwriter and librettist. Best known as the author of M. BUTTERFLY, the first Asian American play to be produced on Broadway, the play ran for two years and won the 1988 Tony, Drama Desk, John Gassner and Outer Critics Circle Awards as well as the 1991 L.A. Drama Critics Circle Award. The play also enjoyed a one-year run on London's West End, and has been produced in over three dozen countries to date. His most recent play, GOLDEN CHILD, premiered off-

Broadway at the Joseph Papp Public Theater, received a 1997 OBIE Award for playwriting and subsequently moved to Broadway where it received 1998 Tony and Outer Critics Circle Nominations for Best Play. Mr. Hwang's other plays include FOB (1981 OBIE Award), THE DANCE & THE RAILROAD (1982 Drama Desk Nomination), THE HOUSE OF SLEEPING BEAUTIES (1983), THE SOUND OF A VOICE (1983), BONDAGE (1992), FACE VALUE (1993), and TRYING TO FIND CHINATOWN (1996). His plays are published by Plume, Theatre Communications Group and Dramatists Play Service. He is currently rewriting Rodgers & Hammerstein's FLOWER DRUM SONG into a new version to be directed by Robert Longbottom, and working on a new play about Paul Gauguin to star actor Armand Assante. Mr. Hwang graduated from Stanford University, attended the Yale School of Drama, and has been awarded an honorary doctorate from Columbia College in Chicago. He lives in NYC with his wife, actress Kathryn Layng, and their son, Noah.

AASIF MANDVI is a writer and performer who was born in Bombay and raised in the north of England, where he began acting at the age of 10. Aasif moved with his family to the United States fifteen years ago. His New York stage credits include DEATH DEFYING ACTS, SUBURBIA and CROSSCURRENTS. His film and television credits include ANALYZE THIS, THE SIEGE, DIE HARD WITH A VENGEANCE, LAW AND ORDER, NY UNDERCOVER, NASH BRIDGES, THE COSBY MYSTERIES and MIAMI VICE among others. SAKINA'S RESTAURANT played for six and a half months Off Broadway at the American Place Theatre before touring various cities around North America and Europe. It is Mr Mandvi's first published work and the recipient of two 1999 OBIE awards.

CHIORI MIYAGAWA is an Artistic Associate of New York Theatre Workshop, where she manages the Writers Fellowship program for emerging playwrights of color, and a resident artist at Dance Theater Workshop, NYC. Her plays include JAMAICA AVENUE (1998 New York International Fringe Festival), FIREDANCE (Voice&Vision Theater), NOTHING FOREVER (New York Theatre Workshop and New Georges at HERE), YESTERDAY'S WINDOW (New York Theatre Workshop), AMERICA DREAMING (directed by Michael Mayer, produced by Music-Theatre Group and Vineyard Theater) and BROKEN MORNING (Dallas Theater Center). She has received support for her work from McNight Fellowship, Binekie Playwright in Residence at Yale School of Drama, Rockefeller Multi-Arts Production Grant, Jerome Foundation, New York Foundation for the Arts Playwriting Fellowship, New York Council for the Arts, NEA, TCG Extended Collaboration grant and others. Prior to becoming a playwright, she was a dramaturg for such major theaters as Arena Stage, Actors Theatre of Louisville, Berkeley Rep, American Conservatory Theater, and The Public Theater. She is a Binekie Visiting Professor at Yale School of Drama and also teaches playwriting at New York University and Bard College.

HAN ONG was named a 1997 MacArthur "Genius" Foundation Fellow at age 29, one of the youngest to ever achieve this distinction. A playwright and performer whose works include THE L.A. PLAYS, THE CHANG FRAGMENTS, SWOONY PLANET, PLAY OF FATHER AND JUNIOR, and WATCHER. His plays have been presented in prestigious venues across the country and abroad, including American Repertory Theatre (Harvard), The Public Theater (NYC) and the Almeida Theatre (London). His writings has been published in CONJUNCTIONS: THE NEW AMERICAN THEATRE and CHARLIE CHAN IS DEAD: AN ANTHOLOGY OF CONTEMPORARY ASIAN AMERICAN FICTION, edited by Jessica Hagedorn. He is the author of the screenplay for a short film broadcast on Los Angeles public television called NOT X.L., and a full-length screenplay called CANTONESE POP STAR, which he is currently preparing to direct. A high school dropout, Mr. Ong was born and raised in The Philippines and came to the United States as a teenager.

PEELING THE BANANA is a New York City based pan-Asian American performing arts ensemble started in 1995 by performance artist Gary San Angel. It uses autobiography and community building as departure points for performance. Peeling the Banana aims to explore various ways to present written work through public performances, ultimately with the goal of digging deep into issues that concern Asian Americans as artists and as members of a larger multi-racial community. The collective has actively sought to include previously under-represented groups in every step of its process focusing on communities traditionally marginalized in the discourse(s) of Asian American art, Peeling the Banana includes Filipino, Indian, Korean, Pakistani, and Thai members, as well as queer and multiple-heritage identified members. Prior performances have included the Joseph Papp Public Theater, Second Stage Theater, Highways Performance Space in Los Angeles, and the Desh Pardesh Festival in Toronto. Peeling the Banana is currently housed within the Asian American Writers' Workshop. Regardless of the physical space where it meets or performs, Peeling the Banana creates a metaphorical space where each participant feels safe enough to challenge themselves both artistically and emotionally. It is a place where individuals are respected. New participants are received enthusiastically without judgment or condemnation, and everyone is encouraged to take risks. It provides, quite simply, a home where participants can explore and express who they really are.

RALPH B. PEÑA is a playwright and actor. Ralph began his theatre training as an actor at the University of the Philippines in Diliman, and continued at the University of California in Los Angeles and at the Circle in the Square Professional Actor's Conservatory in New York as a Birch Foundation scholar. His plays include CINEMA VERITE, KAPE BARAKO, DECEMBER, FLIPZOIDS, and most recently, LOOSE LEAF BINDINGS. His plays have been presented at Theatre For The New City, Henry Street Settlement, The Joseph Papp Public Theater, all in NYC, the New WORLD Theatre in Amherst, Massachusetts, Northwest Asian American Theatre in Seattle, and at the Kumu Kahua Theatre in Honolulu. He is the recipient of a Playwright's Commission from South Coast Repertory Theatre and a panelist for the New York State Council on the Arts. He currently serves as Artistic Director for the New York-based Ma-Yi Theatre Company.

GARY SAN ANGEL is a New York-based Fil-Am performance artist and director. He is also the artistic director and founder of the Peeling the Banana performance troupe. Gary's collaborative performance creations have been performed across the country from Los Angeles to New York. He was a Van Lier Fellow at the Second Stage Theatre in directing and integrates visual art, theater, music, words, and movement to achieve a balance of aesthetic concerns with social consciousness. His work has been seen at the Joseph Papp Public Theater, Smithsonian, Second Stage Theatre, East West Players, Teatro Ng Tanan (TNT), Highways Performance Space, Asian American Theater Company, Japanese American National Museum, and South Coast Repertory.

SLANT is the New York City trio ensemble of RICK EBIHARA, WAYLAND QUINTERO and PERRY YUNG. As a resident company of the world-renowned La Mama Experimental Theater Club, SLANT's work is an original and dynamic tapestry of theatrical satire, live amplified, acoustic and a cappella music, dance, puppetry, and shadow play. Themes and stories derive from pop culture stereotypes, urban and ethnic myths, from stories and visions of previous generations, from contemporary experiences of their very American upbringing while paying homage to the guiding influences of their Asian heritage. Starting with their 1995 debut, BIG DICKS, ASIAN MEN, SLANT has gone on to create 4 more original pieces, THE SECOND COMING, SQUEAL LIKE A PIG, HOTEL CALIFORNIA, and WETSPOT, which they have performed throughout the world. SLANT's self-titled CD of songs and scenes from BIG DICKS, ASIAN MEN and THE SECOND COMING, was independently released in February 1998. SLANT is currently recording their second CD and was recently commissioned by The Joseph Papp Public Theater for a play.

DIANA SON is a playwright whose most recent play, STOP KISS, premiered at The Public Theater, NYC, in December 1998, where it ran for nearly four months. Originally commissioned by Playwrights Horizons/Amblin-Dreamworks, it will be published as a trade paperback by Overland Press/Penguin Press in late 1999. Diana's play, BOY premiered at La Jolla Playhouse in 1996 under the direction of Michael Greif. FISHES premiered at New Georges (NYC) in 1998 and was subsequently produced by the People's Light and Theatre Company. R.A.W. ('CAUSE I'M A WOMAN) appears in TAKE TEN: NEW TEN-MINUTE PLAYS published by Vintage Press and CONTEMPORARY PLAYS BY WOMEN OF COLOR by Routledge Press. Diana currently has works commissioned by The Public Theater and the Honolulu Theatre for Youth. Diana was the recipient of the Brooks Atkinson exchange/Max Weitzenhoffer Fellowship through New Dramatists (of which she is a member).

ELLEN STEWART is the Founder and Director of La MaMa E.T.C., the New York City theatre that began in October 1961 with the vision of nurturing and encouraging the creative endeavors of new generations of artists. To this day, La MaMa remains true to this founding vision, and has presented more than 1,800 productions. Its resident theatre troupe has performed throughout the world, and Ms. Stewart was instrumental in introducing to America some of the world's most influential artists including Andrei Serban, Thaddeus Kantor, Peter Brook, Jerzy Grotowski, Ryszard Cieslak and Ludwig Flazen among many others. She is a visiting professor of the Institute of Drama in South Korea and is a long-standing member of the Seoul International Theatre Institute. Ms. Stewart is the recipient of numerous Honorary Doctorates and awards, including the MacArthur "Genius" Award and the National Endowment for Arts and Culture. She was appointed an "Officer" in the "Odre Des Arts Et Letters" of the Republic of France, and recently received the Les Kurbas Award for "Distinguished Services to Art and Culture" from the Ukraine. In January 1993, Ellen Stewart was inducted into the "Broadway Theatre Hall of Fame," becoming the first Off-Broadway Artist to ever receive this honor. In December 1994, Ellen Stewart was awarded the "Order of the Sacred Treasure, Gold Rays with Rosette" by the Emperor of Japan.

MUNA TSENG is a celebrated dancer and choreographer acclaimed for her seamless fusion of Asian sensibilities and Western abstract forms. Born and raised in Hong Kong, her family immigrated to Vancouver, Canada in 1966. Ms. Tseng has been based in New York since 1978, and has performed throughout the world. In 1986 she founded her own company, Muna Tseng Dance Projects, and has presented many acclaimed productions over the past decade including SLUTFORART (1999), an homage to the life and art of photographer Tseng Kwong Chi (in collaboration with director Ping Chong), AFTER SORROW (1997, in collaboration with Ping Chong and composer Josef Fung), and THE IDEA OF EAST (1996, with composer Tan Dun, pianists Margaret Leng Tan, SouHon Cheung and architect Billie Tsien), among many others.

Ms. Tseng has received fellowships from the National Endowment for the Arts, the New York Foundation on the Arts, five commissions from New York State Council on the Arts and was honored as a "Chinese American Cultural Pioneer" for Distinguished Services in the Arts" in 1993 by New York City Council President Andrew Stein and named "Artist of National Merit" at Washington's Smithsonian Institute.

COPYRIGHTS | PHOTO CREDITS

Tokens? The NYC Asian American Experience On Stage
edited by Alvin Eng

The *NuyorAsian Anthology: Asian American Writings About New York City*
edited by Bino A. Realuyo

Watermark: Vietnamese American Poetry & Prose
edited by Barbra Tran, Monique T.D. Truong and Luu Khoi

Black Lightning: Poetry in Progress
by Eileen Tabios

Contours of the Heart: South Asians Map North America
Winner of the 1997 American Book Award
edited by Sunaina Maira and Rajini Srikanth

Flippin': Filipinos on America
edited by Luis Francia and Eric Gamalinda

Quiet Fire: A Historical Anthology of Asian American Poetry, 1892-1970
edited by Juliana Chang

For more information about the activities and programs of The Asian American Writers' Workshop,
please contact us at:

• 37 St. Mark's Place, Suite B, New York, NY 10003-7801
Tel | 212.228.6718
Fax | 212.228.7718
e-mail desk@aaww.org *web* www.aaww.org

To purchase any of these books, please contact Temple University Press,

• 1601 N.Broad Street, USB 305, Philadelphia, PA 19122
Call toll-free 1.800.447-1656 | Fax 215.204.1128
or visit us on the web at www.temple.edu/tempress